A TEST TO DESTRUCTION

Also by Henry Williamson in
A Chronicle of Ancient Sunlight

THE DARK LANTERN
DONKEY BOY
YOUNG PHILLIP MADDISON
HOW DEAR IS LIFE
A FOX UNDER MY CLOAK
THE GOLDEN VIRGIN
LOVE AND THE LOVELESS
THE INNOCENT MOON
IT WAS THE NIGHTINGALE
THE POWER OF THE DEAD
THE PHOENIX GENERATION
A SOLITARY WAR
LUCIFER BEFORE SUNRISE
THE GALE OF THE WORLD

HENRY WILLIAMSON

A TEST TO DESTRUCTION

'He faced the spectres of the mind
And laid them: thus he came at length
To find a stronger faith his own;
And Power was with him in the night,
Which makes the darkness and the light,
And dwells not in the light alone.'

Alfred Lord Tennyson

Macdonald

A Macdonald Book

First published in Great Britain in 1960
by Macdonald & Co (Publishers) Ltd

This edition published in 1985 by
Macdonald & Co (Publishers) Ltd
London & Sydney

British Library Cataloguing in Publication Data

Williamson, Henry
A test to destruction.—(A Chronicle of
ancient sunlight/Henry Williamson; 8)
I. Title
823'.912[F]　　PR6045.I55

ISBN 0–356–01816–4

Printed in Great Britain by
Redwood Burn Limited, Trowbridge, Wiltshire
Bound at The Dorstel Press

Macdonald & Co (Publishers) Ltd
Maxwell House
74 Worship Street
London EC2A 2EN

A BPCC plc Company

To

GEORGE D. PAINTER

ACKNOWLEDGEMENTS

The author wishes to express his gratitude to General Sir Hubert Gough, G.C.B., G.C.M.G., K.C.V.O., etc., for permission to quote from a letter describing his meeting with General Humbert of the French Army at Villers Bretonneux during the MICHAEL attack in March 1918; and to Captain the Earl Haig, M.C., for his permission to include in the narrative several extracts from *The Private Papers of Douglas Haig*, published by Messrs. Eyre & Spottiswoode (to whom also the author's thanks).

The letter written by the late General Sir Charles Harington, reproduced in part on pages 190, 191, and again on page 201, was originally published in Volume Two, Number 2 of *The Ypres Times*, the Journal of the Ypres League, in April 1924.

A popular song at the time of the story, "Over There" by George M. Cohan, some of the words of which were 'roared out around the piano' (page 42), is used by permission of the holders of the '© Copyright 1917/Copyright Renewal 1945 Leo Feist Inc., New York, N.Y. Rights for British Empire and Commonwealth, except Canada, controlled by Chappell & Co., Ltd., London, England'.

CONTENTS

PART ONE

ANTICIPATION

PART TWO

ACTION

PART THREE

TENSION

Part Four

THE LOST KINGDOM

Part Five

NO-MAN'S-LAND IN CIVVY STREET

Part One

ANTICIPATION

18 FEBRUARY—21 MARCH 1918

Chapter 1

THE STAFF OF LIFE

In the winter of 1917–18 the Great War for Civilization—as it was generally accepted among the elderly and non-combatant of the Christian nations still engaged: Great Britain, France, Belgium, Italy, Germany, Austria, and the United States of America—was about to enter its penultimate phase on the Western Front.

This battlefield, upon which there had been continuous fighting for three and a half years, could be seen at night from aircraft as a great livid wound stretching from the North Sea, or German Ocean, to the Alps: a wound never ceasing to weep from wan dusk to gangrenous dawn, from sunrise to sunset of Europe in division.

During this war there were the terrors of action at the front, as well as mortifying fears arising from comparative inaction at home. Movement is often release from fear; while sedentary suspense can reduce the spirit more than the physical exhaustions of action.

This is a story of the last year of the Great War, and of the year following the first silence upon the battlefield. It has a small beginning, set in a time when all combatants, except perhaps those of the United States—who had yet to share in the general sufferings of the Old World—were coming to the end of their endurance upon both the Home Front, and the Western Front—that deadly area where millions of husbands and sons had fallen, in the coastal sandhills beside the Channel; in the brown, the treeless, the grave-set plain of Flanders; among the slag-heaps and derelict pithead-gear of Artois; upon the chalk uplands of Picardy and Champagne; in the forests of Argonne and Alsace extending to the neutral country of Switzerland—where below mountain peaks, under the snow, wild flowers lay resting as still within their corms and bulbs as the human dead upon the battlefield.

As the great battles of the Spring of 1918 broke upon France and Flanders, so the flowers of the upland valleys arose with blooms as fugacious as human hopes for the outcome of the war, which, it was said everywhere, would decide the fate of the world.

It had been a hard winter, and food was scarce in London, particularly among the poorer or working, and the middle, or clerical and professional classes.

South of the Thames, working-class houses were of yellow brick, built generally in terraced streets for cheapness; while those occupied by the middle classes were usually semi-detached, built of red brick in the nineteenth century, or merely faced with red, for economy, if erected in late Victorian or early Edwardian days; with side and rear walls of the cheaper yellow brick occasionally fused with glass fragments, for greater tenacity. Roads of such houses, built two by two and known as semi-detached, had gardens both at the front and back, the former often protected from immediate view by hedges of privet and occasionally of holly, both shrubs which endured the acid fogs of winter's smoke and mist. Here and there stood lilac and laburnum, bringing colour to limited living.

From such a road, built up the side of a hill just before the turn of the century, a middle-aged housewife, whose life was centred irrevocably around her husband and children, set forth on a cold February morning of 1918 in an attempt to get some eatable food for her family. Rationing had not by then been organized, and life had become more difficult than ever before.

When she reached the hamlet of Randiswell—still so called by older people, who knew the place when it was in Kent, before appropriation by the London County Council—the first thing she noticed was that the tattered poster of Field-Marshal Lord Kitchener on the hoardings before the shops was lying in strips upon the pavement. She saw its disappearance with a slight pang. It had remained there during the years, a figure of assurance that all would come right in the end. Could it have been nearly three and a half years since the stern face, heavy black moustache, extended arm and pointing finger, YOUR COUNTRY NEEDS YOU!, had first appeared when her son was walking beside her in his kilt and glengarry, just before he had gone to France in September 1914? She felt momentarily gay at the thought of Phillip, now safe at home, in category B2. Surely, after four spells at the front, he would not be sent out again?

The billposter, an old man, was slowly moving his long-handled paste brush up and down as he stuck on a fresh roll of paper. She had no curiosity about what the new poster might be, for by now she accepted all things in life: to submit was the only way. One must hope for the best, and be as cheerful as possible, for the sake of others. All was in God's hands; and in the end, she believed, all things would come right.

There was much to be thankful for. Her son, now twenty-two, no longer drank to excess; he had given up that terrible habit, and seemed to have turned over a new leaf. His last letter said that he was learning to box at his camp on the East Coast, and he swam every morning in the sea. So he must be entirely free from the effects of trench fever, if he could safely bathe all through such bitter weather! He was working in the Orderly Room, as an assistant adjutant. It was wonderful news. Papa, too, had got through his bad attack of bronchitis, and was down again in his sitting room before the fire. Yet he was still very weak, and the doctor had said that he must not think of venturing out of doors for a long time.

Now she really must think of food. Things were no longer delivered, one had to fetch everything, and take what was given. Her efforts during the past two weeks had not been very successful. This time she *must* succeed in getting something really nourishing for Dickie and the two girls. Dickie was looking so fagged and pale, after long hours at the office, followed by his patrols as a special. (She must remember never to say 'special' in his hearing: he liked to be called a Special Constable, or rather Sergeant. *I am a sergeant of Special Constabulary*, she could hear him saying. *Otherwise I am certainly nothing special, and never was. Unlike your best boy, Phillip.*)

Poor Dickie, he was so hurt that Phillip never wrote to him nowadays. She had asked him to write sometimes to his father; but after such a request Phillip's next letter usually arrived only after a long interval.

In the Maddison home during the first two weeks of February all that Hetty had managed to get from Chamberlain the butcher and Soal the greengrocer in Randiswell was frozen mutton scrag and some old bones, a few blackened potatoes and one small swede turnip—which meant that on two successive Sundays Richard, the master of the house, had looked with dismay, not far from despair, at what his wife had put before him for his one good meal of the week; and then he had worked himself up and finally shouted that it was her duty to do better; that she had comparatively nothing to do in the house all day, why could she not show some care for those entirely dependent on her? Then throwing down his worn table napkin, he had left the room.

Richard had come back to the table to find another fault: the mutton was old crone! Again he had got up, in impotent protest from a deceived and empty stomach. "Very well, if you cannot do your duty, I must do it for you! I will go without my usual bowl of soup and bread on Friday next, and buy something in Leadenhall Market!"

Poor Dickie! She had tried not to laugh when he had come home on Friday night with a sheep's heart and a wood-pigeon, result of forty minutes' standing in line before one of the shops in the covered market.

"All the same, Hetty, I still think you could do better down here, if you really acted with determination! You are too haphazard, you know, you tamely accept what you are given, instead of demanding the best! After all, if a shopkeeper finds that his customer is taking an interest, he will respond—that is but human nature."

So Hetty had set forth that morning with thoughts of a saddle of mutton, Dickie's favourite dish, to be served with onion sauce, brussels sprouts, and baked floury potatoes. That would, she hoped, make up for the steak-and-kidney pie she had tried, at her younger daughter's suggestion, to make with the sheep's heart and pigeon. Oh dear, that pie.

"Why did you not *stew* my ring-dove in a casserole, pray? And a sheep's heart should be stuffed, with savoury herbs and onions, and then gently baked!" Once again Richard had pushed back his chair and gone out of the room, saying, "I've a good mind to join the Army, 'pon my soul! Oh, I am not joking! I am still not too old, you know, to enlist in the Labour Corps!"

He had not meant seriously what he had said: the remark had arisen from idle fancy after reading an announcement in the paper; but it recurred again and again to his mind in the days that followed. "I'm at the end of my tether," he told himself in the looking glass as he tried to imagine his face without beard and moustache. Could he dye his hair dark-brown, as it had been before his wretched marriage? At least he could shoot with a rifle. And in the middle of the week he announced quietly that he had given in his name at the Recruiting Office in the Strand for the Pioneer Section of the Labour Corps.

"You will soon be rid of me, and what Mr. Turney next door no doubt considers to be my bullying ways! I have made my Will, and left everything to you, Hetty." He had never spoken of his father-in-law other than as 'Mr. Turney.'

Phillip's room in No. 9 Manor Terrace, Landguard Fort, Suffolk, had one window facing west. The glass of this window had not been cleaned for over a year and a half, since the opening of the battle of the Somme, when had begun an unceasing flow of drafts to the Western Front. The frame rattled when the wind blew; the putty holding the glass panes was hard and cracked, fallen in places; the pre-war paint was flaking off. The wooden floor was rough with scratches of hob-nailed boots, and marks of burning coals fallen beyond the flower-pattern'd tiles of the hearth.

Every night since he had lain in his bare room Phillip had hugged himself with the thought that he was warm and dry. When snow had clotted the panes he had drawn up his knees and thought that he was safe from frozen trenches, where hands and feet were pierced as with nails in the added cold of sleeplessness: that he was back in England, and with the Mediators, that he was among friends, that he belonged to the Gaultshire Regiment, that he was now with the finest crush in the Army. Gone was 'the battle of the brain' at night, gone the hopeless weights upon the mind when awakening. To be fit was now the ideal, *mens sana in corpore sano*.

The long wet nights in the Salient during the battles of Third Ypres no longer broke into his sleep: sudden *phew-crash* of 4.2 shell giving time to throw yourself flat on the timber tracks; unlike the 8-pounder, the pip-squeak which arrived in a shower of dust or mud, a mere smokeless amazement unless you were hit and you found yourself without body in a sky-world without dimension; brutal downward droning 5.9s; coarser slower 8-inch stuff; high-velocity railway-guns firing from Wervicq and Menin, sending shells like earthquakes without warning on the cobbles and ruins of the Cloth Hall and Grand' Place of Ypres—rearing mule and crumpling driver, ringing ear-drums and sightless flaming eyes, scorching blast-smell of red-hot iron and high explosive . . . no more sweating entanglements of the mind. Life really was 'Colour and Warmth and Light' come again. Friendship was the sun of living. And the little dog that slept in his bed was part of the new world of zestful fun.

Manor Terrace was a brick and slated row of workmen's cottages built on the edge of the shingle bank near the mouth of the river Orwell. Landguard Camp extended south almost to the estuary, where from the slips and hangars of the Royal Naval Air Service arose the great flying boats which patrolled that area of the North Sea under Harwich Command. To the hutments of the 3rd (Special Reserve) Battalion the Gaultshire Regiment at Landguard came all those men and officers, after convalescence from wounds and sickness, from the various fronts in France and Flanders, Italy, Salonika, and Mesopotamia. Phillip had acquaintance with most of them, since, being assistant adjutant, it was his job to receive each new arrival.

A regulated life had given regulated thoughts. He was in the habit of awakening just before dawn, to lie in quiet happiness with the dog he had bought in Felixstowe. It was the smallest of a litter of fox-terrier pups, the only one with shaggy hair. The owner had let it go for five shillings, saying that it was the 'cad,' or smallest pup of the litter, the last but one to be born. It had been as thin as it was friendly when he had brought it to his billet; but now it was fat—the servants in the end room had seen to that.

Phillip had made up some doggerel verses about it, two lines of which ran

You have been thin and now are fat
Your name should obviously be Sprat.

Soon the buglers would be sounding reveillé. The Colonel had ordered it half an hour later than usual, now that the battalion was composed almost entirely of drafts from hospital: the walking wounded, and the sick, from Third Ypres were now coming in almost every day.

Lord Satchville, the C.O., welcomed all arrivals, speaking to each man by name as he went down the files standing at ease, Phillip beside him reading names from the orderly room roll. The Colonel recognized many of the old soldiers, recalling their circumstances from former talks. What a C.O. to have! Easy in manner, amiable, quiet of voice, always friendly but at the same time impersonal.

The reading of names, and the greeting of returned soldiers, was one of Phillip's many duties as assistant adjutant. He had learned much about the organization of a battalion during his weeks at Landguard Camp; the variety of his duties had given him a personal interest combined with a modest air of authority. And after the day's work there was tea in the mess to look forward to, with plenty of amusing talk; then more work until the bugle sounded for dinner, when in one's best tunic, slacks, and polished brown shoes, the day was delightfully rounded off. After dinner there was auction bridge, sometimes in the Colonel's house, with other invited officers, one of them a newcomer like himself, but who wore the coveted D.S.O. riband, to whom the Colonel had said, "Let me present you to my wife." Phillip had thought for the moment that the 'present' was because he was a Companion of the Order, but Lord Satchville then said the same thing of himself. "May I present Mr. Maddison——"

The disturbing fears about his adverse report after the battle of Cambrai had lessened; he was not the only one, he realized; a week previously the lieutenant-colonel who had commanded the 2nd battalion at Cambrai had been sent home with an adverse report. He wore the Military Cross and South African ribands.

While this colonel had been talking with Lord Satchville behind the closed door Phillip looked him up in the Army List, and saw that he was fourth senior captain in the 2nd battalion, with a brevet as major, which meant major's pay and honorary rank while awaiting turn for promotion. Lord Satchville spent half an hour with him, then as the stellenbosched acting-lieutenant-colonel was leaving, he heard the C.O. say, "I suppose you know that the Professor has gone out, too, over the Cambrai affair?"

The 'Professor' stellenbosched—Lt.-Gen. Sir Launcelot Kiggell, Haig's Chief of Staff, sent home! He felt himself to be in more distinguished company than ever, especially when he learned, through the Orderly Room, that the acting lieutenant-colonel, who for a few days had hung about the camp wearing only a crown, had exchanged into another regiment, where he expected to get a battalion. So there was hope for himself, after all: he who had lost his way on coming out of the battle of Bourlon Wood, taking the transport of 286 Machine Gun Company to the wrong place in that night of flame and gas-shell, before the surprise German attack the next morning, leading to the break-through, and the death of the 'Boy General' of the Brigade, while sixteen perfectly good Vickers guns were miles away when they had been needed in the line.

The notes of reveillé floated through the grey February air. He heard a stir, and knew that Allen, his room mate lying against the other wall, was awake. Allen practised deep-breathing as he lay in bed, slowly drawing in air, and letting it out as slowly. Allen was usually very calm, he said he breathed eight times a minute. Phillip had timed his own breathing; twenty-eight to the minute. He was a shallow breather, using only the top of his lungs, according to Allen. So for two months he had breathed deeply. It had produced calmness. While boxing or running, he was no longer easily puffed.

What was Allen thinking? He was just nineteen, and was on the roster for the next draft. Allen did not know this, and would not think of asking Phillip for information. He was an only child, his father a parson. Still, drafts were not very frequent, now that infantry brigades in France had been broken up into three battalions, which meant that every fourth battalion had been disbanded to feed the remaining three.

Phillip waited, feeling the little dog's silky hair against his throat. Then black and white ears arose. Sprat had heard the chink of cup on saucer. He crawled out of bed and stood up, tail-stump and pied blotched face quivering. Then with a yelp of joy he sprang off the bed to greet the batman entering with the morning tea.

As soon as this was swallowed, Phillip and Allen got into bathing slips, put on shoes and burberrys, and with towels round necks left the billet to trudge over shingle to the sea, now a tarnished coppery-leaden hue with the sun about to move over the far horizon, where a speck in silhouette was the mast of the Cork lightship.

"Looks bloody cold today, Jimmy." Allen's reply was to run into a pebble-jumping breaker. Phillip hesitated, clasping ribs with elbows, while Sprat stood some way behind him: he had been thrown into the water some days before, and now kept well clear. Phillip walked down to the white pebble-rush of a wave's withdrawal, while looking south towards Landguard House, where the Colonel lived. Usually that tall Viking figure, bearded and almost totally enclosed in blue-and-white striped bathing suit of late Victorian pattern—he was said to possess a dozen of such suits, made specially for him in the Burlington Arcade—went into the sea about that time. Ah, there he was, striding down in his white bath-robe. At that moment the rim of the sun blazed upon the horizon. Phillip raised his arms, and diving into a wave, emerged to see Allen apparently making for the Cork lightship.

For Phillip, two minutes in the water was enough. He waited to be swept up the concave of wet pebbles, and holding against the drag of water, crawled out and stood up, giddy for the moment while his heart thudded in his ears. A couple of slow deep breaths, with slow respirations, equalized him with the day; while his skin showed pink, and the golden glow, reward of winter bathing, possessed his being.

He had to shake Sprat off his towel—a thin, war-time affair—whereon the dog had been chewing a bit of flotsam. As he bent down within the towel he noticed that the hairs were beginning to grow again on the insides of his thighs. He must have ridden well over four thousand miles from first to last, during the past year in France. The new hairs were thin and without sharpness, unlike the hairs on jowl and chin, which were made stubbly by constant cutting. Allen's moustache was no more than an eyebrow; the hairs, thin at the end, had been left to grow naturally from the start, for he had never shaved his upper lip; his moustache was soft and thin like that of youths in Italian pictures of the Middle Ages. It was rather attractive, like the faint little soft hairs on an adolescent girl's lip. Did women like young men with soft hairs on their lips, young men unaware of their callowness? It was unlikely, for only the female had beauty, while the male had strength. He looked at his own thin arms and legs.

Allen came out of the sea, and picked his way over the pebbles to him. It was strange that Allen seemed to like his company.

Phillip rubbed his legs vigorously, taking care to hide the ugly purple wound-scars in his left buttock.

A hundred yards up the coast the Colonel's lady had joined Satchville. She wore a sort of crumpled woman's motoring hat down to her ears, held on by a ribbon, and frills round the neck of her dark blue serge jacket. Her bloomers also had frills below the knees. Black stockings and canvas shoes completed the costume; while her lady's maid stood just above the wave line, holding a cloak for her mistress, and, for some reason, an umbrella, although it had not rained for several days. The Colonel was playing ring o' roses with his wife. Then they took turns to dip one another in the waves. They were so free and easy, behind the amiable dignity which both maintained.

Phillip wished that Father and Mother could have been like that when younger . . . far away across the North Sea some of the enemy were perhaps bathing in what they called the German Ocean, before getting into their uniforms as grey as the winter waves which beat upon the coast of England.

"Ready?" said Allen. The two had a competition every morning, to see who could reach the doorstep of No. 9 in the least number of hops over the shingle and roadway. This was the greatest fun for Sprat, who did his best to impede both competitors by jumping around them.

There was a pile of old picture magazines in one corner of the room, collected from the mess sergeant by Phillip's batman. They helped to augment the coal ration, since fires were not allowed to be lit in billets until 5 p.m. each day. The way to burn *Tatler*, *Bystander*, *Illustrated London News*, etc. was to roll them into cylinders, which were stood upright in the grate and fired from below. Flames crept up with the forced draught, and a pleasing column of fire roared while they dressed to a record of Chopin on the new trench gramophone.

In the ante-room of the Officers' Mess, by the door, was the letter-rack, with pigeon-holes lettered from A to XYZ. In the M hole was a letter for Phillip, addressed in pencil, from his mother. He had asked her not to write in pencil; why had she done so again? He kept the letter until he was in the lavatory before opening it, thinking that it was the usual scrappy note; but the contents made him literally sit up.

My dear Son

I hope you are well, and that no news is good news, of course you are very busy with your new appointment. Soon it will be Spring, it will be a good thing when the weather changes. I have some news for you, dear, which I must tell you. Father says he is going to join up, apparently he is not too old for the Pioneers of the Labour Branch, making roads in France or perhaps looking after the vegetable gardens attached to a hospital on lines of communication.

Phillip was soon back in his room, dashing off a letter in reply saying that the Labour Corps worked right up to the front line, that during Third Ypres thousands were killed, almost as many as the soldiers who had gone over the top. He had seen men older than Father working under shell-fire, men who were grandfathers, with white hair. No, Father must not go; he would never be able to stand the life. He wrote with desperation, he must save Father from going through what he would never be able to stand. It was unthinkable.

So, upon reflection, or rather in reaction, was his letter. He tore it up, and wrote another, putting aside his feelings.

Dear Mother,

Please ask Father not to do anything until he has seen me. I may have to go out again to France very shortly; also I may be home tomorrow, Saturday, for a brief week-end. Meanwhile please tell Father that his work on the allotment is helping the country enormously, for if the submarines go on as they have been, sinking ships, we may be beaten on the Home Front. Food is everything. I'll try to bring some butter, I know how hard it is to buy anything nowadays. We in the mess are eating horseflesh for beef, and potatoes are not much in evidence. In great haste, and love to all,

Phillip.

He had pretended, on the whim of the moment, that he might be sent out to France again: the great thing was to stop poor old Father from doing something which he would soon wish he hadn't. Scores of poor old codgers had been hit in the night-long German machine-gun barrages. No, Father must not do such a thing. What would Mother do if he were killed?

And it *was* on the cards that he himself might be sent out again! He wasn't C3, but only B2, and might easily be directed to some base, or lines-of-communication, job in France. Also, he would be passed 'A' at his next board, in less than a month's time. Indeed he was perfectly fit now, so why bother about a Board? He had only to add his own name to the 'A' list, by typewriter, and no-one would know the difference.

It was 8.45 a.m. There was a quarter of an hour before Captain Henniker-Sudley, the adjutant, left his furnished apartments in Manor Terrace, where he lived with his wife. Phillip hurried to the orderly room, and taking down the files, removed his last medical history sheet, classifying him B2, and put it in the stove. After this, he typed his name on the 'A' list. Later in the morning, casually he gave the roll to the sergeant to be re-typed.

When the fair copy was brought in, he checked it with the sergeant, found it correct, and put the old copy in the stove. Then after initialling the new copy he took it to be signed by the adjutant. That evening it was included, the weekly *Nominal Roll of Officers Available for Active Service*, in the dispatch bag to Eastern Command.

When she came to the shops past the hoardings Hetty saw a line of women outside Hern the grocer's; she went on to the butcher's, her smile a little anxious. Mr. Chamberlain, fat, bald, with pink shiny head, raised his cleaver in salute. Mrs. Maddison was much liked in Randiswell, for she had a smile for everyone. "Nothing left fit for you, ma'm!" he announced. "Only tripes and offal. Sorry, my customers all come early now!"

She should not have stayed so long with Papa, or called in at No. 134 to see Dorrie; but Dorrie's youngest boy Gerry was badly wounded, and her sister wanted to try to get to him at Etretat, where Gerry was in hospital. How could she help? Perhaps she might see the authorities at the War Office, instead of Papa, who had said he would go there himself. No; Papa must not be allowed to go out, not yet awhile at any rate. She must pray for help to Saint Anthony.

Hurrying down to the High Street, she had crossed the bridge over railway and Randiswell brook, and was between the Public Baths and the Police Station when flakes of snow began drifting out of the sky, to melt at once, she saw with relief, upon the paving stones. Then, as she was walking under the high-walled garden of St. Mary's vicarage, it seemed that her prayer was answered. She would call upon Canon Hough on the way back! Perhaps he would be able to help.

Going on down past the new row of shops—they had been built in Edward the Seventh's reign, but to Hetty they were 'the new shops'—she heard a bird singing, somewhere high above the discoloured High Street. It must be in one of the trees in the garden of the last old-fashioned house left there with its stucco pillars, before the carriage drive, plastered over with old bills.

There the bird was, on the highest branch of a lime tree, singing into the drift of sleet. She recognized it as a missel thrush, or storm-cock Dickie used to call it, because it challenged the elements bravely in the coldest part of winter. She recalled, with another sigh, how once upon a time, when they were first married, Dickie had been so interested in birds and the country, particularly the butterflies.

Oh, the butterflies in the herb fields of Cross Aulton, when she was a girl, so happy with her brothers, and sister Dorrie! The wonderful colours, section after section of lavender and thyme, licorice and rosemary, chicory and aniseed! And the thrush in the garden, of a summer morning, seeming to say, *Get up, Hetty! Get up, Hetty!* And now, suddenly it seemed, she was nearly fifty years old. Fifty—half a century! How had the time gone by? Mamma and brother Hughie gone, sister Dorrie an invalid; dear, charming Sidney dead of enteric in the South African war—could it be seventeen years since he and Hughie had left in a cab at midnight, for Waterloo station? She could see the stars in the sky now, as the cab went down the road, the horse's shoes striking sparks from the flints, and Phillip staring with tears in his eyes. *They'll die*, he had said, sleepless in bed that night, such a nervous, anxious little child, *I know they're going to die.* And Hubert, Sidney's eldest boy had been killed; and now Gerry, the youngest, badly wounded and in hospital. Thank God that Phillip was out of it. Perhaps the war would be over in the coming year; but they had said that in nineteen sixteen, and again in nineteen seventeen. How quickly all life wasted away! And every life so precious to its owner, the Roll of Honour filling sometimes two columns of small print in the newspapers every day—and no end to it all. Papa, at bezique the night before, had stopped playing to talk of trains rolling day and night across the Rhine bridges, coming from Russia with one and a half million German troops, according to Sir Auckland Geddes, to make a great attack in France. All those poor boys out there, every one with a mother hoping and praying . . .

A sad-sweet smile came over the small face, with its lines of experience at variance with its child-like look: the brown eyes, shrunken within the orbits, filled with tears, the lips trembled; then with cheerful resolution she went on down the High Street, past Electric Palace and Penny Bazaar, and so to the food shops behind the market stalls of the Borough.

Yes, one must always hope for the best, like the bird singing through the sleet. She remembered the baby missel-thrush Phillip had brought home from Whitefoot Lane Woods one day. He had been out with two boys from his school, looking for nests, and one boy had climbed up a tall pine tree and finding only one chick in the nest had thrown it down before Phillip could stop him. It had been hurt, but for three weeks it had lived, and become quite tame; suddenly it had died. Phillip had buried it next to his museum, a hole in the flower bed covered with glass, and put up a little cross over the fledgling's grave. She could hear his voice now, *It isn't a sparrow, but there's not much difference, anyway it fell to the ground, so God must have noticed it.* So thoughtful a remark for one so young: and what a strange mixture he had been, kind and thoughtful one minute, and the very opposite the next, although he had never hurt anyone deliberately, at least never since that sad occasion when he had egged on Peter Wallace to bully poor Alfred Hawkins, for 'daring' to speak to Mavis over the garden fence. How strangely children grew up!

There was her elder daughter Mavis, who now liked to be called Elizabeth. Nothing seemed to satisfy the girl. She was always in a hurry, and nearly always late—and never able, it seemed, to live within her salary from the office. Her bedroom showed only too well the state of her mind. Shoes flung anywhere into the bottom of her clothes' cupboards, underclothes in the drawers tumbled together, bedclothes thrown back in disorder. And yet she had been such a neat little girl, taking pride in having all her clothes just so. If only she would remember not to comb out her brush and roll up the loose hairs and drop them out of the window, where Dickie always seemed to find them, and complain. *Slut*, he had called her, a dreadful word to use before a young girl! Elizabeth had flung herself out of the house, letting the front door bang. But she must not look on the dark side of the moon, as Phillip would say.

Thank goodness for her younger daughter's calm steadiness, but she wished Doris could be a little less brusque in manner towards her father. If only Dickie would understand that Doris's manner concealed her feelings about her cousin Percy's death in the Somme battle, eighteen months before. Doris had never got over it, but being reserved, did not easily show her feelings. But now that Doris had got a scholarship to London University—she was going to Bedford College at the beginning of the summer term—she would meet many new faces, and the change of scene would do her good.

Looking on the bright side, Hetty came to the busiest part of the Borough. But the sight of hundreds of women in the food lines before the shops momentarily overcame her. Then thinking that everyone standing there was like herself, with the same hopes, she took her place before Winner Bros. shop.

She had been waiting in line about ten minutes when an old woman wearing cape and bonnet, and carrying a bass fish-basket from which stuck out the top of a flagon bottle of porter, approached in a rollicking gait, due to the perpetual discomfort of corns consolidated by misfit boots given to her by various mistresses for whom she worked in rotation, charring. She stopped when she saw one of them in the line before Winners', and a feeling of embarrassment came over her, that Mrs. Maddison should have to wait in such company.

None of this feeling was shown in her manner when she stopped before her. "Good mornin', ma'm. The weather is getting better, I feel it in me corns," she remarked cheerfully. "Hope you won't catch cold, m'am, waiting here. But it's the times, m'am. I sometimes wonder what it's all coming to. Still, it's not for the likes of me to say. I'll be along at nine o'clock tomorrow, m'am. How is Master Phillip? Well, that's good news. He deserves a rest, if anyone did. After all, he's done his bit," she concluded, using a phrase that had gone out of common use since the battle of the Somme, when the realization that what Lord Kitchener had said about a long war had been proved right. "Mr. Turney is better after his bronchitis, I hope? Ah, that's promising! Good-day, ma'm."

After waiting nearly half an hour Hetty had an immediate view of the shop. How empty it looked, with its rows of polished hooks holding only here and there a shrunken fragment. She was fourth away when the butcher cried, "Joints all gone, ladies!

Only offal'n sheep 'eads left! Eat a sheep's brains, they'll improve your own!"

There was a jeer behind the humour. 'Meat' for meat was one of his practices, women were cheap. He could now shut up shop for the rest of the day and kip through the afternoon, in preparation for snooker at the Roebuck in the evening. As far as he was concerned, the war need never end.

"'Ow old are them 'eads?"

"Old as their teeth, like you, mother. Want one? Eleven three."

"Garn! Give my 'usband that muck! At eleven three? Think I'm made o' money?"

"Take it or leave it. What for you, lady? Sheep 'ead? That'll set you back best part o' 'alf a dollar! They'll be up tomorrow. I can't 'elp it, lady. You won't get one elsewhere no cheaper. What for you, madam?" The Suffragette in front of Hetty had helped to pass the time by addressing remarks to whomsoever would listen to her, on the subject of Corruption in High Places. It was all a question of the Big Profiteers wanting things to remain as they were, in order to continue their high rate of profit. As for the Ministry of Food, its muddles would be laughable if they were not so tragic.

"One day we are begged to eat potatoes, and showers of leaflets come through the post! The next week we're asked not to eat potatoes—and they come black anyway, and are uneatable. It's all a disgraceful muddle! We ought to organize deputations to Whitehall, demanding equality of price and distribution. Look at the scarcity of sugar in the shops here, compared with the quantity—and the price!—in the West End! Some of the profiteers in our midst are making fortunes! Sugar costin three ha'pence a pound before the war is now sevenpence! As for those awful substitutes called consip and sypgar, what are they but glucose and beet-sugar syrup? Have you bought any honey lately? Half a crown a pound! We have a friend in Somerset who sent us two rabbits—they are five shillings each down there! And the same price for clotted cream! As for eggs, fivepence each, *when* you can get them! And only the other day I was asked a shilling for a cauliflower, quite a small head too! And do you know what grocers are demanding for a tin of peaches? Four shillings and sixpence! There's profiteering for you! What!" to the butcher—"only sheep's heads left. Where are the rabbits?"

"As far as I know, down their little 'oles. Next! Sheep's 'ead, take it or leave it!"

Returning with empty basket Hetty wondered if she could afford some fish out of her £3 weekly allowance for all food, clothing and coal. Papa ought to have some sole, or halibut. But the price was far too high; four shillings a pound for sole, three for turbot.

"Have you any herrings?" The voice was almost defeated.

"Seen none for months ma'm. Trawlers all on minesweepin' these days. And picking up more sailors nor mines."

She remembered Mrs. Feeney saying that she would never touch fish again, from what they were now bound to be feeding on.

Well, there was no hope for it, she must try elsewhere in the afternoon. And going back the way she had come, she saw a familiar figure walking slowly towards her, different only in that now the brim of his dark soft hat was shapeless and pulled down over his ears, while the folds of a long woollen muffler were wrapped twice around his neck, and tucked into the collar of an ulster overcoat extending to his ankles. What was Papa doing, out in the cold?

With head sunken into shoulders Thomas Turney came slowly towards her, tapping a stout lemon-wood walking stick on the pavement. The face looking at her, above the clipped white beard and moustache, was red with a tinge of lilac. His breath came harshly as he stood before her.

"Bad news, my girl," he managed to say. "Yes, he's gone, Dorrie's boy Gerry," as he continued to look at her with his ruined eyes.

"Oh, Papa! I must go to Dorrie at once! But should you be out and about so soon?"

"I'm well protected, Hetty." His trousers below the knees were wrapped in brown paper, tied with string. He spoke on, slowly. "Dorrie's girl Maudie came up to tell me. M' sister Marian is with Dorrie now. I thought it best to wait until I saw you, before going in, Hetty." He looked exhausted. "Well, we'll walk back slowly, shall we? No, I don't need an arm, thank ye."

Upon the Randiswell hoardings, replacing the tatters of Lord Kitchener, was a new notice.

ISSUED BY THE MINISTRY OF FOOD

MOBILIZE THE JAMJARS!
PUT UP THE POTATO BARRAGE!
KEEP THE HOME CRUST TURNING—

back into the kitchen!

In the parks nurses and children still feed the birds with large quantities of bread.

Special Constables report that much bread is still thrown away in the gardens of squares, in *cul de sacs* and unfrequented places.

Our Motto must be:—

Eat as little as we can to keep us in health and *Waste Nothing.* I AM A CRUST. If you collected me and my companions for a whole week you would find that we amounted to 9,380 tons of good bread—WASTED! Nine shiploads of good bread! Almost as much as twenty German submarines could sink—even if they had good luck.

When you throw me away or waste me you are adding twenty submarines to the German Navy.

SAVE MY CRUSTS, AND I WILL
SAVE YOU!
Who am I?
MR. SLICE O' BREAD

While they were looking at this announcement, the billposter was sitting on his pail and eating his lunch. He was pulling apart bits of bread and cheese to put into his mouth, which lacked teeth, when a sparrow flew down and watched him. The man tossed the bird a length of crust, which was seized and borne up to one of the out-jutting tie-bricks in the end wall of the unfinished row of shops.

Thomas Turney pointed with his thick lemon stick. "So much for the bureaucrats in Whitehall!"

Father and daughter went on up the road, which rose towards the Hill; and every step they took seemed to Hetty to be towards the doom that all living creatures shared, in a world of sadness and anxiety. And then, as she thought of the billposter and the sparrow, she felt, as she had felt before in dark moments, that all was well behind the veil of life. And what was to occur when father and daughter reached No. 134 Charlotte Road was to Hetty a confirmation of her faith in life.

In the house over the road from Dorothy Cakebread lived Mrs. Wallace, a Scotswoman, who had lost all her sons in the same battle at the beginning of the war. This woman, distraught after reading the deadly telegram, had cried to Dorrie, whose two boys in the same London battalion had come safely through the battle, "You've no right to have both your boys alive, when I have lost my three!" Now, when Hetty went in to console her sister, she saw Mrs. Wallace sitting beside Dorrie, holding her hand, and heard her saying, "There dear, be brave!" Our laddies are together! They do not want to see us cast down! Our laddies are watching us, I am sure of it! God gives all life, which does not end with death. We are all one with God, in life as in death, dear neighbour."

Chapter 2

WHAT IS COURAGE?

Late on the Friday afternoon a curly-haired, pink-cheeked young man, wearing the red tabs and hat-band of the General Staff, with field boots and spurs, came into the orderly room. Phillip recognized him at once as Devereux-Wilkins, whom he had seen last in October 1915, playing billiards in the Roebuck in the High Street at home. Wilkins, wearing red tabs then, had showed him a wristlet watch engraved as a gift from his platoon at Gallipoli, 'a token of esteem.' The local plain-clothes detectives were after him then, as a bogus officer and possible German spy. He had blandly told Phillip that they must have confused him with his brother, who was a secret agent, and having said that, he jumped on a passing tram for London.

And yet, if he had been bogus then, how came it that he was obviously now a staff-officer? Phillip began non-committally. "I don't suppose you remember me?"

A quizzical look was directed towards him, as though the newcomer was fully aware that this crude opening gambit must be parried by a show of good manners.

"Well, you know, I have met a great many interesting people while with my General," he said charmingly.

"Weren't you an A.D.C. in October, 1915?"

"I was."

"Don't you remember me in the billiards room of the Roebuck in Lewis'm High Street on the night of a Zeppelin raid?"

"I'm afraid I've never been to Lewes in Sussex."

"I mean Lewis'm in Kent, now a part of London. Surely it was you? Anyway, somebody just like you showed me a wristlet watch, which had been given to him by his men, in memory of Suvla Bay."

"You mean this?"

He unstrapped a watch, and passed it over.

"Yes, that's the same one!"

"That belongs to my twin brother. He gave it to me to keep for him before he went on his last hush-hush job."

"Oh, I see."

The other held out his hand for the watch. "Well, my general has been put on half-pay, so I am back footslogging once more."

"But your brother, whom I saw in the Roebuck, told me that he was an A.D.C. to a general," persisted Phillip.

"Ah, he played many parts—it was his job, you see! Rehearsing, no doubt!"

"I see," said Phillip, still puzzled. He was sure it was the same man. "Then it must have been your brother who ordered the local battalion of territorials to parade on Blackheath one Saturday afternoon?"

"Quite possibly. Did it pass off uneventfully?"

"Well, the staff wallah rode up to inspect the territorials on a horse hired from a greengrocer named Soal, and spruced everyone in the uniform of a G.S.O. 2 from the War Office!"

"Sounds just like Aubrey," confided the other. "He used to do things like that, to perfect the art of deception. Rehearsing, as I said. Probably doing the same thing in Hunland at this moment, as a German staff officer." He moved nearer to Phillip and said between his teeth, "Not a word to anyone, mind. I need hardly remind you that under D.O.R.A. all the activities of the secret service are very hush-hush. Between ourselves Aubrey *is* now in Germany, trying to find out the plans of the coming attack."

He said all this so smoothly and confidentially that Phillip felt ashamed that he had any suspicions. All the same, he believed that Wilkins was inventing a yarn. And when he said, with a slight deference in his voice, "I say old thing, I can't very well go on parade in this kit, can I? How about a spot of leave, to get a new uniform?" Phillip knew that he was a sprucer.

"How long d'you want?"

"My tailor might run me up a pair of regulation knickerbockers in, say, four days?"

To see what Wilkins would propose next, Phillip said, "Everyone wears riding breeches now. All you need is a pair of marching boots, and some puttees."

"But marching boots must be made to measure, old thing. I've got flat feet, I'm ashamed to say. I need special reinforced steel arches to my insteps. I suppose you're not wanting a transport officer, are you, by any chance?"

"We've got no transport, no horses anyway. They bring our supplies by lorry."

"Then I must go up and see Lobb, my bootmaker."

"There's a good bootmaker in the town, here."

"But will he give credit, old thing? And can you personally recommend him? Has he the latest orthopaedic knowledge? I'd be no use to the regiment if my feet gave way." He went to a leather hold-all, opened it, and lifted out a cock pheasant by the neck. "Shot a week after the season closed, I'm ashamed to say, but it's yours if you'll accept it. From our Norfolk coverts, don't you know."

Yes, I don't think, said Phillip to himself, as he hid the bird behind some files. He would also ask for weekend leave; it would be a surprise to turn up at home with a pheasant. "Thanks," he said. "I'll see the Adjutant right away." He returned to make out a half-fare voucher. "You've got until 9 a.m. parade, Tuesday morning."

"I'm most grateful to you." But the glance of Devereux-Wilkins rested with some regret upon the tail-feathers of the cock pheasant, as though thinking that it needn't have been given away. Then, to muffle his thoughts, he assumed a musical-comedy air, put on his hat with the suggestion of the bold Beatty-angle, waggled his cane, seized his hold-all (which contained, among other things, a pair of ankle boots and puttees) and with a "So long, old thing," set off back to Leicester Square, to the girl on whose immoral earnings he lived comfortably.

Hetty's faithful charwoman, Mrs. Feeney, was carrying, as a present to the mis'us—a frozen Australian rabbit. It was nearly as large as a cat, and broke some of the stitches of her best bag of black American cloth. It took the place of the bottle of porter, for she would be leaving for her room in a terrace house in Rushy Green at 12.30, and would treat herself to a pint of porter on the way home. Mrs. Maddison was welcome to the rabbit, which she had won in a raffle at the Mission Hall, for 2d. Filled up with happiness at the thought of the mis'us' face, Mrs. Feeney stopped at a butcher's shop near the Free Library to buy herself a couple of pig's trotters, her favourite food. It being early, the shop just opened, housewives were not yet about in any numbers. She stooped to pat a dog with wagging tail and appealing eyes outside the shop. The starving animal crept after her across the sawdust. Mrs. Feeney put down her bag to find her purse—a Highland soldier's sporran with the hairs cut off—suspended for safety between skirt and top petticoat (she wore four, for warmth), and was counting out six coppers for the trotters—a terrible price, she thought, my word, somebody's getting the money—when she saw the dog dragging the Australian rabbit—which for months had been flattened with five hundred others in a wooden box, frozen for the voyage—out of her bag. Then the dog was cantering away in the direction of the Randiswell Recreation Ground, pursued by three other dogs.

She was still very unhappy about it (for Mis'us had not accepted the pig's trotters) half an hour after noon, when she left with a florin for her morning's work; but her mood changed to one of contentment when she saw Master Phillip coming out of Randiswell Station, with the tail feathers of a pheasant sticking out of his haversack.

"My, that's a fine bird, Master Phillip! Your mother will be pleased. Only be careful, don't let anyone take it off'f you, will you now? There's all sorts about nowadays! Oh my, the bag's moving! Is the pore thing still alive?"

"Very much so, Mrs. Feeney. It flew into my carriage on the way up, and I caught it!" He opened one end of the haversack and the black nostrils of Sprat poked out.

"Good heavings, Master Phil, what sort of fessan is that?"

"An Oo-ja pheasant, Mrs. Feeney. It runs on four legs, eats pepper, and flies backwards to cool its exhaust. Look, here he is, Sprat!" The terrier struggled out, and jumped around before beginning to classify the lesser smells of a London suburb.

"How about a glass with me in the Railway, Mrs. Feeney?" They were standing by the late Victorian garish ex-gin palace outside which, late on Saturday nights, in boyhood, Phillip had sometimes seen poor children, without shoes or stockings, huddled together while waiting for their parents.

"Oh, I daren't, Master Phil! Whatever would people say?"

"It's all right, Mrs. Feeney. 'The slums have died in Flanders', as my friend 'Spectre' West once wrote to me. I told you about him, remember? Eight wound-stripes, one eye, and one hand, Mrs. Feeney! His face a black patch, his body a map of scars! Come on, let's drink his health!" They went into the Railway, where he ordered two half-pints of Burton.

"I don't know whether I ought to say it, Master Phil, but I have heard that your father is thinking of joining up. They're taking men up to fifty-five now, Master Phil."

"Yes, I did hear about that, Mrs. Feeney."

"It isn't for the likes of me to remark on it, so you won't say I mentioned it, will you, Master Phil?"

"Of course not, my one and only dear Mrs. Feeney! Have another Burton?"

"No thank you, Master Phil. I must be going. It's been very nice seeing you looking so well. I'm sure your Mother will be pleased. Good day, sir."

When he arrived at his home, Phillip left Sprat in the haversack out of sight, and went in with the bird.

"There now, Doris, my prayer to Saint Anthony has been answered!" declared Hetty, looking at her younger daughter.

"Oh, Mother, do you really think that saints shoot pheasants for people," said Phillip.

"The ravens brought food for Elijah in the wilderness anyway," retorted Doris.

"I expect that Elijah found out where the crows were getting wild currants, that's all."

"Ah, my son, 'there are more things in heaven and earth——' you know."

"I can pluck it and draw it," said Doris. "I learned to do it when I worked on the land last summer."

"This bird was shot last January; it's probably petrified by now. I really meant it to go in a glass case, Mother. My proper contribution to the larder is in my haversack outside. I didn't bring it in, because it's rather high. Just a moment."

He put the haversack on the kitchen floor.

"A rolypoly spotted-dog pudding from the mess! It only wants heating up," as he opened the flap.

The little dog's appearance was greeted with delight, mingled with consternation from Hetty. "What will Father say, I wonder?"

"Anyway, we know what Father's best boy says, Mum," as a growl from the cat sounded under the table. "I won't risk Father's displeasure, so I'm going to ask Mrs. Neville to look after Sprat for me when I go out shortly."

"Oh, Phillip, are you really going again?"

"Now don't worry, Mum. It will probably be a soft job at the base. So you see, Father mustn't be allowed to join up, for apart from anything else, he's the breadwinner. If he went, the office wouldn't pay his salary, as they are paying mine. Now I think I'll just dash down to see Mrs. Neville. I won't stay. I'll go down and try and get some sprouts to go with the pheasant."

"Don't be long, dear, will you?"

"I'll go with you, Phil," said Doris, knowing her mother's dread of Phillip having too much to drink.

"Yes, do, Doris."

"I hope I won't meet the mad soldier again."

"All soldiers are mad!"

As they went down the road together Doris told her brother that she had gone for a walk on the Hill, after working at her History papers, and on the way up the gully a stranger had acted rather queerly. He had stared at her in a peculiar manner, she said, and then looked as though he was about to speak. But all that happened was that his right hand, with fingers stretched, had gone to hide his mouth, with its twisted lips, while he also bent his head.

"He made a sort of clicking noise. Then he followed me up to the Hill, at a distance, and when I turned to go towards him, he moved away across the grass, to the bandstand."

"Some lonely devil on leave, I expect, Doris. No need to get the wind up."

The greengrocer had some sprouts hidden in the room behind his shop; he gave a pound of these to Phillip, saying, "You deserve them, after all your time out in France."

"Oh, I've had a very good war, taking it all round, Mr. Soal."

As they rounded the corner of Hillside Road, Doris said, "There's the mad soldier, outside the Rolls' house!"

"He's a cadet, with that white band around his cap. I'll go and have a word with him."

The cadet sauntered away as they approached; Phillip went on up the road when his sister had gone in with the sprouts. He returned soon afterwards and said, as he brought the visitor into the house, "Let me present Mr. Willoughby, Mother. And this is my sister."

The young man stuttered, after he had saluted Hetty, that he had been a friend of Percy Pickering, and had c-c-come to see his cousin M-M-Miss Maddison, of whom P-Percy had often s-s-spoken. Again the long fingers fluttered to hide the mouth convulsive with words, as he told them that he had been Percy's best friend, and Percy had asked him before the battle of Flers to get in touch with Miss Maddison if he didn't come through, and give her his love. Mr. Willoughby went on to stutter that he himself had been hit later, and had spent many months in hospital.

All this took some time to get out; after which Doris left the room and went upstairs. When after some minutes she did not come down from her bedroom, Phillip, who thought that she should have remained out of courtesy, said to his mother, "Mr. Willoughby and I will go for a walk, and try and get something more for lunch. Also, I must ask Mrs. Neville if she will look after Sprat for me, and there's the question of dog biscuits."

"Don't be long, will you, Phillip?" She remembered not to say 'dear' just in time. "Your father will be home early today." Thank goodness, she thought, that Dr. Dashwood had recently got married, and appeared to have lost his terrible habit of drinking whiskey, and giving large glasses of it to young soldiers.

Yet she need not have worried, she told Papa in the afternoon. The two young men came back in plenty of time, with an extra loaf, half a pound of Cheddar cheese, a large tin of sardines and half a pound of butter, all put into Phillip's haversack by Hern the grocer, who would not hear of payment, so Phillip was going to send him a box of cigars by post from London.

"It turned out better than I expected, Papa. You know how Dickie does not like to see the children's friends in the house, at least at meal times, when he comes home tired. However, he was in a good mood; it was quite like old times."

Thomas Turney wondered what old times, and was about to make some sardonic remark when he checked the thought. Hetty went on happily, "The four young people have gone up to London to see *Romance* at the Lyric Theatre, and Phillip has promised not to be late. Dickie remarked that he saw a great improvement in Phillip's whole bearing and attitude. He seemed much more manly, he said. Oh, I knew everything would come right one day!"

"How old is Phillip now, Hetty?" asked Thomas Turney's elder sister.

"He will be twenty-three in April, Aunt Marian."

"Dear me," said the old lady. "It seems only yesterday that he had his twenty-first birthday party! Time seems to go so slowly, and then suddenly, before we know where we are, it is gone." She suppressed a sigh.

Miss Marian Turney was doing her best to do nothing to upset Tom. Nowadays he was inclined to be so critical of very small things about her. She had been in his house too long, she knew; but where else could she go? Her income was but £8 a quarter, from her father's will. She sat primly upright, ready to speak only if spoken to, as in childhood three-quarters of a century before.

"I asked Phillip particularly to come straight home after the theatre, with the two girls," Hetty was saying. "Dickie is not on duty this week-end, and badly needs a good night's rest. He can never settle down, you know, until he knows that everyone is in bed."

The three came back at half-past eleven. Richard had not waited up for them, but lay on his bed in his blue-flowered dressing gown, twenty-first birthday present from his two younger sisters, Viccy and Dora, in the 'eighties. His carpet slippers waited side by side neatly below the brass bed, ready to be drawn out as soon as three pairs of feet had gone down the passage. When three bedroom doors had been shut, only then would he dare go downstairs and shoot upper and lower bolts of the front door, put the chain across, and turn off the gas-cock in the coal cellar—for safety, should a bomb drop on the house.

Only then would he be able to feel easy, despite the chronic anxiety of his mind aggravated by insufficient food.

In the morning Elizabeth, the elder daughter, said to her mother, "I don't like the look of Bill Willoughby—that awful stutter! There's something wrong with him—he can never look you in the eyes. Like Phillip—shifty, if you ask me!"

All types and ages of junior officers were now reporting to the Orderly Room. Gone were the days of one-man medical boards at Caxton Hall, with their one, two, and three months of sick leave. Three weeks at home after hospital was now the maximum; then back to duty.

On the Monday afternoon a trio of senior subalterns reported to Phillip at the same time: the eldest an Ulsterman, with an arm cut off above the elbow; the other two were Gaultshire men, one with a red weal zigzagging across his forehead and a careful manner of enunciation, as though his tongue were a little thick; the third had a glass eye, looking as though it were about to fall out of the raggedly healed skin of the socket, while the live eye stared fierce as a falcon's.

Phillip wrote the names in the Arrivals book—Docherty, Tabor, and Hedges—all three B2—before taking them in to the colonel, after knocking on the door to ask if Lord S. would see them. Lord S. was always available for such visits.

After they had gone, Phillip was called in to take down at dictation a confidential report by the Colonel upon an officer who had overstayed his leave by two weeks, and then had deserted. He had been arrested in plain clothes by the Metropolitan Police in London, handed over to the Provost Marshal's office at Horse Guards, and brought down under close arrest to Landguard Camp. There he awaited, without his belt but in uniform, a General Court Martial. One of Phillip's duties was to visit him daily in his quarters to ask if there were any complaints, and to replace the officer-guard of the past twenty-four hours.

While Lord Satchville was dictating the excellent record of the officer before his unfortunate attachment to a young woman a year or two his senior, who before her marriage from the musical comedy stage was an actress much remarked for her skill in suggesting innocence and charm, Captain Henniker-Sudley knocked and entered, saying, "General Mowbray, sir!" and withdrawing, ushered in a figure with inflexibly authoritative face that Phillip remembered as belonging to the colonel of the 1st battalion at Loos.

He stood up, and with notebook and pencil, prepared to leave the room, following the adjutant; but Lord Satchville after greeting his guest turned to Phillip and said to the General, "You will remember Maddison, who took command of the First battalion after Captain West had been hit, and captured the Lone Tree position, Mowbray——?"

"Yes," replied the General. "How do you do," as he held out his hand.

Phillip was still glowing with satisfaction, while typing a request to all company commanders for a nominal roll of men who before enlistment were (*a*) boiler-riveters and (*b*) internal combustion engine crankshaft forgers, when Capt. Henniker-Sudley came to him and said, "The Colonel wants you to make notes of the information he is about to be given by General Mowbray, from which you will write a summary afterwards."

Phillip had done a similar job before; and entering the room quietly, without speaking seated himself at a side table, notebook and pencil ready.

Colonel Mowbray, now a temporary Major-General commanding a division on the Western Front, told Lord Satchville that the order coming from Whitehall to reduce all infantry brigades from four to three battalions was considered by all commanders in the field to be a serious mistake, particularly as it was confirmed that preparations for a German attack on the greatest scale were well-advanced.

The voice, grave and modulated, declared that the newly-constituted infantry brigades would not, in all probability, be given time in which to practise and learn the new tactics required with one battalion acting as both support and reserve to two battalions in line. He said that the infantry required training in the tactics of open warfare, but every day and every night large working parties had to be found for the Sappers, to augment the pioneers and labour battalions working in the new Battle Zones now being prepared along the fourteen miles of line recently taken over from the French.

"What are the Battle Zones, Mowbray?"

"One might call them redans extended to enclose sited defensive positions of between four thousand square yards and ten thousand square yards in extent, according to the lie of the land. Each redoubt is self-contained, with ammunition and food stores for the infantry and machine gunners, protected by barbed wire."

"And the preparation of these Battle Zones is only now being undertaken, and mainly by fighting soldiers? Is not the Labour Corps in sufficient strength for this particular work?"

"That is the crux of the matter. For their own reasons, the Cabinet seems deliberately to be withholding reinforcements from the Western Front, while retaining well over a million men here in England, according to Freddy Maurice at the War House."

"When I was in the Lords the other day, Mowbray, I got the impression from Derby that the Cabinet has not altogether ruled out the possibility of a series of raids in strength, coming over from the Belgian coast under cover of darkness, or fog."

"I cannot say about that, of course, but I have it from Charteris at G.H.Q. that agents have identified forty-two German divisions rehearsing, behind barrages of live shell, fifty miles back from the German line. The rehearsals are for a land attack. Then there is the significant fact that von Hutier, who carried out that most successful attack at Riga against the Russians, has been put in opposite Hubert Gough's Fifth Army. It is similar country, down by the marshes of the Somme, to that at Riga. There, of course, von Hutier relied on surprise, keeping his assault troops seventy miles behind his front, and only putting them into the forward areas a week or so before the attack, which was preceded by a six-hour bombardment only."

"Where did you say von Hutier is now?"

"Opposite the junction of our Fifth Army with the French Sixth lying between the Oise and the Aisne."

Phillip found General Mowbray's description of how von Hutier's presence on the Western Front had become detected so interesting that he ceased to take notes, and merely listened. He would remember it better that way. Apparently the name Oskar von Hutier had been spotted in the correspondence columns of a local Königsberg newspaper smuggled with other newspapers into Sweden. Von Hutier had written a letter of condolence to the parents of a Pomeranian Grenadier, attached to the German Air Force, who had been killed *in France*. From that little item Intelligence had deduced the possibility of an attack similar to that across the marshes at Riga, which had broken through the Russian front and ended the war there.

That night Phillip wrote in his journal.

Pomeranian Grenadier, otherwise Prussian Guardsman! What romance in the very sound of the words! I see again the Prussian Guardsmen lying dead in the woods beside the Menin Road in November 1914, some on their backs, one with a knee up, bare cropped head, waxen face, large yellow moustache.

Pomeranian Grenadier, face later the colour of pomegranate, that leathery, unsatisfactory fruit bitten into in boyhood, neither sweet nor sour, looking so juicy but hard-pipped, a cheating fruit.

Pomeranian Grenadier, lying dead in France, gone for ever and ever, while proud parents, hiding grief in *Vur Vaterland und Freiheit*, somewhere on the Baltic coast, had done what my mother did in 1914, when she took one of my own letters to *The Daily Express*. They printed it, but failed to keep their promise to return the letter. I was critical of Mother for not making a copy in the first place, saying that such souvenirs would one day be valuable.

Pomeranian Grenadier . . . Prussian parents maintained by pride because the great Herr General Oberst Oskar von Hutier had written to them about their son, once a boy perhaps living all his true life in thoughts of wild birds in the pine forests along the ice-bound shores of the Baltic, waiting for the spring migrants to arrive, and then the flowers, behind hot dry sand dunes of the coast.

Pomeranian Grenadier . . . lying under a wooden cross, while Mother and Father walk, in black clothes, side by side to the offices of the local paper in the Hanseatic town; and thereby *unwittingly* give away the plan of the last hope of *Deutschland Treu*, and perhaps indirectly cause the defeat of their country: for of course the Alleyman will come over in the usual mass formation and go down under the cross-fire of thousands of machine-guns in the Battle Zones, not to mention the counter-barrages of the artillery.

After writing romantically, Phillip composed a summary of the talk between the two Great Men of the Regiment, typing it out on one of the massive Orderly Room typewriters, with two fingers, like trying to play chopsticks on the piano. While he was finishing this the corporal on duty by the telephone came in and gave him a written message just in from Eastern Command.

Fourteen officers below field rank were to be detailed to proceed overseas within forty-eight hours. This was urgent: it wanted twenty minutes to the dinner bugle. He hurried over to Henniker-Sudley in Manor Terrace, and showed him the signal. Together they went to the Orderly Room, and selected the first names on the roster, which were then typed out by the corporal. The list was signed, Phillip took it to the ante-room and pinned it on the green-baize board.

The following officers are to report immediately to the Orderly Room for railway warrants to London, and to report to R.T.O. Victoria Station at 10 a.m. on Thursday morning, 28 February.

Subalterns clustered round the board, reading the names in silence. Then they were gone, and a silence fell upon the ante-room. He was left alone, with a feeling that the fates of those on the board were already determined, beyond the silence of the room, beyond England, beyond the trench lines in France. A shiver up his spine, the hair of his neck twitched spiky; he hurried out to sign the railway warrants in the orderly room.

Among the names selected by Captain Henniker-Sudley was Devereux-Wilkins. Wilkins left for the night train for Ipswich with the others; but at 6 p.m. the next evening he was back at camp. In his haversack was a large boiled lobster. With this he called on the doctor, a seedy old fellow who had been a professional *locum tenens* in peace time, lacking a regular practice owing to ineptitude and early waste of substance. The M.O. accepted the lobster, and gave Wilkins a chit to the orderly room, declaring that he was suffering from bleeding haemorrhoids and should go to hospital for an operation.

With a feeling that he would meet his fate, whatever it was, Phillip asked Sudley if he might go in Wilkins's place. The adjutant spoke to Lord Satchville, who agreed.

"Inform Eastern Command of the change, and don't forget to send the address of your next of kin, Phillip."

Phillip wrote down the name of his father, but gave the address of his cousin, *Brickhill House, Beau Brickhill, Gaultshire.* This, he told himself, was out of consideration for Mother, should he be killed; she would not then hear directly by telegram. But while he knew it was not the real reason, he did not know the true reason, which was that while he could face the idea of death in battle, he could not face within himself the memories of his formative years.

The last train left Landguard station at 9.15 p.m. He decided not to go home, but to spend the evening in the mess, as it was Guest Night; he would catch the early morning train from Ipswich.

After dinner there was a binge in the ante-room when the Colonel and his guest, Commodore Sir Reginald Tyrrwhitt of the Harwich Forces, a tall man with gaunt face and immense bushy eyebrows, had left. Tray after tray, loaded with glasses of hot Irish whiskey, sugar, and lemon, were brought in by the waiters. Songs were roared out around the piano, including one from a new London revue.

Over there, over there, send the word, send the word, over there!
That the Yanks are coming, the Yanks are coming,
The drums rum-tumming everywhere:
So prepare, say a prayer,
Send the word, send the word to beware!
We'll be over, we're coming over,
And we won't come back till it's over, over there!

Lie-a-beds in cubicles were ragged, wrestling matches became rugger scrums for waste-paper baskets, which were torn to withies. Docherty, the Ulsterman, used his stump-arm like a blunted rhino-horn, keeping all others at a distance. One captain, who had never been overseas since being gazetted early in 1915, an unpopular man with chocolate-brown eyes, was rolled in the carpet and carried half-way to the incinerator by bloodshot-eyed subalterns howling like red Indians. While resting with the carpet load—Captain Despard had accepted it all without struggle—someone suggested the sea, so the carpet went over the shingle and Despard was thrown into the waves. Phillip, who had liked Despard's conversation about music and poetry until something in his ingratiating manner had put him off, suddenly realized that it was the almost naked cowardice in the dark eyes, affecting others, which was responsible for Despard's unpopularity. His own sympathy had been alienated because of his own hidden fear; this, as he realized it, changed to sympathy, so when the poor devil was swung out of the carpet into the sea, Phillip plunged in after him, pretending that it was all a rag. Afterwards he took him into his billet, where Despard, teeth chattering behind fixed smile, got out of his wet uniform, while Phillip made a telescope of the rest of the old magazines up the chimney and set fire to the base. The room flickered, the chimney roared, caught fire, a final blast of lilac and yellow flames rose six feet above the chimney-pot which exploded and a shrapnel-rattling of fragments came down on the roof.

Meanwhile Captain Despard's servant had brought him a change of uniform, and when both had gone away Phillip was sick.

The next morning, with half-dried tunic and slacks wrapped in a groundsheet within his valise, and wearing a tommy's tunic with stars on the shoulder straps, he caught the early train to Ipswich. From Liverpool Street station he sent off two telegrams, one to Lt.-Col. West, 2nd Gaultshire Regt., B.E.F., saying he was on his way; the other to his father at Head Office, telling him that he was going overseas, and love to all at home.

At the beginning of March the old men on the Hill usually met of a morning in the wood-framed brick shelter near the crest, with its view of the Crystal Palace. Spring was on the way, and the talk about food was more hopeful. The new rationing system allowed 15 oz. of meat, 5 of bacon, 4 of butter or margarine per person per week. And, with rationing, prices were now controlled.

"You know," said Thomas Turney. "Just as many firms before this war made their profit out of waste, so a lot of these rascals have made their fortunes out of farthings, which they don't produce, blaming the shortage of coin—11¾*d.* for a sheep's head, 1*s.* 11¾*d.* for unspecified scraps of meat per pound, 'three and eleven three' for steak—now thank the powers that be, all that is a thing of the past."

The fixed prices for mutton, lamb, and beef were 1*s.* 10*d.* the pound, steak 2*s.* 2*d.*

Another of the regulars in the shelter was a Mr. Warbeck, understood to be something to do with Admiralty. Thomas Turney did not think much of the fellow, a man about ten years his junior, a mere sixty-nine or so. He was a bit of a fop, dressed invariably in grey frock coat and trousers, grey spats, grey cravat held by pearl pin, starched wing collar, and white slip to his waistcoat. Grey eyes, bushy eyebrows, a precise manner of speech and the sweeping grey moustaches went with the rig-out of fine Edwardian gentlemen—but he crowned it all with a black bowler hat, not exactly *de rigeur*, even allowing for the war. But it was the fellow's know-all manner, with which he made pronouncements of odd facts he had read in *The Daily Telegraph*, and gave out as his own, that riled Thomas Turney, who had to listen with an appearance of attention to what he himself had already read in that paper after breakfast.

What would it be this morning? For Warbeck had taken a piece of folded paper from one pocket, steel-rimmed spectacles from another, and after rubbing the lenses on his grey silk pocket handkerchief, was about to hold forth. Clearing his throat for attention, he said, looking along the three sides of the shelter,

"It may interest you, Mr. Turney, to know that approximately fifteen million farthings were issued by the Royal Mint last year—thrice the number issued in the year immediately preceding the outbreak of war."

"Extraordinary," said Thomas Turney. "Now can you tell us, from your experience gained at the Admiralty, how the Food Minister arrived at his total of 9,380 tons of weekly bread waste we see on all the hoardings just now?"

Mr. Warbeck was ready with a reply to this attempt to turn his flank. "I know nothing about the so-called Ministry of Food, Mr. Turney, since my work concerns the compilation of Tables of Logarithms for the use of navigators, published by Mr. Potter, for the Admiralty; but, to reply to your particular question, the jumped-up bigwigs and jacks-in-office in Whitehall have to justify themselves as bureaucrats, and also they have to fill up their days somehow. But my goodness, have you considered the utter idiocy of issuing forty-two tons of farthings in the past eleven months, merely to accommodate the petty profiteers who no longer trouble to offer a packet of pins or a box of safety matches in change—and this at a time, mark you, when there is a serious shortage of copper for the driving bands of shells! Winston Churchill at the Ministry of Munitions would, one can hardly doubt, be most gratified to lay his hands on that copper!"

Then, before Mr. Turney could make a frontal attack on the tedious subject of waste bread, Mr. Warbeck turned to someone across the shelter, who had been sitting quietly attentive, and went on, "Tell me, Mr. McDonagh, you are in Fleet Street, is there any connexion between the sacking of 'Wullie' Robertson, our late worthy Chief of the Imperial General Staff, and a ranker to boot—or perhaps one should say to be booted, in the sense of his having been hoofed out—and the fact that Lord Derby has been kicked out of the War Office?"

There was modesty in the eyes behind the gold-rimmed spectacles of the reporter as he spoke, in a voice pleasant with Irish brogue. "I am not on the political side of my paper, so I can hardly speak with authority, Mr. Warbeck, but perhaps it is giving away no secrets when I say that it is generally known in the Street that the considerable friction—which has long existed between the Prime Minister and the Generals—has come to a head. In fact, Sir William Robertson's removal as C.I.G.S. was considered to be only a preliminary to greater changes—had the P.M. got his way."

"Oh," said Mr. Warbeck. "Do I understand that remark to include the possibility that Haig himself may go?"

"That I cannot say, sir. But it is, I think, no exaggeration to say that Lloyd George did consider the replacement of Haig by Plumer—after Haig had refused to take orders from an Extra-ordinary Committee the P.M. wanted to set up to direct the war in France. The Field Marshal is said to have replied—and quite rightly in my opinion—that the man on the spot must decide—not a round-table conference—particularly at a time when the German troops have been set free from the Russian front, and are now known to be arriving in great numbers in France."

This information had a quietening effect. Then the discreet Mr. McDonagh turned to Thomas Turney and said, "How is your grandson, Mr. Turney? When last you spoke of him, he had just returned from the battle of Cambrai."

"Oh Phillip, yes, he has now gone back to France—for the fifth time."

"For the fifth time! He must be possessed of unusual moral fibre, Mr. Turney! Oddly enough, it has often been shown in this war that it is the sensitive type of civilian soldier who has shown himself to possess the greater staying power."

"Yes, yes," breathed Mr. Bigge, a near neighbour of Thomas Turney, a quiet inoffensive man. "Pray proceed, Mr. McDonagh."

"Recently I had to report an Investiture at Buckingham Palace, for my paper. I made it my purpose to take a position near to those who were to receive the Victoria Cross. What, I wondered, was the common denominator in the expressions of these proved heroes? I could determine nothing! There was no characteristic expression, that I could discover. Indeed, I could not help wondering—as I saw the diffidence on some faces, the introspection in the eyes of others—what *was* the secret of courage. One asks oneself—How far was any one man responsible for the quality of moral fibre, or the lack of it, in his make-up? Abraham Lincoln—you may recall—was reluctant to sanction the execution of soldiers for so-called cowardice in the American Civil War. He used to say that a man could not always control his legs. 'How do I know that I should not run away myself?' he once asked."

"Now I come to think of it," said Mr. Warbeck, "did not your grandson, Mr. Turney, once tell us, in this very place, that he had run away at the battle of Messines?"

Thomas Turney felt this remark to be offensive. He decided to ignore it. Mr. McDonagh said, "Yes, I remember that occasion, Mr. Warbeck. I thought then, and I think now, that the remark derived from an unformed sense of courage. And—incidentally—from a condition of self-awareness not usually present in one so young!"

"That's a point of view that I feel Shakespeare would have approved," replied Thomas Turney, leaning the weight of his shoulders on hands clasping the lemon stick. "The boy's mother is a brave woman, generous to a fault where others are concerned. I think that when such people have learned to stand up for themselves——" He checked his words; while the hands, their veined backs delicately wrinkled like cooling wax, clasped more tightly the handle of the stick he had brought back from Greece half a lifetime before. "I wonder——," and he fell into reverie. From thinking of Dickie, and of the voice heard so often in complaint of Hetty next door, his memory led him to scenes of his own behaviour towards his dead wife, and inevitably to the awful occasion when he had knocked her down, and poor young Hetty as well. How then could one judge others?

Voices about him were no longer heard. His breathing seemed to struggle with the congestion of so many broken pictures within his mind. When he came out of the chaos of reverie Mr. McDonagh's voice was saying gently, "Perhaps bravery lies in the blood, and courage is of the mind. Then again, there is the tempering of bravery by courage, which is what we call valour." The voice held a note of diffidence, for this modest man had been quoting from his second leader written after the Investiture. "But after all is said and done, who can judge of such things? We are as Nature made us. No man can escape from himself all the time. He can, of course, raise the best of himself to the forefront, by the aid of prayer, as many in this war have discovered." "The mother is the maker of the child's mind, I fancy," soliloquised Thomas Turney. "Yet there comes a stage when the young man develops traits apparent in his father, which may conflict with the other side of his nature——." The ragged voice was knotted tight by the congestion of breathing. Again his thoughts were devastating. Scenes arose of his eldest son Charley, of the sad quarrels of that summer of seven years ago, Charley opposing him in defence of his mother, so violently that Sarah, God rest her soul, had had a stroke and died. Charley had inherited his own hot temper, how then might Charley be blamed? He sighed, and heard McDonagh saying, "It seems to me, that it is the courage of the mind which produces the great soldier—the man who rises to all occasions under ordeal. But in the last resort, all is fortuitous, it would seem. Without proper food, without sufficient sleep, where would the hero be?" "Ah," said Thomas Turney. "There is little between a man's best and worst but a platter of food!"

"Thank you, thank you, gentlemen," murmured Mr. Bigge, rising with thoughts of his noonday cup of hot Bovril. "It has all been most interesting." He inclined his head in a series of little bobs. "Now I wish you all a very good day, gentlemen!" The sun had gone behind clouds. Thomas Turney felt chilled; and thinking with weariness of the New Will he must make to include Charley, he followed Mr. Bigge down the gully to his fireside in Hillside Road, where, confound it, he would find only his sister Marian, whose silences were almost as unnerving as her pointless remarks.

Chapter 3

MOGGERS

From both sides of the carriage were to be seen, for mile after mile, the wastes of the old battlefield of the Somme. Tens of thousands of wooden crosses stood out of flattened grasses which scarcely concealed shell-holes, edge to edge, extending to all horizons. Not even the brick rubble heaps of villages remained; all had been cleared for road mending. At last the train, running very slowly beside an empty canal bed which, Phillip informed his two companions, must be the Canal du Nord, stopped with a hiss of steam as though it were expiring, followed by a shudder of groans and jolts. They were in the middle of depleted rectangles of every kind of material—iron screw-pickets, rolls of barbed wire, wood, coal, picks, shovels, and vast dumps of salvage. The R.T.O. said that a waggon from their battalion was waiting for them. How far was it? About three miles. Was there a Y.M.C.A. or Expeditionary Force Canteen anywhere? To an E.F.C. marquee they promptly went, Phillip ordering a 5-franc bottle of champagne.

"It's the best way, to get merry and bright on coming to a new crush. One doesn't want to arrive blotto, of course, but just enough to warm the cockles of the old heart," he remarked, as they went out. "How far to camp, driver?"

"The White City, sir? Three mile, as makes no odds."

"But the R.T.O. said it was Corunna Camp."

"Everyone round here calls it the White City, sir. There's ten thousand Toe-rags—Chinks, Sugar Babies, Macaronies, every sort of dago, as well as old Frogs and Jerry prisoners."

"What are they all doing?"

"Making roads, and diggin' 'Aig's 'Indenburg Line, sir."

The braying of mules succeeded the varied human tongues of the White City as the waggon left behind the rows of hutments, and came to acres of horse lines. They pushed through to white-washed flints bordering the road, and arrived at a yellow board on which the regimental badge, a horned wild ox within a star, was painted in black.

Having reported to the battalion orderly room, Phillip was told by the sergeant in charge that only the Quartermaster was in camp. "Major Marsden, Second-in-command, has gone up the line to see the Commanding Officer, sir."

"Is Major Marsden short and thick, with dark hair? I met a Lieutenant Marsden at Loos in '15 with the first battalion."

"That's correct, sir. I was lance-corporal in Captain West's company in the first battalion at Loos, and remember when you took command and led us round the flank past Bois Carré."

"Oh, that little joy ride . . . Weren't you Lance-corporal Tonks?"

"That's right, sir!" The sergeant's face showed pleasure.

Phillip was shaking hands with him, when brassy noises came from an adjoining hut.

"Jerry instruments, sir. We scrounged them out of a dugout at Masnieres last November. Colonel Moggerhanger is trainin' new bandsmen."

"*Colonel* Moggerhanger?" For a moment he felt devastated. Could it be that 'Spectre' West had left the battalion? Sergeant Tonks was reassuring.

"The Quartermaster, sir, has served forty years with the R'g'mint, 'listed in 'seventy-seven as a band-boy, sir. The storeman is sewing on his stars over there. Promotion come through last night, sir."

Phillip went to speak to the storeman, who held up a jacket coloured by many ribands, headed by those of D.S.O. and D.C.M. "I think we'd better find Colonel Moggerhanger, just to let him know we've arrived," he said to Tonks.

"You'll find him in the next hut, sir. The bandsmen are trying out those Jerry instruments. Jerry pinched ours in the counter-attack, sir, at Graincourt."

"Just like this war! We get Jerry's band, and he pinches ours! Come on, chaps, let's go next door!"

"Well, sir, if you'll excuse me a moment——" the sergeant paused. "You see, sir, the Quartermaster can be a bit of a caution, sir. His discharge was due from the 1st battalion when they were ordered to Italy just before Christmas, and he was on the way to Blighty when orders come through cancelling all time-served ranks going home. The Quartermaster is liable to be a little uncertain in temper as a consequence."

Outside the adjoining semicircular shelter of rust and tarred wood Phillip hesitated. "All the same, I think we ought to make our arrival known to him, as a matter of courtesy," he said to the two junior officers with him. His hand was on the handle when the door opened and a big man came out. Phillip stepped back; his salute was ignored as the Quartermaster strode away, muttering curses.

"That's that!" said Phillip.

It was five o'clock. The three had had little food since dinner the night before at Boulogne. "He's the only officer here, apparently, so let's ask him where we can get some grub."

They came upon the Quartermaster talking to what looked

like the transport sergeant. The three saluted again, and Phillip, as senior, went forward. The Quartermaster continued to ignore him. So he saluted once more before turning away to find the cookhouse. "Char will probably be going."

When at length they found the cookhouse, there was Moggerhanger before them. Again Phillip's salute was ignored. They walked on. "This is all rot, you chaps! He may be an honorary lieutenant-colonel, but dammit, we should be treated as guests! Lord Satchville wouldn't behave like this! Leave it to me. You two wait here."

He went back to the cookhouse, and standing at attention, cried out "Sir!" before presenting the Quartermaster with a salute delivered with elbow parallel with the ground, lower arm stiff and rigid and hand vibrating level with right ear in the Guards' manner. The Quartermaster responded with a bellowing cough, followed by hoicking to clear his throat.

"Lieutenant Maddison, reporting for duty, sir!"

The Quartermaster spat into a lime-washed dustbin by the cookhouse door. "Pick the bones out of that," he said.

Phillip took this to mean that they could help themselves, as he led the way into the cookhouse. There they drank sweet tea and wolfed hunks of bread, butter and jam; and feeling optimistic left to look round the camp. On their way they passed the hut in which the band was apparently playing rag-time. Round the corner came the Quartermaster. They walked on pretending not to see him, and had gone a few yards when a voice roared out behind, "Come 'ere, you!"

Phillip turned and went back. "You want me, sir?"

"Yes, you, you long streak of piss on a lamp-post! Don't you know you salute a superior officer when you pass one?"

"Yes, sir."

"Then why didn't you salute me?"

"Well, sir, I've saluted you six times already, but as you didn't take any notice——"

"How the hell d'you know I didn't take any notice? Anyway, what were you in civvy street, a Boy Scout?"

"Yes, sir!"

"All right, you saluted me six times, did you?" He saluted Phillip seven times. "Now you owe me one, you b——r!"

Phillip gave him the Boy Scout's salute.

"So you're a bloody joker, are yer? What's your name?"

"Lieutenant Maddison, reporting for duty from Landguard Camp, sir," as he saluted once more.

"God's teeth, 'ow many more times you goin' to flip about like a Bill Brown? This ain't Caterham," said the Quartermaster, in a voice suddenly mild. "You lot want some tiffin, eh? Well, come with me to the mess. D'you play bridge? Not very well? I don't play very well neither, so that makes us all square. Ker-ist, listen to that bloody din! Like a f——g cattle-yard on market day." Muttering something about showing the little cuthberts where they got off, the Quartermaster kicked open the door and at his appearance there was silence. Coming out again, he grumbled, "They can't even blow, let alone they got no bleedun kissers. I told 'em there'd be some fat lips flyin' about if they didn't get on with it. Would you believe what the little bleeders was playin' at? Seein' 'oo could first blow out the stickin' plaster and soap stuck in the 'oles made by shrapnel!"

About eight o'clock that evening, just as the four had finished dinner of fried steak and potatoes, followed by tasteless gritty prunes, the occasional booming of howitzers became a thundering that rattled the knives on the enamelled plates. Phillip opened the door and stared into a sky flashing with light. Away in the east arose red and green rockets above the calcium flares that told of some desperate endeavour between the opposing armies.

"Close that bloody door!" yelled Moggerhanger. "We don't want no eggs dropped on this f——g camp!"

Phillip shut the door; he was yet to realise that the old man's nerve had gone, that he had had too much war, having served continuously with the B.E.F. since the retreat from Le Cateau; that he had seen too many faces, hundreds of faces, pass before his eyes; and of all the many dead faces, some were now returning at odd moments, as though waiting for him to join them.

"Can you tell me what the British S.O.S. colours are for tonight, sir?"

"Ask my arse." The Quartermaster put bottle and sparklet syphon on the table. "'Ow about a rubber?" He jerked a thumb backwards. "'Elp yourselves. We don't stand on ceremony 'ere. We're the Royal Staybacks, and don't you forgit it!" They sat down. Cards were shuffled and dealt. "Your call, young feller."

Phillip passed. Allen passed. "Well, to test the feeling of the meat, one no trump," said Colonel Moggerhanger, dropping his cards face down on the blanket-covered table to light thick twist in his clay cutty.

"No bid."

Phillip was wondering what Westy was doing. "Your call, Lamp-post." From across the table acrid smoke of thick twist stung his eyes, "Oh, two clubs." Red and green, red and green, was it the British S.O.S.? Had the German attack begun?

"Two diamonds."

"Three no trumps," said Moggerhanger, leaving his cards on the table.

"No bid," said Allen.

"Four no trumps," said Phillip, and spread his hand: ace, king of hearts; king to two of diamonds; queen to four of spades; ace, king, knave, ten, eight of clubs.

"Bon, partner. Quite useful. 'Elp yourself to a spot of old man Johnny Walker."

"No thank you, sir." He left the table, and moved across to the sandbag-covered window in the east wall of the hut. Why hadn't he gone up the line to report to Westy, instead of footling about playing bridge.

"What, you on the waggon?"

"For the moment, sir."

"Got a dose?" asked Moggerhanger, as he scooped in the tricks.

A stream of fresh air was faintly whining through the cracked talc pane behind the sandbag covering. From afar came the crackle of rifle and machine-gun fire. Probably a German raid: he could hear the fast stutter of Lewis guns.

"Ah ha, you went to bed with that arse-piece!" said the Quartermaster, to Allen. "Little slam, partner!" Moggerhanger threw down his last three cards. "'Oo's shuffle? Come on, get a move on."

The third rubber had just finished, nine hundred down, when the door opened and Major Marsden came in. His trench coat was dripping, it was now raining hard. He brought the news that a German raiding party of considerable strength, following on a bombardment with h.e. and mustard gas, had got into the battalion outpost line, and bombed its way up to the main defence line.

"Three of our men were taken prisoner, and I'm afraid our casualties are pretty heavy, mainly from yellow-cross, but there was some blue-cross, too. Eighty odd, all of Bill Kidd's company. The Boche left behind a wounded man, who confirmed that the country for fifty miles behind their lines was stiff with troops marching up at night, and lying doggo in villages by day."

"Wind!" snarled Moggerhanger. "They've been told to say it! Every bloody Hun pinched so far gives us the same ol' tale! It's a bluff! The Germans aren't bloody fools! They know they couldn't get far, with practically no roads over the old Somme battlefield! They'll push up north, the shortest way to the Channel ports! I'll lay you fifty francs to twenty it's all a bluff down 'ere! And what's more, it's stoppin' me from 'oppin' it for 'ome!"

He downed his whiskey, and banged the empty mug on the table.

Phillip looked with concealed scorn at the Quartermaster's face. What did any quartermaster know of the *real* war, when he had slept every night in a bed for years? His fancy played satirically with the red-purple of the old man's face, ruinous and arrogant: the eyebrows, or lack of them, were the Passchendaele ridge of the north-eastern slopes of the Salient, coloured by ten thousand tins of bully beef. Here was the embodiment of the bad old soldier-philosophy—"F—k you Jack, I'm all right."

At midnight, having lost three thousand points by consistent over-calling, and paid out thirty francs, Phillip asked if he might go up the line to see Colonel West.

"What's up, you're so bloody restless, you the Old Man's bum boy?" asked Moggerhanger.

Phillip pushed back his chair and, standing up, said, "You may be my senior officer, Colonel, but that does not give you the right to make such remarks!"

"Come come," said Marsden, gently, as he continued to inspect one of his twin 'Captain' pipes in their case. "We're all friends here. You don't know our old Moggers, Maddison. If he really thought that there was anything like that, he would be the last to mention it."

"That's right, old cock. Don't take no notice of me, I never mean what I say. Isn't that right, Pluggy? You'll soon get used to my ways. I mean no 'arm. 'Elp yerself to a spot of old man whiskey, Lampers. Never let it be said that the talkin' stopped the drinkin'."

"Thank you, Colonel——"

"Cut out the 'colonel'. I'm Moggers." The Quartermaster gave him a prolonged wink. "You'll do, Lampo."

"I'm sorry I lost my temper—Moggers."

The two younger subalterns went to bed, while the three continued to sit by the dull red stove. Outside the wind was blowing strongly, causing little fringes of flame to issue from the bottom of the grate. Two empty whiskey bottles lay on the floor. As Moggers talked on—about his early days as a crowstarver, and then in the Army, Phillip began to feel his underlying steadiness. He had thought him to be dense and dull, like the heavy soil of the farmlands upon which he had been raised; now he saw him as part of the strength and solidity of gault clay, which had made bricks enduring since Tudor times. He felt ashamed of his former attitude towards the old fellow, and thought that such were Mother's people; that he was more Turney than Maddison, the cold-grey-eyed Viking Maddisons. Yet was he really like the Turneys? Was his nature like Father's, or Mother's? What was the difference between mind and nature? Did he have a mixed nature? There was something about both Mother and Father which made him feel only part of himself in their presence. Perhaps he was, as Father had often said in anger, a throw-back.

Moggers was yawning widely, with no attempt to cover a mouth revealing stumps of teeth about as irregular and broken as the tree stumps in the Bois Carré of long ago. Poor old Moggers, a farm labourer's son who had started life as a crowstarver for 6d. a week; dear old Moggers: but where was the original boy of clay, dragging thin young legs behind the seed-harrow strokes, or twirling his rattle to scare the rooks? Since then he had dragged his feet all over the Empire, and now wanted only to rest them before his own hearth—the bully-beef face home at last, roses round the door, and the old women along the street on sunny days working at the lace pillows. How queer—crowstarver Moggy to Lt.-Col. Moggerhanger, D.S.O.

"What yer laughin' like that at me for, young Lampers?"

"I'm beginning to rumble you, *mein prächtige kerl*!"

Moggerhanger obviously took this to be a compliment. His mouth became frog-like as he drew in breath, extended two arms, and started to sing *Nellie Dean* in a surprisingly thin little voice. Then after another drink he was bellowing

Drunk last night,
Drunk the night before,
We're goin' to get drunk tonight
If we never get drunk any more.
When we're drunk we're as happy as can be
For we're all members of the Souse family!
Glorious! Glorious!
One cask of beer among the four of us
Thank the Lord there aren't any more of us
For any of us could drink it all alone
Pom! Pom!

"Them's my sentiments, Lampo! One of the Fireside Lancers, no bloody good to the army no more! That's a bloody fact! Me, who was so'jerin' when your mother's milk was still in you! Khyber Pass, Omdurman, Rorke's Drift, Blennum, Battle of Bloody Hastings, Moggers was in the thick of the bloody lot, and no jam on it like there is today! I began my so'jering with the wildest lot of sods whatever broke their mother's 'earts, let me tell you, old cock!" His head dropped. In a little voice he murmured, "I'm popped," and without further word staggered up on his size-thirteen issue boots and zigzagged from the hut.

"Dear old Moggers," said Pluggy. "Where would we be without him. Don't take any notice of his remarks. He's had a long war, and wants to go home. By the way, the battalion is being relieved tomorrow, I think we should all turn out to welcome them. I'm sending up the drums. Well, I'm for bed. You know your quarters, do you?"

"I think I'll write a letter first, major, before turning in."

"Righty-ho."

He wanted to write up his diary, an act forbidden by General Routine Orders. But there seemed nothing to say when he was alone. He began to feel depressed, his head felt to be swelled, his skin dry and tight. Was he going to spew? He hadn't drunk very much. The yellow-hot coke in the stove was now giving out blue flames when the wind blew down the chimney pipe. He felt sleepy, with no desire to sleep: a feeling of irritability, kept down by leaden hopelessness, held him in faint complaint that the room was thick with the insidious smell of black twist tobacco. A brutal imprint of himself trying to smoke twist in a clay pipe in the Cheshire convalescent home in February 1915 pressed upon him, while his stomach hardened unbearably, so that he got up and made for the door, vainly clutching air for support while feeling himself helplessly to be the centre of a leaning gyroscope. He was scarcely aware of falling backwards, and then the sense of desperately crawling to the door faded.

When he recovered he heard remote voices and was conscious of his chattering teeth and of arms bearing him away. He awoke into candle light, Allen offering him a cup of tea. Recalling something of the night before, he told himself that he was weak, weak, weak; so much for his good resolutions. What would Westy say? His head was aching, tea made it feel less pressed upon. "Who got me here? I suppose I was blotto?"

"You were poisoned by the fumes of that stove. Colonel Moggerhanger found you lying on the floor, he went back when he realized that his own stove had filled his hut with carbon-monoxide fumes."

"Then I owe the old boy my life! And I wasn't blotto after all!"

"No. The M.O. said it was a case of poisoning."

"Thank God!"

"I thought you'd want to be up to see the battalion arrive. They're on the way down."

Phillip was soon shaved, washed, and dressed. Then to breakfast, which he had to forsake half-way through; but returning with emptied belly to the mess room, found that the headache was gone and his appetite, after a bite of bread and butter, keen. Afterwards a visit to the tailor's shop, to have the regimental and divisional flashes—colour patterns—sewn on shoulders and behind tunic collar; and then to join the cadre officers, including the new draft, who were walking out along the track down which the battalion would come.

The sky was beginning to turn pink; flights of scout planes were climbing overhead, already golden in the rays of the sun invisible from below. "Quiet morning," said Phillip. "What do they say, 'Red at dawning, shepherd's warning'?" The wind was from the north-west, already the sky behind them was dull for another day. Sleet wandered down the sky. Then a cyclist was seen through the low haze, coming towards them. He drew up, leapt off, stood to attention, "Battalion just passing Bluet Field Ambulance, sir!"

As they stood under a sky now rising gold in the east but still louring dark over their shoulders Phillip heard the faint throb of drums. After the night of almost continuous gun-fire, the slight sound was strangely moving. Looking back the way they had come, he saw other figures along the track; transport drivers, who had been going up when the box-barrage was put round the Bird Cage and the raid started, had come along to find out what had happened to their chums.

The thin almost feeble wail of the pipes was heard above the throb of side-drums, but still nothing was visible in the frozen mist. The sound died away, then came again; now it was only the drums—*rataplan*, *rataplan*, *ratapattaplan*—swelling and diminishing as though with the contours of the ground.

The head of the battalion appeared suddenly, and he thought the drum-skins must have been damp. In front walked the sergeant drummer: behind the band came an uneven column of khaki figures. When about a hundred yards distant from the camp entrance, upon the area of ground worn bare of grass, now faintly speckled with sleet, drum-sticks were raised, polished brass instruments held to mouths, long silver stick of drum-major held aloft as the band wheeled to a flank. Down came the silver stick, drums broke into roll, and from brass instruments, now brazed, soldered, and patched, came the regimental march, *Colonel Bogey*.

Past the stationary band came the battalion, led by 'Spectre' on foot, his one eye staring ahead under the rim of his helmet. He took the salute, his face white and set. Behind him walked an officer Phillip remembered at Landguard, Denis Sisley, looking haggard and ill. Rows of bloodshot eyes followed, boots and puttees clogged with mud thrust desperately against drag, puffy faces smeared, trousers ripped by barbed wire and bomb splinter, helmets askew, rifles slung, greatcoats gashed, tunics showing dried blood. Was this all the battalion—under four hundred?

In the rear came a limping captain, knitted scarf round neck and covering the lower part of his face, thus emphasising a long nose and dark staring eyes. Phillip saw that a mouth-organ was tucked into one shoulder-strap of his tommy's tunic.

Hetty, going in the back way to play her nightly game of piquet with Thomas Turney, brought a letter from Phillip. "It has just come!" she said, with her gay little laugh. "But neither Dickie nor I can fathom the first part. What do you think, Papa?"

Thomas Turney put on his spectacles, and began to read aloud.

2 Gaultshire Regt.
B.E.F. 27 February 1918

Dear Mother and Father, and all Kind Relations including Sprat and his foster-Mother,

Please enter Roxford Rameses or Northanger Endymion the Second at the Fat Stock Show, from our Vulpine——

He paused. "What's the next word? It's either 'farm' or 'farmy'. H'm. We need a Sherlock Holmes to decipher this——" He read on:

I am sure that either of these boars from our Vulpine Farm will win the first prize, we have in my opinion nothing better in their class. Don't let the bailiff deter you. If in doubt about this, ask Grandpa's advice, for he knows the game not only forwards but backwards. The weather here is cold and some snow has fallen.

Thomas Turney stared at the letter, while Hetty and Aunt Marian sat very still. At last he chuckled. "I think I see through it now! Phillip told me when he was last home that if we took the first letters of every word at the beginning of the first sentence, it would indicate where he was. Now where are we——" He began to spell, "P-E-R-R-O-N-E. That's it, Peronne! But misspelled. There's a map in the *Star* tonight." He showed them. "There you are! And now for Vulpine Farm. Didn't he say that the sign of the Army he served in all last year was a fox?"

"Yes, Papa, the Fifth Army!"

"That's right. Gough's Fifth Army, in a quiet part of the line, right away from Ypres, there it is, Peronne, on the map. So you have nothing to worry about, my girl!"

"I'll just slip back and tell Dickie, Papa. He doesn't say much, but I know he is greatly concerned about Phillip. I won't be long."

Richard was playing *The Sea*, by Frank Bridge, one of his favourite records. He stopped the motor as soon as she entered, believing that she had no feeling for such beauty, and the thought dulled him.

"Peronne, is that the place where Master Phillip is now? Why, it was given up by the Germans a year ago, when they had their 'landslide in the West', as the *Trident* called it. They destroyed a large tract of country, blowing up all buildings, poisoning wells, and cutting down trees, so they won't exactly want it back, will they?" he said cheerfully. "Now that your best boy has found himself a quiet part of the line, take my advice, and enjoy your gambling, Hetty!" He was happy, and yet, somehow, the music did not sound quite the same when he started the turntable once again.

During intervals between his duties Phillip rode a young spirited chestnut gelding 15.3 hands high, lent to him by the transport officer. Away from the incinerated and chloride smells of camp there lay a country of rolling downland little touched by war, except that all trees had been cut down, and long ago become firewood, so that only dead stumps lined the roads. There were no villages, only an occasional heap of rubble.

It was now the second week of March. Despite drafts, the battalion was more than three hundred men under strength. He had been surprised to find that the regular battalion was little different from a service battalion: his mental picture had to be re-made, from one of *sahib* officers, to chaps like himself. A few new second-lieutenants from Sandhurst; others from Cadet centres and the disbanded 8th battalion of Kitchener's Army, or what was left of it after Somme, Hindenburg Line, and Third Ypres.

The Colonel, now that the battalion was out of the line, had the officers dining in mess together every night. The Divisional General was keen on sports for the men—football, cross-country runs, potato-and-spoon races, sack races, riding school for the officers, anything to take their minds for a brief while off their work. On the last of the four days out, a football match was arranged with a north country battalion. This was one of the many return matches between the Mediators and the Pork and Beans, a rivalry in sport going back before the war. One of the company commanders, Bill Kidd, was the Mediators' goalee; he was very fly, flinging himself in extended attitudes at the ball, usually shot at the goal by an ex-pro of a famous Northern cup-tie team. Again and again Captain Kidd managed to frustrate the thick-necked hero of the Pork and Beans, by proving, in various directions across the rectangle of the goal, that a straight line to the ball was the shortest distance between the point of his toes extended through a taut body to his fists diverting the ball. Towards the end of the game more than a hundred Lancastrians were booing Bill Kidd from behind the net, as their own hero, at centre forward, who had a habit of falling on one knee and sticking out a leg to trip an opponent, failed to score. The booing was intense towards the end; no goals were scored on either side; and the Mediator goalee remarked to Phillip as they were walking back, "Good lads, those Pork and Beans, they're all Boche eaters!"

"What about their centre-forward? He played a dirty game."

"Him? He's no Boche eater! He's dodging the column at Corps School, teaches bayonet-fighting and all the milksop stuff of those other highly-paid bastards."

Back into reserve, work-and-carry parties were resumed, twelve hours on and twelve off. For those not on night duty the cinemas clicked every night, and the concert party put on its double bill. By now Phillip had made friends with some of the officers, whose cheery greetings added to life. With surprise he realised that he was the senior subaltern, a bogus old sweat, the riband of the 1914 Star had done the trick.

Mar. 11, Mon. More snow turning to rain. Moggers wasn't far out about my being the C.O.'s odd job man. I am messenger boy (sometimes on a horse), asst. adj., asst. Intelligence Officer, occasional A.D.C. and understudy to Denis Sisley the adjutant. Larks sparring over fields now showing winter wheat beginning to stir. A few peasants back, using ploughs given by British govt.

Mar. 12, Tue. The senior coy commander is a queer bird, usually referring to himself as Bill Kidd, in the 3rd person. He plays the mouth-organ, and has a way of talking all his own. He said to Moggers today, 'My blokes want new greybacks, Moggers. Most of them are walking to the incinerator by themselves', i.e. lousy shirts. He came to the 2nd bn. a month or so ago when the 8th bn. was disbanded. One day, when standing by the padre, he said to a man of a new draft, 'Are you a Boche eater, my lad?' 'No sir, I'm a Nonconformist, please sir!'

Mar. 13, Wed. Denis Sisley gone sick with 'flu to Field Amb. I am acting adjt. Thank God for Sgt. Tonks. After dinner went with 'Spectre' to Wasps Con. party, enjoyable, best item being from Buzz Buzz duet sung by Nelson Keys and Teddie Gerrard, impersonated by Sullivan and sgt. dressed up as Teddie G. in wig, frock, etc. *The blonde who came from Eden, by way of Sweden.* I wondered if Sp. was thinking of Sasha at Flossie Flowers' disastrous New Year's Eve party.

Mar. 15, Fri. Brigadier told Sp. that Gen. Plumer was back from Italy, to take over Fourth Army from Rawlinson (i.e. Plumer's old Second Army). Brig. thinks main German push will come at Ypres, with only a diversionary attack down here, 'which we shall hold'. Sp. does not think so. He saw Mowbray two days ago and was told Oskar von Hutier was commanding 18th Ger. Army from Bellenglise on St. Quentin Canal to La Fère on the Oise, about 20 miles. Von der Marwitz commands 2nd Ger. Army opposite us, and if they push here the *first* objective will be Albert, about 25 miles behind us. Some hopes.

The battalion moved into the rear Battle Zone known as The Aviary. Battalion H.Q. was in a quarry about fifty yards back from the road which led to Corunna Camp and the transport lines. Blocks of stone had been cut to make a bunker, with baulks of timber for the roof overlaid with tarred felt, then sheets of corrugated iron covered by a triple layer of sandbags. There were three compartments; C.O.'s bedroom, orderly room, and headquarters mess connected by a blanket curtain with the cookhouse adjoining. At this end a tunnel had been started into the quarry face, apparently to lead to a series of dug-outs; but this work had been abandoned.

Phillip felt that he would never learn to do all the hundreds of things an adjutant was responsible for, even with the help of Tonks, the orderly room sergeant, who had been a bookmaker's clerk before the war. "I'll be here, on the two-way blower."

"The two-way blower, Sergeant?"

"A manner of speaking, sir. You know the old blower which they used in offices before telephones, sir? You take out the whistle-plug your end, blow down the pipe, the whistle downstairs gives the warning, and then you speak down the pipe? Never seen one, sir, no? Old-fashioned, but I've retained the idea, sir. I suppose from habit. Well, to come back to the organisation in the orderly room, it's my job to prepare the outgoing routine returns, what have to go to the Brigade Staff captain. Of what comes in from Brigade some concerns the province of Major Marsden as second-in-command, some goes to the Quartermaster and some to you, sir, for the Commanding Officer. Generally speaking, Major Marsden takes care of reinforcements and training, with the battalion sergeant major. That roughly speaking is the 'A' side, while Colonel Mogger-'anger looks after 'Q'."

"Who actually makes the plans?"

"The Commanding Officer, sir, in conjunction with the Brigadier, who either holds converse with 'im direct, or communicates via the Brigade-major. Major Marsden works out the details, with the Adjutant, usually. Now if you'll be so good as to deal with this little lot, sir, about the Pig, sir. I'll be be'ind the blanket if you want me. Do you object to smokin', sir? Captain Sisley permitted it."

The excellent fellow retired. Phillip heard the match strike, imagined the sergeant drawing deep at his Woodbine, heard the long blowing out of satisfying smoke. He decided to keep his pipe in his pocket, for it would not do to appear too casual at first, and taking the top sheaf from what Sisley had called the pile of bumff, read it carefully. It was an amazing dossier: no wonder the Staff-newspaper from Corps was called Comic Cuts!

Chapter 4

THE PIG

It began with the findings of a Court of Enquiry presided over by Captain Kidd, late of the 8th battalion. This dealt with the burning of a barn at Senlis, a back-area village where the 2nd battalion had gone out to rest some time before. No direct cause of fire had been found; the barn had gone up in flames while the company occupying it as a billet had been out on a route march. Previous to this, there had been a heap of smoking manure against one wall. The wall was made of *pisé*. He remembered Aunt Dora at Lynmouth telling him that *pisé* was the equivalent of cob in Devon, a pounded mixture of loamy subsoil, lime-ash, cowdung, and straw. Only cob wasn't made in blocks first. The *pisé* blocks had been weather-worn, according to the findings of the court, the cracks between them stuffed in places with straw. It had been decided that this straw had got hot beside the manure heap and finally ignited. The finding of the Court of Enquiry was, according to its President, Captain Kidd, that 'the barn was destroyed by fire caused by spontaneous combustion'.

In the barn, at the time of the fire, had been a sickly pig. It had not been burned, but got out in time, to wander off and refresh itself, according to Kidd, in the battalion latrines. From that refreshment, claimed the farmer at Senlis, the animal had died.

Reading through the dossier again, Phillip saw that it had been travelling quite a lot: from Corps to Division to Brigade to Battalion and back again by various new channels, with some short cuts here and there. He began to laugh; then feeling that he could do better than some of the old jossers who spent their time in a sort of Gilbert and Sullivan outlook, wrote a facetious parody of the whole thing; but on reflection, screwed it up and popped it in the stove. He must be serious, like Mr. Fazackerley Hollis in the office at Wine Vaults Lane.

Min. 1

To East Midland Division. Q.V. 2108. 22/2/18.

For enquiry and adjustment please, reference enclosed letter from farmer at Senlis.

H. W. Shoubridge, Lt.-Col.
A.Q.M.G. Corps.

Min. 2

To 3rd Home Counties Inf. Bde. A/5786. 23/2/18.

Will you please enquire into this lamentable business?

H. F. P. St. J. Holnicott, Major
D.A. & Q.M.G. Divn.

Min. 3

To O.C. 2nd Gaultshire Regt. 24/2/18.

For report as to attached letter.

J. M. Millington, Capt.
Staff Capt., 3 H.C. Inf. Bde.

Min. 4.

To 3rd H.C. Inf. Bde. 27/2/18.

Reference attached, all the billets at Senlis were in an extremely insanitary condition and needed liberal sprinkling of creosol and other disinfectants. The pigs at this billet were allowed to roam at will, and although personally and forcibly warned on frequent occasions, they were always routing about in the latrines and rubbish pits.

D. H. Sisley, Capt. & Adjt.
for O.C. 2nd Gaults. Rgt.

Min. 5

To H.-Qrs East Midland Division. 28/2/18.

Forwarded. Please see Minute 4.

J. M. Primrose-Shaw, Brig.-Gen.
Commanding 3rd H.C. Inf. Bde.

Min. 6

To D.A. & Q.M.G. Corps. Q.V. 2108. 1/3/18.

Please see Minute 4.

It appears that the pigs should have been kept under better control. Latrines are properly disinfected and are not fit places in which pigs should be allowed to feed.

It is not considered that this is a fair claim against the public.

Mordaunt Runnymeade, Lt.-Col.
A.A. & Q.M.G. for G.O.C.
East Midland Division.

Min. 7

To East Midland Division. 4/3/18.

Although, as you say, the pig in question was not well under control, it was probably conforming to the customs of the country. It seems clear that, but for the presence of British troops and creosol, the dead pig might still be alive: in these circumstances the owner should receive compensation for the value of the pig.

H. W. Shoubridge, Lt.-Col.
A.Q.M.G. Corps.

At this point he hid his pipe when 'Spectre' West came in and said, "I want you to come with me round the Brigade Battle Zone at eleven o'clock. You will require a horse; send a chit and ask for Denis's mount, will you? Well, how are you getting on? Sit down. May I borrow some of your 'baccy? What is it, Hignett's Cavalier? That's a good old Crocodile pouch you've got; one doesn't see red rubber nowadays."

"I bought it with my first salary in the City, Colonel. Also a curved 'Artist's' pipe which held half an ounce, and a top hat."

"What, did you smoke your hat? Whole, or in pieces?" He filled his slim curved Loewe 'Captain' pipe. "Evidently you felt the need for conformity and respectability early. Well, keep it up," and having lit his pipe, he went out: whereupon Phillip re-filled his pipe and unfastened the four brass buttons of his tunic, as Denis Sisley had done when the stove got too hot. Light-heartedly he took up the sheaf of papers. Then, remembering the order for a horse, he called the sergeant, who said he would write out a chit and ask him to sign it. This being done, Phillip, feeling himself to be almost a barrister with his first brief, considered further evidence 'In *re* Porcus Porcorum *v.* Rex'.

Min. 8

To A.D.V.S., East Midland Division. *A* 5786. 5/3/18.

Passed.

Will you please express an opinion as to the demise of this unfortunate animal. In view of the habits and customs of this country, it is probable that swine fever is prevalent, and that, should the animal have the seeds of disease in him, his orgy of savoury feeding would only have been indirectly responsible for his untimely end.

G. H. F. Bagshott-Brendon, Major
D.A. & Q.M.G. East Midland Div.

He stared at the signature. Could *Bagshott-Brendon* be the same Brendon who had been A.P.M. at Ypres the previous year? The cove who had all but put him under arrest as a supposed deserter when he had been ordered by 'Spectre' to take a message to Advanced G.H.Q. at Westcappelle? The same old Brendon at Heathmarket in 1915, and Grantham in 1916? He asked the sergeant.

"I've no idea, sir." Phillip felt that his question had been silly. Of course a sergeant could not have known. Now for it. He must reply. The Assistant Director of Veterinary Supplies obviously had ignored double-barrel'd Brendon's Punch-like humour: perhaps the horse-doctor disliked Brendon, for he had replied somewhat curtly, it seemed.

Min. 9

To A.A. & Q.M.G. East Midland Division. 9/3/18

I regret I am unable to give any opinion as to the cause of this pig's death.

If it can be arranged that the body be brought to Peronne I will detail an officer to make a post-mortem.

C. Treraven.
A.D.V.S. East Midland Division.

The next minute was from G.S.O. 1 Division, the senior staff-officer to the General. It declared, very politely, that "as considerable time has elapsed since the pig's death, the course suggested in Minute 9 will probably serve no useful purpose. The claim should therefore be adjusted."

In other words, no more mucking about, get on with it. The writer of the next Minute asked for particulars of age, weight, and breed, so that 'a fair valuation can be arrived at'. Signed by the Claims Officer of Division. Whereupon the gilded and double-barrel'd Bagshott-Brendon had written whimsically to a mere colonel of footsloggers.

Min. 12

12/3/18

Can the O.C. 2nd Gaultshire Regt. claim to be a judge of fat stock sufficient for him to express an opinion?

G. H. F. Bagshott-Brendon, Major
D.A. & Q.M.G. East Midland Division.

The reference to Fat Stock was slightly alarming. Had Brendon, by some remote chance, censor'd his letter home, with the supposed boars being entered for the mythical Fat Stock Show? Divisional Intelligence might have set a trap for him. Putting on a casual air, he took the Minute to the Orderly Room sergeant.

"The Quartermaster may be able to tell you, sir," said Tonks. "Colonel Moggerhanger usually arrives about this time."

"Righty-ho, sergeant. I'll go and meet him. I know absolutely nothing about Fat Stock——" he checked and added, "—in this country. It's rather hot in here, don't you think?"

"Can't be too warm for me, sir!"

Phillip, wearing a driver's issue cape, walked down the road. He passed a Chinese labour company on the way, traipsing along behind a steam-roller. He wondered what use it was, for 'Spectre' had told him that road-metalling was so scarce in the Fifth Army area that stone was being shipped from Cornish quarries, even from Lundy. He was wondering if the quarry was about to be opened up—would chalk do for roads, surely it was too soft?—when he saw Moggers coming towards him, riding his cob and about to be passed by a motorcar. The Vauxhall was going at a speed well over the 12 m.p.h. limit allowed in the Fifth Army area. As it went by Moggers there was a roar of "Stop, you b——r, you! You're under arrest!"

The Vauxhall bore a small pennant on its bonnet, with the three wheat-sheaves of the divisional sign. It appeared to be empty, except for the driver; but as Moggers trotted up to it, Phillip, less than a dozen paces away, saw a cap with a red band under the crown lift itself out of a bearskin coat in the back and heard a little voice from the wrapped-up figure of the Divisional Commander say, "I don't think my driver meant any harm, Moggers."

Colonel Moggerhanger, erect on his cob and staring ahead, said, "Contravening General Routine Orders by exceedin' twelve miles per hour is an offence to be dealt with by the Provost Marshal's office, sir."

"Oh, do you really think it is as serious as that, Moggers?" The voice was gentle, but there was steel behind it. The General turned his head around to look at Moggers.

"I do, sir!"

"I am in a hurry, Moggers."

"I do not consider that is any reason for careless drivin' on the part of your orderly, sir!"

"I am still in a hurry, and if you do not release my driver, I shall be late for the Army Commander's conference, Moggers."

"I regret the momentary inconvenience, sir, but the driver should have considered that before showering me and my charger with trash and muck."

Phillip saw that the near-side of the cob, which was taking advantage of the halt to stale, was dripping with grey mud. So was the Quartermaster's size 13 boot, and the bulky breeches of his off-side leg. Sitting upright, Moggers said stonily, "I consider that the driver should remain under arrest, sir."

"Very well, Moggers, I shall expect you at my headquarters tomorrow. Come to luncheon, and afterwards we'll see what can be done."

With a slight smile and a wave of his hand the Divisional General drove away. Phillip went up to Moggers, whose manner towards him was not encouraging.

"I wonder, Colonel, if you would be so good as to——"

"Not you agen?" groaned Moggers. Phillip was not to be put off; nor was Moggers, who, asked about the Senlis incident, replied with an explosive word relative to the pig. And you, replied Phillip under his breath.

When he got back to the quarry the steam-roller was blowing off a lot of steam among the Chinese labourers whose blue cotton blouses and trousers were augmented by old khaki tunics, bombers' aprons, dark civilian clothing, including cut-up women's skirts; while an assortment of hats upon their heads had apparently been scrounged from house ruins and salvage dumps. Bowler hats; one crenellated top hat; peasants' peaked caps; a tam-o'-shanter, a *pickelhaube*, and several round grey-and-red German pork-pie caps. One man waddled with a sandbag on either flank and fastened over his shoulders by rifle slings, filled with lumpy objects. Seeing Phillip looking at him the man grinned and pulled out a Mills bomb.

"Me Chum Poo, mister. Me done one piecee bad boy Jelly one piecee Millee bomb—bang!—one piecee bad boy Jelly flucked!"

Captain Kidd's loud, slightly rasping voice said behind Phillip, "You be careful, Chum Poo! If one piecee bad boy Jelly catchee Chum Poo mit Millee bombee, Chum Poo flucked pronto, and don't you forget it, you yellow bellee. Now vamoose! Sling your hook! Depart in peace, or else in pieces! Otherwise, in the King's English, piss off!"

The speaker turned to Phillip. "These bastards have a pleasant little habit of sallying forth after an air-raid at night to bomb Jerry prisoner-of-war camps."

"I didn't know China had joined the Allies, Captain Kidd. Are these troops an addition to your company?" asked Phillip, as though seriously.

"God's teeth, I haven't come down to be a Toe-rag ganger, old boy! Have a heart! Now about our shackles next week, when we go into the Bird Cage——"

"Will you excuse me for a moment." Turning to the N.C.O. with the Chinese labourers, he said, "What are these idealists doing here?"

"I had orders to bring them here, sir."

"To report for work to the Second Gaultshires?"

"No, sir, just to bring them here and await orders."

Captain Kidd interrupted. "Look, old boy, I must be off. Will you ask Denis Sisley when he comes back to fix up with Moggers that my men's shackles are no longer greasy and cold when they arrive at night? My blokes are dam' good blokes, let me tell you, and need a real good hot blow-out once a day."

"Oh I see, you mean skilly. I'll try and arrange with the transport——"

"No, old boy, Bill Kidd does not mean skilly. Bill Kidd means what Bill Kidd says, the real and original shackles, none of your broken biscuits boiled up with lumps of bully, old boy! Shackles—you know—as served at the Carlton Grill, cut off the joint and two veg. Fourpence in every good pull-up for car-men!"

"Righty-ho, I'll see Moggers about it."

"Thanks, old boy. You see, we can't spare any scarlet runners from the old coy, so we have to rely on those slack bastards from the White City, otherwise we'd collect our own grub in double quick time. By the way, the name's Bill to my pals."

"Righty-ho, Wilhelm, mein prächtige kerl!"

He told Bill about the encounter between Moggers and General O'Toole, and Bill Kidd said, "Oh, those two crab-wallahs are always having a go at one another. Jimmy O'Toole belongs to the regiment, you know. That monocle he wears conceals a glass eye. His driver's the original Convict 99. Fact, old boy! He was a burglar before the war. On the Somme, he and Jimmy passed a dead Hun showing a gold tooth. Next day, going up the line again, Jimmy saw the tooth was missing.

"'You got that one, Johnson, I suppose?'

"'Yessir.'

"'I suppose someone will take my glass eye, if I cop it, Johnson?'

"'Yessir, I put myself dahn fer that, fer a souvenir, sir.' Good lad, is Jimmy. Cheerio!"

When Bill Kidd had gone, Phillip said to the headquarter-guard sergeant, "I don't like the idea of these iron grapes hanging about the place." He stopped himself in time from adding 'old boy'. "The Chinks are non-combatants. In fact, in those civvy clothes and carrying weapons, they're *franc tireurs*. So get two of your men to collect all the grenades."

He went into the orderly room, and took up the dossier about the pig. With any luck Denis Sisley would be back soon; he had only the grippe, according to the American M.O. attached to the battalion. It was more fun going round with 'Spectre' than dealing with endless chits. He was wondering what to reply to *Minute* 13 when the C.O. came in and said, "Denis has pneumonia, and is being evacuated to the base. That means he's off the strength. For the time being, until a new adjutant is appointed, you will carry on with this job. How do you feel about having Allen as your assistant? Very well, send for him."

Allen was still at Corunna Camp. At a nod from Phillip, the orderly room sergeant went out to tell a cyclist orderly to fetch Mr. Allen. The C.O. then said, "Will you look at this sketch map of the Brigade Battle Zone? It's marked down as The Aviary. We'll look in this morning on the way to the Forward Zone, which we take over on the twenty-second. Here's a smaller scale plan which includes our Forward Zone, the Bird Cage. It would be gracious to send a wire to the Officer Commanding the Fifth Verderers—Sergeant Tonks will know the code word—asking his leave to go round the Bird Cage at 2 p.m. this afternoon. We'll enter the communication trench at the Belvedere. Warn Sullivan to meet us there."

Sullivan, the battalion Intelligence Officer, had the charming manners of one who had had some success before the war in musical comedy. It was he who ran *The Wasps* Concert Party.

"I need hardly say that these maps are not to leave this office, so memorize what you can, of the Bird Cage in particular."

"Yes, Colonel."

He must not allow himself to be flurried. 'Spectre' evidently knew his thoughts, for he said, "It may seem a lot to do all at once, but things will come easier with time. Take each thing as it comes." There was the gruff explosion of a Mills bomb. "What the hell is that?"

"I think it's only the Chinks, Colonel. I've already told off the guard sergeant to collect their grenades——"

They went outside. "What is this steam-roller doing here? What is it, Barnum's Circus? Tell them either to take it away or to damp down the fire."

The Chinese labourers were holding out mess-tins for hot water; it was their tea-time, apparently.

"Get the damned thing camouflaged, and reduce that steam at once!"

The Quartermaster, riding up, was a relief.

"What do you think of our fair-ground, Moggers? Pity you haven't got the band up here too, we might have a dance. Who the devil sent it here? That steam may draw shell-fire. Take your blasted vehicle away!" to the elderly N.C.O. in charge of the Chinese.

"I can do with a roller, to flatten out the brick standings of our new horse-lines in the White City. Corporal, take your men and machine to the Second Gaultshire lines at Corunna, the police will direct you. I'll see your officer, I'm Colonel Moggerhanger. 'Ow many coolies you got? Thirty-two? We can feed 'm. Off you go, make it slippy! Shelling may start any moment now! Don't forget the roller."

Later, he said to Phillip, "Don't see why we shouldn't swing the drippin' on these yellow-bellies, and give our fellers a rest. Camouflage the old stone crusher, eh? They won't recognise it when I've done with it."

The Quartermaster was about to turn away when Phillip said, "Moggers, what shall I say about that bloody pig at Senlis? If you wouldn't mind—I won't keep you a moment—I expect you, too, have rather a lot to do——"

"Don't let the bumff get you down, Lampo! Now you listen to me, m'lad. You think I'm a rough, don't you? A crude old bastard without college ed'jication? Well, you're right! I've had to make my own way, see? And maybe I know what some others don't always know. Pigs, for instance. 'Alf a mo', let's 'ave a wet. We can talk better there. Don't look so anxious!"

Over a whiskey and soda in the mess-room, he continued, "Yes, as I was saying, pigs are choosy feeders, except when they're starved; even then I say you won't catch 'm feeding on latrines. Those with scarlet runners creepin' up to their lug-'oles and corns on the seat of their pants know sweet fanny adams about pigs. I grew up with pigs, I've slept with pigs, and while they didn't object to my presence, all the same they're choosy, and like to be clean."

Stretching out his 13-size feet he poured himself another drink and with manner now gentle told Phillip, who waited with assumed interest for him to come to the point, about the habits of a farrow of little pigs with their sow.

"I've seen each squealer doin' its little job right away from the old gal, for as I told you, Lampo, it's the nature of a pig to be regimental, in other words, to keep itself decent. No livin' creature likes to live in its own muck. The pig, I'll have you know, possesses a very sensitive nose. In the Sudan I saw one once what was trained like a pointer dog by some Buddoo sportsman who fancied himself shooting quails that way."

Allen, lumpy with full kit, looked in; hesitated. "Good morning!" cried Phillip. "Come in!"

Allen saluted; Phillip, after a nod from the Quartermaster, took the salute. "Sit down. Colonel Moggers is talking about pigs."

"That's right. Well, as I was saying, that pig was as good and as patient as any dog in the Duke's Abbey trials. Intelligent? Wasn't it, tho'! It grunted slightly when it sniffed a covey in the cotton fields. No, that pig at Senlis didn't die of us, Lampo, it died of natural causes, and you tell that to your pal Brendon who I'll probably see at lunch tomorrow. But count me out of it, I'm fer 'ome any day now, and don't want no stain on my crime sheet." This with a wink at Allen. "Well!"—heaving himself up—"I must be gettin' back, Lampo."

"Decent old boy, when you know him," said Phillip, when the Quartermaster had gone. "Now about your job." He concluded by saying, "The orderly room sergeant is a tower of strength. Don't be hesitant about asking Tonks any questions. Come with me, and meet him."

On his return from behind the hanging blanket Phillip saw 'Spectre', who said distinctly, "Will you kindly ask for Brigade exchange to put me through to Shiny Night. No, don't do it yourself, ask the telephone orderly." When the call came he heard 'Spectre' ask for the Commanding Officer. So *Shiny Night* was the code name of the Verderers. Damn, he should have put the call through before.

Now for a reply to Brendon. But a picture of Sullivan singing in the concert party persisted: the fascinating duet from *Buzz Buzz*. He tried to recall the words.

Some of the time, you think you love a brunette,
Some other time, you love a blonde
Who came from Eden, by way of Sweden.
They may be short, they may be tall
Some of them sigh (and some of them fall),
But you love somebody, somewhere, all of the ti-i-ime.

Pig, pig, he must get rid of the Great Porcine Mystery. My dear Watson, Sherlock Holmes speaking this end. It's my delight on a shiny night to meet you at the Belvedere. Bring your wooden stethoscope and of course your wooden head, Brendon—who came from Eden, by way of Sweden——

There was half an hour to 11 a.m. Now—concentrate. But the thought of even an impersonal communication with Bagshott-Brendon—plain Brendon in 1915—filled him with scorn for Brendon with his off-hand manner towards the Commanding

Officer of a regular battalion—and to 'Spectre' at that, with his seven wound stripes, triple D.S.O. and double M.C.! Brendon of course would get the O.B.E.

Min. 13. 20/3/18

D.A. & Q.M.G. East Midland Division.

In *re* Porcus Senlisiensis v. Rex, and with reference to Minute 12 it is the experience of a senior office in this battalion, who has bred and known the habits of pigs for many years, that they are selective feeders with sensitive noses, and while they will eat carrion in some parts of the world, notably China, they will avoid useless feeding as in latrines, particularly when creosol is used.

Under the circumstances the claim is considered to be of doubtful validity, despite which the feelings of the farmer should not be ignored. A 20-franc note is appended herewith as an *ex gratia* payment entirely unconnected with any regimental funds.

P. S. T. Maddison, Lt.
for O.C. 2nd Gaultshire Regt.

"The Colonel is ready, sir," said the groom, looking in past the gas-blanket.

On the way up the line, 'Spectre' said, "I am going to show you round the Forward Zone this morning; tomorrow you will take up the new draft subalterns and make them familiar with what you learn today. It's all at very short notice, I'm afraid, but we have had no time for training. In the days ahead, junior officers will have to rely mainly on their own initiative."

"Is there any idea when the Germans will start, sir?"

"At present their front line is being held by Landsturm troops, third-line territorials. That tells us that the assault divisions are still to be moved up. Also, for about half a mile behind their front line, all roads leading to it have been cratered by our heavies. The idea is that the Boche will repair those damaged stretches only just before the assault. Scout 'planes are flying low over them soon after dawn, watching the destroyed sections. So far they have not been made up." Thank God, he thought, maintaining his air of quiet confidence.

Chapter 5

THE CAGE

They dismounted at the Belvedere, a small ruin near the site of a château blown up by the Germans in the retreat to the *Siegfried Stellung* a year previously, and leaving a prospect of cultivated fields grey with a tinge of green, entered a communication trench. This position, known as The Aviary, lay on comparatively high ground. Two gentle slopes, hardly valleys, passed through it, descending east to the Forward Zone. The particular communicating trench lay beside another in which telephone cables, connecting various headquarters with Brigade and Division, had been buried six feet deep.

Where the junction of many lines came together, star-points of chalk had, before the laying, been visible from the air. They had been photographed by high-flying German aircraft. The position was also under observation from tethered *drachen* balloons 8,000 metres distant, behind the *Siegfried Stellung*.

They passed through The Aviary, and went on to the battalion redoubt, about a mile to eastward. Threading their way down a narrow passage of chalk, they found the two battalion Intelligence Officers awaiting them at a T-junction; thence to the dug-out of the C.O. of the Verderers. They were offered whiskey, but 'Spectre' refused.

From the sketch-map which Phillip had memorized, the redoubt was oval, and about 300 yards across. It was a self-contained fort, with stores of water, food, and ammunition, in its four company keeps, to last for three days. Surrounded by many wire-entanglements, the Bird Cage was isolated from the redoubts on either flank by about 1,000 yards. Machine-gun cross-fire covered the intervening ground, some of the guns being hidden in masked pits fifteen feet deep in the chalk.

This land, like that farther north which Phillip had seen during November, was scarcely marked by shell-fire. It was under cultivation by returned French peasants and had been planted with wheat during the previous October. Then, the downland had been cold and grey with much rain; now it was almost countryside under the sun of the vernal equinox. The wheat-plants, small and spidery beyond the maze of trenches, were beginning to curl with the push of sap. Larks were singing in the sky, borne upon warm currents of air arising from chalk made whiter by the sun. The wheat was growing to the verge of the heaps still being thrown up by thousands of shovels; stalks of corn would eventually rise to the level of the horizontal spirals of barbed wire beyond parapet and parados, which gave to the plateau the name of Bird Cage.

The spirit of Spring had arisen in the men digging along the trenches. Among the working parties many whistled, others were singing; helmets, gas-masks and tunics were laid aside. The party of officers moved past them, the two colonels leading, their adjutants following, after them the Intelligence officers. The tour went from keep to defensive zone, from machine-gun emplacement to aid-post and underground stores in the keeps, which were the company headquarters. The lines were sited so that enemy forces advancing in extended order would be seen in silhouette beyond the protecting wire belt.

Leaving behind the Bird Cage, they passed down a communicating trench which zigzagged through the main defensive line, and came to the outpost line. This was held by posts, each widely separated from its neighbour, and consisting of six or seven men under an N.C.O.

Phillip began to see the tactical pattern of defence in depth: first the outpost, or warning line: then the main defensive line: behind it the Bird Cage. A mile or so behind this was The Aviary, the main Battle Zone. In reserve behind the Battle Zone the Green Line, now being constructed by the inhabitants of the White City. Defence in depth: no more 'thin red lines'.

Standing in the deserted front trench, the adjutant of the Verderers told him that it was safe to look over what was left of the weed-grown parapet.

"There's a good view over the Hindenburg Line from here."

Phillip raised his head to the parapet weeds and looked down a valley to the German lines about a mile away. He saw, on ground ascending to the south, the belts of 1917 German wire streaking with rusty brown the withered grasses of the valley side. In the distance lay green meadows, in which a glint was the St. Quentin Canal. Through field-glasses, freckles of red turned out to be the broken roofs of a village seeming to float on the midday mist.

To the right, the skyline of the old French position was slightly roughened by the remains of a village blown up, said the Verderers adjutant, in the retreat to the Hindenburg Line a year before.

"When last I had a platoon, some years ago now, the front line trenches were held fairly strongly," said Phillip.

"You had wonderful targets, I believe," replied the other, glancing at the riband of the 1914 Star on Phillip's breast.

They moved on to an outpost. The Verderers C.O. asked the platoon commander questions.

"What are your duties in the event of an attack?"

"Each of my posts has orders to withdraw separately to the main line of defence in rear, sir."

"You mean to The Aviary?"

"No, sir. To the main defence line of the forward zone."

"Where is that in relation to the battalion defence zone?"

"It lies in front of the support line, sir."

"You mean the Bird Cage?"

"No, sir. The Bird Cage lies behind the support line."

"Do your section commanders know their lines of withdrawal in the event of an attack in force?"

"Yes, sir. I've rehearsed them in the dark, wearing gas-masks."

"How many times?"

"Twice, sir."

"What is your name?"

"Longmire, sir."

The colonel of the Verderers turned to his adjutant. "See that every other platoon east of the main defensive line practises withdrawal wearing gas-masks once every night at staggered times, will you?"

They went back. 'Spectre' again refused whiskey, asking for soda-water with lime-juice. The Verderer's Colonel, who had a slight Midlands accent and wore waxed moustaches, urged him to have some whiskey instead; and when 'Spectre' said he never drank it, remarked, "Go on? I should have thought"—with a glance at his guest's gongs—"that a Band of Hope tipple wasn't much in your line."

"I find it keeps me in good shape, Colonel," replied 'Spectre' equably.

On the way back he looked suddenly tired, thought Phillip.

The two sat down in a passing-place for stretcher-bearers. The sun was now warm, the air buoyant. "Well, Phillip, what did you think of the defensive measures?"

"May I speak my mind, Colonel? Well, to tell the truth, I was rather surprised to see so few dug-outs, but then I understand that there has been no time so far to make them."

"What else occurred to you?"

"I thought that some of the keeps sheltering company headquarters wouldn't stand a direct hit by a four-two, let alone a five-nine. Then, the machine gun emplacements, although camouflaged, are cruder than in 1916. I expected pill-boxes with at least two feet of ferro-concrete head-cover. Those I saw had only corrugated iron sheets over them, held down by sandbags. Others in The Aviary are still only sites marked by notice boards."

"What do you deduce from that?"

"I couldn't help thinking that it was a poor copy of the German redoubt system on the Somme, less the deep dug-outs, less the concrete, less the ten-foot trenches with fire-steps, less the trench-sides revetted with willow hurdles."

'Spectre' was silent, then he murmured, "I will tell you in confidence that in the Fifth Army there are only eleven divisions holding a forty-two mile front. There is one division in reserve. As you know, Haig has been systematically starved of drafts from home. In spite of having to break up one battalion in nearly every infantry brigade, all divisions are far below strength."

Phillip recalled that 'Spectre' had had a Staff billet at G.H.Q. until three months previously. It all seemed pretty bad. "What about the Yanks? Couldn't one of their battalions be put in with every British brigade, as we Terriers were in 1914? We'd have been lost without the regulars to nurse us at First Ypres."

"I heard that Haig suggested that to General Pershing, without result. You can't put an old head on young shoulders. No, the trouble with reinforcements is that Haig has many enemies, who think he's a fool because he won't compete with the glib tongues of the *arriviste* politicians, or play off one against another in the Frocks' game. So here we are, short of men to complete our defences. Even barbed wire is hard to get, and at a time when it is known in Whitehall that the Germans have brought up more than forty assault divisions, including those in support, opposite Gough's eleven depleted and tired divisions holding forty-two miles of front. Five fresh Germans against one tired man in the army of what you call the Mud-balled Fox."

"I heard General Mowbray tell Lord Satchville that, just before I came out." In momentary panic he thought, It's going to be another 'red little, dead little army'. Should he go sick, and get away in time? But it was no good in England any more. God, he was still windy.

"What a thing it is," went on 'Spectre', "for a Commander-in-Chief to have a positive enemy in front of him and a negative enemy behind his back! They say that the onlooker sees most of the game. He does; but unless he has experience of playing the game, he will not understand what the antagonists are going through. But that is the classic pattern of human life in all known literature. Well, we'll have to make a fight of it where we are now, and so allow Gough to withdraw his main forces behind the line of the Somme. Yes, I said behind the Somme: for it's no good holding the banks of canals and rivers, they merely provide easy targets for enemy gunners. Open warfare does not necessarily mean disastrous warfare. On the contrary."

He tried to get rid of flatulence, while Phillip stared at a lark in the sky. "I didn't want that lime-juice, but if one refuses a drink some of these new colonels take it as an offence."

"Sir, did you say Gough's *main* forces?"

'Spectre' laughed drily. "Yes. His main forces consist of one division in reserve—perhaps eight thousand bayonets—against the *stosstruppen* of perhaps twenty *divisionen* making the original assault, and reinforced by twenty more in support. Yes, Fifth Army has one division in reserve. But there are G.H.Q. divisions in further reserve, no doubt."

"Then it may be a good thing if we have to retire some distance, because then Haig will be able to counter-attack, as the Germans did at Cambrai, into the base-angles of the re-entrant?"

"Precisely. Open warfare is necessary for victory."

Peace came upon Phillip. He sat at ease in the warm sun. All would be well while 'Spectre' was with them. Gossamers were now crossing the tops of the communication trench. Pictures of faraway springtimes appeared and faded in his mind, while into the air arose the sounds of pick and shovel, men talking, a tenor voice singing *Roses of Picardy*. He saw that Westy's face looked paler than usual, and wondered if he were like Moggers, tired to his very bones—an eye out, a hand gone; shell splinters through left thigh, calf, and ankle; bullet through top of lung. He had been with 'Spectre' when he had copped that lot; what the earlier wounds, at Festubert, and then at Hooge, were he did not know. Could it be that he had been emasculated? Was *that* why he had been in hopeless love with Frances, and later on, apparently unable to do anything with Sasha, the free-for-all girl at Flossie Flowers' hotel? Since that New Year's Eve party, when Westy had come into his bedroom and found Sasha there, and had walked out of the hotel, Westy had been, not exactly distant, but aloof. The fact that he was incapacitated would not alter his longing to be loved, only his power, or potence they called it, to be natural. Was that his secret, the 'grievous wound' of King Arthur before the sword Excalibur was lost forever?

"Do you know what this war is about, Phillip?"

"Well, I don't believe what the newspapers say, Westy."

"It is caused by the vindictive self-will in France, in England, and above all in Germany."

"Why above all in Germany?"

"Because of their geographical position, and large tracts of sandy soil which will not grow wheat. Hence the Germanic migrations of the Middle Ages."

A gossamer touched Phillip's forehead. He looked across the bay to where Westy, his eye closed, sat with uncovered head a little forward, and wrists crossed on lap. The still figure was to windward of the gossamers, and in fancy he held to the thread across his forehead as coming from Westy. He remembered the myriad gossamers making tunnels to the sun on the stubble fields around Billericay in Essex, where he had gone to the funeral of the Zeppelin crew burned to death with their craft so long ago. Poor Westy, he thought, closing his eyes against stinging moisture; he was worn out, but with a mind still as clear as glass, and as rare as unbroken glass upon the battlefields. As adjutant, he must take care of the old fellow.

Had gossamer thought passed between them? For the pale blue eye opened. "Surely you were boarded B2 until the middle of March, Phillip?"

"Yes, Colonel."

"So you applied for another board, did you?"

Phillip hesitated, then told the truth. "I put down my own name on the 'A' list."

"Why?"

"Well, sir, you know how it is."

"I do know how it is. But do *you* know, I wonder?"

He did not know what to think, much less what to say, at the peremptory tone.

"I—I think so, sir."

"I told you before that you call me 'colonel' unless we are on parade. I will be frank. You were in a position of trust, and you took advantage of that position in the orderly room at Landguard to send in a false return?"

"Yes, Colonel."

"Did you connect your action with the fact that, while living with your people in London, you gave the address of your next-of-kin to be in Gaultshire? Now think of the question! Have you connected those two actions of yours? There is no objection, in so far as the Regiment is concerned, why you shouldn't choose to come from the county. There may be good reasons for it—feelings of consideration, for example, in order to avoid the direct impact of possible bad news."

When there was no reply to this question he went on, "It is my affair to ask about this, as your Colonel, Phillip. For what a Commanding Officer has to determine above all is, how far are his officers to be relied upon."

The spectre of his own weakness, dismissed from his mind innumerable times, with accompanying uneasy thought that one day he would be found out to be bogus, possessed Phillip. Now it had happened: he was seen for what he really was, a liar and ashamed of his parents and his birth-place.

"You've met my parents, haven't you, Phillip?"

"Yes, Colonel."

"Oh, drop the 'colonel' when we are alone. I am Westy to you. As you know, my people keep a pub in the City. My father, before that, was a soldier in the ranks. He joined the Army because he could not find work. His three sons went in due course to the Board School. One of his sons, through scholarships, reached the University. There he met other men belonging to a class above his own. One day this diffident undergraduate overheard, by accident, one of those young gentlemen say to another, 'One cannot possibly ask West to join us, he isn't a gentleman.' Now I'd like to ask you this: Would you say that remark was snobbish?"

"No, Westy, because it was based on the facts of living as they were then."

"In what way?"

"Different classes have different interests, and different perspectives. Just as the ordinary soldier in the ranks can't really enter into the world of the regimental officer, or the ordinary regimental officer enter the world of the staff, anyway at Corps or Army level."

"Good! Did you think that out for yourself?"

"No, Westy. You told me when we were walking up to Broodseinde last October!"

"Good! Now the true Phillip is speaking. Tell me, do you think that remark I overheard about my not being a gentleman had any affect on my home life?"

"No, I don't think it would have had any effect on you."

"Well, it did. From that moment I became conscious of myself as others saw me. I watched myself. I tried to listen to my voice. Once I even went to have a gramophone record made of it, privately, but funked it when I got to the place. I became critically conscious of my parents, in my mind at least. But I loved them, and so would not have had them different from what they were. Do you understand?"

Phillip nodded, unable to face the other man. He dismissed a thought to look piteous, or contrite. If he was going to be sent to a company, as a platoon commander, well, that was that. If he were killed, he was killed. But he wasn't ashamed of Father, really; only of his ways, and his——. He could not face his thoughts, which were beyond the thought of death.

"Fear," said 'Spectre', "can take many forms. Imposture, including braggart bravery on occasion. Then there is fear of not being good enough, which leads to *hybris*, the building up of a false self-showing. The war was brought about, one might almost say, by the massed falseness of the European nations. The truth, of course, is that of Christ. 'Thy neighbour as thyself', not to be scorned for one's own faults showing in him, but to be helped, through one's self-understanding, which is love, or God."

Phillip still sat with averted head. 'Spectre' knew what he was feeling.

"Don't look so unhappy, Phillip. The fact that you have adopted Gaultshire is in itself an indication that you felt more at home there in the formative years of your childhood."

Phillip looked up gratefully. "It was a wonderful place, Westy! Like a story book. The country, I mean, and the brook, and the

Duke's moors. My Mother, too, was so happy there. She came from the county," he added.

"Phillip, I've been damnably clumsy, do forgive me. I think I 'see Shelley plain'. That is all I wanted to see, only I approached with a boss shot." He crossed the trench to put a hand upon the younger man's shoulder. "Now tell me, how do you feel about being with the infantry, after your long spell as a transport officer?"

"I think I shall be all right, Colonel Westy!"

"I'm scared stiff sometimes, I don't mind telling you, Phil. It's only the thought of the men that keeps one going." He sat down and clasped his hands under his chin, shutting his eyes as though praying.

The tenor voice had ceased its plaintive singing of *Roses of Picardy*, to 'Spectre' an ironic longing for a land of myth: did the singer realise that he was in Picardy? Gossamers were now glinting red and blue as they twisted and drew out.

"Hundreds of thousands of money spiders crossing the Bird Cage, Phillip, all trying to get their money out while the going is good."

He remembered his father telling them as children, on one of the Sunday walks to Cutler's Pond, about the gossamer spider, which he called Linyphia. Father had used Latin names for butterflies, too, which he had collected as a young man. He saw himself on a chair taking Father's butterflies from their wooden boxes. What an awful boy he had been to poor old Father. Father telling them on that Sunday walk how each Linyphia rose up on a silken kite, first having climbed to the top of a grass bent or dead thistle, and the warm air took him up, up, up, away, away, hundreds of feet up in the silent singing wind from the south, now drifting across Picardy and Artois into Flanders and away, away, to the chalk cliffs of the coast, and over the sea to England. But millions would die on the journey. How strange everything was when you thought about it, strange and almost terrifying; but if one could only see it glass-clear, one could also sense beyond the gossamers, to the spirit of eternal beauty.

"I never thanked you for what you did for me on the Passchendaele crest last October, Phillip."

They sat peacefully in the warm sun, three yards of intensely white chalk between them. How quiet it was, no sound of gun-fire. The last day of winter, tomorrow it would be Spring, the twenty-first of March, the sun climbing higher every day, and giving everything a smaller shadow until noon: and 'the first minute after noon is night'. Who wrote that? It was startling; it was like the stroke of death. Had he read it in *The Oxford Book*? Ah—

Love is a full glowing and constant light
But his first minute after noon is night.

Uncle Hugh used to say that everything had its shadow, and your shadow went everywhere with you; it stayed with you, it foreshortened when you were asleep, it arose with you, but when you were dead it did not last long, but broke up with you. Yes, it remained your shadow until leaving you it was given back to the earth of your genesis, and then your earth-bound self drifted on like a gossamer, beyond the wooden crosses of the dead.

When they got back to the quarry 'Spectre' said, 'Will you put yourself in Part Two Orders tonight to be adjutant with the rank of acting Captain, Phillip."

Mar. 20. Wed. Moggers today had steam-roller painted black and yellow stripes, with Gaults. badge on front. Chinks poshing up camp. Brigadier and others to dinner, including Moggers and M.O. I put up my third pip!

That was the last entry Phillip made in his personal diary while he remained in France. The Brigadier brought one of his new colonels, recently sent up from the Pool, who seemed very anxious to hear every word spoken by so experienced a soldier as 'Spectre' West. It was his first battalion command. Also among the guests was the colonel commander of the brigade of 18-pounder field-guns which covered the right flank of the Bird Cage, and the Brigade padre who, since he wore the riband of the Military Medal, had served in the ranks. Towards 10 p.m., as they were playing bridge, the clerk on duty in the adjoining office came in with a message marked *Urgent*. Phillip, asking to be excused, unfolded it while the other three at his table put down the cards. His heart raced as he stared at the single code-word RAINBOW. Should he interrupt the game, now that *Prepare for Attack* had come over the wire? Better wait. He took up his cards, hardly knowing what he was playing. The game came to an end without his revoking.

"Ha, they went to bed with that ace, partner! That's four spades to us. Game. Honours, partner?"

"Oh, queen and knave, partner."

Scores had hardly been jotted down when the clerk returned. "Brigade major on the telephone, sir, asking for the Brigadier."

Probably the same message, he thought; let the old boy announce it.

"Well, it looks as though it's coming at last," said the Brigadier, quietly. "Division reports that two companies of Warwicks raided the Boche trenches beyond Fayet, and brought back a mixed bag of prisoners from nine battalions of three Regiments, just come into a sector held this morning by one Landsturm Regiment. They all said the balloon goes up tomorrow, bombardment to open 3.30 a.m. Berlin time. Confirms what the Hun pilot said when he was brought down two days ago, and also those Alsatians from the trench mortar battery. Still, you never know—per'aps they were all told to say it. I have an idea that the real push is coming up north, in Flanders. Much shorter to the coast up there."

The guests stood up. "Well, it's been a jolly evening, most good of you to ask us, Colonel. Good night, and good luck!"

When they had gone 'Spectre' said, "Warn all companies, and don't forget to clean your teeth. It may be your last chance for a week or more."

The night was starry and still. Mist lay in thin strata over fields dim under the moon just past its first quarter. He rang up to warn the company commanders in Brigade reserve at Corunna; all transport waggons to be loaded with spare kits on returning from the ration dumps. The Maltese cart must arrive in the morning for the officers' mess boxes. Then he wrote up the War Diary. Afterwards he sat unmoving at the table so long that 'Spectre' told him to get down to it.

With the telephone on the floor beside him he got into his blanket bag, but not to sleep. Thoughts chased through his head until he fixed his mind with the idea that Spring was coming, warm dry weather, it would not be so bad as First Ypres. But supposing it was the main push, with forty fresh *divisionen* against a half-prepared zone . . . but there was the Green Line, some miles in rear. It would mean a withdrawal, similar to that of the Germans in March '17, when they went back to the *Siegfried Stellung*. Then, there was practically no fighting. Still, forty *divisionen* packing the rear areas wasn't exactly like the mud-balled Fifth Army in the valley of the Ancre. Perhaps the idea was after all to lure the Germans across the derelict areas of the old Somme battlefields, with their inefficient roads, lack of water-points and shelter, and cut them off there.

His mind dwelled upon scenes in the Bird Cage. Westy had said that he did not want his parents to change in any way. Would he himself have been any different if he had loved Father? He tried to imagine loving Father, but at once the picture faded out, like a broken bioscope film. Sudden darkness. Another picture, of Father in his armchair, long-bearded narrow lion-face reading bits out of *The Daily Trident* to Mother about the Hun Hordes massing in France. The film broke again; he could not get near Father. There was always the distance between them, a vacuum. He could never remember when it had been otherwise. Father had never kissed him, or held him warm. There had never been a warm Father. He tried to think of Father as a man, with bare legs and arms and stomach; but all that would come was Father bathing in the sea at Hayling Island, in a blue-white ringed costume to his knees.

Mother's face was approachable, but it would not come really near. It hovered with insistent thoughts about him, so that he found himself struggling to dismiss the face, to get clear to think apart from entangled feelings. Suddenly he imagined himself shouting *Mother leave me alone!* He began to feel hopeless, irritated, remorseful, and hollow. He struggled against dissolution, while darkness seemed to be drawing him down, whence other thoughts arose, dangerous weak thoughts because he might yield to the blue eyes and fair soft hair of the blonde who came from Sweden offering peace in her soft, warm beauty. He must get up; but he lay there, in weak indecision, longing to blend, to be merged into her floating spirit body; and was saved from further rumination by a spot of light dancing towards him, while a leaden weight of apprehension settled upon his solar plexus.

"Are you awake, sir? Urgent message from Brigade has just come through."

The circle of light was held as he unfolded the paper.

BUSTLE.

His heart gave a thump. Sergeant Tonks was saying, "With your permission, sir, I'll repeat to CAB, CART, and WAIN."

"Right, sergeant."

"Will you tell the Commanding Officer, sir?"

"I think I'll let him sleep. He can't do anything now, and God knows what sleep he'll be able to get in the next few days. Let me know when the three companies report from Corunna. Better put in a relief telephonist, and get some kip yourself. Oh, just to check this. CAB, CART, and WAIN are to report here at the quarry before going into the rear zone of The Aviary. No. 4, TUMBRIL, will of course remain at Corunna, prepared to move at five minutes' notice."

"Very good, sir."

"And you'll be informing Brigade as soon as the three companies leave here for The Aviary?"

"Right, sir, I'll tell the signaller."

"No, I'll telephone the B-m myself, of course. I'm going to get up now. I can't sleep anyway."

He went out into the chill of the night. Stars overhead were still visible as he walked up the road beyond the quarry, and down again. He returned to talk to the sentry, then up and down the road interminably until voices and marching feet edged the night against the tinny notes of a mouth-organ. Mist made the figures blurred upon the road. It was CAB, led by Bill Kidd. The Brigade padre was with him. Bill had apparently decided to be very regimental. His words were exhaled with whiffs of rum.

"'A' Company, Captain Kidd reporting, sah!" he barked. "All present and correct! Nominal Roll prepared for the Orderly Room Sergeant, sah!" Having got rid of that, he changed his part. "Congratters my mad son on your third pip! Lovely day, what? Too blasted quiet for Bill Kidd's liking. Bill Kidd knows where he is when the old Johnsons are floppin' about!"

"Johnsons?"

"Aye, Johnsons! Coal Boxes! Black Marias! Angels of Mons and all that stuff. A shout! A scream! A roar! Black in the face!" He coughed, bending down to keep attention upon himself. "Sorry for the rust in the old organ pipes." He adjusted his 5-ft. length of thick, loosely knitted worsted scarf, weighing about 4 lb., flung twice round his neck and almost hiding his chin. "That's better. Keep the old vocal chords warm. Well, old boy, I'll give you a buzz when we're all safely tucked up in the old keep. Chin chin, see you later."

He faded back into the mist, and the last Phillip was to hear of him for two days was a rasping, "Come on, you crab wallahs, do an allez!" and then the thread of mouth-organ music grew faint, to nothing.

Phillip stood with the padre by the sentry's brazier. "Quite a character, Bill Kidd," said the padre. "The men would follow him anywhere. The only thing he appears to be afraid of is French cartridges!"

"How is that, padre?"

"Well, as you know, most of the fellows after some time out here get superstitious fears. With Bill it's French cartridges. This particular hoodoo began, I gather, when some of the boys in the 8th battalion in Oppy Wood found some French cartridges, and carried them as souvenirs. First one, then another, was killed by shell-fire. Then in that raid a week or two ago, four men who had them in their haversacks fell under a direct hit. Bill plays his harmonica to overcome the hoodoo."

Talk came round to the Germans. "They're sportsmen, most of them," said the padre. "I remember a stretch of the Menin Road between Hooge Tunnel and Clapham Junction, I expect you know it? The road there at that particular section, you may remember, was still under direct observation after we had captured the pill-box at Clapham Junction. My job during the battle was to bring stretcher cases down the road from Inverness Copse. Most of the troops and carrying parties went up and down under the right bank, and were under constant fire from everything, but when I went down on the road itself with the wounded, the Germans never fired their machine guns. It wasn't chance, I'm pretty sure, for on three occasions they laid off when stretchers and walking wounded were going down."

Phillip warmed to the padre, telling him of similar experiences at Loos, again on July the First, and at Passchendaele.

"Oh yes, they're sportsmen; the pity is that our newspapers don't publish such things, but I suppose the people at home wouldn't understand, that's the tragic part of it. Well, I must be off, but before I go, do let me tell you the story of our Chaplain-General, Bishop Gwynne. I was riding with him on my way to Third Army School at Auxi-le-Château last summer, when he told me about a chaplain in a battalion of the London Regiment who insisted on going into the trenches with the boys. He had a board outside his dug-out with the words *The Vicarage* painted on it. One day a Cockney passed and said to his pal, 'Blime Bill, who'd have thought to see a bloody vicarage in the front line?' At that the chaplain popped out his head and said, 'That's right! Now you've seen the bloody vicar, too!' 'And,' said the Chaplain-General, 'that's the kind of chaplain I'm trying to get them to send out to France.' Cheerio, Maddison, and all the best!"

Phillip waited until the other two companies had been checked in, then went back in high spirits to report their departure. 'Spectre' was still lying on his back covered by blankets on a stretcher, his boots sticking out like those of a dead man. "Numbers One, Three, and Four Companies have left for the Aviary, sir. It is nearly 4 a.m. The order to Man Battle Positions came in just after 2 a.m."

"I heard it."

A hand came from under the blankets, and took his, the pressure remaining upon his fingers for a few moments, then 'Spectre' said,

"If you feel you have been made unhappy by your father, think that it was because your father has been made unhappy, too."

"I understand, Westy."

A stumped wrist—the black-gloved dummy had been taken off—crossed with the hand and gave a double clasp. "Bless you, dear boy. Now get some sleep. We'll be leaving for our advanced headquarters at 4.30."

Fully clothed beside the security of the telephone, Phillip lay calmly still. There was little under an hour to go. Then messages began to arrive, and no sleep was possible, or desired.

At 4.30 a.m., as he was slinging haversack, field glasses, map case, water-bottle, revolver, etc. he felt the chalk under him beginning to tremble. Then the air was rumbling. He went outside and stood in a light-pattern of thousands of great scissors flashing to the Galaxy.

An hour later, soaked with sweat, the battalion H.Q. party was inside the 30-ft. deep dug-out of the inner Zone. There, sitting on the floor beside the telephone, Phillip managed to make some notes for the C.O.'s use when he had time to write up the battalion War Diary.

20/21 March	
midnight.	Bde 'phoned gaps found by patrols in German wire.
2.07 a.m.	BUSTLE from BDE. Sent to all coys.
3.15 a.m.	CAB, CART, WAIN left Quarry for Aviary.
3.30 a.m.	R.F.A. Bde reported putting down bursts of fire on enemy assembly places.
4.09 a.m.	CAB, CART, WAIN reported in positions.
4.10 a.m.	Bde informed of above.
4.30 a.m.	Bn. hq. party left for HOOK.
5.20 a.m.	Arrd. HOOK. Gas masks worn; much yellow cross and phosgene.
5.30 a.m.	Gas and h-e reported on all coy keeps and posts.
6.30 a.m.	No contact with Bde, or CAB, or CART, or WAIN. Power buzzers also dud. Gas now yellow cross.
7.35 a.m.	No contact by land line with Bde. Runners sent out.
10 a.m.	Fog lifting. Incessant m-g and rifle fire from east, direction of Bird Cage.
12 noon.	Sunshine. No contact with Bde yet. All coys holding positions, but report flanks in air.
2.15 p.m.	Sullivan (I.O.) sent to Bde with report. Our casualties estimated 200. Bird Cage garrison coming into Aviary. Asked for TUMBRIL to be sent up.
6 p.m.	Sullivan's runner came back reporting S. killed by shell. Runner wounded and incoherent.

At 6.5 p.m. Lt.-Col. West ordered Phillip to report the situation to Brigade, which had moved to its advanced headquarters in the Quarry. 'Spectre' gave him a sealed envelope for the Brigadier.

Part Two

ACTION

EVENING, 21 MARCH–22 APRIL, 1918

Chapter 6

RETREAT

The sun was going down south-west of the wooded Sydenham heights, upon which stood the familiar Crystal Palace, as Richard crossed the Hill that evening. In the old days its glass roof had often gleamed with little flecks of fire, reminding him of his boyhood in the West Country; but now the panes of the roof were painted black, lest they guide enemy aircraft into London. And so, he thought, was life; come almost to darkness.

In the City the news had broken at mid-day that a great battle was raging along a 50-mile front. Phillip, in the Peronne sector, must be feeling, as he put it to himself, 'the full force of it'. He must be the first with the news, breaking it gently, lest Hetty imagine the worst, as she tended to do nowadays.

With long strides, carrying a copy of *The Pall Mall Gazette* folded under one arm against the crook of his umbrella, and bowler hat in hand, he crossed the Hill, went down the gully—putting on his hat before reaching Hillside Road—and with a dull feeling of arrival, opened his front door. At once he felt disappointment, then vexation, at the sound of his father-in-law's voice. Having wiped his boots on the mat, he unstiffened himself to be amiable, and looking round the kitchen door, said "Good evening, Mr. Turney", while his glance took in an open copy of the Liberal paper *The Star*, from which his father-in-law had apparently been reading.

"I am afraid I have interrupted you," he said, withdrawing his head.

"Oh no, Dickie, Papa was just going——"

"The news is good, I fancy, according to Bonar Law in the House this afternoon, Dick."

Richard, having hung up black hat and black umbrella, opened the door wide, out of courtesy, before facing the other man.

"Well, Mr. Turney, all I can say is I hope that Bonar Law knows what he is talking about. Castleton in the *Trident* has long urged that there be changes in the High Command."

"That may be so, Dick. For myself, I cannot help thinking that if only Asquith had remained we might by now be at peace. No good can come of the war now, that I can see."

"If I may venture an opinion, Mr. Turney, it was Asquith and his Liberal Government before the war who insisted on cutting the Army estimates, thereby causing so many regiments to be disbanded. Had that not been so, we might have had a just peace by now."

Thomas Turney, cloth cap pulled down over bald head sunken into heavy coat collar, went back next door, where his elder sister Marian, upright in her chair, awaited him. Always stiff, always attentive, she irritated the old man. Why did she always watch him like a cat watching a mouse! Why didn't she read a book sometimes? He had gone to see his daughter with a view to advertising for a housekeeper. He felt Marian was destroying him. She was the eldest of the family, and had always tried to mother him. It was time she went elsewhere.

Marian Turney suspected this, but was too reserved to say anything to her niece about it; even as she concealed the belief that she was going blind.

"The macaroni cheese is ready in the oven, turned low as you told me, Tom. Would you care to have your supper served now, or will you have it later?"

"Wait a minute, woman! Can you not let me rest still a moment? And if supper is to be served now, how can I have it later? You waste words." He sat down, after struggling to remove his ulster coat, having refused her help. He was thinking of Phillip; and of Charlie's boy, young Tom, with the South Africans.

In her sitting-room, while Richard ate sausages largely made of bread and gristle, Hetty waited to hear the latest news. It was not so much that she dared not to ask her husband, but that behind her reluctance hovered the spirit of fear which had long settled into a feeling of dread whenever she thought of Phillip: a feeling which, accumulating during the day, usually broke blackly into the sleepless small hours of night, a period only to be endured by prayer, which brought relief, usually, half an hour or so before she had to get up at 7 a.m.

Richard, having finished his supper, put the bits of gristle in a match-box for the cat—later. Zippy was anxious, too, for sometimes its benefactor left the match-box beside the clock for long periods. On such occasions it would utter a faint *me-ow*, and Richard would say gently "You must learn patience, Zippy," and continue the reading of *The Daily Trident*, which blanked out his face to the cat.

"Where are the girls, Hetty? Have they come in yet?"

"Elizabeth is going to Nina's for supper, and will be home about nine o'clock, Dickie, while Doris has gone to see a friend who lives in St. Margaret's road. She won't be late, I'm sure."

"Oh. Is this another young fellow?"

"Oh no, Dickie! Mary is one of the girl students at Bedford College."

"Does Doris still hear from that young fellow—what's his name—Willoughby?"

"I think he writes to her occasionally, Dickie."

"Who are his people, d'you know?"

"I don't think Doris knows. He lives in Essex, I think she said."

"H'm. Well, it's none of my affair, I suppose. Is it, Zippy?" He rattled the match-box, while the big yellow neuter cat me'ow'd inaudibly. "You must learn patience, Zippy!" He put the box on the chimney shelf before changing boots for carpet slippers. Thus comforted by the sign that master was not going out, the cat settled down before the coke fire, the words *learn patience* causing it to think of food. It began to purr, almost inaudibly.

After reading a third of the paper Richard took out his half-hunter gold watch and compared its time with that of the clock on the marble shelf above the fire-place. "Eight o'clock, Hetty. Time for you to forsake me, isn't it?"

"Oh, I've just remembered, how silly of me to forget! Might I see the thing about Bonar Law——?"

"But surely your father read it to you?"

"Oh no, Dickie! Papa came in to talk over an advertisement for a housekeeper."

"H'm," said Richard, remembering the circumstances of the last housekeeper's sudden departure. "You'd better be careful——" His sense of good taste prevented him from saying what he thought.

"Oh yes, of course, naturally! But perhaps when the better weather comes——" She, too, stopped her words, lest he think the worse of her father, should it mean Aunt Marian's departure.

"Here you are," he said, offering the evening paper, which had remained beside him on the table. "You worry yourself needlessly. Why didn't you say you wanted it before?"

Knowing that he liked to read bits from the paper, she asked him to tell her what it was, and got the reply, "Better read it for yourself, then there can be no mistake about the need for a compromise peace with that old woman Asquith kowtowing to Prussian militarists!" And feeling better, Richard dropped the match-box on the floor for Zippy to try to hook open. Soon the box was skating all over the linoleum, the cat playing happily while knowing that sooner or later the box would be opened by *Dickie*, a name it knew as well as its own.

> I may tell the House that this attack has been launched on the very part of our line which we were informed would be attacked by the enemy if an attack were undertaken at all. Only three days ago we received information at the Cabinet from G.H.Q. in France that they had definitely come to the conclusion that an attack was going to be launched immediately. I do not feel justified in saying that it has not come as a surprise, and those responsible for our forces have foreseen, and have throughout believed that if such an attack came, we should well be able to meet it. Nothing that has happened gives us in this country any cause whatever for additional anxiety.

She could not understand what Bonar Law, the Leader of the House of Commons, meant by these words, except in the last two lines, which relieved her feelings; and with some cheerfulness, which Richard did not fail to notice, she went out of the room and by the back way into her father's house to play piquet.

As Phillip made his way from shell-hole to shell-hole bullets were coming from all directions. He passed a howitzer being pulled on to the road by a caterpillar tractor. Wounded men were lying about. He spoke to many, saying, 'Help is coming', while wondering what he could do to keep his promise. Very lights were white-blurring through the mist to his left front as he hastened, sometimes lying down at the imminent shriek of a shell, on the way to the Quarry. There he delivered 'Spectre's' letter, and gave what information he could to the Brigadier, including the fact that the Germans appeared to be behind the right flank. Then he went across to the Aid Post, where the M.O. and his orderlies were obviously overworked. He returned to Brigade headquarters, and after a drink of hot sweet tea said he must be getting back. The Brigade-major told him to take it easy, and stand by for the time being.

At 8.30 p.m. the Brigadier discussed with his Brigade-major a message which had been brought by despatch-rider, *The Battle Zone will be held to the last man.*

"Sir——" began Phillip, but the Brigadier impatiently flipped away words with his hand.

"Sorry, sir." He went outside the sand-bagged shelter, and suddenly felt very cold. Mogger's arrival was cheering, until Moggers said that 'Pluggy' Marsden had been killed by a shell that morning.

"I am sure that we ought to retire, Moggers——"

"Now don't try and do 'Aig's job for 'im, Lampo."

He left Moggers. At 9.14 p.m. Allen appeared. He reported that the Germans were in the right flank redoubt. The Aviary was under heavy m.g. and mortar fire from two sides. He was sent back with the Brigadier's order to hold on.

"Can't I go, too?" Phillip asked the Brigade-major.

"Not at the moment, Maddison."

Deep depression overcame Phillip. He passed a cold night in the Quarry, wondering off and on if 'Spectre's' letter to the Brigadier contained an adverse report.

At dawn mist lay thickly, hiding all objects beyond forty yards. The Brigade-major showed him a message from Division, signed by Brendon, saying that every opportunity should be taken to counter-attack the enemy probably assembling under cover of fog. "Can't you see old Shotbags picking his teeth after breakfast, while wondering if his effort to win the war will get him a gong, Maddison?"

Phillip said 'Huh', while thinking: What is happening to Westy? It was senseless to allow them all to be killed. That was what the Germans wanted. He recalled a newspaper phrase—'*the anvil of Verdun*'.

Shortly after 11.0 a.m. a motorcycle despatch rider appeared through the salvoes of five-nines and shrapnel now regularly plastering the road. It was a Fifth Army Order 'to all commands'. The B-m. showed it to Phillip.

> In the event of serious hostile attack all troops will fight rear-guard actions back to forward line of Rear Zone (Green line) stop Most

important that all battalions should keep in touch with each other and carry out retirement in complete co-operation with each other message ends.

"That's what we've been waiting for, Maddison. Will you get it through to 'Spectre'?"

Papers were being brought out for burning. Phillip was slinging bandoliers of S.A.A. over his shoulders when a grey-faced subaltern, accompanied by three other walking wounded came into the Quarry and incoherently, through chattering teeth, managed to get out that a German machine-gun was covering the exit from the Belvedere. With the Brigade-major's permission Phillip set off with Sergeant Tonks carrying one of the two Lewis guns which had been set up above the Quarry to cover the road. He took a canvas pannier, with spare drums and a couple of Mills bombs. Some time later, after nipping from shell-hole to shell-hole, they heard, shockingly near in the mist, the shattering reports of a German gun.

Writhing over the grass in the direction of the noise, they saw it mounted on its sled on the edge of a crater. Tonks sited and fired a drum right into the back of the team. Pushing himself forward, all teeth and sweat and fixed staring eyes, Phillip flung himself into a shell-hole and pulling out the pin of a Mills bomb stood up to throw it after counting off three seconds. After the explosion he looked up and saw a large dog twisting round and round. It seemed to be biting itself near two Germans holding up their hands. Wrenching free his revolver he went forward, beating out with his teeth the tune of the blonde who came from Eden by way of Sweden. Then he was looking down at the knocked-out gun, its barrel ragged and steaming beside Germans writhing or still. He became aware of two sets of held-up arms, and from him came a hysterical cry *Mein prächtige kerls*!

Tonks came up. The two prisoners were young and small, with oversize coal-scuttle helmets. Tonks said, lifting back his tin hat, "Would you believe it, sir, that's what's been pushing our boys around!"

The dog was tearing at its own intestines, its muzzle was bloody, it was yelping. Then he saw a wounded German turning over to draw a pistol. He shot him in the head, then took a pot shot at the dog's head. He missed, felt wretched because the bullet had broken the lower jaw. Its screams were unnerving; he shot it from two feet, it rolled about, and went limp. "Message dog," said Tonks. "Poor sod," as he took the pistol from the dead German. "I'll have that," said Phillip. It was a Parabellum, with a leather wallet of ammunition. He gave his Webley to Tonks. Meanwhile men were beginning to scramble out of the end of the communication trench and coming towards them in the mist. He placed some in an arc around the exit to give covering fire if necessary.

All had happened so quickly and easily that it seemed scarcely to be over. But a salvo of whizzbangs scattering chalk brought back the need to hustle.

"Quick, you fellows!"

They were the survivors of three battalions, from both Bird Cage and Aviary.

"You take charge, corporal! To the Quarry! Now you! You! You! Back you go. Keep together under the senior N.C.O. Sort yourselves out later on. Now you! You! You!" He waited for the last men to come out. To his immense relief, 'Spectre' was among them.

"Divide these men into groups and put each group under an officer or senior N.C.O. and tell them to make their own way back to the Quarry."

"I have already done so, sir."

When they got to the Quarry, the Brigade staff had left. Then down the road appeared a German squad, marching at ease.

"Do we want them, sir?" asked Tonks.

"No," said 'Spectre'.

Tonks fired from his hip, the figures scattered into the fog.

It was growing dark when they reached the Green Line. There they stopped short, to see a position marked by up-turned sods with occasional notice-boards. So much for the bloody dago slackers of the White City! Having cursed them, 'Spectre' ordered pits to be scraped out with entrenching tools. There was some relief when Moggers brought up a hot meal. "The Boche is through down south." By this time, 10 p.m., stragglers from other units had been embodied in the battalion, while patrols had been sent out to get in touch with units on the flanks. The right-wing patrol came back to report "No-one within a mile," so the two remaining Lewis guns were posted to form a defensive flank facing south.

It was curiously silent in the mist. Where was Brigade? An officer patrol had failed to find the new headquarters.

"The trouble with us," said 'Spectre' to Phillip, as supper was being prepared, "is that our tactics of defence are out-of-date. We were ordered to form a defensive flank to cover the ground left open by the retirement of the Irish on our right. This in effect meant a narrowing of The Aviary, because we had to draw in Bill Kidd's company. So the gap was widened, allowing more Boche to get past. We were held in by that Boche machine gun at the Belevedere. It was fortunate that you came up at the right moment."

"I brought the order to withdraw, after the Brigadier had sent up Allen telling you to hold fast."

"I anticipated it. There is no point in allowing one's forces to be neutralised."

"You know, sir, I couldn't help thinking when you told me in the Bird Cage——" He stopped. The thought had gone, with his vitality. He felt cold and dispirited.

Boon put out two enamel mugs of tea thick with condensed milk. With the glow of the drink came optimism, to 'Spectre' as well as himself apparently, for he said, "What were you going to say, Phillip?"

"The idea has always been 'to stand fast and kill Germans'. But surely if we had a planned retreat, it would put the Alleyman at a disadvantage? I remember when we got through the Hindenburg Line at Cambrai the Germans drove into the flanks of the salient we'd made in their line, and cut off a lot of our troops. Therefore, if we went back a long way now, wouldn't we be in a position to do the same to them on a big scale?"

"That's the classic movement, Phillip, that every Commander dreams of. But the question now is, how much ground can we afford to give up, before the limited railway supply system comes under range of the Boche guns?"

"Back to the line of July the First?"

"Yes, but no farther. Amiens, and its railway junctions, is the vital town. By the way, I want to talk to your two prisoners, when they've had their grub."

After a good dose of rum in their tea, the two were ready to talk. 'Spectre' spoke to them in German.

"Vogelkäfig! Nein, die Schlachthofe, Herr Oberst!"

"Ja! Ein Uberschwemmung von Englishes, Herr Oberst!"

After the interrogation 'Spectre' said, "They say, in effect, Phillip, that the Bird Cage is misnamed. It should have been Slaughterhouse. The other man's description is more picturesque, 'the Flood-breaker'. I should call it a temporary dam, that got washed away! Apparently they lost a lot of men, but prisoners treated well usually try to please. They belong to the 440th Reserve Regiment, you may note. Not the leading *Stosstruppem*, but the second-rate followers-up. They say their transport is largely civilian carts and farm waggons. Even dogs are used to draw ammunition in those little Belgian trolley carts. They'll have some fun presently, if we go back behind the Somme battlefield, and they have to cross it. Water, too, should be quite a problem."

Tonks, acting R.S.M., was given the pass word for the sentry groups. Men were lying about, sleeping, when Phillip accompanied 'Spectre' round the posts, to be challenged in unfamiliar dialects.

"Oo are yer?"

"'Stag'."

"Commanding officer."

"Pass, Stags."

"'Alt, thar!"

"The voice of Nottingham," said 'Spectre'. "Are you the the Foresters?"

"Yaas, sa'."

"A fine regiment," said 'Spectre', moving on.

"Oo be 'ee?"

"Stag."

"Aw, you'm a-right."

"Almost we might be in a Dartmoor fog with Sherlock Holmes," said 'Spectre'. "No need to tell me that you come from Devonshire!"

"Aye aye, zur, zurenuff!"

"One of the best of the line regiments," he remarked to Phillip, who was admiring the way 'Spectre' aroused interest in these unknown men.

At 1 a.m. when they returned he told Phillip, "I'm going to lie down for an hour. Wake me if anything comes in."

There was a challenge, a light held low. A party approached.

The senior Colonel said he had taken over when the Brigadier had been wounded in the Quarry. Maps were opened. While they were talking Phillip prepared to sign and detach the casualty and other returns, already written out by Tonks in a Field Message book, and to hand them over to the staff-captain accompanying Colonel Calvert. It was only when the party had gone on that he remembered the two prisoners who were now sleeping curled up together.

Battalion H.Q. was chosen, two hundred yards behind the Green Line, in a sunken farm-track four feet or so below the level of the surrounding arable fields.

"What is our strength?"

"Five officers and one hundred and eighty-six other ranks, Colonel. I had no details of casualties, so I returned the total of eighteen officers and four hundred and thirty-three other ranks as missing."

Remotely behind their position, from the south, flares were rising so far away as to belong almost to another war. At 3 a.m. a despatch rider thudded up with written particulars of a new line to be occupied 'in the event of an ordered withdrawal'. With it was a rough cyclostyled map, marking the line in blue, west of the Canal du Nord. Phillip acknowledged the message, and decided to let 'Spectre' sleep on. Should he send out scouts to find the position of the new line? But could they do so in the fog? Everything was so silent—the calm before the storm. The acting Brigadier had said that fresh German divisions had been put into the line.

Just before 6 a.m. the first low-flying Fokker biplanes were heard above the mist. 'Spectre' said, "I don't want any of these aircraft to be fired at, and tell all company commanders to withdraw their men two hundred paces to the rear. This position is certain to be marked on their gunners' maps."

They had hardly got back when shells began to drone down. They lay in extended order across a grass field. Behind them, according to the map, was the Bois de Gurlu, the new position. Mist dissolved everything beyond thirty yards.

"The Kaiser must think that God sent this weather especially for him. Hardly a 'place in the sun', is it? There's one consolation, if we can't see the Boche, he can't see us."

A motorcycle was approaching.

"Sounds like a twin-cylinder J.A.P., sir. One of ours."

"Keep it covered."

A sidecar was attached to the motorcycle. The driver delivered two envelopes. While Phillip was signing for them 'Spectre' opened one. "We're to fight a rear-guard action to the new line, which is wired. Have you got a compass?"

"Not on me, sir."

"Then why not say 'No'?" replied 'Spectre' sharply. He opened the second envelope, while Allen put his compass on the grass in front of Phillip. The needle trembled as it settled to the north.

'Spectre' folded the second message.

"I have to leave you," he said quietly. "Colonel Calvert has been killed. Phillip, you will take over command of the battalion."

Before he left 'Spectre' said, "Treat a battalion as one large company, divided into four. You may feel at first that everything depends on you alone, but your company commanders will support you." Then he said, "Keep touch, in so far as you can, with the battalions on your flanks. We are in for a long and trying rear-guard action. Remember that the enemy will know no more and no less about you than you do about him. Probably he will be a damned sight more confused!" He said, "Don't forget that negative information is often as valuable as positive. I'll keep you informed as often as I can, and I expect the same in return, from you."

They shook hands, then the side-car was gone in the mist. The clatter of the engine had hardly ceased when a scout came out of the fog across the grass to say breathlessly that the Germans were approaching the Green Line.

"I saw machine-gunners in front, carrying the guns, sir!"

Phillip swallowed to get rid of the dryness in his throat; and breathing deep for calmness, said after a few blank moments, "Allen, we're for the Cork lightship! Send runners to the companies with orders to get back, keeping line as far as possible, until they come to the wood. Then get inside and line the edge and await my order to fire. Come with me, Sergeant-major!"

"What about these two Jerries, sir?"

"Bring 'em with us. They can carry a stretcher." God in heaven, everything depended on him.

With relief he remembered the Grenadiers holding their fire in the Brown Wood Line in November 1914, until the Prussian Garde du Corps was right up to the wire. He waited, resisting panic thoughts to urge everyone to get back to the wood, his mind opaque as the fog dulling the world of wet grass and a few ghostly thorns along the sunken track. Seven headquarters details and the two prisoners were waiting near him, hanging on his orders, his feelings. "How far away is the wood? About a mile away, would you say, Sergeant-major?"

"That's about it, sir." He didn't know, either.

They waited. At last an irregular line appeared, men in groups, others lagging behind. Some were puffing fags. There was nothing to worry about, really. What was to be, would be. Until then, to hell with worry.

"Lead on. Hold all fire until further orders. Pass it down. Quietly does it."

"Aye aye, sir!" The reply came from a ramshackle bare-headed figure among them, long scarf round neck, ends hanging low and loose. Tremendously cheering sight!

"Good God, where've you sprung from, you old devil?"

"Hunland, old boy."

"What happened?"

"Well, as a matter of fact, old boy, I was given such a bloody awful breakfast," the voice drawled casually, "that I decided not to stay." The manner reverted to that of the battalion k'nut. "I ask you, old boy! Acorn coffee! Black bread! Sausage made of old boots! Cor, you ought to see their cavalry on cab horses! And their tanks! Towing Randy Ruperts! Fact, old boy! Bloody balloons towed on a cable stretched between two tin pantechnicons! What hopes they have of seeing anything in this fog, God only knows, and he won't split! Where's the Old Man?"

"'Spectre'? He's commanding the Brigade."

"Who's in command, Pluggy?"

"Pluggy copped it yesterday morning. I'm temporarily in charge of things. Not so loud, if you don't mind."

"Right-ho, old boy. What am I supposed to do? Return to Home Establishment, as an escaped prisoner of war?"

"D'you want to?"

"Not in these trousers, old boy. Where're we making for?"

"Edge of Gurlu wood. Here, on the map. Will you look after the right flank, Bill? I'll stay here and look after this end. By the way, no firing until I give the order."

"Righty-ho, old boy." Kidd disappeared along the line.

Phillip walked on, Allen holding the compass. Sooner than

expected a dark shade in the mist. Thank God, right direction! Coils of concertina wire, trees beyond. Where could they get through? He felt alarm. Damn, he should have sent scouts ahead, to find out. "We'll have to get over as best we can. It's only one coil." It wasn't easy, it was terrifying, spikes against cloth. A sergeant hurried up, "Gap over there, sir!"

"Oh, good! See the men through, will you?" He must stand there, be the last through. He took out pipe and pouch, filled the bowl; waited, imagining sudden figures, shouts . . . *stop being windy!* Now think: Germans advancing at, say, two miles an hour. Mile in thirty minutes; thirtieth of a mile in one minute. Roughly fifty yards a minute. Four hundred yards away when reported to be crossing the Green Line. Eight minutes' grace.

"Get a move on there, my lads!" The red-faced sergeant had a stubby fair moustache with waxed spikes.

"Have you seen the Regimental Sergeant-major?"

"'E went off wi' Captain Kidd, sir. I think that's about the lot through, sir."

Why had Tonks gone with Kidd? Of course, he was responsible for ammunition. Would Brigade have a dump? Where was Moggers? They should have brought their ammo. boxes with them. God, he'd left them behind! Through the wire, he resisted panic feelings to run the last few yards. Be calm. Loosen the jaw. As they entered the wood a pheasant crowed, flapped, flew away east. God damn the bird, giving them away! Men lying down. Keep calm, calm, calm. He went down the edge of the wood, telling men on no account to fire until the Germans were at the wire, which was forty yards out in the field, just visible. He leaned against an oak dripping with splashes, and heard himself repeating to a nameless subaltern what the R.S.M. of the Coldstream had said on 11th November 1914 when dishing out ammunition in the wood off the Menin Road, "It'll be a good thing when all this is over, and we can get back to real soldiering." A blank face looked at him. Of course, his remark must seem stupid, pointless.

"Anyhow, this fog will make Jerry blind. They don't know we're here. Keep your men quiet."

"Very good, sir."

He walked under the dripping trees, hearing a Gaultshire voice saying as he passed, "That's Lampo. You know, the one 'oo bounced old Moggers."

More confident, he trod on the wet brown and buff leaves half hidden by new green growths of dog's mercury and bluebell plant, to the end of the line, less than three hundred yards. To Allen, following, he said, "Send out two runners to try to find who is on our left flank. If they see no one after a quarter of a mile, to return and say so. Meanwhile get a Lewis gun posted here, to cover the gap in the wire. According to this map, the wood is wired for about a mile. But where we are along it, God knows. No, wait a moment. Tell Tabor to post the louie gun to form a defensive flank. I want you to act as adjutant."

Allen went away, to return and say, "Captain Kidd has the Lewis gun team, just inside the wire, sir."

"He's mad," muttered Phillip, as they went back to the right flanking company.

They sat on a fallen tree.

After some minutes a hare came lolloping over the field towards the wood. It sat up, ears erect, just inside by the first trees. It crouched in shapeless fear; sprang up and rushed away into the wood. He tried to light his pipe. The tobacco was packed too tight. He pulled out the mouthpiece, and as though with great care fitted vulcanite and bowl into the blue velvet spaces of the case. He must do it properly, before drawing the Parabellum from its holster. When this was done, his mouth now being dry, he stood up, conscious of sweat drops under his arm-pit. Then with a flash of hare-fear he saw figures moving towards the line of barbed wire. Faces turned to where he stood beside an oak trunk. The line of dim figures stopped. German voices. They had found the gap.

"*Vörwarts*——"

"Rapid fire!" His voice sounded weak and reedy.

Rifle reports rang in the ear. Dim figures were jumping sideways. He heard the Lewis gun rattling. There were shouts, screams, a slow dissolving of movement. It was over.

"Pass word down, patrol going out! Quietly does it, men," for they were jubilant. "Pass the word down, patrol is going out!" He didn't want to be shot by Kidd. They waited. Then a voice in front said, "Shut up, you bastards! No bloody kamerade stuff to Bill Kidd!"

Phillip went out with Allen to the wire. Wounded Germans were lying on the ground, some twisting about. "Shoot the bastards," he heard Kidd's voice saying.

"No! Leave them! D'you hear?"

"Keep your wool on, old boy! I'm not wasting ammo. on Huns, although they did bayonet some of my wounded in the Bird Cage," came the drawl from the other side of the wire.

"What about identification?"

"I've got it taped, old boy. Sergeant, cut off a couple of those shoulder straps, and give them to Captain Maddison."

While Phillip wrote a report small fires were being started to boil canteens. Smoke was hanging in the mist when the hare rushed back again. Shots were heard and the thuds of stick-bombs to the left. The flanking Lewis gun opened up. The sergeant with the waxed points on his moustache ran up, red-faced. "They're coming, sir! They're in the wood on the left!"

Later that morning, south-west of where Phillip and his men were retreating, the Commander-in-Chief motored in his black Rolls-Royce flying Union Jack pennant on bonnet to see Sir Hubert Gough, over whose *château* at Villers Bretonneux hung the banner of the Red Fox. There he learned to his surprise that the troops of the Fifth Army were already *behind* the line of the Somme river.

That night the Field-Marshal wrote in his diary,

> Men very tired after two days' fighting and the long march back. On the first day they had to wear gas-masks which is very fatiguing, but I cannot make out why the Fifth Army has gone so far back without making some kind of a stand.

From Villers Brettoneux the Commander-in-Chief went on to his Advanced Headquarters at Dury, a few miles south of Amiens.

> General Pétain arrived about 4 p.m. In reply to my request to concentrate a large French force (20 divisions) before Amiens, P. said he was most anxious to do all he can to support me, but he expected that the enemy is about to attack him in Champagne. Still, he will do his utmost to keep the two Armies in touch. If this is lost and the enemy comes between us, then probably the British will be rounded up and driven into the sea! This must be prevented even at the cost of drawing back the North flank to the sea.

From Dury he returned to G.H.Q. at Montreuil, whither the Commander of the Second Army had been invited to meet him.

> I arranged with Plumer to *thin down* his front; when he has done this I shall be glad to see the Divisions thus set free near the Somme. It is most satisfactory to have a Commander of Plumer's temperament at a time of crisis like the present.

Chief of Staff of General Sir Herbert Plumer also wrote a description of this meeting between Haig and the Commander of the Second Army. He was Major-General 'Tim' Harington.

> The situation was serious. Here was the great wedge we had heard about trying to force itself between the French and British forces. I accompanied my Chief to the Field-Marshal's headquarters at Montreuil. We guessed why we had been summoned. I think the most interesting study I know is to watch a Commander in a crisis. I have watched many. Some get worried, some get cross, some are quite calm, some just breathe confidence amongst those around them. In the great Commander all that is best comes out. He rises head and shoulders above all around him, for it is then he realises that his Subordinate Commanders are there to help him, and with their loyal help he can face any situation. I was, though a junior officer, to be a witness of just such a scene. We knew what terrible responsibility must be resting on Sir Douglas Haig and what he must be feeling as we entered the room. He greeted us exactly as if nothing had happened. He was calm, cheerful and courageous. I marvelled as he took us over to his big map and unfolded to us the latest situation. It was a heartrending story as one thought of our poor Divisions fighting for their lives to stem the tide of overwhelming numbers of Germans. He told us the story in as calm and clear a manner as if he had been describing a situation in a war game. When he finished he said: "Well, Plumer, what can you and your Second Army do for me?" I was now to witness a scene between two great men in a crisis. First of all my Chief, with 14 divisions holding 33 miles of front including the Passchendaele Salient, without a moment's hesitation said: "I'll give you eight Divisions at once." The Field-Marshal then said, "That means you must give up Passchendaele." "Not I!" answered the stout-hearted Commander of the Second Army in a tone I shall never forget. It was a wonderful moment. These two great men with their arms linked in front of that map—the one faced with awful responsibility and with the heart of a lion, the other just offering to give his Chief everything he had and more, but with a fixed determination not to give up one inch of ground to the Germans in the process.

Within a few minutes of that scene we were on our way back to Cassel full of hope and courage. I have visions of railway time tables by day and night. Division after Division left us for days. We did not stop at eight. Of our original 14 divisions which we found on our return from Italy, all but two left us, and in their places we got the tired and sad survivors of the Divisions from the 3rd and 5th Armies—the troops on whom the weight of the German advance had fallen. Poor fellows. They had indeed had a hard time and had earned a rest. Alas, they were not to get it. Our line was very thin; as an instance, the Messines-Wytschaete ridge, instead of being held by four strong Australian Divisions, was held by three weak and tired British Brigades from the South. By this time we were receiving information of a probable German offensive in the North . . .

"Listen to this!" said Richard sitting in his armchair of green Russian leather. It was a bitterly cold night; his coke fire, halved by extra fire-bricks, burned dully. It was his last free evening before resuming duty with the Special Constabulary. "Can Prussian effrontery go further? Here in the evening paper is a copy of the Kaiser's telegram to the Kaiserin, Hetty!

"Please to be able to tell you that by the Grace of God the battles of Mouilly, Cambrai, St. Quentin, and La Fere have been won. The Lord had gloriously aided. May he further help.
"Wilhelm.

"He makes no mention of Peronne, you will be glad to hear. Still, we must hope for the best, old girl. According to the map in the paper, the whole line is going back to the positions held before the Somme battles." He put the paper before his face, suddenly overcome by the thought of the 'wild boy', who——

"I'm just going out for a little while," he heard her saying.

That Saturday night in the officers' mess of the 3rd or Militia (reserve) battalion of the Gaultshire Regiment at Landguard Camp, sixty miles north of London, songs were roared out around the piano. A long list of officers to report for overseas at Victoria station the next morning, without leave, was pinned on the green baize board. These had already departed; the singers were those who now awaited with tremendous zest and excitement tomorrow's list. Already 800 other ranks had left, most of them half-trained boys of 18½ years, sent overseas under emergency powers granted by parliament to the War Cabinet.

Over there, over there, send the word, send the word over there!
The Yanks are coming!
The Yanks are coming!
The drums rum-tumming everywhere!

Hetty had not gone next door to play her nightly game of cards with her father—that selfish old man, in the thoughts of Richard, who invariably kept his distance by addressing his father-in-law as 'Mr. Turney'. Dreading what Dickie would say if she had told him where she was going, Hetty had dared to go down to the High Street, to pray in the Roman Catholic church, to burn three candles for Phillip, her brother Charlie's boy Tommy, and her younger daughter's friend Robert Willoughby, all somewhere in France.

Chapter 7

FOUR DAYS—OR YEARS

The escape of the 2nd Gaultshires from the Bois de Gurlu was ragged as it was hurried. Germans were advancing through the centre of the wood. As they got through to open space a machine-gun began to fire blindly into the thinning mist. The bullets passed over their heads. There was no attempt to give covering fire; they fled, to be met with rifle fire from unseen troops lining a road in front of them. They went prone, the firing ceased, and Bill Kidd's voice was heard shouting through the mist, "Don't be such bloody twotts! Come on, you crab wallahs." They went on, to see Kidd talking to a major of Pioneers, who with "an assortment of semi-noncombatants", as Kidd said later, had come up from the Canal. "That's where we're due, old boy. I've got all the dope from 'Spectre', and was on my way to tell you."

He and Phillip examined a map. "About there." Bullets were now buzzing past. "We ought to get a move on, old boy. If the fog lifts, we'll be in full view of Jerry, as the ground slopes up from here."

"Where's 'Spectre'?"

"Over there, across the Canal, just this side of the river. Christ, that sounds like the bridge being blown!" An echoing rumble had come from the west. "We'll have to swim for it, old boy!"

"How far is it?"

"Couple of miles or so. We ought to get cracking."

"Well done, Bill."

They had gone about a mile, in artillery formation, when a Staff officer ordered them to extend north of a village on the crest of the slope. Then he galloped away west. They rested, while Phillip saw with alarm that the mist was thinning. Scouts reported that the brigade on the left was withdrawing, so he gave the order to go back.

They crossed over the railway and came to the Canal, which had deep concreted sides. Below lay stagnant water. To Phillip the Canal looked to be unfinished, like its section farther north, which passed through the old Hindenburg Line of 1917. Which way? Where was the bridge? Then above the mist thinning overhead two Fokker biplanes roared, firing down at them. When they were gone a small bright light was left hanging in the sky.

"Get over as fast as you can, men!"

Troops of other battalions were coming up to the bank. He heard the voices of Yorkshire and Northumberland. Some slid down the concrete and started to wade, holding rifles above helmets. Shouts for help came, the water was too deep.

There was a bridge lower down, a breathless scout reported, by the village. They turned about, coming to rubble heaps, and beyond was the bridge. Woolly bears were now bursting above where they had left. They crossed over with indifference.

A couple of hundred yards beyond the bridge stood 'Spectre', with the Brigade-major, who was giving directions to the mixed-up men of various battalions. He told Phillip to go on to the river Tortille, get across it, deploy a couple of hundred yards west of it, and dig in. "Any troops coming back may try to pass through you. Take command of them."

When they got there, the bridge across was down. "Those twotts of Sappers again," remarked Kidd. Some of the poplars beside the bridge had been tipped over by the blast; upon these they crawled above scummy water. When they came to the new line they flopped down, exhausted.

"Get some head-cover up, men. Jerry will have light machine-guns." Phillip told the wing company commanders to form defensive flanks before going back to his post a hundred yards behind the new line—the remains of a mangold clamp. Could the cooks boil up some sort of soup, to kill the taste of bully beef? There were no dixies. He spent the night going among the men in their shallow scooped-out cubby holes.

It was a cold night, stained by the glow of flares far behind them, and the pink mists of fires. The battalion was now made up of remnants of seven or eight different units. They suffered from thirst, and chewed slices of mangolds. Rumours came from nowhere: there was to be an armistice: Haig had shot himself: the French Government had fallen.

Weary challenges were called out in the darkness, to be met with enquiries. "Are you the Seaforths? Have you seen the Second South Africans? I'm looking for the Leicesters, sir. Can you tell me . . . ?" Sussex, Herts, Northumberland Fusiliers—soon the whiskey bottle was empty.

"It's my idea there's a spy about," said one elderly lieutenant, who wandered in, wearing pince-nez spectacles. "He asked me who I was, and when I told him Tunnelling company, he said 'Please me by doing an allez, you base wallah', in a gutteral voice."

"Sounds to me like the one and only Bill Kidd, mein prächtige kerl! Had he a swashbuckling manner, and a hoarse, whiskey voice?"

"You speak German?"

"About six words."

"Who are you?"

"Fred Karno's Boy Scouts. D'you mind not shining that torch in my eyes?"

"Where d'you come from? What are those men doing in German uniform, anyway?"

"Oh, let me introduce you to our mascots, Sauer and Kraut!"

"I'm not satisfied! You've got a German pistol!"

At this point Bill Kidd came up and said in a cockney voice, "Cut out the paraffle, old boy, and bring up some more ammo. We want it!" He spun a Mill's bomb in one hand, like a googly bowler practising with a cricket ball before beginning an over.

"I was only asking."

"And I'm giving you an order!"

When the darkness thinned shells began to fall. Then came the fog-muffled popple of a German machine-gun, slow and deliberate. Some time later, by the louder noises on the left it appeared that the Germans were advancing. Orders came to remain where they were and make a stand. They yawned and dozed. The water-party came back from a village (ruined) a mile behind them with no water in the petrol-cans.

When the fog thinned they saw they were on a long slope ending to the west in a grassy fringe which was the beginning of the 1916 battlefield. To left and right small groups of khaki figures were moving up the slope.

The order came to withdraw: the entire northern wing of the Fifth Army was by then overlooked by the enemy on a hill near Peronne. This meant accurate shelling and destruction of all positions; so back once again. They came to a railway, and crossing over took cover at the edge of a burnt-out wood, with one year's new undergrowth pushing through tangles of rusty wire. Phillip sent a runner to 'Spectre', to say they were in position, 'in Railway Wood'. Two hours later the runner returned with an order to remain there and hold on 'at all costs'.

On Palm Sunday morning the London terminal stations of Waterloo and Victoria were thronged with khaki figures. Some were accompanied by women of all conditions and ages—mothers, sweethearts, concubines, sisters, and—rising to the occasion—more than one prostitute hopeful of enduring love. The faces of the women revealed every kind of expression; all shared one emotion. A few showed forced cheerfulness; others, with set faces, pretended to be calm—well-dressed women, these. All were staring beyond the moment, bracing themselves for the coming moment of farewell, determined not to let down their men—many of these from the middling suburbs. The majority, ill-fed, permanently anxious since childhood, had the strained white faces of respectable working class women. A few showed tear stains, as, irregular in breathing, they felt the shadow of death upon the parting.

The parting came sooner than expected. No civilians allowed past the barriers to the platforms! Military police barred the way. Little cries were stifled behind strained faces which assumed a mask of courage, even of gaiety, here and there; but among the less inhibited women of the soldiery there was sobbing unrestrained, with little attempt to put on a brave face. They stood with children in arms wailing, as pressure increased before the gates of wood and iron, guarded by elderly porters and young women, wearing red ties, all trouser'd, cap'd, and tunic'd, beside old ticket collectors with long coats and more formal stiff hats. The screech of boilers at pressure arose under the black-painted glass roof, where a few pigeons and sparrows were flying, plumage dulled by soot and smoke. Goodbye, goodbye! Clear the gates! Make way!

Hour after hour, morning, noon, and night, the troop trains left for Dover and Folkestone; while, on the other side of the station, hospital trains began to glide in with their quiet loads of wounded. No reporters came to ask questions.

That night General Pétain arrived at Advanced Headquarters in the Château at Dury to see Sir Douglas Haig. The British Field-Marshal explained the situation. The British Third Army under General Byng was confident of holding on to the First Army near Arras with his left, while his right was yielding ground in an orderly manner to conform with the Fifth Army withdrawal. Nine fresh Divisions were on their way from the North. With these he hoped to strike a blow southwards if the Germans penetrated to the region of Amiens. Meanwhile the outcome of the present situation depended on what the French would do in the Fifth Army Area south of the Somme.

The German advance appeared to have gone past Railway Wood on the left flank, while the attack in front had been repulsed. The question was, What to do—go back or stay where they were? Leaving Bill Kidd in command, Phillip, having cut himself a thumb-stick, and accompanied by an Irish orderly to whom he had taken a fancy, set off along the railway track, which curved around the edge of the wood, eventually to cross a road. They went on up the road, which rose before them, hoping soon to be able to look around. Phillip saw what looked like a platoon retiring from the line three hundred yards away, and hurrying after them, ordered the subaltern in command to turn about and report to Major Kidd in the wood. Then going on up the road, suddenly from a ditch beside a haystack Germans jumped up, one firing at him from a few feet away. The report rang in his ears, the flash knocked him over, and he found himself lying on the road impersonally curious as to whether or not he was dying, so strange was the feeling. Then he knew when he was helped to his feet what had happened: for the cloth around the left breast pocket of his trench coat was hardened as though scorched, the bullet must have passed under his arm as he started at the sudden appearance of the Germans. In relief at being alive, with O'Gorman his runner, he exclaimed, "Ha, mein prächtige kerl, ist mittagessen fertig, bitte?" which was about all the words he had learned from his German nurse of long ago.

This drew laughter, and a question in English, "Eggs and bacon and orange marmalade, with tea or coffee, which is it, Herr Hauptmann? First may I say what you are from, what regiment I mean?"

"From a Composition battalion, Herr Offizier. All kinds—Jocks, Irish, Midlanders, North Country—the Plum and Apple Jam battalion, the men call it."

This brought more laughter, as a tin of Plum and Apple jam was held up, one among several pork-and-bean tins which the German squad had been eating under cover of the haystack. "Much bean, no pork! Hunt the Slipper, yes, you may find it in one of your games, but find the pork, where is it?"

"It's one of the mysteries of the war, Herr Offizier! Have you tried our Plum and Apple jam?"

"Ja! It is goot, yes?"

"For the first year, but after that——" More laughter. He began to feel light-headed and hoped they would not notice that he was trembling.

An officer came down the road on a horse; they jumped to attention. A few sharp words—Phillip thought he must be a staff officer by the way the young German *leutnant*, who wore the silver-black riband of the Iron Cross in his second button-hole had stiffened himself to attention while being spoken to.

The morning passed timelessly for Phillip, as he watched the preparations for an attack. Companies appeared, all the men wearing light grey puttees (he thought that they must be short of leather in Germany, no more knee-high boots). Many carried light machine-guns as they loped along the road, perfectly grouped in sections. At a certain moment they deployed, no orders were apparently given. The line advanced and lay down, another followed and also lay down; then teams of mules appeared—captured British donks by the look of them—hauling light trench mortars and heavy machine-guns on sleds, and boxes of ammunition also on sleds. Meanwhile Fokkers were flying overhead, circling as though awaiting the signal to advance. Ahead of the first line patrols were going forward in staggered groups. At a certain moment they extended also in staggered line, while the aircraft turned west, flying low, apparently to bomb and machine-gun the British line of defence. The German artillery had been firing for several minutes before this happened, gun shells screeching overhead and the heavier big stuff moaning up into the sky. White lights burned low above the horizon, the artillery ceased, and with the increased hammering of machine gun and rifle fire he suddenly felt depressed and miserable. To end the war like this—perhaps never again to see Westy, and all because he had been unable to delegate, because he must do everything himself and behave like a Lone Scout, instead of a real Commanding Officer . . .

General Humbert had already arrived at Fifth Army Headquarters at Villers Bretonneux, near Amiens.

I said (wrote Gough) I was very glad to see him come to support the line, and eventually take it over as previously arranged, and my men were struggling against terrific odds. He replied, however, 'Mais je n'ai que mon fanion', referring to the small flag on his motor-car. This was not exactly the amount of support that the moment seemed to require.

One French Corps Staff arrived with a few candles for a dozen Staff Officers simultaneously to study maps and write orders. Verily we all had to improvise much.

Only two of the promised French divisions arrived, and without artillery. The infantry of one of these two divisions, after 15 hours in lorries and a 20-mile march, had only 80 rounds per man.

It was after midnight when the Field-Marshal wrote in his diary

Pétain struck me as very much upset, almost unbalanced and most anxious. I asked him to concentrate as large a force as possible about Amiens astride the Somme to co-operate with my right. He said he expected any moment to be attacked in Champagne and he did not believe that the main German blow had yet been delivered.

He said he would give Fayolle all his available troops. He also told me that he had seen the latter today at Montdidier where the French reserves are now collecting and had directed him (Fayolle) in the event of the German advance being pressed still further, to fall back south-westwards towards Beauvais in order to cover Paris.

It was at once clear to me that the effect of this order must be to separate the French from the British right flank, and so allow the enemy to penetrate between the two Armies.

I at once asked Pétain if he meant to abandon my right flank. He nodded assent and added, 'It is the only thing possible, if the enemy compel the Allies to fall back, still further'.

From my talk with Pétain I gathered that he had recently attended a Cabinet Meeting in Paris and that his orders from his Government are to '*Cover Paris* at all costs'. On the other hand, to keep in touch with the British Army is no longer the basic principle of French strategy. In my opinion, our Army's existence in France depends on keeping the British and French Armies united. So I hurried back to my Headquarters at Beaurepaire Château to report the serious change in *French strategy* to the C.I.G.S. and Secretary of State for War, and ask them to come to France.

After more than a hundred hours without sleep, Bill Kidd, now in command, felt himself to be separated from his body, a wonderful feeling. He seemed to be floating at times; only his legs kept him down. After all-day firing from the Railway Salient he had withdrawn under the direct fire from advancing Germans into an undulating area of old shell-holes tangled with sere grasses and rusty barbed-wire. His men needed to rest for half an hour every mile of retreating westwards under cover of darkness; he never rested himself. Almost savagely he drove himself to be better than his 'real self', as seen through the eyes of others in the old days—when in a uniform of gold and silver *ric-rac* sewn all over a long-skirted ex-coachman's coat, and wearing an ex-bandmaster's peaked cap made splendid in the eyes of small boys by additions of more gold braid, Mr. Kidd had stood outside one of the lesser picture palaces of North London, chanting such names as Bill Hart, Theda Bara, Nazimova, Sessue Hayakawa, Charlie Chaplin and other heroes and heroines of the flicks.

With not always concealed scorn Bill Kidd made comments to his men on 'Posh Percy', the men's nickname for the Divisional Commander, General O'Toole—whom Bill Kidd suspected of being bogus, like himself.

Plain eyeglass screwed into socket holding glass eye, shaven, wearing slacks with *polished* light brown shoes, sometimes the dapper figure of Jimmy O'Toole appeared out of nowhere while long-range bullets passed tiredly overhead. Sometimes he offered cigarettes from a gold case to regimental officers; but red-tabs were, as before, of another world—of eggs-and-bacon with coffee for breakfast, and a bed to sleep in every night.

When strafing Fokkers appeared Bill Kidd cursed loudly the absent 'Flying Corpse', not knowing that all scouts were patrolling east to bomb and rake a *feld-grau* road congestion, the counterpart of their own.

Smoke of dumps rose up by day; fires stained with pale rose the nights of endless lunar light veiled in mist until the coming of day revealed the column slouching onwards, to reach the ultimate stand upon the old front line of early 1916.

Bill Kidd could not rest; he had to see to everything. His life in daylight was a series of right angles that crumbled along a base and then down one side, as first they strung out from the road to fire from hasty positions at oncoming distant figures which disappeared, giving them time to scramble back to another temporary position until the cold red ball of the sun went down, when, with backs to the enemy, they trailed to the road, to limp away west, under the chiarascuro of the moon, with half an hour's rest for every mile covered, with always the blond stain to their left front, the silent remote rising of lights which marked the deep German penetrations down south towards Amiens.

"Come on, you crab wallahs, do an allez!" Many had to be kicked awake, goaded to their feet.

> *Monday, March* 25 Lawrence left me (wrote Sir Douglas Haig) to telegraph to Wilson (C.I.G.S. London) requesting him and Lord Milner to come to France at once in order to arrange that General Foch or some other determined General who would fight, should be given supreme control of the operations in France. I knew . . . that he was a man of great courage and decision as shown during the fighting at Ypres in October and November, 1914. General Wilson, C.I.G.S., arrived about 11 a.m. from London. I gave him my views in the presence of my C.G.S., General Lawrence. Briefly, everything depends on whether the French can and will support us *at once* with 20 Divisions of good quality, north of the Somme. A far-reaching decision must be taken at once by the French P.M. so that the *whole* of the French Divisions may be so disposed as to be able to take turns in supporting the British front as we are *now confronting the weight* of the German Army single-handed.

Phillip and his runner had been left in the charge of two *soldaten*, one of whom had a pistol, which he kept pointed in their direction as they sat on the ground. The other soldier had his rifle and bayonet. The attack appeared to have gone forward; other prisoners appeared, with more guards, until several hundreds were gathered there, apparently a collecting post. All had the buttons cut off their trousers, after equipment had been shed. They were kept, without food, until the moon arose, then they were marched up the road, coming to a village with the name *Maurepas* on a white board visible in the moonlight, and British traffic boards with arrows pointing the way to *Bapaume*, *Peronne*, and *Albert*.

Towards the end of the night British shells began to drone down. 9.2 inch. shells burst in the ruins and hutments, and at once Phillip said to O'Gorman, "It looks as though our guns are pulling out, first popping off all their shells." Just as he spoke a salvo fell about them, the guards flung themselves down with most of the prisoners, who kept down as more shells womped into the road.

"Now's our chance, follow me," said Phillip, as he slithered down the ditch on hands and knees, followed by O'Gorman. Then creeping round a half standing wall they got up and ran away, to fling themselves into an old grassy shell-hole. The going was difficult, and hot with sweat they made for the road. There they took off their helmets, and taking direction from the dimming moon, made for lower ground, in what Phillip thought was the direction of the wood.

A fire was burning in the village behind them; they kept their backs to it, and walking on, sometimes falling over old twists of wire, came after about a mile to the railway, where they stopped and sat down, seeing the glaze of the last light-balls growing pale in the west. The battalion had either been cut off and annihilated or got away and was now somewhere beyond the line of lights wavering on the horizon. It was dangerous to expose themselves so they lay in a shell-hole and went to sleep, to awake into full daylight.

"We'll have to stay here, O'Gorman, until it's dark."

"Very good, sorr."

But Phillip was not content to lie still; he must explore. Crawling from old shell-hole to hole through wet draggling weeds and grasses, he stood up after a while, and seeing a dead soldier went to look at the body, its face a brick red from bullets through throat and chest. Farther on were two more British dead, lying as though they had been running when shot. Turning over the bodies to get at the haversacks for food he saw where the line of a machine-gun burst had caught them below the shoulders. Going on, he came across the shattered wooden handle of a stick-bomb, with its white bead still on the string which had pulled the detonator. There, around a crater, lay other bodies, and a Lewis gun tilted off its pronged rest.

He picked it up, sat down to examine it, removing drum and working the cocking handle, forgetting to remove finger off trigger, so that a single round went off. This drew O'Gorman, who came crawling through the grass, "Are you all right, sorr?"

"Yes, and so is this louie gun! Collect those drums . . ."

With cigarettes, matches, water-bottles, and rations from the stiffies, they went back to their original shell-hole and set up the gun; and, not able to eat, dozed.

Phillip awoke with the smell of smoke in his nostrils. By the sun it was about 4 p.m. Looking out of the hole he saw that the grass was on fire to his left front. Gazing intently through the tunnel of his left hand he saw a line of dark figures working forward behind the smoke. And behind them, again, was a group of Germans man-handling what looked to be a small field-gun. It went out of sight, then reappeared, men turning the wheels by hand.

He woke up O'Gorman. The two watched together. When it was about 800 yards off he decided to open fire. It disappeared after twenty rounds, half a drum. They had two other drums; he decided to lie low. After a minute he looked through the grasses again; the gun was smaller, and only when a whizz-bang wopped and spat a hundred yards or so in front did he realize that it was now pointing in their direction.

Another wop and spit, this time nearer. A third shell kicked up turf and a pencil of dirt beyond them. He fired another burst from the louie gun. A fourth shell made its vicious little upright jag and spit, forty yards short. It seemed so funny, almost a private war. He lay back laughing.

"Think of it, O'Gorman, they're shooting at *us*!"

"You're right, sorr!" replied the Irish boy, seriously.

"But don't you think it's *funny*?"

Whiz-bang! "Ha ha, fancy choosing *us*, out of the whole Fifth Army! Come on, give us another drum!"

The wheeled grasshopper disappeared. He sat and laughed until his ribs ached. "I believe we've hit it!"

"Yes, sorr," replied O'Gorman, serious as ever.

Phillip felt suddenly exhausted. He lit a fag, one of the thin Indian cigarettes which had been issued lately, tasting as though made of old tea-leaves. It was bitter; he flung it away, and tried to sleep. "Keep a look-out, O'Gorman, I'm for a spot of shut-eye."

"Very good, sorr."

He floated through time with the blonde from Sweden, who at first was Lily. He tried to drag himself to her, she was view-less, he could not see her, he could not remember who she was, he must write to her, but who was she, he had not written to her to explain why he had not turned up, but where had it been, where, and when was it? His eyes opened to dull dragging failure, and though he knew then that he had been dreaming, yet who was it he had forgotten, and where had he met the nameless, beauteous one?

"They're comin' agen, sorr. With horses, sorr."

He was in the same place as before.

"Horses?" Forcing himself to turn to get on his knees he saw the gun drawn by a team against the skyline galloping towards them. He depressed the louie sight to 600 yards, and holding the black tube steady on the rim of the shell-hole squeezed the trigger and held it back, while the horses reared and one went down, overturning the gun, which was dragged out of sight.

"Poor bloody horses."

"Yes, sorr."

Later, as they lay there, the crackling of rifle-fire broke from the north. Bullets buzzed over them, coming from behind.

"We're between the lines, I think. We'll have to wait until it's dark, then do an allez."

"Yes, sorr."

As the sun dropped to the west it became colder. They dozed, lying together for warmth, until dusk came, when they got up, stiff and weary, to face the trek to the river. The Somme, he told O'Gorman, was somewhere south of where they were.

That seemed to be the best way to get through, so they walked by the moon, allowing for its westerly drift.

The broad valley sloped gently down. Some time later they heard voices in front, and the rolling of wheels. Obviously this was German transport, since it was well east of the flare-line. When within fifty yards they hid, and taking a chance, went across in an interval between horse waggons. About a mile farther on there was another road, also in movement. They crossed again without being seen, and still making south, came to a third road, which passed through the ruins of a village. This area, Phillip whispered, had been fought over by the French in the Somme battles, for rusting Creusot shells lay about.

Avoiding the place, they turned west and picked their way in the timeless haze of the moon up and down and across the grassy wilderness of the crater-zone of 1916. No longer did Phillip care if they were challenged and taken prisoner again: the desire for sleep was such that often he fell over and did not know he had gone down until the moon was revolving over him.

O'Gorman sometimes stumbled, too. They held hands and through the daze of his mind Phillip determined to keep the youth from all harm, so trusting and simple was he, probably believing in him as he himself believed in Westy.

After one rest—they needed to sit down frequently—he said, "I'll bet you forty francs to a centime that we'll be back before dawn, O'Gorman me boy. And what's more, as an escaped prisoner of war, you'll be able to apply to go home. That's in General Routine Orders."

"Yes, sorr?"

They were now above a great bend of the river, with its marshes below extending to an infinity of mist white under the moon; and in pauses of desultry gunfire and the occasional passing throb of Gothas on their way down the course of the river to bomb Amiens with its railway junction and yards at Longueau, they could hear the cries of waterfowl splashing below, and the whistle of a mallard drake's wings overhead. Dreamlike was the white night of water and the lily-lights of the armies; how strange it was that this was the greatest war ever known in the world, and he, Phillip Maddison, was part of it.

They went on more slowly. Phillip felt that he had known O'Gorman all his life. Together they would get through.

"It's rather fun being together, isn't it, O'Gorman?"

"It is that, sorr."

Luck was with them, or the Germans were as tired as themselves, for they simply walked through any posts there were, or were not, above the river; and being challenged in a Manchester voice were told to advance, to the cocking of a Lewis gun handle, and found themselves among men of the Cheshire Regiment.

By noon that day Phillip had accosted several Staff officers, some bobbing on unaccustomed bicycles, or astride nags, to ask them—come to give orders to stand on unknown lines upon a mapless landscape—where the Division was. None seemed to know. He described the appearance of 'Spectre', and was sometimes irritably dismissed. Cavalry was moving up a track; he wondered if he would see his cousin Willie, but they were Canadians, not the 10th Hussars. Followed by O'Gorman he went on across the ruinous tract of the old battlefield, featureless except for distant charred stalks of trees and a line of wheeled slowness moving towards the western horizon of nowhere.

At Maricourt a host of redcaps; stragglers being stopped, questioned, coloured regimental and divisional flashes noted, paybooks inspected, before direction to wired-in enclosures. Officers and men alike.

"Good, now we can find out where our crush is, O'Gorman."

"Yes, sorr."

"Let's sit down here," said Phillip, coming to the low remains of a brick wall. Folding his arms, he dozed, floating beyond a voice speaking for what seemed a long time until he was jerked back to daylight by being struck on an arm.

"Stand up!" An A.P.M. was pointing at him with a cane. "Stand up, both of you!" Recognising the voice, Phillip looked up through screwed eyes and said, "Good morning, Major Brendon, how are your plans working out?"

"Are you trying to be impertinent? Stand up when you speak to me!"

Phillip felt cold anger as he got up, and holding himself limp, assumed a Satchville expression of mild impersonal geniality.

"Why are you not with your unit?"

"I'm trying to find it, Major. Perhaps you will help me? Second Gaultshires, amalgamated with No. 1 Composite battalion, in your Division."

"Why are you not armed, but wearing only fatigue dress?"

"My runner and I were taken prisoner two days ago, and we escaped, Major." He answered questions satisfactorily, and was told that the Division, now known as West's Force, was in support east of Suzanne, holding the heights above the great ox-bend of the river.

There towards evening he found 'Spectre' and made his report.

"We're being relieved tonight, Phillip. 'Gentleman' Jimmy was killed this morning. The Division now has twelve officers, counting you, and six hundred men. Bill Kidd is still with us. He took over when you were pinched. Would you like to stay here, or get back and carry on?"

"Would it upset Bill Kidd too much, sir?"

"I asked you a question."

"I think I'd like to return to the boys, in that case. By the way, can you tell me if my orderly, O'Gorman, as an escaped prisoner, has qualified for Home Establishment?"

'Spectre' looked at him sharply. "Did you tell him he was?"

"Well yes, I did, sir."

"We'll have to see about that later. Does he want to go home?"

"I haven't asked him, sir."

O'Gorman said, "I'll stay, sorr, if you will have me for your batman."

When Phillip told 'Spectre' this, he replied, "Good. But we'll need new N.C.O.'s when we get back to real soldiering." He smiled as he said this. Phillip had never seen him smile before; he was filled with a warm glow, so that for the moment his fatigue was gone.

It was not quite the same feeling when he met Bill Kidd, who greeted him with, "Christ! I thought I'd got rid of you, old boy! What a war! Have a spot of old man whiskey. We've got bags of the stuff. In fact, we're known now as the Whiskey Fusiliers, thanks to Moggers, and if I may say so, to Bill Kidd."

Whiskey was forbidden to all except officers; drunkenness was a crime which, if coupled with dereliction of duty, might lead to the death penalty. They had come upon during the retreat, at Hardecourt beside the railway, a store which had supplied E. F. Canteens in the days of static warfare. By Kidd's order a G.S. waggon had been loaded with several crates, including such brands as Johnny Walker, Highland Dew, Grant's Teacher's and mellowed Auld Scottie. Round about midnight an issue was made from a special water-cart, the first of three linked together and brought up by Moggers, the outfit being drawn by a sight now familiar along the Suzanne-Maricourt road, which later became legendary: a steamroller, camouflaged with black and yellow vertical stripes, driven by a Chinese labourer festoon'd with Mills bombs.

The water had been brought from the river near Suzanne, but there was little to spare for the mules or light-draught horses. The grey canvas troughs of the old war had rotted, pipes laid down beside the road in the fabulous days of Kitchener's Army had opened at the seams during the frosts of a forgotten winter.

"Don't get pissed, you lads, or you'll get Bill Kidd shot. And leave a little drop for Sauer and Kraut. Come on you wheezy crab wallahs, do an allez!" Followed faint mouth-organ music, light-years away from the blonde who came from Eden, by way of Swe-den, Swe-den, Swe-den, Swe-den, one foot forced in front of the other, under the foggy light of the moon.

"Well done, Bill. You're a better man than I, Gunga Din!"

"Ger't yer!"

"I've got some bon news. We're due for relief tonight. How many do we muster now?"

"Four officers and sixty-two other ranks, old boy. Our heads are bloody but unbowed, our ribs are broken but unbent, as the poet said."

A division from Second Army arrived, and West's Force was withdrawn into reserve a couple of miles back on the high ground above Albert, from where could be seen, in the words of an R.F.C. despatch rider on a P. and M. motor-bike, 'a huge black mass of Germans stretching back as far as Cambrai'.

Blistered, bearded, with eyes stinging and bloodshot, they dropped asleep on the ground amidst an old tenantry of rusted helmets, water-bottles, leather-equipment, and wooden crosses near the Glory Hole, site of old mine explosions and the draining of a summer's sighs. Even a fusilade of near pistol shots did not rouse them; nor the shouting of an R.A.M.C. captain on a motor-cycle, threading his way down the road, "They're coming!", to the posts put out along the road—and asleep.

All night the procession of infantry, weary mules and horses, lorries with steaming radiators, civilian carts and dryly bellowing cows passed down the road into Albert. Overhead aeroplanes droned and dived, dropping bombs and sweeping the straight road with bullets, while parachute flares with their brilliance paled the moon above this human ebb-tide of an Army outnumbered five to one.

In the morning the survivors of No. 1 Composite battalion awoke to dull awareness of weighted bodies. Led by their tall, thin commander, they shuffled on to Albert, destination of the night before. In areas of cleared ruins, beside the river which ran through the centre of the town, were groups of Nissen and elephant huts. Among them was a welcome sight—an Expeditionary Force Canteen, the first of its kind seen intact since another war. But it was closed.

"Wait till I get round to the back, old lad," muttered Bill Kidd, his face almost black with a week's beard.

Later in the day Phillip stood beside 'Spectre' in the Grand' Place, watching faces of various shapes and hues going by. Upon all was the same expression—an acceptance of something beyond themselves. Sallow-grey under a week's growth of hair predominated: the fought-out men of the scattered and seldom co-ordinated rear-guards. Among them was to be seen the occasional yellow, black, or coffee-coloured faces of foreign labourers, sharply in contrast to the dead-white skins of very old Picardian peasants sitting expressionless, half-cocooned in swollen cotton bags as sunless as their faces—suffocating mattresses, sleeping and grinding and dying family heirlooms stuffed with the feathers of generations of semi-miserable cocks and hens, birds mis-called domestic, born in captivity and expiring in betrayal after a life as shut-in as those of their masters.

"What a scene for some Tolstoi of the future!" said 'Spectre', feeling that he would not live to fulfil the hopes that had lain behind his eyes since the spring of 1915. In his pocket-book was a quotation from John Donne, which Phillip was shown, later, by Westy's mother.

> Thou knowst how drie a Cinder this worlde is
> That 'tis in vaine to dew or mollifie
> It with thy tears, or sweat, or blood.

"Have you still got your two prisoners, Phillip?"

"Yes, Colonel. Disguised a bit, though. I didn't want Sauer and Kraut to get bombed by some Chink or other."

"What do you propose to do with them?"

"Employ them as stretcher-bearers, and spare-time cooks."

"What do you mean when you say 'disguised a bit'?"

"Camouflaged, sir. We found some overalls in a busted tank when we collared the Louie guns from it."

"Well, keep an eye on them until we know where the Corps prisoners' cage is to be set up. We can't take risks. Moggers tells me that his convoy was raided, well behind the firing line, last night."

"I don't think it could have been Sauer and Kraut, sir, they were tied up."

"You know that's against the Geneva Convention, surely?"

"Well, only their trousers were tied. Tonks thought of it. He fixed telephone wire inside their trousers so that, if they tried to crawl away, they'd leave them behind, the other end of the wire being tied to Tonks' wrist."

"Oh, I wasn't thinking of them in connexion with the raid on Moggers' convoy. That may have been the work of Broncho Bill, the Australian actor, whose speciality, you may remember, is lifting newly-washed breeches from any A.P.M.'s clothes' line. According to your friend Brendon there are two gangs of deserters operating now. They've been living in the devastated area for a year and more, existing on what they can raid from convoys. A cavalry troop was sent by Army to round them up last winter, after shots had been heard, apparently some rival gang raiding another. The troop couldn't do much, owing to hidden wire in the grasses hiding the shell-holes. Now come with me down to the railway embankment. Albert is to be held, with the line of the Ancre to Miraumont, up to Achiet, and thence to Arras. Albert is the hinge between Third and Fifth Armies. We are now under Third Army, by the way."

"What has happened to Gough?"

"What is left of his Army has been placed under the French."

They walked to the railway which ran north through the valley to Arras, by way of Achiet-le-Grand, or did, until the arrival of Spring upon the battlefield. Here, among sidings piled with stores, was a congestion of motor ambulances which had evacuated the field-hospitals. Row upon row of wounded men were lying on stretchers, blankets, ground-sheets, and on the earth itself.

The driver of the Red Cross train was looking anxious about getting away in time, for, said 'Spectre', who wore the blue armband of a brigade commander, "The Boche is concentrating west of Thiepval", which was on the high ground about four miles away, above the valley.

After looking at the crossing places the two men went back to the Grand' Place.

"I'll report your care of the two prisoners, Phillip. Brendon, back again with the Provost Marshal's side, is no friend of yours, I fancy. Meanwhile, hang on until you hear from me. It's possible that we'll be relieved tonight, but keep this under your hat."

After 'Spectre' had gone Phillip felt a great loneliness. Above the red-brick ruins of the church hung the legendary Golden Virgin holding down the Infant Jesus; the Figure would remain hanging there, it was said, with the rust running down the twisted iron framework to blind the eyes of God until it fell, a sign that the end of the war was near. Again he thought of Lily Cornford, his love in that far summer of 1916, and of Father Aloysius, the chaplain-saint, whose deaths had once seemed to have altered the course of his life. Now, the 'statue', as the men called it, seemed ordinary.

Towards noon howitzers sent up from the Fifth Army gun park began to fire overhead from across the valley in the direction of Thiepval. Back in weedy pits dug before July the First! There was no end to it. If they were ordered to attack, his men would be merely targets. They had had only six hours' unbroken sleep during the past six days. Out of twenty-three officers and six hundred and fifty-nine men at Corunna Camp only three officers—Moggers, Kidd, and himself—were left. Three junior subalterns had been attached: their names he could not remember, only their faces and badges, and that with an effort—acorn of Cheshire, knot of Staffordshire, grenade of Fusilier. One company was commanded by a sergeant. The rest were Lost, Stolen, or Strayed, like the advertisements for horses and cattle he had, in another world, read in *The Kentish Mercury*.

Behind closed eyes he was a boy biking along a white dusty lane, making for the dappled woods of Spring, happy, happy, happy with Desmond. The picture was stricken; everything had an end; the opening of a flower brought about its own death. Before the flowering of Lily, he and Desmond were the greatest friends who had ever lived, their friendship was to last for ever and for ever in their lives.

Phillip was not experienced enough to know that physical exhaustion can bring forked thoughts which should be cast, lest they divide and reduce the spirit.

From the riven friendship with Desmond he passed on to present disaster, saying to himself, What use have I been as a so-called 'commanding officer'? What lives have I saved by my taking thought? Not one. Then to the other prong: If I had not been with them, would it have made any difference?

He lay there in dejection, his back against a hay bale which had fallen off a waggon, his mouth foul with saliva, body sweating at moments for no reason, arms and legs like independent even mutinous lumps, utterly reluctant ever to get up again, his back as though broken across, heavy-aching when motionless and painful when he moved. Then he saw a Staff officer approaching, one of many who had been about in the town that day asking questions, taking notes, conferring among themselves: a sight inducing feelings of contempt verging on hostility, feelings the more impotent because he knew they were of his own weakness. He knew that familiar figure, but who was it? He worried that he could not recall the name, or where he had seen it, yet he knew the figure well. Was his memory going? He *must* remember, for the figure was coming to speak to him. He ought to get up, but he had not the power, he felt like crying because he could neither move nor remember.

Chapter 8

PRÄCHTIGE KERL!

The approaching man was about forty-five years of age, of stocky build moulded softer by office work, flaccid with too much food, inclined to testiness from too much pipe smoking of strong tobacco. And now, enlivened by events, his confining desk-work reduced to a few notes, a bow-fronted figure was moving in a new freedom, swinging a walking stick—a sight the more remarkable because it was of a world beyond the general feeling of lassitude and disintegration in the civilian-vacant town of Albert-sur-Ancre on that Wednesday afternoon of 26th March, 1918.

Phillip, lying between two slabs of fallen brickwork, saw the rim of the moon, one orbit short of its full gleam, moving up through the pocked and splattered brick walling of the Church, with its grey stone coigns; then almost with a start he recognised upon the approaching figure a pair of junior infantry officer's knickerbockers of the kind of serge material in the tailors' shops in early 1915. He knew those lower legs, thick at ankle and rising steadily thicker to the knees and enwound by puttees the tapes of which encircled the top of the calves and not the ankles as became a mounted staff officer. Those knickerbockers, puttees, and pointed yellow boots had been worn by the orderly officer of the day when he had squirmed and struggled and thumped his way past trouser'd legs on the floor after one guest night; one pair of boots, puttees, and knickerbockers amidst forty or so pairs of brown shoes below creased slacks on the parquet floor of the ante-room of the officers' mess in Godolphin House, Heathmarket, in June 1915, after a subaltern's courtmartial and consequent mass-ragging of his naked self, squirming below yarring voices and lambasting arms because he was an outsider; and when all was over, it was Brendon who announced with amused contempt, 'Maddison as a soldier *non est*', a remark the more cutting in retrospect when Phillip had come to realise its truth.

Was dear old Bagshott-Brendon wearing his old knickerbockers, instead of his usual shining field boots and spurs, to conciliate the troops like, it was said, Haig wearing an ordinary driver's issue coat?

"Wonder what he's after," asked Kidd, as the three policemen went by. "Looks as though Old Shotbags thinks he's on the front at Brighton, twirling that tanner walking stick."

26 March. 2.55 p.m. 1/243/W.F.

To O.C., No. 1 Composite Battalion.

Division reports a gap for some miles between BEAUMONT HAMEL and HEBUTERNE. Enemy forces in strength are almost to SERRE, two miles south of HEBUTERNE. Unless otherwise ordered by any senior local commander you should remain where you are to delay any attack debouching from direction of AVEULUY approximately 2500 yards on line of Ancre north of your present position. In the event of enemy penetration, go back by AMIENS road turning off right-handed (i.e. in westerly direction) along valley road to MILLENCOURT. My h.q. are in white cottage approx. 2000 yards from AMIENS road. One of the two runners bringing this will remain with you as guide.

H. J. West
Lt.-Col. i/c West's Force.

Keep it up, you're doing well. H.J.W.

26 March. 3.00 p.m. 1 Comp. Battn. B/7/1.

Your 1/243/W.F. received. Orders are noted and will be carried out, i.e. We shall remain here as rear-guard to delay enemy attack but not to engage the enemy, but withdraw with harassing fire with view of making for MILLENCOURT road and your h.q. 2500 yards from switch off AMIENS road.

Some long-range shelling in ALBERT, firing haphazard. As I write enemy aircraft is flying over so-called town.

P. S. T. Maddison, a/Capt.
i/c No. 1 Comp. Battn.

Personal message tremendously appreciated by all here. P.S.M.

He wondered as he lay there whether he would get command pay of 5s. a day, for the period of his being the C.O. Acting captain, 12s. 6d. a day, plus 2s. 6d. field allowance. One pound a day, not bad. Then there was his office pay, with the rise of £10 due at Ladyday, it would be £100 per annum. He was getting £350 a year! What tremendous luck, he had £100 in War Loan, and about £70 at Cox's. He must send some cash to Mother, £10, for a present, as soon as he could get near his valise; if it hadn't gone west. Well, it wasn't a bad war, taken all round. He drank more whiskey-water out of his bottle. Not a bad war at all!

They continued to lie there. A draggle of troops came down the Bapaume road, passing through the Square, some to hesitate before Battle Police halting them to ask questions, and directing them to the Stragglers' Post, a wired compound on the Amiens road. Motor-cycle despatch riders thudded and bounced across the cobbles, pulled up, asked where this or that unit was, and went away, no wiser. Sparrows hopped around, pecking at biscuit fragments thrown out by the resting men. Then shells, with reassuring long-drawn descents denoting extreme range, began to raise pink and black spoutings above the ruins.

Phillip sent off the Fusilier to find out what was happening. He returned after an hour to say that a major commanding a scratch force had told him that the Germans were over the river higher up, by Mill Causeway, and were 'pouring down through Thiepval Wood'.

After discussing this with Kidd, Phillip decided to leave a Lewis gun post with one company behind the ruins of the cathedral wall, to cover the left side of the Grand' Place. The other companies to get over the stream, by the iron footbridge which still stood, and line the bank to form a defensive flank facing up the valley.

"Meanwhile we may as well get some tea for the chaps, Kidd. Tell Sauer and Kraut to get a fire going."

The smoke of the fire drew various figures to it, hopeful of at least a mug of char. Before the dixie came to the boil a runner arrived from West's Force, with cheering news: the battalion was to proceed to BRESLE, there to refit and await the arrival of reinforcements. While tea was being dished out, an officer in a burberry came up and said, "My God, have you heard the news? Paris is in flames from bombardment by new, long-range guns! The German cavalry is almost into Amiens! All the supply railways go through there, so we're just about scuppered!"

"Wind," retorted Kidd. "And—piss!"

"My God, you'll soon see! There's thousands and thousands of fresh Germans coming down the road!" He pointed north-east.

"And they'll all be bloody lucky if any get back again, and don't you forget it! Hi, you, come here! See here, I don't know who you are, or what rank you are, but if I see you talking like that to anyone else, I'll put a bullet into your backside!"

They were drinking tea when there arrived the swishing whoop of a shell simultaneously with a crack overhead and a burst of yellow smoke which hung there during the clatter and crash of masonry—the almost forgotten woolly bear, German h.e. shrapnel. When the smoke had cleared the leaning figure on the broken campanile was not to be seen.

"What did Bill Kidd tell you? Golden Virgin has come down! The bloody war's going to end this year! And we'll be relieved this very night, I'll bet a hundred francs to a centime on it!"

The windy officer came back, and eyeing the tea, asked if he might consider himself attached to the battalion.

"So you're lost, eh, my son? Nasty questions to follow, what? Blime, I can't get over the old gel coming down all of a sudden like that! There's something in it, or my name isn't Bill Kidd!"

"What are you doing here?" asked a voice behind them. Phillip turned, and saw Brendon with his myrmidons.

"Don't be so damned silly," replied Kidd.

"Stand up!" The A.P.M. pointed with his stick.

Kidd remained where he was, resting an elbow on the ground.

"Stand up, you!"

"Why don't you come and join us?" asked Kidd. "Or perhaps you've shot your bags, old boy?"

Phillip went up to Brendon. "This officer is over-strained, Major Brendon. He was taken prisoner in the Battle Zone, he escaped, and has been in action ever since. Then I was taken prisoner, and for two days he commanded the battalion, until I got back."

"Who the hell are you, anyway?"

"My name is Maddison. I spoke to you at Maricourt the other day, remember?"

"Good God, man, I've spoken to thousands of men like you during the past few days!"

"Also, sir, we served together as junior subalterns, with the 'Cantuvellaunians' at Heathmarket in the summer of 'fifteen."

"Maddison, did you say? The name is familiar."

"I recognised those breeches and boots when you came past here earlier on. You wore them when you were in Captain Rhodes's company."

"Ah, I've placed you now! You're the young pup who was ragged for misbehaving yourself in the Belvoir Arms! Yes! And you stole my horse at Ypres last October!"

"I borrowed it, Major."

"What are you doing here?"

Phillip showed him 'Spectre's' letter.

Brendon gave it back with a mildly ironic air. "I think that's all I want to know. Oh yes, you were adjutant of the Gaultshires, I had a saucy chit from you about a pig—at Senlis, wasn't it?" Brendon now assumed a manner reserved for what he called pukka sahibs, genial and fruitily mellow. "Odd how we always manage to run across one another, what? Yes, I remember that dossier, quite a relief in the masses of paper we wretched G.S.O. Twos have through our hands. At least you fellows are spared the paper side of a war. We burned tons of dam' paper when we left those blasted cold huts at Moislains. Have a cigar?" He opened a large leather case.

"Thank you, Major."

They were puffing away when a motorcycle thudded up. Brendon read the message.

Half-way through he remembered to say, "Do forgive me," in his sahib-to-sahib voice. He read it again. "H'm. I shall have to ask you for help, Maddison. The Sappers who were to have blown up the Canteen can't be located, so I've got to see that the hut and all stores are destroyed. Can you let me have a dozen men?"

The door of the E.F.C. was guarded by a corporal of the A.P.M.'s staff. "Got to be done, my boy, but a waste of good stuff, what?" He took aim with his revolver at a bottle of Martell's Three Stars on a shelf, and missed. The M.P.'s looked at each other, and the sergeant gave Phillip a guarded look of appeal. Brendon tried again, causing another hole to appear well above the row of bottles.

"Did you clean my revolver after its last use?" he said to the corporal, who was also his soldier-servant. Sometimes, when speaking to his inferiors, Brendon referred to this man as his valet, to give the impression that he had his services before the war.

"Certainly, sir!"

"Well, it doesn't look much like it."

He broke it, spun the barrel, snapped it to again and clicked the trigger rapidly. "As I thought, the striker mechanism hasn't been oiled. There is a six-pound pull at least on this trigger, it shouldn't be more than four."

While Brendon was slipping back the cartridges, Phillip said, "Why not leave all this for the Alleyman? A drunk German is as good as a casualty."

Brendon dropped in the sixth .45 shell, raised the Webley, and took aim at the bottle. The bullet was thrown higher than the others. It seemed so funny to Phillip that he began to sway with suppressed laughter.

"What's the joke?" Brendon cocked an eye at him. Phillip, imagining Brendon as a fiddling Nero, exploded. His laughter ended as abruptly as it had begun. It was tragic, really. Nobody knew what they were doing, or what it was all about, British or Germans. Not to hurt the other's new feelings of semi-respect for himself he replied, "I was thinking of the Staff's respect for good brandy, sir."

"Well, it has to be done, my boy!" Brendon aimed again, a bottle dropped in pieces. "That's better!" He handed the pistol to his servant to be reloaded. Hardly had this been done when the door banged open and the M.P. on guard bawled, "There's Germans all along the skyline, sir!"

Brendon and his redcaps were soon gone. The sound of bugles playing a march, and singing, floated down from higher ground. Phillip, before going back to the rest of the battalion, seized a hoe-handle, one of several new poles in bundles against a wall of the canteen. He decided also to take a case of whiskey. As they walked across the square, two men carrying the wooden box, bullet streams were swishing by overhead. They appeared to be coming from the high ground of Méaulte from the south, and to be crossing with other flights from the north, from ground rising steeply above Aveuluy wood. Some struck the cobbles, to whine up and sing away into the marshes.

Bill Kidd proposed a rum ration right away. When this had been dished out, water-bottles were topped up with whiskey. They were then ready for anything.

"Why not go up and meet the bastards, old boy? Better than growing mushrooms on the seat of our pants down here."

They set off along the Bapaume road, Phillip leading, using the hoe-handle as a walking stick. The column was little more than the strength of three platoons. He and Kidd were each carrying 2,000 rounds in bandoliers slung across their shoulders. The Germans came on in column. Extending on both sides of the road, and lying down, the Whiskey Fusiliers opened fire. The Germans scattered. Walking along the line to give out bandoliers, Phillip found most of the men asleep. He had to prod them with the hoe-handle.

"We must get back, Bill. No point in dossing down here. This good pull-up for carmen is too noisy."

Eighteen-pounder shells were now bursting white four hundred yards ahead of them. While the men were being kicked awake by N.C.O.s and senior privates, the range was shortened. *Swish—crack!* fifty yards away, the rattle of shrapnel balls into the ground. "Our own guns are on to us. Come on you crab wallahs, do an allez!"

Back in the old position near the Cathedral, Phillip re-read 'Spectre's' letter. His orders were clear: to delay any attack debouching from AVEULUY.

This village, he knew from living in the valley during the winter of 1916–17, was on the left bank of the river; the wood was on the other bank. The enemy was across the river. Should they withdraw? The alternative was to be cut off. He must make up his mind. He decided to wait until the m-g barrage slackened; but it increased. They remained. Dusk came on. Scouts came back with reports of many Germans entering the town on all sides east of the river. When night fell Phillip realized that all ways of withdrawal were ringed by flares.

In his room within the Château at G.H.Q., Montreuil, the British Commander-in-Chief was writing in his diary.

> *Tuesday*, 26 *March*. We must estimate that the enemy has *25 Divisions still in Reserve*.
>
> At 12 noon I had a meeting (at Doullens) between Poincaré (President of France), Clemenceau (Premier), Foch, Pétain, and Lord Milner. It was decided that AMIENS MUST BE COVERED AT ALL COSTS. French troops we are told, are being hurried up as rapidly as possible. I have ordered Gough to hold on with his left at Bray . . . I recommended that Foch should *co-ordinate the action of all the Allied Armies on the Western Front*. Both Governments agreed to this. Foch seemed sound and sensible but Pétain had a terrible look. He had the appearance of a Commander who was in a funk and has lost his nerve. I rode about 5 p.m.—as I was going out I met Milner and Wilson. They spoke to me about Gough. I said that whatever the opinion at home might be, and no matter what Foch might have said, I considered that Gough had dealt with a most difficult situation very well. He had never lost his head, was always cheery and fought hard. Gough had told me at Doullens that Foch had spoken most impertinently to him regarding the leadership of the British Fifth Army.

At this meeting, one of the 'frocks' from Whitehall took the Chief of the Imperial General Staff aside and asked how he could best help.

"By leaving the soldiers alone," replied the C.I.G.S. to Lord Milner.

No. 1 Composite battalion, occupying two hundred yards of the west bank of the river, lay in moonlight which seemed to be shedding pollen upon pink flowers of frost growing in glitter upon the ruins about them. Sentries stood swinging arms, and blowing upon painful fingers. Phillip had put a piece of matchstick under his left eye-lid, to keep himself awake.

Fires were burning in Albert, up by the river; probably, he thought, the British hutments. Curiously stratified layers of mist, after arising from the river and creeping over the Grand' Place, diffused the light of flames.

Were they surrounded? Occasional flares—German parachute 'lilies' larger and whiter than the British Very light-balls—indicated that the Germans held the railway embankment four hundred yards behind them; but how far down through the western suburbs to what he imagined from the map to be the level-crossing over the Amiens road, were they?

Another arc of lights began to arise around the south-eastern outskirts of the town. The second jaw of pincers! But the jaws were not entirely closed. Was there a gap there? Were their own troops holding on to a sort of bridge-head across the Amiens road? Perhaps for a counter-stroke against the German forces down south, in the event of them getting to the railway troop sidings outside Amiens? Ought he to try to get through the gap? Without their helmets, to lessen chance of immediate recognition? The freezing mists would help them, anyway the Germans were as balled-up as themselves.

Phillip had brought back with him a dozen bottles of *Auld Scottie* from the E.F.C. after Brendon had gone, following on the suggestion that a German drunk was as good as a German out of action. Five of these bottles had gone into the water-bottles of the men, well diluted. The rosy glows seen through fog of smoke were now being transferred to the battalion. And also it would seem, to many of the Germans, judging by the singing and excited shouts in front. He discussed this with Kidd and the Fusilier acting-adjutant.

"You know, this reminds me of my grandfather reading the prologue from *Henry the Fifth* when I was a boy. The word 'umbered' made me shiver. I looked it up in the glossary of my sister's Shakespeare school prize, and it said, 'discovered by gleam of fire'."

A burst of cheering came from the direction of the E.F. Canteen.

"Look here, old boy," said Kidd, acting-parts of devil-may-care and *pukka sahib* raised by the whiskey, "how about sending up Bill Kidd with a party to bomb the bastards? Quite frankly"—his voice now took on a drawl—"I don't fancy myself sitting here and listening to bilge from a bloody silly play by Shakespeare, who was probably Bacon anyway, and who knew damn-all about soldiering, old boy."

"Well, for one thing a bombing raid would give away our position."

"What's the idea, then? To remain freezing here on our arses until morning comes, and then put up the white flag?"

"'Spectre's' orders are to hang on to delay any attack, and then——"

"To hell with that for a tale! The chap on the spot is supposed to show a little initiative, old boy, take it from Bill Kidd! I don't care a damn if you are my superior officer, or not! I've had my captaincy with the old Eighth a damn sight longer than you've had yours with the regiment, after being kicked out of the Machine Gun Corps, and don't you forget it!"

Phillip did not reply. Kidd's deterioration after rapid whiskey drinking was repellent: an underlying coarseness of part of his nature showed itself in roughness of contempt of those he felt to be weaker than himself.

The Fusilier subaltern, whose name Phillip couldn't remember, said with a slight stutter, "Didn't Henry the Fifth cross the Somme not far from here, sir, on the way to Agincourt, or was it Crécy? I'm a bit rusty about my history, I'm afraid."

"Christ, you two make me sick!"

Phillip said, "I am now going to look around by myself. I leave you, Bill, in charge until I return." He took off helmet and equipment. "On no account allow any firing, but remain quiet until I return. I shan't be long. But if I do not come back, your orders are to make for the Amiens road, leaving your helmets here. Leave in twos and threes, as casually as possible, with rifles slung. When away from the Square, have the men close up, but not in any regular formation. Straggle out a bit, as though you are a German relief party. I'm pretty sure that it's as big a mix-up with them as it is for us. The only chance of getting back is to move slowly through their outposts. They won't know who you are in the mist, if you go casually."

He set off, hoe-handle tapping the ground as he walked towards the Square.

He imagined the wraith of Father Aloysius braving the mort blast of machine-guns and shells in no-man's-land of July the First, that blue morning with the sun glaring into the eyes of the attacking troops, and rising up to shine upon the dead. He saw himself setting out from the wood below Wytschaete on

Christmas Day 1914, on a bicycle, passing the football match between German and British: and pedalling along the cobbled road of the Messines ridge down to Ploegsteert wood, free-wheeling with the thought that no harm could come to him on the day of Christ's birth. He had not the same callow confidence now, but he must go on. Fearfully he kept close to the ruins adjoining the Grand' Place. Before him hundreds of figures were silhouetted against flames, some sitting down, others standing. Laughter, talking, the crash of an empty bottle, a few cheers. What were their officers doing? He could only hope that none were among them. By the excited shouts and bursts of singing, they were young soldiers, of the 1920 class of Sauer and Kraut, ready to welcome any thought away from that of death.

He went back whistling the Blonde from Eden as he approached a row of faces umbered against the black desolation of moonlight.

To Kidd and the Fusilier he said, taking them apart, "They're unarmed, so far as I can see. With Kraut as interpreter, we might take them prisoner. Make it clear that anybody who shoots without my order will be court-martial'd for it. The whole plan exists on the idea of maintaining the spirit of a damned good binge. Have you got your mouth-organ?"

"You bet your life I have!"

"Well, don't play until I tell you. Now, Kidd, go and tell the company commanders will you?"

After the conference Kidd said, "You're really mad, old boy, but I'm mad too, so count on me."

"The main point is that those Jerries will be unarmed. D'you know *Over the waves* waltz?"

"Sure thing. We've got it on the old polyphone at home."

"So have we! Play it when we get up to them."

"Right you are, old boy."

At 2 a.m., at a time when only an occasional shot was to be heard or flare seen, they set off, bare-headed, rifles slung over shoulders. Phillip and Kidd walked in front with the two mascot prisoners. When within forty yards of the crowd, Phillip halted his men. It was a moment of annihilation of the old, a moment of life and death in balance. As though in a sleep-walk he touched Kidd's shoulder. The weak notes of a cheap pre-war German mouth-organ, 'dumped' under Free Trade and bought in a Penny Bazaar at Dalston for a Christmas present for a wild street urchin, arose among the noises of the Square. Soon voice after voice was softly joining in the tune which had been heard in South German towns, Swabian villages, from the strings of violin and piano in wine-shops and hillside arbours trellised with vines on Bavarian hillsides, in beer-gardens shaded by linden trees in Berlin—a tune of boyhood's lost summers of the old world.

Leaning on the hoe-handle, he cried out, "Mein prächtige kerl! Ihre krieg ist beenden!"

"Ja!" cried Kraut. "Waffenstillstand! Zugreifen sie bitte zu! Zusammenkommen! Auf Parade!"

They fell in, and led by the mouth-organ, passed through the Square, and on down the Amiens road. They saw no one as they came near the plashes of the Ancre, to enter white layers of mist which rose higher as they went on, until only their heads were showing like a string of corks bobbing upon a moonlit sea, whence came the tenuous music of a mouth-organ, accompanied by the chipping cries of water-fowl among the charred stumps of the poplars in the marshes. No challenge rang out, no shot was fired. And so through the German line.

Remained the British outposts.

"Play *A long long trail.*"

The moon was now fearfully bright.

At last—"Who are you?"

"Gaultshires!"

"Give the password."

"Shut your f——g mouth, or I'll shut it for you!" hissed Kidd in his fiercest Cockney.

"Pass friend!"

"Bairnsfather, old boy, pure Bairnsfather!"

Tinny and feeble, generated by the last thrust of the whiskey-water from a nearly empty bottle, a music-hall air arose from the column shuffling and dragging itself along the road to Millencourt. At last—a white cottage on the right of the road. "Fall out." Movement disintegrated upon the earth. Its leader, gaunt and puffy-eyed, moved through a dream to 'Spectre' West.

"Well done. Take a pew."

"Thank you, sir. I'll see that my chaps are settled in, and come back, if I may."

The Brigade First-class Warrant Officer reported one hundred and forty two prisoners.

"May they remain here tonight, sir? They're just about as done-in as my chaps."

"We'll see to it."

It was warm in the cottage, he sat on the floor, flames in the fireplace lapped painfully into him through his eyes, he was asleep.

Holding the pale buff Field Postcard, the visible answer to prayer, Hetty hastened next door to see Thomas Turney.

"Phillip is safe, Papa! He says he is well, and a letter follows!"

"Thank God."

"Amen," from Aunt Marian.

The old man was agitated by thoughts of his Will, and the urgent need, in the little time left, to make up for his ill-treatment of his son Charley; for Charley's son Tommy had been wounded in the battle, with the South African Brigade. Tommy had given the name and address of his grandfather as next-of-kin.

The *Daily Telegraph* correspondent in that morning's paper declared that the South Africans had saved the flank of the Fifth Army by their stand at Combles, half way across the 1916 battlefield. They had destroyed an entire German division before they were over-run, and had fought to the last man.

"I must send a cable to Charley, Hetty. Poor fellow, he will feel it keenly."

He fingered the gold ring, set with a large white diamond, which held his neck-tie together. This cherished possession should go to Charley, with his house. That night he wrote and told his son this, in the letter following the cablegram to a P.O. Box number in Cape Town.

Two days before posting the printed card to his mother, Phillip wrote the last entries in the War Diary of No. 1 Composite Battalion.

23 March. In action.
24 March. In action.
25 March. In action.
26 March. In action.
27 March. In action. Withdrew from Albert at 2 a.m. with 142 prisoners, handed over to West's Force near Millencourt at 4 a.m.

At 2 p.m. we marched in drizzle to Bresle, where No. 1 Comp. Battn. was handed over to A.P.M. at the Stragglers' Cage. There its temporary members were sorted before being returned to their original units.

P. S. T. Maddison
Lt. a/Capt., 2nd Gaultshire Regt.

It was a poignant moment: they had been through much together. Phillip, as he walked away in the rain now falling, heard cheering. He turned and saluted the faces behind the barbed-wire fence. Thank God he had kept back O'Gorman.

At Bresle a draft of nearly four hundred men arrived with nine officers from the I.B.D. at Etaples for the 2nd Gaultshires. Most of them were 18-year-old boys, with but six months training. There were a few old soldiers, combed out of base jobs after wounds which had kept them out of the line since 1916 and 1917. Some had blank faces, and dead almost furtive eyes.

At Bresle could be heard the continuous noises of battle, upon which were borne many rumours; some were confirmed by the night summaries from Corps. The MICHAEL attack, which had begun on 21st March, had gone deeper towards Amiens against the remnants of the Fifth Army, now under the command of the French General Fayolle.

By the icy-cold evening of 28th March it was known that the MARS attack had been launched that morning upon Arras, and been repulsed with heavy enemy losses.

The next evening, Good Friday, they heard that Third Army, which had taken over the northern sector of the Fifth Army, held the line of the Ancre; that the French, below the remnants of the Fifth Army, had lost Montidier; while the Fifth had gone back seven miles towards Amiens, and the vital railway junction at Longeau, a mile east of that town, was now within range of heavy German guns. Would they be sent south? Phillip felt the old dreads of going into action, the more fearfully now that he was away from the line.

Easter Sunday was cool and showery, with bright spaces in the day. Moggers, from whom most of the news came, said that night that General Gough, with his headquarters, was in charge of preparing lines of defence well to the rear of the battle.

It was after midnight when orders came, *Prepare to leave camp on the morrow*. Before this, Moggers had offered to bet Lampo a bottle of whiskey that the Division was waiting to go north to join Second Army.

On April 1 the 2nd Battalion the Gaultshire Regiment, led by its German Band (instruments shining in the sun and to hell with Hun aircraft) marched over the hill to Baizieux and down again to Warloy, through country untouched by war. After a halt to rest for an hour—both old and young soldiers were soon showing distress—they went on up the long rising road to Varennes, coming in late afternoon to the railway sidings at Ascheux, so much larger than when Phillip had arrived there from England with Jack Hobart's machine-gun company sixteen months before.

The long train came in, to stop with shrieking greaseless jolts and nervous high notes of a copper horn. The journey was slow. It took the best part of two days, with many shuntings into sidings to let other troop trains pass down to the Somme. The old soldiers, never enthusiasts, their bodies now gone to salvage and their minds to compost, slept or smoked, having few words; the new boys showed interest and even excitement in all they saw, shouting out to placid civilians what they would do when they got at the Germans.

Along the coast of Northern France the engine of the Chemin de Fer du Nord dragged its train, rolling slowly over the bridge crossing the Canche below Étaples, with its views through dirty windows of woods and distant sands.

"If Longeau is put out of action, we'll be for it," said 'Spectre'. "This line will be the only way through," as they passed a battery of anti-aircraft guns.

At least the journey gave two nights of sleep out of the cold; but the party spirit declined as they crossed the Pas de Calais.

To Phillip this was familiar country, seen from a railway carriage window—flat green fields divided by polders or dykes marked by rows of decaying willows; St. Omer, headquarters of Sir John French in faraway 1914, now surrounded by canvas tents, wooden hutments, and picket lines of horses. St. Omer, still a town very nearly untouched by war, still part of the old world of comfort almost beyond imagination—yet a boring, dull place to officers in jobs done on chairs, who slept in *beds* all night, who, if they got wet, could change and dry their clothes before a fire, perhaps on a clothes-horse. . . . Mother before the kitchen fire, reading Grimm's *Fairy Tales* to them by candle-light, beside the washing on the upright wooden frame.

A long wait in the sidings of the station; then, at last, to the thin cries of the horn those shuntings, jolts, clash-bang-groan. They were going north, passing through the west-east line of the Monts de Flandres—a row of gravel hillocks rising out of the level green plain, above the most westerly of which, Cassel, flew the banner of the Second Army. To the east, and the firing line, the low mounds of Vidaigne, Noir, Rouge, Scherpenberg and Kemmel, crossed the T of the Wytschaete-Messines Ridge—from which in one direction might be seen the English Channel, and in reverse direction the Flemish plain almost to the Dutch frontier.

They had to wait an hour at Hazebrouck. 'Spectre' was angry that this period had not been used for making tea, for each company had brought a couple of large dixies.

"It's your business to find out these things from the R.T.O., who presumably knows how long any wait at his blasted station will last! There's plenty of boiling water in the engine!"

Phillip had already talked with the R.T.O., and been told that troop trains were now passed on from station to station, their ultimate destinations not being known; he supposed this was because enemy agents were active. Phillip thought it best not to argue the toss with Westy, and said, "Very good, sir."

In old newspapers, the first seen for a fortnight, it was possible to see what had been happening, from the maps. The war-correspondents' accounts had long been discredited: in them the lightly wounded were always cheerful and sure their own side was winning; larks sang through the barrage (they did, but heard only by eggs-and-bacon-with-coffee ears, well to the romantic rear); the Germans were always disconsolate and knowing they had lost the war (the proud and 'arrogant' prisoners were never interviewed, only the hang-dog kind). Now, reading Bonar Law's announcement in the House of Commons of the opening of the 21st March assault, 'Spectre' cursed and threw down the *Daily Trident* of 22nd March.

The train-wheels whimpered to a stop outside shabby Poperinghe, crowded by camps; clanked on past a siding near hospitals and the graves of the years; and finally shuddered, with blow-off of steam, at a camp siding. Here they saw the mulberry face of Moggers, who told them that Hubert Gough had been removed from command of the Fifth Army.

"Now if only they had said to me instead, ''Op it, Moggers, you're for 'ome——'"

"It could not be Haig's doing," said 'Spectre'. "It's those damned 'frocks'!"

"The hounds of Whitehall have done what the Alleyman couldn't do, and torn up the mud-balled fox!" said Phillip.

"That's the sojer's life, Lampo. Up with the rocket, and down with the stick."

While Moggers was speaking, an adjacent mule laid back its ears as though preparing to lash out with hind legs at the Quartermaster. Moggers uttered a roar of anger and rushed at the mule, giving it a kick, amid laughter from the onlookers.

It was like old times again—almost.

Chapter 9

ST. GEORGE I

It was known that other German attacks were mounted, ready to be launched. MARS had been repulsed at Arras; MICHAEL was held along a front west of the Ancre to Villers Bretonneux, seven miles east of Longeau railway yards. There remained to be launched the thunderbolts of ST. GEORGE I and ST. GEORGE II in Flanders; VALKYRIE north of Arras to Lens; ARCHANGEL north of the river Aisne. And so, *Nach Paris!*

Such were the German blows planned to weaken, and finally to shatter, the Armies of the Allies in the West.

The object of an attacker in war is to pierce the steel front of his opponent, and, entering into softness, to disrupt and stop delivery of his supplies—food, ammunition, reserves. Thus the defender's fighting soldiers starve, and resistence crumbles.

But if an on-driving attacker goes too far forward in his destructive impulse, without entering into softness of the administrating services, he lays himself open to a side-blow or blows which may stagger him and in turn cause a break in his own supply services.

The situation in Flanders during the first week of April 1918 was that VALKYRIE and ST. GEORGE I were mounted, and preparations for ST. GEORGE II were well forward.

When they reached camp Moggers went sick. He had been subdued ever since they had come out of the line. The M.O.

suspected an ulcerated stomach and sent him down to the base. One more link with the old battalion was gone: how far away were those days of peace and quiet at the White City, how callow he must have been to resent the fun of Moggers when first he had arrived there. But ghosts had no place in Flanders among so many new faces. Legends, yes; the past was gone and seemingly forgotten, save the funny stories, the legends retailed in Y.M.C.A. hut, E.F. canteen, Officers' Club, and Battalion mess.

Coates, the R.Q.M.S., wearing both South African ribands with those of 1914 Star and Long Service Good Conduct—the rooti or bread-eating medal—was promoted Quartermaster with honorary rank of lieutenant. He became the centre of respect among new young officers listening to the legends of the great Colonel Moggerhanger, tales covering the years from the Retreat from Mons to the March Retreat. How the General of the Light Division, a cavalryman appointed to command what was left of it after four days of continuous fighting, wept in Moggers's arms before going off his head with the strain—of being in Moggers's arms. How the grey-haired guardian of the electric light plant at Combles, on being given by Moggers a sled-hammer with which to smash his engine just after he had painted it red, white, and blue, had locked himself in with his engine and had refused to come out, although the South African Brigade was fighting an entire German division just across the way. Only when the Springboks, having fired off all their ammunition and lost nearly all their men, had surrendered to a German colonel who said, 'Why didn't you surrender long ago, why did you have to kill so many of my men?' did the engineman unlock his door and allow his engine to be smashed, while remarking to Moggers, 'There'll be trouble over this, you'll see, when they find out.' How Moggers, coming upon an old mash-tub near Maricourt, had had it trundled into an orchard and had a fire lit beside it to heat a score of petrol cans filled with water for a hot bath into which he had climbed, his 18-stone body as white as a lily and his face as red as a beetroot. There he sat, in full view of the troops, 'a sight for sore eyes', while his batman scrubbed his back with a loofah. Moggers gave his own Parabellum to Phillip before he left, to replace the one lost when he was captured.

Phillip felt less anxious as he got the hang of a battalion's organization. He visited the snob's shop, where boots were repaired; the M.O.'s hut, where more than one old soldier was trying to swing the lead to get to the base: with gleat due to chronic gonorrhoea, flat feet, piles, or other hopeful complaints; the tailor's hut adjoining the Q.M. stores, where three bespectacled men were busy sewing on to jackets the coloured flashes of battalion and division; the cookhouse, where bad rations were shown to him, dried vegetables salvaged from bomb damage at the base, mouldy bread, reasty bacon, compressed slabs of Australian rabbits with heads, scuts, and fur still attached, once frozen in bundles but now in parts deliquescent; the picket lines, where mules still thinly rectangular and mud-rashed gnawed at their neighbours' rugs, being on half rations of oats and hay; the bandsmen's hut, the carpenter's hut where wooden traps were being made to catch the grease in water from the cookhouse drains, to be sent to salvage for eventual use in the making of high explosive.

Once again it was masses of paper-work for Phillip, sitting in the orderly room smoking one of his twin Loewe 'Captain' pipes sent out from home.

He had forgotten the padre, a newcomer, an elderly pale man with a nearly grown family at home, judging by the photographs in leather frames in his cubicle.

"Do you think I should visit the men in their huts, Captain Maddison?"

"It is good of you to suggest it, padre, but later on, perhaps. All this night work, you know, leaves them pretty exhausted. I'll tell Colonel West of your suggestion."

When Phillip returned to the orderly room he had a shock. 'Spectre' had been given command of the Brigade. A new C.O. was on his way up from the 'colonel's pool' at the base. He arrived on the evening of the 5th April, a big man, with reflective brown eyes, an amiable country gentleman who had been a major in the Special Reserve battalion when war broke out. After serving for five months in France he had gone home in December 1915 with jaundice; upon recovery he had been posted to the depot in Gaultford to supervise the training of recruits. He was about fifty years of age, Phillip considered.

The next morning 'Spectre' took him up the line, held by another brigade of the Division, with Phillip in attendance as adjutant. During a routine strafe of shelling the new C.O. repeatedly crouched down in the communication trench. He apologised again and again, saying that he would soon get acclimatised. After returning he had a private talk with 'Spectre'; and when he went back to the pool next morning, Phillip was given temporary command of the battalion.

This did not please Captain Kidd, who appeared at the orderly room with an official request, in writing, to be allowed to see the Brigadier. What he said Phillip never knew, but he suspected that Kidd had complained of his inexperience as a battalion commander; for 'Spectre' afterwards rang up Phillip and suggested that he might like to put Bill in Part Two Orders as acting-Major and Second-in-Command. This was done, and Bill Kidd put up a crown.

That night Phillip went up with the working parties, accompanied by Bill Kidd. One party went into No-man's-land to put up wire. It was quiet. No flares went up from the German trenches. Kidd came to Phillip, whispering, "I don't like it, old boy. What does it mean? I have a feeling the bastards are creeping up and any moment we'll get it, from the flanks. You ought to have told Tabor to put out flanking parties, you know."

"Naturally, I arranged that with the C.O. of the Moonrakers holding this sector."

"What are you going to do about it, stay here until we're scuppered?"

"What do you suggest, Bill?"

"Might send a patrol forward, to listen at the Boche wire."

"Would you like to go?"

"Me? I don't give a damn!"

"Very well, go forward by yourself, taking your runner, and come back here and tell me if you hear anything."

No-man's-land was about 300 yards at that sector. The wire concertina coils were being placed roughly a third of the distance before the Moonrakers' front line. Kidd was soon back.

"I heard them talking, old boy. They're bringing up the old minnies. I swear it's that. I heard bumps, like oil cans being pushed down. We ought to shove off, old boy. Any moment now——"

"Yes, you're right, Bill. I'll tell Sergeant-major Adams to get the word passed down, to return to the Moonrakers' trench. Most of the wiring is done, anyway. Get a move on!"

The forward working party was going down the communicating trench from the front line, while Phillip and R.S.M.

Adams walked on top, when low flashes arose behind them, followed by dull thuds. They turned and watched. Within a few seconds great fans of light arose, and then the crashes of the minenwerfen drums of ammonal. "We'd better get down, sir."

The two slid down into the trench, and had joined the men hastening back when red and green rockets arose, and soon the British barrage was swooping and screaming overhead, the shells bursting in and above the German front line.

Later when Phillip was reporting to 'Spectre' he was told that nine minnies had been reported by the Moonrakers. "Bad luck, you'll have to get the wire replaced tonight. Many casualties?"

"None, thanks to Bill Kidd. He put up a good show. He went forward alone, and heard them dropping the drums into the wooden mortars. The Alleyman must be hard up for material, he's improvising again, on the 1915 patterns, sir."

Kidd was in high spirits, helped by whiskey. Phillip thought that Bill had been giving Tabor his version of the matter when he returned from the orderly room, for his voice tailed off and then was silent a moment before he recovered himself to say, "Bong! A faint hissing! A dull thud! Crash! And the moon shone bright on Charlie Chaplin! Hullo, old boy, what did 'Spectre' say?"

"He said nine minnies had come over, and that you'd put up a good show."

"Well honestly, old boy, someone had to use some savvy—— I ask you!" as Bill Kidd glanced at Tabor.

On the night of 7/8th April Corps Summary of Intelligence said that there were now 199 German divisions on the Western Front. Of these, 88 had been identified as engaged in the MICHAEL attack, while 31 remained in reserve, and fresh.

Dining with 'Spectre' at Brigade H.Q. that night, Phillip learned that there were two Portuguese Corps, of two divisions each in the line, south of Armentières.

"That is where the Boche will push," said 'Spectre', adding that, behind the enemy front along that low grazing country, intersected by canals, dykes, and waterways, the roads had been observed to be full of transport, with train movements from Lille, Roubaix, and Tournai. Much artillery had come north, according to R.A.F. reports.

Phillip was returning with the R.S.M. through the misty darkness of the moonless night, having visited the battalion working and wiring parties up the line, when gas shells began to swoop over along the whole front. They splashed yellow, oily liquid from the soft bursts. No high explosive fell. Out of damp darkness there swooped the softly spinning containers, each *woo-er-woo-er* followed by a slight *pop* on arrival.

He telephoned the Brigade-major, his acting-adjutant, the Fusilier subaltern, Gotley, having gone up with the working parties. These parties were made up of more than three-quarters of the battalion strength. 'Spectre' told him to get all the sleep he could.

"You can do nothing until your men come back."

He could not sleep, but lay with the old helplessness of himself, in command of an untrained incoherence of men, whose officers he hardly knew: a 'crush' of unfamiliar faces, most of them very young, a mere mixture of shoulder numerals officer'd by various regimental badges worn only a few weeks after leaving cadet battalions at home. What would happen if the attack came while they were up putting out wire and doing other jobs under the R.E.? He got up, and wandered about, box-respirator at the alert, wincing in his mind at every flash in the sky, dreading the imminent crash of the Boche barrage.

At last the working parties came in. Some of the young soldiers were crying, burned about the face and hands with mustard gas, which had raised blisters, some of them half-an-inch thick. Forty-two other ranks went to the Aid Post.

If Phillip—one among many junior officers at that time to find themselves in command of scratch battalions—was worried, so was every senior officer in France and Flanders, up to the British Commander-in-Chief. The previous afternoon Sir Douglas Haig had conferred at Aumale with General Foch, now the Supreme Allied Commander. Foch had issued a directive for a joint French and British offensive between the Avre and the Somme—the northern 'hinge' of the MICHAEL salient. All signs, said Haig, pointed to the imminence of the VALKYRIE and ST. GEORGE attacks against tired British divisions, in the line between Arras to Ypres.

Haig found Foch 'friendly but immovable'. While the conference was sitting, a note was passed to Haig. It was from the commander of the British Fourth Army, who wrote that he could not carry out the attack, as directed, unless he had two more divisions. General Pétain, also, had asked for 11 more French divisions. Foch held to his plan, and ordered that preliminary movements for the counter-piercing of the MICHAEL bulge should be made the next day, 8 April.

The following night more working parties from the 2nd Gaultshires left camp to collect picks, shovels, screw-pickets, coils of wire and other dreary weights for their work in the Battle Zone. As on previous nights, they went through Kruisstraatpolk, south of the Canal, to the Damstrasse and Pheasant redoubts near the White Château about a mile behind the front line. The sky flickered with gun-fire. Shortly after 4 a.m., hot tea with rum was dished out to the returned soldiers. Some of the young boys refused it through exhaustion; a few were crying. When they had dropped to sleep, some still in equipment, upon the hut floors, Phillip went back to his hut, to lie upon a stretcher bed. Hardly had he curled up when he heard the bubbling rumble of a barrage down south. He got up to listen in drizzling mist, thanking God that it was not falling on their front.

Had VALKYRIE been launched upon the Lys plain? What if the attack was a feint, and the real push was coming against the Salient?

With knees drawn up to chin for warmth, hands shut tight, he lay in his bag of stitched blankets across the wooden bars of the stretcher, seeing the formless discolorations of the 1917 battlefield, edged by the splintered wooden stumps of the Menin Road and living again the terrors of the nights upon the timber tracks. He breathed deeply to calm his mind, waiting for daylight to come; then getting up, he went out into the cold dampness of fog, and returned feeling that now he could sleep; but hardly had he dozed off when O'Gorman came in with a mug of hot sugary tea made a sickly yellow by tinned milk.

The fog hung low upon the Salient that morning, blotting out the deadly landscape. The working parties of the night before slept on until 10 a.m., then opened their eyes to less than nothing, for all was to do again, without respite—cleaning rifles, puttees, boots, uniforms, then drill intended to give some effect of coherency in what inevitably was to come. They grumbled, "Lampo's all spit and polish, like the rest on'm."

Phillip felt their dullness to be beyond him. What could he do, to bring some kind of regimental spirit to this near-mob of mixed up Scots, Irish, Londoners, and others with dialects and habits from a score of different British districts and homes? He spoke to Bill Kidd about it.

"You tell me what line to take, and I'll follow it, old boy," replied that individualist, shortly.

"You're a lot of help, I must say."

"I'll do what you tell me—sir!"

In the afternoon it was known that the Germans had broken through on a 9-mile front, from Bois Grenier south of Armentières to the old 1915 battlefield of Festubert. The Portuguese had left their trenches and fled in such panic that some of them had stolen bicycles of a Cyclists' battalion sent up as reinforcements. About this Bill Kidd, who had dumped himself in the orderly room, was savagely sarcastic.

"When last seen, all those bastards, poxed up to the eyebrows with old man siff, were making for the red lamp district of Hazebrouck," he said. "Their officers live on the fat of the land and treat their men like bloody pigs."

"Every single one?"

"That's what Bill Kidd said, old boy, and that's what Bill Kidd meant. They've let down the B.E.F., that's enough for me!"

Phillip knew that rather ugly mood of Kidd's when he had been drinking. Unable to resist the desire to give balance to the other man's emotionalism, he repeated, "Every single one, Bill?"

"You 'eard!" retorted Kidd, a rasp in his tone, showing the yellows of his darting eyes. "Christ! Sitting here in the mist waiting to be scuppered gives me the guts ache!" He shoved a pile of typed papers over the edge of the table.

Gotley, the adjutant, got up and said, "I have to see the Quartermaster, sir, if you'll excuse me." He went out.

"Look here, Kidd, aren't you going a bit too far when my adjutant has to make an excuse to go out to avoid embarrassment?"

"Not far enough for Bill Kidd, old boy! I'm not concerned with the delicate feelings of a bloody clerk, anyway."

"It doesn't help, you know, chucking Gotley's files about.

"What's the odds, old boy? We'll be burning this bumph before long."

The telephone buzzed. Kidd listened, put it down. "What did I tell you? Get ready to push off at an hour's notice! I'll go and warn the companies." He shouted out for the R.S.M. "Where are you, you old skrimshanger?" To Phillip, he said, "I may as well take the old lad with me," as he went out. He came back to say, "I'll warn the transport to get loaded, and tell Coates, the Doc., and that bloody priest."

This last for the middle-aged, nearly bald C. of E. parson who had been sent to them the previous morning.

"You won't talk like that about the padre before the men, will you, Bill?"

"My dear old boy, I pay respect where respect is due."

"So do the men."

No orders came that day to move. After a rainy night with unceasing gun-fire and further exhaustion for the cold and dispirited working parties the bombardment swelled to a continuous storm of light and noise upon the Salient, extending from the south. Dawn with its nihilism of grey was filled with cauldron bubbling. Orders came to be ready to move off immediately. 'Spectre' rode up through the mist later in the morning.

"The Boche has got into Messines, Phillip. We've given up Armentières. The Brigade is to be put in the line. How do you feel about your men?"

"As you know, sir, we've had neither time for company nor for battalion training. The fatigues have exhausted my young soldiers."

"It's hard on them, I know. Get them to feel that we're all in it together, Phillip. Are you satisfied with your officers?"

"Oh yes, sir."

"How is Gotley shaping?"

"He's a good chap!"

"Now for the tactical situation. We are being lent pro. tem. to the Scottish Division, to help hold the high ground from the Menin road to Wytschaete. As you know, the ridge extends to Messines, and overlooks the railway junction at Hazebrouck. By holding the northern end of the ridge, we shall overlook the Boche west of Messines. Let your men know this. Give them an idea of the supreme importance of holding Wytschaete. By their holding on, they will be saving the Second Army, which in turn will help to save every soldier in the B.E.F. If the B.E.F.

is driven back to the coast, as it may well be if Wytschaete is lost, we may be scuppered. That means we may experience, across the Channel, what Belgium and France have suffered. I know it's the old stuff, but it's true. If we lose Wytschaete we'll lose Hazebrouck, which is the junction for all our supply trains. If that happens, a few of us may be confined in the bridgeheads of the Channel ports, but a million more will find themselves in the prison camps of East Prussia. Tell them this, Phillip. Tell them also that if we stop the Boche, *as we shall*, the German decline will be as rapid as their present onrush, for they're using up all their reserves of men and material in two or three tremendous gambles. Tell them that Haig has said that if we hold the Germans here, they are as good as sunk by the summer. Tell them that no battle is so bad as the fear which paints it in the imagination beforehand. And above all—above all, I repeat—let them know that you understand how they feel. You've been through it, tell them about yourself, take them into your confidence. This is the end of trench warfare, the beginning of mobile war, the beginning of the end, tell them. Tell them that our losses of guns and ammunition on the Somme during the past fortnight have almost been replaced. That's one up for Winston Churchill! By the summer the Germans will be showing the first cracks, and 'when the leaves fall we shall have peace'. Do you remember that saying of the Kaiser in nineteen fourteen, used in the Raemakers cartoon, with the German dead lying in the marshes of Pinkst?"

After 'Spectre' had finished speaking, Phillip said, "You can count on me, sir."

Leaving Gotley in the orderly room, he went round the huts with Kidd and the R.S.M., a newly appointed sergeant from the base named Adams, with two wound stripes and a Military Medal. "Attention! Commanding Officer!"

Imitating the genial, impersonal manner of Lord Satchville he told them first to sit down. Then in his soft voice he told them that, despite all appearances, this was the last year of the war, in which the Germans would be defeated.

"Our Brigadier, the one and only Westy, has just told me what I am going to tell you. This is the Germans' last win-all, lose-all attempt.

"Now 'Spectre', we all call him, has been on Haig's staff at G.H.Q. He knows what he is talking about. Through him, I met Sir Douglas Haig once, when I had come out of battle last year, just below Passchendaele. Haig asked me to tell him what I thought. Well, I was only a lieutenant then, as I am now, except for this acting rank, and I was rather scared at finding myself face to face with him. But I felt his kindness, and when he asked me to speak my mind, I did so. I told him exactly what it was like up there, with sixteen stretcher-bearers needed to bring in one stretcher through the mud. I told the Field-Marshal what the men on the spot said: that it was murder. But they kept on, and got to the crest, from which they had been overlooked for years, when every waggon and column of men in the Salient below was shelled."

Conscious of Kidd's sceptical gaze upon him, he went on, dreading a break in his thought. "I wish there was time to get to know every one of you individually. I realize that you come from different regiments, each with its special memories of home. That's the link that has been cut, connecting each one of you with happy memories of pals."

Damn Kidd looking at him like that, the conceited bastard.

"Now look here, you chaps, things aren't too bad, you know. Hundreds of thousands of Yanks are on their way to France, while tens of thousands of our chaps from England are coming over the Channel every day. The tide will turn, if only we can hang on."

His voice must sound thin and husky, how feeble he must appear, all pretence of affability now gone, a strain in his manner, the faces regarding him without expression.

"Now I want to tell you something about myself. I think you must be feeling as I felt at your age, but after the first shock of going over the top, things weren't so bad as I imagined. I was windy as hell, white in the face and all that. We all were. But soon we didn't give a damn for bullets, only about one in a thousand hit a man, and most of those caused minor wounds which were blighty ones. But the worst part, however many times a chap's been over the top, is the first half minute."

Was there a slightly sardonic look on Kidd's face? Had he made a fool of himself? Exposed his own weakness, by saying too much? He felt his words to be coming nervous and thin, that he had lost the point.

"Well, we're all in this together, boys. Each one of us must think, not of himself, but of his pals. We must stick by our pals, which means our country. Our country is our people, remember. It took a war like this one to bring that home to everybody. Out here, we have regiments, a bit mixed up at the moment, but all the chaps I've seen and served with during the past fortnight were damned good men. And you must realise that I am only another man like yourselves, quite useless unless you stand by me. I won't say that you'd be no good without me, for that wouldn't be true; but it is true that I'll be no good without all of you. I promise you I'll do my best, at all times, never to let you down."

Weak, thin, what was he saying? Everyone would surely see through him as nothing at all. "All right, Mr. Adams, let them sit down awhile," he said to the R.S.M., who had been ready to jerk them up to attention.

"Very good, sir."

A lance-corporal ran to open the door. Phillip smiled at him and said "Thank you, corporal" as he went out, followed by the other two to the next hut. At the door he hesitated, then told Kidd that, as second-in-command, there would be a lot to see to: so he would go on alone. When Kidd had gone, he said to the R.S.M.: "I've been trying to remember where I've seen you before!", as he regarded the man's splendidly alert face.

"Sir! With your permission! Charing Cross Station, September '16, sir! I had the privilege of being addressed by you as I stood in a hospital train, gunshot wound in arm, sir."

"I remember. You told me about Major West, as he was then, with the Seventh battalion in the White Trench. And I asked you what you *really* thought about the war, and you replied, 'We're all in it', which just about summed things up."

"That's right, sir!"

"Well, Mr. Adams, I have an idea I'd like to go round the rest of the huts alone. That is, if it won't in any way impair discipline, so if you agree—and do say what you think—I'll do that."

"Very good, sir!"

"But do you think it will be all right, really?"

"I do, sir! And thank you, sir, for what you've done. In my opinion, since you asked for it, sir, your visit was just what the young soldiers needed. It will give them something to put their sights on, sir!"

"I hope not!" laughed Phillip. "I thought it was the Sergeant Major who had that place in their thoughts, at least on the parade ground!"

"Beg pardon, sir, it was a slip of the tongue."

"It was a very good slip, Mr. Adams! We'll have to do that act together when we start up The Wasps Concert party again. Now I mustn't keep you. What you've said makes me feel much more confident. I'll be able now to finish the round by myself."

The R.S.M. saluted and went off. Phillip entered the next hut where, after opening the door, he waited outside to give the sergeant in charge a chance not to feel caught on the hop.

"Thank you, sergeant. Let your men sit down, will you?"

At the end of the visits he was in fervent mood, telling himself that when they went over, he would go with them, in the first wave; and leave Gotley to send back reports to, and transmit orders from, Brigade; doubt came with the very idea. For if he were killed, was Kidd to be trusted? How far was the Mad Major, as the men called him, genuine fire-eater, how much was it put on? Which came first, Kidd's idea of himself, or the idea of care for the battalion as a group of men to be moved in adjustment to situation, reserves held back 'to putty up', as 'Spectre' said, holes in the line. His Boche-eating idea would lead to all being thrown away via Kiddish bravado.

A little uneasy from these thoughts he returned to the orderly-room, to study the Situation Map which had come in from Brigade, while new thoughts rushed across his struggle to concentrate: how far was all care and thought foredoomed, a battalion being but a pawn among hundreds of pawns: to advance into machine-gun and mortar fire would be suicide, yet the fates of his men were already settled: to die or not to die was no longer in his hands. If only he could feel detached, be like Father Aloysius, upheld by prayer on July the First: but then the padre had had no responsibilities, no fears of being a dud, he had had only to climb over the parapet and walk forward, reading his breviary, his 'little book' as the men called it, his lips moving with prayer, upheld by the courage of a non-combatant whose only duty was to comfort others, and in doing so bring comfort to himself.

Major Kidd returned. He had the rather dark, slightly strained look, on the edge of rancour, which showed that he had been drinking. Sitting down, lighting a gasper, inhaling deeply before blowing out a lot of smoke almost in Phillip's face, he said through his back-teeth, after a quarter glance at the other man, "Look here, old boy, as your senior in so far as service goes, I think I ought to tell you that it isn't done to dispense with your R.S.M., when you inspect the men's huts, for whatever purpose. I suppose you know that in every unit the R.S.M. is responsible for discipline?"

"Has Adams been complaining to you?"

"If he had, old boy, I wouldn't tell you. As a matter of fac-ct," he drawled, "if you want to know, I haven't seen Adams since I was practically dismissed by you in front of the men."

"Surely not."

"Oh yes I was! And furthermore, old boy, it's not my business to tell you how to run this battalion, but I consider it my duty to say that what you told the men, in my hearing, was defeatist. No bloody good at all! As a matter of fac-ct, old boy, you had the poor little bastards nearly pissing themselves with wind-up. You breathed defeatism, old boy, you *breathed* it!"

"Have you ever heard of neutralising fear?"

"What's that when it's at home—Shakespeare? I believe in straight talk. Be a Boche eater, old boy!"

"Very well, talk as straight as you can," replied Phillip, with concealed irony. This man was a fool.

"By your leave, I will. I think you had hell's own bloody luck at Albert that night, but it was the sort of fluke that happens only once in a lifetime. By all the rules you laid yourself wide open in every direction. You got away with it, but if those Germans had been normal Huns, who are bloody good soldiers, let me tell you, you'd have got the lot of us scuppered! And furthermore, old boy, if that had happened, and you and I remained alive at the end of the war, you'd have damned well got a court-martial! Bill Kidd's telling you!"

Phillip thought to avoid a clash. Drunk men, he had already decided, revealed the dominant trait of their make-up. Kidd was a rather coarse person at base.

"What do you think is the right way to get to know apprehensive young soldiers at short notice?"

"Apprehensive my foot! Give'm the old one-two, every time, old boy!" Kidd moved his arms like a boxer, left jab, right hook. "Soft soap's no bloody good, old boy! You want to stir 'em up, give 'em something to remember when the old Jack Johnsons start comin' over! You know—— A shout! A scream! A roar! Black in the face!"

He coughed raggedly, muttered about having been gassed at Oppy Wood, and after much rasping, chest-thumping, and bending down went on, "This isn't a bow and arrow war, old boy. The men today don't want your On! On! You Merry Bastards, Defile not your Mothers, and all that bilge of Shakespeare's, but some good scrappin' stuff."

"What would you suggest, then?"

"What they want is definite direction. Like this, old boy. 'The second bayonet man kills the wounded. You cannot afford to be encumbered by wounded Huns lying around your feet. The army provides you with a good pair of boots. You know how to use them!" Or this. "The Huns come in holding up their hands! The Lewis gunner accidentally keeps his finger on the trigger'." As Phillip was silent he went on, his eyes dark and darting, "Ever heard Major Campbell lecturing on the 'Spirit of the Bayonet', with Jimmy Driscoll acting the Hun rushin' at him with rifle and bayonet pointed for the thrust? 'I side step! I grasp rifle at butt and upper band simultaneously! I twist to the horizontal! I fetch my knee into his bollocks so! He yells blue murder! His head comes down! I release my right hand! I point my fore and third fingers! So! I stab his eyes!' And if his old woman has been set by some skrimshankin' weed in munitions, he won't be able to see the little bastard! That's the stuff to give them! Turn 'em into Boche eaters! Take it from Bill Kidd! He knows what he's talkin' about!"

"I think you must have been Horatius in a previous incarnation, Bill."

With R.S.M. Adams and Gotley, Phillip walked up to Wytschaete to look around.

Two hours before midnight, under a clouded sky made ruddy by near and distant fires, the battalion left camp and marched towards the gun-flashes illuminating the horizon of the Wytschaete ridge. Wearing issue tunic and trousers, webbing equipment, haversack, Parabellum pistol, water-bottle, and carrying a rifle, Phillip led nearly six hundred men towards the ruins of Vierstraat, along a track avoiding the cross-roads, remembering 1914 days as a picnic, hot baths in the brewery, slight figure of Prince of Wales with walking stick cheered as they marched along the then almost undamaged road. He tried to dismiss all thought leading to despair that this was the end, and all so hopeless——

Brigade headquarters was in a farm. He felt apprehension when he saw 'Spectre', standing by the remains of a brick wall, talking to the Divisional commander. Were they to be put into an attack? He gave the word to halt, and seeing the Brigade Major standing near, with the General's galloper, went up to them. "I think the Brigadier wants a word with you, before you go up, Colonel," said Captain Rogers.

He felt a nervous quaver, almost of hysteria, as he imagined himself giving an account of everything to Mrs. Neville. "There was I, not knowing a damn thing about anything, being treated with great respect by someone double my age, as though I were a real colonel!" He felt like crying out, "I can't go on!", as the horizon was rended by the bursting of 5.9s along the ridge.

"The last information we had was that Wytschaete was held by an officer's patrol of about forty Lochiel Highlanders," said 'Spectre'. "You are to reinforce them, but remain under my orders. Your job is to get beyond Wytschaete, cross the road along the crest and hold the village. Your left flank will rest on this road, your right extend south of the village. You will seek and maintain touch with your flanking units, the 'Moonrakers' on your left and the 'Hadrians' on your right. The Germans are in some confusion, we don't anticipate much, if any, opposition. The Boche isn't what he was; these aren't storm-troops, but a second-rate lot, from what I hear. I'm sending three guides, and if you'll get your adjutant to detail eight good men as runners, they'll be able to find their way back to our headquarters here, Bassieje Farm. Is there anything you want to add, Rogers?"

"I think it would be wise, when going up the road, to keep a hundred yards between companies. Now if you come inside a moment, I'll show you where you should establish your advanced headquarters."

On a table of four ammunition boxes was spread a map. "Somewhere here, south of Wytschaete, east of the Wulverghem road. There are a number of old pill-boxes there. You'll let me know as soon as you are settled in, won't you? Then we'll run up telephone and buzzer wires."

Carrying shovels, balls of wire, screw-pickets and other clobber the Gaultshires went along a track gradually rising to a horizon stained as though with milk; then, as they plodded on, hot and sweating under greatcoats, they saw the top of the white trellis of flares rising beyond the crest of the ridge, revealing by its light 'Lampo' standing beside the road.

Phillip watched the silent young faces looking apprehensively about them, little bunches of friends keeping together to avoid the devastation of private thoughts, while heads bobbed under the aimless swish of bullets, and, thank God, wide of the track, shells bursting luridly in the wastes beyond. To the inexperienced, with shovels, elbows and even hands held before them, their living now in hopeless fragmentary flash-thoughts of homes and mothers, all things must appear lost to them for ever. How could he comfort them, give them a feeling of unity? An insistence of repeated words broke into his reverie. *Pass the word up from the Battalion Sergeant-major, Mr. Gotley has been hit.*

The leading company halted, the young soldiers crouching down while from traversing machine-guns cracks of bullets passed a few feet over, while they listened to that strange officer, 'Kiddo', so near to and yet so far from them, telling them what they would do to the Boche. "The Boche never dares come near the Mediators! Shall I tell you blokes why? The Mediators never take prisoners! The Boche smells the Mediators a mile off, never forget that, you crab wallahs"; while, as though in hopeless hope, the same overlapping words came up from the lower darkness, towards the milky stain beyond the ridge.

"Pass the word up from the Sergeant-major, Mr. Gotley has been hit."

The adjutant had been detailed, with R.S.M. Adams, to bring up the rear of the battalion. This was Major Kidd's place, as second-in-command, but Major Kidd had placed himself in the lead when Phillip had gone forward with O'Gorman.

Phillip went down to the rear of the column. Gotley was lying on a ground-sheet beside the track. He had been hit by several ricochets off the cobble road. The ragged flight of metal had torn his webbing equipment and tunic, and some fragments had entered below the stomach. "Water—for God's sake—water!"

"Don't let him drink," said Phillip quietly. "Get Mr. Gotley back to the aid-post. Where are the stretcher-bearers?"

"I have them here, sorr."

White arm-bands gleamed. "Put two morphia tablets under Mr. Gotley's tongue. Tell the M.O. at the Aid Post."

"I'm so—sorry, sir." The voice was feebler. Phillip knelt, to seek the other's hand. It was a clenched fist.

"You'll be all right, old chap."

"I'm—so—sorry, sir." Paroxysm of suppressed in-gasping sobs. A low mutter, almost a sigh. "Tell—my—mother—to—come." Phillip opened the fist, pressed palm and fingers between his own. The fingers sought to hold his hand, clawing at the loose skin of the back, where scars of phosphorus burns were still painful. He leaned over Gotley's face, saying steadily, "Your mother is coming." He repeated the words, again and again, willing the twisting face to be calm, to accept the truth he himself felt in his words, beyond the chaos of the present. The hand now lay trustfully between his hands; from the open mouth dropped two white tablets. The hand lay limp, the arm allowed itself, in final duty, to be placed under the blanket of the stretcher.

"Take Mr. Gotley to the aid-post at Kruisstraat."

In comparative quiet the battalion went on up the road to the Grand Bois. But how different, he thought, from when he had lived there with the London Highlanders in December 1914. Ahead should be the ruins of the red-brick Hospice, the local workhouse still more or less intact in those days. The leading company was passing the vanished wood on the left of the track when an increase of bullets swished over.

"Get away from the road, and lie down! Pass the word down!" They scattered, all except Bill Kidd, who remained standing in the road. Ignoring this attitude of defiance, Phillip sat down beside the leading company commander, Tabor.

"It looks as though the Germans have got past the Lochiel patrol, Tabor. Perhaps your company, and Dawes', should deploy to the right, a yard between each man. Can you spare Naylor to act as my adjutant?" Naylor was a dark, rugger-playing youth from the 3rd battalion at Landguard.

Having been instructed what to say, Naylor was about to go back to tell Captain Dawes of No. 2 Company what was to be done, when Phillip called him back. "I think you should go down and give the order to Three and Four Companies. Just a moment, Naylor."

The new acting adjutant waited. Phillip could not think what to say, with Kidd, now lighting a cigar, a few yards away. He *must* think. At last, conscious of Kidd's unspoken scorn, he forced himself to say, "They will follow on, behind Numbers One and Two, who will be in columns of platoons. That is, the first two companies will advance in line. Then Number Three will follow, platoons in line. Number Four behind Number Three, also platoons in line." What was he saying? He tried to concentrate. "I don't know if that's a text book drill, but the idea is for three lines of advance, only the first in extended order. Companies Three and Four are to reinforce the advancing line, if necessary." What a sardonic brute Kidd was, conceited and selfish. "The company commanders will have to use their own judgment: the idea is to get to the top, ready to meet an extended advance of the Germans, and the two following companies to be ready to reinforce the front line." He felt desperate, that he was near panicking, sending untrained troops over a terrain of old shell-holes in which coherence might be lost. Forcing away Kidd's silent contempt, he got up and went to Kidd, and forced himself to say conversationally, "What do you think, Bill?"

"You're the C.O., not me!"

After a further period of silence, Naylor said diffidently, "Shall I go along and ask the company commanders to see you here, sir?"

From the upright figure on the road came one word. "Christ!" followed by footfalls going towards Wytschaete.

"He's hungry," said Phillip to Tabor. "The Cannibal Kidd after a Boche for supper." Then to Naylor, "Yes, ask all company commanders to come here, will you?"

"Very good, sir. After delivering my messages, shall I remain at the rear of the battalion, sir?"

"Yes, will you?"

"Very good, sir."

The men continued to rest. Some were smoking. This was against orders—but had not Bill Kidd deliberately lit a cigar? He was a bit of a rotter, a 1917 soldier, coming out in the late spring, and after a few weeks in the trenches at Oppy Wood, getting home with phosgene gas. Obviously he played to the gallery over that gas. He was a show-off, the sort who was ostentatiously brave—just like himself—when others seemed windy. And yet, was he perhaps right in protesting silently against an unnecessary order. The machine-gun long-range fire had lasted only a minute. Supposing the delay in getting to the crest enabled the Germans to re-occupy Wytschaete?

It seemed to be taking a very long time for Adams to come up with Hedges and Whitfield. Meanwhile the Germans were massing, according to Corps Intelligence, along the Oostaverne line. That position was a couple of miles east of the road along the crest; he remembered it from going nearly there in June of the previous year, when Plumer had taken the Messines Ridge. Oostaverne—the West Tavern—was at least an hour's march away from Wytschaete. He told Tabor this.

"I see that the German regimental commander of the troops there is called von Spee, sir."

"Where did you get that, Tabs?"

"In 'Comic Cuts', sir."

"I missed it. Von Spee, did you say?"

"Yes, Colonel. I remember it, because that was the name of the German admiral at the battles of the Falkland Islands. We had a geography lesson at the time, and were told about it."

"When did you leave school?"

"After the summer term of 'sixteen, sir."

"Yes, I remember that battle. Craddock's squadron tried to engage the *Gneisenau* and *Scharnhorst*, while the sun was in von Spee's eyes. Von Spee held off until sunset, when Craddock's ships were silhouetted against the western skyline, making clear black targets. My God, I wonder if this Oberst von Spee will try and emulate his famous relation's idea, and attack over the crest as the sun is rising, and dazzling our chaps' eyes? We couldn't see a damn thing, hardly, when we went over on July the First, with the sun in our eyes! I wouldn't mind betting that's what'll happen!"

Time dragged a little less; and when the company commanders came up, with the R.S.M., Phillip passed round his whiskey'd water-bottle, first offering it to Mr. Adams.

"No, thank you, sir, I never touch it."

The company commanders refused, so Phillip did not drink.

"I'll go briefly over what we have to do. I propose to extend from here to the south, and then move up to the ridge. The going may be a little rough. It isn't essential to keep to extended order all the way, but try not to arrive there bunched. Half sections can trickle through, but don't lose touch with your flanks. The road here is the left flank. When you get to the village with your companies, Tabor and Dawes, feel your way through the ruins to the main road east of the village. There dig in. I shall be on the left flank here, going up the road. Hedges and Whitfield will you bring up your chaps behind the leading companies? Keep in touch with one another. Is that clear, boys? Any questions? None? Righty ho, carry on!"

He waited for ten minutes to allow Dawes and Tabor to deploy, then walked slowly up the road with R.S.M. Adams. When they got to the ruins of the Hospice, Major Kidd appeared having come, apparently, from the village beyond.

"I say, old boy," he said, controlling quick breathing, "may I have a word with you in private?"

The R.S.M. went back a few yards, with the runners, and Kidd said, "I won't mince matters, I'm not a Shakespearean what-not, old boy. I'll come straight to the point. I may be blunt, that's Bill Kidd, often broke but never bent. You ought to know that by this time." He smelt of whiskey.

"What is your point? That you're supposed to be with the cadre at Byron Farm?"

"Does it not occur to you, old boy, that it's my job to know where the battalion is going to hang out? Furthermore, as your number two I may have to take over at any moment?"

"*My* number two? You behave like Bill Kidd's number one, number two, and all the other numbers."

"There's another thing, old boy. The Brigade-major's orders to you were clear, I think. 'Go up the road, a hundred yards between companies.' Right? Right! But at the first whisper of a rikko you give orders to deploy, not in face of the enemy, old boy, but his arse! There are twenty Jocks holding Wytschaete, and you do a deployment that would have shamed the Dogpotter Volunteers of thirty years ago. You don't know your job, old boy, and that's a fact!"

"Well, I would say you don't know yours! Why not go back to Byron Farm? I'll send a runner to tell you where battalion headquarters are when we've established them. Meanwhile our job is to establish contact with the Lochiel patrol."

"I know where they are!"

"You've found them? Then perhaps you'll take me to them?"

"Why should I?"

"Do you refuse?"

"Now listen, old boy! Do you want to be taken to them, and then to say, 'When I've found my little lot, I'll bring them to you'? What sort of a crowd d'you suppose they'd think the Mediators are? The Royal Staybacks?"

"You're boring me, Kidd."

"What the hell d'you think you're doing to me? Let me tell you something, old boy. You've sent our fellows slapbang into the two Peckham mine craters, each a hundred yards across and filled with water fifty feet deep! That's what you've done, and unless our blokes are prepared to swim, the only way round will be taped by the Boche with machine-guns."

"Did you know that, before they left?"

"Of course I did, old boy."

"Then why didn't you tell me?"

"You didn't ask me. You prefer to run the show yourself!"

"What do you suggest now?"

"That's entirely up to you. You're the C.O., not Bill Kidd."

"I am asking for the opinion of my second-in-command!"

"Right, I'll give it, old boy! It's this. I'll put a bullet into you if you muck up this crush!"

Phillip opened the flap of his Parabellum, and was pulling it out when Kidd said, "Now go easy, old boy! You don't put the wind up Bill Kidd with that sort of act, you know. The Mad Son may lose his wool, but not Bill Kidd! Can't you take a joke, old lad?"

"Yes, can you? I wasn't serious."

"Nor was I, old boy."

"Let's get this straight, Bill. I realise how you feel. You're senior to me as a captain, I know. But after all, I *am* in charge of the battalion. We're all in this together. I need your help. What do you think we should do?"

"Carry on, old boy, and to hell with the Boche!"

Phillip held out his hand; Kidd, with a hearty grip, almost crushed his fingers. "Count on me, my Mad Son! Only you must admit that it's the funniest dam' way of getting quickly to a position already held by blokes of another lot that I ever did hear tell of! Let's get a move on, for Christ's sake."

It was 3.30 a.m. The headquarters party, led by the two senior officers, now arm in arm, reached the square of the village without incident. An anxious half hour followed, while they waited for the leading companies, tensely, for the dawn was not far off. While they waited, many streams of bullets hissed over in the passive diminuendo and crescendo of traversing fire. Obviously they were fired from the reverse slopes of the ridge.

"The Boche is chancing his arm, old boy. He's on his last legs. 'Spectre' was saying last night that had old Fatty Ludendorff had the sense to keep pushing down south, he'd have won the war by now. And the Old Man knows what he's talking about, and don't you forget it! 'Spectre's' the finest bloody infantry soldier in this war, bar none, and by rights he ought to be C.G.S. to Duggie Haig! You know he protested to Rawlinson before July the First, that the Fourth Army plan was wrongly based, don't you?"

"Yes. I was serving under him when he was stellenbosched."

"It was a question of the depth of the German dug-outs. Apparently the Staff didn't know they were thirty feet deep."

"I know. He advised that the plan of slow advance be changed to a swift assault."

"Exactly! And what made me bloody mad with you, old boy, was for not carrying out 'Spectre's' orders! Hullo, there! Mediators? Stout lads!"

As figures approached, Bill Kidd began to play his mouth-organ, to the tune of *Colonel Bogey*.

"Well, thanks for your help, Wilhelm mein prächtige kerl! Perhaps you ought to get back to Byron Farm now?"

"Not on your life, my Mad Son of a Gun! I'm responsible for training, you know, and this is the place to train the lads to be Boche eaters."

Kidd waited until the other companies arrived, and then, telling No. 4 (Hedges) to remain where they were, led the others through the brick-heaps of the southern environs of the village and so to the Ypres-Messines road running north-south along the crest. Hardly had they settled into shell-holes when the scouts Phillip had sent out returned breathlessly saying that they had heard many German voices in front of them. Within a couple of minutes, as light began to filter from the east, a file of figures was seen to be approaching the road.

"Will you let me deal with them, Phil?"

"Carry on, Bill."

"Fix bayonets." The word was passed down from Kidd. When the figures were within fifty yards he jumped up, waving his revolver and yelling "Come on, the Mediators!", ran forward. He was followed by a ragged line shouting in release of fear. At once the dim figures turned and made off.

"Come on you crab-wallas, do an allez!"

A light machine-gun was found on the ground. Scouts, under Kidd, went down the Oostaverne road, stopping at an old pill-box at the junction with the Messines-Ypres road.

"We should hold this as an advanced strong point, old boy. We could then outflank any attack, north or south from where we are now. What d'you think?"

"All right. I'll get in touch with the Hadrians on our left, and tell them we've filled the gap between them and the Moon-rakers."

The pill-box at the road junction had been made in the cellars of the Staenyzer Kabaret, a brick-built buvette where, before the war, peak-capped peasants in sabots had clopped in to drink calvados, rhum, and café-cognac, and smoke their own brown, rank tabac. It was a two-storey pill-box, the upper portion having been made originally for an artillery observation post. Some of the original brick walling still hid the massive concrete; and through splayed slits, cased in wood, pointing east, south, and north, machine-guns could be fired only a few inches higher than the surrounding ground level.

"It's a gift," said Kidd.

Here four Lewis guns, with the captured German gun, were set up to form 'Kidd's Post', as it was called. The outpost line, in shell-holes, spread out on either side of the Kabaret, three hundred yards in front of the village.

Later in the grey morning mist as Phillip was going with Naylor along the line, he saw Kidd walking forward to look over the near-level wilderness of the old battlefield extending down to Oostaverne. While he was standing up about two hundred yards in front of the outposts a Fokker flew over low and fired at him. Instead of dodging, Kidd stood still. The biplane turned, and coming down low, opened up again. While bullets kicked up earth all around him, Kidd jerked an arm with two-finger insults at the pilot. As the Fokker flew away they heard him shouting, "Green Hun, you can't shoot straight! Go back and tell Fatty Ludendorff to put you on a course!" Then lighting a fag he strolled back, to arrive coughing and doubled up, to say after a pause in his rusty voice, "You young Boche eaters can laugh! Wait until you cop a packet of rotten eggs!" More laughter, and cries of "Good old Kiddo!"

Greatly relieved at the unity Kidd had inspired, Phillip went back to send off the situation report: Contact made on both flanks; enemy patrol in strength from OOSTAVERNE WOOD repulsed; one light machine-gun captured; STAENYZER KABARET occupied; four (4) columns of enemy troops in vicinity of OOSTAVERNE, apparently assembling for attack; liaison established with LEMON R.F.A., MOONRAKERS, and HADRIANS; red rockets for artillery SOS barrage, green rockets to mark outpost line in position; *morale* good; Casualties to 8 a.m. 1 officer killed (2-Lt. Gotley), 3 o.r. wounded.

Towards noon the sun, a silver shilling in the early hours, became a golden sovereign. More Maltese-crossed aircraft came over. The young soldiers loosed off with their rifles, and shouted insults in imitation of 'Kiddo'.

The Fokkers were followed by a bombardment which caused some casualties. Early exuberance gave way to seriousness, which showed itself in individual hollowing out of cubby holes, and in a few cases of dejection because pals had gone west, after moans and distraction. Phillip went specially to the shocked-bereft, more than once putting an arm round a boy's shoulders, saying, "You'll be all right. Don't imagine too much, this won't go on for ever. This is Jerry's last hope. Don't be afraid to talk to me, that's what I'm here for, among other things. We're all in this together." He felt that he had learned 'Spectre's' secret of letting fear pass out of him by thinking of others, at the same time feeling that he had deserted them when he went back to his headquarters in the comparative safety of Wytschaete.

These headquarters were in a pill-box taller than the usual *mebus*, as the Germans called them. Apparently it had been made by some Saxon regiment in the quiet days of early 1916, for in the lintel over the entrance was carved, in careful Gothic lettering, the word SASCHENFESTE. Arriving there, he found that it was already connected by land-wire with Brigade at Basseije Farm. And he had forgotten to tell the Signalling Officer to get this done! A moment's reflection dissolved self-reproach, as he recalled 'Spectre's' words, *You will be supported by your officers, you needn't think that you must do everything yourself.* And, *Don't be too anxious.* Other lines, said the S.O., also Intelligence, were being taken out to both flanking battalions, and the three companies.

The fourth company was in battalion reserve. Sitting down to a cup of café-au-lait prepared by O'Gorman, he began to feel in control of the battalion. Also, twenty-five bob a day, plus command pay of another five, wasn't to be sneezed at. Then there was blood money, one hundred and eighty days' pay for the first year of service, ninety days' pay for each succeeding year or part-year. He was working out what he would be worth if the war should end by Christmas, and should his acting rank be confirmed, when a call came from the left-flanking battalion. The Moonrakers' colonel said that 'almost black masses were moving up from the Oostaverne position'.

"I'll come along at once."

He went with R.S.M. Adams, leaving Naylor at the telephone, who sent a runner after him, when he had gone less than a hundred yards, to say that reinforcements, consisting of tunnellers, were on their way up to be attached to the battalion 'to putty up any holes', in the Brigade-major's words.

Phillip returned, and told the Moonrakers' colonel that he must put off his proposed visit. The absence of enemy shelling was disturbing. He spoke to all company commanders, and to Kidd in the Kabaret pill-box.

"I've had a dekko, old boy. They won't get past here."

The tunnellers arrived. They had sallow faces, and said at once that they hadn't fired a rifle in the war so far. They looked windy, very naturally, said Phillip aside to the R.S.M. "Treat them kindly, Mr. Adams."

"Trust me, sir."

After the tunnellers came a Motor Machine-gun Battery in sidecars attached to motor-cycles. The major explained that they were Corps troops, sent up because Wytschaete was to be 'held at all costs'. He had seen the Brigadier, and had his orders to find and prepare his own sites in the village. "It means we act more or less independently, sir, on movement orders from Major Montgomery, G.S.O. 2 at Corps. 'Puttying up', as they say."

Phillip showed him the company positions on the map. "We've got a 'mad major' called Kidd in the Staenyzer Kabaret, at the junction of the two roads, just there. He's liable to do anything, even rush out with bayonet men to meet the attacking Germans, so don't scupper him by mistake. Have some coffee?"

"No, thank you, if you'll excuse me. We must get cracking. I'll get my guns up in position, and then send the sidecars back here, if it's all the same to you."

"Righty ho. Good luck!"

They rushed bumping over the rubble tracks; the sidecars returning just before red and green rockets began to rise above the dust and smoke of the German bombardment. British shells were soon screaming past, overlaying the massive hammering of the Vickers guns. Phillip waited until the racket died down, and then went up, after hearing by telephone from two companies that the attack had collapsed two hundred yards short of the line. On the way he met Bill Kidd coming down with a dozen prisoners, and a lance-corporal with fixed bayonet. What had his eccentric No. 2 decided to do now?

"Hullo, you Boche-eater? Going to supervise the cooking of your next meal?"

"These lads are prächtige kerls, old boy. They've got guts, they came right up to the Kabaret, where they chucked their last phosphorus bombs, then began to help their wounded pals. Good lads. Bill Kidd's not handing them over to the slops until they've had their shackles. I've ordered my boys, by the way, to help with their wounded, under the Sky Pilot." This was the nickname of the Brigade padre, who had put up the M.C. riband in addition to his M.M.

"Well done, Bill."

"Thank you, sir!" To this unexpected reply was added a salute, the act being copied an instant later by the prisoners pulling off their forage caps and springing to attention. Phillip responded as punctiliously, and returning to headquarters with Kidd wondered how he could have got on without him.

"I'll take these lads down with me to Byron Farm, old boy. Just to have a look-see. I've left Hedges in the Kabaret, to carry on."

"I see. You'll be needed at Byron Farm, Bill."

Bill Kidd however, if he had had any intention of remaining with the cadre, did not stop away from the line for long. He heard of a pair of limber wheelers killed the night before, and returned to ask Naylor to find him a butcher.

"At once, or sooner, old boy. There's hundreds of steaks on those horses. Both were bled out slowly, real kosher meat."

Naylor telephoned Tabor, many men of whose company had been butchers in civil life, apparently. One was told to report immediately to the Saschenfeste.

While Kidd was impatiently waiting for the butcher, the battery of Motor Machine-guns was still in Wytschaete. The sidecars were parked near headquarters, the guns being east of the church, a hundred yards or so from the Messines road. When the butcher arrived, Kidd, learning that the man could drive, took two of the sidecar outfits, driving one himself while the butcher drove the other down to Byron Farm.

An hour later they had not returned. Meanwhile the major commanding the battery had come angrily into battalion H.Q.

"I'll have you know that we are Corps troops!" he said angrily. "We've been ordered to go to Hill 63. Here's my authority." When Phillip had read it, the major went on, "I'll have to leave two of my guns, with their number ones and drivers, behind. This may be of interest to you, in the circumstances." He held out another piece of paper. "As you can see, it's a special order signed by Major Bernard Montgomery, G.S.O. 2 at Corps, saying that we are on no account to be considered as other than under Corps orders. You may care to explain to him why you have contravened his order, sir." The major saluted stiffly, and departed, leaving behind two Vickers guns and four of his men.

Kidd had taken the sidecars without telling Phillip. When he returned, a couple of hours later, with about four hundredweight of steak, and Phillip told him what had occurred, Kidd replied, "Good! We can do with two Mark Ten Vickers! You know what little old Napoleon said, don't you, old boy? 'The tools are to him who can use them'."

"There'll be a row, Bill. They're Corps troops."

"My dear old boy, there's going to be a much bigger row up here, and don't you forget it. Why worry? We can use these guns, and also the emma-gee wallahs!"

The sun went down behind the western Flanders plain, with its low rises which were Kemmell, Scherpenberg, and other *monts*. It was a lowering moment between the twilight of the day and the rising of flares, after the sweatings of action: a moment when the spirits of each man drew into the loneliness of a world seeming always to have been, and to continue to be, for ever in sweat, squalor, and cold. At least for himself, thought Phillip, there was a roof, the alert face of trusty Adams, the reliability of Naylor, O'Gorman, Bill Kidd, and the four company commanders.

Now to go on his rounds. He set out, walking with his hoe-handle, feeling that while he had it to hand, all would be well.

A purple mist lay upon the Flemish battlefield, like an exhalation of old blood unredeemed, the spirit of despair beyond recognition by those at home, of life abandoned by the departing sun. It was good to see Bill Kidd's cheerful face, and to be shown by him a sketch, adorned with comic figures where flanking Lewis guns were placed to protect Kidd's Castle. An inked notice on the wall, with *Under New Management*, announced the name-change.

"I've marked down here a couple of Boche emma-gees, old boy, to be bagged tonight. Here they are, on this sketch. Now mark ye how Bill Kidd findeth ye olde Spandaus! These young Boche fall for the gag every time. They want me to train them! Bill Kidd is now about to have a private conversation with a bloke two hundred yards east of the Messines road."

He raised the safety bar of a Vickers, and having done something to the belt, pressed the thumb-piece. *Ta-tata-ta-ta*, as he fired a single, followed by a double, then two single shots.

"It's the old Bangtitty Bang Bang technique, Lampo. Not everyone knows the trick of single and double-shot pooping. Half a mo', wait for it!"

Back came the German reply, *Ta-ta*. "That practising churl was out in '15, I'll bet a month's pay! Now I'll show you how a Class '18 or '19 gunner replies." He moved to the other Vickers, on its tripod pointing through the northern splay. Again he fired five syncopated shots. A score of staccato cracking replies whipped into the concrete wall outside. "Class '19, old boy! Gives himself away every time. Bill Kidd's telling you, he knows, old boy, he knows!" with almost childlike *naïveté* that was suddenly endearing.

"You know, Bill, I think you're the perfect hero of the old *Gem*, *Magnet*, and *Union Jack* Libraries!"

"Did you read them, my Mad Son?"

"I did indeed! Those ha'penny weeklies will win the war!"

"You've said it, old boy! But don't forget old man whiskey. Have a spot. Help yourself."

After a couple of spots Phillip let fly at one of the enemy machine-gun posts, and got back, as Bill Kidd said, a certain amount of Class '20 dirt.

Chapter 10

BILL KIDD'S HOUR

Early next morning, through a tremendous reverberation of distant barrage fire, he went round the line again accompanied by O'Gorman, who had polished the hoe-handle with ox-blood boot polish. The day was damp and misty, hanging drops on the eyelashes. They returned under vaporous cover to breakfast of steak rissoles fried with chopped onion. A root of this vegetable had been found hibernating among the ruins, an onion larger than a coconut, which had nourished itself on a fallen chimney heap. It had been kept intact to be shown to him before being cut in half. It was five inches in diameter, but a bit soft in the centre from re-growth.

"It's the mixture of soot and mortar which an onion likes," explained the cook, a man of Gaultshire, home of champion onions.

"Let's send the other half down to the Brigadier, with the battalion's compliments," suggested Phillip to Naylor.

At noon the sun broke through the mist. Flies were moving from corners in the concrete roof of the Saschenfeste, where they had held torpid during the winter—big, slow-buzzing insects. 'Blue-arsed flies', the men called them, obviously bred upon the 1917 battlefield.

"There's a tremendous buzzing of Plumer's bluebottles in here, can you hear them?" asked Phillip, after the Brigade-major had telephoned to say that the Brigadier was on his way up. "I'll hold out the transmitter, then you may hear them."

"Not ours, unfortunately," said the voice of Captain Rogers, mistaking what had been said. "It's the Boche plastering Hill 63, I'm afraid."

"I expect that's all they hear in their drain," said Phillip, to Naylor. "It amplifies gunfire like hell, I wonder they can stick it."

Brigade advanced headquarters were under a culvert—where the Wytschaetebeek, now diverted, had once crossed under a farm road—immediately north of the Petit Bois.

When 'Spectre' arrived he gave further details of the Brigade-major's announcement. Hill 63, near Ploegsteert, was being heavily attacked. He showed him the position on a map. Below Messines the British line was in the shape of a rectangle, almost a redoubt, with the Germans around all sides of it.

"A curious position, Phillip, for our fellows are still up there." His gold pencil indicated Messines. "But if Hill 63, over there, is taken"—a couple of miles to the south—"we'll have to go back from most of the Ridge, pivoting from where we are here."

"I see, General. We are to stay in Wytschaete?"

"Yes. Our orders are to hold this village in every event."

A chill of weakness moved up through Phillip, as 'Spectre' went on to say that a tremendous fight for Hazebrouck was going on.

"Hill 63 is the key, it overlooks the plain to our main railway junction at Strazeele. At the same time, the high ground here is, if anything, more important. If the Boche gets Wytschaete, we'll have to leave the Ypres Salient." He paused. "I don't for a moment think it will come to that. The Boche tried in 1914 and failed, again in 1915, and he'll fail now. I thought I'd make sure that we understood one another about the plan of withdrawal, should Messines be given up. In that event we shall withdraw to the Peckham Switch line, which, as you know, hinges here, at Wytschaete, and goes on down past Boegart Farm, south-west of where we are now. There." The pencil-point lightly touched a pillbox on the Wulverghem road, about half a mile SSW of Wytschaete.

"I understand, sir."

"How are your men shaping up, Phillip?"

"They're in good shape, due to the presence of Bill Kidd. He really has done wonders in bucking them up. He deserves the M.C."

"Put in your recommendation, I'll endorse it and send it on. Meanwhile you may care to know that the Divisional Commander, when I saw him under the Scherpenberg this morning, told me that he was very pleased with the 2nd Gaultshires. So, I need hardly add, is your Brigadier."

"Well, sir, all credit is due to Bill Kidd."

"By the way, did you authorise anyone to swipe those two Motor Machine-gun sidecars?"

"That was a bit of a misunderstanding, I'm afraid, sir."

"That's an understatement. That battery comes under Corps troops, and moves on orders from Mont Noir. You'll get badly strafed by 'Monkey' Montgomery if you allow things like that to happen. Get the guns sent back immediately."

"I'll see to it, sir. By the way, we'll all be pleased if you'd stay to luncheon."

"I'd like nothing better."

Phillip went outside to ask Naylor where the two sidecars were.

"Parked behind the Saschenfeste, sir."

The drivers were by the cookhouse, hoping for steak and chips. When Phillip returned, 'Spectre' had written out a message.

"Have this chit taken, with the guns, to Major Bernard Montgomery, Ninth Corps Advanced Headquarters, on Mont Noir."

"The two Vickers are in the Staenyzer Kabaret, sir."

"I'll add to my message that they were taken to break up an attack."

They had lunch outside the Saschenfeste. Three upholstered mahogany chairs were brought into the sun.

"You've got more luxurious quarters than I have. We possess only two kitchen chairs down our drain."

Oxo-cube soup; fried fillet of horse-steak with onion rings crisp and almost black; 'spinach' (boiled young nettles) and café-au-lait out of tin mugs.

"'A good pull up for carmen', Phillip! Give your chef my congratulations."

Before he left, 'Spectre' led Phillip apart. "Bill Kidd's all right up to a point, but his chief concern is to demonstrate what a fine fellow is Bill Kidd; the very opposite of your own attitude. If there was a place for a clown on the establishment of a brigade, Bill would fill the job excellently. One should be something of a snob in one's assessment of others, Phillip. I don't mean in the class sense, of withholding altogether the common touch, but in the sense of not allowing oneself to be imposed upon by Tom, Dick and Harry. To do so is to lose caste. I wonder if you know what I mean?" concluded 'Spectre', kindly, with a rare smile.

"I think so, sir. I've always been told that I have no reserve."

"To be *too* generous, *too* sympathetic to the faults of others can be a greater fault against oneself. Now I must leave you, I have to visit the Hadrians and the Moonrakers. It was an excellent lunch. Do tell your new quartermaster how I enjoyed it."

"Quartermaster? Oh, I see! Yes, I'll tell the Boche-eater, I mean horse-eater, General!"

They laughed; everything was going to be all right. But when Phillip was alone once more in the Saschenfeste, he could not control his trembling.

"Send a signal to Captain Tabor, to come here, will you?"

He sat down again, feeling heavy. His eyes were stinging. Damn, was he going to get the virulent kind of influenza which had taken twelve men already down to the field ambulance hospital? He simply must not be ill, now. Picking up the telephone, he saw two instruments, one overlapping the other. He put it down again, and resting head on hands, closed his eyes to rest until Tabs should arrive, but the past began to unwind through his mind, the remote world of 1917 when Jack Hobart was alive. He saw himself riding on Black Prince up the green slopes of Hill 63, which overlooked for miles the flat-lands of the river Lys. The western slopes of the Hill were in part hollowed out to give shelter to a brigade, in connecting chambers known as the Catacombs. From the eastern side of the almost level summit, just before dawn of an early June morning in 1917, he had watched the mines go up under the Wytschaete-Messines ridge. Nineteen mines, holding altogether a million pounds of ammonal and TNT, rising like gigantic yellow and red chrysanthemums, the explosions rocking the earth and causing German reserves in faraway Lille to run out of their billets in terror under a crimson sky, while Plumer's three thousand guns opened for the most successful British attack so far in the war.

Now it was happening in reverse, he thought, as he set out with Tabor, commanding the support company, to look around the ruins for extra strongpoint sites to be wired ready for use. Above the red-and-grey rubble undulations of Wytschaete was an outstanding mound upon the site of the church, which had been knocked down brick after brick, section of wall following arcading, coign, and corbel, by shell after shell until nothing but a debris of masonry and splintered wood remained to settle with the elements. Under the tumulus stood a large concrete shelter, with 4-foot-thick reinforced roof, which had apparently served as a German dressing station in 1917, said Tabor, who had had the entrances cleared, but not what had been found inside. The tremendous bombardments of June had choked the entrances into the original crypt, and what had served as a German dressing station was now an ossuary of bones and uniforms, decaying gas masks, bottles, surgical instruments, Red Cross armlets and other litter left by large carnivorous rats which, now that shells were falling again, ran squealing along their runs and into tunnels in the rubble.

"What do you think, sir, shall I get the place prepared for my company keep?"

"It would be another death trap, Tabor. The Alleyman's sure to have it taped. Better to avoid it, don't you think?"

Tabor looked relieved. "I wasn't looking forward to cleaning it out."

"You know," said Phillip, as they went on, "these brick mounds will act as cushions to high explosive, and limit, to some extent, splinters. No, I don't think that crypt will be a healthy place, Tabs, it will draw all the heavy stuff. Keep clear of it. Well, so long!"

He left Tabor at his company headquarters, and refusing a drink, went on to visit Hedges of No. 2 company. They went down to look at the Peckham Switch line, which was being strengthened and wired in preparation for possible occupation by No. 2 company, when the two front-line companies would withdraw through them. It was a warm afternoon on the lower slopes of the Ridge, which were as yet in dead ground, otherwise not under observation by enemy gunners. Hedges was told about the situation, and given the battalion code word for withdrawal, SPARHAWK.

Accompanied by O'Gorman, he went to visit the colonel of the Moonrakers, and hurrying back, called at the Hadrian headquarters; then back to the Saschenfeste, as the guns, which had been thudding and booming continuously to the south since morning, suddenly swelled to barrage intensity. This was followed by comparative silence. Had Hill 63 been taken? Confirmation was soon coming over the wire. Hill 63 was gone, the southern end of the Ridge was to be evacuated.

Rapid fire of British batteries on the south-western slopes of the Ridge suggested that they were firing off their ammunition before pulling out.

"Brigade-major on the wire, sir."

He sat on the floor by the D3-converted telephone box, and heard that Merville had fallen, that German patrols were pushing out into the Forest of Nieppe on the way to Hazebrouck. At once he sent a runner with a written message to Bill Kidd, warning him to prepare to withdraw into Wytschaete, to the position already prepared for, and known by, him.

Heavy shocks of dumps being blown up on the plain of the Lys buffeted the air of the Saschenfeste, seeming to make momentarily solid the ear-drums, up to half a minute after tremors had been felt through the floor. At 5 p.m. he was told that the Brigadier was asking for him.

"You should come back, as soon as the light goes, from the road along the crest," the voice of 'Spectre' said through the itching of the wire. "Keep touch with the Moonrakers and Hadrians on your flanks. Have you been over the Peckham Switch?"

"Yes, as far as Boegart Farm. All my company commanders have been warned, I'm about to send out the code word to withdraw to their prepared positions."

"Where is Bill Kidd?"

"He's forward of the left-wing company, Whitfield's, which is east of the main road, sir. Kidd is in the Staenyzer Kabaret, with those two Vickers guns. Oh, blast, I've forgotten all about them."

"Is he on the wire?"

"He was, but the line's been dud, I'm told, for the past two hours."

"Try again, and put me through."

The signals corporal tried again. "No reply, sir."

Phillip told 'Spectre', adding, "I'll go up myself and see him, sir, and let you know at once."

With a sergeant and two runners and his personal orderly, O'Gorman, Phillip went along one of the many worn and winding footpaths through the brick-and-mortar mounds to the eastern end of the village, past the square, with its miasmic bone-yard under the church; and crossing the road at the eastern end of the village—the Ridge road—distinguishable by patches of cobble and broken rusty lines of the steam tram, continued on down the Oostaverne road to the Kabaret. No *claquement* of bullet came their way across the wastes of No-man's-land, suggesting that Kidd's occupation of the pill-box was well-known, and he was to be scuppered at the right time.

"Bill, we've got to get back to the Peckham Switch. Hill 63's gone, so is Messines."

"All the more reason for staying here, old boy! An Englishman's home is his castle, you know. Besides, has it occurred to you that this place gives observation on Messines? So forget your Sparhawk tripe, old boy. Have a spot of old man whiskey."

"The order has come from 'Spectre'. We're holding on to Wytschaete at all costs, but hinging back from the church to Boegart Farm."

"We're also holding on to the Staenyzer Kabaret, old boy."

"The Alleyman is in Merville, and making for Hazebrouck."

"As I said, old boy, all the more reason for stopping here. What about Haig's 'Backs to the Wall' message? You sent me a copy last night, surely you read it first?"

"Naturally."

"Well, it's our backs to *this* wall, as far as Bill Kidd is concerned. Read your copy of *Infantry Training Manual*, if you've ever heard of it, old boy, and you'll learn that the bloke on the spot often knows a damn sight more than any Staff wallah miles away out of it. After all, Staff wallahs can only act on what reports are sent back to them, then they cough back more or less the same ideas."

Phillip forced himself to treat Kidd's remarks in the manner of Jimmy O'Toole dealing with Moggers.

"Do tell me what is your idea, Bill."

"I've told you! Bill Kidd's boys are here and here they stay!"

"But aren't they my boys too, Bill?"

"Oh, dry up!"

"They're Tabor's boys too, Bill. What is more, Tabs has asked me if he can have them back."

"You give me the guts ache, old boy."

"There's another thing, Bill. I sent you a message to return these Vickers guns last night."

"They're more use where they are now. I've had this pillbox wired, a hundred yards away on three sides. Any Boche coming over will get it in the neck. Enfilade fire, old boy, pop-pop-pop, all the old ninepin stuff they gave us on the Somme, now about to be returned, with interest!"

"I have to tell you officially that the line is ordered to swing back. You are now five hundred yards east of the new line."

"I've got deaf ears, old boy, like Nelson's grandmother. Have a spot of Haig and Haig, old boy, and stop nagging! You're worse than a bloody old woman. Your hand's shaking, what you been doing, wanking yourself in the Saschenfeste?"

"Perhaps you speak from experience?"

"I gave it up, old boy, when I lost my potato-water!"

"Oh, damn all this kid's talk, Bill. You've got to come back."

"I won't!"

"But we need you for further entertainment. You're our *morale* raiser, now that the Alleyman is so persistent."

"Boche, old boy, Boche! Alleyman went out with jam-tin bombs, Lee-Enfield long rifles, crypts of German churches at Sydenham filled with machine-guns, hard tennis courts made before the war to take 17-inch Krupps hows. to bombard London from Guildford, Asquith having shares in Krupps, and all that milksop 'Sapper's' stuff. No use for Alleyman, old boy! I'm a Boche eater."

"This pill-box will be crumped to hell, you know."

"Then we'll find better 'oles outside, old boy! It's no good naggin' at Bill Kidd, I told you. Bill Kidd's a Boche eater!"

"The horse steaks you brought up are good enough for me!"

"I got up the shackles, old boy, and if it had been left to you, we'd have had damn all! Now look, I'm fed up with all this yap! Bill Kidd's busy, so buzz off, like a good little man." He glared at Phillip. "So you need me for further entertainment, do you? Who d'you think I am, Harry Tate? Right, old boy, here's some further entertainment! Let me tell you this! Bill Kidd was *born* in the county! He *belongs* to Gaultshire, see? I don't need to supply myself with a bogus address of so-called next of kin! You lie like a dead mule, my Mad Son! Now hop it, for Christ's sake. I've got a job on." He sloshed whiskey into a mug, and drank.

"So have we all, Bill. I think you'd better come back. It's an order."

"You can stuff it, old boy, where the monkey put the nuts! This is the only order I recognise!" He held up his cyclostyled copy of the Field-Marshal's *Special Order of the Day*.

"Don't get sozzled, Bill."

"Piss off!"

It was growing dark by 8 p.m., the time ordered for the withdrawal to the Peckham Switch. Phillip had seen both colonels of the flanking battalions; he had arranged with Tabor and Dawes the times of bringing in their company outposts, and filing back through the companies occupying the new trenches, and so into support. All papers in the Saschenfeste had been burned, but the wires to Brigade were not yet cut. Signallers waited to do this, to carry away their D-3 converted boxes and power buzzers.

At 8.15 p.m. the Germans put down a barrage extending from the Menin road east of Ypres to the Canal, thence south along the Damstrasse to the Wytschaete-Wulverghem road. Obviously they had anticipated the intended withdrawal, but not the time. After the high explosive and shrapnel there was a pause. By this time the forward companies, except two platoons virtually held prisoner by Major Kidd, had withdrawn to the new line. Soon after 8.40 p.m. gas shells began to fall with soft down-spinning sighs into the low rubble undulations of Wytschaete. Phillip was then on his way back to the Saschenfeste. From the low ground to the south, across wastes of decayed life that was the battlefield there arose the most melancholy, the most desolate noise of the ruined nights of the war, the rising and falling howls of Strombos horns.

Wearing his respirator, he arrived sweating hot at the Saxon fort, and pushing aside the heavy gas-blanket, sat down on an ammunition box and pulled off the rubber mask. About him were men with greenish faces, for the only light within the shelter came from two dips of rifle-cleaning flannel in tins of whale oil, burning fitfully and casting shadows on the walls of cold sweating concrete. The air within was acrid with smoke of ration-box wood, for an attempt had been made to light the stove after a hock bottle on several joined pull-through cords had been hauled up and down the rusted chimney pipe. At least resinous smoke overlaid the smell of sweat and unwashed bodies.

Wooden frames had been made for chicken-wire beds; from somewhere O'Gorman had scrounged a round table-top, and fixed it to biscuit boxes.

"Let the Brigade-major know that the withdrawal is complete, and tell him that we have left an advanced strong-point in the Staenyzer Kabaret, with two Vickers and protecting parties in shell-holes with Lewis guns and rifle grenades on its flanks. If he wants to know why, I'll speak to him."

"Very good, sir." Then, "Brigadier on the wire, sir."

Phillip told 'Spectre' that Bill Kidd was repeating his stunt of going forward to the wire in front of the Bois de Gurlu, when he had caught the Germans in enfilade and broken up the attack there. 'Spectre' listened, then he said, "Come down and see me as soon as you are clear of the Saschenfeste."

The new advanced headquarters of the battalion were to be behind Boegart Farm.

This conversation with 'Spectre' had, of necessity, been overheard by the headquarters staff. As he put down the instrument, Phillip saw R.S.M. Adams look at Naylor, with a half-suppressed appeal. They know I'm going to be stellenbosched, he thought, before saying aloud, "I think I'll lie down for a spell." Would they think that he was saying that, before going sick? He felt cold and thin. After a couple of minutes unrest upon a wire bunk he got up, and taking the hoe-handle, which was by now a mental protection against disaster, he said, "You know what to do, Naylor? Destroy everything here before going down to Boegart Farm. Report to Brigade as soon as you arrive, and confirm telephonic communication with the companies. And don't forget the flanking battalions."

"Very good, sir? We'll see you at Boegart, later?"

"Oh yes, indeed! I shall be back within the hour." R.S.M. Adams looked as though he wanted to say something, but again resisted the impulse. Phillip went out, with O'Gorman.

All wires having been cut and then dragged about, and the telephone removed by the signallers, a couple of Mills grenades were thrown into the opening of the Saschenfeste, to set off loose phosphorus bombs left lying on the floor and so to explode what ammunition boxes had not been carried away.

It was then that the R.S.M. spoke. "Sir," he said to Mr. Naylor, "there are times when silence is not golden. Permission to speak, sir."

"Yes, Mr. Adams?"

"Sir, I don't like seeing anyone so good-natured as the Colonel being put upon, sir. With your permission, sir, I'll go up now and bring back the men in front of the Kabaret outpost to the Peckham Switch. That's the Colonel's orders, sir, direct from the Brigadier, sir."

"Yes, Mr. Adams, I agree."

"I'll go at the double, sir."

Phillip heard the muffled explosions in the Saschenfeste as he hurried down the Vierstraat road. Byron Farm was now Brigade advanced H.Q. 'Spectre' came out of the sand-bagged shelter when the sentry announced the visitor. 'Spectre' and Phillip were standing in the open when salvoes of gas-shells began to flop down. "We'd better get inside, Phillip——" the Brigadier was saying when there was a loud swoosh, followed by a snapping noise as a yellow-cross canister struck 'Spectre' on one of his legs and its contents splashed over the face of Phillip with what seemed to him to be an enveloping rush of crimson.

Unknown to himself, Major Kidd was alone in Kidd's Castle as he smoked gaspers furiously by the light of a solitary candle. His mouth was feeling, as he told himself in the current phrase, like the bottom of a parrot's cage. He was reading a cyclostyled foolscap sheet.

SPECIAL ORDER OF THE DAY

TO ALL RANKS OF THE BRITISH ARMY IN FRANCE AND FLANDERS

Three weeks ago today the enemy began his terrific attacks against us on a fifty-mile front. His objects are to separate us from the French, to take the Channel Ports and destroy the British Army.

"Stale news, old boy," he said to an imaginary audience of Bill Kidd's face imposed on that of Sir Douglas Haig. He spat out a wet fag-end, caught it expertly, and lit another from it.

In spite of throwing already 106 Divisions into battle and enduring the most reckless sacrifice of human life, he has made as yet little progress towards his goals.

"Throwing the ball towards a goal is neither cricket nor football. Won't do, old boy. Must put that straight for the lads." He poured out more whiskey, and after rumination upon nothing added another stub to the pile cremating itself beside the candle.

We owe this to the determined fighting and self-sacrifice of our troops. Words fail me to express the admiration which I feel for the splendid resistance offered by all ranks of our Army under the most trying circumstances.

"No good, old boy. If words fail you, then get someone to do the job properly. Bill Kidd, forward please! Yours in humble duty, Sah!" as in imagination he saluted the Field Marshal about to pin a Victoria Cross, with bar, upon Bill Kidd's tunic.

Many of us are now tired. To those I would say that Victory will belong to the side which holds out the longest. The French Army is moving rapidly and in great force to our support.

"We've heard that one before, old boy, about the Froggies!"

There is no other course open to us but to fight it out. Every position must be held to the last man: there must be no retirement.

"That's the stuff to give 'em!" The glass bottle-neck of Haig & Haig rattled yet once again on the rim of the tooth-mug.

With our backs to the wall and believing in the justice of our cause each one of us must fight on to the end. The safety of our homes and the Freedom of mankind alike depend on the conduct of each one of us at this critical moment.

D. Haig,
F.M.,
Commander-in-Chief,
British Armies in France.

General Headquarters,
Thursday, April 11th, 1918.

"Not quite right, old boy. Permit Bill Kidd to show you."

After an hour or so, the following was written in Major Kidd's Field Message book.

LATE NIGHT EXTRA!

To All Ranks,
KIDD'S FORCE
re SPECIAL ORDER FROM SIR D. HAIG

(1) This sector will be held, and all ranks will remain here until relieved.
(2) The enemy cannot be allowed to interfere with this programme.
(3) If Kidd's Force cannot remain here alive it will remain here dead, but in any case it will remain here.
(4) Should any man through shell-shock or other cause attempt to surrender he will remain here dead.
(5) Should all guns be blown up, all ranks will use Mills grenades and other novelties.
(6) Finally the position as stated will be held.

W. Kidd, Major
I/C Kidd's Force
B.E.F.

He had finished reading it through, when he was interrupted.

Intent on his work, he had not noticed that it had become comparatively quiet behind the double gas-blanket.

The candle had burnt low beside the bottle.

Major Kidd was lighting another gasper, before hooking on a bag of Mills bombs, a knobkerry, a couple of daggers, and a revolver to his person when he heard footfalls coming down the steps of the dug-out. Thinking of his runners, he yelled, "Come on you Boche-eating crab-wallahs, do an allez!"

The blanket-curtain was pushed back at one corner. The barrel of a Parabellum pistol was pushed through. Other footfalls were audible.

"Hop it, my Mad Son!" said Kidd. "This is no time for fart-assing about! And don't play any more dam'-fool games, or you're liable to get hurt!" Then Major Kidd saw that the sleeve behind the pistol was *feld-grau.*

"Your 'Boche-eating crab wallahs' have already gone down the 'Allee'," said a precise voice in English. "What you call 'communication trench'. Put up your hands, Herr Marmaladeating Englander!"

"Well, blow me down," said Kidd. "Back with the old kamarads! Have a spot of old man Haig, Herr Deutschlanderfodder?" as he pointed to the bottle.

The German *hauptmann* took up what Kidd had been writing. He read it, smiled and said, "'Hurraparadismus', I observe. What your comic papers call 'swank', I fancy?"

"That's right, Herr Kanonenfleish. How about that spot? Better have it now, Bill Kidd's boys will be coming back, and don't you forget it!"

From the C.C.S. at Kemmel—"Nobody sit down on the grass, it's contaminated with gas!"—lorries for the lightly wounded and minor mustard-gas cases went to one of the three hospitals outside Poperinghe adjoining railway sidings and named Dosinghem, Bandaghem, and Mendinghem.

"This way the mustard-gas cases. Line up here."

"Do you think I could be taken to my General. I am——"

"This way, sir. Into line. Now left turn. Hands on shoulders of the man in front of you. Lead on in front, follow the orderly——"

The orderly was a German walking wounded, black-bearded and with a Red Cross arm-band. As the line shuffled away Phillip was just aware of a voice saying, "We've had bloody thousands in, and no sleep for two days and he wants his General!"

Nearly an hour's wait. Screams and cries. Men writhing on the ground, clothes torn off, almost naked men with blisters like half-deflated children's pink balloons. "Water! Give me water, someone! For Christ's sake, give me water!" Noises of retching—strainings in convulsive gasps as though life were serpentine trying to crawl out of bodies in froth.

"Are you there, O'Gorman?"

"Yes, sorr."

"Try again to locate General West, will you?"

"I will, sorr. Do you stand here, I will be back, sorr."

With anguish he had to move on, his turn to see the M.O. Where was O'Gorman?

First the anti-tetanus injection; then examination of eyes. Painful light. Shrinking back. "Stand still, I won't hurt you." Soothing lanoline; cool bandage.

"I must be with my General, doctor. Would it be possible——"

"I'm afraid you'll have to wait until you get to the base, Colonel."

"But it is most important, doctor."

The doctor respired violently. He too had had no sleep for two days. "Perhaps you don't know that the Germans have reached Merville, and are only a couple of miles from Bailleul? Do you want to get away or don't you?"

"I'm sorry, doctor."

"All right, all right, don't apologise. And for God's sake don't argue, man!"

Waiting. Obedience. Swimming, weeping pain. Slow shuffle to railway siding. Then a miracle, O'Gorman's voice saying, "Follow me, sir, I've got it taped."

Leading Phillip by the hand the batman took him through several lines of tents to an area where the sickly smells of blood and iodoform, ether and carbolic struggled with the nidors of pus, urine, and excreta; where surgeons were stripped to their breeches' tops, with sweating torsos and set faces working away amidst the cries of the demented as fresh ambulances arrived with their formless loads, splashing mud from wheels over close rows of stretchers, their occupants with tunics and trousers stained dark in patches, occupying the only clear spaces. O'Gorman led him towards circular-saw-like screams of broken men being lifted up to operating tables only just cleared of other bodies, but not of mud and blood, white tables in line whence came the steady frettings of hand-saws cutting across fractured bones. "Mother! Mother!" came the wild cry of a boy without feet, as he saw a silver saw in a doctor's hand.

"Here, you!" said a voice of authority, beckoning to a man in the line of anxious blood-volunteers. Phillip imagined, within the red nightmare of his mind, the tunic being peeled off; arm bared; cut made above elbow; stifled cry; tube thrust into vein. Blood gushing, volunteer (hoping to escape battle) staggering, whimpering. "Lie still!" Drip of blood into container. Spider with fly in web, horror of boyhood 'sport'. It was too much. Had he not been upheld by the need to find 'Spectre', he would have sunk down and given up. The presence of the faithful O'Gorman (equally faithful to his own idea of getting back to Blighty with the 'Karnel') held him to the idea beyond the fireballs of his eyes, the Vesuvius of his chest.

"The Gineral can't do much talkin', sorr, he's after being given the morphia. Here he is, the Gineral, sorr, at your feet." He recognised the voice of Boon, 'Spectre's' soldier servant. "Will you bend down, sir, he cannot move, sir."

A hand came out from under the blanket, Boon took Phillip's hand, and guided it to his master's hand, feeling emotional that 'Spectre' and 'Lampo' were together once more.

"Westy, I must tell you——" He choked, the fire-balls of his eyes broke.

As the long, slow Red Cross train was crawling south-west towards the railway junction at Hazebrouck, through which all trains to and from the bases had to pass, the German guns bombarding Bailleul five miles away seemed to be shaking the coach. Bailleul was directly east. Five miles to the west rose the *mont* of Cassel; the railway lay between the two towns. The wind being slight, when the train passed through an area of wood smoke, fumes entered the white dormitory reawakening fear and pain that it had been set on fire. There was the sound of sobbing. A grey-headed orderly said again and again, as he stepped over stretchers, "Don't take it to heart, laddie, don't take it to heart. It's worse for the boys in the line." He was speaking to a youth of 18, who was overcome temporarily by the never-ending work and, above all, by the moans and smells.

Long wait at a junction. Where were they? He did not like to ask, the orderlies were so busy. Voices heard in the White City passing by open door—African, Chinese, Italian. Were they being shipped home, to dig trenches along the East Coast? O'Gorman told him: they were going to work on 'La Belle Hotesse', a redoubt being prepared from behind Hazebrouck to St. Omer, through the 'forest of Nipper'. He meant Nieppe. "They say there's going to be a fourth line, called the Beebee line, sorr."

The foreign jabber receded. Another train came in. He heard neighing, clop of hooves, unharrassed cries of command. Cavalry. Going or coming? O'Gorman did not know.

The hospital train crept forward again, to the shake of greased couplings. It was being shunted. Another long wait. Anti-aircraft guns popped, there was the crump of bombs. "What time is it?"

"Eleven o'clock, sorr."

Drubbling quiver and head-buffeting of guns increasing.

"'Tes like to be on the Ridge, sorr."

He listened, relieved to be by the open door. Cool air. Wounded being brought to the siding. No room. The young voice crying again, old voice repeating, "Don't take it to heart, laddie, it's worse for the boys in the line." Why couldn't he vary it? Words grated like a blunt saw across his head.

In the grey light of dawn the train stopped finally at a siding along the coast. Blessed warm sugary tea, cup after cup of it made him feel wildly cheerful and safe as the liquid relieved the salinity of the weeping raw patches of flesh, while he lay temporarily at peace, awaiting turn to be put with other stretchers into the Ford ambulances.

Boon came to find him—to say goodbye. No more personal servants, except those specially enlisted valets of peace-time, were being allowed to go home with their officers.

"Good luck, sir. You'll keep an eye on the General for me, won't you, sir? Thank you, sir. God bless you, if you'll excuse me saying of it, sir."

"God bless you, Boon."

"Very good, sir."

It was a sad moment. "Well, cheerio, Boon. It's been a long way since Loos. No, not goodbye, au revoir!"

"Au revoir, sir."

"We'll have a pint together when we meet next."

"Thank you, sir."

Flames roared again in Phillip's head, this side of darkness.

With his mouth-organ Major Kidd was entertaining a group of captured British soldiers behind barbed wire. The cage was beside the railway at Kortrai, whither they had been marched, during unknown days, on their way to Germany.

The spirit shown by one of the temporary officers of the *passé* Army of the drowned Lord Kitchener was not uncommon in the British Expeditionary Force at that time, when action had brought relief from cowering thoughts of trench warfare.

In some ways it was easier for those upheld by the vanity, courage, or prominence of an idea beyond themselves, expressed in the freedom of bodily action, than for the military business mind confined more or less to rooms, tables, paper, telephones and other details of a life of comparative inaction. But any life of service for others generates its own courage, or sense of responsibility.

Major-General Harington, M.G.G.S. to General Plumer at Cassel, has broadly described the April crisis of the Second Army; so while 'Lampo' and 'Spectre' are lying at a base hospital, and the 2nd Gaultshires, commanded now by the senior acting-captain, Tabor, are fighting in the re-upheaved ruins south of Wytschaete, let the spirit revisit the Flanders plain to the hill of Cassel, with its yellow gravelly slopes topped by the village through which ran seven roads.

Here in the last Spring of the Great War were brick buildings with faded paint and broken-tiled roofs, and cracked *pisé* barn walls, grouped together a hundred and fifty metres above the Flemish lowlands. From Cassel could be seen lesser hills of the *Monts de Flandres*—Kemmel, Rouge, Noir, Scherpenberg, and Cats—soon to be the scene of attack and counter-attack seeming without end to those in, and beyond, the fighting.

Twenty miles east from the big telescope on Cassel Hill lay Passchendaele, a village site little more than fifty metres above sea-level.

> If we could only hold in the North (wrote Major-General Harington) the tide was bound to turn in our favour, but could we? Our resources were indeed slender. There were no fresh troops to come. Units

were formed of men who had been through the terrible experience of retreat and drafts of inexperienced men from home. All had suffered severe casualties. Units had never had a chance to re-form.

We were discussing the situation at a Staff Conference when an A.D.C. came in with a message to say that the Germans had re-occupied the Messines-Wytschaete Ridge; *our* Ridge, which ten months before we had captured with such pride. Here we were, the same Commander and Staff, sitting in the same room and places in which we had planned that successful operation, being told that it had all gone.

I watched the Army Commander's face. I wondered what the effect on him would be. I knew what it meant to him. I saw him in a real crisis. He never said a word, but told me to continue with what I was saying on something quite different when the A.D.C. interrupted.

The Wytschaete-Messines ridge was a loss, but more was to follow. Where was it going to stop? The enemy got into the village of Locre, at the foot of the Scherpenberg. Still we held the Passchendaele Salient at Ypres. After all those years of security (in Flanders) it seemed incredible that places like Armentières, Nieppe, Ploegsteert Wood, Bailleul, Bac St. Maur, Fleurbaix etc. could ever fall into enemy hands. Yet that was happening, hourly and daily.

As we knew later, the German Commander-in-Chief had scored a bigger success than he expected and had persuaded the German High Command to give him more and more troops. The goal of the Channel Ports was all he saw. He influenced the High Command. The latter succumbed to a strategy which has led many a campaign to disaster. The troops employed were drawn off their main objective. The pressure about Amiens lessened—the wedge between the British and French Armies got more blunt.

Our Second Army line was a very curious and dangerous one at this time. Still we kept our fist out in the Passchendaele Salient with the enemy almost astride our communications. Every time I told the Army Commander that our line was broken in two or three places his grand courage made him reply that it was better than being broken in four or five.

I think now of a conference in my room. The Army Commander was with me standing at my desk examining the map. I knew what he was feeling about Passchendaele. We both knew that the limit had been reached. We should have to come out. The risk was too great. No more help could come from anywhere. Meteren was in flames. Hazebrouck was threatened. At last I summoned up courage to say what I had feared for days.

"I think, sir, you will have to come out of Passchendaele."

"I won't!"

The next moment I felt his hand on my shoulder. "You are right, issue the orders."

He knew it all the time. We both did. We did not speak about it. He went off to his room. We were both much relieved.

The spirit of surrender, however, to the enemy did not last long: as far as I remember something under five minutes.

The old bulldog spirit then came back. He wanted to make quite sure that, in our orders to be issued for the evacuation of the Salient, we were going to hang on to Ypres. As a matter of fact our plans for evacuating were all complete in every detail and had been for some time. He never left anything to chance in that respect and saw that we, who were privileged to be on his staff, did not either.

He then went off in his customary way to see the subordinate Commanders who were going to carry out the difficult task of evacuation. Such an operation is always nasty and liable to be upset. However, we slipped away without the enemy being aware of it. Our line was then close round Ypres—in truth with our backs to the wall.

A rusty rotten train, on its way into Germany, squeaked and clanked into a siding at Kortrai, to similar but diminished music from Bill Kidd's 'marf-orgin'.

"Don't worry, lads, Bill Kidd's boys will come and fetch us! Come on you crab-wallahs, do an allez!"

An American hospital at Étretât, 14th April, towards evening. The day spiker, going round the George Washington ward, stops as from a swathed face and chest comes a dry croak. "Bottle—please——"

"Sure, buddy, I'll bring you one right now."

Fiery, scalding urine, only a few drops, yet once again. Shame for an empty bottle. More stinging. Try again. Nothing. "So sorry."

"You don't have to worry, son."

With slow articulation, "What—day—is it?"

"Still the same, buddy. Sunday, April fourteen, I guess."

"Any—news of—the Peckham line?"

"I'll ask when the night relief comes on dooty. Now just you try resting up, colonel."

Aeons of flaming suns rolled in the orbits of his eyes.

"That place, what was it now, White Sheet Hill? Yeah, the British have gone back some more, I guess. Now you don't have to worry yourself, buddy, that White Sheet Hill is taken by the Heinies."

When the orderly had gone Phillip sobbed within the flaming hell of his bandage mask, but no relieving tears fell, only gummy stabs of 60-pounder flame.

Chapter 11

HETTY GOES TO WAR

Thomas Turney was standing, as he had stood many times before, just inside the kitchen of No. 11 Hillside Road.

He never sat down in there; nor did he enter front- or sitting-room when he went in to see his daughter; for the old man went next-door only when he had a problem on his mind.

Nowadays he had ceased to talk about the decline in value of his stocks and shares: that was inevitable, accepted as part of the common burden of the war which those behind the fighting men must accept.

On this April morning he stood just by the larder door, his watery eyes fixed upon his daughter's face.

"Don't you think we should go, Hetty? The poor boy is all alone——"

"Oh, I don't see how I could possibly leave Dickie, Papa!"

He said "Oh," and then summoned himself to say, "Doris, isn't she home now for the Easter vacation, Hetty? Couldn't she be left to look after the house for a day or two?"

Hetty looked unhappy. For so long had she been accustomed to worrying about her husband that it had become a habit; and like all habits, good or bad, hard to break.

"I have seen Dawson," he said, referring to the local branch of the London, City, and Midland Bank, where he drew cheques for his housekeeping—his main account was near his stationery and printing works off High Holborn—"Dawson says that all can be arranged through the Y.M.C.A. The Government provides tickets, and also rations, the Y.M.C.A. looks after everything else. I've asked him to try to get two tickets reserved, for the time being. He'll telephone Whitehall."

Thomas Turney had had a telegram the day before, informing him that his grandson, Tommy, Charley's boy, was on the

Dangerously Ill list at the South African hospital at Abbeville. A letter had arrived that morning, inviting him to visit the wounded soldier.

"I think I ought to wait to hear what Dickie has to say, Papa."

"Yes, of course, Hetty." He constrained himself from remarking that Dickie might for once think of others before himself; but for many years now the old man had learned to submit, to accept things as they were. So he checked his thought: of course Hetty must wait to consult Dickie. Poor fellow, he had been nervy ever since he had been blown into the gutter by that Zeppelin aerial torpedo which had fallen in Nightingale Grove, and been covered with powdered glass, when on duty as a 'Special'. In any case they couldn't go before the next morning, there was no hurry, the tickets were reserved.

Richard objected at once. The thought of having to look after himself dismayed him. Then there was, to reinsure his protest, the thought of submarine danger in the Channel, Gotha raids on all bases mentioned in the communiqués from G.H.Q. It was out of the question! He could not face the blankness of coming back to a silent house, of having to prepare his own meals after arriving home, fagged out, late from the office. Besides, there was his allotment to think of. England might soon be starving! He was about to put his foot down, as he thought of it, when Hetty said first, "Elizabeth and Doris will see to things, I am sure, Dickie."

"Oh, you are, are you?"

Elizabeth, he thought, could be relied upon to do nothing that did not please herself, while in the presence of his younger daughter, Doris, with her taciturn reserve and curt manner of addressing him, he never felt comfortable.

"I think I might manage for myself, if the girls would rather be alone. Why can't they go next door, if Mr. Turney's mind is set on taking you away?"

"Oh, I am sure everything will be quite all right, Dickie. Doris will be able to manage, I will tell her all there is to be done."

After supper of fried cod steaks and bread-and-margarine pudding (with currants) his thoughts had come round to the idea of a few days of freedom. He and Zippy the cat would enjoy themselves, and he could always play his gramophone!

"Well, take care of yourself, old girl! We don't want to lose you, you know, if you think you ought to go!" he joked, varying the words of a popular song.

At 9 o'clock the post-girl's double knock came on the front door. Before the war there had been six deliveries between 8 a.m. and 9 p.m.; now there were only three. Doris, sitting silent at the table (she was reading Modern English History) got up quietly and went to the door. There was a letter to her from Willoughby, and a telegram addressed to Richard Maddison. She returned with composed face, to give the telegram to her father.

"The girl is waiting to see if there is any answer."

Richard opened his ivory-handled pen-knife, and with the back of the long blade carefully slit the orange envelope, then as carefully removed the folded message. He glanced at it; laid it on his knee; stared ahead at nothing, before saying, "Good God." Then, he found, he was unable to speak.

"What is it, Father?"

"Read it," he sighed, passing the bit of paper, which half-folded itself, held so lightly in the limp fingers of the long thin hand.

"It says only 'blinded temporarily', don't forget, Father! Anyway it must be a mistake, for it says 'Lieutenant-colonel P. S. T. Maddison', and Phill's only a full loot. Oh yes, and look there—it has been re-directed from Beau Brickhill, so it obviously went to Aunt Liz's first! They've got Phil mixed up with some-one else."

Richard examined the form, then decided to send a reply asking for confirmation: but on second thoughts he considered that the War Office would be closed, or the department which dealt with such routine matters.

"Now, if you please, do not tell Mother about this matter, until I am able to make enquiries tomorrow, and find out the facts."

"Then shall I tell the girl there's no reply, Father?"

"Yes, if you please."

Doris returned to her study of the Chartist riots and Reform Bill. But the words had no meaning. Nor was Richard able to take in what the leader of *The Daily Trident* was about. Could there have been a clerical error? The initials were correct; only the rank and address were in error. '*Temporarily* blinded and in hospital'. Might that not be a gentle let-down? Then the awful thought. Supposing he *is* blind . . . it would mean having Phillip on his hands, living at home, for the rest of his life. Terrible! A variation of Hugh Turney always about the place! He shrank from the word *burden*; poor fellow, he had done his duty, and was lucky to have got out of it with his life. Of course. Even so, the thought persisted, to be brushed aside as unworthy, but to recur again and again: he would no longer be able to call his home his own!

But—the boy, blinded in battle! Whatever was he thinking of?

He tried to read his newspaper, but the words meant little or nothing; he left the room, and went into the scullery, to wash up what Hetty always called the tea-things. He had not done this for years, while his wife was at home; now, in the light of a candle, he lived again a scene of his early married life, when Phillip was a baby and he had nursed him during many anxious nights because his mother was ill and could not feed him; so he had taken on the little fellow, while addressing envelopes, by the light of his dark lantern, and Hetty slept upstairs. The little fellow had been comforted and once had smiled at him! The years of misprision fell away; Phillip was still his boy—and now he was blind. Oh, how could he have been so selfish as to think that he would be a burden in his own home, after all he had gone through?

He went back to the sitting room, having washed and wrung out the dish cloth and hung the drying cloth neatly on the clothes-horse—leaving the place cleaner than he had found it—with new resolutions.

"I suppose you wouldn't care for a game of chess, Doris?"

"No thank you, Father."

Silence. Then, "You've heard about your Mother's proposal, I suppose?"

"Yes, Father. I think she ought to go."

"Oh, you do, do you?"

"Yes, Father, I do. Mother deserves a little respite sometimes."

"From what, pray?"

"From all of us."

Richard was rebuffed. He had intended to ask her advice, but now retired behind *The Daily Trident*, wherein he read that many soldiers were being *temporarily* blinded by mustard gas. This relieved him greatly, and when Hetty came back from her nightly game of bezique—it had alternated every week with picquet throughout the war—with 'Mr. Turney', he told her the good news, adding that 'her best boy' had somehow got himself described as a Colonel. Elizabeth had come in with Hetty, and she said, "I bet he gave that rank to some orderly, and sent the telegram himself, just to swank! How like Phillip!"

"But you don't know that, dear," replied Hetty. "I hope you won't go telling people that."

"Well, it *is* just what he'd do!" she cried querulously. "You *always* make excuses for him, don't you?"

She turned and went out of the room, leaving the door open. At once Richard got up and shut it, to sit down again without a word. Just like that selfish creature, always strutting about in new clothes, thinking only of her own appearance! He snorted when Hetty said, "Mavis, I mean Elizabeth is very tired, Dickie. She has been to the Spring Sales, and needs her supper. I'd better go and see to it."

Hetty had hardly left the room when Doris got up, closed her book, put back her chair, opened the door, "Good night, Father," and shutting it with a slight bang—she could never remember to turn the handle first—went upstairs to bed.

Not one thought had she taken about her correspondent in France, Willoughby, that evening, except vaguely in connexion with the face of Percy Pickering. Now in the darkness of her bed she lay and wept silently, as she had wept during many of the past five hundred and sixty-seven nights, the coming of which she had longed for during each day since Percy had been killed.

Thomas Turney and Henrietta his younger daughter travelled with about a hundred other civilians in what looked to be a very important boat, for beyond the railings shutting off the forward part of the boat were to be seen many red-banded caps among the officers. They landed at Boulogne in the late afternoon, after a queasy journey for her (*mal de mer*, as Hetty had thought of it since Convent schooldays in Belgium) and were taken to the Hotel Bras d'Or, which was run by the British for relatives of the D.I.—as the Dangerously Ill were spoken of.

Hetty was almost like a girl again, travelling with her father 'on the Continent'; only now the scenes no longer had for her a background of gaiety. A slow train took them along the coast to Abbeville, outside which was the 1st South African hospital. It was late when they arrived at the relatives' hostel in a poor-looking street in which, surprisingly, was a small château within a courtyard out of which rose a great chestnut tree.

Within the *salle à manger* was a long table, or series of tables, at which was served a plain dinner of meat, cabbage, and watery black potatoes on a soiled table cloth, its presence there contrasting with the former life of the house, as shown by the tapestries upon the walls, the *armoires* holding delicate glass and china, the candelabra hanging from the ceiling, and—so reminiscent of Thildonck days—sacred poems, written in purple ink, in delicate thin Italian handwriting, others woven in silken thread on perforated white card-paper. The presence of the shabby table-cloth was soon explained: the guests were of all classes, only a very few being of what she thought of as good families; the majority were working-class people. Poor things, she thought, all of them.

She could not sleep in the strange bedroom, but lay awake, the candle burning beside her for company. Would it last through the darkness, this little gleam, so faithful that it seemed to have a soul? Once she blew out the flame, to save the candle's life, and became aware of the rolling of trains passing continuously, far away, an undertone of the war which now seemed so vast and terrible, an evil spirit controlling millions of men and women, something quite apart from themselves; and somehow the lost light of the candle was as though she had killed a friend. Kind, thoughtful Dickie had given her a box of matches to bring with the candle, saying that both would be scarce in France. She revived the flame, and it was Dickie's kind thought in the rising gleams; the thoughts of others, too, for the small flame was trembling all the time with the distant gun-fire; then it was blinking at the nearer *thump-thumthump-thump* of bombs. She could bear it, with the flame of loving-kindness glowing upon the *prieu-dieu* on the wall and the tapestry of the four-poster bed which reminded her of *Mère Ambroisine* and her schooldays at Thildonck.

And yet—and yet—was there a strange smell in the room? Or was it her imagination? She sat up, and it seemed to be stronger. At last she could bear it no longer, and getting out of bed, began to search about the room. Tracing the smell to a cupboard, she opened the door to see, staring at her with glass eyes glinting in candlelight, a stuffed spaniel. This was a shock; but it became horror when she saw, running out of various holes in the body, at least a dozen mice. She shut the door at once, and put a chair against it; even so, she could not stop herself from thinking what would happen if it opened in the night.

It now became a matter of endurance, centred round the life of the candle. Would it last the night? The darkness seemed congealed behind the heavy curtains across the shuttered windows. She felt she could not breathe, while the image of the stuffed dog being slowly pulled apart under its hair by restless tiny mice was, in some way she could not determine, part of the war.

She prayed, and feeling calmer, dropped asleep, to awaken with the candle still burning beside the bed-head. Its light was welcome, and she got up happily and pulling back the curtains saw that it was already day, with the sun shining on the leaves of the chestnut tree, and flowers in white-washed tubs around the courtyard. German prisoners were down below, sweeping the cobbles; she peeped at them, strange objects from another world in their lead-grey uniforms into which large blue patches were sewn, and their small round grey caps with red piping. She felt a slight fear, but when one smiled up at her, and touched his cap, his eyes nearly as blue as Phillip's, the remoteness of vague war-conceived ideas left her, and she smiled back happily, thinking that they had mothers, too.

After *petit dejeuner* they went to the Y.M.C.A. in the Place Amiral Courbet. She thought the canteen women's uniforms very neat, grey skirt, coat, and triangular badge. It was surprising to see English newspapers on sale there. One had heavy black headlines—METEREN IN FLAMES. The Germans claimed thousands of prisoners, but the Americans were pouring into France.

"It will be a race against time, I fancy," remarked Thomas Turney.

There was an hour before the 'bus would take them to the hospital, so they walked into the town, seeing the collegiate church of St. Wulfrum partly destroyed by bombs, its window spaces filled by wire frames supporting mica sheets. A notice on the door proclaimed that *bougies* were *interdit,* obviously lest they show light at night to the Gothas.

It was a sad visit to the South African hospital. The D.I.

Ward sister, in her pale buff and navy blue uniform, told them that Corporal Turney was very ill indeed. Both his thighs had been removed almost to the pelvis. He was unconscious.

"Gas gangrene develops so quickly. A stick bomb went off beside him as he was firing his rifle, and his legs were badly torn, with compound bone fractures. They were removed above the knee in a clearing station, but sepsis had already set in."

He lay with mouth open, and eyes closed, his face a greenish-grey. Hetty only just recognised in that face a trace of the boy who had played with Phillip, and once, had taken all Phillip's birds' eggs to bed with him, hiding them under his pillow. Phillip had been very kind, she remembered; he was heart-broken, but he had not said much to Tommy, four years younger than himself.

"I'm afraid we may lose him," said the nurse.

The next day they went to the funeral in the cemetery outside the town. There were other coffins in the G.S. wagons drawn by black horses, with soldier drivers on the seats. Almost white coffins, of deal. The yellow mounds of clay recalled Randiswell cemetery, the graves of Mamma and Hughie. It was all the same world, of course, and God still watched over it, with Mary and Jesus and all the saints, whose beauty of spirit was born of suffering, she thought as she and Papa followed the coffin up stone steps past the cypresses of the civilian cemetery. How it all came back to her, the childhood dread of French cemeteries—the iron frames above graves adorned with black and white silver crucifixes on mauve wreaths made of beads.

Beyond was the military burial ground. There they waited. Something seemed to be not right among the chaplains in uniform: apparently some of the coffins had got mixed up, and as two were Nonconformist, one Roman Catholic, one orthodox Jew, and the remainder Church of England, it took time to determine which was which; and when this was done, the order of burial had to be arranged in accordance with procedure laid down by G.R.O.—first C. of E., then Nonconformist, Catholic, and Hebrew. She wept, she could not help it, it was all so sad, the bewildered mourners, the open distress of some, the voiceless grief of others.

After a rest in the little château in the Rue Duchesne de Lamotte, containing so much elegance within, while in the gutter outside its sewer moved with grey deadness, she went for a walk with her father. They came to a river, and looking down from the bridge she saw the water flowing swiftly cold on its way to the sea, and heard, with a shock, Papa saying that this was the river Somme.

What (wrote General Harington) was to be the next phase of this drama? The enemy did not leave us long in doubt. With Castre, Fletre, Meteren, all in his hands it was soon obvious that Strazeele and Hazebrouck were next on his list. We were forced to leave Cassel, except as an advanced headquarters. We were near the climax. If we lost these towns, we should be in a very serious position. We had very extensive and valuable railway plant at Strazeele; Hazebrouck was the keynote of our railway communications. It was indeed a race against time.

Sir Douglas Haig had ordered the 1st Australian Division, under Major-General H. B. Walker, up from the south to our rescue. It was due to arrive at Hazebrouck at 2 p.m. How we counted the minutes and how disappointed we were at hearing that all the trains were delayed! The trains had to come via Etaples—the only route left. The enemy knew this and made a determined bombing attack on the bridge at Etaples, missing only by inches. The trains were delayed; the whole course of the war might have been altered by those inches.

Few people knew what a race it was—all the officers, N.C.O.'s, servants, cooks and policemen of the Second Army Schools were indeed putting theory into practice around Strazeele. They were determined to hold on till they heard the whistle of the trains bringing relief and they did so.

The first trains of the Division arrived some nine hours late. From the moment Walker and his men arrived we never looked back. The onslaught into the Flanders plain had expended itself.

Richard had good news for Hetty when she returned. Doris had loyally kept the secret of the telegram; and now he had a letter to show her as well, written by Phillip, the sentences rather like a jig-saw puzzle, but obviously he was in good heart and spirits.

"Oh, and he was at Boulogne when we were there! If only I'd known! Papa and I could have seen him!"

"He'll be home before very long, I'll be bound. Well, tell me all about it."

He listened in wonderment, asking many questions. It had never occurred to him that, except for war-time conditions, life was going on ordinarily in France and Belgium.

"Now tell me how *you* have been getting on, dear."

"Oh, I've managed, thank you."

Richard had enjoyed his little holiday, as he thought of it. The two girls had breakfasted next door with Miss Turney, and also supped there; his breakfast had been prepared for him on a tray, and he ate 'in solitary splendour' in the sitting-room, with the eastern sun shining through the open french windows, and birds singing outside. An oasis in his life; he had worked at his allotment for an hour every evening, and returned to listen to Elgar, Wagner, and his favourite records of Frank Bridge's *The Sea* in the sitting-room; and there had been the May number of *Nash's Magazine*, as well as *The Daily Trident*. The news was better from France, too: the Germans had been stopped.

"I see by the paper," he said, sipping his cup of hot water before going to bed, "that I've lost my chance of joining the Labour Corps as a Volunteer. From now on it's to be conscription, and I'm out of it by one year. This Military Service Act has been rushed through both Houses and the Royal Assent has been given by Commission in the King's absence. Listen to this, Hetty, 'Every male British subject . . . who has attained the age of eighteen years and has not attained the age of fifty-one . . . shall be deemed to have been duly enlisted in His Majesty's Forces for general service with the Colours or in the Reserve for the period of the war . . .' Yes, I've missed my chance at having a go at the Germans, just as I missed the chance of becoming a fruit farmer in Australia as a young fellow. Now it is too late. I am a half and half creature, a mere cog in a machine. Still, I suppose the Army is composed mainly of cogs." The idea appealed to him, and thinking of himself in uniform, with hair dyed (he had bought a bottle of hair restorer) and moustache like that of Sir Douglas Haig, he went on, "I should have liked to have been a sniper. What are you laughing at?"

Her sense of fun had upset the picture of himself; he closed up at once behind his paper. She was laughing at him, because he was old and done-for.

"I wasn't laughing at you, Dickie——"

But she was, and he knew it. "I am glad you find me amusing, that's something in my favour."

"I know you would be a very good sniper."

"Well, I won't go so far as to say I will be, but I might have been. After all, I have my first-class marksman's certificate, you know."

"Yes, dear, of course, naturally."

He retired hurt behind his newspaper.

She felt like crying. If only he could sometimes laugh *with* her, how much easier life would be. The idea of Dickie as a sniper had been funny, for the poor man had been just that all his life—sniping at this and that from behind the entrenchment of his newspaper—Lloyd George and his 'ninepence for fourpence', Churchill, Ramsay Macdonald, the Suffragettes, George Bernard Shaw, Free Trade. She smiled from her cross, feeling suddenly exhausted, and going up to the kitchen, stumbled on the stairs, and with a slight whimper stood still in the unlighted scullery, her place of retreat where she could think her own generally sad thoughts.

The smell of burning toast drew her back to the kitchen, to draw the curtains and open the bottom of the window, for across the top of the window ran the hot pipes from the boiler to the hot tank in the bathroom, and Dickie said that the cold air coming in cooled the pipe. She saw a star shining above the arch of jasmine between the two houses, and thought that the same star was shining in France upon the yellow heap which was the grave of Charley's boy; she heard again the shivering boom of guns 'up the line', she saw the cold clear waters of the Somme which had come down from the battlefield; and closing her eyes, prayed without words to the Virgin Mary, Mother of God, while tears moved in silence down her face.

"I suppose," said Richard, when she returned to the sitting-room with a tray of toast (scraped brown) and a boiled egg, "we shall be having Phillip back in England before long. I heard in the City that many men of the Fifth Army have come back, and all tell the same terrible story of the way things were mismanaged over there by General Sir Hubert Gough."

The Major of the American hospital at Etrêtat was about to come round the ward with the Colonel from Paris. The Major, with Senior Sister, the young 'loo-tenant' doctor, and the nurses had all been busy seeing that the ward was one hundred per cent freshened up.

Phillip stood by his bed, in felt slippers and dressing-gown, awaiting their coming. The bed had a large white bow tied on the head rail, denoting milk diet. He felt like a pouter pigeon, eyes lost under feathers of lint and cotton, throat and chest big with bandages. The water-blisters had gone down, the raw flesh itched. At night gloves were tied over his hands, lest he scratch, and develop septicaemia. He was not a pouter pigeon, he was a dodo, misshapen with blobbed wings and reptilian clawed feet, for his toe-nails needed cutting. He tried to curl in his toes when being washed in bed by the ward nurse (who was the very blonde who came from Sweden, *via* the United States) lest she see them, and he fell in respect in her eyes. He could not see her face, but from what others in the ward said, she was very beautiful; another Lily, her voice low and gentle.

Senior Sister came into the ward for a final look round. "Don't you want to be in bed to meet the Colonel, young man?" Her question was the equivalent of the English veiled request, "Don't you think you ought to be in bed——" but Phillip did not know this.

"No, thank you, Sister," he replied with a little bow. He wanted the Colonel to see that he was now quite fit to leave the ward. He must get to 'Spectre', by hook or by crook.

Senior Sister went away, with what a story-writer in *The Saturday Evening Post* would have called 'a little *moue*' at Ward Sister. Such high-toned British dignity! The young British colonel insisting that he stand in the presence of a United States colonel! Admiration, amusement, mingled with her wish for symmetry—beds aligned, drapes seventy five per cent drawn back, pillows at forty-five degrees to lines of necks, arms parallel above coverlets, Old Glory and Union Jack crossed above the chimney piece at the correct angle of forty-five degrees, while below on the shelf lithographs of President Wilson and King George of Britain stood together, divided only by a framed Manifesto on Moral and Ethical Principles issued by the Daughters of the Revolution.

The moment came. He waited, pulsating more, right arm sweat glands unexpectedly closed.

"Glad to know you, young man. How goes it, as the British say?"

"I am quite fit, thank you, sir. I was wondering if I might be transferred to the ward where General West is, now that there is a vacancy."

"So you've found that out, have you?"

"Yes, sir. My orderly, that is my striker, told me. Of course

I don't want to cause any trouble, but the General is my best friend."

"Wale, what do you think, Major?"

The Major looked at the Senior Sister, then at the chart in the Ward Sister's hands. Temperature 102 the night before, 99 that morning. Pulse 92. Respiration 70. He saw pus encrustation on the eye bandage removed for his inspection, he touched the livid swollen lids, noting that hyalin was already running down one cheek. The raw blistered flesh on neck and chest was weeping, too. He listened with his stethoscope. Heart intermittent, mucus in respiratory passages, probably incipient bronchitis. Against that, no pneumococcal trace in the stained colloidal smear revealed under microscopic examination.

"Wale, I guess I've got some noos for you, Colonel," he said, his pronunciation similar to that of 17th century English. "You are doo for embarkation to Britain on the boat this afternoon. We have to lose all of you. Do not thank me, sir. We require every bed for a convoy doo in tomorrow, I guess, as our common enemy now appears to be making his all-in effort. Meantime you sure must keep those eyes occluded. I think we have gotten rid of streptococcus, but conjunctivitis remains."

"Is mustard gas made from mustard, doctor?"

"Mustard gas is a compound called dichlorodiethyl sulphide, sir. The Germans call it Yperite, maybe with the hope that by its aid they will capture Ypres, or as they call that old town, Yper, which some of their cartoonists, I observe, are delineating in the shape of a skull, which has to my mind a pathological fear-fulfilment. Yes sir, dichlorodiethyl sulphide is no simple compound. At this moment of so-called prog-ress our chemistry research men find it indestructible, that is, they cannot yet provide an antidote for use upon damaged tissue. But they will, we may be sure. Goodbye, Colonel, give my regards to London, England."

"Sure thing, Colonel. And please accept my thanks for what you and your kind helpers have done for us British here. By the way, sir, will General West be on the same boat?"

"Surely, but the General's a very ill man, with gas gangrene, I guess."

The hospital ship *Persia*, a small boat brought into service for the emergency, was convoyed by two destroyers. Sitting below the deck on canvas-covered forms all round the steel walls were the lightly wounded and walking cases. Others lay or sat upon the floor for the two-hour crossing. The officers' ward led from this; there were other wards, those amidships on the first deck were for the stretcher cases.

Phillip, sitting by a porthole, was waiting, with renewed hope and annulment of hope, for an opportunity to ask O'Gorman to lead him to Westy. His anxiety grew as the ship left harbour and became dread of being sick before others, the more so because he would not be able to find his way to the lavatory, and, behind a locked door, be safe to vomit, and lie down unseen. Should he ask O'Gorman to take him to the lavatory now, or wait in the hope of feeling better? The orderly had said it was a fine day, the Channel like a mill-pond; perhaps lack of sight had put out his sense of balance, for the ship seemed to be rising and falling.

He sat there, trying to force his mind to believe that sea-sickness began in the imagination, like fear: thrust away nervousness, and he would not feel sick. After all, the little levels in the human ear could not really be upset while he was sitting down. So it was a case of mind over matter.

"Send Private O'Gorman, my orderly, to me, will you?"

"I'm here, sorr."

"Oh, thank God! Go and find where General West is, will you? Leave your rifle and clobber here, beside me. Say I sent you if anyone tries to stop you. Then come back here as quickly as you can."

"Very good, sorr."

He felt better. It was a case of mind over matter, he told himself. But the word *matter* started another train of thought: yellow matter—pus, stink of cordite, mortar and brick dust—hot oil engines. If only those around him would not talk so, and smoke, smoke, smoke; the combination from irritating became menacing. What a fool he had been to send O'Gorman away. He would never get back in time. The crisis was near, water was gathering in his mouth, fatal sign. He was reluctant to call out for a bowl, and it was too late now to ask to be taken to the lavatory. How weak he was, always going against his intuition. He should not have sent O'Gorman to find Westy.

The ship was beginning to creak. The cork life-belt was too tight round his chest. It was pressing against his breathing. He would not be able to lower his chin to be sick. He must ask for a bowl. Acrid smoke from the man smoking a ghastly Belgian cigar on his left. He must get away. He stood up, and was flung down by the greatest world-splitting noise. It seemed to break him into a million atoms. He did not feel the blow of his head hitting the deck. He lay there, vomiting, while remote voices began to speak only to fade again. He did not care, but lay in a semi-coma until awareness returned of shouts and cries around him. Then a loud megaphone command.

"Every man is to remain where he is."

The beat of the engine stopped. There was a roar of steam, the *whoop whoop* of whistles which he thought vaguely must come from the destroyers.

Feet were moving overhead. An authoritative voice called out, "Everyone on the upper deck! Take your time. Every man to move in an orderly manner. The ship has struck a mine, there is no danger."

"Any more for the 'Skylark'?" cried a wag, as Phillip knelt up, trying to find where he was by his hands.

He was helped on deck into fresh blowing air. "Wait here, please, sir. Everything will be quite all right."

"Yes, I am sure it will. Do you know where Brigadier-General West is? He's a stretcher case."

"He'll be taken care of, sir. Now you wait here, sir, until they get the boat off of the hooks."

Too many voices were talking at once. Was the deck sloping? He asked the voice next to him, and heard that the explosion had torn a hole in the engine room.

"The boilers might go up any minute now."

The deck lurched. There were cries from the line of waiting men.

"Keep your places, men. Help is coming. The boats will soon be lowered."

Westy had a big wooden cage around his leg, how could they get him into a boat? With immense relief he heard O'Gorman beside him. "The Gineril be on the upper deck, sorr. That's the one above us. We're on 'B' deck, sorr. We'll have to swim for it, by the way things is lookin'."

"We ought to get to him. He won't be able to swim with his leg like that. Take me to the companion way."

"Very good, sorr."

O'Gorman guided his hands, steadied him up an iron ladder nearly vertical with the listing of the ship.

Boots were scraping and scrambling. Floats were being unlashed. The boats along the port side filled with men were no longer hanging over water.

"Wait here, sorr, while I take a look for the Gineral. I'll spot him by the red about his tunic."

The ship was taking on a steeper list, men crowding the rails steepened the angle. More words through the megaphone.

"Attention, all men! Help is coming from the escort destroyers. Let every man see that his cork-jacket is properly fastened. Those of you who can swim should take to the water, to ease the manning of the boats. There is no need for alarm. All will be picked up."

It was now five minutes after the mine, wallowing in the ebb down Channel, had struck amidships to starboard.

At the beginning of the sixth minute the order was called out, 'Every man for himself!' Phillip pulled off the bandages in order to find his friend. Instantly his eyeballs were stricken by an explosion of light. With blood dripping from the lids he stood there giving himself up to defeat, until a voice told him to sit down, slide to the rail, and then jump into the sea.

The *Persia*, taken off the Salonika run during the emergency, sank in seven minutes after its rusty plates had touched one of the horns of the mine. Some of the patients went down with the ship, but most of them, with Phillip and 'Spectre', were picked up by the escorting destroyers. Phillip was none the worse for being a quarter of an hour in the sea, but 'Spectre' was drowned, the wooden cage around his leg having kept his head low. He had been wearing a cork life-belt on entering the water, but was without it when picked up.

Later O'Gorman said to Phillip, "The Gineral, sorr, he fleeted off av the stracher, he was w'arin' av his cark belt, but his sharp eye saw me misself without one, for I had gone to watter without it, sorr. The Gineral he guv me the order to put on his belt, sorr. The Gineral he barked at me, sorr, and offered me a court-martial thin an' there unless I obeyed him, so I obeyed the Gineral's order, sorr, and put on the cark belt he untied from around his own chest, sorr, the white man that he was. May his soul rest wid the Holy Mother of God Herself, sorr."

Part Three

TENSION

May—September, 1918

'For what peace of mind can any man have if his honour is no longer in his own keeping?'

The Anatomy of Courage,
by Lord Moran.

Chapter 12

EVASION

A letter from Phillip at last! And oh dear, the words slanted about the page as though he was learning to write all over again! Still, it had arrived on his birthday, with such wonderful news: he would soon be able to see again. The writing paper was embossed with heavy black lettering, *Husborne Abbey, Gaultshire*.

"Just fancy, Papa! Phillip is in that lovely place, in that beautiful park, with all the deer, the bison, and the other animals! Oh, I am so proud of my boy, so is Dickie! I expect someone will be able to read my letters to him!"

"You could get there and back in a day, if you were to make an early start, Hetty."

Other ideas were in the air, buoyant with the song of birds. Doris was going up early to London, to be with two friends of hers in the Women's Land Army; there was to be a procession through the streets of London, and a review afterwards in Hyde Park. Hetty wanted to go, too; but could she leave Dickie? He, elated by the good news of Phillip, agreed at once; he intended to work in his allotment in the afternoon, and could get his own tea.

"You go and enjoy yourself, old girl!"

After a light lunch Hetty and her elder daughter went down the road to catch a 36 'bus to London. At the corner, where the lilac bushes were in bud, they saw Mrs. Neville sitting at her open window. Sprat, Phillip's terrier, was looking out beside her.

"He's always there when I go by," said Elizabeth. "I bet he's not happy with her, but always looking out for Phillip to come."

"Hush, dear, Mrs. Neville may hear what you say."

They crossed the road, to tell Mrs. Neville the news. Mrs. Neville had also had a letter from Phillip that morning; but she dissembled, knowing how wrapped up 'the little mother', as she thought of Hetty, was in her boy. However, she made one mistake which was detected by the sharp mind of Mavis under the would-be aloof façade of Elizabeth.

"Oh, I am *so* glad to hear the good news, dear! And in the Duke's hospital at Husborne Abbey, too! He'll be well looked after there, and have the best of food. That horrible burning gas, I suppose *we'll* be using it next! Tell Phillip that Sprat is quite happy, won't you, and looking forward, as we all are, to seeing him again. I shall miss my little companion very much, he is quite a companion, you know, so understanding and intelligent. He's a little rascal, too. If I read too much, and don't give him what he considers proper attention, he jumps and up knocks the book out of my hand! Then he fetches his tennis ball, and gives it to me, so prettily. Well, I must not stop you, it's a lovely day for the procession, isn't it?"

As the two walked on down Charlotte Road, under its chestnuts opening their sticky buds, Elizabeth said, "I don't trust Mrs. Neville, with her smarmy manner all put on. Why couldn't she say straight out that she had had a letter from Phillip, instead of pretending like that! I knew it at once, didn't you, Mother? It was obvious as soon as she mentioned Husborne Abbey! You didn't tell her what hospital he was in."

"What does it matter after all, Elizabeth?"

"Well, I can't stand hypocrisy in any form!"

A twinge of helplessness came over Hetty, to be avoided by "Well, why shouldn't Phillip write to Mrs. Neville? After all, she was kind enough to look after Sprat while he was away. And I expect Phillip wants to know how Desmond is getting on." At the same time she could not help a pang because Phillip had always seemed to prefer Mrs. Neville's flat to his own home.

"Oh now, you know very well that he and Desmond quarrelled over that girl, Lily Cornford, two years ago! Ever since then Desmond won't speak to Phillip. No wonder! Look how he deceived his best friend!"

"Really, Mavis, I mean Elizabeth, you should not say such a thing!"

"It's true, anyway! You see, *you* don't know Phillip like I do!"

"I told you before, dear, that you are inclined to be too critical of others. It only hurts yourself, you know. One must try to live and let live. It's the only way, I am sure."

"All right, you tell that to Phillip when he comes home! You are always taking his part against me! You favoured him as a child! It isn't fair!"

"That is not true, my girl! I have no favourites, as I've told you many, many times in the past. All you children, and your Father, are equally dear to me." Immediately she regretted having been so unkind (as she thought) to her child, whose troubles and perplexities she knew so well; and behind all her care was a dread that she might have one of her attacks. She must be careful not to upset Elizabeth in any way.

By now the beauty of the spring day was made remote by care; but once they were on their way, and past the Obelisk, she felt happy again, living in the variety of life all around her in the streets—people whose feelings she could secretly share, their hopes and kindnesses to one another, their tragedies endured so bravely, their happy little family moments. Ah, there was the Old Vic, with its wonderful, wonderful plays of Shakespeare, week after week despite all the war-time worries. Yes, the war had brought people together in so many ways; God indeed did work in His own way, to bring beauty and love into the lives of everyone: if only they could see it was true!

And the Thames! Hetty had never ceased to feel the wonder of the river, every stone and brick beside it part of history. Oh, life was truly wonderful! But more was to come on this buoyant Spring day. Suddenly through the dusty glass window of the tram was to be seen the procession, lined up along the Embankment, just about to start off. The two got down at the next stop, and waited under the speckled shadows of the plane trees for the head of the column to pass.

"Oh dear, I do hope Doris has not missed it, Elizabeth."

At the head was a tall girl carrying the Union Jack. She wore a smock with breeches and leggings, and on her head was a turned-up felt hat on which was pinned a rosette of red and green. How healthy she looked, with her coiled golden hair! Behind her walked another girl carrying a duck, with a notice round its neck, *I have laid* 31 *eggs in* 34 *days, and I am still doing it.*

"Poor thing," exclaimed Elizabeth. "I think it's a shame to make fun of a dumb creature!"

"Doris will be so disappointed not to be here."

"Oh, Mother, stop worrying!"

Next came light-draught horses, pulling wagons and carts, all brightly painted, while the horses' coats gleamed and their feet were dark with oil. In the wagons were more land girls, singing songs as they stood among sheaves of corn set in patterns of beech and box branches, and clusters of primroses and daffodils; while above them were banners, 'Come with us into the country', and 'Join with us and work for Victory'. How Dickie would have loved seeing it, she thought, instead of being cooped up in the office. Still, he was happy on the 'rods', as he called them, of his allotment.

"There you are, Mother, I told you not worry!" cried Elizabeth. "There's Doris, you see, in the queue! Look, over there, one of those girls singing!"

The wagons had passed; and among the girls carrying rakes, spades, shovels, and hoes, and wearing smocks, knickerbockers, high-legged boots and felt hats, walked about fifty girls in ordinary clothes, but with rosettes pinned to their jackets and blouses. Could that be Doris? Surely not, for her hair was bobbed.

"Of course it's Doris! I shall get my hair bobbed, too."

It was quite a shock for Hetty: why, Oh why, hadn't she told her mother that she was going to cut it? And could she really have joined up? Oh dear, what about Bedford College? She ought to work for her degree in History, if she was going to be a schoolteacher. She sighed. "Such a pity!"

I have lawns, I have Bowers,
I have fruit, I have flowers,
The lark is my morning's alarmer;
So jolly girls now, here's God speed to the plough,
Long life and success to the farmer!

Doris saw them as she marched by, and waved gaily.

Let the wealthy and Great
Roll in splendour and state,
I envy them not, I declare it;
I eat my own Lamb,
My Chickens and Ham,
I shear my own fleece and I wear it;
So jolly girls now, here's
God speed to the plough,
Long life and success to the farmer!

By the time Hetty arrived at Hyde Park, to walk among pens of lambs, pigs, and poultry, to see happy faces and clear eyes, and to be told by her younger daughter that she had joined for six months—"Only until the autumn, Mummie!"—and that she would be able to work at her books at night, she felt that the only worry now was what Dickie would say.

The girl took home with her a copy of *The Landwoman* which she put on the sitting-room table, near the corner where her father usually sat in his armchair. When Richard came home, having worked until nearly 7 o'clock, he took it up, and was at once interested in an item that said the plague of moles in the country was due to all ferrets having been sent to France to kill rats in the base warehouses, and in the trenches.

"H'm," he remarked. "Whoever heard of ferrets being used to kill moles? It's the mouldiwarp catchers who have gone to France! Where did this come from?"

"Doris brought it home, Dickie. Some of the girls at London University have joined the Land Army just for the summer. They are going to do their studies in the evening, and on wet days."

"That's a sensible idea. Why doesn't Doris go, too? It will do her the world of good."

"I'll tell her what you say, Dickie."

"Oh, it's nothing to do with me, really. It's for her to decide, she's of an age to make her own decisions now."

He took up *The Daily Trident*, to read a forecast that the new Budget, to be announced on Monday, would contain a rise in Income Tax. Richard was already paying 2*s.* 3*d.* in the £, his annual salary being within the £160 to £500 class, at £350. And when on the Monday evening he read in *The Pall Mall Gazette* that there was not only no increase in tax for him, but an extra allowance of £25 had been given for a wife, he felt quite optimistic.

"Well, Hetty, it may interest you to know that you are worth more by £25 today than you were yesterday!"

"Well, I am glad to hear that I am of some value after all, Dickie."

"Oh come, may I not make a joke for once in a while?"

"Yes of course, dear, naturally!"

"Well—— Just a moment. Ah, I see! The £25, after all, is but a nominal sum."

"I thought it was too good to be true."

"In practice it will work out at, let me see, a saving to the household of just under £3. Against that, all letters will require a thr'penny ha'penny stamp instead of a penny. Tobacco is up, that doesn't concern me any longer. The stamp duty on a cheque is to be raised to twopence. However, Doris being under eighteen years of age and still at home will entitle me to the same allowance as last year, £25. Of course, if she joins the Land Army, this relief may not be allowed."

Hetty was silent.

"What is the situation, do you know?"

"I joined on Saturday, Father," said Doris, coming into the room.

"Oh?" said Richard, looking at his wife. "You didn't tell me that, Hetty."

Her fatal desire not to upset anyone was once again the cause of upset. "Why don't you tell me these things? Why are you so—— Why do you hide them from me? 'Pon my word, you treat me in my own house as though I were a bully, who cannot be told a blessed thing!"

"Well, you can't, Father."

"What?" He turned in his chair to look at Doris. "What do you mean by that remark?"

"That you are always bullying my Mother."

"Doris, how dare you," said Hetty.

"Leave the room!" shouted Richard. "Leave the room immediately!"

Doris got up, gathered her books, and walked out of the room. The front door closed.

"She shall not enter my house again until she has apologised!"

"Yes, Dickie. It was wrong of her to say that. It is all my fault. Please don't upset yourself. I'll bring in your tray. It's a herb omelette, Doris got some eggs specially for you from the Parade on Saturday."

"Oh. Then why didn't you tell me before?"

"Doris wanted it to be a surprise." She wept. It was always the same. Everything went wrong, however hard she tried. Perhaps the best thing she could do was to die.

"Oh, for heaven's sake don't turn on the water-works! Why can't you think straight? You are afraid of me, I know it. But your fear creates these situations, you know." He went on, protestingly as usual, "I am far from being a bully by nature. But it is my duty to try and see that things happen in an orderly and upright manner in this house." He felt hopeless.

"It's all my fault, Dickie. I should have told you, of course. Please do not take any notice of what was said by Doris. She is still terribly hurt by Percy's death. She doesn't say much, but she feels things the more because of it. She's been working very hard, too, at college, to be a credit to her parents."

"Well, we all work hard. I work hard, but I don't complain! I do what I am supposed to do, as a normal thing, and accept what comes along with as good a grace as I can."

"I think you are right about her working on the land, Dickie. It will tone her up."

"I never said that, but I certainly hope it will. Where's she gone now?"

"I expect next door."

"No doubt complaining to Mr. Turney!"

"Oh no, she wouldn't do that. Doris is very loyal, you know."

He sat down again, and took up the paper. "Loyal, is she? I had not noticed it when she was here a moment ago."

"It's her nerves, I think. She also feels she isn't wanted."

"By whom, pray?"

Hetty felt a desire to laugh. It would be fatal. "I'll get your supper, Dickie. It's all ready in the oven."

"In the oven? What, an omelette? What am I supposed to do with it, pray? Repair the soles of my boots?"

She could laugh now. Richard was mollified by the success of his joke.

"The gas is turned very low, Dickie."

"Well, I haven't had a herb omelette for many years now. Where did the herbs come from?"

"Doris brought them with the eggs."

"Oh, she did, did she? Well, I expect she will do well on the land. After all, it's in her blood, on both sides of the family. Now let us see what this celebrated herb omelette looks like, old girl."

While Hetty was out of the room he looked at the Roll of Honour. Under *Infantry* his eye ran down to the words *Gaultshire Regt*. Nothing about Phillip; it would be too early; the lists were delayed, he had heard, lest information be given to the Germans. But there was one name which held his sight in that column of small print under KILLED: (*temp*) *Lieutenant H. F. Turney*. Some relation of Hetty's, no doubt. It raised her in his eyes;

and when he heard her coming, he got up quickly and opened the door for her, allowing her to pass, before closing it, as though he were still a young man, and she were the young woman he had wanted to marry.

Later, Doris apologised, formally and stiffly. He had meant to be affable about it, but her curt manner discomposed him. He could say nothing until she was almost out of the door, when he said, "Please try to close the door gently this time. Each time the lock is banged it is like hitting it with a hammer."

Noiselessly the door was shut; he gave a sigh, and found that he was reading Bonar Law's Budget Speech again without any feeling about what he was reading.

Day in the Royal Tennis Court ward of the Duchess of Gaultshire's hospital meant relief from night—but day brought another kind of endurance, voices talking, talking.

"—as I was saying, Garfield chucked himself at the machine-gun, and that's how he lost his testicles——"

"They're off, as the monkey said, sitting on the circular saw——"

"That's not funny, Brill."

"—hard luck on his wife——"

"Steady on, you fellows, Garfield's just coming——" Silence. Then the voice of Major Henniker-Sudley continued, "No, I couldn't agree that that war correspondent's account was propaganda. I saw the New Zealanders arrive on the 27th of March. They were in tremendous form—shaved, boots polished, webbing equipment khaki-blanco'd, even tin hats oiled. The wounded called out from the ambulances, 'Gawd 'elp Jerry now'."

The man in the next bed, Brill, was always discussing someone called Colin. "Colin slept with the Admiral's wife when he went on leave. She told him he reminded her of her son. Any old excuse——"

The fool didn't understand. He thought of Sascha, 'all things to all men', she had said.

The gramophone on the end table was a relief. It played always about this time, and the same record, sung by Clarice Mayne, accompanied by 'That' at the piano.

Give me a little cosy corner, and the boy that I love——

But why didn't the fool change the needle, and put back the regulator to 78, instead of playing at 84?

—*And the boy that I love.*

The record began again, the needle grating as it jabbed the wax. It was a relief when it stopped.

"I hand it to the doctors in this war. It was hell for them at the C.C.S. at Merville. Rasp, rasp, rasp with the silver saws, filling a tall wicker basket every quarter of an hour, legs and arms taken away by orderlies, who looked as though *they'd* had the treatment! They had the *effect*, without the action, if you understand my meaning."

"I saw one of those young soldiers come in who'd shot himself through the wrist. The bloody fool didn't know enough to do the job properly by putting a sandbag over it, before pulling the trigger. The M.O. saw the scorchmarks, half way up his elbow."

"What happened?"

"The doc took off his forearm, before the A.P.M. came round and spotted an S.I.W."

"He deserved a court-martial. Why should that little tick get home to tell the tale ever afterwards, with a pension?"

"I don't quite see it like that, you know, Brill. He shouldn't have been sent out in the first place, in my opinion. You can't *put* guts into a man if nature hasn't done it first."

"You've been reading that book again. What the hell you see in poetry beats me."

"It's damned good stuff, the first to tell the truth in this war. Haven't you felt like that, during a counter-attack?"

"Of course I have, but I don't talk about it, let alone bleat about it afterwards. Who is he, anyway? Sounds like a Jew to me."

The voice of Henniker-Sudley said, "The Sassoons are Parsees, Bombay merchants, I fancy."

His mind wandered, came back with a start when at the other end of the ward, another voice said, "'Spectre's' old man dropped a farthing in the grave as they fired the volley. Curious custom, that, to start the dead man off with something in the next world. It's in all races, they still put out food for the pixies on Dartmoor, and the fairies in the Isle of Man."

"The last pay of a soldier, when he's for the town's end," said the voice of the man who had been reading the book.

Phillip wondered what 'the book' was, as he lay with eyeballs stung by tears. He dreaded the time coming when the bandages would be off, he could not face things again.

Eleven o'clock beef-tea came round. In fifteen minutes the Duchess would arrive.

"If they give us any more of this bloody broth, I'll cat my heart up. They say the Duke has had nine and a half pounds of beef shin brought into the kitchen every day for the past thirty years. No wonder he looks like something out of a cave."

"I'm told it's mostly bison meat now. Too strong for my taste. Still, mustn't grumble. You should taste the grub in Devonport Military Hospital."

"Couldn't be worse than Netley, old man. I was there last time I was hit. It was——"

"I was at Osborne first, in the Isle of Wight, but got the shove to Devonport. Robert Loraine, the actor, was there. Flying bloke. I got the push after three of us had got lost down a passage, and found ourselves in the Royal Family wing. Then the Queen came along. We didn't recognise who she was until she sailed up to us, and said 'Out of my way'."

"Doesn't sound like Queen Mary to me. Are you sure it wasn't Queen Alexandra, I've heard she was always late for any appointment? They usually say, 'Make way', the equivalent of a Commanding Officer's order when passing through troops."

A rough voice came loudly from the other end of the ward, "The man who wrote that book is a f——g good man, and don't you forget it, Brill!"

In the silence the voice of Henniker-Sudley said equably, "Do you mind being more careful with your language, Garfield?"

"I thought you told me there wasn't no rank in 'ospital, major."

"It's a question of manners, particularly if one wears the riband of the Victoria Cross."

"They can keep the bloody thing for all I trouble, I didn't arst for it!"

"You're too good a soldier to let yourself down like that Garfield. There are young ladies working in this ward."

Distant voices, a door opening; shuffle of carpet slippers as those up, in dressing-gowns, stood by their beds. The low, bird-like voice of the Duchess, shy, remote, carefully quiet because she was partly deaf, coming down the ward, saying, "Good morning—Good morning." Murmurs where she stopped. "Good morning." She was coming nearer.

"Good morning. How are you today?"

"Much better, thank you, your Grace."

"Are you sleeping well?"

"Yes thank you, ma'am."

The Good-mornings receded, the far door shut.

The scabs on neck, face, and chest had ceased to crack and weep, the cuckoo was singing all night and all day when he was allowed to get up. After two days of shuffling about he knew his way blindfold around the ward, knowing his whereabouts by the various angled patterns of voices, and thereby what to avoid, and, always with relief, to find his way by rubber-shod stick, down the flag-stone corridor to the lavatory, the throne as the high, box-like apparatus was called.

Then to laze about on the terrace in the sun; to be taken for a walk by one of the V.A.D.s, as he thought. At first his arm was lightly held, a delightful voice asking questions about birds, as though she were greatly interested.

Across the open spaces of the grass he stopped to listen to the off-tune calling of a cuckoo. The notes came clear as air, no longer muted by the glass windows and walls of the ward.

"That's a queer sort of call, don't you think?"

"In what way does it seem queer?"

"The notes seem flattened, somehow."

"Perhaps the cuckoo feels flat."

"You're laughing at me!"

"Why should I laugh at you?"

The tone of her voice made him uneasy, and he attempted to pay her a compliment. "Wordsworth wrote of the cuckoo as a wandering voice. Now, I suppose, I am wandering like a cuckoo, but guided by a more charming voice."

She ignored this pretentiousness, and said, "Doesn't a cuckoo lay its eggs in other birds' nests?"

"Well, some naturalists think it lays its egg first, then carries it in its bill to the selected nest of its dupe."

"That can't be much fun for the cuckoo, surely?"

"On the other hand, I've actually seen a cuckoo squatting across a hedge-sparrow's nest, and when it had flown away, I found a larger grey egg among the hedge-sparrow's smaller blue eggs."

"I think it's much more sensible to lay one's egg in a nest already warmed for one."

He felt foolish; and had to resist the impulse to say something startling, to break the restraint. They walked on in silence, while he wondered how he could get away. No longer was his arm held, obviously a sign that he had bored her. At last they turned back, to his relief, and as they approached the great hollow square of buildings, which increased the sound of their feet on gravel, she said, with a return of her former resilience, "You know, I fancy that Uncle Boo'n would be most interested in your cuckoo theory." At the door of the ward she said, "You know, as a family we're rather inclined to be that way!" She said, in her original gay voice, modulated and charming, "It has been a *most* interesting talk. Au revoir!"

"I must thank you——"

Thank heaven he had not asked her name, or any questions of a personal nature. Obviously she was one of the family. Left alone, he was dejected by what he felt to be his dullness. Of course she had not asked his name, or given her own; he was only one of scores of temporary members of the regiment; such people were not introduced to their class. The walk for her had been but routine duty, 'walking' a patient in the same way that a hound puppy might be 'walked'—looking after it until it was strong enough to join the pack—back to the regiment and the war in France. And the sooner, the better.

He wanted to scream—he had made a fool of himself.

Night was broken dark rocks which he could never cross to the other side. Always the same dream, his legs dragging and finally held in black glue, a nightmare from which he awakened in terror, his body slippery with sweat, while his mind began to writhe through scenes which he tried to straighten, to find their true meaning, to connect them coherently, to resolve them into one simple sentence of truth. He must begin again. Now face up to what had happened. Begin at the Kabaret Staenyzer. How far was Bill Kidd's refusal due to an obvious lack of respect, in turn due to his lie about his next-of-kin living in Gaultshire? How had Bill Kidd found out? Surely not through 'Spectre'? No, 'Spectre' would never betray a confidence. But had it been a confidence? Was a reply to what in effect was an official question a matter of confidence? Leave that for the moment. Begin again at the Kabaret Staenyzer.

If he had insisted that Bill Kidd come back, used his authority instead of drinking whiskey with Bill Kidd and being matey he would not have needed to go and see 'Spectre' about it. But had he gone to see 'Spectre' at Byron Farm at his request, or had 'Spectre' asked him to go down, perhaps for another purpose? To tell him that he was being relieved of his command, that he was a washout for not enforcing his, 'Spectre's', order. Whichever way it was, he was to blame.

Black depression weighed him down. He was on the rocks. What would they think of him in the regiment when they found out? It would be almost a relief, then he could resign his commission, and volunteer to go back in the ranks. In any case he must ask to resign his commission, 'for private reasons', then they would ask no questions. As soon as his bloody eyes were all right. But—would that not be going too far in the other direction? Was it not a sort of showing-off, a kind of inverted bravado, like the bicycle ride on Christmas Day, 1914? But had that been bravado? It had seemed a simple possibility, while the other fellows and the Germans were all streaming back to play a football match. Other scenes, at Heathmarket . . . disastrous exhibitions of bad form. O God. Oh, what a fool he had been all his life, a prey to sudden mental picturing, so that he did silly things which he never really wanted, or even meant, to do. *Picturing*, a pale word like rolled warm putty, breaking off when rolled thin, Father's putty taken to make little balls, to fire out of his brass cannon at Mr. Bigge's window next door, pale putty-picturing like a pale snake, moving without purpose through the dark rocks of the ward shattered by silence until the pale snake of his thoughts was twisted in desperation by the longer snake of the snoring of Brill in the next bed, Brill who was always talking about Colin this and Colin that. It went on and on, he tried to resist it by breathing deeply, but the air indrawn would not go in easily, he could take only small breaths, as though a part of the lungs were shut off. He must lie limp, and pray. The battle of the brain was so much more deadly than the battle of physical movement; perhaps all battle came first in the mind? Clear the mind, and there is no battle. 'Be still, and know that I am God'. But the snoring sawed through all resolutions, and he shouted silently at Brill to stop.

Thank God, the night sister was coming down the ward. He could hear her slippers. She spoke in a whisper to the snorer, shook his shoulder. Brill sat up and said, "I wasn't snoring, honestly!"

"Turn round," she whispered, then her slippers were sweeping away. Soon Brill was snoring again, bubbling thickly with the boiled blood of the black bison in the Park. He wondered if they ever ploughed with oxen, now that so many horses were in France. He forced himself to think of oxen teams slowly plodding o'er the lea; but they were snoring blood as they lumbered over the black rocks; bubbles of blood blew from their eyes, ears, and nostrils in a hot varnish of sweat. At last he could bear it no more and lifting the bandage over his eyes, peeped through clotted lids, and with a shock of joy saw a row of brilliant lights down both ends of the long table dividing the middle of the ward. At once the snoring diminished for him, and he stood up, repressing an impulse to shout, "I can see the lights, sister, I can see!" Then to enjoy his new freedom the more he sat on the edge of the bed and closed his eyes, or rather squeezed the lids into place with his facial muscles, and lapped in happiness, put back the bandage and got between the sheets, to lie with arms under head, and after a while to lift the bandage sufficiently to allow him to see the winking lights of the candles all along the promenade of the ward, between bowls of flowers which were like railed-in gardens, while the shadows on the walls were familiar and comforting for he was in England, he was free of the war, and of the disasters of the past. He began to cry with relief, he felt that 'Spectre' was with him, telling him that he was forgiven.

He thought back to the scene in the Bird Cage, on the calm sunny morning before the twenty-first of March, and heard 'Spectre's' words again, saying that a father needed his son the more that his life was wasted away; and the beauty of the lights along the promenade of the ward, the wind in the trees of the park, murmurous through the open tops of the windows was like the sound of the sea first heard in childhood, when Father had found a gold watch on the shingle of Hayling Island, and taken it to the police, who had returned it to the owner, Father saying that he did not want his name to be mentioned, or to claim any reward. Father had always been an honourable man; he, his son, had been like Bill Kidd, but without Bill Kidd's guts.

The lights were blurred, as he struggled for recovery, with the determination that he must not let his thoughts worry, like Shelley's hounds, 'their father and their prey'.

In the morning he was taken to the operation theatre to be X-rayed through chest and back. To his surprise the Duchess worked the apparatus, which Major Henniker-Sudley, in the ward afterwards said was the first privately to be installed in the country before the war in her 'pet' cottage hospital. The Duchess had qualified both as radiologist and radiographer at the London Hospital in Whitechapel.

That afternoon he was taken out in a vehicle with four small wheels, judging by the noise on the gravel drive. It was drawn by a Welsh pony called Clunbach, led by his guide. He sat in the back seat, feeling the leather upholstery to be dry and cracked, needing saddle-soap. There was a small child in the 'brougham' —as he thought of it. She was with her nurse, taking a picnic tea to one of the lakes.

"I've never ridden in a bro'ham before," he said to the nurse.

"No, sir?"

Perhaps it wasn't a brougham, but had another name.

He could feel the child's presence beside him, and tried to picture her from the name used by the nurse—Melissa. Not knowing what to say to the child, he remained silent. When they stopped, he got out first, and stood still.

"I think this is about the best place, out of the wind, don't you?"

"Oh yes."

"I'll get the hamper out of the broo'am."

"Oh, let me——"

"No, you must rest. Nanny, will you spread the hammer cloth?"

He sat on one corner of the rug. When they were all sitting he said, as cheerfully as he could, "I've been trying to determine our position from the fixed point of that off-tune cuckoo's voice, and what I imagine to be its echo glancing off the long southern front of the Abbey."

When there was no reply, he said, trying to make a joke of it, "I suppose you must think me a terrible bore——"

"Oh lor', no! I think it's all most interesting. How you think of it, I simply *can't* imagine!" Then, as though to reassure him, she said casually, in a voice partly wooden with *hauteur*, "Most of the family is inclined to prefer birds to people, y'know. Uncle Boo'n and Aunt May would spend their lives watchin' them through glasses all day, if they could."

He sat silent once more, struggling with feelings of insufficiency, which prompted him to go away at once; and after many mentally-suppressed attempts to do so, he got on his feet, all control gone, and had walked a few steps over the grass when her voice said, "What wonderful hearing you have! Fancy hearing them all that distance off." He stood there, and after a period of time heard voices. When they came near she said, "You're just in time for tea! How awf'ly nice of you to come!" He recognised Brill, Garfield and others from the ward, but when a clear baritone slightly nasal voice cried, "Phillip! My dear old son!" he felt free at last.

"Denis!" He projected himself towards the voice, while distantly conscious of how-d'you-do's, and the spoken name of Lady Abeline. "My dear old son!" repeated the clear, endearing voice, "Let me sit beside you, and hear all your news! You know that Tabor's commanding now? He's done very well, so I hear. Bad luck about 'Spectre', wasn't it? But of course, you were in the same ship."

"I—I—was in another part of it."

"I heard about it from O'Gorman. He's here, you know, at the command depôt at the other end of the park."

"O'Gorman is?" He felt faint.

"I expect you'll be seeing him soon, when Lord Satchville comes on leave. The Duke, who, as you probably know, commands the depôt and wants to hold some sort of regimental Court of Inquiry, to try to get posthumous recognition for 'Spectre'."

Sisley looked at the bandaged face beside him, taut from prominent cheek-bones to thin line of jaw, at the fingers twirling and twisting a stem of grass; and changed the subject. The poor chap was still too shaken to talk about it, he told Major Henniker-Sudley afterwards.

When the bandages were taken off Phillip saw that he had no eyelashes, and that the lids were a thick bright pink like the new skin of his nose and face; while his beard that had felt to be so soft was black and ugly. The face staring at him with distaste looked as if it were suffering from some loathsome skin disease. Smoked glasses added to the complete villainy of the picture. "You swine!" he said to the face; no wonder that the child in the 'broo'm'—not *bro'ham*!—had been too frightened to speak. At least he would not inflict his boring presence on them at any picnic parties in the future.

He discovered a friend in Major Henniker-Sudley, who had got a shrapnel ball in the shoulder within the first half-hour of going into action in the final German attack before Amiens. They went for walks together, and to his delight Phillip learned that Henniker-Sudley had a copy of *The Oxford Book of English Verse*. 'Hen' lent him a book by Conrad, *Victory*, which, he explained, was nothing to do with the war. One morning this new happiness was riven when 'Hen' said, "The Duke would like to have a word with you, about Harold West. Don't be put off by his manner, he always was a bit of a recluse, you know. He's wrapped up in country matters, especially birds and fish and that sort of thing. Rather in your own line, I gather. Odd about that cuckoo singin' out of tune, isn't it?"

Phillip started to make excuses. "I—I—what about my beard, 'Hen'? I don't think I—I—I mean, shaving——"

"My dear fellow, I don't think it will matter in the least."

When he was recalled to the operating theatre, enlarged photographs of what looked like shadows were being examined by two doctors. Questions were asked. Did he at times feel a restriction in his breathing? Were there, to his knowledge, any blue-cross shells falling that evening, with the mustard gas? Had he taken in gas before, at any time? He had? A touch of chlorine at Loos? Perhaps, as his medical history sheets were apparently mislaid, he could remember the particulars? That 'touch of chlorine at Loos', what did he mean by a touch? Any retching? No, only sickness. Did he feel puffy after walking, or taking exercise? When lying in bed? Possibility of emphysema, murmured one doctor to the other. Now, would he tell them if he had to *force* his breathing sometimes? He did? A developing emphysematous condition, the younger doctor murmured. Had he ever had broncho-pneumonia? No? They looked at the photographs again, pointing to one place with a pencil. They drew apart, and spoke together. He heard the younger doctor say, "There might possibly be an incipient emphysema, the over-distension of air-cells——"

They returned. The senior M.O. said, "How long have you been overseas? Just about two years in all. I see you were out in 1914. This was your fifth time? You need a long rest, to build you up. I don't think there's the least need to worry. What you need is plenty of sunshine, and good food. Convalescence in the west country, take everything easy, laze about. Do you fish? The very thing. I'll put your name down for convalescence. They'll fix you up with a place to go to, in London. And, as I said, take things easily. The intermittence in your heart is most likely due to flatulence, consequent on strain. We'll give you a tonic; in the meantime, take it easy in the sun, and enjoy yourself."

It was wonderful to see one's shadow again.

Everything he saw had a beautiful shape, and colours all made perfect patterns in a manner never seen before. They absorbed sounds; voices of men and birds were part of their patterns. Print on a page was miraculously clear. On the way to the throne was an old notice, printed, he at first thought, from wooden type, but on closer scrutiny the lettering must have been based on metal, for the hair-lines were so fine: work of craftsman like Father, who wrote always meticulously, every letter clearly defined.

The notice on the wall was to do with the servants, who obviously had to jump to it; by the long letter *s* as a tall *f*, the notice had been put up in the 18th century.

RULES *and* ORDERS, *to be* OBSERV'D *in this* HALL, *without* EXCEPTION

		d.
1.	Whoever is last at Breakfast, to clear the Table, and put the Copper, horns Salt, Pepper, &c. in their proper places . . . . . or forfeit	3
2.	That the Postilion, and Groom, shall have the Servants hall cloth laid for Dinner by one o'clock, and not omit laying Salt, Pepper, spoons, &c. . . .	3
3.	That the knives for Dinner, and the housekeeper's room, to be clean'd ev'ry day, by the Postilion, and Groom, and in case one is out the other do his business in his absence, be it which it may . . .	3
4.	That if any Person be heard to swear, or use any indecent language at any time when the Cloth is on the Table	3
5.	Whoever leaves any powder, or pomatum, or anything belonging to their dress, or any wearing apparel, out of their proper places	3
6.	That no one be suffered to play cards in this hall, between six in the Morning and six in the Evening .	3
7.	Whoever leaves any pieces of Bread, at breakfast, Dinner, or Supper	1

He read on, imagining that the strict life behind the green baize doors would have pleased his father. The hall was to be decently swept, the dirt taken away; water to be pumped every Wednesday; no Provision to be put in any Cupboard or Drawer; Table cloth to be folded after all meals & put in the Drawer for that purpose; anyone detected 'wiping' knives on the Table cloth; anyone taking plates to the table, to be 'seen to set them for dogs to eat off'; 'no wearing apparel or hat box be suffered to hang in the hall, but shall be put in the closets for that purpose'—fined 3d a time; and it ended with WHOEVER DEFACES THESE RULES, IN ANY MANNER 5s.

When he was back in the ward an aged footman, whose face was vaguely familiar, came and said, with a bow, "His Grace presents His Grace's compliments, sir, and His Grace requests the honour of your presence in His Grace's Lignum Room at eleven o'clock this morning."

"Oh, thank you. My compliments to His Grace, and I'll attend upon his Grace at eleven. But how does one get to His Grace's Lignum Room?"

"I'll come and take you there, sir, five minutes before eleven."

"I've met you before, somewhere, I think?"

"I was Colonel Mogger'anger's batman, sir, at the White City. I come home with 'im, sir."

"Of course, I remember now. Dear old Moggers! Well, I'll see you here at five to eleven. Don't be late, you crab wallah, or it'll be three dee up your shirt!"

The crab-wallah returned to the minute, and led him down several passages to a green baize door, through which he passed to a corridor lined with sporting prints on either wall almost to the ceiling. Down another corridor lined with butterflies in cases. Here an elderly butler took over from the footman, leading him on to a red-baize door, behind which stood the chamberlain, an equivalent, he thought, of the Senior Regimental Sergeant-major. With great dignity this individual, resplendent in crimson and gold, led him to a tall door made with what seemed to be teak-wood, or possibly *lignum vitae*, since it resembled the round boxes in which string was pulled in ironmongers' shops to tie up parcels. Before the massive door the chamberlain paused to rap loudly on the door, afterwards opening it by turning a handle of what looked like gold. Stepping back, he announced in quiet tones, "Lieutenant-Colonel Maddison of the Mediators, Your Grace"; whereupon he bowed slightly to the guest, and with a sweep of the door closing backwards, left him in a tall room with an advancing figure of medium height, wearing spectacles above a heavy moustache rather like a sturdier Rudyard Kipling.

The Duke held out a hand. "Good morning, Colonel Maddison. Pray sit yourself down."

"Thank you, Your Grace."

The Duke was wearing the blue patrol uniform of a full colonel of the regiment. He re-seated himself behind his desk. Phillip waited, entirely calm. His mind was made up: he would tell the truth.

The Duke said nothing. From afar, Phillip heard the out-of-tune cuckoo singing in the remote world. The Duke stared at his desk. He seemed to be considering what to say, consulting chin with hand; plucking at loosening skin with finger and thumb, until he reached a decision; only to reject it while regulating the two ends of his moustaches in an upward direction. Phillip continued to feel calm. This man was more nervous than himself. He wanted to help him; but remained silent, sitting back in his chair, and with detachment removed his smoked glasses, to pass his hand across his eyes. That would suggest something to the Duke.

"Are you gettin' on well?"

"Yes, thank you, sir. It's wonderful to be back in England, as Browning said, now that April's here—or, rather, May!"

"Who?"

"Browning, sir, the poet."

"Oh yes, of course."

There was another fairly long interval. Putting on his glasses Phillip said, "Harold West and I used to discuss poetry in France, sir."

"Really."

Phillip became aware of several clocks ticking away in the panelled room. He must wait for the Duke to speak.

"You knew Colonel West, of course?"

"Yes, sir. I met him at Loos."

"Where?"

"At Loos. The battle in September, 'fifteen."

"Oh yes, of course. Loos, yes. Mowbray was wounded, I remember."

He heard himself saying, "It was from Harold West that I first heard of the traditions of the regiment, sir, or rather the spirit of the county." Oh, what a fool he must seem, talking so stiltedly.

"Really."

More prolonged racing ticks of half a dozen clocks.

"You are gettin' better? No after effects?"

"None, sir."

The Duke's forefinger and thumb seemed to spend much time with the Duke's post-Crimea guardee moustache. Suddenly Phillip remembered having read in *The Field*, when at school, of the South African cuckoo, which sang more slowly than the ordinary cuckoo, and the first note was lower, nearer in pitch to the second.

"I wonder if you can tell me if a South African cuckoo has ever been recorded in Gaultshire, sir?"

"What?" Ducal head was raised off shoulders, fingers forgot moustache, ornithological eyes grew larger behind spectacles. "What makes you say that?"

Phillip told him. "It's only an idea, sir. But the slower singing, and the notes close together——"

"Remarkable. You did not mark its exact whereabouts, I suppose? Only by ear? Most interesting. Have you read Frank Buckland's writings?"

"Yes, sir, but not since I was a boy."

"A wonderful man, indeed. Yes, one's hearing is improved, of course, when the sight is in abeyance, the auditory nerve is quickened. *Cuculus gularis*, indeed. We have a record of *glandarius*, the so-called Great Spotted Cuckoo, which inhabits, as you know, south-western Europe and the Mediterranean countries, extending through Syria and Asia Minor to Persia, and migrating in the fall into Africa, as far as Cape Colony. Let me show you."

He sprang up, and pulled out a volume, one of several on a shelf, while humming words to himself. "Here we are, Lydekker's *Royal Natural History*, volume four. H'm, ha. At the beginnin'."

A stubby forefinger pointed at an engraving—"Crested cuckoos. H'm. Hawk-cuckoos. Ha. True cuckoos . . . the tail-feathers lack the transverse bars of the hawk-cuckoos. That's our fellow, *gularis*. Where is it calling, you say? West of the house. Probably down by the Satchville brook, the moor, as we call it. Well, I am most grateful to you, Colonel—ah—Maddison. Thank you, indeed."

The Duke held out a hand, while pulling a crimson bell-pull with the other. "We must foregather again. Do you shoot?"

"Yes, sir."

The door opened, the chamberlain stood there, bowing.

"Good morning," said the Duke.

All the way back, past the butterflies and sporting prints; and at the green baize door stood the butler, with a three-tiered trolley whereon stood bottles; while beside the butler was the aged footman with a mahogany tray of cigars, cigarettes, and packets of tobacco.

"I'd like a glass of beer, please."

"I must regret, sir, that I have no beer to offer you. Beer at the Abbey, sir, is brewed only for polishing his Grace's floors."

"I'll have a peg of whiskey, I think."

He drank his whiskey and seltzer, selected a cigar, which the butler cut and pierced with a gold cutter; and, accepting the light of a taper from the footman, he thanked them and went through the door into the familiar echoes of the stone-flagged passage leading to the Royal Tennis Court of pre-1914.

Now the ward lights shone with friendly gleams, the little flames moving in the night airs which brought the songs of nightingales; but they were nightingales in the Croiselles valley before the Hindenburg Line in May 1917 that he was listening to, straining his mind to re-enter the past, to bring it back, even for one moment of life. Croiselles was again in German hands, so was Mory Copse, St. Leger, and Ervillers where his picket lines had stood, and Black Prince had whinnied to see him coming. He felt again the urge in his innermost being to be back, but there was little hope now, with part of his left lung drawn together like a scab.

Life was pleasant; he felt that he belonged there. The night-dreads were for the moment gone; a diet which included a bowl of chopped cabbage, seasoned with butter, salt, and a little pepper, had cured his constipation. He looked forward to the late evening, and the nightingales: almost the best period of the twenty-four hours, when the night sister had taken over and gone out for her supper, leaving the ward like a deep pool, with twenty tallow candles standing in water within their glass bulbs, each the shape of a tulip, shining down the length of the refectory tables which, joined together, made forty-five feet in length. Before the war the tables had stood in the servants' hall, or one of the many rooms of their quarters, for there had been very nearly a hundred of them in the Abbey then—coalmen, watermen, footmen, chauffeurs, grooms, stablemen, as well as all the kitchen staff, the butchers and poultrymen, the maid-servants and other women employed about the place, including the laundry, and the men in the brew-house. The Duke had been a model employer, insisting that his steward pay good wages to his estate workers; and if any man in any of the villages was out of work through no fault of his own, a job had been found for him. His generosity, said 'Hen' Sudley, was in the Whig tradition; the Duke had sold much of his off-lying land to the tenants, believing in progress. How little Uncle Jim Pickering at Beau Brickhill, an avowed Liberal, had failed to understand the Duke! Lloyd George again, 'Mr. "George"', as 'Spectre' had always spoken of him, who had broken Gough, and damned the Fifth Army.

It was said that before the war two men were continually employed boiling down deer fat to make the tallow tapers which lit the corridors behind the green baize doors—nearly half a mile of passages which connected the servants' quarters, kitchens, stables, etc. One man's full-time job had been to clean and polish the globes with methylated spirit.

After midnight many of the tapers were smoking. Each glass tulip was clear half-way up, then smoke tinged it; so they had burned behind the green baize doors for centuries. With the herds of deer and bison which roamed the Wilderness within the demesne walls were emus, gold and silver pheasants, peacocks, jungle fowl, and other foreign birds, all of them living wild within the sanctuary of six square miles of the Park.

And yet, underlying all, was a tragedy. The only child of the Duke, his son, was alienated from his father. The Marquess of Husborne was a conscientious objector. The two never met; it was forbidden to mention the name of the heir at the Abbey. He was a Socialist, and thought that the money system of the country was all wrong, and responsible for the war. What an extraordinary thing to think. The other great interest in his life, 'Hen' Sudley had said, was wild animals and birds . . . as with his parents, the Duke and Duchess. What was the reason for it: could it be that, underneath everything, it was as in his own home? Surely not, for such rich people lived entirely different lives. Perhaps if 'Spectre' had not died, he would have known what was the matter, for 'Spectre' had hated the war, too, and saw only ruin in it. Aunt Dora had the same ideas, so had cousin Willie—it was all part of the tragedy of the world.

He had finished *Victory*, and the first story, *Youth*, of another volume lent by dear old 'Hen'. Joseph Conrad was a noble writer, who knew the underlying truth of things. He was now half-way through *Lord Jim*: had 'Hen' specially urged him to read it, because he suspected his secret? How much did he know? Did the Duke know, as well? Was that why the Duke had not spoken about 'Spectre'? Because he had not liked to broach the subject? Was it being kept for the Regimental conference?

The lights, which had burned clearly down the ward, were beginning to thicken and glare. He hid his face under the sheet, but sleep would not come.

Chapter 13

HIGH SUMMER

As the month of May advanced, thoughts of the Regimental conference gave Phillip dyspepsia, and brought a return of cold sweats, embarrassingly under the arm-pits. He believed that the conference was being called solely to deal with the matter of finding out why 'Spectre' had been drowned unnecessarily; the fact was that a certain number of senior officers of the Regiment were either on leave from the front, or doing duty at home, and the Duke had invited old friends and acquaintances to spend a weekend at the Abbey, to enjoy what amenities were remaining from the war. The private golf course was ploughed up, put down to beet-sugar—a crop introduced before the war by the Duke, as an experiment, together with new strains of Irish rye-grass, white French wheats, and (a failure) the sweet potato from Virginia (which he believed was the original tuber brought into England by Walter Raleigh) and other seeds; but there was still the fishing in the several lakes which were stocked by rainbow trout reared beside one of his rivers in Scotland. Tennis, the original game played with lop-sided racquets and leather balls stuffed with feathers, was out of the question; the covered court was a hospital ward. It was not the season for deer-drives, fox-hunting, or shooting; but there was still cricket to be played, and watched, in the area of the Command depot; and towards the end of the month the Mayfly would be up.

He needed a new tunic, and went to London to get one made by a tailor recommended by Denis Sisley. All he possessed was the tommy's tunic, brought over from the depôt, and his original knickerbockers and puttees bought early in 1915 at the Civil Service Stores; and a service cap, the inner band stuffed with newspaper, lent by 'Hen'.

From St. Pancras station he took a taxi to Piccadilly Circus, and there decided to walk down to the Embankment and see the sights by Charing Cross and Trafalgar Square. After a cup of coffee in the Corner House he walked on down Whitehall, seeing that the Stars and Stripes was flying over No. 10 Downing Street, beside the Union Jack. Hawkers on the kerb were selling little flags for the button-hole. "Old Glory—a penny each—only a penny! Buy Old Glory, sir!" He bought one and stuck it behind his lapel; and walking towards Westminster, saw that the same two flags were flying from a tower above the Houses of Parliament. Had there been an advance in France, of the two Allies? Everyone seemed to be fairly jubilant. Then he heard that an American regiment was to be reviewed by the King at Buckingham Palace before going to France.

It was so fine a morning that he walked on to Mr. Kerr's shop in Cundit Street, which Sisley had told him was a little way down from where it joined Regent Street. He walked through the Park, seeing the wildfowl on the lake, and thought that London could be beautiful—the water, the trees, the wide grass-lands with their flower-beds and old elm-trees. He had to ask his way to Piccadilly Circus, then knew the way up the curve of Regent Street, with its Regency stucco buildings and pillars painted yellow, rather faded, and quite a different place by day than by night.

Entering the tailor's shop, he was greeted by a pleasant-faced man with a quiet, "Good morning, sir."

"I'd like a tunic, and a pair of riding breeches, please."

This request produced in the middle-aged man a mild suggestion of enthusiasm subdued by deference as he held up a finger. At once a figure detached itself from among shadowy bolts of cloth and came forward with an impersonal smile.

"May I have your burberry, sir? Thank you." It was deftly removed, and given to the secondary figure. Mr. Kerr, with a glance at the shoulder-strap badges, turned slightly, and said, "The barathea, Mr. Brown."

At these words the figure hauled a bolt off the pile, using apparently all its strength, then held it upright a moment before lifting it as though about to toss the caber; then, changing his stance, he let the roll descend in a half spin which caused two folds to fall upon the carpet, thus revealing a pride of new cloth, which caused Phillip to say without hesitation, "I'd like that one."

"If I may say so, an admirable choice, sir. Barathea is, as you know, a tenacious cross-weave, and worn by members of the Foot Guards."

Mr. Kerr inquired if his visitor had recently returned from 'out there'.

"About a month ago. I'm in the same hospital as Captain Sisley, who gave me your name."

"Ah, the Mediators, sir?"

"Yes."

"We had Captain Sisley in here with us a few days ago. Now if you will allow me, I'll take your measurements."

The tape went round his chest. "Thirty-six, Mr. Brown."

"A nice man, Captain Sisley, sir. Neck, fourteen. Now your waist. Twenty eight." Mr. Kerr paused. "Are you up to your usual weight, sir?"

"I'm normally eleven stone four pounds, I think."

"If you'll come with me——"

The scales balanced at nine stone, nine pounds. "I'll allow a couple of inches on chest and waist, sir, to be on the safe side. Wounded, sir?"

"Mustard gas."

"Wretched stuff, isn't it? Now for the breeches, sir. Mr. Brown, the cavalry twill!"

From another bolt were shaken waves which settled soft as sand minutely ribbed aslant the electric light, which cast shadows almost imperceptible between the twills. Then the bolt was turned round, so that the light relieved the shadows, causing Mr. Kerr to exclaim: "A beautiful cloth, sir, don't you think? Like a field of loam, ploughed north and south, with the midday sun behind one. Do you know a well-ploughed loam, sir? It crumbles in the hand."

"I'll have this cloth, Mr. Kerr."

"I knew as soon as I saw you, sir, that it would be your choice. Infinitely superior to a more commonplace cord, which is suitable enough for the administrative services, no doubt, but Bedford cord lacks *dash*, sir."

"I know what you mean. I think I'd like to farm after the war."

"A number of officers now serving feel that way, sir. Now I'll take your measurements, if you'll undo the two lower buttons of your tunic."

Afterwards he invited Phillip into his office, a glass box among bolts of cloth and brown paper patterns hanging on the wall with partly hand-stitched tunics; and opening a large leather cigar case, offered a Corona. Phillip selected one. Mr. Kerr offered to cut and pierce one end, and when Phillip put it in his mouth, struck a large match, holding it until the wax had burned away before offering the flame.

"I have some rather special old whiskey, thirty years matured in the wood, and soft as milk. 'Dew of Benevenagh', sir. May I pour you a peg? Perhaps you will add your own soda. That glass is a real tumbler, by the way, you will notice that the base is oval."

Phillip began to enjoy his first visit to a gentleman's tailor. The whiskey *was* as soft as milk, with the power of the sun in it. The cigar, too, was gentle, burning evenly and leaving straight ash. The bluish smoke coming away in skeins that were pleasant to watch.

"The secret is in the storage in cedar wood cabinets at the correct temperature. Odd, isn't it, that only the soil and climate of Havana can produce the perfect leaf. So you lost all your kit in the March affair, and again in the Flanders push? My word, you've seen some sights, I'll be bound. London was greatly shaken, you know. You read about the Maurice debate, no doubt? If it had gone against him, Lloyd George would have had to resign, no doubt about that. He turned the tables on his critics very cunningly, I thought."

"I haven't seen any newspaper since I came back. In fact, I thought I was going to lose my sight!" laughed Phillip, accepting his second tumbler of 'Dew of Benevenagh' and soda-water.

"Mustard gas can be pretty horrible, I understand. You are fortunate, sir."

"Well, here's to your health, Mr. Kerr!"

"And to yours, sir!"

"You were saying something about Lloyd George nearly having to resign, Mr. Kerr?"

"Oh yes, the Maurice debate. General Maurice is, or was, head of the War Office, as you know. He wrote a letter to *The Times*, saying in effect that Haig had been starved of reinforcements, although the Cabinet had received ample warning that the German attack was coming; and yet Lloyd George had persisted in retaining a million and a half troops here in England. There's been a lot of talk about that letter, in fact, it's not too much to say that it shook the country. The Asquith Liberals, led by Asquith himself, put down a motion of no confidence, based on General Maurice's letter."

"You know, Mr. Kerr, I heard about this from my Colonel, Lord Satchville, when I was adjutant in the reserve battalion, last February. And it was Mr. George, damn him, who broke Hubert Gough, when we in the Fifth Army had held the Germans from breaking through! It wasn't Haig, you know, who sacked Gough."

"So I understand, sir. Well, as I was saying, the Maurice debate, as the papers called it, was expected to provide some fireworks, and it did, but in the other direction. Lloyd George sent his critics spinning by reading from the document which had come from General Maurice himself, giving him the comparable figures for our troops with the B.E.F. in January 1917 and again in January 1918. There were more men in France at the later date, declared Lloyd George, and General Maurice's own figures proved it. He waved the letter to a packed House. Someone went and told Maurice, who said that the figures were not those of the second amended list he had sent to the Prime Minister. Lloyd George replied, 'I am quoting the General's own figures! Here they are, signed by the General himself!', as he waved the letter."

"And it was the first list of figures, and not the corrected one?"

"I have heard that, sir."

"It must have been, for we had fewer men in the B.E.F. last January than we had a year before! It's obvious, because all infantry brigades were broken down from four battalions to three, throughout the entire B.E.F.! Even then, most battalions were far under strength."

"Yes, I've heard the same thing from a number of officers. Lloyd George is a slippery customer. I did hear that when Asquith resigned, after Lloyd George had intrigued against him, all letters sent to 10 Downing Street to the Asquith family were marked 'Gone Away' in blue pencil, and returned through the Dead Letter Office of the G.P.O. Not quite the thing, was it?"

Mr. Kerr looked at his watch. "If you're not doing anything better, would you care to be my guest at lunch? I know a chop-house not far from here, where one can still get a chump chop and some excellent Stilton cheese——"

At the senior officers' meeting, held in one of the many large rooms crammed with gilt furniture, and hung with pictures in gilt frames on walls lined with watered crimson silk, the Duke, in the uniform of a Colonel Commandant of the Depôt, took the chair. With his cousin Satchville on his right, his adjutant on his left, he spoke about the circumstances of General West's death. There was, he read from a paper before him, a proposal to place a mural tablet in the Cathedral, by permission of the Dean and Chapter, in memory of their fallen comrade. A suitable place would be near the corner where the Regimental colours of past generations were reposited.

Also, he continued, it had been suggested that a Fund be raised, to which all ranks could contribute, to provide for Harold West's parents a sum to help them in their declining years. As they knew, Mr. West the father was an old member of the Regiment, having served in India, Burma, and China, among other stations, and all his three sons had given their lives in the service of their King and Country. In due course members of the Regimental Officers' Association would be informed as to particulars.

While he was reading, Phillip, with concealed impersonal glances, was trying to recognise who was present; he recalled some of the faces from the book of photographs in the ante-room at Landguard. There was Major-General Mowbray, grave and courteous in silence; Colonel Vallum, who had played rugger for

England, and won the Victoria Cross at Neuve Chapelle; Lieutenant-Colonel K. T. F. S. ('Knock Them For Six') Percy, who having captained England at cricket had found immediate promotion in Kitchener's Army—thereafter his senior rank prevented his being sent to the front, since he lacked experience of command in action; Lieut.-General the Earl of Tyrone, Colonel of the Regiment, a Guardsman commanding a corps in France; and dear old Moggers, in what looked like a home-made civvy suit, whose arrival on a diminutive Levis motorcycle, wearing a bright green velour hat too small for him, the brim turned down all round as in the pre-war fashion, had suggested to Phillip a bucolic Pan half disguised as a red toadstool springing up in the woods through the moss.

He recognised about one fifth of the faces, the others were strangers, all wearing South African and 1914 ribands after their decorations.

"It has been proposed that Harold West's last act, inspired, like his behaviour in all circumstances, by the highest qualities of chivalry and selfless devotion to others, be brought to the notice of the appropriate authorities for His Majesty the King's Commendation. Would anyone care to make any observation on this proposal, before I ask for a show of hands?"

Phillip stared at the carpet. He tried to breathe deeply, for steadiness. Why had he been asked to attend: was he supposed to second the motion, if that was what it was. Why had he come, he had no proper place there, his acting rank ended when he was gassed. If only he could get away; he couldn't breathe in that atmosphere. And the shameful sweating under his armpits had started. Why had he not put a handkerchief pad there, instead of lending his only clean one to Brill?

His heart thudded in his ears as a voice said, "Has it been determined why O'Gorman was not wearing his cork belt when the mine struck the hospital ship?"

The Duke turned to his adjutant, Major Mills, who said, "The matter was not raised at the Court of Inquiry, sir." The roof of Phillip's mouth dried, the sweat dripped fast. The Duke was saying, "It can be presumed that Private O'Gorman, in the arduous circumstances, found the somewhat bulky cork-belt in the way while helping to lift the stretcher down the sloping deck, which was then canting at about thirty degrees."

"Can you tell us, Maddison?" said Lord Satchville.

He must say something. That he was in another part of the ship at the time, as he had prepared, should the dread question come. Now his mouth opened, but he could not speak.

"I think it might be accepted," went on the Duke, after an interval of silence, "that in consideration of all the circumstances, the matter be allowed to remain in abeyance. It was unfortunate that Private O'Gorman was without his life-jacket, but on the other hand, had he not, with commendable sense of duty, gone to the aid of Harold West, it is unlikely that he would have taken off his jacket. Perhaps the Colonel of the Regiment would give us guidance in this matter?"

"I agree, Duke, with the line taken. What useful purpose would be served by an inquiry at this time? Maddison, I understand, was temporarily blinded by mustard gas. Nevertheless he sent his orderly to help Westy, as all of us who were privileged to know Harold West called him. A most commendable action, in my opinion, after the order of *sauve qui peut*."

"Hear hear!" They were praising him. He hid his face with his hand to conceal tears. Afterwards Lord Satchville came up and said, "I haven't had an opportunity before to tell you, Maddison, of my personal satisfaction in how you have borne great responsibilities in the field, and to offer you my congratulations."

The luncheon extended the ordeal. He dreaded that the stain of sweat under his arm-pits would show through the tunic borrowed from Denis Sisley, and kept his arms almost rigid by his side. It was a simple luncheon: thick brown soup, the usual salty 'boiled blood', followed by slices from a haunch of venison, tasteless and pale-green in colour. He sat between Moggers and Vallum. Claret was served. The Duke, Phillip noticed, was not eating venison, but a grilled fish with pink flesh, obviously a trout, brought in by his special butler on a trolley and served to him by his valet, who also put a dish of spring onions before his master. The butler dropped a bit of ice in his wine: rather strange, he thought, since he had always heard that red wine should be drunk at room temperature. After the meat there was a hot caramel pudding, with chilled cream ladled over it from a large golden bowl, and a variety of stewed raspberries and strawberries in jelly, presumably preserves, also with unlimited cream. The Duke had no helping, but munched his spring onions.

He felt more at home with his neighbour, Colonel Vallum, a massive man with a big head, strong jaw, and modest manner, when he told him, almost as a confidence, that his hobby was painting wild flowers, 'when I can get the time'. Vallum went on to explain that he was a clerk, employed at the War House, 'all paper'. He wore with the dark red V.C. riband, the D.S.O., 1914 Star, Legion d'Honneur, Croix de Guerre avec palme, the Montenegrin eagle, and Coronation Medal.

"I was a schoolboy at King Edward's coronation, and got it for shouting at him as he walked by underneath, on his way to be crowned. I had this in my pocket—it always brought me luck." He put a small object on the table between them. "D'you know what that is?"

"It looks like a piece of yellow phosphorus, but it couldn't be that."

"It's a piece of pancake I grabbed during the Greaze in School Yard."

"Oh, you were at Westminster, sir?"

"Yes."

"I went to school at Blackheath."

"Rugger?"

"No, soccer."

"Before I got the shape of a rhinoceros I used to play in the Rectory field at Blackheath—you know it, of course." He made crumbs with his bread. "You did well in France, Maddison. I was reading about you before I came down here."

Moggers winked at him. "I told yew yew'd do, Lampo, old son."

I didn't—*drip*—I didn't—*drip*—I didn't—*drip-drip-drip*.

"Gentlemen, let us rise and drink the health of His Majesty the King!"

One Monday morning he went up to London to see Georgiana Lady Dudley, who, bright and gay as when he had seen her last, marked him down for the next vacancy in a private convalescent home in the West Country.

"So you are home again, Colonel Maddison! Let me see—last time it was?—of course, in the early summer of 1916! And how are you? Much better? I *am* so glad! Last time, let me see, you went to——? Of course, Lynmouth! Dear, dear Lynmouth! I remember how we set out one day to go there from Watermouth, with dear, dear Bobo Curzon, and the coach wheels skidded all the way down that awful hill! I do hope you will not find Falmouth too relaxing after Lynmouth, it's much flatter, too! If you come across the Tregaskis at Carligan, do remember me to Zoe Tregaskis, won't you? They have such lovely gardens. South Cornwall has almost the air of the Riviera, don't you think? Oh yes—your address? Hus'b'n Abbey. And how is the Duchess? Tireless as ever, I expect, in her hospital? Goodbye, Colonel Maddison!"

Had she really remembered him, or was she helping life along with grace and kindness? Both, probably: it was the only way to live. He wandered down to Piccadilly, a place entirely of memories: gone the uniforms of the Allies in those early days and nights, when he had been with Desmond and Gene. He felt himself to be almost a ghost. What to do? Go down to see Mother? By hurrying, he could catch the 12.30 from St. Pancras, and be in time for Lady Abeline's picnic. That darling child Melissa, smiling blue-eyes and honey-coloured hair, Melissa the honey-bee, Melissa whose nurse insisted on her wearing white gloves in the park, Melissa—Lily and her dreaming, azure eyes.

To be with the four-year-old child was happiness, sans memory, sans thought. To him came the old desire, no longer frantic but with acceptance that it would never be, to find rest in the tenderness of eyes, hair, warmth of arms, the near-delirious softness of dove-like breasts. He stood still, resisting, resisting the near-terror of loneliness in this city of many streets filled with wheels and faces pressing upon the eyes, and the laughter of passing strangers. He bought a paper to look for a theatre matinée, and was held by bold type on the front page: a new German attack on a wide front down by the Chemin des Dames at Rheims. The Wolff Wireless Bureau claimed a break-through, with thousands of prisoners, both French and British, and hundreds of guns. British divisions so far down the line? They must have been tired troops sent south to rest.

There was no end to it, he thought, giving the paper back to the newsboy. For a moment he wondered if he should go to the War Office, and ask to be sent out immediately, saying that he was perfectly fit.

The paper did not say who the British troops were, of course, although nowadays some regimental names were mentioned by war correspondents, usually long afterwards when prisoners had been taken. Anyway the Germans knew as much as the British High Command knew about the German dispositions. Should he go at once to the War Office, say he was perfectly fit, and ask to be sent out again, as a subaltern perhaps? Those 18-year-old boys . . . at least he would be able to help them in a small way. But they would not be able to do anything, he was officially still in hospital.

He went to see Mr. Kerr in Cundit Street, and told him his news.

"Falmouth, that's a pleasant place. I suppose you'll be wearing plain clothes most of the time? They do a lot of sailing down there. The oaks up the river Fal will be showing their best at this time of the year, too. How are you off for flannels, and a tweed jacket, sir? I mention it now, so that we can have all you require in the way of fittings at one time."

"Yes, I'll want a tweed jacket, and some trousers—grey flannel, I think."

"I'll show you some patterns."

They went to the back of the shop to the bolts, Phillip thinking that if they had been found in Wytschaete, they would have been soiled and lousy within twenty-four hours. He was rather amused by Mr. Kerr's concern for their qualities, as though there wasn't a war on; but another side of him took it all in. "We've been fortunate enough to get hold of some very decent Donegal tweeds, in spite of all the controls and shortages. I wonder what you will think of this peat and sedge mixture? It's a summer weight, and will go well with any trousers."

"Yes, I'd like a jacket with patch pockets made of this, also two pairs of white bags. And while I'm about it, I think I'll have another tunic, for the summer."

"I have a light-weight serge here, made from the wool combed from a pedigree flock of Border Cheviots. A very active little animal, the Border Cheviot, as resilient as the heather——"

Phillip approved this cloth at once, and ordered a jacket with slacks to match. No cuff badges of rank: he'd probably come down to commanding a platoon, when he went back to France again, he told Mr. Kerr.

"Yes, sir?" said Mr. Kerr, lightly. "Would you prefer cloth rank badges on the shoulder straps, or gilt and enamel? We've also got some in dull bronze? They're in three sizes . . . here we are, sir."

The smallest were scarcely more than a quarter of an inch across. "I'll have this size, Mr. Kerr."

"In gilt or bronze?"

"Bronze."

"They'll be hard to distinguish, sir. Perhaps you want that?"

"I think I'll have them medium size, in gilt."

"That would balance up the jacket, sir. Now the buttons. You'd prefer the usual gilt, or leather? I always think that the smaller round leather button looks well with a fine serge cloth, particularly for a mounted officer."

"Yes, I'll have leather buttons."

"Small leather buttons, Mr. Brown. I think that covers all for the moment. We'll have everything ready for fitting when you come up to town, on your way through to Cornwall."

At the door Phillip heard the distant thumping of drums, and a waft of brazen music.

"There's a parade of some of the girls in war jobs in Hyde Park this afternoon," said Mr. Kerr. "It should be quite a sight. More war babies to follow, I suppose——" He looked blandly at his customer. "Well, who is to blame them, sir?" as he bowed out his customer.

Phillip went to Hyde Park and saw rank upon rank of regiments of girls—in uniforms brown, grey, white, red, and khaki. One company were Little Red Riding Hoods, covered from head to foot in scarlet. "They make our gas-masks, sir," explained a constable. Others wore red caps with white jackets and loose white trousers, others the same garb with blue caps. "Also from Woolwich Arsenal," explained the constable. Phillip knew the V.A.D. nurses with their blue dresses and white aprons, the bus-conductors in dark blue trousers and brown holland jackets, the Post Office girls with bags slung over shoulders, other girls in dark blue uniforms from the electric trams. There was the Land Army—might Doris be with them? He went close, but could not see her, then along a line of Foresters in brown jackets and bright green caps. He drew smiles and glances from some W.A.A.C.s, but hauteur from the senior service (female) W.R.E.N.s, as he looked for blue eyes and fair hair, a soft glance to feed him, the more beautiful the more that the hunger for love weighed upon him, for the face of—a Lily.

Older women officer'd them.

"Company! For-r-rm—fours! Right tur-r-rn! Quick—

march!" The drum thumped out its *boom-boom-boom—boom, boom, boom*—from the brass instruments curled sunflower-petal music; he walked, fifty yards distant, beside the marching column that led the way to the broad walk under tall and spreading elms, where pigeons strutted and coo'd.

"Mind the low railings, girls!" said a smart young lady W.R.E.N. officer. He watched them go.

It was June, it was high summer, nobody there heard the guns, nobody saw rifles thrown forward as ghosts left bodies sinking at the knees, heads falling forward upon ruined fields under the Monts de Flandres, or among old and rotting heaps of sandbags from which the chalk had long since broken, above the Somme and the Marne.

Chapter 14

ALGERIAN WINE PARTY

Phillip went up to London again, while awaiting authority and railway warrant to proceed to Falmouth. It was towards the second week in June when he said goodbye to the Duke and Duchess, and was driven away in one of the half-dozen 1907 Silver Ghost landaulettes. He told himself that he must not tip the chauffeur, having seen the notices put up on many of the walls beyond the red baize doors asking guests not to give money to the servants. He was a sort of guest, so the pound note folded in his trousers pocket was creased and recreased as he rode behind the glass partition to Bleachley junction, where the London train was stopped whenever the Duke requested it, since the line ran through his land.

A luncheon basket had been provided; it was put in the carriage for him by the chauffeur. Out came the pound note; the grateful smile made it a pleasant journey, familiar as far as Exeter; then it was strange country onwards beside the estuary of the Exe, and the railway continuing along the coast to the red rocks of Dawlish to Teignmouth; and along another estuary where salmon fishermen were hauling their nets. After Newton Abbot was green country with cider-apple orchards, giving way, as the train rushed westwards, to purple and yellow tracts of moorland about which he recognised, with excitement, the granite tors of Dartmoor, with their memories of *The Hound of the Baskervilles*, the blue paper-covered *Strand Magazines* in the drawer below the linen-cupboard in his bedroom at home.

The sun was beginning to descend ahead of the engine; and seemingly drawing the train in its descent to lower fields, until the slate roofs and towers of Plymouth came into view. Over another bridge, more salt water, and he was in Cornwall at last! The engine was throwing out smoke; he closed the windows, while the laboured piston-thrusts indicated another ascent to the western redoubts of Dartmoor, and then, running freely, descending once more to a strange country which reminded him of Loos, only these heaps towering into the sky were white: they must be the china clay learned about in geography books in that remote time called schooldays. He imagined battle among the near-impregnable spoil heaps with their muffling effect on high explosive shells, and safety for the machine-gunners in their deep dug-outs. Then the slaughter: it would be like the slaughter around Kemmel Hill, where the German dead had lain in thousands, after Wytschaete had been evacuated. And living in the past with the imagination, he found that the train was slowing before St. Austell station; and puffing onwards into the sun, still high, they came to Truro, and a country of woods and green pastures, and near the end of the journey, for here were wooden ships, beside the muddy saltings of a creek over which the train rattled.

And so at last to Falmouth, and crimson rambler roses along the station railings, where a fluttery old lady (as he thought of her) came smiling obliquely, as with shyness, towards him.

"*Can* you be Colonel Maddison? But you are so young! Do forgive me, but I was expecting someone quite different, and wearing uniform. I *do* hope you had a pleasant journey? Jack will take your bags. It is rather a long way round by motor to Tregaskis, so I do hope you will not mind crossing over by the ferry? I have a taxi waiting, to take us to the pier. How *very* nice to see you, Mr.,—I mean Colonel—Maddison."

"Well, I was only an acting colonel, so I am really only a 'Mister', my substantive rank is lieutenant, Miss Shore."

It was a brief run down to the pier, where the fresh-faced Jack, who wore a sailor suit and round cap with white band, smilingly took his bag. Phillip was delighted with the idea of crossing over the harbour in a small steamboat, with its vertical boiler and open furnace door glowing with logs, thrown in by a boy. The ferryman was obviously an old sailor, with a peaked cap and white beard. And looking about him as the boat beat its way across a few hundred yards of water, he saw out to sea, in the broader area of the harbour, two old wooden men o' war, relics of Nelson's day. Miss Shore explained to him, in her gentle fluttering voice, that the nearer vessel was a school for sailor boys, run by someone with a name sounding like Mr. Barley Swann.

"He is so good with the poor boys he looks after, many of them without fathers since the war," she said happily. "I do hope you will like our little place, Colonel Maddison—no, Mr. Maddison, of course, I must remember not to say 'Colonel' mustn't I? Here we are, Jack will drive the governess cart."

They moved slowly up a street past white-washed cottages, and entering a drive, arrived at a stone-built house among the trees on the top of the hill.

"I am afraid we cannot let you have a room to yourself, but you will find Major Wetley quiet and understanding. Would you like tea? I am sure you must be famished after such a long journey. Now tell me, I have been simply longing to ask you, are you musical? You are! There, I felt sure you were! Let me play you a beautiful record, while they are bringing tea."

Miss Shore wound up a cabinet H.M.V., and from the open doors came the strains of *In a Monastery Garden*. "Would you care to control the tone?" She held out a black cable, with a sort of plunger on the end. "If you push, it will play softer, or louder if you pull out the plug. It's so much more like the real thing then, I always think. Now I will leave you awhile, to amuse yourself with it."

Phillip softened the music, then for an experiment pulled out the nob, so that the mixture of organ strains, bird-notes, bells, and chanting voices swelled out, filling the room. He tried to push in the control, but found it was stuck. While he was wondering how to free it without breaking anything, a tall captain in trews came thudding down the stairs, glengarry on head, and crossed over the room to stand above him, and say, "Must you make that hideous row! It's time those blasted monks were called up!" and going to the gramophone, the scowling captain jerked the needle off the record. "I've had enough of that bloody old woman's sentimentality," he muttered, as he strode out of the house.

"Ah," said Miss Shore, coming back a minute or two later, while he was still trying to free the plunger. "It was *so* kind to stop the record. It is so beautiful, I think, don't you. So peaceful."

"It's my mother's favourite record, Miss Shore."

"How wonderful! Yes, it belongs to a time gone by, when there was peace in the world. Ah, here's Nurse with tea! Let me introduce you—Miss Goonhilly—Mr. Maddison. Now do you prefer cream or lemon with your tea? Lemon? Help yourself to sandwiches—these are cucumber, and those patum—and tell me all about your journey!"

After tea, Miss Shore said she thought he looked tired, and he ought to go to bed. Nurse Goonhilly would bring up his dinner on a tray at half-past seven. "I shall be dining out tonight, with Mr. Barley Swann, in the *Foudroyant*, his training ship, you know. The more distant ship you saw is the *Implacable*. Mr. Barley Swann is hoping, after the war, to fit that up too, for the older sailor boys. Tomorrow morning Doctor Bull has promised to come and see you; there are plenty of books for you to read meanwhile. Now if you will come with me and Nurse, we will show you your room. I *do* hope you will like it."

The room was large, facing west. Its white walls were glowing with the sun still high over the trees beyond the lawn. After the northern outlook of the Tennis Ward, it was blankly open to Phillip.

"Have you many other patients here, Miss Shore?"

"Oh yes, all our beds are now filled; we can only have fourteen patients at a time. The others are out and about somewhere; this is Liberty Hall, but we ask for notice if anyone is going to be out for luncheon and dinner, for the sake of the staff, you know. Lights out are at half-past ten, with all our guests, as we think of them, in by ten. That is one of the conditions imposed by the authorities, you know. Nurse will show you the bathroom. Dressing gowns and bathrobes you will find in this cupboard, with towels. Would you like a glass of hot milk, or some Benger's Food, to stay you until dinner? Do ring if you want anything, won't you? We shall meet again after breakfast! Ah, here is Jack to unpack your things. Until tomorrow morning, au revoir, and pleasant dreams!"

He was unable to read; a feeling of claustrophobia grew with unbearable thoughts of 'Spectre'; he stuck it until dinner arrived —vegetable soup, fillets of plaice cooked in milk, and chicken with new potatoes and small carrots—and then began to put on his clothes while trying to control an inner trembling, which spread to his hands, while he sweated coldly. He must get out of the place. Why the hell had he submitted to being sent to bed? He could not breathe; no wonder the tall Scotch captain had been so sullen. Why did they always shove one into bed as soon as one arrived at a convalescent home? If you were fit to walk about in hospital, surely to God a man was fit to walk about in a country house?

The blatant sun, burning the treetops, glared into the room. It was all he could do to unknot his shoelaces. His finger stuck in the back of a shoe, he pulled it out violently, and shoved on the shoe with a knife-blade, afterwards throwing away the knife; then forcing himself to pick it up he put it back on the tray and tip-toed to the door, opening it to listen. It was like *Alice Through the Looking Glass*—Nurse Goonhilly—Mr. Barley Swann—Major Wetley. What a collection! He sat down in a chintz-covered armchair, and tried to breathe deeply, to find calm. It was no good. He must get away. Damn the old woman, what was the point of sending him to bed? He dared not leave the room, and sat there trembling.

The sun had gone down, with gulls flighting silently over the trees, when he opened the door and, with invisible sparks running through him, went down the stairs. Voices came from a room beyond the large hall where he had had tea; he listened outside, then dared to open the door.

Inside was a pianola and a half-sized billiard table, looking as though they had been hired in the town by an elderly spinster lady to "keep your boys at home", as the pre-war advertisements ran in popular magazines. Beyond the billiard table three men were sitting at cards. Wine glasses stood on the table. As soon as the door opened the glasses were removed, while heads turned in his direction. "It's all right," he said, much relieved. "I'm only one of the patients. Came this afternoon."

"Ah, you've got out of bed without the Goonhilly knowing, you naughty boy!" replied one of the card-players, an elegant youth with gold hair parted down the middle. "We're playing cut-throat. How about a foursome, Major?" to the dark-haired elderly man opposite.

"Anything you like, Swayne." Major Wetley turned to Phillip. "Do you play?"

"I play auction. I don't play poker."

"Nor do I," said the dark man, in a Midland accent. "Come and take a pew. How about a glass of wine?"

"Not at the moment, thank you, sir."

"I don't blame you," said the gold-haired youth, with a mock simper.

Phillip kept his amiable expression at this remark. They drew for partners. He and the elegant young officer drew highest. Sitting opposite his partner, Phillip noticed that Swayne wore a service uniform similar to that of the Foot Guards. Remembering the Guards officers of 1914, it was therefore with some surprise that he heard the young ensign say, after the major had cut to him, "The senior officer present having neglected to introduce us, partner, let me do it for him. My name is Swayne. This extraordinary-looking fat cove here is called Coupar, otherwise Copper Nob. Have some Algerian wine. It's the major's birthday, so he's responsible. God, it's filthy muck you've bought, major! I'd rather drink the Goonhilly's disinfectants!"

"I told you, it's all that shop 'ad, Swayne."

"But why buy wine at a grocer's, major?"

"This is Falmouth, not London, Swayne."

"And this is red-ink, not wine, major."

"You're drinking it, I notice."

"Worse luck," with a simper in Phillip's direction.

"You don't 'ave to drink it, Swayne. Any as wants to can help themselves. There are four more bottles."

"You old poisoner!"

Phillip said to the major, "I should of course have told you that my name was Maddison before I sat down, sir."

"Oh, we don't stand on ceremony 'ere," said Major Wetley's mild Midland voice. "'Elp yourself to a glass when you fancy one. There's a spare glass o'er there."

"The major comes from a place where they had no names, only numbers, didn't you, major?"

"Anything you say, Swayne. Whose call? Oh yours, Swayne, since you dealt."

"Well, give us a chance to look at my bloody cards, major!"

Swayne gulped some wine and said, "I've got a hand like a foot, so no bid."

The major studied his hand for some time. At last, "I'll venture one diamond."

The fourth player, Coupar, had a fat body below waves of oily copper-coloured hair crowning a big face with thick features. He sat biting his nails as he stared at his cards, then said musingly, "I wonder what you meant by calling a diamond, partner."

The major was still studying his cards. "My original call was only a conventional feeler, you know, partner," he said across the table.

"A 'conventional feeler', is that what you are, you dirty old man?" said Swayne.

"Now now!" said the major.

"Surely during your sojourn in Aly Sloper's Cavalry you have learned that Portland Club rules forbid information being passed to a partner directly?"

"Very well, I pass, Swayne," said the major.

"The correct phrase is, 'No', or 'No bid', major," said Swayne.

"Two no trumps," said Phillip.

"Three diamonds," said Coupar.

"I'll double three diamonds," said the major.

"But you're my partner!" exclaimed Coupar, indignantly. "You can't do that!"

"The major can do what he likes. He's the senior officer present," tittered Swayne.

"Why can't I double my partner's three diamonds if I want to?" said the major, mildly.

"It's not in the rules of the Portland Club," said Swayne.

"Three no trumps," said Phillip, filling his glass again, and draining it.

"Do you usually toss off your liquor as quickly as that?" enquired Swayne.

"Usually much faster, partner."

"Good man, 'elp yourself to more," said the major.

"I double three no trumps," Coupar said.

"No interest."

"Content," said the major.

"Four no trumps!"

"What are you used to, poker?" asked Swayne, across the table.

"He pokes anything," said Coupar.

"Are you trying to be offensive to my partner, you nail-biting dogsbody? You Aly Sloper's Cavalry cad!" asked Swayne.

"Did you hear that, major? He's insulting the Army Service Corps!"

Phillip got a little slam, and while the scores were being written, offered to fill the glasses for Major Wetley. A drop fell on the sleeve of Swayne's jacket.

"Mind my uniform, you four-flushing card-sharper!"

"Swayne's a fop, an immaculate base-wallah, did you know?" remarked Coupar.

"Who the hell are you calling a base-wallah?"

"That's just what you are, Swine," said Coupar. "'Mind my uniform'. D'you call that a uniform? Where did you get it from? Willie Clarkson's?"

"I happen to be an ensign in the Honourable Harquebus Corps."

"What's that when it's at home?"

"Only the oldest corps in the City of London, you ignorant fart."

"Oh yes, you fire flintlock muskets from a forked hand-rest, don't you, on Guy Fawkes' Day?"

"Don't let the talkin' stop the drinkin'," said Phillip, emptying his glass.

"Shall we continue playing in accordance with the rules of the Portland Club, partner?" said Swayne blandly.

"Yes, let's be posh," said the major.

"'Posh'? I don't understand thieves' slang, major."

"You would if ever you'd been in the ranks, Swayne."

"But I have been in the ranks, major."

"In what lot?"

So far all had been in fun; now it looked as though Swayne was turning nasty.

"*Lot?* What were you in civvy street, an auctioneer, major? Oh, you mean what *regiment*! I *do* beg your pardon, major! Naturally, the Army Service Corps would never have heard of the Honourable Harquebus Corps."

"Oh yes, I 'ave. I've seen your fellers in the Lord Mayor's Show. As I said, it takes all sorts to make a world."

Coupar roared with laughter, while Swayne said, suddenly very quiet, "What were you doing when the Lord Mayor's Procession went by, major? Selling souvenirs on the kerb, with a hawker's licence and little tray?"

"Oh bollocks to you, Swayne," said Coupar.

"We don't want to know what you had for breakfast, you pox-doctor's clerk!"

Almost grimly the major took the other pack, shuffled and cut to Swayne, who dealt. Phillip found Mr. Bones the Butcher among his cards. Someone had been playing *Happy Families.*

"God's Body," said Coupar. "Did I deal this sewage? Definitely no bid," as he swigged his glass of wine.

"Doubled," said Phillip, filling the glasses.

"Bloody fool, you can't double nothing," said Swayne.

"Yes you can. Double nothing is nothing."

"You mean, 'No bid' I presume, partner?" Swayne shook his head as though sadly, and said, "This fellow drinks his bath-water."

"YOUR CALL, SWINE!" yelled Coupar.

"It's mine," said the major. "I can't do anything."

"Try eating oysters," said Swayne. "And your reply will then be, 'content'."

"How kind of you to correct my ignorance, Swayne."

"Impotence, major."

"Five no trumps," said Coupar.

"You're all bloody mad," said Swayne.

"I'll bid eight no trumps," said Phillip.

"You're blotto. There isn't such a call!"

"But I've just made it!"

"It's not 'in the rules of the Portland Club'," mimicked Coupar.

"All right, I'll make it nine no trumps!"

"I'll double that," said Coupar.

"That isn't 'in the rules of the Portland Club', either," said the major. "Is it, Swayne?"

"*You've* never been inside the Portland, major!"

"Where's that?" asked Coupar. "Among the harlots around Paddington, you ponce?"

"Ask the major, Copper Nob."

"I've stood just about enough from you, Swayne," said the major. "I've just about had enough of your swanking ways!" The major looked quite pale.

"Don't take any notice of old Swine, he's pissed as arseholes, major."

"Tell me, partner," said Phillip, challenging Swayne, "Do the Portland Club rules *expressly* forbid a player calling nine of a suit?"

"I've just told you."

"You said 'it stands to reason'. Does it also stand to the Portland Club rules?"

"I don't suppose they do, any more than they state any other negative, such as 'you don't gargle with your wine', or——"

"Drink your bath-water?" suggested Coupar.

"Very well, I call ten no trumps!"

"And I double ten no trumps," retorted Coupar, banging his fist on the table so hard that a glass jumped off.

"Redoubled!" cried Phillip, balancing his glass on his head, in imitation of Major Maurice Baring at Advanced G.H.Q. in 1917.

"Steady on, lads," said the major. "Miss Shore won't care for a rough 'ouse."

Phillip laid down his cards, including Mr. Bones the Butcher.

Swayne jumped up, bawling, "This man's a card sharper!"

"Come on, get a decent pack, and stop mucking about, everyone," said Coupar. "Where's the booze? Christ, the bottle's empty! You've swigged it all!" to Phillip. "What are you here for? Dypsomania?"

"That's right, he's dipped it too much," said Swayne.

"I kept two bottles in reserve," said the major. He went down on hands and knees before a grandfather clock in a corner of the room. "One club," his voice said, as he bumped into the case, which set the weights within thumping, whereupon the works began to click and whirr and the clock struck fifteen times.

"I told you, everything about this place is dippy," sighed Swayne, looking as though he were about to renounce the world. "The f——g clock's just called fifteen no trumps!"

"Steady on, Swayne!" said the major, still on hands and knees before his secret cellar.

"It's Maddison's call," said Coupar.

"Sixteen no bumps!" as the major came back with two bottles.

"Half a tick," said the major. "We don't want to leave evidence about, in case Miss Shore comes in," and taking the empty bottles, he hid them inside the clock case. Then he refilled the glasses; Phillip put his back on his head.

"Your call, major," said Swayne, winking at the other two. He had dealt the major all the court cards during the visit to the clock.

"One club," said the major.

"No bid."

"No."

"No."

Phillip led a small heart. Coupar, the major's partner, immediately spread his cards as though opening a fan on the green baize table. "Yarborough," he said. "Bad luck, partner."

Major Wetley took out his pipe and began to fill it. He lit the tobacco and puffed steadily until a cloud of smoke hung over the table. Then he examined the fuming crown of tobacco, and with the matchbox tamped it level.

"Take your time, partner," said Coupar. "We've each got another two weeks in this 'ere skrimshankers' 'ome."

"The major starts off with a gas attack," said Swayne. "It only wants a few belches to complete the picture of a genuine old Aly Sloper's Cavalryman's idea of a battle."

"Let me tell you this, Swayne," replied Major Wetley, putting his pipe on the table, "I never had a single bearing, big, little, or main, run in any one of my engines in my convoy the whole time I was in France! And shall I tell you why? 'More haste, less speed' was my motto, and I had the loyalest lot of drivers any man could wish for."

"Yes, at six bob a day pay!" said Coupar. "They stuck loyally to their cushy jobs, of course they did! And pinched the soldiers' rum and rations!"

"You deserve the O.B.E., major," remarked Swayne, as the major, taking up his pipe, puffed furiously to keep the damp tobacco alight. "My God, what are you smoking? 'Wayside Returns'?"

"Don't you like it? It's 'Tortoiseshell Shag', Swayne."

"Well tortoises don't shag very quickly as a rule, I'll agree."

"Quite a lot of it is smoked among pore people." The major belched several times. "Pardon. I've got indigestion."

"Come come, major, this isn't Rowton House! Although I'll admit it's beginning to smell like that stately 'ome."

"Oh, so you've lived there, Swayne, have you?" said Coupar. "I happen to like 'Tortoiseshell Shag' and also it's cheap, Swayne."

"You're not 'pore', major. You've got plenty of money. What is it an A.S.C. major gets, twenty-four bob a day? And no mess bills to pay! You must be 'rolling in t' brass', major."

"Twenty-four shillings a day don't go very far when a man's got two boys to educate, Swayne. You're only a young man, and won't know what responsibility for a family entails."

"I don't want to know either. Where are your sons at school, Harrow?"

"You know perfectly well that a man like me would not be able to afford such an education for his sons, Swayne," said the major, putting down his pipe again. "Now I'll ask you a question, Swayne. Where were you educated?"

"He wasn't," said Coupar. "He's the most ignorant sod that ever broke his pore mother's heart. 'Swing, swing together'—all bloody crooks in 'lovely summer weather'."

"Where were you, Copper Nob?" asked Swayne.

"Epsom."

"Never 'eard of it. Oh yes, of course, 'Where the salts come from'. You look as though a dose would do you good. Where were you, major?"

"I was educated at the Polytechnic, Swayne. And talking about Epsom salts, I feel I could do with some now. This wine is beginning to play Old Harry with my interior economy." He tapped his stomach.

Coupar gave him a hearty slap on the back, which shook the cards out of the major's hand and on to the floor.

"Christ, the old four-flusher! He's got every court card in the pack and only called 'one club'!"

The major collected his cards, "Ah, that's better," as up came wind. "I feel better now. Thanks." He began to re-sort his hand laboriously, before laying the cards face up on the table.

"I don't see as 'ow I could lose a trick. Any'ow, I'll risk it."

"Four arse-pieces, four kings, four queens, and the knave of clubs," remarked Swayne. "What a nerve you've got, major! Trust the A.S.C. to be cheese-paring! They pinch most of the troops' rations as it is. One mouldy club! 'What did you do in the Great War, Daddy?' 'I "won" the fighting soldiers' rations, dear, I never went faster than eight miles an hour, glued to the wheel, eyes sweeping the road ahead, and then when I got to my journey's end I called one club.'"

"Too true, I never exceeded eight miles per hour with any of my lorries," said the major. "So you're right there, Swayne."

"Otherwise the horrible harquebusses would have been shaken to bits," laughed Phillip.

"Who the hell are you grinning at?" said Swayne, looking at Phillip. "What 'lot are you from', as the major would say?"

"Oh various lots, here and there."

"You don't mind my asking?"

"Not at all. I used to ask personal questions myself."

"That's got you, Swine!"

Ignoring Coupar, Swayne went on, "Have you been out?"

"I think so."

"Where were you?"

"Oh, here and there."

"Royal Staybacks, weren't you?" said Coupar, winking.

"Were you ever in the firing line?" persisted Swayne.

"For a short time."

"Who were you with?"

"I kicked off with a battalion of the London Regiment."

"Oh, the Gor' blimey boys!"

"What's the H.H.C. then, if they're not Gor' blimey boys dolled up?" said Coupar, winking again at Phillip.

"If you want to know, the H.H.C. is recruited among gentlemen."

"With obvious exceptions," remarked Coupar.

"Anyway, which battalion of the London Regiment were you?" went on Swayne, staring at Phillip.

"London Highlanders."

"The real stuff," said Coupar. "Not like Swayne's Saturday Afternoon Wet Bobbed Brummagen Fireguards. Look at him! Look at old Swine! Just take a look at him! Look, I ask you! Look at his bloody face! Saturday afternoon guardsman, guarding what, you may well ask! Sweet Fanny Adams! He fancies himself in that tunic, obviously. Doesn't know what a perfect twott he looks in it. Look at the silly sod! Did you ever see anything like it? Got as far as the base and came home with corns on his arse!"

"If I look a twett, you look like a bloody horse-collar, with that wide grinning mug," said Swayne, flushing. "At least I didn't go sick as soon as I got to the base with non-existent rheumatism!"

"Like hell I did! You had trench fever in Piccadilly as soon as they combed you out of the Pay Corps!"

"You bore me, Coupar. Come on, shuffle the cards. What's the score, partner?"

"Suck it and see," answered Coupar, hurling the scoring pad at Swayne. Cards followed. Over went the table. Swayne removed his belt. Coupar began to tear off his tunic, thus exposing a soft front of chest and belly in one contour.

"Steady boys, mind what you're at," said the major, looking up from probing his teeth with a pencil point.

"Permit me to help with your sons' education," replied Swayne, emptying his pockets of loose cash, and throwing the coins into the major's lap.

Phillip, wine glass still on head, waited for the scrap; but once his shirt-sleeves were tucked up Coupar seized the remaining full bottle of wine, together with an empty bottle, and began a juggling act.

"Steady on," said the major, as the full bottle fell on Swayne's toes.

"You bag of guts, you did that deliberately," shouted Swayne, kicking Coupar on the rump, so that he fell sprawling.

"By Jesus, I won't stand for that!" he yelled, getting up.

Phillip put down his glass and got between them. Swayne turned on him, Phillip squared up to Swayne. Coupar picked up the card table and drove at both. All three collapsed on the floor.

"That's enough!" said the major, absent-mindedly breaking the pencil point between his teeth. "No rough housing, boys. You know the unwritten rules of hospitality." He tried to blow the point out, producing hissing noises in Swayne's direction.

"Ah, it's always the unwritten rules that count in life, major," retorted Swayne, getting up. "As, for example, the unwritten rule that a field officer is protected by his rank from hearing from his juniors what they really think about him and the chemical muck he calls wine!"

"Well, you've said enow' about my wine already, Swayne, but if there's owt else worryin' you, out wi' it, man!"

"Your rank forbids, major!"

"There's no rank in a convalescent home, we're all equal 'ere as far as I am concerned, Swayne."

"Very well, in my opinion you're an absolute outsider." Swayne, his eyes bloodshot, glared at the major. The major looked down, saying nothing.

"Hold hard!" said Phillip. "I think you should apologise to the major for that remark, Swayne, which was in gross bad taste!"

"'Gross' is pronounced with a long 'o', as in 'grocers'," said Swayne. "Who are you to tell me what is good taste, when you can't even pronounce the King's English?"

"Will you fight?"

"*Touché*, what?"

"Put up your hands!"

"Oh, don't let's have quarrelling, boys. It's all my fault, so I ask pardon of all. I'm afraid I don't know much about red wine. They told me where I bought it that it was the stuff they drank in the Foreign Legion. It's rather on the acid side, I think. I've got some bicarbonate of soda upstairs. If you'll excuse me, I'll go and get some. I find it a good standby."

The major staggered away, hissing and sucking, and came back with a wooden pill-box, which he offered round. Phillip put two tablets in his glass, then took them out and ground them up between finger and thumb; and when he dropped the pieces into the glass, the red wine fizzed and changed to green.

"It's bloody conjuror's wine!" said Swayne. "I thought the major had a look of the Mad Magician about him. If this is what they drink in the Foreign Legion, no wonder they go periodically *cafard*." He put three tablets in his mouth. Phillip drank his green wine. Coupar chewed away. Soon all four were belching.

"That was it," said the major. "Acidity! Flatulence! It's all my fault, as I said just now."

"After all, the French make petrol out of this stuff for their *camions*," said Swayne.

"Alcohol, or what they call *alcool*, surely," said Phillip, recalling mechanics in a comic French film carrying huge cans lettered *alcool*, in the Electric Palace when he was a boy. "Well, thank you for a jolly good birthday party, major."

The major looked grateful. Not to be outdone, Swayne said with a gracious manner, "My dear major, I do apologise for my stupid remarks. It was a most amusing party. Would you all care to be my guests at the Pier Hotel across the water, and crack a bottle of bubbly?"

"Thank you very much, Swayne, but I think I'll go to bed, after I've cleared up this little fracas. It's just as well Miss Shore was out, I think. Don't you bother, I can do it. I'll get rid of the bottles, too, and wash out the glasses."

"How about you, Maddison?"

"I'm supposed to be in bed, Swayne, so I think I should stay here. By the way, were you at Bullecourt in May '17? That was where Bill Whiting got his V.C."

"I was there, in Bill's company!"

"I heard about it, I was with the M.G.C. then. Your chaps put up a wonderful show. But then the H.H.C. is a *corps d'élite*!"

"With the London Highlanders," bowed Swayne. "No ill feelings?"

"On the contrary!"

"Come on Swayne, before Miss Shore gets back."

"I can't bear that bloody old woman!" said Swayne, winsomely to Phillip. "Have you met her yet?"

"Oh yes."

"Well——!"

When the other two had gone, the major said, "I usually brew myself a cup of tea at this time, would you care to join me?"

In the wardrobe at the other end of the Major's bedroom Phillip saw fishing rods standing in one corner. The major said he spent some of his time fishing for pollock and codling, and had had some good sport off the rocks by Pendennis point. Soon they were like old friends. The major told him he was born in Staffordshire, and had had a haulage business before the war. Had Phillip been to the Potteries? Or read anything of Arnold Bennett's? He was a fine writer, and his *Five Towns* novels would become part of English literature. He offered to lend him a copy of *Clayhanger*. While the tea was brewing, Phillip glanced at the book, saw a passage about the fires of the kilns glowing in the smoky night, and decided that he must read it.

"I managed to get half a pound of Orange Pekoe, one of my little luxuries," said Major Wetley. "I had a brother in the tea-trade before the war, in Mincing Lane, who always sent me a box for Christmas. Now I drink China's best in his memory. Tell me, what do you make of Swayne?"

"I've met people like him before, who were not really sure of themselves, and so they take it out of others——"

"You've got it, Maddison! Swayne's people keep a large jeweller's shop in the county town, where my wife comes from, so I know all about him. The Swaynes fancy themselves, and tell people that they are *county* jewellers—you know, imitating the high-class county folk. Well-to-do shopkeepers are terrific snobs, you know. The Swaynes sent their son to Eton, and in my opinion, unless the world changes after the war, Swayne will find himself neither one thing nor the other. Hullo, do I hear the soothing strains of *In a Monastery Garden*? Miss Shore must be back. You'd better hop into bed!"

Phillip listened at the open door: footfalls were coming up the stairs. There was no time to undress, so he got into bed as he was, pulled the blankets around his neck, and pretended to be asleep.

Nurse Goonhilly came in, carrying a tray with a glass of hot milk. "Are you awake, Maddison?"

"Oh hullo, nurse."

"I'm sorry if I woke you up. Here's something to drink. Now sit up and take it while it's hot, like a good boy. Why, you've got your jacket on! Are you feeling cold?"

"I feel cold sometimes, nurse."

"Well drink this, and I'll get you a hot-water bottle. It won't take long. I'll bring you some bed-socks too."

He flung off his clothes while she was out of the room, pushed them under the bed, and leapt in, having heard the tap in the bathroom turned off. He was only just in time.

"Now sit up and drink your milk, while I put the bottle at your feet. Why, you were in your coat a moment ago, now you're in your vest! How did that happen?"

"It may have been some R.A.M.C. orderly—you know 'Rob all my comrades'."

"Nonsense! we've not any of that sort here. Why, you've put it under the bed! I hope you aren't going to run a temperature on your first night. That won't do at all. Here, put this under your tongue, and don't talk. Where are your pyjamas?"

"I think they're in my bag still."

"I told you not to talk!"

She looked under the bed, and pulled out a pair of trousers. "Well I never! Do you always keep your trousers under your bed?"

"Always, nurse. Ever since Cambrai last November, when the Germans pinched my best Y.M.C.A. breeches——"

"Oh, I don't want any of your tales! Trousers under the bed in England because the Germans did something to your precious breeches! Don't you try to tell the tale to me! I'm too old a bird to be caught with salt on its tail." She opened the bed, and pushed in a stone bottle wrapped in red flannel. "Come on, shove down your feet! Don't curl up like a spider. I'm not going to tickle them. Now put the thermometer back under your tongue, and don't talk this time, or it won't register properly." She shook out the trousers, and began to fold them. "Why, you've been sleeping in them, what a thing! You're not in the trenches now, you know. Such a nice new pair, too, you ought to be ashamed of yourself. No talking, now! Not until I take out that thermometer from your mouth." She put away coat and trousers, turned the socks inside out, and laid them on a sofa. Then his shirt, and short cotton pants. Removed the thermometer. "Ninety-nine point two. There, you see what comes of skylarking about downstairs, when you're supposed to be in bed! I heard you, and a fine old time you were having, judging by the row inside the smoking room. Lucky for you Miss Shore didn't come in and catch you at it! Now drink your milk, and be a good boy and put on your pyjamas, and be quick about it, while I go round the other rooms."

Chapter 15

RELAPSED HERO

8 July, 1918. *at* Tregaskis House,
Flushing,
FALMOUTH.

Dear Father and Mother

The above is my address for the next few weeks. I arrived here the day before yesterday, and am now fully recovered from my slight indisposition. By the way, we all wear plain clothes here (or mufti as some I.A. officers call it) and as there is no rank in a convalescent home, please do not put any regiment, etc., on the envelope, or any rank, just P. S. T. Maddison Esq. (my substantive rank is Lieut., of course, but that should not be put on the envelope). And please do not give my address to anyone at all, as I can't write letters in reply, so keep it from *everyone*, even Mrs. Neville. When I leave here, after a Board (Medical) I am entitled to three weeks' leave at home, when I shall see you. Until then, please keep the secret of my whereabouts.

There are a number of M.L.s here, fast submarine chasers, built in the U.S.A. and Canada, each with two 250 h.p. petrol engines and capable of doing 40 knots (a knot is a sea-mile per hour, not, as Kipling wrote, 'knots per hour'). I can't say any more, for obvious reasons. Yesterday there was a bit of a row, because a certain Scots captain went out with one, having made friends with the skipper, an R.N.V.R. lieutenant, and came back very late, after midnight, having been almost so far as the Scillies, on a hunt of a U-boat. I have heard of other 'mysteries' in that connexion, but will say no more now.

How is Gran'pa and Aunt Marian? Give them my love. Also Elizabeth and Doris. And Mrs. Bigge and Mrs. Rolls. Tell Mrs. Neville I am looking forward to seeing her when I come home, and give her my most grateful thanks for looking after Sprat for me. I have written a brief note of thanks to the Duchess of G. for her kindness & hospitality.

I share a room with an elderly fellow from the A.S.C. and this morning we went down a path through the woods to the private quay and boathouse belonging to the estate. The water is warm, and we bathed. We wore long dressing gowns of white towelling, which are provided. The home is run by Miss Shore, a middle-aged lady who pays for everything from her private income. She lives in Campden Hill, in W. London, and rents this place from a Miss Tregaskis, daughter of the late Lord St. Austell.

There are all sorts of officers here, infantry, gunners, flying corps, tanks, etc. I must dash now, I am with a party going to sail in a quay-punt, a half-decked yacht of sorts, rather tubby and very stiff in a breeze. It holds six, and belongs to an old sailor called Tonkin.

Love to all,
Your affectionate son
Phillip (with one 'p')

P.S. My correct address is as above; not c/o.

Major Wetley wrote in a diary every night, after his cup of tea, an act which led Phillip to buy a commonplace book in Falmouth, in which to record his impressions. His journal had been lost in Flanders.

Hired a rowing boat this afternoon for 1*s*. an hour and rowed to the *Implacable* at its moorings in the Carrick Roads. It lies high in the water, with only a bowsprit left of its former spars and masts. Riding there, with its regular segmented gun-ports, and cracked and peeling brown paint, it looked like a gigantic cockchafer. (I saw one of these insects after the capture of the Pilckem ridge by the Welsh last August, when they routed the Pomeranian Grenadiers, to whom the Kaiser had sent a number of cockchafers, their emblem.) Making fast my boat, I climbed a stairway built up one side, and walked about on deck, noticing that no seagulls appeared to visit there. There was an ominous feeling about this half-rotten 'Frenchie', as Tonkin called it when we sailed round it in the quay-punt. The *Implacable* was one of the prizes taken by Nelson, or handed over afterwards, and so was never used with the British fleet: originally it was the 74-gun *Duguay Trouin*. Going down into the admiral's room, with its windows like the sides of a great lantern projecting over the stern, I had a feeling of its utter vacancy, as though all life had gone out of the ship when it was surrendered, leaving only a cold hostility.

Below the top deck was an under-deck, with ports for the cannons now boarded up. It was a cramping feeling to walk there, one's head held down lest it scrape the rough boards above, or rather slabs of massive wood the seams of which were a little ragged with oakum and pitch. Down below again was a crampingly low under-deck, also supported by rows of teak stanchions, set close together to bear the great weight of the decks above. The hammocks must have been slung here in olden times. The place had a grey, inhuman look increased by the roughness of the wooden ceiling and equally rough floor. Neither looked ever to have been holystoned, perhaps the officers never went to inspect the crew's quarters. I could feel the spirits of men broken here, all tenderness turned into violence except in a few rare souls who were probably derided at first, then in steadiness gaining the respect, even affection, of the majority. They were hard times in those days; we are still on the fringe of them, but the war has taught us many things that will not be lost.

Church on Sundays is optional; nobody goes. I rowed a mile or so up the Fal, to picnic on the rocks of a little bay where were thousands of small yellow shells, among others. The oaks came down to the line of high tide, and I thought that a man could live in the woods for weeks without being found. One could make a cave there, and have a fire at night, the smoke being led up through a hollow tree. After the war, perhaps, I may come here, and live on fish.

One of the M.L. captains, a lieutenant of the R.N.V.R., sailed a hired yacht, and invited two officers—any officers—from the convalescent home to go out with them one day. Phillip went with Swayne. After sailing across to St. Mawes and picnicking, the young married couple invited them to 'take tea' with them at their hotel. Staying at the same place was the elderly skipper of a tramp steamer, who had been commissioned with the rank of commander, R.N.R. He wore the D.S.O. riband, and was said to have sunk a U-boat in the North Atlantic off Ireland while commanding a 'Q ship'—outwardly a defenceless sailing ship being abandoned by her crew, while a submarine stood by to sink it by placing explosive charges in the ship's hold—thus saving a torpedo. But under a dummy boat upturned on the Q ship's poop was a six-pounder. When the submarine appeared, the halves of the dummy boat were flung aside, and the gun-crew went into action.

The Germans soon knew of this trick, and some commanders stood off out of range and sank the 'decoy' ships, crews and all, with their heavier gun.

Phillip and Swayne were told of this hush-hush action by the R.N.V.R. lieutenant, after introducing them to the captain and his wife; and when the two old people had gone upstairs, 'to have a lie down before dinner', as Mrs. R.N.R. said, Mrs. R.N.V.R. remarked, "Don't you think it's rather an odd idea to give a man like that, before the war only the skipper of a tramp steamer, the Distinguished Service Order?"

"Why not?" asked Phillip, "if he sank a German submarine?"

"But he wouldn't have been commissioned if there hadn't been a war. In any case, the D.S.O. should be reserved for pukka naval officers, who are gentlemen."

"Oh."

"And what does that 'oh' mean?"

"Well, what *is* a gentleman?"

"'What *is* a gentleman?' Well, really——!"

"I was thinking of an uncle of mine, years ago. One morning he employed me as honorary unpaid private secretary to write a letter at his dictation."

"What has that got to do with it?" asked Mrs. R.N.V.R., on her face the slightly haughty air she had worn in the presence of Mrs. R.N.R.

"It was entitled, 'What is a Gentleman?', and was a contribution to some letters then appearing in *The Daily News*. My uncle wrote that a party of friends were in a bar drinking with the landlord after closing hours. They were pretty merry, and making a bit of a noise, when a resident in the hotel came to the door and complained. The landlord then came back and, standing before them unsteadily, said sternly, to his drinking companions, 'If you cannot conduct yourselves as gentlemen, I must ask you all to leave at once'."

"Well go on, finish the story!"

"That's all there is."

"But I don't see any point in it!" complained Mrs. R.N.V.R.

"Well, now I come to think of it, there isn't any point," said Phillip, regretting his concealed satire. "Thank you both for a very good party!"

"Come again," said Mrs. R.N.V.R. without enthusiasm.

"Yes, rather! It's been awfully jolly."

"Topping!" said Swayne, adding as they left the hotel, "If you ask my opinion they're a couple of pure bloody unadulterated snobs! That old skipper was a *real* sailor, not a dolled-up nincompoop like that Wavy Navy fop who, I wouldn't mind betting, was never nearer the sea than the winkle stalls at Southend before the war!"

There was so much to do, life was glorious; to awaken in the morning, to realise you were in England, in a bed with white sheets and a carpet on the floor, the sun shining on the lawns below, where thrushes hopped. To get out of bed, put on bathing robe, and your footsteps in the dew left a darker green track among dewdrops glittering and winking sapphire green, blue, red and sometimes a purple glint in the low sun rising above the line of the woods; and walking down the path through the trees to the private boat slip, to dive in and swim around with your two regular bathing companions, young Sandhurst subalterns who, friendly and open, yet held themselves back from full intimacy with one who had no class consciousness and no criticism of others; an odd bird always a little remote and at times almost childish—putting a stone in each wet bathing suit, or broken sticks in their shoes—this senior subaltern who wore the 1914 Star, and three wound stripes, and spoke of poetry as though it were the greatest thing in life; who said that he had kept going through Third Ypres on a bottle of whiskey a night, but who now, when they went together into the hotel bar on the pier at Falmouth asked only for ginger beer.

One morning Phillip went into a drapery and haberdashery shop in the High Street, ostensibly to buy a pair of white socks, in order to scrape acquaintance with the pretty girl sitting in a little glass sentry box, to the roof of which were led overhead wires from the various counters. Told by an elderly assistant that they did not deal in men's wear, he lingered, saying that he wanted also to buy some hair ribbon for his sister, for a birthday present. While being shown various rolls of velvet, silk, and cotton in many colours and widths, he wondered if he dare send the girl in the glass office a note, by what he thought of as the Wooden Overhead Egg-shell Post: for small wooden shells, containing bills and cash, were shot from the various counters by spring triggers, to speed over the wires and stop above the glass office, and drop into a wire basket. The wooden shell was unscrewed, paper and cash taken out; receipted bill and change sped back to its counter.

Dare he risk being thought a bounder by enclosing his card in a wooden egg? He dared not; and left the shop looking straight ahead, with three kinds of hair ribbon.

The next afternoon when he went in for more ribbon, another girl was in the glass box. The elderly assistant at the ribbon counter asked him if he had managed to get his white socks.

"I'm afraid I didn't." He was about to leave when the girl in the box came out and told him where he could find a shop which sold men's wear. Upon his saying that he was from the convalescent home, she replied, "Father and Mother feel that my sister and I ought to do our bit by helping to cheer up wounded soldiers. We hire a boat for the summer, and perhaps you and others from Tregaskis House would like to come for a picnic up the Fal?"

He arranged to go the next day, and to take one of his bathing companions. Formality was soon dropped. Beth, the elder girl, was fair-haired and eighteen, quite old, thought Phillip, because of her grown-up manner; Editha, too, who was sixteen and had recently left school, had a grown-up air about her, but she played the piano and was interested in poetry, knowing some of the works of Tennyson, Wordsworth, and best of all, the *Songs of Innocence* by William Blake.

For the next four afternoons he called to see Editha, being invited into the apartment above the shop, where was a railed-in roof-top terrace leading out of french windows—a sunny place with views over the harbour and beyond to St. Anthony-in-Roseland, where a white octagonal lighthouse rose above the sea, no longer showing its beams because of German submarines. The dreaded Manacle Rocks were five miles westward.

He had tea upon the terrace with Editha. Her mother, Mrs. Sithney, a kind old lady (as he thought of her; she was forty years of age) left 'the two young people to themselves', after coming to say how d'you do. It was all fun, thought Phillip; and forgot all about Editha when a new attraction arrived at the convalescent home—three children on bicycles from one of the country houses in the district, for a picnic party arranged by Miss Shore on board the *Foudroyant*.

Two of the children were twins, sixteen years of age, and different in every aspect except a merry outlook on life. Both had developed mumps at the end of the Whitsun vacation and had remained in quarantine at home. The boy, a naval cadet, was small and dark; his twin sister was big and fair, with yellow hair falling over her shoulders. The third was a cousin, a girl of ten, with a face and self-contained expression that promised beauty later on. Phillip was immediately attracted to them, and became the fourth child of a quartet seeking fun and adventure.

A picnic to 'the Frenchman' was arranged—Miss Shore, Mr. Barley Swann, Swayne, Coupar, two other officers, and Nurse Goonhilly sailing to the hulk by quay-punt, while Phillip and the children were towed in the dinghy, already deep in a friendship which was to last forever in his mind, a memory of golden days and laughter—diving from the platform below the companion-way leading up to the massive deck of the ship, exploring the lower decks, one under the other, in deepening gloom until they sat, arms around one another, above the ugly yellow bilge water rocking with the tidal motion of the great and ruinous wooden hulk. It was a melancholy moment saying goodbye, after lingering until the last moment in lengthening shadows; to watch the bicycling figures ever turning to wave, to hear the last far cry of 'Don't forget to come over early for lunch to-morrow, will you?'; but his spirits recovered at the thought of bridge in the games room.

14 July

The Tregaskis twins came over after breakfast to take me to lunch at Carligan. I walked a couple of miles to their place, while they rode bikes, one on either side of me, each a hand on my shoulder. Squire T. was at Truro, their mother homely and friendly. She was brought up in a large Irish family. We had cottage pie then strawberries and cream. Afterwards the twins planted me in a large leather chair in their father's study, while I wondered what he would say if he came in suddenly, finding them rummaging in the drawers of his desk to find me a cigar, while I sat there, wearing a sort of dark Napoleonic hat which B. had dared me to wear, saying that it had been bought by her father, years ago, when he thought he was going to be appointed High Sheriff, only he wasn't. We explored the outbuildings, and there was an old motor-car under a dust-sheet weighed down by bits of straw, etc. from starlings nesting in the roof above. We took it off, and tried to start the engine, J. having got a can of petrol from somewhere. I cleaned the plug, then the make-and-break, flooded the surface-carburettor, filled the cylinder with gas, called out, 'Contact!' while J. switched on. It fired, and thumped away, sending out clouds of blue smoke. I switched off, and looked at the oil level, it was well up, so asked if we ought to be doing what we were. B. said her father never gave it a thought; the De Dion hadn't been driven for years. Anyway, I thought we ought to ask their mother, so her brother J. asked her and returned saying, 'It's all right to drive it'.

We pumped up the tyres, which were a bit cracked, and rather gingerly I tried the gears, after we'd shoved it out of the shed. The clutch worked smoothly so we set off around a field. Mrs. T. having no objection, we went back to Tregaskis House to tea. Miss S. was a bit anxious at first, thinking I'd pinched it without permission, but on being reassured said gaily, 'Come along in and have some strawberries and cream', which we did, to the strains of *In a Monastery Garden* muffled by the doors of the cabinet being closed, as the control plunger is still stuck at loud.

Afterwards I took them back home, and put the De Dion Bouton, now renamed *Boanerges*, in the shed.

After dinner Miss S. took me aside and said with a sigh, "Such a pity, that Captain T. drinks." Then she said, "Oh, I am no better than a scandalmonger! Please never repeat what I said. What I intended to say, only please do not be hurt, is that I know what happened on the night of your arrival, and while I do not wish to blame anyone, I must tell you that it must never happen again. You see, I have known so many friends go to the wall through intemperance, young men with all the world before them, who ended up by sleeping on the Embankment, and earning an odd copper by holding horses' heads in the Strand."

The three met every day; then the twins were gone back to school, and he felt desolate until, remembering the Sithney girls, he took the penny steamboat across to the Pier and walked up the High Street to the shop. Editha was sitting in the glass sentry box. He lingered a moment in the doorway, regarding those bright brown eyes, the high forehead from which the brown hair was brushed back to fall, below the black ribbon at the nape of her neck, over the shoulders to her waist. Her ears were a delicate shape, and close to her head—an endearing sight. The nose was slightly aquiline, her teeth, fine and regular but slightly protruding, or so it seemed, for he had seldom seen her except when she was smiling at some gentle thought, or at him.

The female shop assistants, a contented and elderly lot, were watching the couple. Their faces showed pleasure. Miss Edie had been their favourite from her babyhood up.

"Good morning, Phil!"

"Good morning, Edie! I must make a purchase." He was wearing a blue cornflower in his buttonhole, given him by Miss Shore that morning. Having bought a yard of black garter elastic, he took the flower and put it in the wooden egg with the bill and sixpence, then whizzed it over its wire. He watched her take out the flower, and make as if to pin it to her blouse; but changing her mind, she put it among the marigolds in the glass vase before her, and taking 1½d. from the till, whizzed it back in the wooden egg with a radiant smile.

"I'll be off duty in five minutes. Do go up if you'd like to." While he was sunning himself on the terrace beyond the french windows Beth came out and asked him if he were free on Sunday afternoon to come to tea. "And stay to supper if you feel like it."

"Music afterwards? Oh good!"

"Mother and Father only allow hymns on Sunday, you know."

"I like hymns. Such as *Rock of Ages*, *Lead Kindly Light*, and *Many Brave Hearts are Asleep on the Deep*."

"That's not a hymn, that's a song!"

"How about *Annie Laurie*?"

"You're being deliberately irreverent, aren't you?"

"Well, not altogether. A love song is in a way a hymn. What about *The Song of Solomon*? That's a love song."

"But it's in the Bible, and it foretells the love of Our Lord's Mission on earth."

"So does poetry, Beth. It all leads to God."

"Are you being serious?"

"Perfectly. The purpose of God on earth is to create beauty in all His forms; you can see that in evolution, how birds' feathers are beautiful, when once they were skin-wings."

"I agree with you there. 'All things bright and beautiful, all creatures great and small'. Do you call that poetry?"

"Of course. Just as the harmonium is music, or the song of the crow is music."

"Now you're being sarcastic! I believe you are really a wolf in sheep's clothing!"

"No, I'm a ram in wolf's clothing!"

"Whatever do you mean by that nonsense?"

"I mean that the crow is a faithful bird, and sings in a little under-voice to his mate on awakening, every morning. Or to the sky, for happiness that another day is starting. The same thing! If he hadn't got a mate, he would be cawing for one."

"Really, you do talk nonsense at times, Phillip!"

He felt deflated; what to him was an observed fact, was to Beth obvious nonsense. He felt he had let her down in her estimation of himself; and this idea, which he had not really believed, came again when Editha arrived with her mother to sit with them. Mrs. Sithney stayed until tea-time, during tea, and after tea, crocheting away, saying little, but occasionally putting in a question obviously to satisfy curiosity about his origins, if not his intentions. He invented information.

"My father used to go over a lot to Brussels before the war," he told her, thinking of what Mr. Jenkins at home had told him years ago about himself, "to see his silkworm factory."

"You mean a silk factory, do you not, Phillip?"

"Oh no, it is, or was, a silkworm factory. Father had an idea that he could invent a method by which silkworms could be trained to spin their silk direct on to bobbins, and so save their time and the factory's in one go. I'm talking nonsense, really." Obviously he had put his foot in it; Mrs. Sithney sat silent, as though disapproving. No, he wouldn't accept for supper on Sunday; not after all the family had come back from chapel on Sunday afternoon.

"Well, thanks so much, Mrs. Sithney. It has been so enjoyable. Don't take me too seriously will you? As a matter of fact, the silk people *are* trying to find a substitute for real silk. One of the fellows in the convalescent home, Captain Courtauld, whose people live at Nottingham, tells me that chemists are actually trying to find substitutes. Goodbye, Edie."

"I'll come to the door with you." Downstairs she said, "Mother is a very truthful person, and doesn't understand your fancies, Phil. I do," she breathed, squeezing his hand.

It was a little after six o'clock when he reached the pier, to see the penny steamboat chuffing away to Flushing quay, so he went into the long bar of the Pier Hotel and ordered a double whiskey, sitting by himself and reliving old times with Jack Hobart and Freddy Pinnegar in the Angel at Grantham in the autumn of 1916, and with 'Spectre' a year later in Flossie Flowers' pub in Jermyn Street. What was a girl's innocent face compared with such friendships, such times together, gone for evermore? And yet—that tremulous hand-clasp, the gentle voice, *I do*.

That evening sky and water burned with sunset. He remained on the quay until red became purple, and crossing over on the ferry boat, got back to Tregaskis House when dinner was over, to hide among the trees when he saw the others strolling on the lawn with Miss Shore, enjoying the warmth and colour of the day's end to the strains of *A Monastery Garden*. Dodging back from tree to tree, he hastened unseen down to the quay, and on impulse hired a boat with an outboard motor, and set out to cross the bay to the lighthouse with a two-gallon tin of petrol-oil on board, which cost him £1, for petrol was no longer publicly sold. It had come from one of the crew of an M.L. There was a nice pub in St. Mawes, where he had taken Wetley one evening, and they had had a good time in the Rising Sun. Now Wetley was gone away; life was always like that, everything ending, every parting a little death.

Not finding what he was seeking in the Rising Sun he went back to the boat and made for the lighthouse at the entrance to the Roads. Could he make the Scillies on two gallons? Or rather one gallon, for he would have to come back. Grant-Browne, the rude Highlander, had spent a couple of nights in the Scillies, with the crew of an M.L., and been sent away on his return by Miss Shore. What about navigating the Manacles? If he went down, well, he would go down and be with Jack Hobart and 'Spectre' West.

There was a fort near the lighthouse, and as he was passing, the boat lifting and dropping in the choppy tide, a siege-gunner with a megaphone called out, "Go back! Go back to harbour!"; so turning round, he had the wind with him, and enjoyed the rolling of the boat, then the plunge, waves riding him high before the drop and wallow in each succeeding trough. Thoroughly exhilarating!

"My Gor', us thought you wasn't comin' back, midear!" said the boat owner at Flushing quay.

He got in without being seen, and going up to his bedroom, unobserved by the others in the lighted drawing-room, went to bed and read *Clayhanger* until Nurse Goonhilly came up to tell him shortly that it was after midnight, and his light must go out. Paraffin was rationed she said, and the batteries were low. "You ought to know better, *Colonel* Maddison!"

In the morning, after breakfast, she said, "Miss Shore would like to see you in her boudoir, *Colonel* Maddison!"

"'Colonel'," tittered Swayne. "'Boudoir'! What next?"

"Yes, '*Colonel*'," repeated Nurse Goonhilly. "*And* 'boudoir'! You'll see, Swayne."

"You sound like a duenna out of *The Boccaccio*, Goony dear."

"I don't want any of your cheek, Swayne."

"'Swine', you mean," said Coupar. "This kipper is dried up, Goony darling. Can I have a boiled egg?"

"You're lucky to get anything, Coupar."

"Brigadier-General Coupar, please," said Swayne. "Or should it be Lance-Corporal? I hear Mr. Barley Swann is now a Rear-Admiral. Very much rear." Then, as the nurse went out, "Doesn't get his greens, I fancy. Oh, so pure, in a monastery garden!"

Phillip went to see Miss Shore in her room, with its many photographs in silver frames among vases of flowers. He was prepared for a reprimand.

"So you have been hiding your light under a bushel, Mr. Maddison!" she said, with a shy smile and movement of head that swept his face momentarily with a glance almost coy. "Did you see yesterday's *Times*?"

"No, Miss Shore," he replied, puzzled.

"Then I am the first to congratulate you? How splendid! I say it with all my heart! I am so proud to think that one of my 'young men', as I think of you all——" Miss Shore, almost overcome by sentiment, fussed with a tiny laced handkerchief—"But you must see for yourself——" She gave him the newspaper folded back at a column headed *The London Gazette*, with its sub-heading *Decorations and Awards*.

"There *you* are, dear boy! I *am* so proud——"

"Good heavens! There must be some mistake!"

It was unbelievable! But there it was, under the section *Distinguished Service Order*—His heart thudded.

"A letter came for you yesterday by the second post, but you were not in all day, so I kept it for you, as it had the Royal Cypher on the envelope!"

"Will you excuse me if I open it, Miss Shore?"

"*Do*, please! Oh, I am *so* excited!"

Within a covering letter was a sheet, typed with a blue ribbon, in italics.

Awarded the Distinguished Service Order. (*temp.*) *Lieutenant* (*A/Lt. Col.*) *Phillip Sidney Thomas Maddison* (*attd.*) 1*st Gaultshire regt, Commanding* 1*st Composite Battalion, British Expeditionary Force in France. For conspicuous devotion to duty and gallantry. Throughout the operations in March* 1918, *he displayed marked courage and determination as a leader, especially at Albert on the night of* 26/27 *March in an attack on superior German forces in the town, resulting in the capture of many prisoners, followed by a skilful withdrawal through encircling enemy forces. It was entirely due to his example, courage, and determination that the Battalion did so well in the face of outnumbering enemy forces.*

He is an extremely keen and resourceful Commanding Officer.

He did not read all of this, but glanced at the sheet of paper, before dropping it on the table; then recovering his manners he offered it to Miss Shore, saying, "I don't deserve it. The man who wrote that is dead, owing to me."

When he had told her part of the story, she said, "I, too, have lost dear friends, and reproached myself afterwards that, if only I had known what I knew later, I might have been able to help." She yearned with sympathy on the *chaise longue*. "But you are so *young*! Do, *please*, believe me when I say that Time will heal the memory—meanwhile, I ask you, most sincerely, not to be too hard on yourself!"

"Miss Shore, do the others know about this?"

"I have told no-one. Oh dear, I thought you would be *so* glad, and proud, to learn that you had been paid such a wonderful tribute! And at your age, how splendid!"

If only he had gone down with Westy.

At two o'clock on that Sunday afternoon, having drunk seven double whiskeys in the Pier Hotel by himself, he walked out at closing time and knew that he had only a short while before he passed out. He managed to get to the Sithney's side-door, and with a feeling that all below his head was without weight turned the handle and, with the door safely shut behind him, gained enough hope to haul himself up the stair-rail to the landing, where, locking himself in the lavatory he knelt down and all dissolved in his mind except the remote need to remain on his knees waiting until froth and nausea gave way to further need to hide. Time went by without knowledge of its passing. At last he got up, shuddering with cold, and made his way to Editha's bedroom, where he crawled under the bed and became unconscious.

When next he was aware of himself he heard the sister saying, "Oh Phil, how *could* you, and on Edie's birthday?"

"Don't tell anyone," he managed to say.

"They know already. Edie came in, and I heard her cry out before she fainted."

He crawled out, and got on his feet. "It's no use saying I'm sorry, I know, but I *am* terribly sorry."

"Why did you do it? And on a *Sunday*——"

"I don't know. I'll go. Oh yes, I must first apologise to your parents——"

"I don't think that would mend matters. I'll tell them that you have, though."

"Is Edie very upset?"

"Yes, very!"

"Might I see her for a moment?"

"What good would it do, Phil? You must never see her again."

"Very well, but please tell her I am truly sorry."

Under the tan of summer her face was almost as pale as his own. "Goodbye, Phil. I'll come and let you out——"

"No, I can do it. Really——"

"No, I must make sure that nobody will see you."

She peered into the street. It was quiet and empty, people were at their tea. "You realise that you've made it quite impossible, don't you, for you to see Edie again?"

"I always seem to make things impossible. Well, thank you all for your kindness to a rotter."

When he got back to the house he avoided the room where they were having tea, and, creeping upstairs, locked himself in his bedroom. When Nurse Goonhilly knocked on a panel, he lay still on the bed.

"I know where you've been! And a nice way you chose to celebrate your success! The whole town knows of it! What did you want to do it for? Come on, open the door, and drink this warm milk."

When he would not open the door she went away; and returned with Miss Shore, followed by other footfalls. He heard Swayne suggest a ladder to the windows. Coupar capped this by saying, "How about fetching the Fire Brigade, Miss Shore?"

"Oh dear, do you think he might set fire to himself? I have heard of such things happening."

At this he got up and opened the door.

The next morning Miss Shore told him that he would have to go away. She could not risk a recurrence of what had happened, she said. He listened to an earnest and embarrassing lecture on the evils of drink.

"I had a very dear friend, he was very dear indeed to me, when I was young, but he drank, Colonel Maddison, and today he is holding the heads of horses! No, I am afraid we cannot give you another chance. In any case your time is nearly up. Dr. Bull has arranged for you to be transferred to Devonport Military Hospital. You will be leaving this afternoon. I have asked Jack to take your bags in the governess cart to Flushing, and a taxi is to meet you on the pier and take you to the station. I will say goodbye, now. You will *try*, for your mother's sake, to overcome your—your terrible propensity, won't you?"

"Yes, Miss Shore. And thank you for all you have done for me."

Devonport Military Hospital. Patients allowed out 2 p.m.–7 p.m. daily. Prison-like high walls; small area of garden divided off from a smaller area in which the venereal cases were isolated and totally enclosed.

Plymouth Hoe. Broad parade whereon walked or sat seemingly thousands of young officers, of all shapes, sizes and classes; one-third of them intent on trying to get to know the few score of girls in the summer weather. A boring, arid place, until an afternoon in Genoni's Café when a young junior subaltern across the table offered him a cigarette from a gold case. He explained that he was at Durnford Street hospital, that the case was a twenty-first birthday present from his mother. Thenceforward they met every afternoon outside the Theatre Royal.

It was a gay summer friendship by the sea, with nothing to check mutual liking. 'Gibbo', from Eastbourne, and 'Maddo', from south-east London, ate oysters and drank stout in Jones's Oyster Bar; they walked miles up and down Union Street, seeking interest and pleasure; joined the promenaders upon the broad asphalt of the Hoe, laughing and talking; visited Williams' and Goodbody's for tea, saw flicks at the Savoy, Gaiety, the Palladium, drawn by Charlie Chaplin or William Hart; they called, as time of return within walls drew near, at Nicholson's sawdust bar for crab sandwiches, the long bar of the Royal for sherry, the Poseda for Pimm's No. 1 stout, the Athenaeum where many midshipmen were to be seen; or descending to shadier, more attractive places, drank beer in the Golden Lion, the Post Office, the Corn Exchange, the Old Chapel, where port and madeira came from the wood at sixpence a dock glass. In one sailor's pub they were shown the skeleton of a baby in an ebony coffin over the counter—not a place to revisit, they agreed.

Gibbo sometimes stuck on a Charlie Chaplin moustache, while wearing an eyeglass with his usual languid manner. They were photographed together, Phillip with cap on one side of his head, a lieutenant's stars on his shoulder straps, but no ribands on his left breast—thus keeping faith with the undistinguished dead.

It was a tremendous friendship while it lasted; and it lasted all their lives—in Phillip's memory. Soon they were to go their separate ways. In the meantime they met 'Lux', a young Marine who had been at school with 'Gibbo'. The two men talked of Eton, and all Phillip could think to say was, "Did you by any chance know a chap named Swayne?" Lux and Gibbo laughed lightly and replied, "Oh Swayne! Ha-ha-ha, oh yes, we knew Swayne. Have *you* met Swayne?"

He told them all about the Algerian wine party.

"Oh yes, that sounds like Swayne, indeed yes," and all three laughed gently, lightly, together.

Dear delightful Gibbo. One afternoon the sunshine seemed not to glitter. "I shan't be seeing you tomorrow, Maddo, my dear. I'm being boarded, and go home by the afternoon train."

A last toasted-tea-cake at Genoni's, a last dozen oysters at Jones's, two final docks of dark brown sherry at the Old Chapel;

and then the hand clasp, Gibbo saying calmly through his teeth, "Well, all the best, Maddo. I suppose I'll be back in France this time next month."

"I want to get back as soon as I can, Gibbo."

"Pity we aren't in the same regiment, Maddo. It would be fun going over the top together."

"Yes, indeed it would, Gibbo."

"So long, Maddo."

"So long, and all the best, Gibbo."

So long—for ever.

Phillip asked for a board the next day. One among several score of officers, all needed for the coming Allied counter-offensive on the Western Front, he was perfunctorily passed fit for Active Service, and given three weeks' leave and a railway warrant to London. It was 19 July. The mid-day editions of the London evening papers carried thick black headlines of Foch's counter-offensive on the Marne, with sketches arrow'd in the shoulders of the great salient left by the German drive to Paris in May, when the city had been shelled by a long-range gun, and from the Eiffel Tower at night could be seen the lights of the battlefield beside the Marne.

It was too early to go home, so he decided to call on Mr. Howlett, his old manager in the office, and was taken to lunch in the London Tavern.

"I always knew you had it in you, Phillip. Downham's a colonel, too, you know, so is young Sparks of the Accident Department at Head Office. He's got the M.C. as well as the D.S.O. I often wonder how you young fellows will settle down to office routine after the war? It can't be long now, the Germans are very shaky over raw materials, the Blockade is having its effect. Well, I shan't be sorry, apart from everything else, it's been a hard grind to get through the work. We've lost a lot of fellows, you know, over eighty have been killed in the various branches in London and the provinces. I saw your father the other day, he always comes in to pay his midsummer premium. You have some commission due to you, I'll keep it until you come back, shall I?"

"Thank you, Mr. Howlett. Will Downham be coming back to the Branch, d'you think?"

"I see no reason at present why he won't be. He was in the other day. He's commanding a Young Soldiers' battalion at Colchester."

If Downham comes back, I won't literally be seen for dust, thought Phillip, imagining the new Norton motorcycle he had ordered, the first on the list of post-war deliveries. He would go down to the West Country, and live alone in the woods. This feeling came again that evening when he went down to Mrs. Neville's flat. Seeing him, Sprat almost curled tail stump to nose; the little dog looked most unhappy until suddenly it ran up the stairs and hid under the table.

"I know how he feels, Mrs. Neville."

"It is only for the moment, Phillip. Time restores, you know, as well as heals."

He looked at her sharply. "Why do you say 'heals', Mrs. Neville?"

"Oh, no particular reason, dear," she said gently. His eyes had a fixed remote look; the scarred skin of his face seemed stretched over nose, cheek-bones, and jaw. "Things will seem a bit strange at first, Phillip, they're bound to." She went on, after a few moments of unhappy silence, "I understood why you didn't reply to my letter, congratulating you on your—award, is that the word? Also, you must have had a great many letters of congratulation."

"Five, Mrs. Neville. One from Freddy Pinnegar, one from Mr. Howlett at the office, and one each from Gran'pa, Aunt Marian and Uncle Hilary, who asked me to get in touch with him."

"You will, I suppose?" She knew from Phillip's mother that Hilary Maddison had bought back family land in the West Country; and that he had no children of his own.

"I don't know, Mrs. Neville. How is Desmond?"

"Oh, *my* son can be relied upon to look after himself, you know that! He's guarding the East Riding against German raiders, or was when I last heard. I've no need to worry myself over Desmond!" She went on to ask about his parents. "I expect Father is *very* proud of you now, Phillip! I often see him going to his allotment in the evenings, wheeling his barrow-load of tools. He was very pleased to see you, I expect?"

"I don't know, Mrs. Neville."

"Of course he was, dear! Your Mother came down here,

waving Grandpa's *Telegraph* when you were in the papers. I can tell you, it was quite a local sensation. Did you hear that?"

The terrier who had been shivering under the table crept out, and lifting up its head, uttered a long, cooing howl. Then turning away, it went to its rug under Mrs. Neville's bed. Phillip got up.

"Well, I mustn't keep you, Mrs. Neville. Goodbye."

"Phillip!" She turned in her chair, round-eyed. "What is the matter, dear? I've felt all the time you've been here that something is worrying you. Won't you tell me? You know that you can trust me with your confidence, surely, by now?"

He dropped back into his chair, all sharp bones she thought, knees sticking out of trousers, thin wrists, neck and bony skull. She caught her breath with the pity of it.

"I wish I hadn't come home," his voice said levelly, behind the half-shaded face.

"You felt like that when you came home after 1914, dear. It will pass."

"Do you know, Mrs. Neville, I've *always* felt more or less like this since I was a child, and Mother had scarlet fever! Mavis and I went away to stay with Uncle Hilary and Aunty Bee. When Mother came to fetch me, I hid, and wouldn't kiss her. You know, to be truthful, I never really got back my old feeling for her again. At the time I didn't know why I felt that I wanted to pay her out, for having me sent away. My feeling for my father had already gone by then. It wasn't his fault, or Mother's. It isn't Mavis' fault that she's what she is. But the truth is, I can't bear them any longer——"

She began to feel swelled with pain as she looked at him; something *had* happened to him: the old Phillip, gay and full of fun, who could always laugh at himself, was gone. She wanted to comfort him, but was impotent to say or do anything, and from the swelled feeling tears oozed, to run down her cheeks. "Sprat knows, Phillip," she managed to say. "Look at him, the little dear, he knows what you are feeling." The dog had crept back into the room, and was staring at his old master. "Make a fuss of him, dear!" she cried.

"I don't want to," he said. The dog was now hiding its head in her skirt. "I must go now, Mrs. Neville."

"Come and see me again, Phillip. I'm always here, you know," she managed to say, with an attempt at gaiety.

Chapter 16

ROSES AND REWARDS

He went back after only four days of his leave to Landguard. To his relief, Denis Sisley was in the orderly room.

"You're entitled to put up the cherry ripe riband with the blue bars, you know. Oh yes, rather! No need to wait until you go to Buck House. By the way, on Wednesday the Colonel is taking a bunch of the old sweats to Husborne for Minden Day. He's away in London at the moment, but you're to attend the party, so let me see that manly breast properly adorned."

"Minden Day?"

"First of August. You'll have to eat your rose in the evening, washed down by bubbly. It's an old custom, and apparently not done to ask why."

On arrival with other senior officers of the Regiment at the Abbey Phillip was led to a large bedroom with a four-poster bed, a thick blue carpet which muffled his footfalls, and, among other furniture, a writing desk inlaid with lighter woods in an intricate pattern of flowers, above which was a level top behind a gilt trellis. Here stood a large gold bowl of red and yellow roses, flanked by candlesticks of the same metal, each nearly two feet tall and fluted above stepped-up bases. His room was behind the red-baize door preserve. Wonder at his position possessed him; how had it happened? With no belief in his own powers, he thought of himself as evasive of all real life, unlike other men, who got to and held their positions by deliberate force of will. Everything so far in his life had happened in spite of himself, all was due to a series of flukes. He had known that when having lunch with Mr. Howlett during which the idea of going back to the Moon Fire Office after the war had been unthinkable.

A double knock on the door. "Come in!" The door opened, and Colonel Vallum entered.

"Hullo, Maddison. I've come to offer my congratulations."

"Thank you, Colonel."

"Vallum to you. How are you feeling? All the gas effects

cleared up? Good. What wonderful roses. I've got some in my room. That's an old moss rose, you don't see many of them today. Good to see you again."

"When do we wear our roses? Tonight?"

"Tomorrow. One of each colour, on the left side of the service cap. They've been practising Trooping the Colour all this afternoon. A bit ragged, inevitably, but these boys are coming on nicely."

Phillip wanted to ask what the origin of the roses was, but forebore: he imagined that it was an incident similar to that when the Cherrypickers got their nickname, after eating cherries on their way up to some old battle. Perhaps it was Minden? He did not like to ask, so powerful a personality was Colonel Vallum to him, with that rock-like steadiness behind massive imperturbability; before which Phillip's inner core of diffidence revealed itself in the sudden remark, "You know, sir, I feel a complete fraud to be here. I did nothing, really, it was all a tremendous fluke—Albert, I mean."

"I think we all feel like that when we think about ourselves." Behind the held-back glance of grey eyes was friendliness. "These things are after all a tribute to the Regiment." The speaker noticed Phillip's glance at the maroon riband, with its miniature bronze cross: the ten-thousandth glance he had had to endure with equanimity. "After all, nothing is ever done without one's men. Otherwise such things would have no justification, as I see it, in modern war. And talking about flukes," went on Vallum, "Minden was a classic example of a battle won almost by chance. As you know, in the Seven Years War, Austria, France, Russia, Sweden and Saxony combined to knock out Prussia under Frederick the Great. In the end we went to help Prussia, sending the equivalent of a small expeditionary force of infantry and cavalry. There was a gale blowing on August the First, 1759, and our infantry advanced through a mistake in delivering an order against the French flank. We went up through some rose gardens, and helped ourselves, whence these"—he pointed to the blooms in the silver gilt bowl—"and caught the French on the hop. The cavalry under Sackville didn't follow through, so the infantry went on to victory by themselves. So here we are!"

"Have you read, by any chance, the poems called *Counter Attack*, sir?"

"Oh yes. I read them in course of duty. I'm Intelligence at the War House, for my sins."

"What do you think of them, sir?"

"Oh, I think we've all felt like that, at one time or another. I'm no judge of poetry, but I heard Winston Churchill at White's talkin' about them the other day. 'Cries of pain wrung from soldiers during a test to destruction', were his words. Well, I must bathe, and dress for dinner. See you downstairs. By the way, Maddison, I asked you to call me Vallum."

August the First opened calm and clear. Phillip was awake, and reading Joseph Conrad's *Heart of Darkness* when bugles sounded Reveille. Almost at once came the sound of drums; he went to his open window; the band was approaching the Abbey from the park. Entering under the Gate House, they marched round the courtyard upon which his windows looked. Under the sun, now burnishing the sloping roofs and chimney stacks of the far side of the Abbey and casting shadows on the cobblestones behind the Drum Major twirling his gold stick, the walls resounded with the crash and blare of the Minden March. The side drummers wore white leather aprons, the bass drummer a leopard skin. All wore roses in caps and upon the cords of the drums. He saw heads leaning out of windows to left and right, some above pyjama coats, like himself.

When the band had marched away under the arch of the Gate House he flung on burberry and made for the bathroom, where he quickly shaved while water gushed from a massive silver tap into the deep and narrow bath, set on a lead base to trap and lead away splashings. The bath, enclosed in mahogany, was deep enough to drown two people at once. He filled it a third full, over a foot deep, and got in, to lie down, pull himself up and soap himself quickly, then dipping again, stood up and dried in a huge towel while the water gurgled away down the trap. Others would be wanting the bathroom; he was out within three minutes of entering, to see Vallum walking down in bath-robe and red Algerian slippers without heels, like those brought back by Grandpa and Mr. Newman from their travels years ago.

The Trooping the Colour took place at the other end of the park, on the parade ground of the Command Depôt. The G.O.C. Eastern Command took the salute on a dais, the senior officers standing behind the Colonel of the Regiment; behind them were other officers from the hospital. Everything looked new—the pressed tunics and trousers of the troops taking part, roses in their service cap bands, rifle butts gleaming with oil, the Colour adorned with roses. He quivered, near to tears; shook back his feelings, while his mind burned within ancient sunlight of Somme and Bullecourt, Poperinghe, the Bull Ring at Etaples, the white chalk parapets of the Bird Cage, the brown desolation of the Messines Ridge. *Posterity, posterity!*—a sentence from Francis Thompson's essay on Shelley ran in his head with the beat of the drums—*posterity which goes to Rome, and weeps large-sized tears, carves beautiful inscriptions, over the tomb of Keats; and the worm must wriggle her curtsey to it all, since the dead boy, wherever he be, has quite other gear to tend. Never a bone the less dry for all the tears!*

And now it was ending; and he wanted it to go on, for ever and for ever, in the sunlight which was shining on the dead, in the spirit which carried all who had walked away from love at home and found a greater love in friendship of men like Father Aloysius in the land of pain and destruction; but it was over; and the battalion of Young Soldiers was marching away, the column getting smaller against the dark hutments of military servitude.

The officers and sergeants waited on the men's dinners, the tables set with vases of roses and pint glasses of ale, roast pork, baked potatoes, batter pudding with chopped sage and onions, and then plum duff with dates instead of currants. Then to a cold luncheon in the sergeants' mess, after which the Colonel of the Regiment proposed the King, and the Duke made a speech, congratulating the Regimental Sergeant-major, one of the original Mons sergeants of the First battalion, with his Military Cross and Distinguished Conduct Medal ribands, and five wound stripes.

To rest; and at night a dinner in the Great Hall at Husborne, over a hundred officers, Phillip at one end of the high table, eating a rose petal by petal and washing it down with champagne which (Lord Satchville told him afterwards) was cider, matured in bottle for twelve years in the cellars, and 'indistinguishable from all but the best vintages in the caves of Rheims, where expert cellarman turn the bottles, with a special flick of the wrist, every so often, with inherited skill'.

Landguard was anti-climax, but for a few hours only. Soon he was at home in his old billet in Manor Terrace. There was bathing from the shingle bank, tennis on the courts of Felixstowe, and bridge in the ante-room after parades. He was now second-in-command of a company, with the acting rank and pay of a captain.

There was to be a tennis tournament at Felixstowe in the third week of August. There were dances at night in the Felix Hotel—to waltzes, fox-trots, and one-steps on the gramophone; a string quartet played for tea every Saturday and Sunday afternoon. By now the actualities of war had passed beyond memory, as day followed day as hot and bright as that almost forgotten summer of 1914.

For the war was going well at last. On the 8th of that month had come the British counter-push, with tanks, a brilliant victory for the Australians, New Zealanders, and British divisions. In the first step, tanks and infantry had penetrated beyond divisional to corps headquarters, taking many prisoners, including German generals, and guns. Monash, who from being a civilian in 1914 in Sydney was now a Lieutenant-General, had planned the attack, with Haig's approval. He was now spoken of as 'the finest General produced by the War'. This was John Monash, a Jew, who could have taken Passchendaele a month earlier than it was taken, according to 'Spectre', Phillip remembered. Ah, if he had lived, and not been knocked out, where would Westy not have got to?

The Yanks were no longer coming (on the piano). They had come. The submarines were mastered, the last Zeppelin had fallen in flames, the Gothas had done, and had, their worst. Every dinner in the mess was a party. The morning sea was warm, glittering under the sun of 7 a.m. Even Sprat had learned to swim.

Young officers arrived from the Command Depôt in dozens. Their faces were hardly observed, their names unknown—except on the company rolls—a brief moment, and they were gone—and new fresh respectful young figures were herding quietly in the ante-room, rising to their feet whenever Phillip entered. He wished they wouldn't.

It was not the same war any longer: the names in the casualty lists no longer dismayed one. Movements forward were in miles where they had been in yards—the same yards, forward and back, a dead man in every other four square yards. And if the old Hun—almost a term of affection—if the old Hun wasn't beaten by the end of the year, he was done for anyway. Germany could no longer win. So eat, drink, and be merry, for tomorrow this life will be over: and then——

War Office,
Whitehall.
28 August, 1918.

Sir,

I am directed by the Secretary of State for War to inform you that you are Commanded to be received at Buckingham Palace for presentation before His Majesty the King at an Investiture of the Insignia of Honours, Decorations, and Awards at 11 a.m. on Monday, September the Sixteenth. Field Service Uniform will be worn.

I have the honour to be,
Sir,
Your Most Obedient Servant
etc.

"You do shoot, don't you, Maddison?" said the Colonel, as Phillip left for a week's leave on the Friday before the Investiture. "My cousin the Duke has asked me to bring two guns for a partridge drive at Husborne on Saturday week. Very well, I shall accept for you, and expect to see you at the Abbey at six o'clock next Friday evening."

Phillip travelled to London with several other officers, including the handsome Colin Keith-Thomson, an actor before the war, who had returned to the regiment after being seconded to the R.F.C. for two years. After 350 flying hours in scout machines Colin had gone to hospital with 'flying sickness debility', and a Military Cross for shooting down 5½ E.A. or Huns as enemy aircraft were called. Now, a footslogger again, he was a little *blasé*, and slept through most of the journey. He was also going to Buck House.

It was agreed, after the 'show', to have luncheon together at the Café Royal, and then go on for drinks to the Joystick Club, a furnished house rented from a peer by some officers of the R.F.C. Colin was a member; there were no rules, he said, except that fighting drunks were scragged. Apparently it was a wilder Flossie Flowers'; the peer's butler had locked up all the glass, china, plate, *objets d'art*, etc., and rolled away the Aubusson carpets. Otherwise the house was as in pre-war days.

"You'll be most welcome," said Colin, awakening as the train drew into Liverpool Street station, to Phillip. "Bring some pumps, we'll probably end up at the Grafton Galleries. There's always a shake-down afterwards. Do come along, and bring a girl if you like, we can put her up, too."

Phillip called at a gunsmith's in the Strand, to look at second-hand 12-bore guns. He chose one with 36-inch damascus barrels, of a pair which had become separated. What knowledge he had of shot-guns had been absorbed from used copies of *The Field*, from the Free Library during schooldays. Some damascus barrels were hand-forged, from old horse-shoe nails beaten flat with iron wire, he had read; while those beaten out by Joe Manton, a classic name, were the best in England. Was it a Joe Manton, he asked; to be told that it was not, otherwise it would be priced considerably higher than £20. This gun was made by one of the best Yorkshire gunsmiths, for grouse.

The taxi was waiting on the kerb. He decided to go home in it, the driver agreeing to the ten-mile run there and back after seeing his rank badges; nor was he disappointed, for he got a five-bob tip in addition to the legal fare.

To Phillip it seemed like standing just over the edge of the world, as he watched the cab turning the corner, leaving him with new valise, leather gun-case, and cartridge bag on the asphalt by the faded green gate. So much had happened to divide him from the boy with dreams of hitting sparrows in the Backfield with catapult and dust-shot wrapped in tissue paper, and baking them in clay, in the embers of his fire hidden in a deep crack in the slope of wild grasses. What was the reality of his life now, in this uniform, with this gun-case?

He must avoid being seen, or spoken to; he pushed his way through the gate, with its old name *Lindenheim* faintly showing under the paint of 1914, before Mrs. Bigge next door could pop out and congratulate him. There she was, the lace curtain pulled aside, waving. He saluted her, smiled, and went on. He is so eager to see his mother, she thought happily.

Hetty, who had been waiting in her bedroom, hurried downstairs when Mrs. Feeney called out, after opening the door, "Master Phillip's come, ma'm!" This delay had been planned, for Hetty did not want to appear too eager. She must behave with restraint, too, in the manner of his admired Duchess. But it was the first time she had seen him in his new uniform, his light serge tunic with leather buttons, *two* ribands, and small gilt star and crown on each of his shoulder straps. She glowed with love and pride, and was near to tears as she stood on the second stair from the bottom, a little above the level of his head; forcing herself to the restraint of, "Well, I hope you had a pleasant journey?" Then her restraint broke, and she said the very words she had, for days, been telling herself that she must never utter, "Oh, we *are* all so proud of you, Phillip! Aren't we, Mrs. Feeney?"

"Yes ma'am, the whole neighbourhood is," and the charwoman went back into the kitchen, to leave the mis'es and her boy alone.

"I have something to show you, in the front room!"

On the table were newspapers, with photographs of him. He picked one up, and after a glance put it down. The next, *The Borough News*, had a snapshot reproduction of him as patrol-leader of the Bloodhound Patrol. 'The boy is father to the man.'

"Did you get the snapshot back? It was from my album, wasn't it?"

"Not yet, but the man has promised to send it back."

"That's what the reporter on *The Express* promised to do with my letter in December 1914, but he didn't send it back, did he?"

"I'll go and see them again, dear. You're quite right. I'm keeping all your other letters, with these papers, for your own little boy, one day."

"I shall never marry."

"Ah, my son, just wait until the right girl comes along!"

"Oh, Mother—please——"

"Well, how are you, anyway?"

"Very well, thank you. How are you?"

"Oh, as well as can be expected—— Quite well, really!"

"I think I'll just go down and see Mrs. Neville. No, I'll change first."

She stopped herself from saying, But you're only just home, and said instead, "Wouldn't you like something to eat first? I've managed to get a chop specially for you, from Mr. Chamberlain."

"Oh really, Mother—we all have *lots* to eat—— But thank you all the same. Where is Father? On the allotment?"

"He's gone to get some new potatoes, specially for you, dear."

"Well, it's most awfully good of you all, but really, as I said, we get plenty of food in the mess. I may be able to send you some partridges next week. I've been asked to shoot with some friends."

"How splendid. I wondered what the gun was for."

"Oh, Mother, what do you think a gun is for?" He saw her face on the edge of weariness, or despair. "You can't say a thing to me, or Father, can you, without being ragged? I'm sorry. Of course it was a fair question, considering the state of Mr. Bigge's greenhouse! Are those airgun holes still there? What a little swine I was in those days, taking Father's gun without permission, and shooting at anything I saw. How are the girls?"

"I'm expecting Doris home any moment, she is coming from Norfolk, where she has been pulling flax."

"Then she must have been on the same train as I was! I wish I'd have known, I could have given her a lift in my bone-shaker. How long is she home for?"

"Doris has got special leave until Monday night, in order to go up to London with us all on Monday."

This was a jag. "What, are you all going to the Old Vic?"

"Well, dear, we thought you would like us to be there when you receive your decoration." She felt unhappy, he was staring at the carpet. "I mean afterwards, of course."

"Who is 'we'?"

"Well, Phillip, we won't get in your way, of course. But as it is such beautiful weather, I thought it would be nice to see the sights."

"Who is 'we'? Father?"

"He won't if you don't want him to, of course—I think he will expect to be asked, perhaps."

"Who else?"

"Oh, Grandpa and Aunt Marian, and the two girls, of course." As he remained silent, she went on, "At any rate, think it over, dear. It was only our idea, but we don't want to stand in your way if you have any other plans."

The fact was that the family-party idea had arisen out of new hope; Hetty and Richard had lived almost buoyantly since that day when he had come home early with a copy of *The Times*, to say almost casually, 'Have you seen the paper, Hetty? *Our* best boy is something of a dark horse, evidently!'

"What about Elizabeth, the butterfly out of the Mavis cocoon?"

"Of course your sister must look her best, Phillip. She has ordered a new frock and hat specially for the occasion. She is very proud of you, as we all are."

"Really!"

Mrs. Feeney, bonnet'd and cape'd, looked round the door. "I'm off now, ma'am. Good luck, Master Phillip, for Monday!"

"Thanks, Mrs. Feeney." When she had gone he said, "I think I'll change, and go for a walk, Mother. Wish I'd brought Sprat—but among other things, he might have upset Mrs. Neville."

"How very thoughtful of you, dear! You *are* so much more thoughtful now, you know! Indeed, in some things *too* thoughtful. There, I didn't mean to criticise you! Come on, give me a kiss."

A brief moment of communion, a temporary freedom from the little ego for Phillip. She said, happily, "Father will be back at a quarter to eight, and Elizabeth too. Doris should be here any moment now. They are such nice lamb chops. Chamberlain let me have four, as it was a special occasion."

"Four? There are five of us. You're not having one yourself, *as usual*, I suppose?"

"Well, Phillip, meat never agrees with me at night. I have to be careful nowadays what I eat. Oh, and before I forget! Gran'pa wants to take us all to lunch at Simpson's, in the Strand, afterwards. It is only for once, after all. And he is so looking forward to it, so don't disappoint him. Dr. Dighton tells me his bronchitis must be watched carefully. Gran'pa did ask your father to come, but he says he has so much to do at the office."

"Father's always hated the old boy's guts, hasn't he?"

"Your language, Phillip!"

"All right, Hetty. Father has always shown a marked disinclination to converse happily with his semi-attached father-in-law. Is that better?"

There was another reason why Richard was self-withdrawn just then. He had asked Hetty to say no word about an incident which had caused him such humiliation that he had been seriously thinking, as he told her, of resigning from the Special Constabulary.

On the last day of August, 14,000 Metropolitan and City policemen had gone on strike. They wanted recognition for their newly formed Trade Union, increase of pay to keep pace with risen costs of living, and reinstatement of a constable who had been active as an organiser of the Union. Thousands of policemen in plain clothes, wearing favours of red and white ribbons, had hung about Whitehall; there were near-violent arguments between constables and civilians; and fearing chaos, particularly in traffic, the Special Constabulary had been called out. Many had refused to appear. Among them, at the Randiswell Station, was a neighbour of Richard's, Mr. Jenkins. "I'm keeping out of this." Richard had reported for duty, and been sent to the City. Traffic being self-regulated, Richard and other Specials were drafted to Downing Street, where many of the policemen in plain clothes were assembled, ready to hustle the newcomers, to the accompaniment of one of their number with a baritone voice singing *Annie Laurie*, and two members of the Police Union playing the bagpipes.

A detachment of the Scots Guard was waiting behind the closed gates of Scotland Yard; and, facing Downing Street in the quadrangle of the Foreign Office, another detachment of Grenadiers, armed and wearing steel helmets, only too ready to have a go at the slops.

Boos and cries of *blackleg* arose; one of the crowd, who was said afterwards to be not a member of the Police Force, struck Richard in the throat. Fearing for his eyes—he was wearing the long-distance spectacles he used when rifle-shooting on the range—Richard struck out with an antiquated straight left. Cries of 'Coward!' arose. He was mobbed, and when finally detached, without tin-hat and spectacles, he had two rents in his tunic which looked to have been started by a razor, and his lower lip was cut and bleeding. Two soldiers led him away, while another soldier in hospital blue cried out, "If you want to fight anyone go out to France and fight the Germans!" Then he heard, "Dirty blackleg, taking bread out of coppers' mouths!"

Altogether it was not a happy experience; but when Richard was led into the Horse Guards, where a reporter spoke to him, all he said was, "I consider that a man in the course of his duty is not called upon to make a complaint."

That evening the deputation, which had been to see the Prime Minister, came out waving caps. "We've won!" The members were carried shoulder-high down Whitehall. On condition that they went back to duty at once, wages were raised 13/- a week, and pensions were to be given to widows. There was no house-breaking during the day; later, Thomas Turney's reporter friend on the Hill suggested a reason why no shops had been pillaged.

"I fancy it can be traced to two causes, Mr. Turney. First, to the smooth working of the rationing scheme, now on a national basis, and second, to the general fatigue, physical and mental, of this appalling war."

"Well, you may be right, but in my view the causes of crime go deeper than the material circumstances of one generation. But perhaps you are right. I can only say that I hope so."

"You will try and remember not to be late, won't you, Phillip."

"Yes, Mother, I shall try and remember not to be late. May I borrow your newspapers?"

"Of course, naturally! Only bring them back won't you?"

"Yes, Mother, I shall bring them back. Your orders shall be obeyed in every particular."

Mrs. Neville said, "I know how you feel, but it is perhaps the greatest moment in Mother's life, dear. Yes, I should say the greatest, because, you see, everything is known. Marriage and giving birth are events of mixed feelings; but a son's success, to his mother, is unalloyed happiness—yes, that is the very word. It is pure gold. Of course I realise your feelings, too, but it will be only for once, Phillip. You see they are all so proud of you, and it has almost made me weep to realise how much Mother has so been looking forward to it. She's bought a new hat, and a coat and skirt specially for the occasion! She's like a child, so eager and excited. Have you had any tea?"

"Yes, thanks. We had some, waiting for the connexion at Ipswich."

"Who is 'we', Phillip?"

"Oh, some of the chaps I came up with. We had arranged to have lunch together on Monday, and go to the Grafton Galleries in the evening."

"I see! And you want to be with your friends, of course! Well, can't you meet them after the lunch at Simpson's?"

"I don't know where they'll be, nor do they—you know what such parties are, liable to end up anywhere. No, I'll go to Simpson's, but I do wish Mother had let me know beforehand, then I wouldn't have made this other arrangement. Still, she's never had any social life."

"Well, her life has been all hard work, you see, dear."

She looked out of the window. "Do my eyes deceive me, or is that Ching coming down the road? Surely he can't be coming here? Yes, he's crossing over!"

"Damn him! He sticks to me like a leech!"

There was a knock on the door. "Let me go down, dear, and get rid of him."

"No, I'd better see him."

As he got up she said, "Don't you let him persuade you to go with him to Freddie's bar, Phillip. I hear that he spends a lot of his time down there."

"No fear! I never want to see Freddie's again!"

Before the door was fully opened, out came Ching's hand of welcome. "I just want to offer my congratulations, Phil! I saw your name in the office list for Monday, and came over hoping to find you at home. I'm in luck!" He saw Phillip looking at the silver Disabled Badge in his lapel. "Yes, I've got a pension now, and it calls for a celebration. How about coming down to Freddie's?"

From the top of the stairs Mrs. Neville called out, "Come on up, Ching. Don't stand there on the doorstep."

Ching moistened his lips with the tip of his tongue, and promptly stepped over the brass threshold. "Put your things on the stairs—we don't stand on ceremony here," but Ching had already hung up his purple velour hat over the newell post. "Come in and find yourself a chair, Ching. I've known of you as 'Ching' from the days of the Bloodhound Patrol, when you and Phillip and Desmond used to go on your Saturday afternoon escapades——"

"Ah," replied Ching, dolefully. "They were the days." He moved a hand in an arc across his eyes, as though brushing away memory. "Lots of things have happened since then." He held his head for a few moments in silence. Then, "I suppose Phil's told you all about me?" He looked from face to face. "I mean, about this?" He pointed to the badge.

"I don't remember Phillip telling me anything, Ching."

"Well, I may as well tell you, then. I'm a fraud, and I don't mind who knows it."

"We're all frauds at times, Ching."

"Anyway," went on Ching, ignoring Phillip's attempt to ease him, "what happened was this. I couldn't stand any more, and when we had to go over a second time at Inverness Copse, I thought out a new way of pretending to be shell-shocked——"

"You told me about that the last time I saw you, in December, in the High Street, Ching. You're not the only one, by a long chalk. No need to go on."

"Anyway, what happened was this, whatever I told you then." Ching's voice was now low, as though from the shaky base of his being. "I thought that to get away with it I'd have to do something pretty original, so when the Colonel came round with the adjutant, as we waited at the cross-roads——"

"Yes, you told me that. Do you find it easy to settle down to office work now?"

"Half a mo'. Where was I? Oh yes. Well, when the C.O. came round I pretended they were two Jerries, and ran at them with my bayonet, shouting like hell, and what's more, at the time I believed it——" He gave a hollow laugh—"almost! Anyway, they stared at me, and seeing a shell-hole between us, I pretended not to notice it, and charged through it and managed to go in head first into the mud. They pulled me out, and I pretended to have had a fit. That's how I got home."

There was a pause, while Ching rolled his head in his hands. Then Mrs. Neville said, "I'd say that you *were* shell-shocked, Ching! In any case, you were obviously in no fit state to continue."

"I was never in a fit state for anything, really. Anyway, I got back, and now they pay me eighteen bob a week for life. It pays for my weekly rum ration, three bottles a week. Why not? I'm no good to anybody, no girl will look at me, and when I tell people the truth, they either turn away from me, or say, as you did just now, Mrs. Neville, that I'm a case of genuine shell-shock. Oh, it's no good trying to tell me that the remedy lies in my own hands," he went on, seeing that she was about to speak. "Everyone tells me that. What have I got to live for? I ask you?"

"You could live for others, surely?"

"What others? The whole world's run on hypocrisy! I'm a

hypocrite, I don't mind admitting it, but most others never admit their hypocrisy. You ought to see our office! When I tell them that the Russian revolution is a good thing, and has got rid of hypocrisy, and the sooner we have a revolution in England the better, they can't face up to it, but tell me either to shut up, or that I'm shell-shocked."

"We were all more or less shocked before the war," said Phillip. "I know I was."

Ignoring this remark, Ching said, "Well, I won't bore you any longer." He looked at his watch. "I'm going down to Freddie's."

But he sat on there, talking in the same strain until Mrs. Neville, who was looking out of her open window, exclaimed, "Why, there's Doris, just turning the corner!" She waved. "Doesn't she look well! Come on up, Doris!" she called down. "Phillip's here. He's just leaving to go home, come up a minute, do!"

Doris brought with her brown face the spirit of harvest fields, talk of corn sheaves set in stooks, of flax pulled and tied by hand under the sun. Ching stared at her—bosom, hair, cheeks and finally her eyes, without remark; then he seemed about to say something, for his tongue moistened his lips; almost immediately he became dull. "So long, everyone," and with that he went out of the door and thumped down the stairs.

"You want to be careful of that feller," said Mrs. Neville softly, as Phillip left with his sister.

"Oh, he's quite harmless, Mrs. Neville."

"I wouldn't altogether say that, Phillip. There's something about master Ching——"

When he returned home Hetty said, "Oh yes, the luncheon at Simpson's, Phillip—Gran'pa says you are not to worry if you cannot manage to be there. He quite understands that you may want to be with your friends. We thought of going up early, as there are bound to be a lot of people outside the Palace."

"I suppose I should have applied for tickets for you."

"Perhaps we shall see you afterwards; but if you don't come I am sure we shall understand."

He left by an earlier train on the Monday morning to avoid being seen in uniform, and after walking the length of the Embankment from Charing Cross to Blackfriars and back again, thinking of Francis Thompson and the nights of the poet's dereliction under the arches of Waterloo Bridge, while panic slowly moved up despite exterior calmness, he took a taxi down the Mall. In front of him, beyond the stone island of the Victoria Memorial, were many people lining the railings before the forecourt. Beyond, over their heads, he could see red draping in front of the stone steps of the Palace entrance; and as the taxi bore to the left, rows of chairs in front of a red dais.

The taxi drew up behind others, to await its turn at a side gate. He gave the driver a pound note, and looking out, saw that the cabs in front had brought wives, mothers, and sometimes children, with those in uniform. It was too late now to ask for tickets for Mother and the others. When he got out he saw that he was the only one without relations or friends. His invitation was scrutinised.

"Members of the Armed Forces receiving Honours this way, please."

"Ladies and gentlemen accompanying Recipients of Honours that way, please."

It was twenty minutes to eleven. A Staff major checked names outside a door. Inside was a board with an arrow pointing down a corridor. There was an official every few yards to direct them. After a long walk, reminding him of the great barrack-like passages of Husborne, he emerged into daylight at the far end of the building, and walking round the outside of the north wing with others saw before him two areas of wooden chairs, the larger area already half filled with civilians. The chairs of the nearer area were numbered. Two Grenadier captains, each wearing a red brassard embroidered with the Royal cipher, and carrying a nominal roll, checked the numbers on the letters of appointment with the names on their rolls; and again when a man was in his seat.

There was a further check when a major arrived to thrust into each tunic breast a hooked pin.

By now the band of the Grenadiers was playing almost softly in the great forecourt. Phillip was calm and composed, observing without emotional distraction the exteriors of others about him.

It had been a quiet Sunday (church in the evening with Mother and the girls) following hours of darkness awake under tyrannous thoughts. At the worst moment, at 3 a.m., the devil had percolated most of his spirit: he must get away, vanish, go out on the tide from London Bridge: he was a hopeless hypocrite, he had condemned Ching for the same reason that Downham had threatened to have Moggs shot for cowardice when the Gothas had bombed the hutments in the oakwoods north-west of Poperinghe a year ago: Downham's fears had been put upon shell-shocked Moggs, his scapegoat. He was a worse coward, for not speaking up to clear O'Gorman's character at the conference. He had ordered O'Gorman to leave his rifle and equipment beside him, before he had sent O'Gorman to find 'Spectre' on the top deck. In the circumstances, I ask leave to be allowed to forego this award and to resign my commission. I cannot allow O'Gorman to be known henceforward as the man whose carelessness was the direct cause of Harold West's death. It is no excuse to say, or think, that he had gas gangrene, that he might have died anyway. Is it not possible that the salt water might have checked the sepsis? So, gentlemen——Bah! I am a snob, the truth is that I do not want Mother and my sister Mavis to be outside the Palace because I am ashamed of their lack of restrained impersonal manners. But who am I to criticise them? I hail every Tom, Dick, and Harry as a bosom friend. No reserve. WHAT ABOUT WESTY AND HIS PEOPLE? *I have not yet been to see them.* I have *never* been any good. Downham found me out in a lie on my first day at the office, when I pretended to have shot wildfowl in the Blackwater estuary when I had never been there.

But these torments had lifted with the light, and the familiar cheeping of sparrows on the roof ridge next door; optimism arose in the glow of a cold tub; and later, when he went down to see Mrs. Neville, she, as befitted a special occasion, got out the bottle of brandy kept for air-raid emergencies since 1915. Soon laughter was filling the room as she proposed to Phillip that Wakenham should do the thing properly. "Can't we find that rascal scoutmaster of yours, Purley-Prout, and get him to come? And Mr. Jenkins, wearing that yachting hat he puts on to cut his hedge in? What about old Mrs. Tinkey downstairs——?"

"Don't forget Dr. Dashwood!"

"He's had a baby, did you know? Yes, he married the Randiswell baker's daughter, and now he's a father! It hasn't sobered him yet!" she shrieked.

"Seriously, Mrs. Neville, I *would* like Mrs. Feeney to come."

"Ah, she's an old servant, you see, dear. An old servant gives one an air." With a shriek, "Can't we get the Lanky Keeper on the Hill to dress up as your butler? And how about me coming as your old nurse?"

The Wakenhamites—Gran'pa Turney, Great-aunt Marian, Hetty and Elizabeth—took a taxi from Charing Cross down the Mall, and got out at the Victoria Memorial, in front of the Palace. Steps led up to this monument and its terrace, where already many people were standing in position, with a view over the iron gilt-topped railings of the forecourt.

They saw two groups of chairs within the railings, the left group half occupied by civilians, while the right group, nearer to the Memorial from which they looked, was for soldiers in khaki, obviously those to be presented to the King.

"Surely," said Thomas Turney, "we should be included among the relatives over there?" as he pointed with his unrolled umbrella.

"I don't think Phillip was given any ticket, Papa."

"I'll go and see if I can get some," the old man replied. Immediately Hetty became anxious, being unable to go against the will of her father. But with Marian beside her she managed to say, "I think we shall see quite well from here, perhaps, Papa?" But Thomas Turney had already made up his mind.

"Wait here, Hetty. I'll not be long."

She watched him crossing to the railings by the main gates, where a tall policeman bent his head to listen before giving direction with sweep of gloved hand towards a distant gate.

Unaware of their arrival, Phillip was sitting on his chair. It was nearly half-past eleven by his wristlet watch, the band was playing softly, with no brass, only wood-wind, while he strove to steady his thoughts. The band stopped; there was a stir among the civilians on the flank, heads were moving sideways, some rising up only to subside, he observed while still looking to his front. Faraway in the other world beyond the railings arose a woman's voice, others took it up, tossing it in pieces, shrill tern-like cries around the atoll of the Victoria Memorial, sea-bird-shrill cries before a storm, clamouring, rising up together . . . the picture broke before cheering. Then prolonged stentorian cries of command pierced the cheering. He stood up with others rising before and around him to attention while drums rolled and massed trumpet notes arose with the Royal Salute.

The King, dressed in the uniform of a Field-Marshal and followed by his Aides-de-Camp, appeared under the arch in the centre of the Palace front. He took the salute, gloved hand to red and gold cap, remaining so until echoes of throat-tearing command to stand at ease had died away over the murmuration seeming to come from the walls of the Palace.

The chaps getting the V.C. were in the front row, they were to go first. Two of them, ahead of the generals and other brass hats, were readjusting cap peaks, after pulling down their tunics. Could they be nervous, too? Garfield was one of them; he had a devil-may-care look, and no wonder. The thought of Garfield, now a eunuch, calmed him. He himself was really very lucky!

The figures in front began to move away, led by the V.C.'s, in single file, unspeaking, each one going towards the pool grouped twenty yards away from the King. Then, to clapping on the left, the foremost figure walked stiffly towards His Majesty.

Phillip sat still, until it was his turn to join the file on the right of the chairs. He took off his right-hand glove, and slowly rubbed a moist palm on the reassuring roughness of barathea. Time hung heavy; each clapping of spectators caused anew anticipatory qualms, with the corrective will to remain calm.

One by one the senior colonels in front left for the pool. It was near his turn to move forward now. He cleared his throat, breathed deeply for calmness. The terror of open space, with only one before him as protection, was restricted by thinking that at least no machine-guns would open up. He heard before him the murmur of the gruff, near-guttural King's voice. The salute, the step back of the other fellow—now he must go. The scenery dissolved. He saw the Queen's upright figure and expressionless face a little back from the King's movements as the bearded figure half-turned to glance at dark blue velvet held by an Aide—hang right arm limp, open fingers. No move forward until *after* name was called. Why hadn't he got tickets? The officers before him had turned left, after leaving the King twenty yards or so, to sit near their people. He would have to go there, too, lest it attract attention to himself—a bogus, lonely soldier. Damn! he always allowed imagination to prey upon him before anything occurred, when it was never so bad as imagined.

Quite a nice day for it, really. Not a cloud in the sky. Now for the high jump——

"*Lieutenant, acting Lieutenant-Colonel Phillip Sidney Thomas Maddison, The Gaultshire Regiment*——"

Swallow saliva, proceed—proceed—stop. Right turn. Wait for the King to turn before saluting.

Blue eyes almost naked with weariness within creased pouches of skin held his gaze. He found himself saluting automatically from booted brittleness upwards.

The blue eyes came out to him, giving a feeling first of endearment, then of calm self-possession, of modesty which prompted him to lower his eyes before that weary blue gaze. The King turned, looking down upon the dark blue velvet tray upon which lay the cross of white enamel embossed with a gold crown on a green mound. The King turned it over with gloved fingers, and Phillip saw green and red on the enamel of the reverse side, below the deep cerise glow of the riband enclosed within bars of cornflower blue.

The King took a step forward, coming close to him, so that the beard with its streaks of grey was below his downward glance as he stood there, pressing slightly forward to aid connexion between riband and pin. Then the King, stepping back, said in a deep, slow, throaty growl, "Are you gettin' on all right now?"

"Yes, your Majesty!"

Pause. He felt that he was holding the weary blue gaze in the modesty of his own regard.

"How old are you?"

"Twenty-three, sir."

The King turned to the Queen, and said something, of which the only word he caught was 'David'. She smiled, and her face was suddenly kind and gentle. The King's gloved hand came out to him.

"The Queen and I are glad that you are gettin' on well."

"Thank you, sir!" he said, and stepped back to salute in jubilant relief. A turn to the left, a ripple of clapping, he was walking away on air. Across the courtyard the order was lifted off, and put in a case, then the pin was removed, and the closed case given to him. A slow salute from the Grenadier major, he responded as slowly, and went quietly to sit down in one of the back rows. There he saw Colonel Vallum, Major Henniker-Sudley and 2nd-Lt. Garfield. Vallum came over to him and murmured congratulations.

"You're expected to join us at the Café Royal for luncheon, you know. Colin and the others will be here soon. Wonderful day, isn't it. I've just heard that we've made a big advance in France, and there's a good chance of gettin' through the Hindenburg Line, and finishin' the war this year."

"By Jove, that's good news!"

After a pause he said, "I wonder if there's any chance of my getting out to France again, as a subaltern."

"I doubt it. You're back in B2, aren't you? But I can tell you that officers of the rank of captain and under are wanted to serve in India. In fact, it's already gone out to Eastern Command. I think the engagement terms are for two years after cessation of hostilities. Your adjutant will have details when you get back to Landguard." The idea of remaining in the army made him happy. But this feeling left him when, with five others of the Regiment, he walked through the gate, and saw Mother, Grandfather, Great-aunt Marian and sister Elizabeth looking at him, as they stood beside a man with a camera, obviously from some newspaper.

While Hetty had been waiting there, fetched with the others by her father because there was a better view through the railings, she had thought of her brother Hugh, and of Dickie—and, by contrast, how wonderfully her son had succeeded in life. The world of the spirit, which flowers through success after tribulation, was upon her as she watched her son before the King, so confident and upright as he stepped back to salute, to be joined by two officers who, said the policeman on duty, were holders of the Victoria Cross. Her son, on whose behalf she had suffered and hoped so much, protecting him from the weaknesses of his character which at times had seemed more than she could bear—now he was a success before all the world.

She awaited him, smiling and tremulous, a little anxious lest she say the wrong thing, and admit her pride to others, and telling herself that she must not attempt to kiss him in public. Elizabeth stood beside her, prepared to defend her 'little Mother' should Phillip criticise her by look or word. On the other side of Hetty stood Thomas Turney, wondering if his grandson now had the character, reinforced by his experiences in command, eventually to take his place in the family business, to be the one he needed—at times desperately when he felt death to be very near—to carry on the firm of Mallard, Carter, and Turney. His other three grandsons were dead, and Joey, his son, had no aptitude to manage even a department, let alone the ability to meet and reorganise for the new conditions which would inevitably arise after the hostilities were ended. How boyish Phillip looked, walking unsteadily—poor fellow, he still looked a bit shaky, and thinner than ever, his eyes staring like a hawk's as he came towards them. Then the boy stopped, and said something to one of his companions, who wore the hat of a Staff officer.

"Yes, of course!" said the Staff officer. "We'll see you later! Au revoir!"

Phillip saluted him stiffly, and turned towards his people with a forced smile.

"I am so sorry I didn't get you tickets——"

His sister looked at him sceptically. He was reduced by that look to his old life; there was change, 'Spectre' used to say, but never progress in human affairs. The soul, and the body, were evolved to their peak. He remembered 'Spectre' quoting Spenser, '*For soule is forme, and doth the bodie make*'.

"Well, Phillip, how do you feel after all that?"

"Oh, much the same, Mother."

"May we see the medal, dear?"

"It's an order, Mother."

"Yes, of course, how silly of me."

He opened the case, and gave it to her. "Oh, isn't it beautiful!" She could not stop herself from saying, "You have made me very, very proud, my son."

The deliberate tone of voice, less fluttery than he had dreaded, was touching. "Well, Mother, such things are really a tribute to the men, you know."

"Ah!" exclaimed Thomas Turney. He seemed shaken, and sighed, before saying, "Phillip, I must congratulate you. I am an old man——" His voice stopped.

Phillip had not seen him like that before. "Thank you, sir." He felt almost gay.

"You'll be coming to luncheon with us, m'boy?"

"Yes do, Phillip," put in Aunt Marian. "It will make us all so happy if you will."

"Mother, the photographs——"

"Oh yes, I almost forgot, Elizabeth. Phillip, do you mind if the man takes some?"

"Oh, Mother, you haven't been saying anything about me, have you?"

"Of course not, dear. He's from the local paper, the *Borough News*."

He felt relief. If it appeared in the London papers, it would be bound to be seen, and perhaps O'Gorman would be interviewed, and then—— "All right, so long as it's *only* for the local rag."

"Oh yes, of course, Phillip. I shall buy some prints afterwards, and send some away, to Aunt Dora and others in the family."

The photographer came up. "Would you mind, sir, a family group? I won't detain you long. First, I'd like one of you standing between your mother and sister, holding the case, and showing them your medal, sir."

"Well——"

"It won't take a moment, dear."

"Oh go on, Phillip!" said Elizabeth, as he hesitated. "Don't pretend to be shy!"

The photographer arranged the three figures. "Could you and your mother hold the open case between you, and the medal in your hand, as though you're offering it for the inspection of this young lady. It's the usual pose, sir, I've taken scores like that. I might place one in *The Tatler*, and other weeklies, so if you don't mind I'll take one or two poses."

Phillip looked at his mother, saying with his eyes, *Only the Borough News, Hetty?*

Four different poses were taken. To Phillip, depressed after the strains of the morning, it was a disaster from the roots of his being. The hopes for a new life, desperately maintained at times, were discarded as he resolved to go straight to the War Office and ask to be sent to the front immediately. The shadow took the place of the impostor, a shadow arising from an event which, while not forgotten, had as yet no connexion in his mind: an event which had appeared to lay darkness evermore around him when, after the mumbling of Father's voice coming up through his bedroom floor had ceased one Sunday evening when he was small, his mother's red tam o'shanter above her overcoat had come round the door, in the twilight as he lay in bed unkissed, Mother weeping as he watched her standing there, all his life dulling away while he lay still and heard the whisper, *Your father does not want me any more, so I am going away for ever, Sonny.* Then she had gone away down the passage and he had heard her footfalls on the stairs, the front door had closed quietly. He had waited for her to return, lying still, his eyes wide in the darkness. Mother had died, his feeling was deeper than tears. Without knowing it, from that night the four-year-old child had gone forward into life always a little apart from his mother, as he had already departed from his father.

The photographer was writing down Hetty's address, for specimen copies to be posted, when Thomas Turney got the idea that he and his grandson should be photographed together. In the course of time, he thought, such a record might well grace the walls of the Board Room of M., C., & T.

At last the posing, clicking, and spool-winding was over. "Now we'll get a cab to take us to Simpson's. I expect you could do justice to a good meal, Phillip? Mustn't deny the inner man, y'know, as Napoleon knew very well."

They sat at one of the tables along the wall, with tall wooden partitions between each table. It gave a feeling of privacy, almost of intimacy, with the rest of the world shut away. The trolley with shoulder of mutton and vegetables came round, kept hot by spirit flames; the chef, all in white from tall starched hat to apron extending to his boots, carved the meat, with its browned skin covering a layer of fat, into thick slices, while a smart boy, bony of head and thin with quickness, in similar laundered white uniform spooned on each plate red currant jelly, a braised onion, and three small boiled potatoes—a delicacy allowed in any restaurant or hotel only one day a week by order of the Food Controller. Hetty had her ration books ready, one meat coupon each for the meal, but after Thomas Turney had tipped the chef with a crown piece these were waved away.

"I've ordered a bottle of claret, will you tell the wine waiter——" Tom Turney was saying to the chef, when Phillip said quietly, "I rather fancy that he's waiting just behind you, sir."

The ritual of smelling and tasting was observed; the wine was not corked. Hetty said, "Just a little, please, only a little"; Phillip thought, All the more for me; Aunt Marian put her hand firmly over her glass, thinking of her lumbago; Elizabeth asked for half a glass only, being afraid that it might bring on one of her 'attacks'; Thomas Turney said, "Fill it up", not wanting his grandson to get the taste of too much liquor. Then, tucking one end of his napkin into the top of his 'weskit', the old man proceeded with one of his four main enjoyments of life—food, reading before his fire, daily walk and talk in the shelter on the Hill, and his evening game of picquet or bezique with Hetty. Once there had been sleep; that was now broken, and through the breaks came the twin torments of the night, the senses of past failure, and regret.

"Excellent saddle, Marian. Oxford Down and Hampshire cross, more substantial than South Down, I fancy."

Blackberry and apple tart followed, Thomas Turney eating his portion with a slice of cheese, in the country fashion. No coffee; it was mainly roots of chicory and dandelion, ground up, he declared, going on to propose a visit to the factory in Sparhawk Street. "I've told Hemming that we might be coming along."

Hetty looked at Phillip. "Will there be time for you to meet your friends afterwards, dear?"

"Oh, I don't think I shall go now, Mother."

After his first glass of claret he had felt easier, almost at home with them, a feeling marred by the thought that he had behaved badly by cutting the Café Royal luncheon. He could hardly turn up just as they were leaving. It was always the same: he could never keep to what he had made up his mind to do. The Bill Kidd fiasco at the Staenyzer Kabaret from which so much had followed, including the gas-shell outside Byron farm, up to his presence at that very moment in the eating-house in the Strand, was but one sequence in his aimless, ragged living. He should have accepted definitely for one party or the other, instead of falling between the same old stools.

"I must go back to the office," said Elizabeth. "I'm supposed to be in by two o'clock."

They took a taxi to Holborn Viaduct, where Thomas Turney, having paid the driver to take his grand-daughter on to Haybundle Street, led them up Farringdon Street.

"You look tired, Phillip," said Marian Turney, when they had climbed the steps to High Holborn. "You must not do too much yet awhile, you know."

After the visit to Sparhawk Street they had a cup of tea in an A.B.C. shop and caught a tram on the Embankment by Blackfriars, and so over the river and down the dreary streets to Camberwell—where Thomas Turney remarked sorrowfully on the changes which had taken place since the 'eighties, 'when your dear Mother and I set up our little house together here, Hetty' —and southwards to the Obelisk and the familiar stop at Randiswell road. At least there would be Mrs. Neville, Phillip thought, as they walked slowly home.

"I think I'll just drop in and see her, Mother. Thank you, Gran'pa, for a most enjoyable time."

"What did you think of Emm, Cee, and Tee, m'boy?"

"Carrying on nobly, sir."

"Yes. There'll have to be changes, after the war, to meet new conditions."

"You'll be coming home later, won't you, Phillip? Father will want to see you, of course."

"Yes, Mother. Oh, before I forget, you'd better take this bauble." He gave her the case, with the 'badge of the Order', as it was officially described, while wincing momentarily at memory of those ghastly photographs.

He crossed over and rang the bell of the flat. Heavy footfalls came down the stairs, the door was opened by Desmond, whom he had not seen for nearly two years, since the death of Lily Cornford. His old friend, much sturdier, brown of face, and with a light brown moustache, looked at him impassively. Then, "Come up, Phillip," called down the voice of Mrs. Neville. "You're just in time for a cup of tea."

"Thank you, Mrs. Neville. How are you, Des?"

"Well, thank you. And you?" He moved aside to allow the caller to go up first.

"Quite fit, thanks."

The constraint remained until Mrs. Neville had an inspiration. "Here, what am I thinking of! This calls for a celebration! Get out the brandy bottle, Desmond, and let's drink to the end of this dreadful war, and all it's responsible for. I've got a syphon of soda left, thank goodness."

Desmond poured out the drinks. He offered his mother a cigarette, then Phillip. "Oh yes, I've taken to smoking!" cried Mrs. Neville. "Well, here's to your very good health, and I do congratulate you, Phillip. My, you two boys do look smart!"

"I had to wear this," said Phillip, almost apologetically to Desmond, as he touched a shoulder strap. "I can take it off now, thank God. So we're level now—congratulations on your second pip, Desmond. Where are you stationed?"

"Oh, in Yorkshire—inland from the Humber."

"Come on, let's clink glasses, all together!" said Mrs. Neville. They drank. "Now come on, Phillip, tell us all about it!" Her voice became creamy. "Where was the Investiture held, dear, in the Throne Room, or perhaps in the garden, in such beautiful weather?"

"In the forecourt, Mrs. Neville." He drained his glass.

"Give Phillip another drink, Desmond."

Desmond emptied his glass, before refilling the two.

"Desmond is engaged to be married, Phillip!"

"Mother! I told you in confidence!"

"I'm a bit hard of hearing," said Phillip. "What did you say, Mrs. Neville?"

"Only unofficially, Mother. I don't want it to get about. He added, "I haven't told even Eugene."

"Ah, dear old Gene!" said Phillip. "I haven't seen him for ages!"

"I think," said Desmond, "that Eugene feels you have dropped him."

"Nonsense!" exclaimed Mrs. Neville. "Phillip has been out in France practically all the time!"

"I hope to go again soon. Colonel Vallum, whom I saw today —he's at the War House now—says the war will be over this year. I'm supposed to be seeing him, with some other chaps of our crush, tonight. They're going to the Alhambra, then to the Grafton Galleries. I don't really want to go."

"Why not, dear? You deserve a little fun, after all!"

"Oh, I don't know. I can't dance. Also, I haven't got anyone to take."

"A girl, you mean? But there will be plenty at the Grafton Galleries, from what I hear! Go and enjoy yourself. Who is this Colonel Vallum?"

"He's a regular, Mons and all that, and got the V.C. at Festubert. Stout, rugger-playing sort, has the D.S.O. as well, a *real* hero."

"I'll leave you two to talk, while I get the tea!" Mrs. Neville said.

Desmond sat back in his chair, one hand over his eyes. "I'm meeting Gene tonight."

"I would like to see him again, sometime."

When Desmond did not reply, Phillip wondered if Desmond

were truly in love, if so, surely he would be different; he would be free. At the same time, Desmond always had been very reserved. Ah, he had been too hasty in his judgment!

"Why not come up tonight, and we'll have a drink together, before you go to your friends?" said the near-expressionless voice.

"If I shouldn't be in the way——"

"Well, I've just asked you to come, haven't I?"

Large cups of weak tea, that innocent liquid, freed them all.

"How is my—I always feel he is mine—dear little Sprat? You know, I miss him more than I ever thought I would. He was *such* a companion! I am sure he understood more than what was said to him. How is the little pet?"

"Oh, flourishing! The servants look after him, but my batman tells me that Sprat is on the alert all the time for my return."

"You weren't serious about going back to France, were you?"

"Well, I *was*, but I don't suppose I'd stand much chance. I'm B2 anyway, for three months. According to one of our colonels—the real ones—temporary officers, captains and below, are wanted for the Indian Army, so I'll put my name down when I go back. One has to agree to serve for a period of two years."

"Well, dear, if you want to find a home for Sprat, you know he is always welcome here, but I don't think I could face another parting from him." Mrs. Neville wiped an eye. "You see, I live rather a lonely life——"

"I'll give him to you, Mrs. Neville, whether I go or not!"

"Well, don't decide now, Phillip——"

It was time to leave. "What time shall I come for you, Des?"

"I'm meeting Gene at the Monico bar at a quarter past seven."

"Oh, I'd forgotten. I ought to stay to see Father. He may be late. If I miss you at the Monico, where will you be dining?"

"Oh, at the Pop, where we used to go."

"Right, I'll see you there, anyway. Au revoir, Mrs. Neville, it's lovely being here again!"

"It was very kind of you, dear, to give up your time to be with us today."

"I owe you so much, Mother."

At this unfeeling remark she seemed to be twenty years younger, he thought sadly.

"You'll be glad to hear that Gran'pa was impressed by your behaviour throughout. He told me when I went in to see him that he has decided after all to let Aunt Marian stay. You didn't know the situation? Well, old people get on one another's nerves at times. Marian was the eldest of the family, you know, and had to look after the younger children, and I think your grandfather was a bit of a handful, and didn't always take kindly to his sister's restraining hand. So he has always rather tended to resent her presence, I suppose it is very natural, in a way. But don't imagine that he is selfish, or unkind; on the contrary, he has always been good to all his children in their troubles."

"Yes, I know. He stuck to poor old Hughie, didn't he. And look how Father's sister, Aunt Victoria, kicked out Uncle George Lemon when *he* got syphilis. Shoved him out to Australia!"

"Phillip, don't let your Father hear you talking like that, whatever you do. Your Aunt Victoria's circumstances were a little different from Papa's, and in any case, who are we to judge others."

"She used to judge me, anyway. And doesn't she say the Turneys are Jews?"

"Please, Phillip, never mention that before your Father!"

"I don't suppose I'll see him. I'm going up with Desmond to meet Eugene, before going on to the other fellows. Desmond is friendly again, thank God. By the way, is my old uniform here? I can't very well wear these crowns any longer, it will look like showing off."

"Yes, I've got the first tunic you had made at the Stores, Phillip. It has cloth badges, on the shoulder straps, I can take them off if you like."

"Thanks. I don't want Father to see me in this fancy dress. I'll change into slacks, meanwhile will you sew on those cloth stars on this jacket? You can see how they go on—point to point, not parallel. Many thanks, dear Hetty!"

When he came down Hetty told him that his father was home. "He's in the sitting-room."

"Oh, lor!"

Richard got up immediately his son opened the door, and held out his long thin hand. On the worn brocaded tablecloth at his corner lay the open case and the white enamelled cross. "Well, old chap, I must congratulate you! I've been looking at it. Mother assured me that you would have no objection——"

"No, Father, of course not."

"It's a beautiful piece of work. I must show you your grandfather's Crimea medals sometime."

"Did he—er—have any luck?" asked Phillip eagerly.

"He had campaign medals. I have them in the vault at the Bank, they will be yours someday. Have you seen the *Pall Mall Gazette* tonight? Rather a libel, I consider; it looks as though you haven't washed your face since you came out of the trenches!"

"Good heavens, why did I grin like that? And my cap's on one side. What a bounder! I didn't really want the beastly thing taken."

"Would you like a glass of sherry?"

"Well, as a matter of fact, Father, there's a sort of regimental dinner tonight, and I ought to be off now."

"We'll expect you when we see you, then. I expect you'll be back fairly late? Mother has given you a key, has she? I see. I've got to be on duty tonight. By the way, I saw your Uncle Hilary the other day. He asked me to give you his congratulations, and to say that he'd be very glad to see you at his club, the Voyagers. He will be there until the end of the week, if you care to look in, he said. Well, I must not keep you. Oh, before I forget—would you like me to clean your double-barrel for you? Mother tells me you are going to shoot partridges."

"Thanks. Oh, by the way, there's just a chance I may stay in town, Father. One of our chaps who was in the Flying Corps has the entrée to a club, and can put up people. We're all going to a dance later on."

"Well, you're only young once, but look after yourself, old chap, won't you?"

Part Four

THE LOST KINGDOM

"A man may bear a World's contempt when he bears that within that says he is Worthy. When he contemns himself—there burns the Hell——"

From a diary written at Sebastopol, 1856, by Augustus Williamson, Lieut. 30th Foot.

Chapter 17

NIGHT FLOWERS

At half-past eleven that night Phillip was walking alone down an unfamiliar London street, trying to clear his mind of the confusions of the evening. The street was nearly empty; in front of him walked another figure, solitary and small between the shaded lights of lamp-posts. What an evening—almost every moment of it wasted.

First, the reunion at the Monico bar. Desmond and Eugene both had two dry martinis each, for which he paid, as in the old days. Gene told them about his latest bird. "I'm working on her now. She's engaged to a chap I know, but says that isn't going to stop her having her fling. She's a sport, has a fairly well-to-do father, but works in a factory to help the war effort."

"Where?" asked Desmond.

"Out beyond Finchley. She wears trousers while there. I tell her that I don't mind a girl wearing trousers, provided she takes them off occasionally."

"And has she?" asked Desmond.

"She will, I think." Eugene gave some details which Phillip thought were rather crude; but then Gene was a Brazilian. "I'd like you to see her, Phil. How about asking her to come along?"

Phillip thought this a bit off, but he said, "By all means."

When Eugene returned from the telephone booth he said: "Leonora asked if she could bring her young sister along and I said it would be all right. We'll go to my flat afterwards. I shall have to get a bottle of crême-de-menthe. I suppose you couldn't lend me a bradbury, could you?"

"Yes, of course." Phillip had two fivers, and to get change (for he didn't want Gene to borrow the fiver) he said, "How about another before we go?" The change came with the drinks. "If you could make it two, old man?" Having put the pound notes in his case, Eugene, who had been looking at his rank badges, went on to say, "I thought you were a colonel now, Phil."

"Oh, that's all done with, Gene."

"But I've told Leonora you are a colonel. What shall I say to her when she sees that you're not?"

"Tell her that I went up with the rocket and came down with the stick."

"But—I saw it in the paper!"

"Acting rank in the field only, old boy. You'll have to use your own ammunition on your bird."

"Still, you've won the D.S.O."

"It came up with the rations, Gene. They dish them out to figureheads. But the real heroes——"

He told them about Garfield. "My God," said Gene, "fancy chucking yourself on a machine-gun instead of a woman. It just shows how mad the world is."

Phillip determined to slip away as soon as he could after dinner. He had outgrown his life of the days before the Somme. "Come on, you crab wallahs, do an allez."

They crossed Piccadilly Circus. Swan and Edgar's bombed and boarded up, the press of figures coarsened, rough, formless; the bright lights gone with the keen and simple faces of '15 and '16 long since dissolved from the bone, and 'dunging with rotten death' the loams of Picardy and the clays of Flanders. He passed wondering faces of Americans under wideawake hats, a few shocked behind their eyes after returning from the St. Mihiel salient. At least there was fugacious light and warmth inside the restaurant, the string band playing the barcarolle from *Tales of Hoffman*.

"The Yanks should have been brigaded with our fellows for the first kick-off. And it was damned unfair to ask them to make a salient out of a salient at St. Mihiel, Vallum told me."

Eugene glanced at him, and went on telling Desmond about someone called Roy Cohen.

"Roy Cohen, did you say? Is he an insurance broker in Piccadilly? Well then, he's the one who used to come into our office in Wine Vaults Lane. His father bought up all the old Metropolitan Police uniforms, and had a factory in Houndsditch!"

"That's right. They've opened a shop, Cahoon Brothers, just off the Strand, and sell second-hand uniforms, boots, et cetera. Roy tells me it's a gold mine."

"How did you meet him, Gene?"

"Through Leonora Spero. In fact he's practically engaged to her, she says."

"But if she's engaged, how can she——"

At this Desmond withdrew his face from the circle, his lips screwed into sardonic detachment.

The small Italian waiter was hovering. "Hadn't we better order now, Gene? I expect he's thinking that the manager will strafe him. People down there are already waiting for tables. We got here just in time. What will your friends want to eat?" The waiter put the menu before him. He passed it over.

"Do we need coupons for steaks?" asked Gene. The waiter nodded. Desmond said he had plenty, so four steaks were ordered. He explained that he commanded a gun detachment, and had as many leave ration-books as he wanted. Also railway warrants.

"I make them out for a station beyond my destination, and so they never get back to the Paymaster's office. Coming this time to London, I made out my warrant to Folkestone, saying I was breaking my journey, so the inspector handed it back to me."

"How about going back?"

"Oh, I make out another one to Northallerton, and get out at a station before York, where my headquarters motorcycle combination meets me and takes me to the detachment."

"That's a good wheeze, Des."

"I can let you have some warrants if you like."

"Thanks all the same, but I don't think I'd be able to use them. I mean," as sardonic aloofness returned upon the other's face, "it's a short journey from Ipswich to Liverpool Street, and to buy a ticket from Landguard to Ipswich, then to go on by warrant——"

"There's no need to explain. I fully realise the change in you since the old days. You weren't so particular about riding to Fox Grove on a penny ticket from Crofton Park then. In fact, you taught me that it was the thing to do."

"You're perfectly right."

At first the arrival of the two girls did not make things easier. He disliked their dark almost jet eyes, and the rather fat fingers of the older girl, Leonora, who began by being arch. When he spoke to her she opened her eyes wide so that they gave out a sort of flash, while with full red lips parted she showed off her fine even teeth. Finding him unresponsive, she turned to Desmond, while her sister sat demurely, long hair brushed straight to her waist, between them. The only thing to do was to finish the bottle of wine as soon as possible and get another, so that the stream of reverie flowed and he was moored, fairly happily, off a bright little island imagining faraway scenes against the talk of Desmond and the young girl, and Eugene with his hand on the knee of his *inamorata* under the table, while instructing her about his favourite Italian operas. By the time the cheese came round, five bottles of Spanish-Algerian Château Victoire Burgundy had been taken away. The younger girl had drunk none of this, but sipped her Cyderette with little finger extended, as befitted being up West.

"Have a liqueur," urged Eugene. "Crême-de-menthe? It's not alcoholic, or barely so. For me, a brandy and a good cigar just rounds off a dinner. Waiter! Then we'll go back to the flat and have coffee."

"Well, honestly, we mustn't be late, Gene. Rebecca has to go to school in the morning."

"You won't be late."

"Are the others coming?"

"Sure thing."

"The colonel? He's a nice boy." Leonora looked naturally across at Phillip. "He has such lovely eyes. What's been the matter, Phillip? You look so sad." She put her arm across the table, and laid her hand on his. He looked into eyes which were no longer bold, but softened by the wine, and turning over his hand, clasped hers.

"Here, change places, Gene, I want to be next to Phillip." She settled beside him, and taking his hand between her two hands, felt all of herself from the waist up going into his eyes. "You have beautiful eyes, Phillip," she repeated. "What's the matter, darling?"

"Oh—just life!"

"Don't go away from me! Look at me! I may be tight, but I know what I want when I see it. Oh no, don't take that the wrong way. I'm not that sort of girl, cross my heart!" She drew his hand to her chin, lightly touching it, then to her bosom, and laughing, said, "No further!" as she lifted his hand and kissed it.

Eugene had watched this exhibition with mixed feelings, among them admiration that his hero had impressed his friend, and satisfaction that Phillip had drawn her out, thus bringing Leonora nearer his bed, as he told Desmond later that night, while the two undressed in Eugene's attic flat opposite Paddington station.

"Sex is the root of life. All poetry and music comes from that. There's no such thing as an ideal love. That comes from being afraid of the real thing. All girls are the same underneath their clothes. I once did a lot of good to a girl who had been jilted by an officer. She told me that he was always wanting to have her, and when she gave in he gave up before getting half way, and then chucked her. She was still a virgin, and so unhappy that she spent hours going back over the past trying to find out what had gone wrong, to cause him to chuck her. I told her that if she had had any experience it wouldn't have happened. In Brazil, I told her, a girl was complimented when someone in a crowd pinched the cheeks of her bottom, while in this country, she would be angry and call a copper. Well, this girl asked me what she ought to do, so I told her to leave it to me, who had the experience. You have to be gentle, of course; all this caveman stuff is a masturbator's dream. That was what was wrong with this girl's *fiancé*, he had flogged his mutton too much. How did you get on with your bird, Des?"

"You tell me how you got on with yours."

"I got there. I knew I would when she fell for old Phil. I wonder what he's doing at this moment?"

"Oh, probably telling the same platonic tale to some prossy or other. Tell me what Leonora said about him."

"She cried when I told her that he had got his D.S.O. by flinging himself on top of a German machine-gun, so that he was maimed for life."

Desmond grunted and groaned with laughter. "You're a cunning sod, Gene!"

"But it's all the same thing. It's all sex! She didn't love Phillip, her behaviour was due only to the fact that he was a mystery to her, and it piqued her——"

"Then *you* piqued her!" Desmond laughed. "I wasn't so lucky with mine. She was too tight."

"Nervousness," said Gene. "She'll be sorry she couldn't before long, and won't rest until she has. That's where I'll come in, while you're shooting at raiders coming up the Humber."

There was a Curfew Order, so called, that restaurants and hotel dining-rooms be closed at 10 p.m. Shortly after this hour, having paid the bill, and said goodbye, with the feeling that he was on all accounts the odd man out, Phillip had gone to the Alhambra, to find that it had just closed, the hour being 10.30. He thought of the Café Royal, for coffee in the red plush room with mirrors, visited last during the winter of 1915–16, when it was open at midnight. It was closed, so he took a taxi to the Grafton Galleries, paid off the driver and walked past the door, waiting until the taxi had gone before going back. There was no one there, the door was locked. Should he go to the airmen's club in Berkeley Square, in the furnished house rented from Lord Someone, where the fun went on until dawn and later, according to Colin? Where was Berkeley Square? He set out to walk there, having asked the way.

He had gone down several side streets and arrived at a narrow main road of sorts, marked by dim specks of street lamps. In front of him walked another figure, and as it passed under the small circle of lamp-light he saw it was that of a girl when she turned half round. She was dressed in green. The look quickened him, he wondered what she was like, prepared to avoid an obvious tart and the repellent 'Hullo, dearie'. By lengthening his stride he kept to the same number of footfalls and came level with her under the next lamp-post. There she looked up at him, and he saw that she was young, almost a flapper, with brown eyes and short hair under a knitted green cap.

"Can you tell me where I am, please?"

"This is New Bond Street."

"I want to get to Berkeley Square."

"I'll show you the way. Look!" She held out her arm, and he saw a bracelet on her wrist in the form of a snake, with glistening eye. "Don't you like him? Don't be afraid, he doesn't bite."

They walked on side by side. He felt his blood thicken. Was she——? His heart bumped when she said, "Do you mind?", while her fingers sought his. They walked on hand in hand, past a policewoman.

"I've missed the last train from Baker Street," she said.

"That's bad luck. I'm on leave."

They walked on, she gently swinging her hand in his.

"Do you know any place where we can go and sleep?" he said, at last.

"I know a place at Paddington, if you don't mind the noise of trains."

"You and me?"

"If you like."

He was disappointed. And yet——

"I suppose you've been there with other men?"

"Only once. With a friend."

"Did you meet him like this?"

"Would it matter if I did?"

"Well—no."

They walked on, he making an excuse to take away his hand by lighting a cigarette. Then, "I'm sorry, do you smoke?"

"Thanks." He lit it for her. "I know Eastbourne Terrace in Paddington. I've got a friend who has a flat there."

"Then perhaps I'd better say good night?"

"No, don't go." He seized her hand.

"I think you're sweet," she said.

"Honestly, have you only had one man?"

"Yes, truly. He was my boy, only he cast me off."

They got a taxi, and in the cab he put his arms round her and rested his cheek on her cap, with its little tassel, and gently touched her forehead with his lips, while his heart beat faster as he felt desire for her. "How old are you?" he whispered, lest the cabbie hear.

"Seventeen. And you?"

"Terribly old. Twenty-three!"

They were moving under trees. "Where is this?"

"Hyde Park. I work near here, in Oxford Street. I type on a tall new Remington, the only new one in the office!"

"What will your people say, if you're not back tonight?"

"I'll say I stayed with a friend. Anyway, they don't care."

He was becoming afraid. Perhaps after all she was a tart, and taking him to a house where he would be robbed and perhaps knocked about. At the same time he longed to feel he could trust her, she had such a young and innocent face.

"Look, he does not like you now," she said, holding the silver snake to his cheek.

"I can't quite make out what you are doing here, to be frank."

"My father married again only a week after my mother died, and I don't like his wife," she said, rapidly and tonelessly, as though she had said it many times before.

"Where's this?" He peered through the window.

"The Marble Arch, leading into Edgware Road. Paddington Station's up on the left, about three quarters of a mile. You don't feel very easy, do you?"

"You seem so grown up for seventeen."

"Well, you make me feel grown up. You seem so young and innocent, somehow. Haven't you had much to do with girls?"

"Once, no twice, some time ago."

"Have you been in the trenches? You must have, with those ribands. What are they?"

"Oh, the sort of thing you get over there."

Hoarsely the old driver called through the glass window, "What number, miss?"

"This will do."

When the taxi had gone she said, "Are you sure you wouldn't rather go and stay with your friend? Say so, if you do, I shan't mind." She took his hand. "But he will—Snakey, I mean. He'll bite you."

"I'd rather be with you."

She knocked at a door, they went in, she whispered apart with a woman, who led the way upstairs. His doubts returned. "Here you are, ma'am, you'll find it clean and comfortable, I hope. What time would you like breakfast? Eight o'clock? I'll bring it up to you. Good night, sir."

"Surely you know the landlady?"

"No more than you do. I told her you were my boy, going back to France. Do you mind?"

Under the hanging fly-freckled electric light bulb the room looked bare and shabby. There was an iron bedstead covered by a worn counterpane, a rug beside the bed, otherwise the boards were bare. A wash-hand stand against the wall, ewer and basin, one towel, no soap, water carafe and glass. He avoided looking at her, then catching her face in the looking glass, piquant with large dark eyes, he turned and sat on the edge of the bed beside her, feeling gratification that she was pretty. She looked at him, then held his face in her hands and kissed him lightly on the lips, saying, "You have beautiful eyes."

"So have you."

"It's nice and clean, isn't it? The floor's well scrubbed. Say you like it!"

"Yes, I do, I think."

"Do you mind if I wash first?"

"Not at all."

"I can't sleep if I don't wash. I love cold water."

"So do I. I used to swim in the sea last winter."

"Where?"

"At Felixstowe, on the East Coast."

"Ooh, I'd like to go there, I've heard it's lovely!"

"There's no soap," he said.

"What, in Felixstowe?"

"No, in the soap bowl!" he laughed. This was fun.

"I'll borrow some. Be back in half a mo'." She went out, but looked round the door to say, "Snakey likes you, too!"

While she was out of the room he removed shoes and tunic, then his trousers, hanging them on the bedrail, beside his cap; and got into bed, with its dumpy mattress but clean sheets showing the creases of ironing. His momentary exhilaration was checked by the thought of possible consequences, a thought at once dismissed.

She was soon back, waving a slip of soap. Then in rapid time she took off green jacket and skirt, to stand in her chemise and bend to unclip her stockings; sat on the floor to take them off, and standing up, pulled her chemise over her head. He caught sight of two swelling breasts, then she was naked at the wash bowl, pouring water, stooping to sluice face and neck, armpits, and when the upper half of her body was soaped and rinsed by her hands, she vigorously washed her middle parts. When all was dried, she came over to him and climbed in, saying, "Ooh, I feel good, now. I'm so glad you came along. What's your name?" He told her, adding, "I must wash, too." Off with shirt and vest, and he was naked, keeping his back to her until with a start he remembered the scar on his buttock. Then holding the damp towel before his stomach, he crossed the room and switched off the light, opened the window, and got in beside her, to lie still and feel free from all thought.

Noises of trains shunting, blowing off steam, short whistles, came through the window. He sighed deeply, put hands behind head, and breathed contentedly.

"What's your name?"

"Phillip. What's yours?"

"Stella. Tell me something, Phillip. Are you all right?"

"I feel all right, yes. Do you?"

"I mean, have you anything the matter with you? You know what I mean. If you have, please use something."

"Oh, you mean have I got one of the two things you read about in those large official advertisements in the newspapers? Not that I know of."

"Have you been with other girls on leave? Tell me truly!"

"I have told you. The last one was September, 1916. My young cousin."

"That's all I wanted to know." She seemed happy. "You *are* sweet, you know. I could fall in love with you." She snuggled under his arm. He held her, stroking her head with the other hand. A dear little head, female little head, smooth skin, neck and shoulder and arm of *a girl*. He could not believe in his luck. His other hand moved down to the hollow above the hip, then up the ribs again until he held the firm breast with its small hard nipple in his hand, while he heard her sigh before she turned to kiss his collar bone, then he got down in the bed and put his lips to her breast, afterwards snouting the nipple gently with his nose as he had seen a little pig snout the teat of its sow. But there was so much to explore, the breadth of her back, the shape of her loins, the smoothness of her legs, the delicate small bush between her loins. She put arms round his neck and drew down his face to fit her lips upon his and there was no difficulty, as he had feared in the taxi, in his taking her.

Afterwards they lay side by side, while the arch of her foot stroked his shin.

"You've been wounded, Phillip."

"Only slightly."

"Did it hurt very much?"

"At moments—afterwards. Tell me about your boy."

"He went to France, and I never heard from him again."

"Was he killed, or something?"

"Oh no, he didn't really like me. He came back on leave, took up with another girl, and cast me off."

He turned, and possessed her again. They fell asleep. In the morning when he awakened he saw her sitting up in bed, in her chemise, looking at him. "I was just going to wake you, Phillip. Breakfast will be here in five minutes."

"I'll get up." He saw the line of her bosom. "No, let's hide under the bedclothes." He pulled her down. Both were prepared to look demure when the landlady knocked on the door. A false alarm, for her voice said, "I'm leaving the tray outside, sir."

After breakfast, another jag of lust, started by sight of a chemise with frayed lace edgings, a child's shift; a long look at her face, with its small mole above one eye, the slightest down of a moustache, the skin with pores not yet covered by papier poudre, which, after dressing in her green frock, she rubbed over her face, before screwing the two-inch paper into a ball and putting it in her handbag. He put a pound note beside it, folded eight times. "Do you mind?"

"Can you spare it? I didn't ask for it, you know."

"You're 'not that sort of girl'? I'm sorry—I didn't mean it, truly."

"But you thought it." Meditative gentleness left the brown eyes.

"Yes, of course I thought it, otherwise I couldn't have said it. But it came from long ago, and was a stupid remark, for obviously it has nothing to do with you. Please forgive me."

"All right, I will." She began to put on a stocking, and the sight of her white leg against the black made him push her backwards on the bed. "No, Phillip, not now, or I'll be late for work."

"Damn that Remington."

"I mustn't be late, honestly."

He dressed rapidly and left to pay the bill.

"You'll come back?"

The old woman said, "Will fifteen shillings the two be all right, sir?" He thought it rather a lot, but paid without remark. He met the girl in green coming down the stairs. "I'd rather say goodbye here," she said.

They walked to the end of the terrace. "I go this way."

"To the smart new Remington?"

"Shall I see you again?" she said, ignoring his levity.

"I don't know your address."

"I'll give it you, if you promise to be careful what you write, as my step-mother steams open my letters."

"All right, I won't write, then." He only half meant it, crossed by a self-destroying mood which induced obstinacy in her.

"Please yourself," she said, and walked away. He went along the terrace, with its porticoes of scabby paint, to find Eugene's number; then hurried back. He waited at the corner, and when she did not look back, "Oh well, that's that," he said to himself.

Gene was putting a tin kettle on a rusty gas ring when he reached the top flat. His grey, slightly sallow face looked somehow shrunken in the northern light of the unwashed kitchen window. Desmond, he said, was still asleep.

"Where did you get to, Phillip?"

"I dossed down with a friend. I was too late for the Grafton Galleries."

"I had Leonora. She's a natural *casse noisette*." Phillip connected with with Tchaikowsky's *Dance of the Sugar Plum Fairy* and Leonora's plum-black look.

"Most Jewesses are," went on Eugene.

"I wonder if there is ever a fair-haired one?"

"Peroxide, every time."

"Where was Desmond while you were tactically employed?"

Eugene told him, adding that Desmond was the sort who attracted elderly married women. "He sleeps with one in Yorkshire, who tells him he reminds her of her son."

"Killed, I suppose? I've heard of women like that. I suppose it's the maternal instinct."

"Yes, she gives him decent presents, what's more. Have you seen his pigskin hold-all? Also a pair of gold cuff-links. Then there's the wife of that tenor who was in the Electrical Engineers with him, and gave him his singing lessons free. One night he went outside in the garden, when Des was staying the week-end with them, leaving the two together in the drawing-room. But Des read his mind, after he had let down one blind a couple of inches short at the bottom. Desmond pretended to be reading a book, and saw his friend's eyes staring into the room below the blind. He couldn't help laughing, he said, for old Frank and he had been singing *Vesti la giubba* from *Pagliacci* a few moments before. He reckoned that was his last lesson, he said."

"Just as well." Even so, it was not very nice, to be a guest in a friend's home, and carry on with his wife. "Does he ever say anything now about Lily, Gene?"

"No. I think it was you more than Lily he cared about. But anyway it's all forgotten. Desmond's practically engaged to that girl in Yorkshire. Want a cup of tea?"

It was a cracked cup, and it began to sing like a grasshopper warbler. Or was it his ear? Or his brain? People who heard things, like Moses in the burning bush, had some sort of epilepsy. Perhaps that shell which burst near him and buried him at Messines on Hal'o'en in 1914 was having a delayed action which showed itself after sexual excess. He became worried.

"Want some saccharine, Phil?"

"No thanks. My ear's singing, and yet it seems to come from the cup." He went on after a moment, to screw himself up to mention his fears. "It was that mustard gas, perhaps. Hope to God I'm not going deaf."

"That cup always makes that noise. It's air coming out of one of the cracks in the hard covering, as water seeps into the porous part behind the crack."

His relief was great, and when Gene took a cup of tea to Desmond in bed he began to imagine a story of the clay in the cup, dug from soil made of a thousand millennia of fears and hopes, among them the creeping, skin-winged life that later evolved into a bird with feathers, and a song of joy which it reeled in some Staffordshire wilderness upon which kilns had arisen, to burn with dull glares in the night, and bring phthisis to the former moor-dwellers in their slum cots. Long ago the warblers had died out in the waste land, but the spirit of one bird had survived in the clay, and now was trying to sing itself out of the cracked cup, because it was near to its migration time. But its way across France to Africa would be through areas of fire more terrible than the Staffordshire kilns, and it would perish. Better to remain in the cup until it was broken, when its voice would be lost for ever.

"What's the time, Gene?"

"Ten to nine. I must be off to the office."

"Still got your job in the corset factory?"

"Yes. I'm going back to Brazil after the war, to start a business there." It was sad. He would miss Gene. "Shall we meet tonight?"

"I'm going to Brighton for the week-end."

"Same bird as when I saw you last?"

"No, that's long over. Her niece is the one I sleep with now."

"How many women have you had, Gene?"

"About a hundred, more or less." He lathered his chin. "Afraid I've not got any breakfast for you. I never eat it."

Phillip returned to see Desmond. "When are you going back to Yorkshire?"

"Sunday night. How long are you up for?"

"A week. Doing anything today?"

"Not particularly. I did think of getting a mount at Woolwich, where I did a course recently, and riding on Blackheath. Would you like to come, too? I can get you a nag."

They went down to Blackheath together, and had lunch at the 'Shop' mess, then got two riding-school hacks. He had a bony chestnut, 17 h.h. After cantering on the Heath, Phillip suggested riding up to the Hill. When they got there, he proposed a race around the Warm Kitchen, the level area below the bandstand. Football matches were being played as the two horsemen galloped around the rectangle enclosing three pitches; mud was flung from the hind feet of their mounts about the heads of some of the spectators. Shouts and cries came to Phillip, the usual cockney humour—"Go it, Dick Turpin, you're winning! —Wrong direction, mates! We're not the Germans!—Does yer mother know yer out?" etc. etc. Suddenly it seemed idiotic to be riding in such surroundings, as well as flat, a mere imitation of his 1915 self, showing off, so he led the way down the gulley; but turned back half-way, not wanting to be seen in Hillside Road.

They went back the way they had come, down the northern slopes of the Hill to Mill Lane, small and shabby terrace cottages beside the river Randisbourne, where in the past he had walked to and from school, sometimes with Tom Ching. The place was repulsive with cinder path and empty tins and bits of paper and meat bones in front of ricketty doors with paint flaked away, with squares of cardboard and sack-cloth replacing broken window panes. Children in bare feet were as ragged and dirty as in those faraway days, boys with cropped heads and small girls with pale, blank faces—fathers dead, he supposed, the wretched widows existing on small pensions. Passing by the tall brick mill he stopped to watch the water flume rushing under the culvert beside the unseen water-wheel, sighing as he thought of his father in the early days of marriage peering there with mother, hopefully for sight of trout or roach. The brook was dead, dead, dead, with oily sheens on the black water.

They hitched the bridles of their mounts outside the Rat Trap, a small beer-house bearing outside a rotting sign-board with its official name of *The Maid of the Mill* telling of fairer days before the Kentish stream was Londonised. The beer was dark brown, and tasted of saltpetre, put in to give it a bite; he forced it down, feeling that it was a mistake to have joined up with Desmond, to have tried to bring back the past, to live again as in the old days. In silence they walked their horses up to the Heath, passing the school which he viewed with mixed feelings. It was all too sad: one must never go back.

But tea in the gunners' mess and a couple of whiskey-sodas afterwards revived his spirits, or rather induced a return to pre-1916 flush, before the break with Desmond over Lily Cornford. He made an attempt to get straight with his friend, who by now surely would be able to see that affair in perspective.

"Did you hear that Keechey was sent to prison for getting some old woman to make a will in his favour, under threats, Des?"

"Yes, Mother wrote and told me at the time."

Silence. He tried another line. "I didn't congratulate you, Des, on being engaged, because I understood it wasn't official yet."

"It isn't."

"As an old friend I'd like to say that I wish you the very best."

Desmond sighed. He, too, was weighed down by memories. His father had deserted his mother when he was very young, and had another family in Essex. The girl in Yorkshire he had asked to marry him was second-best: he had always to convince himself, by thinking deliberately that she was pure and simple, that he felt any kind of love for her; he had also to convince himself that he did not mind that her people, small village shopkeepers, were dowdy. He had first noticed her for a slight resemblance to Lily Cornford, the only girl he could ever have loved, to whom he had yielded body and soul until Phillip had gone behind his back and, with his plausible ways, stolen Lily. His new girl was no Lily, not thoughtful and understanding like Lily, but—ordinary. Her brain was that of a simple village girl; so he had deliberately forced himself to be simple, too, to see the world through her eyes. Desmond was at times so lonely that he had seriously thought of committing suicide.

"Yes," he said, in low, languid tones, putting away all feeling, "I thought Keachy going to quod was poetic justice. But all rogues in the end hang themselves by their own rope."

"'There but for the grace of God go I'," laughed Phillip. "Tell me about your lady, Desmond. I'm awfully glad you're happy."

"Oh, there's nothing to tell. She's just an ordinary country girl. My uncle in Nottingham talks of paying for a farming course for me after the war, and then setting me up on my own somewhere. Pansy has a good business head, and is capable of making a home for a farmer."

"I am so glad! Yes, farming's the thing to do after the war. I shall never go back to an office life; in fact, I've thought once or twice of emigrating."

They left the Shop precincts, while Phillip began to feel closer to Desmond; they laughed over Eugene's adventures, and soon their friendship appeared to have reassumed its pre-1916 flush, so much so that Phillip suggested that they go on to Freddie's, although he had made up his mind, nearly two years before, never to go there again. And there was dear old Freddie wearing the same faded yellow straw 'boater', tipping it to each in turn.

The 'No Treating Order', under D.O.R.A. was in force; Phillip got round this by passing Desmond a £1 below the counter.

"Pint please, Freddy!" he said, putting down half-a-crown.

"One for me, too," said Desmond, tendering the note.

"This is on the 'ouse!" declared Freddy, leaning over to say to Phillip, "To hell with D.O.R.A.!" Then in his politest voice, "My sincere congratulations, Colonel!"

"Keep it dark, Freddy."

"I quite understand, sir."

Phillip saw Mr. Jenkins making his way to him, no longer wearing his special constable's hat and arm-band.

"Well done, Phillip. I always knew you had it in you, despite the way your father behaved towards you when you were a boy."

"Oh, I was a pretty awful little rotter, Mr. Jenkins. Not on duty tonight? We've seen the last of the Gothas, I hope!"

"I've resigned, you know, Phillip. I expect your father has told you about the police strike?"

"He hasn't mentioned it so far, Mr. Jenkins."

"Oh yes, I resigned on a matter of principle, you know."

"Well done, sir!"

"I can say the same to you, Phillip. As I told your father, it's no use bullying a small boy into doing the right thing. What is needed, I told him, is personal example in the home. That was after you'd told me, in this very bar, how you'd run away from your first battle in 1914. Remember?"

"I couldn't very well run away this last time, Mr. Jenkins."

"How was that?" Mr. Jenkins came nearer, not to miss a word.

"No one could get past Haig's wall!"

"What was that, Phillip?" Mr. Jenkins inclined an ear.

"The Reserve Position Wall. It lay some miles behind our trenches, solidly built, rather like Hadrian's wall. Of course, it wasn't in the papers, in case the Germans found out about it."

"I don't quite follow you."

"Well, you remember Haig's 'Backs to the wall' order? That was the wall."

"I still don't see what you mean."

"It was an idea based on the Great Wall of China. There was one built in 1915, at Ypres, called the Great Wall of China, but only of mudbags. Well, Haig's Wall grew out of that idea. It was built like the Ramparts of Ypres, of solid brick, nine feet high and six feet thick. We had our backs to it, so you see, no one could run away."

Freddie, who had been listening, nodded. Phillip winked at him, Mr. Jenkins saw it. "Are you trying to be funny, Phillip?" he demanded.

"Yes, Mr. Jenkins."

"Well, take my advice and don't try to be funny at someone else's expense! I try to be pleasant to you, to offer my congratulations, and you respond in a sneering manner. It becomes neither the uniform you wear, nor the honour the King has bestowed on you."

"Honestly, I was only chaffing, Mr. Jenkins!"

"All right, no more said. But it will pay you to remember that the war won't last for ever, when next you try to be funny at an older man's expense!"

Ching was the next to push through to Phillip. Desmond was enjoying himself, an ironic look on his face as he stood a little apart, his back to the mahogany partition. Phillip viewed the imminence of Ching with reluctance, until he remembered the words of Lily on the night of the Zeppelin raid; almost her last words were about Ching. "*He's terribly hurt in himself, isn't he?*"

"I'm glad to see you, Phil, to offer anew my congratulations." He put a florin into Phillip's hand. "Have a double rum with me."

"Well, no thank you, Tom, I've got a very weak head," as he gave back the coin.

"Just one won't hurt you. Rum goes well with beer, it's made from sugar, and beer's got sugar in it."

"If you'll excuse me——"

Ching ordered two half-quarterns. When they came he seized one of the thick-bottomed glasses and was about to tip the contents into Phillip's pint glass, when Phillip lifted up his beer saying, "Your good health, Tom. Tell us your latest news."

Having poured the rum into his own glass and then down his throat without a pause, Ching said, "Are you hungry?" and pulled a paper bag from his pocket. Inside was a large pork pie. "I'm asking four meat coupons for it."

"Where did you get it?"

"It was sent by a farmer friend of my mother. She doesn't eat pork either. It's worth five bob, if not more."

"When did you get it?"

"Came by this morning's post."

"I'll give you four coupons," said Desmond.

"Here's the five bob," added Phillip.

"Now I can buy a bottle of rum! We can drink it on the Hillies after closing time at half-past nine!"

The upshot was that all three went to Desmond's flat to play the gramophone and share the pie, Ching having apparently forgotten his dislike of pork. By midnight Phillip was lying on the carpet half asleep, while the voices of Ching and Desmond came with whorls of Liszt's *Campanella*, a popular rag of the moment, *Yaaka Hula Hickey Dula*, Caruso singing *O Sole Mio*, and *Solveig's Song* from *Peer Gynt*: which mixture, preyed upon by rum, pork, pastry and beer, went to his head with an urgent signal from below to seek seclusion behind the locked door of the lavatory. He came back to sleep upon the carpet, and to awake at dawn to see the horrid black rum bottle standing on the circular mahogany table beside its cork transfixed by a revoltingly large nickel-plated corkscrew. Desmond, also undressed, was seated in an armchair opposite Ching, from whose open mouth came snoring.

"I've got a kettle on for tea."

"Phew! Let's open the window and let out the fug!"

After a cup of tea, he felt bright and happy, and leaning out of the window suggested a walk on the Hill. The three walked up, under the pink flush of dawn upon cirrus clouds. From the crest, as for the first time, London was seen clear to the horizon of the north-west, while north-eastwards lay Woolwich upon the marshes of the Thames under its layers of mist and smoke. But the clear light of morning was not enough to contain Ching who, when they walked beside the lavatory, built like a bungalow surrounded by shrubs and flower beds, climbed over the railings to see what he could find. He reappeared with a can, and began to spray the flowers, returning inside to fill the can again until all the plants had been watered. When he rejoined the other two he shoved his fingers against Phillip's nose, saying with tongue-rolling satisfaction, "Smell that!" Phillip moved back his head, affronted, but not before he had got a whiff of carbolic acid.

"That'll show the LOUSY CIVVIES what we think of them!" Ching bawled.

"If they find your fingerprints on the disinfectant bottle, as well as on the watering-can, they'll put two and two together, and you'll be for it, you bloody fool!"

Yet Phillip knew the feeling which had prompted the vandalism; the same feeling he had had as a boy when setting fire to the dry grass in the Backfield in August, a kind of self-destructive terror, a substitute for courage, a despairing I-don't-care-if-I-die feeling. He might have been like Ching, but for the fact that he had met Westy, Jack Hobart, Lord Satchville, and General Mowbray. What a gossamer was the spirit, between a sense of duty and a sense of nihilism, until death was not the last enemy, but the ultimate friend. Conrad would have understood: or would he? There was not much sympathy for *his* Donkin in *The Nigger of the Narcissus*.

One day he would write a book, and it would have no villains or cowards in it: the failures would be loveless men who had once been unhappy, shadowed small children.

Chapter 18

NIGHTSHADE

A Humberette, hired for the week-end from Mr. Wetherley's garage in the High Street, was rattling over the granite sett-stones of London Bridge, whence by way of Lower Thames Street it entered the smoother jarra-wood block paving of the City streets on its way to the northern suburbs and Barnet and St. Albans and the Telford highway to Dunstable and the turn at the tiny hamlet of Hockcliffe for Husborne Abbey.

The next morning the Regimental party, under Lord Satchville, walked over fields of roots and stubbles, putting up partridges, eight guns in line, no beaters; one of several parties covering part of the Duke's estate. Phillip shot a brace of birds, firing off about forty cartridges. The next day they went to church, and he saw Lady Abeline with her son and two daughters in charge of a grey-uniformed nurse. He spoke to them outside the porch, where good-mornings were generally being exchanged, and bent down to speak to Melissa, feeling that he loved her. Then after luncheon goodbyes were said to the Duke and Duchess, a footman waited at the door with a tray of smokes for the journey. No one took cigar or cigarette, so he imitated them, before leaving for the cross-country journey to Landguard. Should he call in and see the Turneys at Brickhill? The old life was gone, he thought, and turning east, made for the coast, wondering how long it would be before he would be in India, a prospect to be faced without enthusiasm, since it was only an escape—from himself.

And so, with next to no hope, to Manor Terrace, and the old round of bridge, bathing, and the minimum of work.

A few mornings later, as he was about to go out and swim, he had a shock; and with the shock came a memory of what cousin Hubert had told him at the beginning of the war, when warning him not to go with any women he might feel like picking up; how Uncle Hugh, when an undergraduate at Cambridge, had fainted on being told by a doctor that he had got syphilis.

Returning from the lavatory, Phillip sat down on his camp bed. He must see a doctor at once; but not the battalion M.O., for then Lord Satchville would know. He thought of swimming out to sea, the tide setting north up the coast would take his body far out to the Dogger Bank, where it would never be seen again. Mother would grieve, but would think of him as having gone to join his cousins Hubert, Gerry, Percy, and Tommy.

"Anything the matter, old boy?" said Renclair, his room mate, peering at him with an expression of secret happiness deep inside him—a limited happiness, the reason for which Phillip was familiar.

Renclair, two years younger than Phillip, had recently returned to the third battalion after being put on the retired list, without pay for a year, during which time he had earned a small wage as a chorus boy in a musical comedy at a theatre in London.

"Oh no, I just felt a bit giddy."

"Like to try a shot? It will buck you up no end."

"No, I won't rob you, Renclair."

"But I've got plenty by me, old boy!"

Renclair was rather a pathetic character; a bit of a weakling, with a kind and gentle nature that went with feeble will-power. He had been sent home with an adverse report within three weeks of his first arrival in France. Certainly it had been a bad time August 1917, in the rains of Third Ypres, but Renclair had gone into a shell-hole and stayed there during the advance on Inverness Copse; later that day the eighth battalion had been decimated. His colonel had put him under arrest; Renclair had gone home and soon was wearing a pre-war suit and bowler hat (which sat low on his ear-stubs) and now had come back for home service with a fund of stories about the comedian W. H. Berry and a matinée idol called Joe Coyne—all of them kindly stories. Sometimes he sang songs out of the Adelphi show to Phillip, or rather hummed them through nearly closed teeth, while staring at Phillip's face with an expression of dazed enchantment.

I want to go to bye-bye
To rest my weary head
I'm Humhum and humhum and hum hum and hum
Won't somebody put me to bed?

Somebody had put Renclair to bed: a drab little woman whom he had encountered after an evening show, and gone home with to her room in Lime Grove. She was nearly double his age—he had confided his story to Phillip—the only woman, beside his mother (dead) who had loved him. Once a week a letter arrived from her, written in mud-coloured post-office ink with a clotted post-office pen upon the cheapest kind of envelope in sloping child-like writing of a Board School education. From her Renclair had caught gonorrhoea; together they had gone to one of the many clinics whose existence was advertised prominently in all the daily newspapers; together they had been cured. This bond of misfortune and salvation had increased mutual affection, and they had married. But it had not cured Renclair's addiction to drugs.

He acquired tablets of morphine sulphate on forged prescriptions from various chemists in Felixstowe and Harwich; Phillip had accompanied him once to Harwich, waiting outside until Renclair reappeared with an expression of suppressed jubilation, as though he had heard the happiest news, but was taking it quietly. After a shot, usually in the forearm, Renclair simmered happily for an hour or so, before becoming haggard and almost limp. Often Phillip wondered how far his home life had been responsible. Mother dying of cancer, father a regular soldier, who had always disliked his eldest son. Renclair had been sacked from a famous Army school for stealing; he had not gone to Sandhurst, but had a temporary commission not in his father's regiment; while his younger brother, father's favourite 'little man' from infancy, had succeeded where Renclair had failed, and, to Renclair's eternal damnation in his father's eyes, this younger brother had been killed leading his platoon in the April fighting outside Amiens, six weeks after passing out of Sandhurst, where, before abbreviated courses were instituted in the war, he would have qualified for the Sword of Honour.

"Aren't you going for a swim this morning, old boy?"

"I'm in a bit of a mess, Renclair."

"Anything I can do to help? You've only to ask, you know. Yes!"—with a return of secret satisfaction—"I managed to get ten grains yesterday, in a shop in the Butter Market at Ipswich! That's the place, Ipswich!" His eyes had a shine around diminished pupils.

Phillip told him his terrible news. Renclair became almost professional.

"May I see? How long ago, less than a week? No, that's

not old man siff. Not a bit like it. I've seen scores, but never one like that. Nor does it look like old man gunn'k, old boy, but more like barber's rash. Nothing to worry about—it may be married-man's clapp. Why not see Dr. Farina in the town, he's fixed up a lot of chaps. Sure you won't have a bracer? I've got plenty," he said, as he thrust a hypodermic needle into the skin of his own forearm.

After breakfast Phillip got leave to go into town. Dr. Farina was Italian, slim, dark, and popular, almost celebrated, among a certain class of sporting officer in the garrison brigade, for the poker parties he gave on Saturday nights at his villa, providing sandwiches and a sideboard of drinks, the bottles being contributed by the guests.

"Herpes," he said. "It should clear itself up in a day or two. I'll give you some ointment. Come back in a week's time. Meanwhile if you feel any pain, or if a hard chancre appears, an ulcer in other words, come and see me at once."

Phillip left in jubilation, and said a prayer as he walked back to camp, feeling a little mean that he was using God, considering all the circumstances.

After two days the cluster of pustules burst; there had been no pain whatsoever during 'micturation', a term he had read in a medical dictionary in the Public Library. However, from the uretha there remained a very slight discharge, with neither discomfort nor swelling.

When this did not disappear, Dr. Farina prescribed syringing three times a day with a weak solution of permanganate of potash.

After a week of this self-treatment there was no change, so he went to see the doctor again.

"Curious," said Farina. "It should have cleared itself up by now. You say that there is not more than a pin's head in the morning? It may be a small pocket in the prostate."

Since the treatment had begun, Phillip had read several more medical books. A gleet might last for years; one could never marry; children might be born blind; the prostate might close up and cause a stricture which prevented micturition. In a bad case of stricture an operation would be necessary; water could not then be contained in the bladder—which might, furthermore, be infected—indeed the disease could spread to the kidneys and cause death.

"I'll open the pocket," said Dr. Farina. "Sit in the chair, and lie back. It won't hurt."

A silver tube, covered with glycerine, was inserted. "It won't hurt," repeated the doctor. "When I turn this screw, it will gently expand. Ready?"

Phillip nodded, and held his breath. Then with a cry he contorted in the chair.

"Steady on, old chap, you nearly kicked me in the face!"

"Sorry, doctor."

"Yes, it looks like prostatitis. I'll write to MacDougal in Harley Street. He's got a new colloidal manganese which oxidises the blood, which has been successful also in some cases of syphilis. Come and see me in four days' time, when I shall have a reply from him about an appointment."

"Thank you, doctor."

"Keep your pecker up, my boy! You're not drinking any alcohol, are you? Good man. We'll soon have you fit again."

Phillip made a will, leaving his money and medals to his mother; his double-barrelled gun and rods to Desmond; to Eugene Goulart the several IOUs Gene had given him from time to time during the past three years; and Sprat to Mrs. Neville. Then having entered up in his pocket-book the half-quarterly salary of £16 13*s*. 4*d*. due at Michaelmas, he went into the mess, to hear that the expected general offensive had opened along the Western Front. The Hindenburg Line had been broken; Cambrai lay open; the Belgian Army under King Albert had got back the Passchendaele Ridge, starting from in front of Ypres that morning; the French and Americans were going forward; the Bulgarians and Turks were about to leave the Central Powers.

There was excitement in the ante-room, and many requests—Phillip and Renclair going together—at the orderly room to be sent out with the next draft. The adjutant told Phillip that his name was already on the Indian Army list, his application having been accepted. He was free to go to London to get his lightweight drill kit, the grant of £15 having been authorised.

He saw Mr. Kerr the tailor, who made no comment when the offer of a tumbler of Dew of Benevenagh was refused; he had already observed a remote look on the young man's face. Leaving Cundit Street, Phillip went to see the specialist in Harley Street, prepared for intramuscular injection in the thigh. But to his relief this did not take place; Mr. MacDougal, in morning coat, vest, and trousers, said that he would write to Dr. Farina, who would do what was necessary.

Should he try to find the girl in the green knitted ensemble, as she had called it, and warn her to go at once to a doctor? She was innocent of any knowledge of her condition, he felt sure. But where would she be—one of London's four millions?

Where to go? After mooning about he went home. There he locked himself in the bathroom, for the second permanganate douching of the day; but feeling that this was of no use, before he went back he hid the glass syringe, stained brown, on the wooden casing of the bath pipes behind the lavatory pan, where in boyhood he had hidden his first penny packet of five Ogden Tabs cigarettes.

On his return to camp, he found an order awaiting him: to hold himself in readiness to proceed to Taranto in Italy, the port of embarkation for Suez and the East. After reading this, he hurried into Felixstowe, where Dr. Farina told him that the colloidal manganese had arrived from London. He was given an injection in the right buttock, after which he limped back to Manor Terrace, and feeling chilled, got into bed, where he lay in a fever of pain all night, his thigh feeling as though a bullet had gone through it. Renclair made him some tea, put on gramophone records to cheer him up, lit a fire, hummed songs from the Adelphi show, and then, as Phillip groaned and twisted, injected morphia in his arm. Ah, that's better, sighed the patient, while Renclair, his eye-pupils no bigger than black pin-heads stroked his hair.

A week later the ante-room was more than half-empty. Even Renclair had gone with a draft. No embarkation order came for Phillip. News of the crumbling of the Central Powers was filling newspapers; Bulgaria had surrendered; Turkey was asking for an armistice; Allenby was in Damascus; the retreat of the German armies in the West was general from the North Sea to the Alps; there was a mutiny in the German navy at Kiel.

The order to stand by to proceed to Taranto was cancelled. This was followed by notification that no officers were required for the Indian Army. Every breakfast time there were maps in the newspapers, with half-familiar names—Valenciennes, Bruges, Mormal Forest—MONS.

It was over. It was ended. He sat in his bedroom of 9 Manor Terrace, at noon on 11th November, and mourned alone, possessed by vacancy that soon the faces of the living would join those of the dead, and be known no more.

But all was not yet done with. The officers paid an informal visit to the sergeants' mess, where each drank one glass of beer, standing, the gracious bearded face of Lord Satchville rising above all. Phillip drank, too, dreading that his abstention be noticed. At night toasts were drunk in the officers' mess, before all stood on their chairs, one foot on the table, and with linked arms sang *Auld Lang Syne*. At the top table Phillip, his rank of temporary captain confirmed, felt that at last he belonged to the old Regiment of Foot, as he saw before him the rows of 18-year-old fresh faces above standardised uniforms—cut close for economy, factory-made by commercial tailors become rich since the death of Kitchener's Army on the Somme—modest youths, well-trained in the Cadet battalions, polite, respectful—and spared.

Up went the Very lights, scaling the edge of the sea; off went slabs of gun-cotton, mock shells of practice battle, tracers flicked away over the waves until stopped by a calm-spoken 'Hen' Sudley; down went the hot Irish whiskeys; up came the carpets; on went the hunt, scrums for waste-paper baskets across the parade ground and down passages outside the asbestos cubicles—even through some walls. The piano was surrounded, thumped by fists upon the upright case, the strings gave out twangings and occasional dumbness, being stuffed with papers, periodicals, and somebody's boots, breeches, puttees, and tunic rammed in by a hitherto rather solemn red-headed subaltern combed out from the cavalry named Moynihan.

The owner of the clobber came in, swearing. He was a dark Jewish-looking fellow, wearing one wound stripe. Earlier that evening he had thrown a glass of whiskey and soda into the red-haired cavalry subaltern's face. Royle had been drunk, of course, but just a little nasty with it.

Now he challenged Moynihan to a fight. Gloves were found, a ring made. There was but one blow, upon Royle's chin: he staggered back, clawing the air and falling backwards all the way to the door, and beyond to the outer door, where, by the noise, he crashed over the threshold. But those who followed him could not find him. It turned out to be a put-up job; Royle had been a music-hall knockabout before the war, and that was part of his 'business', arranged with Moynihan.

The party ended in a midnight bathe, fully clothed, Phillip leading half-a-dozen of the pack into the sea.

Part 1 Battalion Orders by Lieutenant-Colonel Lord Satchville, G.C.S.I., G.C.I.E., Commanding 3rd Battalion Gaultshire Regiment.

ISSUE NO. 277. Landguard. 19-11-18.

GERMAN SUBMARINES.

Section Order 2725 d/19-11-18 is republished for information—
"Surrendered German Submarines are expected to arrive in Harwich Harbour on Wednesday and following days.
All ranks will refrain from making or taking part in any demonstrations of whatever description."
The R.E. Pier and Harbour Front for 100 yards on either side of same are reserved for Officers and their families during the entry of the surrendered German Submarines into the Harbour. These submarines are expected in batches of 20 at about 12 Noon on Wednesday, Thursday, and Friday next.

Phillip watched with others on the sea-wall. The submarines came in flying the Imperial German flag, red white and black, conning towers open and crews in white standing to attention upon the low decks. From each bow, rising at an angle of about thirty degrees, was extended a great jagged saw fixed to a cable which rose over the conning tower and sloped down to the stern —for cutting and passing through steel nets which were said to stretch from Dover to the French coast. But more immediately startling were the figureheads on the bows—Chinese dragons painted red and yellow, blue and white serpents, black wolves with open jaws, sharks' heads, and even the profile of a red-faced laughing giant. They entered the harbour in line astern, two hundred yards between each craft. Some were rusty; they were of varying sizes; many of them had small quick-firing guns, but one, half as long again as the small fry, had what looked like a 6-inch gun. Not a movement among the crews, only the ribbons of their caps fluttering in the breeze; not a word from the onlookers as the U-boats went by in procession to surrender.

Such weariness; such sadness.

In the New Year the adjutant sent for Phillip and said, "The Colonel is asked to recommend the names of those officers who may wish to make the Army their career. It means an abbreviated course at Sandhurst, and as you will imagine, giving up temporary rank and also a certain amount of seniority. Private means are not essential, the scale of pay as you know has been stepped up, and for an unmarried officer should not present much hardship. How do you feel about the Army as a career, Phillip?"

"I don't think I'm really cut out for it, Denis."

"I think I know how you feel. Lord Satchville, by the way, wants you to accompany him tomorrow as his galloper, and to make notes of what happens when he addresses the disaffected troops at Ipswich. Odd, isn't it, how the Old Man's fame has spread?"

It was a matter of pride to the Gaultshires that their Colonel had succeeded where Generals had failed in the matter of pacifying other camps over demobilisation. The feeling was that the Frocks in Whitehall, eager for five more fat profiteering years in office, had rushed the Khaki election on slogans calculated to snatch votes, such as 'Hang the Kaiser', 'Make Germany Pay', and 'Homes Fit for Heroes', while failing to prepare for demobilisation; not only were there no new homes for heroes, but no concerted plans for the change-over from war to peace. Coal miners had gone, certainly, and classes for heavy industries, but for the great majority of those in other trades, particularly among the youngest soldiers, there was Sweet Fanny Adams; while many who had jobs waiting for them could not get away. It was the old free-for-all, catch-as-catch-can situation over again, summed up in the cynical soldier-phrase, 'F—k you, Jack, I'm all right'.

Battalions were not going on parade; temporary colonels were usually on leave, eager to get back to the City, or the pickings of the Disposals Board sales, while the going was good and the shortages lasted. Some soldiers attempted to form Soldiers' Councils, to take over command; their complaints were justified; who could speak for them? A name was passed about, 'Lord Satchell', which became in the Eastern Command a legend, a token of hope. Wisely the great man, who had been a Governor of one of the Indian States, and had deputised for the Viceroy for one period—the bearded Viking famous as sportsman and rowing blue—Grand Master of Freemasonry—was called to Eastern Command to put the case for the need for patience to the hundreds of thousands of Jacks who wanted to go home to the mis'es and the nippers.

"Will you be going, too, Denis?"

"Too much work here, old boy. You leave for Ipswich at ten ack emma tomorrow, by Rolling Royce."

The character of Lord Satchville had been formed by a single-minded generosity directed upon the problems of others, to simplify their sense of duty. His courtesy was childlike in the pristine sense of the word. It was like the most simple poetry, which concealed the most skill. His manner was invariably kindly, which might by some be taken for softness; his mouth behind the yellow beard was gentle. His great height and appearance helped. Once, on a route march which passed through the town, Phillip's company commander, Major Sir James Poins, a pre-war 3rd battalion militiaman, himself a tall figure with out-brushed moustaches, had said to him, as they marched at the head of the battalion behind the Colonel on his charger: "Have you noticed that every time Satchers goes by a plate-glass window he looks at his reflection?" Company commanders did not ride on route marches; only three chargers were kept for C.O., Second-in-command, and Adjutant, in reserve battalions at that time.

"I hadn't noticed, Jimmy."

"Vanity holds him together."

"What's the difference between vanity and pride?"

"There's a distinction, of course. But Satchers knows he cuts a fine figure, and relies on it."

The amusing thing about that remark was that when Satchville had gone on leave, and Poins had taken the battalion, riding the C.O.'s horse, Phillip had noticed Poins looking at himself in the same plate-glass window when they marched down the High Street.

When the Colonel addressed thousands of men in a camp near Ipswich he asked them to come as near as possible, "for I want to tell you the situation as clearly as I can, in my own words.

"There are millions of men in the Forces, and I am one of them. I think most of us want to get home to our jobs, to live again with our families, to be with our friends and children. Some of you will recall the difficulties of forming so many of us into new battalions, the hardships of living in fields, under canvas, which soon became seas of mud. You have lived through the greatest war in history, when millions like you have gone from their old lives to a strange new life, often beset with discomfort, and in some cases, hardship. These imperfect conditions arose through inexperience. But the character of our nation, which was formed by the overcoming of difficulties, whether it be a footballer who is determined to play better football, a mechanic who will do only his best work, a boxer who trains to win a contest, or a ploughman who takes pride in his horses and his straight furrows—the character of our nation has held us together in this terrible, and at times almost overwhelming period through which we have passed, leaving, alas, so many of our friends and comrades lying upon the field of battle."

The Colonel paused, and blew his nose on a red bandanna handkerchief.

"Now we have a task before us, as a nation, a nation which is composed of us all, every man jack of us, to return our millions of soldiers, airmen, and sailors to a normal life of peace. It cannot be done in a few weeks. If ten thousand men go back to their homes and jobs daily, to send home a million men will take a hundred days. The machinery for demobilisation, and dispersal, cannot at the moment take a great many men, but as every day passes that machinery will be working smoother, expanding as it goes, until more and more men can be returned to their homes, after being given civilian suits, which are now being made during twenty-four hours of every day.

"To take the question of suits by itself: the factories all over Great Britain have been turning out bolts, or rolls, of serge cloth, dyed khaki and blue, for the Armies abroad and at home, and for our sailors. It isn't easy to turn over, in the few weeks since the last bullets were fired, and the last shells have dropped upon the battlefields, to making cloths suitable for civilian life, now that peace has come.

"I am told, and I am only one of hundreds of junior officers commanding a battalion, that the Government wants every man to go back to a job, to help make articles for peaceful living, after more than four years of the factories pouring out materials for destruction. We do not want to see the long lines of men, waiting for work, that we saw before the war. We want better conditions. I think if all of us are patient, and face the problems of peace as we faced them in war, we shall do better than by trying to do too much, too soon.

"It can justly be asked, who am I to talk to you like this? I can reply that I am a man like you, with his own problems, for I am not a soldier by profession, but by necessity, and have tried to do always what I have thought to be my duty. I, too, want to go to my home in the country, to see my new trees, now in their rows in the nursery, planted out, to replace those trees which have been thrown in the war. I want to walk over grass again, to see my old friends in cottage and farm, to talk with them, to do what I can to make their new lives happy, before my time comes to lie in the ground where my parents lie, and their parents before them. But meanwhile there is a duty, to be patient, to await one's turn, which will come when most of my old friends and comrades in the Regiment to which I belong have gone home before me.

"The General Officer Commanding Eastern Command has asked me to come before you today, to speak to you. It remains for me to thank you for listening to me, and to wish you all good luck in the days that lie ahead for us all."

Cheering faces, waving arms; tears streaming down the Old Man's face; Phillip tremulous before the massed emotion.

Temporary infantry officers were invited to stay with the Forces for a period of one year, at increased rates of pay; a captain would receive 18*s*. 6*d*. a day, plus allowances. Phillip gave his name to Denis; and when next he went on leave, called on Colonel Vallum at the War Office, and was taken to lunch at the Naval and Military Club, where Phillip met again Major-General Mowbray, on leave from Cologne. Listening to the two great men talk, he learned much about the retirement of the German Armies from France, which Mowbray said was a marvel of foresight in preparation, and skill in withdrawal.

Phillip wrote the gist of it in his journal.

After we broke the Hindenburg Line, until Armistice, Mowbray said, we took a great number of prisoners, many of them deserters. The Censorship dealt lightly with this, and the bursting point of our Prisoner Camps, in order to keep up *morale* at home and the base.

Our aerial propaganda, by means of balloons with leaflets and other means, was cause of thousands of extra prisoners, virtually deserters.

The Germans deliberately left in our hands tens of thousands of *bouches inutiles*, to be fed and lodged and looked after, together with their own clerical staffs, hospital staffs, service corps, telegraphists; everyone they could spare was left behind to retard our advance, while withdrawing their fighting men—the Army proper and the engineers.

One of the first signs civilians in occupied towns had of intended retreat was sudden departure of the numerous 'camp followers' including *filles de joie*, 'the Frauleins'. The day after Germans evacuated Bruges, Mowbray was lunching at the Café des Milles Colonnes. It was stripped of every scrap of metal, as every other house and building in all towns: door handles, hat rails, gaseliers, fire-irons and fenders, etc. German officers had fed there since 1914. Daughter of proprietor told Mowbray that while 'the Frauleins' were there German officers always seemed to have plenty of money, but after they had left they were hard-up. "Which made one think," commented M.

He said: "The Boche retreat was a marvel of *logistique*. They retired in light order, through undevastated country, where every means of transport was in good shape, and so their retreat was, for an army, at an exceptional pace. As for ourselves, we had to relay every railroad, for all the rails had been torn up. Every canal lock was smashed, water beginning to pour all over the country. Every railway bridge was blown up, blocking the road below it; all river-bridges lay in the rivers, every culvert was gone, all buildings utilisable as quarters and billets were razed. They left not one food building or munition store, only blackened ruins or shattered masonry".

Main roads mined at regular intervals.

"Nothing impressed me more, as I followed the trail of the Boche in a staff motor, than the recurrent remarks of imperturbable Tommies stopping us to report, 'Road mined, sir! You'll have to go round by the fields—she'll go up any minute!'"

He said the sappers did marvels laying down miles of light railways every day, but not half so many as the Boche had taken up the day before, having first "taken his munitions back with him, then lifted the rails, leaving us to bring up our ammunition and stores as best we could, after the long way round from the Channel bases".

"We had also to build forward dumps for food, erect hospitalization units; and also build roads. Our main difficulty was food due to the delays of rolling stock, *when* got going, being blown up by delay-action mines dug-in under the permanent way."

M. was at Roulers late in night of day Boche had left, and came across an advanced detachment of A.S.C. motor convoy.

"Their red-hot stove in a ruined farm-house kitchen was a joy to men soaked by the rain. Things were enlivened by an ammunition dump blazing and blowing up about two hundred yards away. I saw men warming their rations in canteens balanced on the embers around the outskirts of the dump. Among them was an American reporter with a tendency to panic. I tried to persuade him that the stories of danger were a *canard* such as Bompard served out to Tartarin in the Alps. Apparently someone had told him that the farm-house, what there was of it, was mined. When my A.D.C. went away to see that our motor was not standing in the moonlight, and a potential target for bombs, the subaltern in command said to me, "The mine's safe, I think. We found the fuse outside and disconnected it—but the stove might try it a bit high, for the mine lies directly beneath it!"

Vallum said it was not possible, as some stay-at-home critics had urged, to destroy the German Army.

"Our army by then was composed entirely of civilians, most of them very young, and the people at home would not have stood it. The young entry had a good *morale*, but it came mainly from the thought that the war was all over bar the shouting."

Also he said that women had arrived at having a voice in matters, and they had had enough of sending sons, brothers and husbands to be killed.

Mowbray agreed. He said it was hard enough for the young soldiers when they were wanted to keep the Boche at bay, in March and April, but when the time came for the Boche to hold up his hands, it was asking too much of them, especially as we had not got the right type of leaders any more.

"And now," said Vallum, "one reads in the yellow Press that the Germans have fooled us, and the War Office particularly; that we ought to have gone on to Berlin and made a job of sacking it; and that the German Army was in dissolution, all gone Red like the Russians. It may have been so in Berlin and behind the front, but there one finds the weakest elements in any army in a prolonged war."

I thought of Father, reading *The Daily Trident*, in his armchair at night, and holding forth to Mother, and felt more than ever that it was impossible at home.

At the beginning of February the adjutant told him that he was to report for duty at No. 1 Dispersal Unit, Shorncliffe, Kent. Thus, except for a brief time with the 1st Battalion later on, ended Phillip's service with the Gaultshire Regiment.

Chapter 19

GUTTERING CANDLE

In the front room of his house, No. 12 Hillside Road—semi-detached in the language of house-agents, but almost totally attached in the opinion of his son-in-law Richard—Thomas Turney was sitting before a fire. Outside the sun was still high enough in the late September sky to send down its rays unreddened by the lower atmosphere of London south of the river. It was not yet autumn; the weather still held the warmth and brilliance of the first summer of peace-time, the middle months so hot and clear that he had felt, while sitting on the Hill, that he was almost back in the summers remembered in youth—of ripening corn, of meadows forever green as he played with friends, brothers, sisters: golden day following golden day, all thoughts of death denied by the summer sun upon the Hill; and then the picture had tilted, the sky glared, and he was stricken by Spanish influenza, and thereafter his living was wrecked upon the fevered seas of memory: Papa, Mamma, brothers, sisters, long since shrunken to dust and bone in the dry-rot of coffin death. He cried out for the one who would save him—Marian, whom he had sent away.

Thomas Turney had survived the epidemic which was said to have killed more people in Europe than combatants during the four years of war upon the battlefields of France and Flanders. Unknown to him, the virus had taken off Marian, who had lived austerely in a little room in Greenwich, existing on an income of £8 a quarter, from which had been found rent, food, and gas; and although Papa was now 'allowed down' by the doctor, Hetty had not yet told him the sad news.

"Here's your spectacles, Papa, and I've brought you some of your favourite books. You'll soon be out and about again, meanwhile try not to worry, promise me?"

"Have you heard anything about Phillip, Hetty?"

"Not yet, Papa. He has left Folkestone, thank goodness, and is now at Cannock Chase, with the first battalion." She put a volume of *The Letters of Jane Welsh Carlyle* on the table beside him. "Miss Cole will bring in your tea, and I'll be in later, to play our usual game of cards, Papa!"

Thomas Turney did not want to read. He was gone beyond it, he thought with a dead feeling. Until his illness, in the eightieth year of his age, life had been sustained in part by the companionship of books. For more than two decades he had seen himself as a sinner, and had lived much in remorse; yet he had found comfort in the reassurance that he was as other men, as revealed in the pages of Dickens, Hardy, Fielding, Carlyle, and the Brontës; but his chief prop had been Shakespeare. More fortunate than Lear! Wolsey! Richard the Third! Aye, and Richard the Second. He knew that broken king's lament by heart.

> For God's sake, let us sit upon the ground
> And tell sad stories of the death of kings!
> How some have been deposed, some slain in war,
> Some haunted by the ghosts they have deposed,
> Some poisoned by their wives, some sleeping killed,
> All murther'd: for within the hollow crown
> That rounds the mortal temples of a king
> Keeps Death his court, and there the antic sits,
> Scoffing his state and grinning at his pomp,
> Allowing him a breath, a little scene,
> To monarchize, be feared and kill with looks,
> Infusing him with self and vain conceit,
> As if this flesh which walls about our life
> Were brass impregnable, and humoured thus
> Comes at the last and with a little pin
> Bores through his castle wall, and farewell king!
> . . . I live with bread like you, feel want,
> Taste grief, need friends. Subjected thus,
> How can you say to me I am a king?

In the past he had been able to read the Bible to find peace within himself, and fortitude for what he knew could not be far off. When his spirits were raised, he could criticise the Old Testament objectively, saying that the chroniclers of military history and political intrigue lacked a sense of humour; but, he was wont to add to Hetty, who shared his enthusiasm for Shakespeare, it was one thing to be born in a pleasant, well-watered, fertile island remote from enemies, and another to be a nomadic tribe whose security was based on the desert and its own determination to survive by eternal diligence and a sublime conceit in its own superiority over all other Semites. What was a miracle, he had been wont to say in the shelter on the Hill—ignoring the scepticism of Warbeck, whom now he avoided in thought, lest he be quelled by that pedantic, scoffing feller—was that a desert race should have produced inspiration of such quality and magnanimity, as was revealed in one of their number, Jesus born in Nazareth. That they did not accept Him was inevitable, for He was of all time, whereas they were of their own time. God was Love, that was all one needed to realise. Interpretations of dogma by men, professional clerics, did not interest him; and having no care for suburban respectability, he had not gone to Church (except for funerals) since coming to live in what he had called 'a deadly swamp' in the late 'nineties.

He sat by his fireside, on the mid-September afternoon, in a wooden chair which looked too frail to carry him. The arms and legs, and the back shaped like a bullock's shoe, set with arrow-thin spokes, were slender. The chair weighed only a few pounds, but it was strong; except for the seat, which was of elm, the framework was of yew—straight-grained and cleft, not turned—and the design of the frame was such that the pressures or weights that each part bore were carried, by tension, to the four legs and so to the ground. Thomas Turney used to say that the chair was built like a cathedral, which owed its strength to stresses and strains defying the force of gravity. All life could be illustrated by that chair, he would say: the fundamental forces of life in eternal opposition could be used by men for happiness and goodness, or for wretchedness and evil. They were there; and each man was free to choose how he used them in his own life.

Upon the back of the yew-wood armchair hung a closely-knitted draught-shield, a sort of prolonged antimacassar, in brown and yellow worsted, the work of his elder sister Marian. The sight of it, the feel of the thick wool, gave him comfort; dear, patient Marian must come back. He must send her fifty pounds for a present. To Thomas Turney, one generation removed from yeomanry, the chair was as much part of his life as were his own legs and arms. Made in Jacobean times by a 'hedgerow carpenter', it was part of the history of his family, which had been tenants of the dukedom of Gaultshire for more than four centuries. His father, his grandfather, his great-grandfather, all had sat in the chair: they too had known suffering and disappointment. They had endured, and in course of time had handed down their work to their sons. But now—sitting in the chair, clasping its thin wooden arms of yew, once pink, now faded, polished by the touch of many hands—he groaned in spirit. What of his own sons? Charley—Hughie—Joey——

The chair had been of his household since the earliest London days of married life in Camberwell; in the tenacity and strength of the yew-wood were two hundred years of the spirit of the farm-house standing on the blue gault clay two score and ten miles north-east of London. Turneys had farmed such land, according to the records, after the Wars of the Roses; according to that poor, dead, silly fellow Hugh, they were dispossessed of the Le Tournet estates at the battle of Bosworth, since they had supported Richard III. Unfortunately Shakespeare had omitted to mention the Le Tournet knights in his plays of the period; but Hughie had had a wit, once declaring, "The upstart from Stratford-upon-Avon had his limitations, sir!"

His mind wandered. With eyes unfocus'd, he recalled once saying to his dead boy, "Ah, Hughie, if this chair of bow-wood could speak! It would need the pen of Shakespeare to interpret what it would say——!"

"It would no doubt resound like a gatling gun to many a pot-gut overstuffed with crone-mutton, sir." He could see Hugh now, as he sat, thin legs showing under his trousers, crutches extended beside him, his expression relapsed into brooding melancholy for an ambition never even attempted—"One day the world will know me for what I am—a great writer, of love and death and royster and laughter, beyond the lilies and languors of Victorianism". Poor foolish fellow, all words, words, words.

Thomas William Turney was born in 1840, in the troublous times of the Reform Act. Besides the chair, he possessed, equally dear to him, the original duodecimo set of the works of William Shakespeare, which had belonged to his maternal grandfather, an Irish captain of the Royal Navy. The set was imperfect, for Hugh, before his death, had taken at various times one after another of the volumes and sold them to a bookseller at Charing Cross.

In the past Thomas Turney had suffered spasms of anguish, showing in bursts of rage, for this treachery of his own flesh and blood, this betrayal by one who once had been his cherished, dark-haired, quick-witted 'little fellow'. Alas, alas, that he, the boy's father, had been in some part responsible for the poor boy's tragic ending!

He stirred on the chair; spoke harshly of himself to himself as Hugh arose alive in his mind: instantaneously changing from grey-haired cripple groaning into death with tertiary syphilis to disdainful dark-haired undergraduate, to nervous, half-frightened, half-laughing child glimpsed in ancient sunlight. Hughie, Hughie, he groaned, to the ghost tottering, with angry eyes and thin set lips above the dark ramparts of his mind. *You killed my mother!*, and the apparition had collapsed, stick legs and stick crutches, upon the floor by the open door. Tell him, Sarah, tell the boy not to fret away what little life he has left in him; in Christ's mercy tell him, Sarah, now that you are dead and know the truth.

Silence; the face of Sarah had avoided him at that terrible moment, after Hetty had come down the stairs, crying, "She is gone, she is gone".

Ah, had he but shown more understanding, more sympathy, particularly to the children's mother! Too late, too late! If ripeness was all, it involved the withering of the blossom, the death of its heyday beauty; if wisdom was the fruit, to what purpose could it be put, since only the old recognised it? A bitter fruit! His grandson Phillip came into his mind—foolish boy, foolish boy! Would he break his mother's heart, as Hughie had broken Sarah's?

The old man sighed, as he thought of forgiving, gentle Sarah, suffering all selfishness—he winced away from his own part in crucifying her—until she had died of a stroke; he thought of Charley, his eldest boy estranged, living abroad, perhaps never to write to him again, for Charley had not replied to his last three letters, even to the one which had been sent to console him for the death of young Tom. Sarah, poor, dear woman, in her grave beside Hughie, poor little fellow, in the cemetery, slowly shrinking away in yellow clay. Gone also Dorrie, his eldest girl widowed in the South African war, that splendid fellow, Sidney Cakebread, buried somewhere on the veldt; Sidney's eldest boy, Hubert, in the chalk of Artois. He thought of Hamlet's cry in the grave-digging scene.

Imperious Caesar, dead and turn'd to clay,
Might stop a hole to keep the wind away.

"God, who knoweth the hearts of all men," he muttered; and wiped his eyes with his red silk handkerchief. Then, blowing his nose, he felt more cheerful, and went to the sideboard for the schnapps bottle. Hetty had hidden the key in the aspidistra bowl on its mahogany what-not; there the key was, under the plate at the bottom.

The drink made him feel easier. Hetty—thank God for his younger daughter's love and care! His little Hetty, gay despite what she had to put up with from that narrow-minded fellow, her husband, next door. Thank God too for Joey, a good boy from the beginning, never giving any trouble! Not much brain, certainly—but brains were a handicap, unless accompanied by stability of character!

The fiery spirit warming his belly, he reflected upon the scarce-believable fact that he had, very swiftly and in some unaccountable way, entered upon his ninth decade. He must live for the moment always—no corroding regrets. Why, bless his soul, he felt younger and clearer in spirit already!

Yes; but the nights? Those small hours of night when mistakes and stupidities and cruelties of his past life returned to garotte him with the triple bow-strings of remorse, guilt, and despair. Keep the watch-dog, liver, free to see off such spectres! Schnapps was good for the liver, as well as the kidneys. He poured himself another little drop.

It was curious how he was tormented by his *own* shortcoming in the hours before cock-crow; and never by *material* losses. Never once, in the dark and grinding small hours, had he been worried by thoughts of the loss of over five thousand pounds of his capital since the war. That was a regret of the day. It was the seeming little personal mistakes and acts of a man's self that had power to torture his mind, decades afterwards, when they recurred in the lost landscape of night.

During the day, the depreciation of most of his holdings in both equities and commodities dragged at his spirit at least once a week; and, seeking consolation and solution, he usually talked about it with Hetty with another ever-present problem: How should he make his new Will? The trouble was that, as soon as he had resolved what he should do, his doubts invariably rose again to the fore. On scores of occasions, and more, Hetty had listened to his perplexities.

"Five thousand pun' is a lot of money for a man of moderate

means, y'know, Hetty, especially in these uncertain times. That sum means that you and Dorrie and Joey, when I am gone, and your children and their children after you, and Charley's two children in South Africa, will be deficient by that amount of my accumulated energy. That's what money is, you know—stored-up energy. However, our friend Dora regards money as the root of all evil, he-he-he! She may well be able to afford such fancies—she lives on interest of her portion of her grandfather's estate! People who talk of the evil of money might as soon talk of the evil of energy stored in the flywheel of a steam-engine turning a dynamo supplying electric light. But what I wanted to consult you about was this question of m'will, and more particularly, about the debentures of Emm, Cee, and Tee."

During the summer Hetty had concealed her anxiety about Phillip, while Papa went on about his shares in the Firm—of Mollard, Carter, and Turney, Ltd.—printers and manufacturing stationers of High Holborn, London.

"You see, Hetty, if I leave a block to Charley, living as he does in Cape Town——" But with the figment of Charley came hesitation, and contradiction. Why should Charley benefit, when he had proved himself an ungrateful son? Charley had accused him, his own father, of responsibility for Sarah's premature death—— Yet he must be fair to Charley.

"I often see Charley as a little child, Hetty, sitting on m'knee." Then—"But if Charley sells the shares, young Mallard will buy 'em up, and use them to prevent Joey from having a seat on the Board. And then there is bad blood between Hemming and Joey. What a pity it was that Hubert—well, it's no use crying over spilt milk. Hubert was a fine feller——"

And so on—the perplexities and indecisions of an old man after a hard life, having no one in the family with the required energy and application to replace him in the Firm: and thus to allow him a little peace near the wax end of life's candle.

"Well, Papa, I will think over what you say, and consider it carefully."

Which meant that Hetty would, once again, agree with all he suggested; for she did not want it ever to be said by the others, later on, that she had in any way influenced the Will.

That evening it was settled; for the moment. He would leave all his shares in the Firm to Hetty; and his house and diamond ring to Charley, with the use of the income under the Trust Fund until he died, then the capital to be divided between Petal and her brother, Young Charley.

On the table beside them was the small mahogany box, inlaid with yellow wood, holding two packs of cards, with scoring disks of ivory set with dialled figures and silver markers.

"What shall it be, Hetty? Bezique, or piquet tonight?"

"Oh, before I forget, there's a little matter I'd like to ask your advice about——" She went on hurriedly, "But I don't want to tire you, Papa. Shall we play bezique?"

"What's on your mind, my girl?"

She could not bring herself to face her hidden anxieties. Then with mixed relief and alarm she heard him saying, "I see Phillip's little dog sometimes outside in the road, looking at the gate as though expecting to see his master arrive home any moment."

"Yes, I have often had to send Sprat away, now that he belongs to Mrs. Neville. He is such a dear, sensitive little creature, and curls round when I have to speak to him. Still, he is very happy with Mrs. Neville. I often think that dogs have a sixth sense, for he followed the postman up the road this evening—and there was a letter from Phillip, saying that he will be leaving Cannock Chase any day now, to be demobilised at the Crystal Palace!"

"He will be going back to the office, then? He won't like that at first, after his widening experiences, Hetty."

This gave an opening to say what had been worrying her. "I must tell you, Papa, that Phillip in all probability won't be going back to the Moon."

"How's that, Hetty?"

She told her father what Richard had told her; how the General Manager had written to Phillip in March, and asked when he was going to be demobilised. No reply had been received. The General Manager had written again in July, saying that as no reply had been received to his earlier letter, he had to inform Phillip that no further payments of salary would be made; in the meantime he required a reply at his earliest convenience. That had also been ignored; whereupon a third letter had been sent, telling Phillip that as apparently he had no intention of returning to the Office, no doubt he would want to refund the money paid to him during the war.

"Phillip did not answer that either, Papa."

"So he won't be going back?"

"No, Papa, I'm afraid not."

"D'you suppose he squandered the money on that woman in Folkestone, Hetty?"

"Oh, I have never asked Phillip, Papa! I have never broached the subject, after that terrible time last summer."

The 'terrible time' had begun with Elizabeth spending her holiday at Folkestone. It had been Hetty's idea that if she and Phillip saw each other away from their home, it might be the beginning of a new and happier relationship. Like most of Hetty's good intentions, it had had the opposite effect. She knew the letter Elizabeth had written, by heart.

> Everybody down here in Folkestone is talking about Phillip gadding about with the young wife of a General, who is abroad with the Occupation Army in Germany. They are always together. Phillip takes her openly on the back of his motorcycle, sitting on the carrier. She is notorious for picking up young officers, one of whom is that red-haired man we saw on the Hill with Gramps one day, the son of old Mr. Warbeck. He is a horrid young man, and usually the worse for drink, they say.
>
> I can't bear the idea of anyone finding out that Phillip is my brother, so Nina and I are going down to Sandgate this evening to try and find the apartment where we all stayed when we were children—Aunt Dorrie and our cousins Gerrie and Maudie. Please can you send me £2, *by return*, to Poste Restante, Sandgate, Kent, as I have had to buy a new tennis frock, my old one is far too long in the skirt and right out of fashion . . .

After posting the money, which meant that she would have to owe some housekeeping bills for the following week, Hetty had called in to see Mrs. Neville.

"The last time Phillip came to see me, now I come to think of it, dear, I found him very reserved, in fact, not at all like the old Phillip. He hardly noticed Sprat at all—and you know how fond he used to be of him. There, you see? Sprat knows who I'm talking about!"

She patted the sharp-nosed little dog. "Of course, dear, I could tell that there was something on Phillip's mind, but knew he would tell me about it only if he wanted to——"

Ominous words: it must be something awful, for Phillip not to have confided in Mrs. Neville, thought Hetty.

Then Desmond had come on leave, and Phillip had arrived the same evening. When she learned that Phillip was proposing to take Desmond back to Folkestone with him for the week-end, Hetty had gone again to see Mrs. Neville. There she had a heart-to-heart talk. "But please, Mrs. Neville, never never let Phillip know that I have spoken to you, will you."

"I'll have a private word with Desmond, don't you worry, dear."

That Friday evening the two had gone off on the motorcycle to return soon after midday on the Saturday.

Hetty had been in the kitchen, cooking an omelette for Elizabeth's lunch, when she heard the rapid reports of the motorcycle coming up the road. Seeing the set look on Phillip's face she feared the worst, as he and Desmond came unspeaking into the kitchen.

"Mother! Did you ask Desmond to humiliate me in the eyes of my friend, Mrs. Fairfax."

"*I*—Phillip——? I don't understand——"

"We were guests in her house. We dined there, we slept in two camp beds in the attic room, we were given breakfast. When we were about to leave this morning, Desmond refused the hand of his hostess when she offered it. When Mrs. Fairfax asked if he had hurt his hand, Desmond said, keeping his hand in his pocket, 'Oh, you and I do not need to shake hands, Mrs. Fairfax, we know each other too well.' Is that correct, Desmond?"

"Quite correct."

"Did I ask you for a reason?"

"You did."

"Did you give a reason?"

"I told you that I was not free to do so."

"Did you act like that deliberately?"

"I did."

"To cause a breach in a friendship between Mrs. Fairfax and myself?"

"Yes."

"Why did you act like that?"

"To help bring to an end an impossible situation."

"You made it impossible!"

"That may be so. But, in any case, it was quite plain to me that that fellow Colyer, who came up after dinner, was having an *affaire* with her."

"Mother, did you ask Desmond deliberately to humiliate me in the eyes of my friend?"

"Yes, I did ask Desmond to help me, Phillip. I did not want you to ruin your whole life." Her lips trembled. "After all, I am your Mother." She could not keep the tears from falling. "I beg you, my son, to give me your promise not to see this lady again. Will you, for my sake?"

She stood with her back to the gas stove, feeling that all the hopes of her life were in vain; while, as though from a sacrificial offering (Phillip thought later) pale blue smoke from the burning omelette began to arise and add one more layer to the congealed essences of thousands of frying pan and oven experiments which had darkened the varnish of the paper'd kitchen walls.

"No, of course I will not give such a promise!"

She made another effort. "Please tell me, Desmond! Has Phillip been co-habiting with Mrs. Fairfax?"

Before Desmond could reply, Phillip said curtly, "Why must you depend on gossip to know about my affairs? Haven't you had enough from Elizabeth whom you sent to spy on me?"

Tears ran down her face puckered like a child's, Phillip thought, holding himself apart from her feelings, blank within his own suffering. Hardness filled the blank when she said, "Desmond, do you think it would do any good if your mother and I went down to Folkestone?"

Pointing at her, he shouted in sudden frenzy, "Mother! If you do that I will never see you again!"

The front door had been left open; Elizabeth had come in softly, to stand listening. She moved forward.

"Now you know the truth, Mother! You didn't believe me before, did you? Now you can see for yourself what Phillip is really like!"

"Mavis—Elizabeth—please—please—— There, you see what you have done? He has gone away."

"Yes, and good riddance to bad rubbish! Oh, is that my omelette burning? I shall be late for tennis, and Nina and I are in the semi-finals!"

Hetty looked at her daughter, and something in her went blank. She said quietly, "Go now and change and I will do you another." When Elizabeth had gone upstairs she said to Desmond, "I am most grateful for your help."

"I shouldn't worry, Mrs. Maddison. She had obviously done with Phillip, in fact she was trying to get off with me, that's why I refused to shake hands."

It was the brittle hardness, the sudden revelation of a selfishness that sometimes had possessed Phillip in boyhood, that remained to affect Hetty. He was not well. His outburst alarmed her, in that it had reminded her of Mavis when she was in demanding mood, stamping her foot, her voice harsh and near-guttural, until she dared not not give way lest the girl fall into one of her 'attacks.' Mavis had been like that ever since she had been sent away with Phillip, at the turn of the century, to their Aunt Victoria at Epsom, during the scarlet fever epidemic, crying to her outside the door of the sick room, 'Don't lose me, Mummy! Don't lose me! Please don't lose me, Mummy!' Later, she had had fits—the fear-filled face crying 'Mother,' 'Mother,' 'Mother'—the child who had never really been able to stand on her own feet had grown into the young woman—'Money,' 'Money,' 'Money'!

After leaving Landguard Phillip had spent a month at the Dispersal Unit at Shorncliffe. Troops from France had been marched there after disembarkation at the docks of Dover and Folkestone, to hand over arms and equipment and be demobilised. There had been little work to do. He had spent most of the month of cold weather snug in his cubicle reading, and smoking French cigars which could be bought cheaply from the returning soldiers. The books had come from a Sandgate lending library. He had progressed from Galsworthy to Hardy, and back to Conrad—the possibilities of a new world opened upon him as, feet extended to the glowing stove, blanket hung across window, he lay back in a battered Morris arm-chair and began to feel that he had the power to write scenes in the style of those arising from the printed pages.

One night an unexpected visitor called to see him. It was his cousin Willie, filled with the grandeur of a book he had found in a secondhand shop in Folkestone. Willie declared that he was never going back to an office life; on the contrary, after demobilisation he intended to walk to the West Country and live a life next to nature. He read rapturously from the book, which was *The Story of My Heart* by Richard Jefferies. The next morning he left, leaving another blank in Phillip's life.

In April Phillip was appointed to the adjutancy of a Rest Camp just behind the Leas of Folkestone. Just before this, at a dance given by the Dispersal Unit in the town, he had met a beautiful girl who had been brought by a red-headed R.A.F. officer. The three had become acquainted. The R.A.F. officer, who had the scars of a crash on his face, had shown jealousy, revealed in a manner of aloof scorn.

The girl, who said she was Mrs. d'Arcy Fairfax, took a fancy to Phillip, tall and aloof in his 'blues' adorned by two ribands. He thought she was the most natural person he had ever met, and wrote in his diary, early the next morning, that it was wonderful to be friends with such a rare, happy spirit, so understanding and generous, and 'entirely devoid of any ulterior thoughts, since she is obviously very happily married, and has a little girl of her own.'

The Rest Camp was a couple of acres of commandeered buildings, pre-war boarding houses and hotels, used as a hostel for troops coming on leave from, and returning to, the Rhineland Army. Phillip found the work in the orderly-room to be negligible, a mere signing of returns, which took him less than an hour every day.

The first weeks of spring were a time of pleasure, shadowed only by occasional dark thoughts that he was barred forever from physical love: not that he had the least idea of any *affaire* with Eveline Fairfax, quite apart from the fact that she had a soldier husband in the Army of the Rhine—a question of honour. Anyhow, their friendship, he told himself, was not based on 'anything like that.'

The earlier symptoms of infection had disappeared; he had seen no doctor since leaving Felixstowe. He thought that the disease had 'gone into his blood.'

One day Eve, as he called her, had asked him if he had ever had experience with a woman. The question appalled him, for it had been made when she had impulsively taken his hand while they were sitting by the sea and kissed it; and he had felt that poignancy which meant he might be going to fall in love with her. That would be too awful, for he was virtually a pariah.

"Oh, I've just remembered something I wanted to tell you, Eve! You know that the London agents promised me the first Brooklands Road Special Norton they received from Birmingham?

Well, I had a letter this morning, saying it had come, and was at their showrooms in Great Portland Street!"

"Wonderful news, my dear! Simply wonderful! No wonder your mind is preoccupied. I can compete for your interest with old Hardy and old Conrad, but not with a new motorcycle! You might be out of a book yourself—the strong, silent Englishman of fiction, at the same time boyish—oh damn you, why do you mock me!?"

That night she taught him to kiss, gently plucking with the lips before the full conjoined softness which worried him in case his breath smelt of rank cigars and possibly decayed teeth—for he had not been to a dentist during the entire war. The next day he went up to London, to collect the longed-for bike.

The salesman in Great Portland Street said they had taken the Norton out of the window, since so many enquiries had been made about it. He could have sold it fifty times over; so he had put it in a back room.

It was beautiful, long in the wheel-base, with a greyhound simplicity enhanced by the nickel-plated exhaust pipe curving down from the exhaust port to lie parallel with, and eight inches off the ground, and extending to behind the back wheel. The pipe was two inches in diameter, with a note like an organ pipe when the salesman, a pilot recently demobbed from the R.A.F., had raised the back wheel on the stand—the machine weighed only 200 lb.—and pulled over the wheel.

"Lovely sound, isn't it? Two hundred and forty revs on the pilot jet. You can paddle off at walking pace. She'll fire at the drop of the valve lifter. Top speed? Oh, she'll easily run up to three thousand six hundred revs on full throttle. Flexible job, this engine, considering the long stroke and high compression."

"The engine runs with little bubbles of sound!"

He stood back to admire the lines of the machine. The handlebars were set wide for control at speed; the grey tank, flat like a wild-fowling punt, extended back to the saddle pillion, where it tapered off. The pearl-grey of its paint, under a coat of clear varnish, was lined out in red; proudly on the bows the word *Norton* proclaimed the inventor, the capital *N* of which flowed back to cover all the other letters, like a guardian wing.

"One feels like a jockey, lying across the back of a horse. Or a greyhound!" he said, bestriding it, holding the grips.

The salesman pointed out the wide cooling flanges and fins of the cylinder, black with graphite; the new model of the B. & B. carburettor, with tapered needle lifting in the barrel as the throttle opened, thus allowing more petrol to be sucked up through the jet, he explained—giving infinite variation, from tick-over to full throttle. "She lapped Brooklands at 74 m.p.h."

The foot-rests were set back so that the rider's heels tailed off from his body lying forward over the tank like a pulled-out Z, he saw in a wide looking glass on the wall.

"I've got a pair of rubber knee grips, in case you want them," went on the salesman.

Phillip could not find a mark, much less a scratch, anywhere on his splendid Norton, and no signs of wear on the blue rubber-and-canvas belt to the back wheel. How did the Phillipson variable pulley work, he asked.

"It automatically expands to give a lower ratio with the v-pulley on the back wheel when the engine labours."

"What is the top ratio?"

"It's set at $4\frac{3}{4}$ to 1 at the moment. I think you'll find that all right, for traffic down the Old Kent Road. There's not much about on Tuesdays. A touch of the shoe-sole on that outer flange—it's phosphor-bronze, which is malleable as you know—and the pulley automatically opens against the broad coil-spring within the flange. Normally it's kept wound up by the engine thrust. Neat little job, don't you think?"

"I'm a bit scared of its speed. The first time I rode a motor-bike, I went straight into a lamp-post."

"You'll find her very docile. Go easy for the first hundred miles, won't you? The bearings like to bed themselves in gradually, of course. Keep to a steady forty, don't let her labour, and you'll be all right."

"How about petrol and oil?"

"I've put some in for you. The tank holds just over three gallons, I tipped in a can, that should get you to Folkestone with about a gallon left."

"Is this the way out?"

"Yes. Er—just a little matter—— I've got the bill here for you. You paid a tenner, that leaves eighty-two odd quid."

New knee-grips laced criss-cross over the tank, new horn clipped above the throttle controls, receipt in pocket: he wheeled her into the street. He had a 5s. driving licence, the other didn't matter, he had never bought one for his two previous mounts and certainly wasn't going to bother about such civvy nonsense now.

Wheeling her round the corner of the street out of sight of all salesmen, he quickened the pace, dropped the valve-lifter, and vaulted into the saddle. At first, owing to the extended position, he swayed across the road, but recovered, and stopped to get used to the feel of stretching forward on cork grips.

It was drizzling, the surface of the road slightly greasy, he must go gingerly. But by the time he came to a wide thoroughfare he felt at ease, and passing omnibuses and drays, after several enquiries reached the Embankment.

There he stopped, and walked up and down, in doubt about going to see Westy's parents in their City pub. But supposing O'Gorman had gone to see them, and told them the truth? The thought was unbearable; and pushing off the Norton he leapt upon the saddle and opening the throttle with a crackle of the exhaust went down the Embankment a couple of hundred yards before dropping back to a quiet 35 m.p.h. Thence through traffic on wet cobbles to the Old Kent Road and finally home, subduedly to collect an old trench coat and flying helmet. His mother asked if he were going to stay the night, as it was Father's birthday, but he replied that he must get back to duty; and after declining an invitation to a lunch of cold mutton, ate bread and cheese, and with a cheerful goodbye set out for the Dover Road over Shooter's Hill. At the sleepy village of St. Mary's Cray, where cuckoos and nightingales sang outside the post office, he sent off a telegram to Eve, *Falcon flying east hope arrive six tonight please dine with me Corvanos*.

Down Wrotham Hill to the Weald of Kent, the fruit gardens of England; through Maidstone and on to Ashford; at last he was running with closed throttle down the hill into Hythe, round the sharp left-hand corner and along the coast road to Sandgate, where he stopped, and trudged on the brown shingle, trying to think back to a moment of his childhood there, to recover at least a picture of cousin Gerry's face, and his own romantic feelings when Gerry had told him of the wreck of *The Benvenue*. Then he thought that he might miss Eve if he did not hurry; and flying up the hill with the open exhaust cracking at more than four times the rate of a Vickers gun firing bounded over the crest, and closing the throttle, turned right-handed to the Leas, and went along smoothly and almost silently beside the promenade, at little more than fast walking pace; to see, a hundred yards ahead, the figures of Colonel Tarr, his C.O. talking to the G.O.C. Shorncliffe Command, General Shoubridge, a convalescent in a bath chair after double pneumonia. Out of the corner of his eye he saw them looking his way as he passed, and felt relieved that he was not in uniform. Should he have got leave from old Tarr, nicknamed locally the Flapper King? What did it matter, the war was over.

Chapter 20

SPECTRES OF THE MIND

The engine was making deep harp-string notes in the silver exhaust pipe now burnt faintly blue where it left the port. He passed the Pavilion, to see with a shock Eve walking beside a tall, heavy-weight figure wearing the double oak-leaf scroll of a General on the peak of his red-banded service cap. At the same moment Eve saw him and waved. He stopped, and walked over to her, wondering who her elderly companion might be.

She seemed to be a different person, almost formally composed as a lady as she walked a foot apart from her companion, not exactly keeping step with him, but giving the impression of unity with him. As he approached she smiled, and said something to her companion, who had an air of knowing him, almost of expecting him, which was puzzling. He tried to recall where he had seen the big face before.

"Good evening, Mrs. Fairfax!" he said, pulling off his tweed cap with an assumed air of shyness.

"Good evening, Phillip. I've had a wonderful surprise! Lionel arrived home on leave at five o'clock this morning, isn't it simply heaven? We've got a whole ten days together. Lionel, this is Captain Maddison, otherwise Phillip, adjutant to the Flapper King."

"How do you do, sir."

So this was her husband: crossed swords of a Brigadier, two rows of ribands, four wound stripes, friendly face—not at all like the 'we live our own lives' dullard he had imagined from Eve's description.

"We're going to sit by the band, Maddison, why not join us?"

The Bacarolle from *Tales of Hoffman* throbbed from the octagonal glass shelter.

"I think you know an old friend of mine, George Mowbray, who commanded the Home Counties division in France? We travelled together from Cologne. As you may know, he's come home to command your first battalion at Cannock Chase——"

"Oh really, sir?"

"I'm a sapper, and may get posted to the Canal. I was telling Eve that life can be quite amusing in Cairo. You are serving on, I suppose?"

"I'm only temporary, sir——"

Eve's red-lipped smile and bright eyes turned from one to the other. "You two soldier boys don't mind me eavesdropping, I hope?"

"Do forgive me, darling."

"I wasn't serious, I can see you both at once when you talk across me!"

There was a pause, while the 'cellist stroked dark blue plummy notes from a humming G string before moving over to an ecstatic A.

"Let me change places, darling," she said, with a brilliant smile for her husband.

Under the assumption of an open, unsophisticated manner Phillip concealed a feeling of slightly painful perplexity increased by a liking for Lionel and faded hopes of an early dinner in a restaurant with Eve and the dream of taking her on the pillion to the open spaces of the Romney Marshes, free as air, and bathing in the sea off the shallows of Dungeness among the ring-plover and shore-larks. Soon he made an excuse to say goodbye, with thoughts of applying to be sent back to the first battalion; or for a job in the Army of Occupation, anywhere so long as it was not in England.

"We'll be seeing something of you, I hope, before I go back to Hunland?"

"Oh—thank you, sir."

"Call me Lionel. Damme, I'm only a camouflaged major!"

"Thank you, Lionel."

"Come round in a day or two, Phillip," called out Eve and as he backed away she gave him a wink.

Every afternoon for the following three days he went alone to the low country behind the long sea-wall of the Marsh, visiting places he had hoped to visit with Eve, whose image accompanied him every moment of the long sunny days, arising from the vacancy within. At moments he twisted to get free of her image, while knowing that by every thought he was more deeply held.

"Quillie darling, be Mummie's very own sweet girl, and ask Marty to bring in tea, will you?" Eve knelt on the carpet to enfold and kiss her child. Then to Phillip staring out of the window, "When are you going to take me on the Romney Marshes?"

The old woman called Marty brought in the tea, set it down on the leather pouffe by the sofa, and without a word went out again.

"I don't know, Eve."

"What's the matter with you?"

"I think I ought to go away." He took a letter from his pocket. "This came yesterday from a cousin of mine, in Devon. He's left the army, and suggests that I do the same, and go and live with him, and share a wild life. He has an old lime-burner's cottage miles from anywhere, by the sea."

"I should go then, if you feel you'd like to. Is he a nice person?"

"Yes. Full of fun and life. Unlike me."

"Darling, don't get morbid. It's all those books you read. Julian Warbeck got the same way, and seemed to think I was responsible. Personally I think a barrel or two of beer and half a dozen volumes of Swinburne may have had more to do with his state of mind."

"I don't like Jay Double-u, Mummy, and hope he never comes back. But I like Pat, and I like Pillie, too, because he plays with me sometimes on the floor. I like the floor best, and under the table."

"Yes, darling, it's fun to enjoy yourself, isn't it? What's that, Pillie, a photograph of your cousin? Oh, *isn't* he good-looking! Such enormous eyes, and humorous mouth. Where was this taken?"

"Under one of the trees at the bottom of our garden."

"Where is that?"

"Near Blackheath."

"I like your straw boaters. What kids you both look! Willie and Pillie, under the tree at the bottom of the garden. Yes, I certainly like the look of Willie! The name seems to suit that clever little face, full of intelligence."

"Shall I read you his letter?"

"Do, please."

He read only part of it, telling of Willie's life in the solitary cottage above Shelley Cove, with an otter, seagull, and birds he had tamed. It was a beautiful life, said the writer, but lonely at times. He recalled the holiday they had spent together at Lynmouth when on convalescent leave in 1916, particularly the day when they had gone on the light railway from Lynton to Barnstaple and walked down the estuary and round the coast to Cryde bay, 'where those two men were drowned trying to rescue a governess, who afterwards walked ashore.'

"The bathing sounds as dangerous as Cornwall, where Lionel and I went for our honeymoon. Oh, that grim little Cornish farmhouse at Constantine Bay! Lionel chose the place from a map, because of the name."

"How d'you mean?"

"Quillie darling, ask Marty to take you for a walk on the Leas, will you? It's such a beautiful evening."

When the child and her nurse had gone Eve continued, "He made me swear I'd be constant, after calling me his 'wild English rose' to rouse his passion. He'd been used to living with scores of native women, you see, and wasn't quite sure how to tackle a sixteen-year-old bride, I suppose." She laughed. "The weather certainly lived up to the name, it rained constantly for a fortnight! However, it helped to produce Jonquil eight months later. Well, are you going to visit Willie Watt on your beautiful new female Norton, whose heartbeats mean so much to you?"

"Willie Watt?"

"Well, I don't know his surname, do I?"

"Oh, the same as mine, Eve."

From the high window of her flat she watched Jonquil and Martha walking to the Leas. Then taking his hand, she said, "Why are you so aloof, Pillie? Oh, before I forget! I got *The Man of Property* out of the library when Lionel was here, and found it very moving, and life-like. Especially the feelings of Irene, Soame's wife. I know exactly how she felt. I'd have gone straight to Bosinney's side, and damned those bloody old Aunts and Uncles. But she married someone nearly twice her age, and *that* I *do* understand. Darling, come and sit beside me. I do love you so."

On the sofa she put an arm round his neck, her fingers gentle in the hair behind his ears. Then she leaned to him, enclosing him with her arms, and put her head on his chest. "Don't speak. I could be like this for ever with you."

Half a minute later she said, "I can hear your heart beating, Pillie."

He held back his head to look at the back of her neck, where the auburn hair grew away in thick tresses, and felt desire from the innocence of her white flesh.

"Pillie dear, don't you ever feel you want me?"

"Yes, Eve, of course I do."

"Then why don't you make love to me?"

He was shocked; for so far he had esteemed her above Rupert Brooke's 'sneaking lust' felt by Lionel for his 'wild English rose,' otherwise a young girl's virginity. But who was he to judge another, when he was afraid to tell her the real truth: that he might give her venereal disease.

"Pillie darling, you disapprove of me, don't you, in your heart of hearts?"

"I feel first one thing, then another. Anyway, the 'wild English rose' feeling is only—lust."

"Pillie, do *you* feel lust for me? How lovely, darling: Tell me when you first felt lust for me!"

"When you rubbed your bare foot against my shin, when we were lying on the pebbles side by side after bathing that day, soon after I met you."

She kicked off a shoe, and held up a foot. "This was the one. Bad foot! It couldn't help it, honest it couldn't, cross my heart. Naughty foot!"

"I liked the spread of your toes, on the shingle. They looked so natural."

She felt under her skirt, and unfastened her stockings, pulled them off, and threw them across the room. "That's better," she said, spreading her toes. "I used to climb trees like a monkey when I was a kid. I could hold on to branches with these toes."

She lay back, waving one leg, admiring its shape. "I know how a fish feels with its fins. Let's go and have a swim!"

"No."

"Oh, darling, not now. Someone may come."

"I'll lock the door!"

"Do you truly love me?" she said, feeble now. He did not answer, held in tension by a thought to pay her out, since she wore nothing under her skirt. Afterwards, alarmed and weakened by shame, he asked what she was going to do about 'preventive measures.' She said in a hurt voice, "Why do you have to talk like that, and spoil it? You're like Lionel."

"I don't want anything to happen to you."

"I wouldn't mind a baby with your dark blue eyes, Pillie."

"I think you ought to take precautions, all the same. Haven't you any——"

"Really!" She looked at him with scorn. "Very well, I'll ease your mind. On such occasions I usually douche with Lysol, and swish away any little strangers. God, you men are all alike. Go away from me, you and your poetry! Don't you dare to touch me!"

Some weeks later, on returning to Folkestone after taking Desmond back to Wakenham on the pillion of the Norton, Phillip went to the orderly room and saw the Commandant sitting at his, Phillip's, desk.

Colonel Tarr was smoking a cigar and reading, or rather examining a library book which had remained on Phillip's desk, unread, for some months, *Joan and Peter* by H. G. Wells. The presence of the C.O. was a surprise, for Tarr seldom put in an appearance at the camp after mid-day, and never on a Saturday.

It was past the Colonel's time of going to the East Kent Club to read the evening papers, drink a couple of long brandy-and-sodas, and talk with one or another of his cronies at the bar before dining. Throwing down the novel, he said,

"You are doing no good for yourself here, Maddison. I am sending you back to your regiment. You will hand over your office to Captain Browne tomorrow morning, and he will give you the necessary papers for your journey. Good night."

Phillip went to see Eve to say goodbye, and on approaching her flat saw a grey Mercédès-Benz standing outside. Ah, he thought, she didn't think I would be coming back so soon.

After walking about for an hour he rang the bell, and went up to the flat, to be told at the door that Mrs. Fairfax had given orders that she was not at home to anyone.

"I'm sorry, mister, but that was what I was told to say."

"Tell her that I understand. Well, goodbye, Marty."

He walked about until dawn; and after breakfast, having handed over to Browne, and sent off his valise by train, addressed to the first battalion at Brockton Camp, Cannock Chase, Stafford, he set off to cross the Thames by the Gravesend ferry; and riding north passed through Essex and Gaultshire to the Midlands, stopping only for oil and petrol, and so through Birmingham and on to Cannock Chase, where his heart sank deeper when he saw hutments.

Mon. 9 June.

I am attached to a company for duty. O.C. is Lt. Silvester, M.C., a regular. 2d i/c another loot, also reg. Both Lt.-cols. in the war. Drills on square, route marches, bayonet practice, Lewis gun instruction—all dull & lifeless. Know no-one. Camp on high moor of ling and heather, stunted pines growing out of poor soil. Bredon Hill in far distance, seen through glasses when smoke haze of Brum and other industrial towns drifts away east. Bought a new gramophone and records in Stafford.

Mon. 21 July.

Went on leave four days ago. Peace Day Celebrations on 19th. Bonfires everywhere. Couldn't stick the Hill, so went down to Folkestone, blinding all the way, almost no need for lamp, sky ruddy and fireworks going up all the time. E. and I had agreed last May to meet 'whatever happens' on Peace Night. Knew it was no good but went. Saw her in Grand Hotel, with a mob of people. Surprised to see Willie there. She and Pat C. went down to Devon, apparently the day I left Folkestone. E. was a bit tight, and rude to me. Returned to Wakenham, slept under bushes in gully. Cold. Thought of going back to find Willie but didn't fortunately, would have bored him. Had 'Nunhead' nightmare, awoke slippery with sweat.

Phillip stayed in his cubicle, and did not go on parade. At last the adjutant sent for him. Phillip said he was not well.

"You will report to the Medical Officer."

The doctor, a *locum tenens* from Stafford while the R.A.M.C. regular was on leave, said: "You have a dull patch on your left lung. How long have you had these sweatings?"

"Off and on since September 1915, doctor. But much more since I went down with mustard gas—"

"That's enough to have caused a break-down of tissue, and infection by tubercle. Can you give me any particulars of previous wounds or illnesses?"

After this the doctor said, "What do you want to do? Go into hospital, or on leave? Anyone to look after you? Where d'you live? No, London's not too good. How d'you feel about things?"

"Oh, fairly fit, except a bit depressed at times."

"Sleep well? Any nightmares? H'm. The same dream night after night, you say. Tell me about it."

When Phillip had ended his somewhat jerky account, the doctor said, "You know, more ill-health is caused by chronic depressive thoughts, from painful incidents buried deep in the mind, than medical science generally allows. There are two schools of thought about this. The new school, very much in the minority, one need hardly say, believes that the effects of prolonged strain in the war can be delayed longer than was formerly thought. I was an M.O. with a regular battalion for a couple of years, beginning in 1915 and going on until Third Ypres, when I came home fagged out. The former theory was that, as experience is cumulative in human life, so battle experience hardened and acclimatised a man to endure where a partly trained soldier would crack. The contrary is the truth, I believe, for within my experience I saw again and again that a soldier's power of endurance is worn away the more by every battle he goes through. My dear fellow, what's the matter?"

Phillip's tears were momentary. The doctor decided not to press him; he knew already that he had hit the target. "I should think from what you have told me, and from what I know of you, that you have been drugging yourself by returning again and again to France. You have exhausted yourself, by using the war to escape from some underlying repression, probably from your early years. What every man needs is a good wife: in your case, I should say, the need is acute, as in most young men, and the blue-eyed fantasy in your dream denotes this. Have you known someone with blue eyes, someone particular, I mean?"

Phillip told him about Helena Rolls, and then Lily, while the doctor made no comment, but nodded his head slowly as though to himself during the hesitant confession.

"I'll give you a week off duty. It's a fine healthy air up here, keep in the sun, and laze about. D'you read? All the better! Conrad? Grand chap! Great writer! But don't get too tense. Try some P. G. Wodehouse, he's a very skilful writer, you know . . . ever read 'Saki'? He's another with more in him than at first meets the eye! I'll lend you a copy, if you promise to bring it back. Of course you will, but somehow books 'walk,' as they say. Start with the *Chronicles of Clovis* . . . now out in the sun, and lie in the heather. Meanwhile I'll send a chit to the orderly room."

Mon. 4 Aug. *My dream-nightmare.*

Nunhead station (which I used to pass on my way to Grantham on my old motorbike *Helena*, to avoid tramlines). General Gough and Lord Satchville have come at *my request*, to be shown something very important. It is all semi-dark and confused. They wait inside the station, because it is raining, while I go outside to find my motor-car. (The old Humberette I hired from Wetherley to drive to the shoot.) I can't find it because it doesn't really belong to me, although it is mine in the dream. With the two figures is the blue-eyed girl I met at the Duke's house-party, I can't in the dream see her, only know that her eyes are watching me, a sort of Helena—Lily—Melissa beautiful and coolly competent; more tenuous than a flower, a presence rather than an object. But as soon as I am outside the shabby little brown-painted wooden station and see the twisting hill above it I am lost in almost total darkness. Vague figures pass, I try to ask them about my motorcar which I left there, but it is gone, lost, perhaps stolen. Where can I hire a taxi for the two great men, who will be getting impatient, and the blue-eyed girl with them? I see several taxi-drivers with peaked hats but all evade or avoid me. The search for transport goes on endlessly and time-lessly and in a chaos of twilight turning to silent darkness and now I cannot see anyone. Suddenly the road is all mud and the station is gone, but I know it is there all the time, and the gleaming water and mud is not really there and all will be well if I can find the road and taxis on a rank there, although Nunhead never had any taxis because clerks etc pouring out of the station, white-faced, hurrying home on foot, were not the sort of people to afford taxis. The search in darkness goes on timelessly without end and when at last I find my way back to the station it has no roof, the rails are rusty, and General Gough and Lord Satchville are gone.

And when I awoke I knew what the dream meant as I lay in deep depression afraid of the white light if I switched it on. I was wet with sweat and forgot what the dream meant, knowing only that my life was ruined and it was my own weakness that had ruined it.

Withdrawal from all life of the battalion, including the officers' mess—no longer hectic, for these were regular soldiers with careers and ambitions before them—was extended for another week, without seeing the doctor. Philip had not called at his house in Stafford for the 'Saki' book offered him, although daily he went into Stafford for mid-day beer and bread-and-cheese at one or another of the pubs. Every afternoon he went to the same place at the edge of the moor, to sit near a self-sown glade of birches and see the road declining before him to the south. Dimly under the heat arising in the fine harvest weather lay the 'coloured counties' of the song that Desmond used to sing in his light tenor voice, *In summer time on Bredon.*

At last a chit arrived from his company commander ordering him to report at the company office; it lay unheeded on his dressing-table for a couple of days. Then Silvester, a lean, pale-eyed, lithe rugger-playing fellow with very light yellow hair, came to the cubicle. He was curt.

"The Commanding Officer has called for a report from me in the matter of your dereliction of duty."

Phillip asked to see the Commanding Officer, Lt.-Col. Mowbray. He sat at his desk, service cap on head, unsmiling. He wore the C.B. with his D.S.O. and two bars, the Legion d'Honneur, the Belgian Croix de Guerre. He had served in the South African war. He had gone out with the original Expeditionary Force in command of the first battalion. Now he was back again to real soldiering, his face carrying the heat-burns of the African veldt, the rains of the Curragh, the sweats of the Retreat from Le Cateau, of First Ypres, Festubert, Loos and Somme, and of all the weights and tensions of a brigade decimated many times in the Flanders battles of 1917, the Fifth Army miseries of 1918 and his division falling back, falling back, always falling back, and no reserves left. These strains had been temporarily relieved by thousands of pegs of whiskey taken abstemiously, thousands of glasses of port also in moderation, and for relaxation—and his eyes still saw with simple straightness behind their set look.

Lt.-Col. Mowbray said quietly, "I am glad you have come to apologise, Maddison. I am sending in papers for your immediate demobilisation."

"Very good, sir."

Lt.-Col. Mowbray got up and held out his hand. "Goodbye," he said. "And good luck."

Three days later the order for demobilisation arrived. Phillip said goodbye to half a dozen officers outside the mess hut, and pushing off on the pilot jet, vaulted into the saddle, to ride quietly, with the softest beats of the engine, down the narrow stone road to the south; and when clear of the camp he opened the throttle, fleeing on down the road, leaving behind the heather slopes, the birchwood dells, the stunted pines of Cannock Chase and Army life for ever.

Night had fallen when, having passed through Derby and many other towns, he arrived at Beau Brickhill; and turning into the courtyard of the house where in childhood he had found so much freedom and happiness, stopped and dismounted and drew back the Norton on its stand. A half moon hung above the ivy covering the disused stables; cob-webbed window panes glinted in silence.

A shaft of light came through the open french windows leading into Uncle Jim's little office, with the roll-top desk still there, an oil-lamp on it showing the calendars on the wall, many of them going back long before 1914; they were there when Uncle Jim was a boy, his father had hung them up under the boy's eyes, and for that reason they had been there ever since.

Phillip waited in shadow, hesitating whether to call out, diffident about cousin Polly's reception of him after the way he had treated her three years before. Then he saw the thin figure of Grannie Thacker in the doorway, dressed in black as always, tight bodice over the wooden corsets which had been her mother's before her, her skirts below the ankles of her button boots, her hair scrimped into a wispy nob.

Her voice said quietly, "Is that you, Percy?"

He stood still, alarmed lest he shock her. Had she waited, every moment, every hour, of all the days and nights since cousin Percy had been killed at Flers on the Somme: waiting for a miracle, sustained by hope in God's goodness that Liz's boy would one day come home?

"No, it's me—I mean I—it's Phillip."

"I thought at first it was Percy," the voice quavered. "I

heard a motor-bicycle, and thought it must be Percy. Of course, how idle of me. Come you inside, Phillip, and sit you down by the fire, and I will tell Eliza you've come."

"I can't stay very long, Grannie. How well you look. I'm on my way to the Crystal Palace. How is everyone?"

She appeared not to hear, for she said, "So you are staying at the Abbey for the shoot. My, how times have changed."

"Yes, Grannie." It must be wonderful to live outside the flow of time, to live a life of dreams like the sun. "I think I'll go on now. I must get some carbide."

"Percy may have some. I saw his tin on the stable rack only this morning. Come you in, my dear, and sit you down by the fire."

He went into the little room between the office and the kitchen parlour. How small it was, the horse-hair sofa still there, and the *petit point* cushions, with their red and yellow roses.

The kitchen door opened, and Aunt Liz came in, in black from bodice to trailing skirt, small as a pawn on a chess-board.

"Why, it's Phillip, I do declare! What brings you here? How glad I am to see you." She held up her face to be kissed. "So you've left the Army, have you?"

"Well, almost. Tomorrow at the Crystal Palace——"

"I heard from your mother only this morning, she told me you were leaving. Grandpa has been very ill, did you know that? Poor old fellow, he is eighty, and has had this Spanish influenza which is still going about. Polly is at Husborne village, staying the night with her cousin, she will be sorry not to have seen you."

"I'll call on her as I pass through, Aunt Liz."

"We can give you a bed for the night. You know you're always welcome, don't you?"

"It is so good of you, but I must go on, I think. I must get some carbide."

"We have a tin in the stables, you're welcome to a fill up. It was Percy's, and we've kept it there ever since he went away."

"I understand." He lit a cigarette. "D'you mind?"

"No, do smoke. I like to see a man smoking about the house. Uncle Jim won't be back just yet, he's gone to a meeting of the Gas Board, down by the station. I expect you remember it?"

"Yes, Percy and I fished for roach there once, in one of the pits."

"That's right, Phillip! What a good memory you have, to be sure! Now you won't refuse a sausage roll to warm you on your way, will you? Have you had tea?"

"No, I wanted to get through by daylight. I'd love a cup of tea, if I may."

"Of course you shall. And I'll warm up a plate of rolls for you. You always liked them, didn't you?"

When he was eating hungrily, she said, "Polly is going to be married, did your mother tell you?"

"Why no, Aunt Liz! I am awfully glad!" And yet——

"We've known him all our lives, he's one of the Greylands cousins, at the Round House Farm, I expect you remember it? Turneys have farmed that land under the Duke for four hundred years. Yes, George will take it over, now his father is getting on, and the young people will live there."

He called on Polly and her cousin in Husborne village, and had a second meal. A glass of wine, then another one, soon had him back in the spirit of the old days, joking with Polly and Milly, her cousin, slices of home-cured ham on his plate, and home-made gooseberry pickle.

"Dam' good stuff, you girls. Think I'll come and stay here."

"You're quite welcome, to stay the night, Phillip."

"I must press on, Polly, my dear old sporting partner. I wish you everything good in your marriage, my sweetie!"

"I wondered if Mother had told you. Thank you, Phillip."

Polite and subdued, he thought. Surely she wasn't still keen on him? Damn, he must be careful, or she might read his thoughts. "Yes," she went on, "Doris has a beau now, too. You've met Percy's friend, Bill Willoughby, haven't you? Doris sees quite a lot of him, I hear."

"I met him once. Rather shy. A good thing, shyness. Better than being a thruster like me." He drank more wine.

Polly laughed. She had small teeth, very white and even.

"What's your beau like?"

"Oh, he's a farmer. He was in the regiment, you know."

"Oh, then he's all right."

"He's a very good shot, and is asked to shoot over the Duke's land, with the tenants, of course."

"I hit two partridges with four thousand cartridges, two Mills bombs, and half a ton of bird-lime."

They laughed at this. "I wish I had a simple country mind, like you two Sweeties. Laugh at anything."

"Not in the least!" said Polly, tossing her head. "*You* are funny, you see. You always were a funny little creature, I remember. So there!"

"Have you met Bob Willoughby?"

"Oh yes. He came to us and stayed quite often, before he went to see Doris. Still, I'm very glad for Doris's sake, although I think she will never forget Percy."

It was time to go.

Down the lane, past the beautiful village built entirely by the Duke, and his father, and so to Telford's straight macadamised highway to St. Albans, past the winking gas lights of the streets, and on to the distant sky-stain that was London.

It was late to wake them up, so he lay under the bushes on the Hill and shivered all night on the edge of sleep, thinking that at least he was free, that nothing ever again would be as bad as the battlefields, because he could go home in the morning.

After breakfast he sped at between 50 and 55 m.p.h. to the Crystal Palace, was examined by a doctor, told where he must attend a medical board later, and after signing papers noticed that a plate with coins on it had been placed on the desk near him by the corporal, a weedy youth in spectacles.

"What's this for?"

"Some officers like the staff to drink their health," replied the corporal, dropping the 'sir' to the civilian before him.

Seeing an empty plate, Phillip put it beside the other. "What's the idea?" asked the corporal.

"All contributions thankfully received, sir, to my Widow and Orphan Fund. My mother's the widow, and I'm the orphan. Cheerio!"

Resting astride the Norton on the crest of the Sydenham ridge he looked north and saw the grammar school on the hill standing above a grey wilderness of roofs and church spires under the smoke of London. If only it were like Ypres, so that the rubble could be cleared away, and fields of grass and corn arise again; or even lie in ruins like the Cloth Hall, with grass growing on the ruined walls, and wild flowers, and willows, and strange birds returned to a wilderness sanctuary—then there might be hope.

Where could he go, what could he do, where find the bosom of *Eleänore* upon which he might rest, as in the song by Coleridge-Taylor that Desmond used to sing? Or was his longing to be forever like that of Edgar Allen Poe for Annabelle Lee in that lost kingdom by the sea?

Part Five

NO-MAN'S-LAND IN CIVVY STREET

'But the old flags reel and the old drums rattle,
As once in my life they throbbed and reeled;
I have found my youth in the lost battle,
I have found my heart on the battlefield.'

from *A Song of Defeat*, by G. K. Chesterton.

Chapter 21

THE MOUSE

"Can you tell me," said Richard to his wife, while outside the last leaves from the elm at the bottom of the garden were being scattered by the October wind, "if, and when, Master Phillip is proposing to do any work?"

"I think he is looking round, Dickie. Papa would like him to go into the Firm, but Phillip wants time to make up his mind, I think."

Phillip was away on a visit to his Aunt Victoria, now living in the neighbourhood of Hawkhurst. She lived in a cottage provided by her brother Hilary, who had retired from special service with the Navy with the rank of Captain (R.N.R.). Hilary was due to arrive at Hawkhurst two days after the arrival of Phillip.

Phillip came home unexpectedly on the evening of the third day. His father waited to hear about the results of his stay, but Phillip had nothing to say. Only later did Richard hear from Hilary that the visit was 'not altogether a success.'

"Phillip, before my arrival, Dick, went off on his motor-bicycle, without telling his Aunt, and returned at all hours, without explanation or apology. He spent his evenings with the railway porters in the local pub, giving the excuse that they were old soldiers, and he wanted to hear about their experiences in the war. I tackled him about his future, but could get little out of him. Then abruptly, just before dinner, he said he must go, and that was that. We haven't heard from him since."

"He's been behaving queerly since he has been home, Hilary. It's my belief that there is something seriously the matter with him. I found a certain article hidden in the bathroom, some months ago, and it set me wondering."

When Richard went on to say that it was a glass urethral syringe, Hilary replied, "At least it shows that he has some common sense. These young fellows, you know, can't be held back; and as the saying is, If you can't be good, be careful."

"I do not look at it in that light, Hilary. There are others to be considered. I can't sleep at night, with Phillip coming in at all hours. He treats the place like an hotel. But what can one do? I have tried to talk to him, but have found him unresponsive."

"He's not fit, you know, Dick. He has a disability pension, in fact I cashed the money order for him, a little over £6 for the month."

"He never told me that."

"I shouldn't worry, Dick. They wouldn't give him that if he had had venereal disease. I wanted to talk to him about an idea I've had for some time now—of farming the family land I've bought back—under a manager of course—with my two nephews under him, to learn the job properly. I'm no longer interested in farming, but I'm prepared to put up some capital so that the land can be farmed properly by someone in the family. The two young fellows would live with John in the house—he's agreeable—I saw him on my way back from Pembroke Docks. John is rather worried about his boy—told me he had nearly come a cropper with some married woman at Folkestone. That was last September, and I gather John hasn't seen Willie since."

Richard had not heard about Phillip's escapade at the same place; Hetty's anxiety lest her husband find out had been secondary only to her fears for her son.

"I'm sorry to hear that about Willie," said Richard. "He's a decent little fellow, and from what I know of him, I would say that he has been ensnared by some siren. And now they are talking of giving women the vote! Did you ever hear of anything so ridiculous? I don't know what the world is coming to, Hilary! There is that two-faced Lloyd George, only a few months ago promising to bring those responsible for the war to justice, including the Kaiser, and where are his promises now? The Kaiser enjoys his days cutting up wood and living like a country gentleman at Doorn in Holland, living on the fat of the land! As Castleton in the *Trident* keeps on trying to bring home to everyone, 'They'll cheat you yet, those Junkers!'"

Hilary found his elder brother's emphasis a little trying, and made an excuse to take his leave. Part of Phillip's trouble, he thought, was that he had a stick for a father; while the boy's dual nature was due to Jewish blood, from that old reprobate, Thomas Turney.

When Hetty asked Phillip how he had got on with his uncle, he replied, "Oh, he was much the same as usual, asking a lot of personal questions."

"He is interested in your future, Phillip, now that you have done so well in the Army."

"Maybe. But the primary rule of good manners is surely that one does not ask personal questions."

"He is your uncle, Phillip, remember."

"I find it more interesting to talk about things, rather than people. By the way, will it be all right if I pay you thirty bob a week while I'm at home?"

"It's far too much, dear. Are you sure you can afford it?"

"Oh easily, I've got a pension, you know. And Austin Harrison is considering one of my sketches of the Saschenfeste at Wytschaete for *The English Review*."

Walking down the High Street one morning, striding fast while breathing deep to expand his lungs, Phillip saw Julian Warbeck outside the Roebuck, talking to a poor man with a barrel organ in the gutter. He crossed the road to avoid him, but curiosity made him hide behind a vegetable van, and watch Warbeck, who wore khaki trousers and R.A.F. tunic, with wings and rank badges removed. Evidently some deal had been made, for the man touched his decayed bowler hat and set off to haul the wheeled box behind Warbeck.

Phillip followed them, past the Obelisk and over the Randiswell river bridge. They turned up Mill Lane, and stopped outside the Rat Trap. When Warbeck went inside, the man turned the handle, tinkling out the overture to *Cavalleria Rusticana*. Phillip decided to follow Warbeck, and going into the tiny bar, was greeted by him like an old friend, instead of a rival, as he had feared.

"I met your cousin Willie in Folkestone," Warbeck said, in a jovial yet mocking voice. "He was one of the pack after La Belle Amie. Quite an education knowing that woman. Let me see"—he began to count on fingers the more stubby with their bitten nails—"between the daffodil and the swallow there were, to my limited knowledge, 'Naps' Spreycombe; Jay Double-u—the nickname of my unrepentent self; your most respectable Self"—he bowed ironically—"that makes three of us in the Paragon pack. Patrick Colyer, the bogus knight-of-the-air, now doing a well-earned stretch in the glass house; your cousin Willie with the large soulful eyes—five; 'Sandhurst' White, six; Aubrey de la Hay, an actor with no talent whatsoever, seven; and finally Lord Spreycombe, who returned to take the pool after the youngest puppy, Peter White, had given her the supreme satisfaction of shooting himself with her name on his—I won't say bloodless—lips; for as a fact the bullet passed through the roof of his mouth. Quite an achievement, don't you think, for La Belle Amie? You have gone pale, my friend. Why not have a drink?"

Phillip said, after a few moments to steady his voice, "Are you serious?"

"I am always serious. What are you drinking—the only question that really matters."

"Did somebody really commit suicide?"

"He did indeed, Phillip. Your cousin, with the soulful eyes—'Willie'—was not there when they asked for him at the inquest. He was there when Peter White shot himself, but had in the meantime crossed over to Boulogne, emulating Oscar Wilde in another connexion. A curious, indeed a remarkable chap, 'Willie.' He told me that his ambition was to write a Fifth Gospel, proving, among other things, that the Galilean meant something quite different when He said what he was supposed to have said. But at least 'Willie' believed in the dead burying the dead, for he skipped over to France on the next boat. What are you drinking? May I call you Phillip, by the way?"

"Please do."

"I am Julian. My respected father, who has retained many of the ideas of his adolescence well into middle age, still had a high opinion of the works of Byron when the midwife presented me to him, my unhappy mother having died of puerperal fever meanwhile, chiefly owing, my father has repeatedly told me, to the size of my head, which may well have been a euphemism for a part of his own anatomy. Oh yes, Father has been quite a chap in his time. What are you drinking?

"Just a glass of mild, Julian, if you please."

"Mild? My dear chap, you! Our local hard-shell hero drinks swipes! Perish the thought!"

"But not the stomach! Just half a pint, thank you, Julian."

"Certainly, Phillip! Every man to his taste! I will join you in one moment." He raised a pint of Burton and drained it in what appeared to be a gulpless pouring down the throat. Then turning to the landlord, in a voice of extreme courtesy he said, "One small glass of mild for this gentleman, and the same again for me. I have a musical friend outside, would you be so good as to send him out a pint of the same excellent liquor? He has a long uphill future life before him." To Phillip, "It is my respected parent's birthday, and a little music will, I hope, lessen his chronic concern for my so-called working career—in other words, he wants me to find a job in order to save him from forking out the dough. Well, it's a poor heart that never rejoices——" And lifting up his fresh pint Warbeck poured it down his throat. "Ah, that's better! Landlord, the same again, if you please!"

"Have this one with me, Julian!"

Warbeck gave him another slight bow. "I am glad to see some light returning to your eyes, even if it is only a pale ray from swipes." He rubbed his hands together, and expelled a lungful of air. "Yes, it's a poor heart that never rejoices. Now tell me, how does it feel to be a local hero? Do not mistake me, I am serious! Your fame has spread from the pages of *The Kentish Mercury*, 'the boy is father of the man.' You were a Boy Scout, if I recall rightly? The patrol leader of the Bloodhounds? Your photograph, dimly reproduced among the leaves that strew the brooks of Vallambrosa, was next to an advertisement urging the constipated to Take Carter's Little Liver Pills. Fame indeed! Seriously, Philip, your praises were sung in all the old *clichés* of mid-Victorian journalism! How about a pint of Burton, you look quite pale, my dear fellow!"

Phillip, to get away from the grindstone of the other's manner, changed the subject. "Did you see that photograph of a masked ex-officer in *The Daily Trident* the other day? I thought at first that you had hired the barrel organ, for the same purpose."

"Good God no! Still, it's an idea!"

After another pint, Warbeck got the landlord's wife to cut out a rough mask in black cloth, with a piece of elastic garter sewn on; and leading the way through the lane where Phillip had walked to and from school many times, they went up the street to the Hill, the barrel organ following until the man stopped, exhausted.

"Let's give him a hand, Julian."

They helped to push the thing up the steep slope to the crest.

There, behind the garden of the lavatory, Warbeck put on the mask, and with the borrowed broken bowler perched on the top of his large head, got between the shafts and hauled the outfit, head held low, towards the shelter where the old men were sitting. The man remained behind, according to instructions;

Phillip walked along the crest, to cross the allotments on the old tennis courts and so to approach the shelter from behind.

He saw Julian stop in front of the shelter, and slowly turn the handle, while *Won't You Come Home, Bill Bailey* issued like a dirge from the faded green cheese-cloth covering the tired strings of the instrument. When the last *tremolo* had stopped, Julian, with a bow, went forward, bowler in hand.

"What foolery is this?" growled Mr. Warbeck.

"I'm trying to turn an honest penny, Father, as you have been urging me to do daily for some months. Come, Father, it's been a long pull up, on this occasion of your seventieth birthday anniversary. Or is it your seventy-fifth? Don't frown so, Father, it makes you look even older."

"You're drunk again, you scoundrel!"

"On the contrary, Father, I am sober, but it is a good idea, all the same."

"Where did you steal that damned thing?"

"I hired it for the day, Father. You see, I have got a job."

"You are a ne'er do well, a waster! Do you call this exhibition of arrant nonsense a job? You have never looked for a job, unless it was emptying beer down your gullet while leaning on a pub counter!"

"Looking for a job is a job in itself, and requires some thought, as I have explained to you on many occasions, Father."

"What did you pay for this nonsensical object?"

"Five shillings for the day, Father. On credit. I hope you will advance that sum, on the principle that you cannot accumulate unless you speculate. Come, Father, do not let the lack of a mere five bob abort a good intention to add to the gaiety of nations." He went back to the organ, and turned the handle rapidly; then seeing Thomas Turney feeling in his pocket, stopped to go forward.

"Here you are, m'boy. Ah, two of you, eh? Well, Phillip, what are you going to do with that thing?"

"A mere spectator, sir."

Julian pocketed half-a-crown. "Choose your tune, sir. I can produce an approximation of *Cavalleria Rusticana*, *Out Went the Gas*, *The Arab's Farewell to His Steed*, *The War March of the Priests*, *After the Ball Was Over*, *Goodbye, my Bluebell*, or *Floradora*."

Thomas Turney chose *Floradora*, with its memories of Charley and his wife humming the gay, romantic airs when Sarah was still alive, and the world had not changed. The remote, sad-sweet tinkle was followed by *The Arab's Farewell* and a memory of Dickie's voice on summer evenings coming through the open window next door, while Hetty sat at the piano.

The concert came to a premature stop with the arrival of a stout park keeper, who said that all playing of unauthorised music was forbidden by the by-laws of the London County Council which were displayed at every entrance; so the barrel organ was taken down the gully, to be played outside No. 11, and again outside the flat, from behind the upper window of which the face of Mrs. Neville wagged about with laughter.

After handing over the organ in Randiswell, with an extra five bob for the man, Phillip suggested that they take the tram so far as Cutler's Pond. It was by now closing time, a relief, with the thought that he might walk off the cloying effects of two pints of beer. They went up Whitefoot Lane, and through the woods, meaning to cross the Seven Fields to Brumley; and coming out beyond the trees, by Shrofften Farm, Phillip saw before him a great heap of stones, with standards of timber, tin roofed sheds, and other gear, near a notice board with the name of a London firm of contractors. A reservoir was to be made at the highest point, for a new housing estate to cover all the Severn Fields. Thrown oaks and elm trees gave the place a look of desolation.

As they crossed over the condemned green fields, where once flocks of lapwing and fieldfares had gathered, the voice of Julian became tedious, and Phillip felt the front of his head beginning to ache. Julian strode a foot or so in front of his left shoulder, talking away, either about his favourite poet, Swinburne, or one or another of the literary figures known from his immense range of reading—words, words, words, too often delivered in a scoffing manner as he declared that every source of art was materialistic, that all artists were decadent, that all 'musings and hopes for the ideal derived from mere idle sentimentality, having a basis in masturbation.'

"Even Swinburne?"

"Certainly! Likewise Dostoieffsky, Tolstoi, and Beethoven. The slight hollows at the sides of the temple, to be seen in their portraits, show this clearly. But what does it matter how poetry is written, so long as it is written? The oriental races simply cannot understand most of our romantic Western love poetry."

"Then you think that love is entirely based on sex?"

"What else? What free man would want to write of love, when he could enjoy it naturally? Herrick wrote his best verse when deprived of his mistress. He certainly didn't want to write it when he was in bed with her!"

"But the great writers——"

"Mere *folie de grandeur*! Consider Nietschze, and his masterpiece, *Thus Spake Zarathrustra*. It's great prose, but it would never have been written if Nietschze had not been syphilitic, nor would Dostoieffsky have written *The Brothers Karamazov* without the condition of his epileptic fits! As for Francis Thompson, whom you believe to be a great poet, but I know has only a streak of genius, neuralgia and laudanum were the agents which induced him to write. Thompson was also sexually impotent; his *Sister Songs*, with their fawning love for the Meynell girls, Monica and Viola, proves it. But nevertheless he wrote some great stuff.

> Forlorn, and faint, and stark,
> I had endured through watches of the dark
> Th' abashless inquisition of each star,
> Yea, was the outcast mark
> Of all those heavenly passers' scrutiny.
> Stood bound and helplessly,
> For Time to shoot his barbèd minutes at me . . .

Oh, it's great stuff, Phillip! I shall live only for great poetry, by God! Let's get a 'bus, it may be market day in Brumley, and the pubs open all day."

Eight hours later the two, with wet feet and muddy shoes and trousers, were back in the Randiswell, Phillip drooping wearily beside Julian as he talked to Dr. Dashwood, who stood, his face the colour of magenta, before the mahogany counter of the saloon bar drinking the last of his nightly bottle of whiskey. Ten minutes before closing time Phillip went outside with Julian, who after mixing nearly a score pints of beer with whiskey, port, sherry and gin—drinks paid for by others in the bars the two had visited—was obviously going to shoot his bundle. Holding to the iron rail between white-painted oak posts, to which ponies and horses had once been hitched, Julian bent over towards the ditch three times in rapid succession. As he wiped his mouth with the back of his hand, Phillip—who had drunk little, and then only mild beer—said to him with sympathy, "I know how you feel, Julian. I've often felt like that. You've had too much, old boy, that's the trouble."

Straightening up, Julian replied, "The trouble is I haven't had enough!" and went back into the bar. Phillip slipped away home, to let himself in with his key, and tip-toe silently to his bedroom, which was now the end room, facing the garden and the early morning sun. By the window was a card-table, its green baize covering blotted and blotched with ink shaken from an old army wooden pen with a relief nib which he had used when acting as assistant adjutant at Landguard nearly a year before. He was secretly writing a novel with a setting in a far, imagined countryside, with imagined characters derived from memories of his boyhood with Percy Pickering and his village friends at Beau Brickhill and others of his own boyhood, including Cranmer, a ragged boy he had befriended. The foolscap sheets of this romance were hidden under the mattress of his bed, in the fear that if anyone in the house saw them, especially his sister Elizabeth, he would not be able to continue in what he was believing and living in with nervous exaltation as an escape from real life. It would be equally fatal, he thought, as he lit the candle, if Julian knew of what he was doing.

If night was a friend, day was worse than an enemy in its emptiness. With renewed optimism he sought Julian; and after one Saturday mid-day meeting at the Roebuck, when Julian did most of the talking, recounting his amorous and other adventures while with the R.A.F.—most amusing story-telling marred at times by derisive arrogance—they hired another barrel-organ and dressed in pre-war civvy suits, Phillip with his top-hat stove-in and broken umbrella, Julian in a grey frock coat and bowler taken from his father's cupboard and worn with long sheepskin flying boots, hauled the thing on the Hill the next morning, and played it in mockery of the after-church parade with a few silk hats bobbing here and there in the streams of mainly elderly people walking up and down the path along the crest. Inevitably they were turned off by one of the keepers, who said that if they brought back the vehicle, as such it was within the meaning of the by-laws applicable to Open Spaces and Recreation Grounds of the L.C.C., they would be summoned.

Richard heard about this incident, but said nothing to either his wife or his son.

Tues. 4 Nov.

Mother, Doris and I went down from Euston for Polly Pickering's wedding. I wore the suit of khaki barathea dyed navy blue, which I had made in Folkestone (and haven't paid for), with a yellow silk tie bought in the Burlington Arcade. George Turney, her cousin twice removed, appeared after supper, and hung or rather lay about in the billiard room afterwards, a dazy look in his eyes as he slumped back in an armchair with Polly across his knees, fondling her before everyone as though we weren't there, sprawling on the small of his back and murmuring endearments as though he were half tight. I thought it was pretty bad form.

I asked Polly when he had gone off on his motorbike, banging harshly with tappets not properly adjusted, if she had expected him. No, she said, adding that he had not got any friends left, and did not get on very well with his father, and so had come to see her, feeling lonely. I felt like U. Hilary. I asked her, Did she love G.? She said she was fond of him, but did not ever expect to find true love. I asked her if she had been hurt by my behaviour, after Lynmouth in 1916. "I wasn't aware of any particular behaviour on your part," she replied. Later I realized that she had something of the quality of 'Spectre' in her: a clay-like strength. S.'s father was a Gaultshire man.

The wedding. P. was in white wearing her gt-g'mother's lace veil, and carrying a spray of lilies. G. was in uniform, with the M.C. Dozens of small dark farmers, most of them Turneys, black beards, bowler hats, with old-fashioned broadcloth claw-hammer coats, starched collars and dickies, and grey ties. I felt a bounder in my yellow silk tie, bought as a protest against the drab life of a soul-destroying suburb. Thought of writing a novel called *Soot*, but satire is superficial, therefore untrue; all human characteristics, as 'Spectre' used to say, come from environment.

No shortage of food among farmers. The wedding breakfast was spread over three rooms connected by open doors, reminding me of Hindenburg Line at Graincourt—hams, sausage rolls, chickens, a baron of beef, mince pies, cream meringues, jellies, blancmanges, chocolates, biscuits, cheeses. Napkins tucked in necks, the old clod hoppers knew how to do themselves well. I tucked in mine, and felt less a snob.

At the back of my mind a vague feeling that all was not well with Polly; and when later, after she had changed into a going-away tweed coat and skirt, she said to me privately, in the little conservatory where withered bunches of grapes hung above us, that she might need my help one day, I felt that, underneath her calm appearance of strength, her heart had broken when I more or less jilted her in September 1916, at the time when the telegram came that Percy was killed, and Doris and I saw her off at Euston.

Weds. 5 Nov.

Saw Jack Smith. I remembered him as a quiet, rather lonely boy walking home from Wakenham Road School down Ivy Lane, always by himself. He lent me Edward Carpenter's *Towards Democracy*. Most of the sentences in every page were heavily underlined with purple copying-pencil. He asked me to go to their party next Friday evening. He lives with his younger brother and sister in the Randiswell Road in one of those yellow-brick houses built about 1904.

Thurs. 6 Nov.

Walked alone over the old places, and through the woods. Along Shooting Common, and through Brumley and down to Cutler's Pond and so home. Noises of motor-buses, cars, hooters etc. spoiled the tranquillity. I walked through Randiswell in gathering fog, eyes filled with sulphurous specks, which affected my breathing. I felt exhausted, and was sulky and rude to my patient, silver-haired mother. I am conscious of being a perfect swine, *but can't help it.* Her cheeks seem to glow, and she always eats humble pie. I feel hurt as I write; eyes are brimming—yet why am I conscious of the pig I am, and *still* remain reserved and curt?

Thought all day of 'Pauline' . . . and wondering if I shall attempt to portray her as the iconoclast or not, later in the book. No, I don't think so. I find my thoughts still dwelling on her. Girls like her are filled with 'earth' force, the life-force, vital as the sun's ray; that is why they have such a terrible sway over men. At the other extreme, poets have the spiritual fire within them; they are of the aetherial force, perhaps of the after-life. Who knows? God help the clashing of earth and spiritual forces.

I realize that the pain is still deep within my heart. And Eve? Never remembers. The sun's warmth comes again; I may die tomorrow, still the sun will shine. At times I nearly despair. However, I have my *work* to love—my book. Now for more of it!

Fri. 7 Nov.

The Smith's party was pretty awful. Gas fire, cuckoo clock, oleographs of Pear's Annual Faunteleroy child figures on walls, etc. We sat around playing Consequences, Charades, Hunt the Slipper (jokes about smelly feet, etc.) and other wearisome games. When the 'ladies' went out to get supper, Bob Smith the young brother, said 'Come on' to the men and at once they got into a huddle like flies in an attic—except that numbed flies crawl and these men hastened to clot around Bob—eager for what I wondered. An exchange of smutty stories! Jack the elder brother stood aloof, a smile on his face as he glanced rather pathetically at me. I behaved badly, no doubt, also keeping aloof and not troubling to conceal my dislike of this aspect of lower middle class depression or repression. When I spoke to Jack, he asked me rather timidly what I thought of Edward Carpenter, blinking slightly as though fearful of possible derision on my part. I thought it was thin, rather vacuous stuff, the work of a self-enclosed man without real urge to write of the world as it is, with true understanding of opposing forces always in play in nature; but I said Carpenter struck me as one who had seen through the dross of civilization. His face lit up, and glancing round he whispered, "Don't tell the others about it, will you? They won't understand."

Tom Ching came in later, after the pubs had closed. He said his mother had come out of Peckham House, cured, but was v. frail, after a stroke. I walked home with him, he comparatively sober, and rather boring, as he kept saying that he had no friends. "I get such strength from you," he said. I didn't say that what he got from me I felt I had lost. He asked if we could go for country walks together, he wanted to know more about nature, hardly knowing one bird from another. We arranged to walk on Sunday, and explore the Randisbourne above Cutler's Pond to its source.

Had the Nunhead dream again and awoke to see Father by my bed asking what was the matter, why had I been groaning and muttering to myself. I apologized, said it was probably due to indigestion. He said it was more probably because I had nothing to do, except to lie in bed half the morning, turn night into day, etc.

"You should have gone back to the Office!" he said, querulously.

I asked if he had to bring that up now, when the matter was finished.

"Yes, I do! You were in receipt of full pay for nearly five years, including annual increments, and if you did not intend to go back, the honourable course was to have paid back the money."

I said I would pay it back, and he went away.

Downham is now second-in-command of the Wine Vaults Lane branch, under Hollis, old Howlett having retired. Some hopes for me, under D., who must know I know that Teddie Pinnegar nearly shot him for wind-up in Sept. 1917, at Proven. I bear no ill-will to D., but he must dislike me more than before, for knowing what I know about him.

Richard had the morning of Saturday away from the office—the fifth of six Saturday mornings a year given to each of the staff.

Breakfast was to be an hour later than usual, at 9 a.m. It was a sunny morning, free of mist and fog; the south-west wind was blowing. Phillip was up in his room, shaved, washed, dressed, and reading over, with some excitement, what he had written the night before. Breakfast was not yet ready. Hetty had laid the places in the sitting-room, the french windows of which had been opened by Richard to bring in the warm morning air.

Before going down, Phillip opened the top of his bedroom window, and looking out, saw his father below watching Zippy with a mouse. In the kitchen his mother was putting the hot plates on a tray, the eggs and bacon, a special treat for the two men, being already in the chafing dish.

"I'll take the tray down for you, Mother. Are the plates wiped underneath?"

"Oh dear, I nearly forgot! Thank you, dear, for reminding me. I'll just make the tea, and bring down the kettle in a minute. Now where did I put that cloth?"

"Leave it to me. You bring down the tea." He wiped the plates, then peered into the oven. "That's where the specks fall from, you know. This oven contains the mural memorials of a thousand cremations."

"Yes, I'm always trying to find time to scrub it out. Oh, how I miss Mrs. Feeney! She went on working when she had that influenza, you know. And I never went to her funeral! I *would* have one of my bilious attacks at the time, wouldn't I?"

"She was a lovely person, Mother, she had impeccable manners. I always admired her—no, I took her for granted. Still, we all have to die sometime. I'll take down the tray now."

He put it before her place at table, with the silver-plated chafing dish, kept warm by boiling water; and going to the open windows, said "Breakfast is ready, sir."

"Thank you, old man. I'll be along in a moment. I want to make sure that the cat does not lose its mouse."

"Isn't it dead *yet*?"

Zippy was enjoying itself on the lawn, and Father appeared to be enjoying himself equally. The cat would roll on its back ecstatically, clutching the mouse with its paws; and then, flinging it away, lie still while the mouse ran away for its life. The 'wee tim'rous beastie' had got so far as the path below the steps when the cat sprang again and hooked it up in its claws, and was rolling once more upon its back when Hetty appeared at the door.

"Oh, *please* kill it, Dickie!"

"Why?" He looked at her. "May not the cat have its sport?"

"*Please* kill it."

"Why must you always be so sentimental?"

She turned away, with trembling lips. Phillip breathed deeply, to control his own feelings. He tried to think: Did his father gain what his mother lost, as the cat with the mouse? Or did she *thrive* on suffering, as Father had once accused her of doing, 'like a Christian martyr'? He must try and keep his own feelings in balance, resist feelings of hardness towards Father's apparent callousness.

The cat bounded away, and when it dropped the mouse on the concrete path leading to the back door he saw it was a short-tailed field-vole, with little white nipples—obviously a female who had young somewhere in a grass-ball nest. Its fur was wet, he could see that its life was ebbing fast; big or little mammal, the feelings of all were basically the same. He clenched his hands as he saw his mother's face, turning away from the *feld-grau* vole crawling in a slow zig-zag, as though its spine were disjointed.

"Why not kill it, Father, and put Mother out of her misery?" he managed to say.

"Oh come, Phillip! You, a colonel once commanding men, to talk like that!"

The cat rolled on the concrete, watched by Father with what seemed to be simple happiness. Then it squatted on its paws, tail twitching with little jags of lust, watching the vole trying to climb one of the creosoted boards of the fence. While it was hanging there by its paws, a foot from the ground, Mother came back to the open window.

"Oh, do let it go, *please* do, Dickie! Or kill it——" Her voice was weak.

"It's sport for the cat!" repeated Richard. "It's the cat's nature."

"Oh, I cannot bear it," she said, and went away again.

Phillip followed her into the house, his breathing restricted, his father's voice calling after him "Your mother didn't object to eating those birds you brought home from the Husborne shoot, did she? The fact is, your mother takes every opportunity to object to what I do, or if it isn't what I do, it's how I do it!" Then almost amorously to the cat, "Poo-or Zippy! Would they take away your mousie then, poo-oor Zippy." He bent to tickle the cat's stomach, drawing back his hand from the claws. "Naughty, Zippy!"

The cat sprang up, then meeow'd weakly at its master, blinking eyes when Richard half playfully, half angrily, cuffed its head.

Phillip went away from the window to the front room, where he saw his mother sitting in her armchair, her eyes bright with unshed tears, her cheeks faintly flushed, her body seeming smaller than when last he had seen her sitting there, in what was supposed to be her very own chair. He had seldom seen her in it, and never when the children had been in the front room on Sunday afternoons, for usually he and Mavis had made a rush for it.

"Phillip, I can't bear it any longer! I have my nervous headaches almost constantly now."

"I know how you feel. I often feel just the same myself. Father doesn't understand. We all fail to understand one another, it seems. Look how beastly I was to you when Desmond and I came back from Folkestone that day."

"I was afraid you were going to ruin your life, Phillip."

"I know, Mother. But it is not always good to interfere. Yet I understand, Mother, how you felt."

"Thank you for saying it, Phillip."

He stroked her forehead with his fingers, the first sign of affection he had ever given her; she took his hand, and pressed it to her bosom; and felt his movement to withdraw it. To cover her feeling she said, "Do you see where I've put your Order, Phillip? Under that glass dome, where the waxed fruits used to stand? It looks so beautiful, oh I am so proud of it. One day you will want to give it to your wife; until then, I'll keep it for you."

"Oh, Mother——"

Seeing his face, she went on, "Are you sure you feel all right, Phillip?" She thought she must not talk about the war. "I expect you want your breakfast. Oh dear, I hope I have not let the plates get cold! It's silly of me to be so upset over a mouse, isn't it?"

"It's not silliness, Mother. It was the same feeling for which Father Aloysius lost his life on the Somme. Father does not understand about the war," he muttered. He wanted to be alone. "I don't think I could eat breakfast, thank you."

"Oh do try and eat something, dear. If you don't, it may upset Father, and he is so looking forward to his little holiday."

"Yes, I understand, Mother."

The next day, Sunday the 9th of November—first anniversary of the Red Revolution in Germany—was one to be remembered in the Maddison family for the rest of the members' lives. It began much as usual, all discordance subdued until, at mid-day dinner, as Richard was about to carve a half-shoulder of ex-frozen Australian sheep he saw a black speck on the top plate. Putting the plate on one side, he pointed to another example of his wife's carelessness: a trace of dried mustard remaining on the rim of the second plate from a previous meal.

"Who brought in these plates from the kitchen, I would like to ask?"

"I did," said Doris.

"Oh, it is all my fault," said Hetty, "I really must get some glasses."

"Why cannot Doris do the washing up, pray? Or does she, too, need spectacles?"

"Doris has so much to do, Dickie—she is working very hard for her degree——"

Phillip carried the plates back to the kitchen, followed by his mother, while Richard sat behind the cooling week's ration of meat, obstinately determined to punish himself and all concerned by refusing to allow it to go back into the oven.

"It's no good, Phillip, I try to please your father but everything I do upsets him. I can't go on any more," said Hetty, behind the closed door.

"Come on, let's get the plates clean. Give me that kettle of hot water. You dry, Doris. Now, Mother, you should never think in terms of *pleasing* anyone."

"Hear hear," said Doris. "Father isn't worth it."

"I said, *anyone*. It's wrong primarily to *try* to please people."

"Mother isn't so selfish as you," remarked Elizabeth, who had followed her sister out of the dining-room.

"What I mean is, one should put the job first, Mum. That way one becomes an artist."

"Oh yes! Hark at you!" said Elizabeth. "That's what you think you are, don't you? Putting all those ink-blots on Father's card table upstairs, while waiting for inspiration! Just you wait till he sees what you've done! And why don't you go to bed before he does? It worries him, and that affects Mother."

"I walk at night, to get some peace and quiet for my writing, if you must know."

"Is that why you wear that yellow tie, to be seen in the dark? People in Wakenham laugh at you, do you know that? You and Julian Warbeck—both of you going to be great writers, I don't think!"

"Have you been telling people about my writing? I wish you would mind your own business!" He peered into the oven. "As I said, it's coated with the effects of many a burnt offering. I'll scour it out tomorrow. Make way, Elizabeth!" as he hastened out of the kitchen with the plates.

Feeling easier by his son's moral support, Richard went on with the cutting—the art of carving, he remarked, was in abeyance until rationing was ended. At last all were served; knives and forks taken up; cat in position beside the master's chair. The meat was not so tough and tasteless as he had feared.

"You may not long remain the only member of the family to be entitled to wear a medal, Phillip," he said, amiably. "Perhaps you have read in the paper that they are talking of giving the Victory Medal to the Special Constabulary?"

"I'm afraid I haven't time to read the papers, Father."

"Oh! I should have thought that a gentleman of leisure like yourself would have all the time in the world."

"Now you come to mention it, sir, I think I did read somewhere that the Birmingham City Ironmongers have struck a Water Guard Medal, for helping to guard the City water supply 'from malicious interference and contamination by enemy agents'—smoke from the profiteers' factory chimneys, possibly. It has a *moire*, or pale blue riband, I understand, and an inscription, 'Brummagem contra mundum.'"

"Ah, no doubt you are feeling very superior, Phillip! Well, while I do not know about Birmingham, I do know that guarding anything in the war called for constant vigilance, especially during the long hours of darkness."

"Ah yes, spies signalling to Zeppelins, and all that sort of thing," replied Phillip with a straight face.

"Well, they did, you know! They had many ingenious ways of giving information to their masters in the Wilhelmstrasse."

"I suppose German spies could have signalled the whereabouts of the water by placing dead fish at the side of the reservoir, revealing a phosphorescent perimeter?"

Hetty laughed. Phillip's grave manner reminded her of her brother Hugh. But he must not go too far——

"So you still take this spy business lightly, I see! Well, I can assure you that the high authorities, who presumably knew what they were doing, took quite a different attitude."

"'The high authorities'—the 'Frocks'—save us from 'high authorities,' Father. The Fifth Army was nearly obliterated because Lloyd George and Co. refused to send out sufficient reinforcements in January 1918, to the B.E.F., until it was almost too late. We were starved of troops, which were deliberately kept at home, a million and a half, although it was known what was coming. Perhaps Lloyd George will get the V.C. for that, as well as the Birmingham Water Guard Medal!"

"I hold no brief for Lloyd George, Phillip, but according to the House of Commons debate in May, following the German break-through——"

"The Germans didn't break through, Father——"

"As I was saying, I seem to remember reading in the paper that the Prime Minister refuted what you now say, by giving the figures supplied by the head of the War Office, General Maurice, who wrote that letter to *The Times*. As I said, I hold no brief for 'Loud Jaws,' but when he quoted General Maurice's own figures, given by General Maurice himself, to the Cabinet *before* the debate in the House of Commons, his whole case, prompted by Asquith and others, collapsed. For the figures given to the Cabinet proved that there were nearly a quarter of a million more men in France at the beginning of 1918, than there were at the corresponding time in 1917."

"Well, Father, that simply isn't true!"

"Of course, if *you* know better than the Government, there's nothing more to be said!"

"Well, I do know a little about it, Father. At the beginning of 1917 all our infantry brigades were composed of four battalions. Every infantry brigade in the B.E.F. in January 1918 was cut down to three battalions, the fourth battalion being disbanded to feed the other three. Even then, most battalions were far under strength, while a million and a half men were kept back in England. They were withheld because Mr. George wanted to get rid of Haig. The war was very nearly lost owing to the vindictiveness of an outsider for a soldier and gentleman."

"Well, I suppose that settles the matter? You know more than the authorities!"

"The civilian mind invented propaganda, Father, so it is quite capable of faking information from the War Office. What General Maurice said was this: The Prime Minister read to the House of Commons a wrong set of figures, the first set that Maurice had sent him. General Maurice sent a corrected set of figures before the debate, but Lloyd George quoted the first set. He must have deliberately suppressed the second set."

"I can tell you one thing, Phillip, and that is that Lloyd George is going to lose us the peace, in my opinion!" Richard went on vehemently, "I tell you that we should have gone on with the war until we had got to Germany, to give them a taste of what they have given France! In yesterday's *Trident* there is an account of para-military forces being assembled in Berlin, to march through the streets—tens of thousands of them!—with bands and flags, defying the Occupation authorities! 'They will cheat you yet, those Junkers!', as Castleton is always trying to drive home to us. I tell you that we should not have agreed to an Armistice a year ago, but finished the destruction of Prussian militarism once and for all!"

Richard waited as though expecting agreement. Phillip sat still, exhausted. "Well, have you nothing to say further?" as his son put down his knife and fork.

"You are a curious chap," went on Richard. "I can never quite make you out. You have hardly said a blessed word before or since leaving the army, unless, I might add, it was something to the advantage of the King's enemies."

"You mean those in the House of Commons, Father?"

Anxious to change a dangerous turn in the conversation, Hetty said brightly, "Where are you going for your walk this afternoon, Phillip? Do eat your dinner, dear, before it gets cold."

Phillip sat so still that the cat was emboldened to jump upon his lap, and begin to pound with clawed feet. Phillip lifted it up and dropped it on the floor, where it stood still, mewing faintly.

"Poo-or Zippy," crooned Richard. "At least you have a tongue in your head, haven't you, Zippy?"

"I'm rather lucky to have a tongue in my head, too, sir. At least it isn't hanging out all the time."

Richard put down his knife and fork. "I don't quite see what that means, unless you are deliberately trying to be offensive?"

"Oh, I'm sure Phillip did not mean anything of the sort, Dickie!"

"Ah, I was forgetting," said Richard. "You, too, like to take the contrary view to what is generally accepted, don't you, Hetty? You, too, have a soft spot for mice, encouraging them in your kitchen by not seeing that it is kept as it should be. Zippy is wrong to catch mice, and I am wrong for standing up for my country." He pushed back his chair, and looked at Phillip. "Having made that clear, may I ask what you meant by your remark about my tongue just now? I warn you to be careful in choosing your words this time, for I intend to put up with no further rudeness, even if I am only a despised civilian!"

"I merely said, Father, that I was lucky to have a tongue in my head. I was thinking of one of Wilde's Rifles, of the Lahore division at Messines in 1914. This sepoy, or whatever he was, wandered into our lines at twilight, still wearing his turban, but with his tongue hanging on his tunic, since his lower jaw had been shot away that morning. He tried to tell our Colonel something, with signs, and cheered up no end when the Colonel spoke a few words in Hindustani."

"Whatever has that got to do with what we were talking about, I'd like to know?"

"Those sort of things, which were the *real* war, never got into the papers, Father."

"Isn't Phillip awful?" cried Elizabeth. "He's not like any of the other men in the office! He talks like that to upset everybody!"

"Elizabeth, *do* please be quiet! Now, Phillip, tell us where you are going for your walk this afternoon," pleaded Hetty. "I suppose you wouldn't like Doris to go with you? The walk would do her good, she has been working so hard."

"I'm going with Ching, Mother."

"I knew it!" cried Elizabeth, turning unnaturally bright eyes to her mother. "Why does he choose such awful people for his friends? If it isn't Ching, it's Warbeck, both of them rotters, if you ask me!"

"That reminds me, my girl!" said Richard. "Did you take my November *Nash's Magazine* with you out of the house yesterday evening? You did! Then kindly do not do so again! I do not take your things, why should you take mine?"

"Elizabeth only borrowed it for a little while Dickie, to show Nina something. She did ask me first, so it is my fault entirely."

"There you go again! Always condoning what is wrong!"

"Elizabeth, please do not forget to bring back your Father's magazine by tea-time!"

Phillip said to the tablecloth. "Father—please listen. If some student of the future had only *Nash's* and other popular magazines as evidence for a historical study of the war, he would be utterly in the dark to know how our fellows *really* got across to the German trenches during the Somme—or how Ypres was *really* held in 1914—or Passchendaele reached in 1917. He would have no idea of what the war was *really* like—minute by minute—hour by hour—day after night—night after day—week after week—month after month——" He looked at his father's face, and quickly down again at the table-cloth—"or how it happened that hundreds of thousands of faceless bloody half-sacks were left lying near spectral spinneys—rifles swaying in the wind on bayonets—he would learn nothing! nothing! nothing!!!" he cried, getting to his feet.

"What's he going to do now, attack Father?" cried Elizabeth. "What's he saying it all for? Is he mad?"

"Go on, Phil," said Doris quietly.

"Doris, how dare you!" said Hetty, ineffectually.

"Well, I must say I don't altogether like your attitude or your language," said Richard, in a strained voice. "Also, I do not see what all this has to do with what I asked you. Of course men get killed in war—just as we stay-at-homes sometimes got killed in air-raids—the effects of which aren't pleasant, to say the least of it! But the Germans began it, and we had to finish it! I said, and I still say!—that we should have carried fire and sword into Germany, to give them a taste of what they gave others!!"

"The Germans were the same as ourselves, Father."

"Oh! Have you read, by any chance, the Bryce Report on atrocities?"

"There were blackguards in every army, Father. But the great majority of the Germans were brave, decent, humane soldiers."

"You can sit there, and talk like that?"

"Yes, I can!" cried Phillip, starting up again. "Brave!—brave!!—brave!!! Decent!—decent!!—decent!!! Their Government didn't fight with lies! Their newspapers didn't slander Englishmen with print in order to make people sleeping in beds at night determined to keep the war going!"

"If you keep on like this, I shall not answer for the consequences! I warn you——!"

"Have you heard about the German Corpse Factory, Father? Do you know where it went to work, tieing up the corpses 'in bundles of four'! In *Fleet* Street! Only they were in bundles of twelve, for the newsboys to carry under their arms, and they were called *Daily Tridents*!"

"What are you saying? Are you tipsy again?"

Phillip took a deep breath, and said quietly: "Father, I saw some beautiful German graveyards, with carved stones, when we advanced over green country to the Hindenburg Line! I sent Mother some pansies growing on the graves, didn't I, Mother? Not one British soldier who was there believed in the Corpse Factory idea. It was one of a lot of false reports. Incidentally, the British soldiers did some pretty dirty things in France, you know. Did you ever read Willie's letter, which I showed Mother, about the British bombardment, exactly at eleven o'clock on Christmas Eve, 1915, German midnight—blowing poor little devils in mouse-grey uniforms to hell while they were singing carols—and about to come out in No-man's-land to offer us presents of cigars and sausages, as they did in 1914? You never read about that British 'atrocity' in *The Daily Trident*, or any other British paper or magazine, did you? It was always the Huns who were unhumorous and atrocious, and always the British who were chivalrous and humorous, in our newspapers and magazines!"

Richard left the room. He came back to say, "If you keep on in this strain, I shall say something to you for which I might be sorry afterwards!"

"Please sit down, and eat your food, Dickie! Phillip, *please* do not say things to annoy your father!"

"But, Mother, I am only telling what every soldier out there knew at the time! There can never be real peace in the world until we understand other people's points of view! For instance, it is a fact that our Guards Division seldom brought back any prisoners! If they did happen to have some 'Huns' surrendering, the aforesaid 'Huns' were put conveniently in a communication trench and treated to a present of Mills bombs lobbed in, accidentally on purpose."

"What are you saying?" cried Richard. "Are you in your right senses?"

"I'm telling you about *our* 'frightfulness,' sir! At Cambrin, near Loos, in 1915, the Coldstream band played in the trenches, the Germans being thirty yards away. A very pleasant concert, Germans soon singing away, and asking for German tunes. The next evening, the same concert, plenty of Hans' and Carls' and Heinrichs cheering the Coalie band. But they didn't cheer for long, for they lay in bloody rags under a rain of sporting hand grenades. Hubert Cakebread told me that himself! He was there!"

Richard was white in the face.

"I repeat: If you go on like this I may find myself calling you a name that you will not like!"

"*Please* don't go on, Phillip," said Hetty. "*Please* stop—for my sake——"

"It's rather late in the day for you to talk like that!" cried Richard, turning on his wife. "It was *your* doing in the first place that made the boy grow up as he did, neither one thing nor the other! It's all coming out in the wash, now! Everything I tried to tell the boy, you invariably countered!"

"You've made my Mother cry!" said Doris, in a firm voice, staring at her father.

"Mother, don't cry," said Phillip. "I know exactly what Father means, only it wasn't, the war, I mean, as he imagines. No doubt he thinks that my mind is warped by my Jewish streak, but the finest General in the war was an Australian Jew called Monash!"

"I have not said so," replied Richard. "But from the trend of your remarks, it is plain to me that in your eyes the fault can be laid entirely at my door! You who as a boy showed yourself to be untruthful, cowardly, and a sneak-thief, not to mention a bully!"

"Yes, you are entirely right there, Father. You see, when I left home to go into the Army, I had to learn, or rather to unlearn, all over again. I had to start from scratch. The first thing I had to realise, was that men who bullied others did so from fear in their own souls. They used scapegoats, in other words. I found out that the really brave man was a calm man, and he was calm because he had grown up in a calm household, and not been bully-ragged, as you used to say. I found out that men who came from loving homes were invariably steady and courageous, in other words that a sense of honour came from love. I learned this from a Roman Catholic priest, and saw again and again that it was true."

"A Roman Catholic priest!" Richard sat down. "Well, that could explain quite a lot! About your muddled ideas, I mean. But even your Mother's persuasion towards Roman Catholicism would hardly explain how it happened that you came to command a battalion!"

"I also failed to understand many things, until I tried to shed my own preconceived notions, Father."

"Well, that is an admission for which I suppose I should be grateful? What do you think of that, Hetty? Your best boy admits that there are some things that he does not understand!"

"Father," said Phillip, looking at him steadily. "Father, I wish you could believe me that I do not mean to be personal, when I say this——"

"Oh no, *you* are not being personal! Not in the very least! You are merely criticising me in my own house, after living in it for two months, the while more or less treating me as if I did not exist—getting up in the morning late, presumably to be waited on hand and foot by your Mother—in whose eyes you can never do wrong, it would appear—coming home usually nearer midnight than any other hour—in fact, treating the place like an hotel! Now let me tell you this!" cried Richard, rising to shake a warning finger at Phillip. "I have said very little to you in this matter, but if you think I have not known what is going on, you deceive yourself! You seem to think that those whom you despise, or consider your inferiors, have deluded themselves by doing nothing but read magazines during the past four years——"

"I'm sorry, Father, I should not have said that. I was rather intolerant——"

"Perhaps you will allow me to finish saying something I have wanted to say for a long time? It is this! I am tired of being treated in my own house as though I have no right to exist in it! And I will tell you this—it is fully time that you thought of finding a home of your own!"

"Oh, Dickie, please—Phillip is not well——"

"And whose fault is that, pray?" Rising indignation caused a rise in pitch of his voice. "If you think that I have not been aware of what has been going on, you are entirely mistaken, let me tell you! It never occurred to you, I suppose, that innocent people might have been made to suffer because of your condition, to put it at its mildest possible aspect? Yes, you know what I mean, I think!"

"What does he mean, Mother?" asked Elizabeth. "What is Father talking about? What has Phillip been doing?"

"Oh, *do* please be quiet, Elizabeth! What your Father says to Phillip is nothing to do with you!"

"Well, what have you to say?" cried Richard to his son, now silent again. "You don't answer! Very well, I now make a formal request to you that you leave this house by this evening! If you do not leave, if you are on these premises tomorrow night at the latest, I shall have no alternative but to summon you for trespass! Do you hear me?"

"Yes, Father," replied Phillip, getting up and leaving the room.

"Oh dear, oh dear," said Hetty, in tears.

Chapter 22

BY A DYING STREAM

As he turned the corner he waved to Mrs. Neville sitting at her window, Sprat with cocked ears by her side. It was twenty past one; he had forty minutes before Ching, who would be coming down Ivy Lane, was due to meet him at the junction with Charlotte Road.

He felt thirsty, and thought to go into the Randiswell for a pint of mild ale, and perhaps some bread and cheese. One pint of mild, and no more. But he reckoned without Dr. Dashwood, who put his bulk between Phillip and the bar counter, saying, "I insist, my dear Middleton, in doing the honours!"

"Thank you, doctor, may I have a pint of mild ale, please? I'm not awfully well at the moment."

"My dear Middleton, good beer is much less likely to upset one, than swipes! And as your honorary medical adviser, who has your welfare very close to his heart, I suggest the best Burton. A pint of your best Burton, and the usual for me, please, Mrs. Purvis! Well, Middleton, I must congratulate you——"

It seemed ungracious to refuse the dark brown ale, which soon induced freedom from tension. Returning the compliment,

Phillip put down another pint. Then Ching came in, having come from the Bereshill Jack, so named because Jack Cade, a peasant leader in revolt, had assembled his men there for the final march upon London. Ching had been drinking rum since opening time at noon. Now, in the Randiswell, there was a party; and at closing time, with three quarters of a gallon of strong ale to walk off, Phillip led the way to the Recreation Ground, a place trodden dead under gravel paths: of black patches, wide and bare, in the grass; sooted trees, and tarred railings; a slow-moving, poisoned river.

Ching was making an effort to appear sober; Phillip strode on fast in front, dreading a return of Ching's wallowing self-depreciation, which was somewhow in keeping with the L.C.C. park enclosed by ghastly brick houses.

It was not easy going, after they had left Fordesmill Bridge, on the broken-bottled and old-iron'd banks of a narrowing stream which now moved below back-gardens, sheds, and commercial buildings. Soon they were leaping across the bends, once landing short in the water, Phillip to scramble out laughing at the muddy streaks on his own face and that of Ching, who began to look doleful.

"I've got on my second-best suit," he complained. "If I'd've only known, I'd've put on my third-best."

"Only think!" cried Phillip, as they went on with squelching shoes and dripping trousers, "We are free! We can be under a real roof at night! And sit by a fire, and *sleep*!" He would find a shed somewhere, or make a lean-to in Knollyswood Park, and have a fire. "Forward, the crab-wallahs! The Steenbeke used to be something like this, I suppose. No! It was in the country. It wasn't debased by yellow-brick suburbanism creeping out like dry-rot. I wish I had seen the Steenbeke before the war. I wonder if they will ever get it back to what it was, with trout and roach in it. Blast the London County Council! They had no excuse for polluting this Kentish stream! They say that beauty is in the eye of the beholder, but it has to come through the mind, not the pocket. Look at this ghastly muck-up!"

He peered through a gap in a tattered garden fence, to see sickly rows of thin-stalked cabbages, the upper leaves of which had been riddled by caterpillars in the past summer, while the lower leaves were grey with blight, stricken upon a limeless soil.

"'Flow down, cold rivulet, to the sea, Thy tribute wave deliver: No more by thee my steps shall be, For ever and for ever,'" he declaimed to the air.

"F—k everybody except me!" shouted Ching, and kicked in two planks of the garden fence.

"Oi!" yelled a face out of a little window. "Mind what you're at, knocking down my fence like that!"

Ching shoved his head through the gap, crouching and waggling his arms like an ape, then gave the face at the little window a double two-finger insult; while Phillip raised his cloth cap to the face and bowed, and stepping backwards, fell sprawling over a broken galvanised pail half-hidden among tangled grasses.

"Serve you bloody well right!" shouted the face at the lavatory window, as Ching helped Phillip to his feet before flinging the pail into the stream.

"Don't add to the filth in the water, you bloody hooligan!" shouted Phillip. "What the hell are you doing? Come on, let's get on with our walk, or we'll never get to Reynard's Common!"

Ching's answer was to jump into the stream, haul out the bucket, and heave it over the tattered fence.

"Oi!" yelled the man at the window. There was the noise of a lavatory plug being pulled, again and again.

"Poor chap, his ball-cock's out of adjustment," said Phillip. "Come on, get a move on!"

They approached the dying hamlet of Bellingham, with its occasional elm trees, tumbledown field-barns, and yellow-brick cottages dulled by coal-smoke.

"Jack Cade's men assembled here you know, Tom, before they marched on London, not to raise rebellion, but to protest against starvation conditions. Did you know that?"

"More bloody fools they! What did they get out of it?"

"A row of heads stuck on the spikes of London Bridge, I suppose. At least there are no bones here on what, if the City of London lawyers hadn't been so cunning, might have been a battlefield." He stared around, and said bitterly, "It would have been better if they had all been killed here. 'And never a bone the less dry for all the tears,' as Francis Thompson wrote of Keats in his essay on Shelley."

"'Hail to thee, blithe spirit,' bird thou never f——g well wast!" replied Ching.

Phillip went on, "I remember my father telling us children about Jack Cade, when we came here for walks. The brook was alive then, and one winter day we saw wild duck flying down to feed, a wonderful sight."

Scum moved slowly down the surface of the water-course. Ching said, "See those soap-suds? When I ran with my bayonet at the colonel, to dodge the attack on Inverness Copse, I had it all worked out. I munched up a bit of soap in my mouth to make it frothy, as though I was in a fit. Luckily I spewed when I fell in the mud, so there wasn't any evidence left."

"I really don't want to hear, Ching. Let's get on, why must you always stand still when you talk?"

"As soon as I got up the line, and saw hundreds of corpses lying about, I made up my mind to get away as soon as I could," persisted Ching. "I tried eating cordite, to give me a bad heart——"

"I know, I know. You weren't the only one. See those birds over there, like an eyebrow? They're green plover. Thank God they're still about."

"—but all I got from the M.O. was a No. 9 pill. Then I tried to get a few breaths of phosgene when we were carrying up duck-boards one day, but the sergeant saw me lifting my mask, and said he'd get me a court-martial if I tried to swing it that way——"

Phillip tried to jump across to the other side, to get away from Ching, but he jumped short and fell in. He floundered about among old tins, bottles, and nearly went face-down over a bent bicycle frame, but recovered; to be splashed a moment later by Ching jumping in beside him.

"Let's pretend we're in the Steenbeke near Langemarck, Tom! If we raise our heads, we're for it. At any moment the counter-barrage will come down. Listen! *Psst-psst-psst-psst!* Their machine-gun barrage sweeping the timber tracks! That's the Cockroft in front! Our only hope is to keep down until the tanks come up the road to Poelcappelle. Ah, there they are! See the smoke screen?" A train going into Kent was passing to the west side of the brook. "The Jerries are running out!" He stood still. "I don't feel a bit tight, do you? Vörwarts Cutler's Pond! Let's wade there." Perhaps that would take Ching away from his self-accusing memories.

It was too slow, too muddy, too cold, playing this game. He

got out and pulled up Ching, and they squelched onwards, leaving behind the last of the run-out streets of terrace houses. Now the course of the stream lay through cabbage and potato fields, fighting a forlorn rear-guard action against the London County Council he thought. The burst heads of bulrushes gave an illusion of the old brook, and he peered hopefully for fish, sign that the water was not yet dead, but he could see not even a stickleback, which had lived there when he had walked along those same banks, leading his Bloodhound patrol of Boy Scouts, and tried to tell ragged boys from Deptford and Botany Bay not to take them home in jars, to die in airless water: some poor little father fish, faint red marks on its scales, raced away from a small bundle of sticks and drowned grasses, the nest made for its wife to lay her eggs in.

Why had he come back again? All the old life was hopelessly gone; so was his own life, now that he had a chronic disease.

A thousand suns will stream on thee
A thousand moons will quiver,
But not by thee my steps shall be
For ever and for ever.

"Come on, Tom, we must get a move on if we're going to get to the Fish Ponds on Reynard's Common, and see the source of this stream."

They had by now reached the main road, the stream running shallow in a stony bed beside it. Electric trams ground past, to the terminus at Cutler's Pond. When they reached the woods, the real walk could begin. They approached the Tiger's Head, once an inn for carters and waggoners coming in with vegetables by night to Covent Garden market, but now a modernised flash place, rebuilt about the time, he recalled, that King Edward had died.

"Perhaps we could get a drink if we tried the back door," suggested Ching.

"I don't want any, I'm still feeling muzzy. Come on!"

"We might want a drink later. I'm going to try to get a bottle."

"I'm going on. I shan't wait this time!"

Relenting by the railings of the pond, his thoughts returned to the Salient, no bird or animal or even earth-worm could have lived on or in the battlefield of Third Ypres. Were there any watermills in Flanders before the war, or were they all driven by wind? There used to be a windmill on the crest near Passchendaele village; would it be rebuilt, or was it a thing of the past, like the original pond here, which used to have posts-and-rails, and reeds around the edges, before the L.C.C. built a brick wall below the road and crowned it with a spiked iron railing?

At the foot of the wall the muddy bottom was pale with newspapers thrown in; and the old mill-house, where Father had told them that bayonets were ground for the Crimean War, was ruinous and overgrown with ivy. Did nothing remain in the world the same, for year after year, or was all doomed to fall into ruin, and pass away? Was there hope anywhere? Bones and flesh came from the earth, as phosphates, calcium, and carbon; and back they went after a space of time. Must natural beauty die, too?

He strolled to the top of the pond and waited by the road-bridge under which ran the brook coming from a wood which hid a house said in boyhood days to be filled with the lunatics of a private asylum. There Ching joined him, the top of a rum bottle wrapped in a page of *The People* sticking out of his third-best jacket pocket. Phillip felt scorn for this concern with clothes, until the idea came that Tom's father, the bread-winner, was dead, and Tom was probably the main support of his mother. Supposing *his* father had died; where would Mother be then? It was too late now to go back to the office, he thought, as they climbed down beside the bridge and pushed through under-growth along the bank of the stream. Out of sight of the road Ching offered him the bottle.

Phillip ignored him, and pushed on by himself, regretting that he had ever had anything to do with Ching; he had only tried to help him, out of a slight resemblance, in face only, of Ching to Driver Mobbs, a genuinely shell-shocked infantryman transferred to his transport section of 286 Machine Gun Company in 1917. Mobbs had been fundamentally decent; Ching always had been soggy, human fungoid. Perhaps some human beings had pre-evolutionary primeval traits still in their natures; others —the killers without self-knowledge—had traits of tigers and predatory beasts, Zippy-like torture-pleasure which stimulated the sex instinct. Somehow all cruelty was involved with thwarted sexual appetites . . .

"How about a drink?"

"I thought you wanted to know the names of birds?"

"There aren't any left here, are there?" Ching tipped the bottle and poured past his back teeth.

They were being watched. A man in an old-fashioned tweed suit with high lapels and knickerbockers was standing, with the aid of two sticks, on a path leading away from the water. Behind him was a wheeled chair. As Phillip went near he saw that the stranger had dark hair and eyes with a dark look in them. By his attitude, confirmed by his speech, he was a gentleman.

"You have a problem on your hands, I see."

"He's a sort of faked shell-shocked case. And a bore, because nothing about him is real. Morally disintegrated by knowledge that his father committed incest with his own daughter, after having rated the son for the same offence." Phillip felt himself disintegrating as he spoke; for Ching had told him that in confidence.

"A case of paternal idealism gone wrong! Although in my case it is the other way round."

Phillip, now recovered, told himself that he must on no account show curiosity or ask personal questions. The other man observed this and went on frankly, as to an equal, "My father cannot forgive me for having a bullet in the base of my spine."

"Is it still there?"

"Unfortunately yes. But an operation might kill my father's remaining son, which would entirely upset what remains of his hopes of partial immortality of his possessions through me."

Phillip wondered if the set stare in the eyes indicated a mental case, but what was next said made things clear.

"I was hit in the spine by a sniper when going to help one of my men hit by the same sniper a minute or two before. It was against regimental orders, of course, for an ensign of Guards to do that, you follow me? And my father is a soldier, regarding himself pre-eminently in that character, but with a confusion similar to that of Nicodemus, who, you may recall, had great possessions. I am, or was, his heir, my two elder brothers having been killed."

"But you saved a man's life, or tried to——"

The other continued, his eyes glittering, "For a year my father barely endured my presence after I returned home. I was a half-man, he said, as I footled about in a wheeled chair. My occasional clumsiness irritated him until he could not bear the sight of me. If, for example, on entering the dining-room, my dragging feet caught in the carpet edge, or a wheel scraped the door, or my hand caused the soup spoon to rattle, it was the sign for an explosion in my father. Towards the end of his patience he even rated me before his guests, until one night a friend of the family went for him, and there was almost a brawl. The result was that I was sacked, and here I am in the Cads' Club, the unofficial name for this so-called private nursing home for so-called gentlemen. Have you, and your tippling friend over there, come to join us?"

"No, we're passing through. I've just been hoofed out of home, too." Phillip was as frank about himself as the other had been in his story.

"Aren't they a purblind generation, our fathers? Sitting in their damned clubs, talking about having 'given their sons to the war'? I suppose one should be as charitable as you are, and try to see causes of effects, but there is a limit to one's physical resistance." He looked at Ching. "Surely he's not going to finish that bottle? What is it, rum? He knows how to put it away, doesn't he? Needless to say, the Cads' Club is unlicensed. We've got some pretty bad cases of shell-shock here. One fellow, of the Black Watch, goes dippy whenever he hears a tree coming down, and wants to scupper what he calls the British Huns. They have to put him in the padded cell, poor chap. He can't bear the idea of a tree crashing down, after Bourlon Wood. No, not the Cambrai show in '17, but last September, when the Hindenburg Line was broken. You missed that? That's where I got hit, and was lucky not to be burned by the phosphorus bombs they lobbed over among our fellows."

Ching came along, and offered the bottle. The stranger hesitated, then accepted. Phillip drank after him. It became a second party; but Ching's contribution to the conversation was an obstacle, his remarks being based upon his own very limited experience, which to him was 'the truth.'

"Here's our tree-hero approaching," said the man with the sticks. "He's normal today, it being Sunday, and no felling."

A tall man with untidy black hair and large black moustaches passed by unspeaking. He wore a loose-woven tweed suit, bramble plucked and shapeless; and pushing past, hat brim pulled low over his eyes, he continued along beside the river.

"Why are they throwing the timber?"

"They're going to build a new suburb, apparently."

"I knew they were going to build on the other side of the road, but not here as well. What a pity."

"Yes, indeed. Everything is to be swept flat, and the brook, which still holds trout, by the way—farther up by the watercress beds—is to go into the sewer. The only good point about it all is that the Cads' Club will be pulled down, too."

"Did you hear that, Tom? There are still trout in the Randisbourne! So there's hope yet! I thought the poor old stream was dead! Come on you crab wallah, we must do an allez! No, don't chuck the bottle in the river, you ass. Bury it decently." To the crippled man, "We're supposed to be exploring this cold rivulet to its source on Reynard's Common. Goodbye, and good luck!"

Onwards; a little sad that another friendship was to end as soon as begun. Ching was no consolation. Phillip determined that this really was the last time he would see him. And so it turned out: but not quite in the way Phillip meant it to be.

Soon they were through the wood, with a sight of large oaks and ornamental trees either thrown and stripped or marked with blue paint for felling. The brook ran clear through the watercress beds above the wooden mill known in Bloodhound patrol days as Perry's, now derelict; but the cedar tree still leaned over the mill pond beside the road.

Beyond were gaps where willows and poplars had been felled in low-lying ground, and the makings of a new road, bright with red and yellow crushed bricks, lay through the loppings and toppings beside the trunks.

Half a mile from the watercress beds they crossed a wide clearing where stood stacks of bricks and heaps of gravel. The drink had made Phillip lethargic, and he sat down near a wooden hut beside the broken brick road, feeling heavy and ugly, his tongue sour, his head thick. How could he shake off Ching? Where could he go? Down to Devon, on the Norton? Willie was in France; there was only Aunt Dora at Lynmouth. But she had written a letter to him at Folkestone, warning him against 'treading the primrose path.' What had she heard, and how? She was an old maid, and would not understand. Well, for the moment there was no need to decide. He would find a shelter in the woods for the night.

Then Ching's voice, more guttural than usual, said beside him: "How about having a fire here? A match to that heap of shavings beside the hut would soon set things off!"

"What do you mean, set fire to the hut?"

"No one would know who did it. We could always say we found it alight, and were trying to put it out, if anyone came. It would dry our clothes all right!"

"We'll make a fire in the wood over the railway, if you like."

"All right. I'm just going to look in the hut. There might be some beer inside."

Phillip lay back again, until Ching's voice brought him out of his reverie. "I looked through the window and saw an old man inside, reading a paper. There's a lot of shavings round the other side. One match, and it would soon be alight."

"I'm going on alone, if you don't stop talking like a prize bloody fool."

"But I *am* a prize bloody fool, didn't you know that?"

Phillip decided to leave him. He had got through the wire strands of the railway fence when he heard a noise of breaking glass, and looking back, saw Ching running towards him, and smoke rising in the background. As he watched, a man appeared round the side of the hut, yelling to an unseen mate before starting to give chase.

Phillip held down the second wire strand for Ching to get through. "You idiot! We'll have to move fast! Get on with it."

"They can't prove we did it," replied Ching, loosely.

"*We* did it! I like that! Run, for Christ's sake! I can see flames! Come on, damn you, get through! Move, blast you! Don't argue. Follow me."

He ran through the trees on the other side of the railway, and up a path through the wood. After a couple of hundred yards, while the pursuer was still shouting, he had to wait for Ching. But less than a stone's throw away Ching sank down on the path, rolling his eyes and gasping, "Oh my side! My side!"

"Don't do that old stuff on me! Get up! Run, you swine! There's only one man after us. If we keep on, he'll give up, My God, look at the smoke."

Ching lay there, groaning and rolling his eyes; in vain Phillip tried to pull him to his feet, while Ching moaned about his mother, saying she had only just come back from Peckham House, and it would kill her if anything happened to him. "Oh, oh, I can't breathe! My side! It's that phosgene gas."

"You horrible bloody mess, why in God's name did I ever bring you here? If you won't help yourself, then go to hell!"

Phillip set off up the path again; only to stop once more and return to where Ching was lying, the man standing by him. "I think we ought to go and put out the fire," he said.

"Too late for that, my bucko! You come wi' me!"

"It's not too late. Come on!"

"Ah no, you don't play no tricks on me, like that! You be comin' wi' me to the constable!"

"I'll pay for the damage."

"Ah, that you will!"

"I didn't do it, you know."

"You was both the same! I seed you both runnin' away. You're comin' along o' me, mister!"

"What about him?" Ching was apparently unconscious.

"I don't trouble about he. One's enough for me. You was both together. I wor' watchin' of you both, you didn't know that, did you? So wor' my mate, worn't you, Jim?" to another man hastening up.

"That I wor'! I seed 'em both a-doin' of it!"

"You know, there's still time to put out the fire. Take your hand off me! I'm not going to run away!"

"Not this time, you ain't! We'll see to that! Call yerself a gent! Where you from, the sawney house? Don't you try no tricks, now, or we'll crown yer!"

"I told you, I won't run away, and I'll pay for the damage. But why do you refuse to let me put out the fire? It's not got a real hold yet, and we're wasting time, I tell you!"

"Ah, you'll be wastin' time all right, mister!"

Between the two men Phillip walked to the main road, and down towards Cutler's Pond. "I'll tell you again: if you come home with me, I will give you a cheque for ten pounds, to cover any damage. You will have my address, then. Ten pounds should cover the cost of replacing that hut."

They got on a tram, he paid the fares. The men neither assented nor disagreed, and he thought the matter would be settled by his cheque. They got off at Randiswell Road, and had passed the Fire Station and come to the Police Station when suddenly his arms were grabbed and he was hauled up the step, and inside, where he was charged with destruction of property by arson. Asked his address, he said, "I haven't got an address."

"Then where do you live?" asked the sergeant. On being told nowhere, the sergeant wrote down *No fixed abode*.

"May I have a pen, and some writing paper, to communicate with a friend?"

"I shall have to report your request to my Inspector."

While the sergeant was telephoning Phillip remembered that his grandfather had been ill, and thought of writing instead to his mother; but she would be too upset. Mrs. Neville came to mind. He would write and ask her to come down. Looking round the room, where two young constables sat reading sheets from the *News of the World*, he said: "I can't, of course, even suggest offering a police officer any money to take a letter, but could anyone outside be asked to take it, when it's written, I mean?"

"You'll have to ask the sergeant."

"Any objection to my reading a newspaper? I mean, if you've done with that sheet over there."

"There's a Bible if you want it."

"Have you ever thought that parts of the Old Testament are rather like parts of the *News of the World*?"

This attempt at humour fell flat, and he sat unspeaking until the sergeant came back.

"If you wish to make a request to see a lawyer, I shall take notice of it, in accordance with the regulations."

"Very well, I would like to see a lawyer."

But who? Then he remembered a brass plate on the gate of one of the houses in Charlotte Road, with *Solicitor* engraved after the name *Bowles*. "I'd like to see Mr. Bowles, if you please."

After this he was locked up in a cell, and when later he asked if he might go to the lavatory, the constable on duty unlocked the door and took him to a seatless pan in a doorless space, and stood there close to him, apparently guarding against any attempt at suicide. This, added to the fact that all his personal possessions had been taken away—money, pocket knife, fountain pen, tobacco, matches, and note-book—before he had been put in the cell, increased his depression.

At last Mr. Bowles appeared. He was told that he would have to appear at Greenwich Police Court on the Monday, to be charged before the Magistrates. If the charge were proved, the bench might impose a fine, with damages, or a term of imprisonment, or both; or, at the worst, a remand to a higher court.

"It may depend on whether or not we can produce your companion. Perhaps you will give me his name," said Mr.

Bowles. As Phillip remained silent, he went on, "It will not help your case if, on the other hand, you merely state that it was someone else who set fire to the hut, and then refuse to say who he is."

"Then it looks pretty bad for me, sir?"

"That I cannot say at this juncture. You say that you offered to help put out the fire, and that the two watchmen not only refused your help to do what you could, but prevented you from getting to the building to prevent further damage? There again, you will have to produce a witness or witnesses. If you cannot do this, it might be a case for the Petty Sessions. But again, if in the opinion of the magistrates it constitutes more than a misdemeanour, that is, a criminal offence, it may mean a remand until the Assizes, with a wait of some weeks for the visit of the Circuit Judge. In the interim that will involve remand in custody, or alternatively, a remand on bail. That, again, will be decided on any evidence of good behaviour, or testimony as to war service, and such things. How much bail do you think you could raise, or secure from relations or friends vouching for you?"

"I've got about fifty pounds, and a motorcycle worth at least another fifty."

"You have no one—a parent perhaps—you could call on for bail?"

"I don't want to involve anyone else, sir."

"Well, we'll leave that for the moment. Meanwhile I'll call on this lady, Mrs. Neville, as you suggest, and ask her to let your mother know your present whereabouts. I'll come back later on this evening, when I shall know more about tomorrow's procedure at Greenwich. Until then, keep as calm as you can."

When Mr. Bowles was gone, the sergeant came in and said, "Am I right in thinking that you was here once before, brought in by a Detective-sergeant Keechey, during the war?"

"Yes, sergeant. He thought I was a bogus officer. It was in the early summer of 1916, just before I went out to the Somme."

The sergeant had an almost crafty look on his face. Closing the door, he sat down again and leaning forward said in a low voice, "Keechey never thought that, did Keechey! He knew Lily Cornford was goin' with you, and that made 'im mad. You knew Lily was dead, no doubt?"

"Yes. She was a wonderful person."

"She was that. A fine girl. So was her mother." He looked at Phillip sideways, "You wouldn't by any chance be any relation to Special Sergeant Maddison, would you?"

Phillip knew that the sergeant knew, and he answered simply, "Yes." And liked the sergeant when he said, "Of course I knew that, the moment I set eyes on you, sir, but I didn't like to seem too personal like. Oh yes, we all know Mr. Maddison down here at the station. A very highly respected gentleman. And I fancy I saw something about his son in the local paper?"

Phillip's heart thumped. He was for it. After a moment to steady his voice to casualness he asked if he might be allowed to have pen and paper. "I must write a special letter."

"It's against regulations, but between ourselves, I'd like to be of help. The letter must be read by me, of course."

"It would be regarded as a confidence, sergeant?"

"Well, sir, that's the trouble. I'm a policeman, as you might say, as well as a man. And anything that might bear on the present situation, if you understand my meaning, is within my duty. Of course, sir, anything reely private-like, you can count on my discretion."

Phillip knew that if he got a civil conviction his name would be removed immediately from the Register of the Order, so his letter addressed to *The Secretary and Register, Buckingham Palace, London*, begged that he be allowed to 'relegate to obscurity from the Roll, for personal reasons which I beg permission not to disclose, and cease forthwith to be a Companion of the Order'. This was read by the sergeant, who made no comment before it was taken to the pillar-box round the corner. Soon afterwards the sergeant arrived back at the cell with a supper of fried steak and chip potatoes, fried onions, bread, and a large pot of strong tea.

The next morning at Greenwich Police Court Phillip saw his grandfather in a room with Mr. Bowles before the case was called. Mrs. Neville, her face powdered, sat at the back of the court, smiling when she saw him. The charge was read, to the effect that Phillip Sidney Thomas Maddison, of no fixed abode, describing himself as a racing motorcyclist, did, etc. Two witnesses, describing themselves in turn as watchmen, both employed by the same building contractors, told the same story. The foreman's hut was burned out, the first witness got out in time to avoid injury. There was a second man with the accused, but he was a cripple, and had had a fit. The accused had tried to bribe them, after trying to pin the job, beg pardon the fire, on his friend. They weren't having none of that, but took him to the police station.

Phillip reserved his defence, as directed by Mr. Bowles. The case was remanded, bail being allowed of £100 on Phillip's own recognisances and a further £100 surety provided by Thomas William Turney (who put up both sums). Phillip thanked his grandfather, and said that he would pay back the money one day.

"You're not thinking of absconding, are ye, m'boy?"

"Certainly not, sir!"

"Then the money will be returned to me in due course." He added, "In any case it would have come to you, after my and your dear mother's deaths. Now tell me, what made you two do it? Your mother tells me you were out with an old school-fellow. Aren't you going to name 'im?"

"At the moment, if you'll forgive me saying it, everything is rather sub-judice, Gran'pa. Cheerio, I'm going to walk home. See you later, sir."

In the evening he went round to Ching's house. The door was opened by the elder sister, who did not invite him in, but behind the almost closed door said, "We've seen the evening paper. No, my brother is not at home, Phillip. In any case, he would not want to see you. Why did you try to lead him astray? You knew he was not well, didn't you? He has a war pension, you knew that, didn't you?"

"Who is it, Ellie?" said a tremulous voice behind her. He saw the wan face of Mrs. Ching in the flickering gas-light. "Don't let anyone in, Ellie."

"It's Phillip Maddison, Mother. I've told him it's no good trying to see Tom."

"If I cannot see him here, where can I get in touch with him, please?"

"He's staying elsewhere."

"But I must see him!" The adjoining door had opened slightly, as though someone was listening.

"Do you mind if I come in? I can't very well talk on the doorstep."

"What good would it do, Phillip? You can't drag Tom in, you know. I remember when you used to set fire to the dry grass behind your house, again and again, when you were a boy. Why do you do such things? It must be a kink in you. You must go away, please, it's no good your coming here any more. My Mother is very ill, you know, and must not be worried." The door was shut.

Phillip went to call on Julian Warbeck, to be told by Julian's aunt that he was out.

"I see. Well, good night, Miss Warbeck."

"Won't you come in, Maddison?"

"I don't want to embarrass you."

"Good heavens," said the voice of Mr. Warbeck, coming forward, spectacles in hand. "Good heavens, nobody could ever do that, I do assure you, my dear Maddison, after what we have had to put up with from Julian! I am only amazed that he is not about to go to gaol himself! So come in, and have some beer—my beer I may add, that is if there is any left after Julian has been to my own private cupboard—and you are prepared to take the risk of a row of empty bottles. There's at least a fire in the grate, so you will not need to make your own, at least I hope not!"

From the house in Foxfield Road Phillip went to call on his grandfather. "If you promise not to tell anyone, sir, I'll tell you what happened. Only you will promise not to say a word, won't you?"

"I hope you are going to make a clean breast to Mr. Bowles, Phillip. He can't very well help you unless you do that, you know."

"Gran'pa, I think there's only one course open to me. Otherwise it will be three against one. Those two men said they saw me set fire to the hut, and they will be too scared not to stick to their story. Will you give me your word, sir?"

Phillip told him what happened. "So you see, Gran'pa, in all the circumstances, I think it would be best to plead guilty."

"Will you let your mother know what you have told me, Phillip? She is not well, you know, and the strain might be very bad for her health. Do what I ask you, my boy, I beg of you!"

"Yes, I will, Gran'pa."

The old man was moved so that he could not speak; his breathing choked him, he began to cough, long contorted raspings from an inflamed bronchial tube. "I'm—better—alone," he managed to say, in shame that he was old, no longer hale, and suffering.

Hetty went in to talk to her father with a light heart after Phillip had confided in her. It would not do to tell Dickie, she agreed; his rigid sense of what was right and proper would prompt him to say that in the circumstances there could be no two ways about it: Phillip's first duty was to his own family, as it was to his country.

"Dickie says he will not have Phillip in the house, Papa. I wonder if you would mind if he has Hughie's old room for the time being? It is quite safe by now, I feel sure."

The garden room, of tragic memory, had remained unoccupied since her brother Hugh had used it nearly ten years before—almost like last summer to Hetty. After his death sulphur candles had been burned in the room for a week, while all doors and windows were sealed, and the chimney blocked, to make sure that no germs remained; after which the floor had been scrubbed, disinfected with Dodder's Fluid, and scrubbed once more in preparation for repapering and painting. So now Hetty thought that it was fairly safe for Phillip to have a bed there, with writing table and chair, and his own books and gramophone.

It was the best dug-out he had ever had, he declared, and put a notice above the door

GARTENFESTE

He decided to conduct his own case, after much confliction of mind. He did not want anyone to testify on his behalf, but could not bring himself to tell anyone the reason: that a defence, with possible testimony as to his service during the war, might lead to the dreaded exposure of O'Gorman ordered to remove his cork-belt, which led to the death of Brigadier-General West. If he offered no defence, it would also ensure the smallest mention in the paper. If asked about his war-service, he would say that he had served as a private in the London Regiment.

At the last moment Mr. Bowles advised him to plead not guilty. For the man in the lavatory had come forward—"Oi"—prepared to say that he had heard Phillip reproving the second man for behaving like a hooligan in throwing an old pail into his garden. But no: Phillip's mind was made up. He pleaded guilty, and was sentenced to a month's imprisonment in the second division—porridge among the screws of the scrubs.

Hetty was at times almost light-hearted, sharing a sense of innocence with her father while Phillip was away. Richard enjoyed another kind of freedom. He was the more settled in his mind because his former feelings about Phillip's contrary character were justified. It was the boy's mixed blood, inherited from that old Jew, Thomas Turney, who, he thought, had had no Irish mother at all: she must have been a Jewess! Hetty, her sister Dorothy, and Hugh Turney—all had the black hair and brown eyes of that accursed race!

Richard sat alone in his sitting-room at night with the *Strand Magazine*—which he had decided to take now instead of *Nash's*—reading about Jeeves and Bertie Wooster, P. G. Wodehouse's delightful heroes, although they could never fill the place left vacant by Sherlock Holmes and Dr. Watson!

Another worry in Richard's immediate life was Doris. She and her beau, the stuttering Willoughby, spent far too much time in the front room, often staying there until 11 p.m., when Richard wanted to go to bed. What they were doing all that time he did not propose to ask; but was it necessary to turn down the gas, as soon as Hetty had left them? What good could come of a courtship, if indeed it could be dignified by such a word, of two young people from whom, whenever he passed the shut door, in his slippers, perpetual argument seemed to be coming. What were they talking about? There was never any laughter; Doris never appeared to be glad when the young man arrived, as he did, night after night, staying there in half-darkness until he, the master of the house, invariably had to tap on the door and say, as amiably as he could, "It's eleven o'clock, you know!" for all the world as though he were a night-watchman. What sort of manners was this? It was all part and parcel of the new so-called freedom the young were beginning to claim for themselves, pushing aside the older generation as though they had no right to exist.

As for Elizabeth, he had long given up any hope that she would be able to enter into the feelings of other people. She would not do so, of course, until she had her own house to provide for. The sooner she went to live with her friend, Nina, the better. Why Nina had put up with her demands, and tantrums on occasion, for so long, he was blessed if he knew!

And the same with Doris. Let her pass her exams—Willoughby or no Willoughby—and get a job as a school teacher, and make her own life. Then, at long last, he might be able to call the house his own!

Doris and her beau sometimes went to the moving pictures, and Hetty sat alone in the front room, which was supposed to be her very own room, almost her boudoir. Why had she not thought of it before? But the need to economize in gas and coal had prevented her from using her room during the years, she told herself. Perhaps it was selfish of her to leave Dickie alone? He liked to have her near him, to read to her bits from his newspaper, and give to her his opinion on what was happening in the world.

The fact was that Hetty had seldom retired to 'her' room before because she had always cherished the hope that the family would come together again, perhaps playing games together, Dickie joining in as he had when the children were small, and he had offered prizes of butterscotch, usually arranging that each child had a prize.

And yet—Dickie was happy enough in his Sportsman armchair, given by Mamma for a wedding present; and the front room did provide a place for the girls and their friends. Now they were grown up, it was perhaps natural that they should want to wander farther afield, but—— Here she sighed, and fell into a reverie, accepting all things as sent by the dear Lord to try His children.

Hetty wondered about Doris. She had never asked questions, but to herself she thought that the girl could not forget Percy; while Robert Willoughby, his best friend in the army, pleaded with Doris to be allowed to make her happy, by yielding to his—— His what? Hetty became uneasy when her thoughts got so far about her younger daughter. What was it Robert had to offer—his love? Or his demands? Men, she knew, often had ideas which were exaggerated by loneliness, and in such cases they could change utterly after marriage.

Sitting in her room alone, when the two young people had gone out for a walk or to the Electric Palace, Hetty followed a ritual. She put the glass dome on the tablecloth, and polished it before taking out and doting upon the symbol of the true Phillip, who had led his men through such hardships, 'in the face of outnumbering enemy forces'—the Phillip who had been so keen on his scout patrol, and taken such care of the smaller scouts—O, it was the splendour of sacrifice on the battlefield that had led him now to suffer for another's sin in Christian silence!

How beautiful it looked, the Badge of the Order! The royal blue almost purple velvet lining of the open case contrasted with the white satin into which cross, riband, and clasp fitted so exactly. And how the blue-purple velvet glowed in the light of the new Veritas mantle! Getting up from her chair, she held the Badge against the aspidistra, her very own fern which she had had before Phillip—'little mouse'—was born; and she felt that the fern was a sentient being, capable of sharing some of her feelings for its beauty.

On one side of the white enamelled cross, edged with gold, was a green laurel wreath enclosing the Imperial crown, also in gold, upon a red enamelled ground. She turned it over; a second wreath encircled the Royal Cipher of King George the Fifth. Such a shapely, such a pure-looking Cross, the token of honour, which was the same thing as love for one's fellows, which was true courage.

How proud Dickie had been, coming home with a copy of *The Times*—ah, if only he could have understood Phillip—if only he could have sympathised with him when Phillip was a little boy, if only he could have *understood* that a small boy wanted to be like his father, to *copy* him in all his ways, even to taking his father's things—if only Dickie had shown understanding of a growing mind, then Phillip might never have resorted with bad companions; and the tragedy might never have happened.

And yet, who could tell? One of Phillip's faults was that he was too prone to accept other people at their own valuation, instead of using the judgment which Papa said he undoubtedly possessed, but seemed unable to trust.

Beside the Badge, usually kept hidden under the case, was the small ebony and silver crucifix she had given Phillip when first he had gone to war, and which he had worn in France and Flanders, and given back to her—the Cross which had kept him safe, and under whose sign, she believed, he had suffered for another's sin.

Phillip came home on a Saturday afternoon later than he had intended; he had thought to see his mother while she would be alone in the house; but he had lingered with some of the local bogies and off-duty screws in the pub they called the Rogues' Gallery—a friendly yet oddly reserved occasion.

Richard arrived while Phillip was sitting in the front room, laughing with his mother.

"What are you doing here, may I ask? Do you not realise that you are forbidden this house? And what is that object doing on the table, Hetty?"

"I left it there, Dickie, after dusting it."

"Perhaps you do not realise that the recipient is no longer entitled to such a thing, after conviction for a civil offence?"

"I am aware of that, sir. As a matter of fact I applied to be removed from the Roll before I was convicted."

"In that case you may agree that your mother's ostentatious display should be done with, and the sooner the better? Perhaps you will take it away with you, and leave my house?"

"All right, I'm just going, Father. I'm sorry about everything, and the trouble I have caused you."

"It is too late to be sorry. You should have thought of that before you set out to indulge your propensity for liquor. In any case, 'being sorry' was your invariable excuse when you were a small boy. Too often I was lenient in the matter of your underhand behaviour."

Richard turned away, turned round again at the door and said, "Well, I have warned you! Once and for all, I have washed my hands of you, and all your ways!"

"Goodbye, Mother. Don't worry. One day——" His voice broke; recovered. "Please don't worry. I quite understand how Father feels about it."

"You will write sometimes, won't you, dear? And please call in and see Gran'pa, he has something important to say to you."

Having seen his grandfather, who had offered to help him find work, Phillip set out to walk to Blackheath, and down to the river, to cross by the Woolwich ferry, with the idea of making for Hornchurch and seeing where he had been billeted in 1915; but changing his mind when it began to snow, he returned and wandered up on the Hill, where he tried to break in under the bandstand, and make a secret hide there. Thence to the Backfield, remembering his shelter of railway sleepers—his camp before he was a Boy Scout, in those wonderfully happy days of innocence, as he thought of them now.

There was a moon, and by its cold light he climbed the spiked railings, after many attempts to get up, and then to balance without getting the soles of his shoes caught between the spikes. His shoes in the old days had been much narrower, he realized; and his camp, where was it? Were these the thorn bushes, so small? Had they grown at all, in the yellow clay? Was this core of wood all that was left of one of the sleepers? Hopeless even for a fire. Lying down, head wrapped in arms, he breathed deeply to find harmony and sleep; at least he was out of the N-W wind, and free to go where he liked in the morning. He lay there until dawn, when notes of small birds in the thorns, coming with a scattering of sleet, brought memories of far-off days in Whitefoot Lane and upon the Seven Fields, and of other days in snow almost as remote—December, 1916, 286 Company transport trek from Grantham to Newark, redwings piping thin cries in the Lincolnshire meadows, *seek-seek*. He rose on an elbow to look at them, and they flew away. He stood up, stiff and cold, and set off down the slope to the end of the yellow-brick houses he remembered being built when he was a child; and hurrying through Randiswell, face hidden in the collar of his overcoat made from an army blanket, got on a workman's tram to Cutler's Pond.

Large, soft snowflakes were now falling. At the terminus he went into a carter's pull-up, and had breakfast of two fried eggs and bacon, a large pot of tea, bread, margarine and jam. Feeling optimistic he sat by the fire and wrote in his journal.

In the nick.

Meals in hall below balconies leading to flowery dells (cells). Canopy of wire-netting stretched on iron hoops to prevent objects, including bodies, being flung into well below, where we sat at wooden tables pushed close together: the wide boys at breakfast, dinner, and tea. Each had tin plate, mug, and aluminium spoon. Rough music sometimes on plates; complaints usually of poor grub. Forbidden to speak to warder (screw) unless addressed. Language 100% filthy. Some screws ditto. Thicks and tea for breakfast; guff and duff for dinner; water, thicks and cheese, cocoa (milkless) for tea.

Saw familiar face of Devereux-Wilkins. Told by meal mate "The Toff was done for half-inching sparklers" (jewellery) from women he lived with, before moving on. Apparently D.-W. made mistake of taking up with younger sister of former flame, absent-mindedly giving her brooch she had originally given to her elder sister.

"The Toff conned 'is f—g self, see?" gloated the informant, a little Jew who, when not restoring his *morale* by recounting the pinches of others, oozed self-pity, telling me he had been done by a squealer (informant). He stank, chiefly from chewing tobacco mixed with hemp from mail-bags.

Asked me what I was done for. "Arson", I said. Apparently reticence led to rumours that I was a grasser for the screws, reason why I was not in for a stretch.

Didn't speak to D.-W. Didn't want to; probably mutual. Saw him during morning exercise round courtyard, where talking forbidden, but they do.

Had threatened bad time in Mail Bags Two, five days after arrival, my reticence being taken for superiority? Grassing? But timely return of Poxy Paul, pale-eyed, foul-mouthed, pale-haired warder stopped them bashing me against wall while someone held my legs.

The flowery dells.

Trestle bed, palliasse in old stained ticking, 2 blankets, no pillow. Iron-cased door, small grill peep-hole. All my things taken away on arrival, then carbolic bath, and interview with governor (behind him chaplain) curt to harshness. (There had been trouble that morning, I heard later: prisoners confined to cells, screaming, yelling, kicking doors, whole building in uproar, after one had attacked a screw and various fights had broken out.) Gov. asked what I had done; whether served in army, what rank, if any decorations, etc. I said private in London Regt., and no medals. Then dossier put before him. "It says here——" etc. Why had I lied. "For the sake of my parents, sir," I lied. That seemed to satisfy him, for I was taken away and banged up.

Effect of imprisonment.

Occasional upspreading-to-near-panic-screaming feeling as under continual bombardment in trench; feeling of not belonging to yourself any more; realizing the soul indivisible from body, you could not get out of your body, everything pressing on you until fact of being innocent was same as feeling guilty, for guilty or innocent you were trapped in a small space behind grilled peep-hole; cell bare, ugly, soulless, your feet imprisoned in sordid, worn slippers stinking of other men's toe-jam, as you dragged them on way, bogie behind you, to the lavatories foetid with piccalilly evidence of epsom-salts cum dysentery, no plugs to pull only periodical sluicings of all pans in row together, so that if someone had been before you and no intermediate sluicing you had to try and not let the rim of the pan touch you, while Poxy Paul or others of his ilk yelled "Choosy, ain't yer, what you fink this place is, the f—g Ritz, Archibald?" Not allowed to wash afterwards until evening; not exactly good for *morale*.

Watching and reckoning the hours and sometimes the minutes of every day and night until the long long unimaginably long month should be up. And at last it was, and then the idea of being outside was almost frightening: one had become *guilty*.

"May I have some more hot water, please? This tea tastes simply wonderful!"

He was free! He could look back on the Scrubs as an experience for Horace Donkin, in *Soot, or, A World of Half Sun.* Lighting a Woodbine, he added notes for a new beginning.

Put in comic description of Horace Donkin's arrival at orderly room of new unit after commission, on motorbike out of control, via bow-fronted window of Bogspavin House, Oldmarket.

"My goodness, who are you?" asks Colonel at desk over gold spectacles.

"Donkin reporting for duty, sir!"

"Mr. Donkin, do you usually report for duty through a hole in the wall of a house?"

"I have so far, sir!"

"What do you mean?"

"Normal way of arriving in trenches in France, sir. Houses there always completely ventilated ruins, sir. Jerry built and Jerry broken, sir, lack of lime under generally acid soil, sir."

"Mr. Donkin, are you being facetious?"

"No, sir, only factual, sir."

"In that case, report to the adjutant. You'll find him in the next room."

"Find him, sir? Is he lost?"

"Mr. Donkin, will you kindly move on?" looking over specs.

"Certainly, sir, forthwith, sir!"

Donkin pushes bike, leaps on, navigates doors, enters next room ready for action wearing smoke helmet, fires off revolver with flour instead of bullets *a la* cowboy films, shouting, "Be prepared! The old order changeth, yielding place to new! You are my prisoner!" to adjutant. "Have a drink," says Adj. putting down *The Pink 'Un*, "and don't be so noisy. A joke's a joke, but you go too goddam far, Donkin. Obviously you have had no education. Where were you at school, Donkin?"

"I was bricked up in a grey-yellow Board School, later I was bored in a red-brick school. Bricks very old and mellow, genuine

Elizabethan, pitted by soot, birds, wasps, and occasional catapult and pen-knife. School was built on yellow clay, colour of some of the pupils' (and masters') faces. I was said by the Head Master to be so tinted, sir, positively yellow. School prospectus spoke of character being moulded, like bricks I suppose, before being baked. We had some decent fellows, of course, known as bricks. Speaking for myself, I am a half-baked brick, Adj."

"I can see you are a rorty boy, you have no reserve, Donkin."

"That's where I beg to differ, Adj. Permit me to show you." Opens cap on tank, lights match, Adj. peers in, tank explodes, air-raid warning goes, troops march to East Coast, British fleet leaves Scapa Flow, German fleet leaves Kiel, occupies Scapa while British fleet enters Kiel. There is a general exchange of uniforms and opinions, and mass-migration all round. Years pass. Insularity produces in Germans tolerance due to becoming the world's wholesale shopkeepers talking down and through noses to lesser breeds of retailers; while British become claustrophobic and guttural and create armies where they once built ironclads.

"You seem to be enjoying yourself, laughing away like that," said the woman behind the counter.

"I'm writing a book."

She looked at him narrowly. "Are you from over the way, where the shell-shocked soldiers are? An orderly, or something?"

"I'm just an author."

"My, fancy that now! It's going to be a funny book, I can see that."

"Life can be very funny at times."

"You're quite right! Sometimes people forget that, especially round 'ere. There's a lot of talk about the lunatics we've got now, per'aps you've heard of them? At the house in the wood over there." She pointed through the window. "Some's reely dangerous; one big feller tries to stop the trees comin' down. They 'ave to lock 'im up. They say he got messed up in the war. Yes, the big dark feller carries on something awful, just because a few old trees are coming down. Good thing, I say, the place wants opening up, although they say they're goin' to put people here from the slums of Deptford and Woolwich, on the new 'ousing estate. Some say they'll bring a lot of rough behaviour with them, but I say it's time those slums beside the river was pulled down."

"I hadn't thought of it that way. Yes, it's part of the post-war 'homes fit for heroes', I suppose. By the way, have you seen one of the patients in the Home, who goes about in a wheeled chair?"

"You mean the Honourable? Oh yes, he's ever such a nice gent! Real gentleman, he is. The Honourable Stert, they say he is the son of Lord Illinton or some name like that. They say he can't go 'ome, because the Lord don't like 'aving a cripple for a son. You'd think a father would take extra care of a son what was crippled in the war, wouldn't you? But that's only what they say."

"I expect his Father can't bear to think of his being crippled, and the thought of it all the time wears him out, like a bad dream that recurs again and again."

"Yes, I know what you mean. Still, I don't think the old gent can be much cop, in 'imself like, to turn out that pore young man, because he can't help being wounded, can he? I mean to say, it isn't the young man's fault. It's not as though he did it to himself, is it? Still, you never know. I 'ave heard of some what blew off a finger, to get out of the trenches. Still, you can't reely blame them, can you?"

"May I have a cup of coffee, please? And one of those cheese cakes?" He went on writing,

> Westy said, "the slums have died in Flanders". Donkin is dead and millions like him. They arise as flowers from an enriched soil that is forever England and Germany; but also very good manurial dressing for Flemish and French farmers. Were not the bones of Waterloo dug up and collected and ground into phosphates for the wheatfields of East Anglia, only five years after Napoleon was finally defeated?

It had stopped snowing. He left the pull-up, thinking that it wasn't just suburban fathers who could be tyrants, but all classes of men. There was the Marquess of Husborne, the Duke's heir, who since the age of sixteen had been a pariah in his father's eyes, forbidden the house, and later he had become a conscientious objector. And thinking that after all Father had not been too bad—after all, the old boy had had a lot to put up with—Phillip felt a lessening purpose to retrace his steps, as he had intended, to the site of the burnt hut; and arriving at the bridge felt reluctance to go through the wood, the thought of the unhappy war-wrecks made him feel uncertain of himself. Nor did he now want to see the place where Ching had set fire to the hut, as he had intended. The thought of Ching was too much.

He went on up the road, and having left the Mental Home grounds behind, turned into a field which led through a marshy meadow to the edge of the site of the old woods. Once he had seen snipe there, birds of comfort in the old days when he had collected worn copies of *The Field* for 2*d*. each on Friday nights from the Free Library: when the sight of a snipe rising up with a cry like *sceap!* from that *hurt* country—the yellow houses stretching out across fields abandoned to desolation—had power to make him wildly happy and forget his home life, where he had been always naughty and disobedient: doing daring things like widdling against the lamp-post nearly outside Mr. Jenkins's house halfway down Hillside Road, on foggy nights, to get a thrill, but he had been caught and caned on the bare bottom by Father—and after the thrashing he got a better thrill by walking past women on foggy winter nights to the Free Library with his limp little penis hanging out under his button'd overcoat. Why had he done it? There must have been a reason for it. Had he been driving himself beyond fear, to enter a world of so-called heroism?

Later, in the country he had never thought of doing anything like that: only when on pavements, and on foggy nights. Was then all poetry a spiritual escape from pavements, back to nature? No pavements, no poetry, but only happy action? Had any farmer ever written poetry? Richard Jefferies had written beautiful descriptions, the finest he had ever read—far finer even than Hardy—but he had been cut off from the place of his boyhood, to work in towns, in newspaper offices; and so he had pined for nature in passionate longing and homesickness.

No snipe left now; the place was a rubbish tip, the marshy meadow being overlaid for foundations of the houses to be.

O when this my dust surrenders
Hand, foot, lip to dust again
May these loved and loving faces
Please other men!
May the rusting harvest hedgerow
Still the Traveller's Joy entwine,
And as happy children gather
Posies once mine.

Yes, Walter de la Mare had the balanced feeling, so different from Julian's adopted lament of Swinburne.

O love, my love, had you loved but me!

He came to the little bricked cattle-arch and passed under the railway to enter the woods of an old manor of the Cator estate, lying north of what had once been a park and was now still, thank God, a golf course as when first he had known the woods, creeping through them with Desmond to fish for roach in the lake, hiding themselves and their rods in the reeds. Perhaps the golf course was to be sacrificed also, to the Jerry Bros.

By a roundabout way he came to the Seven Fields lying under a shroud of snow. Thin flakes were wandering down the wind, touching his brow and cheek. Fieldfares made their small police-rattle warnings in the woods of Whitefoot Lane, not yet cut down—the birds from Norway were resting on flight to the south. He heard the wild-flung notes of lapwing, high up under the grey sky; and walking up the gradual slope, he heard again the cries of redwings—*seek seek—seek seek* as they flitted before the storm from the N.E. Would they cross the Channel in time to find shelter and food among the seed-pods of the wild flowers which had bloomed unseen during the last silent summer shining so deathly quiet over the battlefields of Flanders, Loos, Arras, and Somme?

How shall I thy true love know, from another one?
He is dead and gone, lady, he is dead and gone.
At his head a green grass turf, at his heels a stone.

The Seven Fields were blotted out in whirls of driven sleet. Forward! Blind in the snow, blind as the boys on 9th April 1917, toiling up the long gradual slope to the Vimy Ridge, to the cauldron-bubbling of guns wheel-to-wheel, to endure light-bubbling nights of cold and terror. But he must not forget the occasional fun when out of the line; do not ever forget the fun. Or the love of man for man, of which the fun was an expression.

Love—unselfishness? Was he now not thinking only of himself? What about his mother? He stood still, eyes closed, trying to clear himself of ragged thoughts; then turned and hurried back along his tracks. He had passed through the barrage; Mother was still in No-man's-land. And Father, too. He was stronger than his parents; he had passed through; he must not, he would not permit his own weakness to destroy that which had been given to him, which he must pass on to those who had not had the chances he had had. Dear 'Spectre' West, was his spirit helping him now? He believed so.

Look thy last on all things lovely,
Every hour. Let no night
Seal thy sense in deathly slumber
Till to delight
Thou hast paid thy utmost blessing;
Since that all things thou wouldst praise
Beauty took from those who loved them
In other days.

He must beg Father's pardon; and then he would go far away into the country, perhaps to the woods above the Fal in Cornwall, and never again make human ties. Farewell, Seven Fields. May the songs of children arise where once the larks sang, and redwings sheltered from the storm.

Church bells were ringing; he went into St. Mary's, passing the yews where once he had stood under the gas light of the lamp-post with Lily Cornford, and sat at the back of the pews, the tears running down his face hidden in his hands as he prayed to be a better man.

Chapter 23

WAX END

"Here comes your Father, dear, back from his walk. You will be most careful what you say, won't you?"

Jingle of keys. One key, the Yale, in the lock. Crack of front door varnish unsticking from paint on door jamb. Rub-rub of boot sole; heel; welts, toe, on mat. Then the other boot. Walking stick hung by the newell post. Now——

Phillip felt throat and mouth go dry. He stood up as Father's head came round the door.

"What are you doing here?"

Richard came in and closed the door behind him, an action from old habit when his son had been a small boy, caught in some misdemeanour.

"I am just about to go, Father. I'm leaving for Cornwall. I only called to collect some of my things. And to say that I am sorry for my behaviour."

"I do not intend to accept any more of your apologies. And while you are here, I will say before your mother what has been in my mind for some considerable time. You know to what I am referring, I expect."

Hetty saw in the eyes of her son, staring in a face pale and strained, a look that reminded her of Hugh just after Mamma had died, and he had come from the garden room, and there had been a terrible scene with Papa in the front room. Was it all to happen over again?

"Oh, what is it, Dickie? Please do not keep me in suspense!"

"Very well, since you ask it, I shall come direct to the point. I have consulted a certain doctor, who has confirmed my suspicions that that fire episode could well be a symptom of a state of mind which is one of the after-effects of a certain disease. You remember my sister Victoria's husband, George Lemon, no doubt? He too showed 'illusions of grandeur,' which I believe is the correct medical term, before he ended as a pyromaniac in Australia!"

She nearly fainted. "Is it true, my son?" she managed to say.

"You mean that I've got syphilis, Father? Well, I haven't got it, and I never had it!"

"How much trust can be put in your word? You never had a sense of honour!"

"That is true, Father," he began tremulously. "I had not the slightest conception of the meaning of the word, as you say." He drew a deep breath. "When I was small, Father, you once accused me of stealing your cigarette case. You told me that if I didn't 'produce' it—your very word, Father!—you would cane me when you came home in the evening. I could not 'produce' it, for the simple reason that I had not taken it, or even seen it. I snivelled in my usual 'creepy-crawly' way all that day, and could not do my lessons at school, or eat any lunch. True to your promise, you thrashed me at night. Then, a week or two later, you found your case where you yourself had put it, locked up in your desk."

He hid his face in his hands, then went on in a strangled voice, "Did you ever apologise to me for your forgetfulness? Did you ever say you were sorry, or even that you had made a mistake? No, Father, you didn't. You had a wretched undersized boy entirely in your power—as powerless as that field-vole you enjoyed watching your cat play with." He gulped, and said jerkily: "I did not criticise you then, even to myself, for you were my Father, and under all my unhappiness I thought of you as being much better than any other man. That is how a small boy looks up to his father, and when that regard is broken for any reason, that boy is like an old rudderless hulk in the Sargasso Sea, practically done for!"

"How dare you talk to me like that in my own house! Get out of here at once! And take your bauble with you!"

"I'll kill myself!"

Gasping with sobs, Phillip ran to the side-table and struck the glass dome with the back of his hand and shattered it; then picking up the badge he hurled it into the fireplace, where it hit the white tiles with their fleur-de-lys pattern. Picking it up he dashed it against the tiles again and again until they were speckled and splashed with blood from his hand. Then he rushed from the room and up the stairs to his bedroom, where kneeling before the fireplace he took from the chimney the smaller of the two revolvers souvenir'd from the Dispersals Camp at Shorncliffe. With shaking hands he slipped a cartridge into one chamber.

While he was doing this, Richard was saying to Hetty, "Why does he bring up that bit about my cigarette case, after all these years? He was only a bit of a boy at the time! I simply do not understand how his mind works!"

He went out of the room, and was taking off his coat when Phillip came thumping down the stairs three at a time, revolver in hand, crying out, "All that we learned in the war, all that men died for, is reduced to less than nothing in this house! I cannot bear it any longer! It is much better to be dead!" Pulling open the door, he ran out.

"Now do you see, Hetty? What did I tell you? The boy is insane!"

Hetty was sitting in her chair, calm beyond despair, all tears run out, when Elizabeth arrived home. The girl saw her mother's face, the broken glass, the blood, and her concern and sympathy for her mother took the form, now second nature to her, of querulous indignation against Phillip.

"Of course he's mad! He ought to be locked up again! He doesn't care a bit about you, Mother! Why do you bother with him? He knows you love him better than you love me or Doris, and so he always takes advantage of it"—an attitude that Phillip had described in his notebook as a robin fighting itself in a looking glass.

Phillip meanwhile was in further trouble. Mr. Jenkins, standing in his front garden, had seen him running down the road while putting a revolver in his coat-pocket. At once he followed at a safe distance. He watched Phillip go across the road and shout out something to Mrs. Neville, who opened her window to speak to him. At that moment Sprat sidled up to Phillip, who stooped to pick up the dog, and held it against his neck with the hand holding the revolver.

"Phillip, what are you going to do?"

"Goodbye, Mrs. Neville! As Desmond told me once, I am too complicated a person to live! How right he was! Goodbye!"

"What are you going to do?" she shrieked. "You're not going to shoot Sprat, are you? Oh my God! Mr. Jenkins, do something!"

"Now, Phillip, be sensible——" began Mr. Jenkins from the opposite pavement. Phillip turned and gave him a steady look. The hysterical mood had passed, and was succeeded by a feeling, not far removed from that of Richard's when watching Zippy with the mouse, to quell and dominate with contempt those who were attaching themselves to his unclear emotions. He crossed the road, one hand in jacket pocket, and slowly walked towards Mr. Jenkins, who began to back away from him, saying, "Now, Phillip! Don't do anything silly! Keep calm, Phillip! Keep a cool head! If you're hard up, I may be able to help you!"

"Help me to another bit of porridge, perhaps?" The arrogant mood had passed, and Phillip was now playing. "Take cover, Mr. Jenkins! Air raid warning has gone! You have the same chance as this dog!"

Thinking he had gone too far, he slipped the cartridge out of the barrel, and threw it over the railings into the grass, before putting the unloaded pistol into his pocket. "It's a lovely day, isn't it?" And re-crossing the road, he walked up to his house, the dog still in his arms.

The door was open. Before his father could speak he said, "I can't go away without apologising for my bad behaviour. And would you like this revolver—it's unloaded—for a souvenir?" He held it out, butt first.

"Come in," said Richard. "How is little Sprat? I often see him, he is a dear little fellow." He held open the door of the front room. "Now, Phillip, I am prepared to let bygones be bygones. I realise that you have had a difficult time. Your Mother tells me that someone else set fire to that shed. I am asking for no names, but I shall be glad if you will help me. Is it true that you shielded someone else?"

"Will you accept what I say in confidence, Father?"

"Of course."

"I tried to stop Ching, in fact I had already left him, with his rather boring ways. He wouldn't even run away, but pretended to have a fit or something. I offered to pay for the damage, and was on my way home to get my cheque book, which I had in my drawer, when the two men suddenly frog-marched me into Randiswell Police Station."

"But why did you not say that at the time? Why shield somebody else, at the expense of yourself?"

"It would have been three against one, Father, and I thought it would look as though I were trying to put it on the other fellow."

"But you had a duty towards your family. Did you not think of us?"

"Of course, Father."

"You really did?"

"Yes, of course, Father," he said, breaking into tears.

"Now now, old chap," said Richard. "I'm not so unsympathetic as I seem sometimes, you know. How about striking a bargain with me? I'll swap my air-gun for your revolver! You always had a soft spot for that air-gun, didn't you?"

"Yes, Father. I used to fire it off, although you asked me not to. I'm sorry!"

"But you were only a bit of a boy at the time, Phillip! It was only cussedness! However, we don't want to bring up the past." When he had washed his hands he said, "I'll have a word with Hilary, and see if he can't fit you in somewhere in his farming schemes. You are fond of the country, and farming is a wonderful life. You'll have to stick at it, of course. Farming is pretty hard work, but once one has settled down to country life, with time off now and again for sporting, why, there's no life like it! What's happening now?"

Cries came from outside. Mrs. Neville, her immense bulk collapsed against Mrs. Bigge's gate, was being attended to by Mr. Bigge, in the frock coat and top hat he had worn at St. Mary's church that morning. Mrs. Neville was hysterical.

"He said he was going to shoot my darling little Sprat! Oh, there you are, Phillip! How dare you! I'll *never* speak to you again as long as I live!" Turning to Mrs. Bigge she said, "I thought I had suffered from the biggest cad on earth, my husband, but anyone who threatens to shoot a dog like Sprat is far, far worse!"

"Hear hear, Mrs. Neville! But I didn't say I'd shoot Sprat."

"Mr. Jenkins said you did, Phillip!"

"With all due respect to a Special Constable, as a finger of the law, Mr. Jenkins is a bloody liar! Tell him I said so! Also tell him I'll put a pellet of my new air-gun through his hedge-clipping yachting cap," he laughed. Then he remembered that he had starred Mr. Bigge's glass-house with pellet-holes in the past, and added, "I'm not serious, of course, Mrs. Bigge."

"You can joke, Phillip," went on Mrs. Neville, "but I shall never, never forgive you for the shock you have given me!"

"I apologise, Mrs. Neville."

"So I should think, Phillip! Don't you ever dare to behave like that again!"

Mrs. Neville went down the road, the little dog frisking around her, enjoying the fun of an unusually interesting Sunday in the suburbs.

After tea Phillip went into GARTENFESTE, and played his gramophone with a soft needle. Hetty had warned him not to let Grandpa know that Aunt Marian had died, for he was still very shaky.

He went up to London the following Saturday morning, to call on Eugene. At the corset factory he had a feeling that he was not exactly welcome; Gene seemed to have nothing to say to him. They caught a bus to Charing Cross, and walked towards Piccadilly, lingering in Leicester Square, each waiting for the other to give direction.

"I'm taking a bird to Brighton on the five o'clock train," said Gene, at last. "So I've got till about half-past three."

"Have you had lunch?" asked Phillip.

"No," replied Gene. "Have you?"

"I've got no money."

"You know, Phil, I feel disappointed in you. I used to admire you quite a lot, and tell my friends you were a D.S.O. colonel——"

"Yes, you told me that, when I turned up at the Pop a mere loot!"

"It's not so much that, but when they read in the *Mirror* that you were—well, in Wormwood Scrubs—I just didn't know what to say. You were a sort of hero to me before, you see."

"Ah, heroes, my dear Eugene! Now there's a real one over there! My God! If it isn't Bill Kidd!!" He ran across the street to where Bill Kidd stood outside a picture palace, dressed as an Arab sheik, sunburn paste, sword and all, but wearing his own extravagant moustaches.

"Blow me down if it isn't my Mad Son! Well, sink me sideways! Once seen, never forgotten! You old crab wallah, you! Got me pinched by Jerry, you double-crossing son of a lamppost! By God, I'm glad to see you, old boy! You got blinded by mustard gas, I heard. Poor old 'Spectre' gone, dammit. You'll never guess who's my assistant, or *trainee*, as the bastards who run this place call him. Your old batman, O'Gorman! Remember him? We often have a jaw about you, and the old days. I got him a job, from the Regimental Association employment register."

"May I present a friend of mine, Mr. Eugene Goulart. Major Kidd. He's got the Military Cross, you see, Gene—and none deserved it more. A real hero!"

"Gar'n!" said Kidd. "You did bloody well yourself, and don't you forget it! O'Gorman tells a different yarn to yours, old boy. He says you saved him from a court martial, by refusing to give evidence about his cork-belt."

"I don't understand!"

"O'Gorman didn't bother to put one on, and 'Spectre' made him put on his, when the mine had sunk the ship. Don't pretend you didn't know that!"

"But before that, I told O'Gorman to take his off, Bill! Together with all his equipment—when I sent him to find 'Spectre'!"

"Well, that isn't what O'Gorman told me, old boy. He said he never had a bloody belt in the first place, and never wore one all the time he was on the ship. And furthermore, my Mad Son, he says it was through you that the enquiry was stopped! He knew you were at the Duke's hospital by the way. He was at the Command Depôt across the park, and pissed himself nightly in case you sent for him to ask him questions."

"My God, and I've been thinking the exact opposite for nearly a year now, Bill!"

"Ger't'y'r!" retorted Bill Kid, preening his moustaches. "Who'r'y'r kiddin'?"

"You! You King of the Crab Wallahs!"

They talked happily of old times, while Eugene stood by, feeling out of it, and also resenting Phillip's delight at meeting such a person.

"What happened to Ah Chum Poo, Bill? Did you ever hear?"

Bill Kidd waited, a look of relish upon his face, while Phillip explained to Gene that the Chinese labourer had driven a camouflaged steam-roller, to bring up water during the March retreat. Gene didn't think it all funny when Kidd said, "The silly f——r got his one-piecee millee bombs mixed up with the coal and blew the bloody thing, with him to b——y! Well, so long my Mad Son! Bless you, dear boy. You were a bloody good C.O., and don't you forget it! I read you'd done a stretch in the old Scrubs, like all the best people, sooner or later. Silly bastards, calling it arson! You ought to have told them it was due to 'fire caused by spontaneous combustion,' like our billet at Senlis! D'you remember my Court of Enquiry findings? That's enough for those inquisitive sons of bitches! Well, cheerio for now, I must do my stunt, I suppose. I'm the door wallah combined with Shagbag the Tailor—the bloody film's about a silly bastard called that! Happy days!"

Happy days with Gene were over, too, it seemed. With veiled irony under his sadness Phillip noted the details of the end of their friendship. After more aimless walking about, Gene finally invited him to have lunch with him in Tiger's Apex House, where they sat at a table for two while Gene studied the menu, finally ordering sausage and mash for Phillip (10*d.*) and a mixed grill for himself (2*s.* 4*d.*). But then, thought Phillip afterwards, it was the same pattern as with Desmond: he had always invited them to be his guests, without actually putting it that way; they had always come, he had always paid. That had been the pattern. Mother had always given way to Elizabeth when she had bullied her for money, and that was the normal pattern to Elizabeth. In nature, the parent fed the young, and the young went to the parent to draw warmth, food, and protection. Until Mother turned against Elizabeth, Elizabeth would treat her the same way, and not learn by necessity to stand on her own feet. The same with Father and himself. Now it was wonderful to feel free of one another.

"You know, Mum, I am sure it was a good thing that all that fuss happened. Honestly, I never knew half the time what I was saying, about the cigarette case, I mean. I suppose it had burned into me so many times when I was a kid, the injustice I mean, and then to be smudged over in my mind until it became a sort of murky gramophone record in my memory, and out it came when Father used the word 'honour'. I felt quite light-headed while I was shouting at him, rather like going over the top."

Later he said, "The spirit of hate in newspapers has rather maimed Father, you know. Also, he's so honest himself that he thinks everyone else is honest, too. That Corpse Factory story was a deliberate fake, you know. And when I think of how our fellows kept on—and the Germans kept on—both in the same hell—and all in vain——"

And later, "Well, it was hell for most of them. I was really very lucky, you know. I learned something out there which people at home have missed. I'm much luckier than Father. He never really had a chance, did he? I mean, look at the way his father behaved towards him! I hope he gets his Special's medal. If anyone deserves it, he does. I've always remembered how he stuck it after that Zeppelin torpedo had knocked him out, and covered him with powdered glass in Nightingale Grove, that night when Lily Cornford and her mother were killed. I think he's probably still shell-shocked, you know."

Phillip wrote to Desmond, now learning to farm as a pupil in Yorkshire, sponsored by the uncles in Nottingham. Phillip asked in the letter if it would be convenient to let him have some repayment of the money lent to him during the past four years. He had kept a careful account, he wrote, and the total was £39 10*s.*; which of course, he added, did not include the dinners and theatres they had been to together, as Desmond had been his guest.

Back came an answer on an unsigned postcard.

> £39 10*s.*! Think again! For I should hate to have to write to the Duke of Gaultshire and tell him that one of his guests was a swindler!

Desmond must still be very bitter to write like that, thought Phillip, before the fire in his dug-out, snug in the rainy night. A tweed blanket—one of half-a-dozen taken as souvenirs from No. 6 Rest Camp, two of which had been made by a tailor into overcoats—hung across the french windows. He sipped tea made in his 1908 scout's billycan. A pity about Desmond and Eugene, but it was his own fault—he had made the nest warm for those two cuckoos.

By day he walked many miles into Kent, sometimes with Julian. Then one morning he read in a newspaper in the Free Library that a new Club for writers was to be formed in London, with premises in Long Acre, where once a week young authors and journalists might foregather to discuss literary matters and listen to lectures by famous writers.

Thither the next Thursday evening Phillip went, and this led to an idea of becoming a journalist in Fleet Street; which in turn led to Thomas Turney, after summoning all his strength to leave his fireside, taking his grandson to the City to introduce him one

February morning of a biting north-east wind to a former Lord Mayor, Sir Timothy Vanlayitt Sterneau, from whose firm M.C. & T. had long bought their paper.

Phillip thought that the only word to describe Sir Timothy was the Victorian word *dignitary*. He was a living effigy of Elgar's *Pomp and Circumstance March*: not a ridiculous figure, not at all, as Julian Warbeck would have seen him, but one certainly oozing the comfortable spirit of gold transmuted from the sap of many primeval trees turned first into wood-pulp then into paper.

"May I introduce my grandson, Lt.-Col. Phillip Maddison, Sir Timothy."

Tall silk hat with curly brim, unnaturally dark curly moustachios and eyebrows, thin face the hue of thousands of grilled rump steaks, frock coat revealed under greatcoat with astrakan collar, pointed boots shining black under grey box-cloth sides fastened by small flat buttons of mother-of-pearl—surely a concession to Edwardian fashion by a Victorian? Protruding starched white cuffs and crested gold links, immaculate pink nails, ridged and polished on long fine fingers—two of which, after the Dignitary had bent down to listen to Thomas Turney introducing his nephew, immediately felt into a waistcoat pocket and fished out a pasteboard card, simultaneously with fingers of the other hand seeking elsewhere a gold pencil with diamond slide—thumb pushing out the lead—card poised——

"I'll give you my card to take to Lord Castleton's Chief Private Secretary in Foundry House Square. You are Colonel——?"

"Oh, Mr. Maddison now, sir. I was not a regular soldier."

The City dignitary gave him a smile of brown and gold teeth and said, "As you wish, Mr. Maddison," and having written on the pasteboard and held it out, acknowledged Phillip's raised bowler and strode away down Ludgate Hill.

"You'll find Foundry House Square—down by—the river." Thomas Turney struggled for breath. Finally, "Be—modest in your—approach, m'boy—and temperate in—all you do."

The shaking, rasping struggle for breath began again. At last, wheezing and gasping, the old man managed to say, "I think—I'll take—a cab—home." Phillip called a taxi, gave the address, and helped in his grandfather. The last words he heard from him were, "Guard well thy tongue."

Phillip followed the taxi round the corner down to the Embankment, and turned into Upper Thames Street, and so to Foundry House Square, and the principal newspaper of Lord Castleton. Walking up steps he went through a heavy mahogany door, to enter a hall with a long counter at one end, behind which stood men scrutinizing forms and talking to callers about filling them in. His heart sank. Would he have to work behind the counter, at one of the many tables all so close together? Beyond was a glass house, with the words CLASSIFIED ADVERTISEMENTS MANAGER on it.

He was shown to a lift, taken to an upper floor and into a small office where sat a pale, clean-shaven young man wearing pincenez spectacles, stand-up collar, bow tie, and dark vicuna jacket. He was writing on a pad, and continued to do so until, throwing aside his pen, he looked up and said, "Mr. Salusbury isn't in town, he's with the Chief in Kent. Anything I can do for you?"

"I'd like to write for your paper."

"Do you know the Chief socially?"

"No, sir."

"Know Sir Timothy?"

"I had an introduction, sir."

"Ex-soldier? What were you?"

"A private in the London Highlanders."

"Where were you at school?"

"Heath's, sir."

The young man stuck out his jaw diagonally. "How much?"

"It's at Blackheath. I was there five years, leaving just before the war."

"What d'you want to write about?"

"The countryside—or the war——"

"The war's over. Well, I'll see. Half a motor." He lifted a telephone, spoke briefly, and said, "I'll take you to Mr. Linnett-Jones. After you."

Down a corridor and through an open door, and there behind a desk sat a small man with agreeable blue eyes and greyish hair with whom Phillip at once felt at ease. After some talk, during which Mr. Linnet-Jones sat quite still and composed, in contrast to the jumpy young man Phillip had first seen, he was told, "We have nothing to do with the editorial side, here we are concerned only with advertisements. They are the main support of a paper, you know. There is much competition between newspapers, for what is called advertising revenue. I see you're wearing a B.N.C. tie?"

"It's the Mediators, sir, I fancy?"

"Yes, the gold stripes are slightly thinner than Brasenose. What rank did you finish up with?"

"Captain, sir."

"I'll take you down to see our Classified Advertisements Manager, Major Pemberthy. Perhaps he can fit you in."

They went down the stairs to the hall, and through the counter to the glass box. There sat a big young man with kind and gentle manner transcending ordinary courtesy, who asked him if he would like to work as an advertisement canvasser in the House Agents' and Auctioneers' section of his Department.

"Very much, sir, thank you!"

"Then you can do your writing in your spare time."

"Yes, sir."

"I thought you were a writer as soon as I saw your face."

It was arranged that he should start in a week's time at £4 a week, then Phillip was taken to a smaller office at the far end of the hall, introduced to the senior canvasser, and left with him. Mr. Brown said:

"We're going to run a weekly Auctioneers' and Estate Agents' Register, the idea being that a reader of the paper, perhaps in a Free Library, desirous of obtaining a property in the suburbs, will see the Register, and write to the agent in the desired district. I will tell you more when you come here to start." Mr. Brown brushed up his moustaches, looked at some papers on the table, and said, "I expect you know the Chief?"

"I met Lord Castleton when I was a boy at Brighton. He asked me to call and see him when I had left school. That was before the war."

"You know who Major Pemberthy is, don't you? He's the Chief's godson. Yes! Son of the Chief's great friend, Max Pemberthy, the author."

"Max Pemberthy, who wrote *The Submarine Pirate*? I read it years ago; wonderful stuff!"

"Fine yarn, I agree. You saw Mr. Linnet-Jones too, didn't you? Nice feller. What did you think of Colonel Cow?"

"Colonel Cow?" Phillip kept a straight face.

"Young feller-me-lad, but don't say I said that, with *pince-nez* glasses."

"He didn't look much like a Colonel!"

"They made him one when he was put in charge of selling war-surplus goods. Sold millions of pounds' worth of stuff, lorries by the hundred lot, they went like hot cakes. Yes, Cow got an O.B.E. for that. His job here is to suggest schemes of layout-space to big commercial concerns, to get them to advertise more in the paper. Some old readers won't like it, of course, but the times are changing, or should I say *is* changing, ha ha. It's the Chief's idea to popularise the paper; he dropped the price from fourpence to a penny, you know. So long, old man, till Monday week!"

Now that he was hopeful again, Phillip confessed to his mother what had happened to him eighteen months before. He was surprised that she was so calm. In fact, she did not behave like the Mother he had known.

"I think if I were you I should go up and see the specialist in Harley Street again, Phillip," she said quietly, "and let him examine you. Then you will be quite sure, and it will relieve your mind."

He went the next morning. A man-servant showed him into a waiting room. At last he was before Dr. MacDougal.

"It may have cleared itself up by now. To make sure, I will give you an injection. This will cause recrudesence of any latent infection." When this had been done, he said, "Take home this bottle, and let me have a specimen of your water on first rising tomorrow morning. It is important that it is the first water you pass."

The next morning Phillip took up the specimen, and left it with Mr. MacDougal—as he preferred to be called—who told him that he would write to him. Phillip left his cheque for £2 2*s*. face down on the table.

23 Feb.

MacD. said only slight trace of streptococcus infection. He will send a vaccine to my doctor here, for two weeks' injections to clear it up.

After hearing verdict (by letter, which I asked Mother to open) I went to London to call on Westy's parents. Found them very friendly. Told them why I hadn't been before, and they understood. My grandfather is dying. I have never seen anyone actually die of old age; scene will be important for my scheme of a long family novel. I want to get hold of my grandmother's diaries for this before anyone can burn them. They are locked up in T.W.T.'s desk in his bedroom.

She died before the war, and when home for the summer holidays I saw her the moment after she had died, when my Mother had come out of the bedroom crying, *She is gone, she is gone*, running downstairs to tell her brother Hugh, an invalid to whom something terrible had happened when he was a young man, what, I did not know then; but I was sternly forbidden to go into his room at the other end of the house by my father, the room where I write this now. After watching the nurse tie up my dear Grannie's jaw, without emotion beyond curiosity, I listened on the stairs to my mother in Uncle Hugh's room, where I imagined her crying beside him, while he sat on a couch, his paralysed legs showing the outlines of bones inside his trousers, at different angles to the floor. *He killed her, the devil*, I heard him saying, and then on crutches he went to see my grandfather. A little awed by this time, I crept down and listened outside the door to terrible accusations by my uncle, while Gran'pa sat still, breathing heavily.

My uncle had been left his mother's diaries in her will. There were about a dozen leather-bound books, each with its small brass clasp and lock. Sometimes when I visited the garden room he would play his violin with poignant longing and sweetness, making the tears come in his eyes, and in mine too. At other times he read to me from the diaries, intimate accounts of her early life, the bringing up of her children, and later unhappy confessions about Tom and her growing sons.

When Hugh died, without leaving a will, the diaries presumably went to my grandfather, so now my mother may have them. I shall want them, for having read Galsworthy, I recognize the importance of all details of past living that the diaries contain—details of a similar penetration which are lacking in the Galsworthy family story. It is *detail* which makes books last, true detail. I hope to write, one day, a family triology of novels which will bite deeper than Galsworthy's satirical yet officially respectable family novels. All members of my family, as I see them, with the exception of Mother, are part of mass neurosis (from which I am not free altogether) which is the underlying cause of the war. But I must not stress that, or other aspects (as, e.g., Galsworthy seems to find property the root of evil) for attitudes of mind pass away, while simple details, almost 'small beer' details, as in Hardy at his best, give the true feeling of living. Soames is obviously somebody Galsworthy hated, and perhaps feared (the same thing?)—and yet, if I put Ching and Mavis in the books, how can I get round to their true or underlying natures? Both are essentially selfish, living only for themselves. Effects of causes, or heredity? Or both?

My uncle Joseph Turney, the 'fool' of the family (who was, says

Mother, 'dropped on his head when a baby') has just arrived. He brought his son, 18, Arthur, but would not let him come into this room. Perhaps he thinks I am a second Hugh, as I am, in a way.

There are now two nurses in the house, as well as Miss Cole, the housekeeper. Must break off now: Miss C. has just come to tell me I am wanted upstairs. "Please go, quietly, won't you, and you must be prepared to find Mr. Turney much changed."

Later.

The curtains were drawn across nearly all the windows, shutting out the view over the grassy slopes of the Hill, set with silver birches and other trees. I saw my mother and uncle standing mutely by the bed, in a dim light, holding hands like children. That is just what they are, I thought, two good little children standing sadly by the bedside of their 'dear Papa' who is going to leave them.

Seeing me, my mother came towards me. I could see she was crying. I put my arm round her (she is a small woman) and tried to feel as I thought I ought to be feeling; but no emotion arose in me, or passed between us. I have been cut off emotionally from her ever since my first return from the war early in 1915. I wanted to say to her that death is as natural as birth, and to trust in the truth that is the spirit of life, and so to reassure her and give her strength; but to my dismay I could not speak, but found the tears rolling down my own cheeks.

Grandfather in bed was now writhing and muttering, clawing the bedclothes and evidently finding great difficulty in breathing. His face seemed very dark as it twisted about on his shoulders covered by the white nightshirt. He was 80 years old, and the flame of life was hovering over the wick fallen at wax end.

Now he began to gurgle, as though being strangled. One nurse stood by the bed, moistening his lips with something on a sponge. Seeing the sad and innocent look on the face of my uncle—who is short, like my mother—I went to him and put my arm through his, while holding my other arm round mother's shoulders. Suddenly there began a fearful struggle. Gran'pa had been a man of powerful physique, and now he was wrestling for life. It reminded me of some wounded men who clung screaming to those who would help them (against orders in an attack), gripping with a grip that could only be broken by the aid of a blow from entrenching tool handle or rifle-butt. Some men badly hit in the body hooked on to the legs of passing soldiers, and dragged them down in their instinctive terror of death, or loneliness. Holding firmly to my relatives, who were deeply affected, I watched the suffocating face. It was almost as though some force were tearing the life away from the contorted, garrotted body; with a prolonged noise, half snore, half cry, ending in throaty bubbling, the struggle ceased, and my grandfather was dead. I was more affected than I thought I would be.

Later.

I did not like to ask then about the diaries, so said nothing about them. This morning, while Gran'pa is lying in his coffin, I asked Mother, who said that her brother had taken them away to burn them, because, she said, he wanted to 'protect his father's memory'. I was angry when I heard it, because, I told her, apart from personal and local details, they contained many interesting details of travelling, to Africa, Canada, and North America, and smaller journeys by carriage and dog-cart in Gaultshire, where he had been born, and had scores of relations, many of whom were sketched sharply, so that they were immediately visible to me when a boy listening to Hugh reading to me. Apparently it was the record of the old boy's marital infidelities, and the account of Hugh's misfortune, that had caused Uncle Joe to take them away to burn them.

That evening Phillip went to London to a meeting of the Parnassus Club in Long Acre. He was accompanied by Julian Warbeck, who insisted on calling at several pubs on the way up. The meeting took place in an upstairs room of a ricketty house. The lecture was on *The Decadence of the pre-Freudian Novel*, by John Crowe.

The Chairman was the lady founder of the Club, a doctor's wife from St. John's Wood. She began by saying that Mr. Crowe's powerful, almost—she might say—revolutionary novel as set in Cornwall, the country of his adoption. Mr. Crowe was a genius, from whom a very great deal would be heard in the future. He had been many things in his life, all of which had given him valuable experience; he had also been a policeman, who had resigned from the Force when he saw what brutal suppressions, chicanery, and bullying went on behind the blue lantern. He wrote plays as well as novels. His plays in her opinion were better than Shakespeare's, because nearer to universal truth of the ordinary man.

Mr. Crowe then rose to speak. He wore a red tie and had an untidy mass of grey hair. Before the war, he said, he had acquired an acre of land on the coast beside a small bay in West Cornwall, where he had built with his own hands a cottage, mathematically a cube. The roof and walls were made of corrugated iron, which he said, he had covered with tar, and so had roused the ire of the local middle-class nonentities who considered that the country belonged to them by right of their money.

Several people laughed, but he went on, "This was a one-man attempt to strike a blow at bourgeois domination of architecture, to show up the decadent monstrosities of suburban villadom springing up like toadstools along the coast to house retired *petit bourgeois* urban business gents with no eye for true beauty, but only for the pretty-pretty based on puritanical sex-suppression, the sort of men like a late Lord Mayor of Birmingham, or it might have been Cardiff, who caused a Greek marble figure of a nude woman, on the stairs of the Town Hall, to be draped from the neck downwards in a Kate Greenaway length of material, because, said the Mayor, 'Every time as my wife cooms up these 'ere stairs to see me in me parlour, she 'as to turn away 'er 'ead for very shame'."

More laughter. Julian, beside Phillip, began to gnaw his nails, while uttering little grunts of disdain.

"That pot-bellied business gent should have been tarred and feathered," went on the lecturer, adding that no doubt Freudians would see in his own tarred cottage a symbol of revolt against such materialists. "Perhaps it was! But I left out the feathers!" More laughter.

"We in this Club, as artists—writers, painters, musicians, sculptors, even journalists—have a duty to isolate ourselves from these materialists who now fill Parliament with rows of hard, stupid faces, putting money first, and denying all true expression of the inner life of the people. We need to come back to the simple truths of nature. My cottage, which as I said was inevitably criticised by the local bigwigs, is nevertheless strictly in keeping with the bleak landscape, and the bleaker inhabitants, of West Cornwall. We need not only regional artists, not only regional protests against the invasion of the pretty-pretty, but an attitude of unflinching realism expressing the beauty of stark human truth. For the war has blown to hell all the old fanciful ideas of the pretty-pretty, the romantic nonsense based on sexual inhibition."

He sipped water.

"During the winter I live in Willesden, and see more beauty in the railway lines from the bridge above the Junction than there is in Tennyson's 'haunts of coots and fern——'"

"'Hern'," called out Julian, projecting the word meticulously through his front teeth. "'I come from haunts of coot and hern.'"

"'Hern' or 'fern', it's all tripe to me! Anyway, what is 'hern'?"

"A heron," said Phillip, thinking that the lecturer wanted to know the answer.

"Perhaps you are thinking of Coutts, the hard-faced banker?" enquired Julian, satirically.

"Order, if you please, at the back!" said the lady who had founded the Club. "In any case, Tennyson is a wishywashy poet. But shall we allow the lecturer to finish what he has to say before we have a discussion? Do go on, please, Mr. Crowe."

"Yes, as I was saying, I see more beauty in railway lines, mathematically correct, and laid by the sweat of the underpaid worker on whose back the plutocrats live, than in pseudo-lyricalism—the stale old symbols of frustration in wet and squelching walks through a bleak countryside—after which the Georgian poetaster has his muffins and gold-laced slippers by the fire, and then imagines something he has not seen, a mere titivation of his imagination. For the working men and women who live there, or exist there, are condemned to live in primitive conditions, and so they are in a mess, psychologically speaking, where every life is a stone from which when you turn it over lots of filthy little things crawl out, metaphorically speaking. Incest is common, inbreeding has produced idiocy——"

"Speak for yourself," remarked Julian, in a loud whisper. "Where were you born?"

"No more interruptions from the back *if* you please!" said the Founder.

"I was born in Willesden, if you want to know!" said the lecturer. "Anyway, what has that got to do with what I am saying?"

"Then why don't you write about Willesden? You and Herr Freud might together turn over some of those beautiful railway sleepers."

"Mr. Maddison, I really must ask you to tell your guest to leave if he cannot behave himself!"

Phillip did not dare to reply, he was shaking with silent laughter.

"Beauty is in the eye of the beholder," continued John Crowe. "An irregular row of dustbins down a back area of a town holds more beauty for me than a Turner sunset, or all the piffle in J. C. Squire's umpteenth volume of *The Georgian Book of Poetry*.

Who reads real new literature like T. S. Eliot's *The Waste Land*? Or Wyndham Lewis's *Tarr*, and *Blast*? Who reads James Joyce, or D. H. Lawrence? Or the works of Barbusse or Lenin? Instead, trash reigns, such as the music of a mushroom baronet called Elgar. What is his music but the expression in sound, or rather in noise, of the black top hat, the black frock coat, the black Rolls-Royce, the black hearse, the black-robed priest with his black-bound Bible? To me, they are all outward symbols of ingrowing toe-nails of the mind!"

"Do you include your black-tarred residence in West Cornwall? Or is that a bunion?" asked Julian.

"I treat that remark with the contempt it deserves!" cried the lecturer hotly, "as coming from a bourgeois reactionary. But I shall not attempt to argue with him. Ladies and gentlemen, my point is that all the arts of the Victorian and Edwardian eras were decadent, and it is up to us today to use new forms which are in keeping with the new renaissance. Take painting. I say that the daubings of Lord Leighton are no better and no worse than the Lord Tennyson in his *Idylls of the King*—work only fit for the dustbin, the work of mushroom peers tamed by the hypocritical *haute bourgeoisie* with their gods of hypocrisy, respectability, and humbug, all based on money, with their overladen tables, over-staffed flunkies, and over-loud jewellery on their wives, concubines, and mistresses! Freud is the answer to these parasites upon the arts! In the future," he cried, running a hand through thick grey hair, "poetasters and decadents like Tennyson, Swinburne, Francis Thompson, Alfred Austin, Wordsworth, and even Shakespeare himself, with his ragbags of plots, will be seen for what they are, feeble men who were sexually ignorant and certainly decadent, whose works should be put in their proper place, which is a clinical museum, among other exhibits of the dark ages, such as the Iron Virgin of Nurnburg, the thumb-screw, the rack, the—the——"

"Tomahawk," suggested Julian.

More laughter.

"That remark isn't so frivolous as the speaker intended, for the tomahawk is equally barbarous with the bomb, the bayonet, and the gas-mask, all symptoms of a hypocritical Christianity, paternal tyranny, and the boiled cabbage with roast cow-beef on Sunday!"

"What about beer?" enquired Julian, as the lecturer sat down.

"Are you for or against beer as a symbol of hypocrisy, respectability and humbug?"

The lecturer popped up again. "I don't drink beer myself, but I would defend to the death the right of anyone else to drink it if he wants to!"

"Have you finished, Mr. Crowe?" asked the Founder.

"He looks thoroughly finished from here," declared Julian. "If he ever began," he added.

"You are a joker, I see," remarked the Founder, "and do not take Literature seriously. Fellow members, we have listened to Mr. Crowe I am sure with great interest, and some of you will be wanting to give us the benefit of your views, no doubt."

Julian stood up. He had arrived with seven or eight pints in him, and had passed, in the process of assimilation, from scoffing to humorous-truculent mood.

"I have listened with growing amazement to the dismal cawings of Mr. Crowe, and I have three observations to make. One. When Mr. Crowe uses the metaphor of *ragbag* to describe Shakespeare's plots, I can only regret that the corvine and carnivorous lecturer has no ear for music.

"Two. This disciple of Freud has had the infernal impudence to suggest that Swinburne is not only not a true poet, but that he is decadent and *bourgeois*. I can only say that I have never heard such infernal impudence combined with such utter bosh ever before in my life, and the sooner the lecturer buys a pair of nail-scissors and tackles his own spiritual feet, and then puts himself and all his works in one of his beautiful dustbins, the better it will be for the world in general and this club in particular, otherwise it has no hope for today, let alone for tomorrow.

"My third and last point. The speaker is himself an example of the common *petit bourgeoise* non-conformist attitude rejecting *petit bourgeoise* morality which begins in the home. Apart from that, I would like to ask, why is it always the middle-classes which damn the middle-classes? Now I am going to get some beer."

"And I hope you will not come back!" said the Founder.

"Don't worry, madam," retorted Julian. "The wild stallions of the lady novelist's stock-in-trade will not drag me back to this rookery."

Thomas Turney was buried beside his wife Sarah, his eldest son Hugh, and his daughter Dorothy in the yellow clay of Randiswell cemetery, among thousands of white marble tombstones and wreaths of withered flowers on new clay mounds; for many people in the district had died of what was called the Spanish influenza.

Afterwards the Will was read by Joseph Turney, the youngest son, to near members of the family—Hetty and her three children; Joseph Turney's wife, Ruth; and his son Arthur, who had left school recently and was now in the Firm; Aunt Liz and Polly Pickering, visitors from Beau Brickhill, who had come to offer comfort to Hetty, and to Maudie, the lonely daughter of Sidney and Dorrie Cakebread. Cousin Maudie was a young woman of Phillip's age, dark like her mother, and with Dorrie's quiet and reflective manner.

They sat in the dining-room with its heavy mahogany furniture, familiar oil paintings, and the pair of ebony elephants with ivory tusks—the absent Charley's gifts of long ago from South Africa—standing on the dark green marble shelf above the fireplace, while Joseph Turney prepared to read the Will. Mr. Leppitt, the solicitor, had not been invited to do this, Joseph declared in his somewhat huffyfluffy voice, for the sake of economy.

"In the absence of Leppitt I cannot tell you the value of my dear Father's estate, until it is proved in course of time, but in my opinion it should reach an expected total of between thirty and thirty-five thousand pounds."

"I didn't know Gramps was so rich, did you?" said Elizabeth to Phillip.

"I never thought about it," he replied, hoping that he had not been left anything.

"The Estate is subject to certain duty-free legacies. Our dear Father appointed myself and Hetty to be the trustees, with Leppitt, I need hardly add." He cleared his throat loudly. "My dear Father has left £500 and his house 'Wespaelar' to Henrietta Eliza Maddison. He has left his diamond ring to our absent brother Charles, in Africa; and £500 and his house in Cross Aulton, where I am domiciled, to me, Joseph Fitzgerald Turney. Excuse me."

He took a red silk handkerchief from his breast pocket, and having unfolded it, fitted it to the end of his long nose, from the nostrils of which brown hairs protruded and touched his moustache. Having blown a trumpet note he folded the red handkerchief, put it back in its pocket, and said: "What about a glass of sherry? Liz? Hetty? I know Ruth won't, so it's no good asking her. Arthur, help the ladies. Ruth, did you remember the Osborne biscuits?"

"Yes, and I brought some charcoal biscuits for you as well."

Hetty refused a glass of sherry, saying it did not agree with her liver. "Do you mind if I ask Miss Cole to make some tea, Joe? Or shall we wait until you have finished? What do you think? Oh, very well. Elizabeth, be a good girl and ask Miss Cole, will you, dear."

"I want to hear the Will read, Mother! It's all very well for you, you know what's in it already!"

"Uncle will wait for you, I'm sure."

"Quite so, Sis."

Phillip was already at the door. He had never heard his uncle address his mother like that before; he saw them again as two rather pathetic small children, beginning life all over again without their Papa.

"Tell Miss Cole not to put in more than three spoonfuls, will you, Phillip?"

"Don't forget one for the pot," said Joseph. "For luck," he added.

"Ask Miss Cole for a jug of hot water as well, will you, dear?"

"Very well, Mother."

"Has Gramps left Miss Cole anything?" asked cousin Maudie, while Phillip was in the kitchen.

"Why should he have?" exclaimed Elizabeth. "Miss Cole has only been here a short time."

The housekeeper, a small demure spinster, invariably dressed in 30-year-old clothes, with dyed hair so thin that the amplifying ginger pads lying flat on her skull showed through, had been sitting quietly in the kitchen since her return from the funeral, wondering about her future.

Phillip, bringing in the tea-tray, heard his mother saying—"Perhaps after all we should add ten pounds to a year's wages, making it up to fifty pounds for Miss Cole?"

"Oh, when are we going to hear about the Will?" complained Elizabeth.

"All in good time, niece," replied Joseph, his lips black with charcoal biscuit as he sipped sherry. "There's a point I think ought to be raised, Sis, first. I propose, with your concurrence as co-Trustee, I need not add, to ask Leppett to agree to name a lump sum for his professional services in winding up our dear Father's estate. Some attorneys, as no doubt you know from reading your Dickens, hang on and on just to feather their own nests."

"Very well, Joe, I will leave that to you to discuss with Mr. Leppitt."

Tea-cups were passed round, while Phillip helped himself from the decanter.

"Has Gramps left you anything, Mum, beside the £500 and this house?" asked Elizabeth.

"I'll try to tell you, niece, if you will give me half a chance," said Joseph, as he finished his second charcoal biscuit, taken to absorb wind and other impurities in the stomach. "My dear Father has provided for all of us." He rinsed his mouth with tea, and wiping his lips on the red handkerchief, took up the Will once more.

"To begin at the beginning. My dear Father was primarily blessed with five children, two daughters and three sons. One son is no more, I am sorry to say. That leaves four children to be accounted for——"

"Three, because Aunt Dorrie is dead as well as Uncle Hugh," Elizabeth reminded him.

"Quite so. I am coming to that. The law presumes nothing, may I remind any who do not know that fact? Very well. My dear Father, when he made his Will, knew that Hugh, our poor unfortunate brother, had of course predeceased him. And, in the interim of the Will being signed and witnessed, our dear sister Dorrie also passed away, last June, eight months before our dear Father's own death——"

"We all know that!" whispered Elizabeth to Doris. "When is he going to come to the point?"

"—according to the Will, Dorrie was to have enjoyed an income from the Trust fund, *pro rata*. It is now my duty to explain that, having predeceased our dear Father, Dorrie's income is no longer to be paid from the Trust, if you follow my meaning. I hope that is clear to all?"

"Then, Uncle Joseph, since Aunt Dorrie is dead, Maudie's share of the capital will be paid to her in a lump sum out of the Trust, I take it?"

"Exactly, Phillip. You took the very words out of my mouth. I was just about to say so. I'll repeat——"

"Oh no!" said Elizabeth, and she laughed throatily to herself.

"Quite so," said the huffy voice. "Quite so. Our dear sister Dorrie having gone to join her very dear parents in heaven, the capital sum due to provide her with an income for life will be paid over, in due course, after the Will is proved, to Dorrie's surviving children, that is to say, to Dorrie, *in toto*, because——"

"You mean Maudie, Uncle Joe?"

"Quite so, Phillip. Maudie, who is here with us today. Ralph, Dorrie's second son, was cut out of my dear Father's Will after he became a Mormon."

"What, Gramps a Mormon?" laughed Elizabeth. "Well, that's what it sounded like, you know. Didn't it, Mother?"

"Uncle is referring to your cousin Ralph, Elizabeth——"

"Quite so, Hetty. Maudie, who is with us today, as I said, come from her duties at the Hospital, will in due course, as I have already indicated, receive one quarter of the value of the Trust fund—roughly eight thousand pounds."

"Aren't you lucky!" cried Elizabeth to her cousin, who continued to sit with downheld eyes. "Well, why don't you say something?"

"Well, you see Mavis, I have not got a mother," replied Maudie quietly.

"But you will have all that money!" persisted Elizabeth. "Just think what you can do with eight thousand pounds!"

"Hush, dear," whispered Hetty.

"Why should I hush? Gramps wanted her to have it, didn't he?"

"Maudie won't be able to have her share until the Will is proved, I need hardly say," went on Joseph. "Nor will my brother Charley's daughter Petal and her young brother. For this reason. My dear Father's wish was that my brother Charley's share of the capital should be paid direct to Petal and to her youngest brother, I forget his name."

"Charley," prompted Hetty.

"Oh yes, young Charley. Thank you for reminding me, Sis. The two children will benefit by about four thousand pounds each in due course. Until young Charley is twenty-one, the interest of his share will go towards his education." He sipped his tea.

"Will you sell this house, Mother?"

"I shall have to see, Elizabeth. This is hardly the time to talk about such matters, dear. Hush, your Uncle has not finished yet."

"Two fourths of the capital of the Trust fund will remain on trust to provide an income in equal shares between Hetty and myself, during our respective lifetimes. After we are gone, the capital is to be shared among our children." He cleared his throat again. "There is one more legacy I must mention, while I am about it. To Phillip, my dear Father left his steel engraving, after the portrait of David Garrick by Gainsborough, now at Stratford-on-Avon, his gold cuff-links, and his volumes of Shakespeare. That is all." He sat down.

"Nothing for any of the other grandchildren?" asked Elizabeth.

"You can have the engraving, the cuff-links, *and* the books, if you like," said Phillip.

"Is the engraving a rare and valuable one, Mother? Didn't Gramps say once that the steel plate broke after only a few were done?"

"That is so," said Joseph Turney. "I understood from my dear Father that only a dozen or so proofs had been pulled when the plate broke. Now may our dear Father and Mother rest in peace until the Judgment Day."

Phillip saw tears in his kind grey eyes. Mother was crying, too, sitting quietly beside Aunt Liz, and holding hands with her cousin and friend of more than half a century.

"Joey, how very careless of me! I quite forgot to ask Hemming to come back with us! Papa would have expected it, I am sure. Oh, what must Mr. Hemming be thinking?"

Mr. Hemming was the Managing Director of the Firm.

"It's just as well you didn't, Sis," said Joseph. "I consider that his letter, which I received this morning, was out of order on two counts. He should have waited until our dear Father was buried before writing to offer his congratulations to me, on my appointment to the Board in my dear Father's place. He only did it because he knows that you and I have a large block of voting shares, of course. Then again, the letter should have come from Stringer, the Secretary. I shall not reply to it."

Phillip moved over to his uncle, and said quietly, "Surely Mr. Hemming is only acting on a decision of the Board? And as Managing Director, I think he is paying you a compliment, as the late Chairman's son, by writing a personal letter."

"That may be as it may be, Phillip, but I shall not reply to Hemming."

Phillip was persistent. "But surely it is a matter of courtesy to reply?"

"Possibly. But I prefer not to discuss the matter."

"Yes, I am wrong in interfering, Uncle Joe. I've just remembered that I never answered the letters from the Manager of the Moon Fire Office, about my going back to my job. Please forgive my interference."

"I thank you for your kind thought, Phillip."

Phillip went with his young cousin Arthur to the Gartenfeste and put on the record of the prelude to *Tristan und Isolde*, with a loud needle, leaving the door open in the hope that all would respond to the music. But only his mother came down, to say that perhaps it would be best not to play the gramophone so soon after Gran'pa's death, for the sake of the others.

"But it is beautiful spiritual music, Mother, with the theme of deathless love."

"I am sure it is, dear, but the others may not understand that."

"Then ask them down, and I'll explain it. People say *Tristan* is sensual music; it isn't! Listen to the yearning of Isolde, faithful unto death!"

"Yes, I know Phillip, but——"

"You *don't* know," he said, and lifted the tone-arm.

When Hetty had gone back, his cousin said, "I don't think you should have spoken to Aunt like that, you know, Phillip."

"I thought you were musical?"

"So I am, but I also try to consider other people's feelings."

"Such as my feelings now? But who am I to talk? I try to improve your father's manners, while my own remain imperfect, and you do the same to me."

"Well, I don't think it is at all the same thing, Phillip."

"Perhaps you're right, Arthur. How's the Firm going?"

"In my opinion, it wants modernising. Everyone is going on in the same way as when Grandfather started it, forty years ago. All our customers are old men. We ought to go out for new business, and install new machinery."

"You must do that, Arthur."

"I intend to."

"Good for you. 'The tools are for him who can use them,' as Napoleon said.

"I thought Napoleon said, 'Not tonight, Josephine,'" sniggered Arthur, to which Phillip made no reply. He had hoped to make a real friend of his young cousin.

The diamond ring left to Charles Turney of Cape Town could not be found. It was neither in the steel safe beside the desk in the dead man's bedroom, nor in the desk itself. It had not been deposited with the Bank.

"Perhaps it will turn up," said Hetty, adding, "I must pray to Saint Anthony."

The ring, with its large pink diamond worth several hundred pounds, was never found; and its loss, together with the fact that 'Wespaelar' had been promised to Charley in a letter from his father when Charley's son Tommy had died of wounds in April 1918 was the cause of much heart-burning, leading to final estrangement between Hetty and Joseph on the one hand, and Charley on the other. Later, Phillip attempted to resolve this deadlock; but in vain.

Meanwhile, in one corner of the front room a conversation of sorts was being carried on between the two cousins, Elizabeth and Maude.

"I suppose you'll be giving up nursing, now that you have more than enough to live on, Maudie?"

"I don't think so, Mavis."

"But why not? And please call me Elizabeth. I hate 'Mavis'!"

"Sorry. Well, it's my job, and I like it."

"What, in Whitechapel? Among all those common people?"

"I don't think of people like that, Elizabeth. They are in my care, you see. In fact, when one knows them, they are rather wonderful people. Well, I must be getting back now, I'm on duty at six o'clock. Goodbye, Aunt Hetty, thank you for all you have done for me. Goodbye, Aunt Liz. How long are you staying?"

"Just for a couple of days, Maudie, to be with Hetty. It is so nice seeing you, dear. You must come and stay with us at Brickhill when you can spare the time, won't you? Just send a card saying when you can come, you will be very welcome."

"Thank you, Aunt Liz." The women kissed; Joseph embraced his niece. Phillip said he would walk down with Maudie to the station.

"I agree with what you said to Mavis, you know," he said. "I had the good luck to know many East Enders at Ypres, in 1914. They were wonderfully kind and steadfast. 'The slums died in Flanders,' as my great friend West said to me. One day I shall write a book about them, and him."

Mrs. Neville, sitting at her window, her little dog beside her, waved to them as they passed.

"You should come up and see my ward, Phillip. You'd find a lot to write about there. Lots of 'copy.'"

"Well, thanks for suggesting it, but it's already in my head, Maudie. I feel so much of the old life that has passed away, particularly when I am alone in Gran'pa's house at night. Ah well, friends meet but to part, I suppose," he said, as the train came in. "Keep your heart high, cousin! One day I shall bring back the old faces and the old places we knew, which may seem to have been destroyed, but their spirit is still in the sunlight. Cheerio!"

The train went under the bridge, and he turned back, feeling a sense of power with which to face the future, because now he understood what had not always been clear in the past. No man could be destroyed, once he had discovered poetry, the spirit of life.

November 1958—March 1960
Devon

A TEST TO DESTRUCTION

is the eighth of a sequence of novels to be known collectively as

A CHRONICLE OF ANCIENT SUNLIGHT

"This will be in its entirety one of the most remarkable English novels of our time. . . . It is amazingly rich in all the living detail of a swiftly changing society; the characters are drawn with such loving sympathy and such firmness of imaginative outline that we are entirely absorbed by their vicissitudes. We are apprehensive for them, we are relieved; we rejoice and are sorrowful; we are angry, and we understand and we laugh and laugh again. To be able to do this with us is the novelist's supreme gift. . . . I believe it is high time we awoke to the splendour and scope of his effort and achievement in *A Chronicle of Ancient Sunlight*. Begin with The Dark Lantern and read on: you will be the richer for it."—JOHN MIDDLETON MURRY ("The Novels of Henry Williamson")—*Aylesford Review*.

"His soldiers, officers and civilians speak with a voice of a doomed generation yet with a vivacity and historical truth that make the living seem, in Yeats' words, more shadowy than they. It is a feat of recollection that has something in it which is akin to genius. If one can judge by *Love and the Loveless*, it seems certain that when the story of Phillip Maddison is completed it will compose a chronicle which will be of permanent literary and historical value. There are not many works of fiction of which one can say that."—GORONWY REES (reviewing *Love and the Loveless* in *The Listener*).

"Mr. Williamson's capacity for re-creating, after some forty years, the living detail of an epoch is continually astonishing."—*The Scotsman*.

"They are adding up, book by book, to one of the few truly great achievements in twentieth-century fiction."—MAURICE WIGGIN (*Sunday Graphic*).

"The important historical monument that Williamson is building in intensely felt words."—KENNETH ALLSOP (*Daily Mail*).

The first seven novels in A CHRONICLE OF ANCIENT SUNLIGHT *are as follows:*

THE DARK LANTERN

The courtship and marriage of Richard Maddison and Hetty Turney. "There is a magic about this book. . . . This excursion into a Late Victorian suburb and merchant materialism is unexpected and it is as genuine and affectionate as it is accomplished."—JOHN BETJEMAN (*Daily Telegraph*).

DONKEY BOY

Phillip Maddison—the early years. "Vibrant with light and shade. Mr. Williamson's study of a sensitive child, yearning for love and understanding, is masterly."—FRED URQUHART (*Time and Tide*).

YOUNG PHILLIP MADDISON

Youth's singing season—the schooldays of Phillip Maddison. "How well Mr. Williamson conveys all the secret thoughts and doings of boys, living lives that are all heights and depths. Magically he suggests the era by subtle description."—JAMES HANLEY.

HOW DEAR IS LIFE

The last summer of the old world and the coming of war. "Mr. Williamson's prose is like sunlight and clear air; and then, when necessary, it has the taste of fear in the mouth, the terrible beauty of life on the edge of the abyss."—GEORGE D. PAINTER (*The Listener*).

A FOX UNDER MY CLOAK

Fear and the quest for courage—the time of Loos. "What matters about *A Fox Under My Cloak* is its being a work of unquestioned genius—that its characters and situations are created straight from living truth."—W. GORE ALLEN (B.B.C.). "Unforgettable battle scenes."—MICHAEL SWAN (*Sunday Times*).

THE GOLDEN VIRGIN

The year of the Somme. "It is difficult to know which to admire the more, the skill of the characterisation or the art by which the character is subordinated to the theme without contrivance and without loss of humanity. . . . The contrast between the tenderness of youth and the cruelty of war is most effectively described."—*The Times Literary Supplement*.

LOVE AND THE LOVELESS

Passchendaele—a soldier's tale. "A strong, sad, courageous novel which re-creates, with great fidelity, the sense of the ordeal which was life for an infantry officer on the Western Front in 1917."—JOHN CONNELL (*Evening News*).